SCHOOL HOUSE IN THE WIND

A TRILOGY BY ANNE TRENEER

UNIVERSITY
of
EXETER
PRESS

First published in 1998 by
University of Exeter Press
Reed Hall, Streatham Drive,
Exeter, Devon EX4 4QR
UK
www.ex.ac.uk/uep/

Reprinted 2002

British Library Cataloguing in Publication Data
A catalogue record of this book is available from the British Library

Hardback ISBN 0 85989 511 4
Paperback ISBN 0 85989 512 2

Typeset by Exe Valley Dataset Ltd, Exeter, Devon

Printed and bound in Great Britain by
Short Run Press Ltd, Exeter

CONTENTS

ACKNOWLEDGEMENTS

Brenda Hull and Patricia Moyer would like to express their gratitude for the continuous and lively support of the late F.L. Harris, the distinguished Cornish educator and historian, who was for many years the Director of the University of Exeter Extra-Mural Studies programme in Cornwall and who is mentioned by Anne Treneer in the trilogy.

We also wish to thank the Revd Cyril Treneer, priest and poet, Anne Treneer's nephew, for his generous and creative encouragement.

We thank all of the members of the University of Exeter Press, the intelligent and supportive readers who recommended the reprint, and most particularly Simon Baker and Genevieve Davey for their subtle, patient, consistent and imaginative editing and supervision.

INTRODUCTION

by Patricia Moyer

This first complete one-volume edition of the three books of Anne Treneer's autobiographical writings gives readers something rather special. At various times it has been possible to get a copy of the first part, *School House in the Wind,* but *Cornish Years* and *A Stranger in the Midlands* have been out of print for many years, and difficult to locate except in library reserved collections.

Many readers will be new to the writings of Anne Treneer, attracted by the Cornish, Devon and Midland settings of the texts. Others will be interested in the autobiographical form and its particular relevance for women writers. Some will be more concerned with Treneer's fascinating history of education from primary schools to training colleges, the universities of Exeter, Liverpool and Oxford, grammar schools in Cornwall and Birmingham, and timely references to adult education. Anyone interested in poetry as writer and reader will find a rich source of pleasure in these texts. But whatever your interest, you are privileged to be able to read the works in a unified format.

This edition of the three volumes contains a short biographical sketch as well as a full bibliography, both prepared by Brenda Hull. The bibliography will give you a clear indication of how much other material in other forms and genres was produced by Anne Treneer. You will have the pleasures of searching out these other writings and beginning to learn more about Anne Treneer's work. Readers may browse, researchers may explore, and eventually Treneer will receive the recognition her work demands.

*   *   *

With extraordinary assurance and continuity, Anne Treneer's autobiographical narrative moves throughout the three texts from her beginnings as a student in her father's two schools; to her acceptance in the Pupil Teachers' Centre at St Austell in 1906 (which became St Austell County School, attended a few years later by A.L. Rowse); to her training at the Diocesan Training college in Truro, including her period as an unqualified teaching assistant in small village schools in Treverbyn in Cornwall and in Exmouth in Devon; to her academic studies at Exeter University College, her external London degrees and her Camborne grammar school position; to a research fellowship at Liverpool University, her return to teaching, then to Lady Margaret Hall, Oxford, from 1929 to 1931, for research and a further degree; and to her prestigious and accomplished career as a teacher at King Edward's School in Birmingham.

This is a remarkable educational and social history of the period 1891 to 1947. It is an astonishing achievement for a young woman from a modest if cultured background, quite comparable to the heady achievements recorded by A.L. Rowse in his autobiography *A Cornish Childhood* (published in 1942, two years before the first of Treneer's trilogy appeared in 1944). We do not know how much Treneer was inspired to write her own version of a Cornish childhood after reading Rowse's, but it is reasonable to speculate that she was stimulated by his work as well as by the general wartime awareness of the transience of cultures. She refers to Rowse's book in a footnote in *Cornish Years* when she is describing the new St Austell County School building:

> The school at a later stage is memorably described in Mr A.L. Rowse's book *A Cornish Childhood*; but by then, under an

authoritarian head master, all was changed. Mr Raynor had tried to run a free school. (*Cornish Years*, p. 177)[1]

Treneer's educational growth was achieved some years before Rowse's, with the additional problems of needing to qualify to move from the rural to the town environment and also of being female in an educational world still strongly gender biased. Of her liberation through education Treneer herself writes: 'Exeter is my true, my most beloved College; Liverpool University was a good foster mother to me; and Oxford set me free'. (*A Stranger in the Midlands*, p. 401).

The first volume, the book actually called *School House in the Wind*, is the most condensed and stylised. Treneer, as narrator, has almost completely merged her individuality into community and family, giving us a gentle elegy for the Cornish world of her childhood. So selective is she as narrator, however, that much of what she describes from the end of the nineteenth century and the early years of the twentieth century is still to be found in the Cornish environment at the end of the twentieth century.

As narrator of the second volume, *Cornish Years*, she is rather more of a social historian, while not relinquishing the archetypal completely; she gives us Cornish interludes within the main action, which is in Devon, Liverpool and Oxford. The narrator of the final volume of the trilogy, *A Stranger in the Midlands*, is a local historian, teacher, and an experienced writer with professional ambitions and experience, living in Birmingham but still deeply connected to Cornwall. All these narrators are naturalists and poets.

It is interesting that even a decade ago Treneer's achievement could be underestimated in unexpected ways. Charles Causley, in a review of the 1982 reprint of *School House in the Wind*, expressed some annoyance that Treneer was writing about a middle class environment in Gorran and Caerhays

---

[1] All page references for quotations of Anne Treneer's autobiographical writing relate to the pagination of the present single-volume omnibus edition.

rather than about the sharp reality of the lives of fishermen and their families in Mevagissey. This is to misunderstand or to underestimate the sharp reality of life as the daughter of a genteel schoolmaster and church organist, and its own realities of low income living in an agrarian rather than a fishing environment. Besides, how to be a fisherman's daughter when your father is the schoolmaster first of Gorran then of Caerhays village schools? Although many aspects of the social world Anne Treneer describes may be gone or transformed, yet the natural world she also depicts is flourishing still in her two Cornish parishes. In the oblique style characteristic of Treneer's writing in these memoirs she conveys a profound sense of the relationships between parents, children, siblings, friends and the rural community.

Treneer refused to write any autobiographical work after 1952 (or about the period after 1947) although she lived on, and continued writing in a wide range of forms including poetry, review, essay and biography, until her death in 1966. Other forms of writing became the desired genre. The series of memoirs/memories that comprise the trilogy remain highly selective and somehow austerely determined. It is as if there never was any notion of continuing beyond 1947. Any efforts to urge Treneer to resume her autobiographies were rapidly deflected.

★　　★　　★

Autobiography is one of the more mysterious of genres. It is not just that the narrator's voice is constructed by the author, emphasized here by the variety of narrative stances throughout the trilogy. It is also that linear time can be deceptively emphasized by readers and writers of autobiography. Treneer's memoirs foreground places, periods, styles of living, rather than personalities. The individuation is obviously there; sketches and vignettes of numerous persons are included. Yet the characters written about are viewed much more in their communal sense than in any particularized psychological framework. We can say the same for Anne Treneer as reticent narrator. She retains control of the narratives without revealing much at all about herself. Thus some of the traditional associations and expectations of autobiography are displaced continuously as we read the series. The trilogy illustrates several postmodernist insights about the reticence of autobiography as a genre in which the subject continually withdraws and eludes definition. Anne Treneer is both reticent and elusive.

Treneer uses the first person singular, of course, not in the confessional, tell-all mode, but rather as a narrative device. Although she changes tone and style considerably between the beginning of the first volume and the conclusion of the trilogy, she also provides numerous links between the volumes: there are back-glancing references to earlier sections of the trilogy and some forward-looking pointers.

Contemporary theory poses some exciting questions about autobiography. I do not wish to move into an abstract discussion on theoretical issues, but I would like to quote one lucid statement which I find most particularly suitable in considering Treneer's autobiographical writings. Katy Deepwell is writing about Barbara Hepworth and the importance of women's autobiographical statements:

> ... in a culture where women's words are readily dismissed as 'personal' rather than analysed for their theoretical or philosophical content. Autobiography as a form never reveals the pure presence of the subject, in spite of its claims to do so. Not only are its forms highly conventionalised and codified narratives from birth to the present day, but it presents the history of its own subject as moving relentlessly towards its present position. The disjunction across time between the months or years in which the work is conceived and written as opposed to the selective past life experiences which the seemingly-present narrating voice of the author claims to represent serves to illustrate this point.[2]

[2] Katy Deepwell, 'Hepworth and her Critics', in *Barbara Hepworth Reconsidered*. Critical Forum Series, Vol. 3, ed. David Thistlewood. Liverpool University Press and Tate Gallery, Liverpool, 1996, p. 75.

Deepwell's comments give us a helpful frame in which to place the rather intricate dates involved in and between the three volumes published in 1944 (*School House in the Wind*), 1949 (*Cornish Years*) and 1952 (*A Stranger in the Midlands*). It helps us understand the tensions between the time of writing and the period written about. The frame also gives us some clues as to why the year 1947 assumes such importance in the texts.

If we reflect on Deepwell's descriptions, we perceive the 'disjunction' between the period 1942–1951, when the three books were composed, and the period 1891–1947 actually covered by the three texts. The history does indeed move 'relentlessly towards its present position' in writing up to the year 1947, which for the purposes of *A Stranger in the Midlands* is the constructed present. Thus we have approximately 55 years from which highly selected episodes are described from a point in time whose maximum distance moves inexorably from 51 to 60 years later. The disjunction involved in writing during the last years of the second world war and the five or six years just after the war's end about a period beginning in the nineteenth century is obvious. We could do even more elaborate mathematical tables for each book to illustrate this paradigm but that would be to miss the point which is simply to alert us to some of the complexities of autobiographical narration.

This sort of disjunction is more familiar to us in novel writing, when an author frequently sets a text in a period considerably before the present without being completely historical. What we take for granted in novel writing and in reading novels is often neglected when we read autobiography or biography. It is noticeable in the trilogy, for example, when we move from the nineteenth century forwards until nearly the present time of writing (late 1940s to early 1950s), that the tone, perspective and narrative devices alter considerably.

There are envelope style references in each of the texts which take us out of that time into the future or the past. When riding Dart is compared to speeding on her Velocette from the Midlands we move from the 1890s to the 1930s without noticing it. The first chapter of *Cornish Years,* titled 'Two Parishes' (meaning Gorran and Caerhays), throws out a casual 'recently in Indiana' which takes us out of the second book's time clear to the end of *A Stranger in the Midlands,* which describes her preparations to visit the United States. While in Indiana in 1947 Treneer and her brother Maurice 'walk together in memory the deep hidden lanes', the woods and the harbours of the Gorran area, taking us back to the time of *School House in the Wind.* There is a reference forward to the middle of World War II and to her father's death in 1943 in the last chapter of *Cornish Years* which is titled 'Two Parishes Again', another example of Treneer's circular technique. There is also in this chapter a summary of the Birmingham years. Earlier in this second book of the trilogy we find in the Liverpool section a reference to:

> . . . Miss L.K. Barrie, head mistress of Wallasey High School at that time, and later of King Edward's, Birmingham, sitting on a divan in front of the fire and saying very little. She was like an island; a piece of silence surrounded by conversation. But when she did talk she made me see parts of Scotland in my mind's eye as vividly as I could see Cornwall. She had a great gift for delineating wide tracts of country and making the colours glow. Next to walking myself over open country I liked to hear her describing it. Her words were springy as heather.
>
> (*Cornish Years,* p. 321)

We meet Miss Barrie again when Treneer is interviewed at King Edward's High School for Girls at Birmingham and throughout *A Stranger in the Midlands.* Hers is one of numerous skilled character descriptions in a picaresque or continuously shifting framework which uses many of the techniques associated with fiction.

Both *Cornish Years* and *A Stranger in the Midlands* end in 1947. The final chapter of the whole trilogy, titled 'Off Again', returns us to the beginning in describing the response to *School House in the Wind,* in crediting her brother Maurice with this suggestion that she write it:

During the war it was impossible for me to travel from the
Midlands to Cornwall as often as formerly, but I found that, by
writing a page or two of *School House in the Wind* I could whisk
myself into Cornwall, into my country childhood. When the
book was published, it appeared that it had power to whisk other
people too.

(*A Stranger in the Midlands,* p. 606)

This casual description of the first book of the trilogy does not
of course convey its rich spiritual and intellectual context, but
it does take us in the familiar circular route back to Cornwall.
The 10 chapters of *School House in the Wind,* the 18 chapters of
Cornish Years and the 25 chapters of *A Stranger in the Midlands*
are all crafted in an integrated style with persistent weavings
and links between the texts, so that it is particularly appropriate
for them to be published now as three books in one. Yet the
linear approach still reveals the numerous spaces, lacunae and
fragmentations typical of the fictional techniques used in
autobiography.

*   *   *

The story of a self in autobiographical form is also, perhaps
primarily, a fiction, a selection of episodes constructing a
portion of a life. Treneer's disciplined style, her somewhat
austere (yet often humorous) stance, and her stylized approach
to writing result in texts situated in a past that is never
nostalgic. As we perceive the trilogy in its crafted, fictional
aspect, we can more fully appreciate Treneer's skills in the use
of narrative devices familiar in high quality autobiography. It is
in this context that Deepwell in her discussion of women's
words suggests that autobiography with its particular kind of
'truth' can be an empowering form for women in our culture.
The personal once again becomes the political. Even if the
subject is partially absent, or only partially present, the
authorial voice becomes an authority.

Fictional amalgamations of linear events merge into one
account. In *School House in the Wind* in particular, narrative

unity is formed by the seasonal account. The delicious and subtle changes in the Cornish seasons are detailed throughout the text. Her flower descriptions alone could fill an anthologist's collection, not to mention those of grasses, trees, bracken, butterflies, dragonflies and the entire range of her treatment of wind, air, and all forms of water.

It is in the two central chapters, five and six, of *School House in the Wind* that we find the central seasonal metaphor developed with her particular combination of liturgical and pagan time, 'the Church's year'. The naturalist's seasons merged with a Wordsworthian style of existentialism focus our attention on being and time. Chapter five ends with a description of harvest on so many levels as to be almost medieval:

> Hay harvest was often not in full swing until July, that is until after the longest day of the year. But it is with June that I chiefly associate it; with the climax of the year's progression. In the rhythm of rise and fall which governs all things it is the rise which exhilarates. To mount, to reach the maximum height, to pause for an infinitesimal moment before the inevitable decline! I have heard that the soul can only float out of the body with the ebbing tide. The fall of the year, too, seems appropriate for a flitting. Who could die in the up-swing from January to June? In childhood one feels immortal all the year round; but even then June was, in some indefinable way, the highest pitch of the swing-boat.
>
> (*School House in the Wind,* p. 74).

The months of the year are stylized here rather like those in a medieval book of hours. Many of Treneer's analogies lead us into elegy in the style of this passage. The harvest festivals of September in the next section are presented in the context of the earlier reference, a linking and circling technique often used by Treneer. Harvest also illustrates her persistent use of literary reference:

> We rejoiced in the harvest in a way best expressed in Hopkins' 'Hurrahing for Harvest'. Barbarous in beauty the stooks arise. My heart leapt to it when I first read those words.
>
> (*School House in the Wind,* p. 83)

Treneer's readers are given some help here, but in fact we are expected to know our Hopkins and Wordsworth references well enough to recognize them when they appear as assimilated parts of her sentences. Yet in the style of late modernism the statements are clear enough even if we do not recognize the references.

Certainly emotion, event, cultural context, and individuals in Treneer's work are recalled, reformed in meditative tranquillity with more than the usual state of awareness. Treneer's narratives attempt to recreate the carefully selected original experience in a manner which is well described in the familiar and powerful description by William Wordsworth in the Preface to the second edition of *Lyrical Ballads* (1800). It is remarkable that such a precise description written at the beginning of the nineteenth century should so relevantly convey a method or process used a century and a half later; Treneer's writing practice and theory is brilliantly indicated here:

> I have said that poetry is the spontaneous overflow of powerful feelings; it takes its origin from emotion recollected in tranquillity; the emotion is contemplated, till, by a species of reaction, the tranquillity gradually disappears, and an emotion, kindred to that which was before the subject of contemplation, is gradually produced, and does itself actually exist in the mind. In this mood successful composition generally begins, and in a mood similar to this it is carried on; but the emotion of whatever kind, and in whatever degree, from various causes, is qualified by various pleasures, so that in describing any passions whatsoever, which are voluntarily described, the mind will, upon the whole, be in a state of enjoyment.

Chapter six of *School House in the Wind* has a preface poem, the complete version of Treneer's 'To Cornwall in all Weathers', in which the months are equated with the love of the familiar chant-poem 'I love my love in/a/with . . .'. Here the months are archetypes in a hymn of praise. Readers seem expected to retain the preface poem in the form of a meditative exercise while reading the chapter. The poem frames and interprets the chapter. Here is one of the most innovative of Treneer's techniques, and one which clearly relates her to nineteenth century novel-writing style.

This narrative device of the use of poems by Treneer herself as chapter headings is used consistently throughout *School House in the Wind* and *Cornish Years,* where the poems are sometimes identified by title, although author Treneer is never indicated. These prefaces may function as a subtext in tandem with the chapter title itself, a significant subtext which may not be directly mentioned in the main text of the chapter and which points an ironic contrast to the prose writing.

The Dart chapter, for example, which forms chapter three of *School House in the Wind,* is prefaced by a three-stanza elegy for the 'frisky shadow' of Treneer's beloved pony Dart ending with:

> Does he stop by muddy Rush-pool to drink,
> Dredging it up through his lips so clever?
> No! rushes and pool and pony and child
> Have vanished for ever.

The chapter itself includes detailed descriptions of the live, living, moving pony, his activities, residences, all the manners of being with him from wild gallops to trots in the cart to St Austell. There is no reference within the chapter to his death, his absence, or to the memoried icon of the poem. There is rather an amusing description of a drink at Rush Pool with Dart very much alive. The poem is left as a signal or flag to mark the elegiac nature of the memoir we are reading.

The later disappearance of the pony who was so much a part of Treneer's idea of family—'he was really included with my brothers and sister'—is connected not only to the loss of childhood vision but to the death of the narrator who can in the poem only touch the pony with her 'ghostly hand' and who is now separate also from the natural world of rushes and pool. This contrast between the gentle threnody of the framing poem and the energetic vitality of Treneer's prose chapter is very typical of her style. The entire trilogy is frequently elegiac in tone. Treneer uses techniques such as the laments of nature, exclamations about the incredibility of death or changed conditions, and the vivid recreation of the absent which are common to elegies.

In *A Stranger in the Midlands* there are no preface quotations before chapters at all. Treneer does, however, occasionally refer within the text to her own poems. In these instances she clearly identifies the subject about which she was writing; she then quotes her work acknowledging it as her own. It is a quietly radical change in style. It is also in *A Stranger in the Midlands* that she reproduces the letter from Edward Garnett about her poetry: 'This was by far the most exciting letter I ever received in relation to any work of mine'. Garnett was interested in her book on Doughty, especially in her comments on style and words. When he read her poetry, Garnett wrote:

> Yes. You are a poet and you have found your own individual way to enshrine, delicately and finely, sensations and feelings not commonly discerned and centred so truthfully. I like all your poems except the Epilogue. I am left speculating whether you may go further along the track and become known as the Poet of the Body's Feeling—by extending the field of your perception and analysing your sensations and emotions in the same aerial, delicate, flying style.
>
> Here your strength lies in the fine exactness of your perceptions and the grace and beauty of your phrasing.
>
> (*A Stranger in the Midlands,* pp. 540–1)

There are other indications in *A Stranger in the Midlands* that the narrator now acknowledges herself as a professional writer of biography, reviews, essays, literary criticism, poetry and autobiography. Indeed this third text is much more autobiographical in the documentary linear sense than the first two. Garnett's perception of Treneer as poet is certainly cited for authority, but the narrator's stance as professional is clear throughout the last volume of the series.

The title poem of Treneer's collection of poetry published in 1942, 'This World's Bliss', is one of those Garnett meant when he spoke of her work. There are poems in this collection about the body as a leaf, the body running, the body slanting to and in the wind, the body swimming, sleeping out, running, smelling, waking, questioning, hearing, feeling, darting, riding, loving, dying. Garnett's speculation about Treneer's being a poet of the body's feeling is intensely pertinent to her style. This particular poem is used as a preface poem to chapter six of *Cornish Years,* a chapter about Treneer's period of study in the earnest Victorianism of Truro Training College, for whose teachers she conveys much respect. It is quite an ironic juxtaposition to have the detailed, sometimes caustic, descriptions of the events at the College within the context of one of Treneer's most philosophical body-poems. She quotes all eight couplets of the poem in this chapter heading, giving it weight and significance:

THIS WORLD'S BLISS

I dreamt I skipt from skin and bones
Into the starry mansions.

Yet knew I'd give my soul to be
Once more of the old earth, earthy.

To hear a blackbird singing clear
With a gross unpurged ear,

And with an uncelestial nose
Savour the sweetness of a rose

Run with the wind; my Holy Ghost
Has never known the Angelic Host

My daily bread and rarer wine
Small traffic have with the divine.

O who would, for immortal ichor,
Change his warm blood, and earthly liquor.

And, dear my Lord, what I love is
Not other, but this worldes bliss.

It is as if Treneer inserts yet another narrative voice into the text of the trilogy in these poems, a lighter, airier philosopher-poet who picks up the threads of the prose discourse and weaves them into a structured prologue statement and then flies away until the beginning of the next chapter. Treneer even manages to include one of her skilled medievalisms by the spelling of 'worldes' in the last line of the poem. The impact on the style of the prose is quite powerful for the reader who retains the poem in mind throughout the chapter.

Within the prose sections Treneer uses the idea of poetry to describe natural formations in Cornwall. The first volume is dedicated

TO CORNWALL

Great rocky scroll, graved by the wind,
Cut by the bright blades of the sea.

In a sense all three volumes seem dedicated to Cornwall, although there are specific dedications to family members: *Cornish Years* to Treneer's sister Susan, and *A Stranger in the Midlands* to her sister-in-law Helen and her brother Maurice, Helen's husband. Still the powerful words of the initial dedication inform the entire trilogy. Cornwall remains the desired, the dominant place with all other places seen in relation to it. I am reminded of Virginia Woolf's comment about *To the Lighthouse,* when she wrote that however much the book was about her mother and father, St Ives in Cornwall was really the central character.

The conception of the rocky scroll is continuously evoked in Treneer's emphasis on rocks; rocks and poetry are related in her vocabulary:

Pordenack is like a good poem, never disappointing to return to, grander than I remembered, with always some fresh aspect to show. It is formed of cubicle rocks, pressing and flattening one another, in massive pillars. The deep groovings lend to individual rocks a peculiar expressiveness . . . The rocks between Pordenack and Carn Boel help us to appreciate sculpture. Here again is felt the thrill of related shapes, the tenderness, the strength or the impudence which can be implicit in poised masses.

(*Cornish Years,* p. 354)

Treneer's descriptions of West Penwith include her full range of perceptions in natural history, social and cultural history, and in literary awareness. Her imagery reveals her as a modernist for whom the boundaries between poetry and prose are flexible and tenuous. Her syntax and grammar, however, remain traditional.

Treneer returns again and again to stones as Cornwall's poem. She speculates about time and how it is possible to 'slip out of it into a sea of other time'. She quotes sources about the functions of the stones as memorials, altars, and meeting-places:

> This does not preclude the idea that the stones were set with due regard to the movements of the heavenly bodies. The feeling that the same spirit is in the round ocean and the living air and the heart of man and the ancient heavens did not find expression first in Wordsworth. Antiquaries are like editors, a little apt to bury the poem beneath the comment. And the erected stones are Cornwall's poem. They are in keeping with the natural stone fantasies of coast and carn and, harmonizing thus with the character of the land itself, they express it as it has never been expressed in words.
>
> (*Cornish Years,* p. 361)

⋆　⋆　⋆

The trilogy presents a disciplined and precise record of an educated woman's voice during an important period of twentieth-century feminism. It is practically a cliché of gender history that we continue to view each period from the late eighteenth century to 1960 as 'early' feminism, largely because so many of the issues of rights, responsibilities, and definitions seem to recur. Here is another instance where the disjunction between the period in which these texts were written needs to be perceived in relation to the period about which Treneer is writing.

We do not find evangelical proclamations about property owning, employment selectivity, even the struggle to gain suffrage and other voting rights, in these texts. Nor indeed do we find discussions of sexuality, depression, reproduction or contraception. But the memoirs are nevertheless a valuable contribution to our understanding of the position of an independent, working, unmarried (and delightfully unconcerned with locating such a relationship for herself), well educated woman who lived from 1891 to 1966. What we do find are portrayals of a wide range of intellectual women through several historical periods, including two world wars.

The series could in fact be redefined as war writing, since the two world wars of the first half of the twentieth century are central to their conception and execution. The perspective of nineteenth-century, and early twentieth-century rural, village, market town, and cathedral city life given by the rapid changes Treneer was living through during and after the Second World War is sharp and clear in these texts, memoried but never sentimental. This general social consciousness includes numerous gender perceptions.

In one of her sharpest comments on gender Treneer is writing about the repetitious and intensive bombing of Coventry and then of Birmingham, ironically begun shortly after the return to Birmingham of the King Edward's High School group from their evacuation centre at Cheltenham:

> It is impossible for a civilian, and a woman civilian at that, to describe war impersonally and objectively. I think a woman is chiefly obsessed with the incredible folly of it.
>
> (*A Stranger in the Midlands,* p. 562)

Treneer makes both subtle and direct references to gender throughout the trilogy. Her descriptions of children's games are delightfully gendered:

> Girls would watch the boys play marbles, and back their champions, and sometimes play themselves. But it was not a girls' game. There was considerable distinction between boys' and girls' games. Boys never had skipping ropes; whereas we girls played 'All in together this frosty weather' for hours. Our hoops were different. Girls had wooden hoops and sticks; boys had iron hoops with iron crooks. Cap'n (if in a good temper)

would lend me his iron hoop. Iron was associated with boys. In a
sense they were shod with iron, for most of them wore hob-nails
in their boots, and could strike fire from the road flints as Dart
could. I was ambitious for a pair of hob-nailed boots, and tried
to persuade John Parnel to put some hobs in when my shoes
were mended. The nearest he would come to it was 'boot
protectors'—little iron lozenges cunningly shaped. I can
remember, as if it were yesterday, my joy in these protectors.
When old John Parnel handed my shoes with the protectors in
he said, 'There, my handsome, now you'll make the stones bled.'

(*School House in the Wind,* p. 126)

An entire monograph could be written on this section: on
difference, on the feminine as audience, on iron envy, on
participation and observation. It is a characteristic mark of
Treneer's style that the humour and exuberance carry us
buoyantly through the social comment, which is nevertheless
pervasive.

When the family leave Gorran to go to Caerhays School
House to live, one of Treneer's first actions on having a
bedroom of her own as distinct from sharing with her sister,
Susan, is to 'set up a bookcase with all the boys' discarded
books in it'. This is reminiscent of numerous stories in fact and
fiction about the education of young women and their
relationship to texts, tutors, and the general education of their
brothers. She is alert to the history of women's education, a
history in which she participated in its twentieth century phase.
She writes movingly and wittily of a previous period in
describing the background of Miss Edith Elizabeth Maria
Creak, who was the first headmistress of King Edward VI High
School for Girls when it opened in 1883:

. . . she was one of four girls who went up to Cambridge. Under
Miss Clough, these four were the first students in what
afterwards grew into Newnham College. Lectures were available
to them only by courtesy and, although they took examinations,
they might not be awarded a Cambridge degree. That privilege
took another seventy years, pretty nearly, to achieve, so devilish
an innovation was the teaching of women in Universities
thought to be. I suppose it was feared we should grow uppish,

and so we have. I often wonder what Queen Elizabeth, Emily Brontë, Christina Rossetti and Jane Austen would have been like if they had gone up to Cambridge, and whether there is any significance in the fact that both Virginia Woolf and Dr Edith Sitwell were privately educated.

(*A Stranger in the Midlands*, pp. 417–8)

Treneer of course had an education, as well as a room, of her own; yet her story is most definitely a girl's own story developing through the trilogy into a woman's story—a woman living in a community of women connected with teaching. These women are studying, travelling, teaching, writing, talking, reciting poetry, directing splendid school productions of Shakespeare and other dramatists, caring for evacuees, playing music, enjoying each other's company, and leading lives of remarkable and well-recorded independence.

Treneer's description of wit in women is particularized about one Cornish colleague, Marjorie Pascoe, initially, then expanded to include Treneer's sister, her mother, and witty women in general:

Sudden sparkles of wit pleased her a second before she uttered them, so that she smiled in advance; I have known no more inward, yet free and illuminative smile. But it is impossible to re-create in a book a witty woman; wit dies on the pen. Even Meredith could not succeed in it. Marjorie's wit was born of the moment and was gone with it. Yet wit serves a woman well, not withering with her beauty. My sister Susan has it, my friend Marjorie has it; so that living with either of them is never dull; the unexpectedness of their replies is the only factor I can see in common between them and my mother, who also had a happy wit.

(*Cornish Years*, p. 292)

I imagine that, like many descriptions of others, this particular passage also portrays Treneer's own wit. One gendered example appears in the section on Cornish saint stories and the holy wells, stones, and crosses which remain. In a fine passage on the natural setting of the well at St Leven near Madron village, Treneer shows us the trees, the remains of a building where 'the sky itself is roof', and a still, green area where the well 'is a well of quietness':

> Some say that St Madron was a woman, and it is a sanctuary a woman might have chosen; though it was probably a man, for men as a rule have more time to be saints. Had I been Madron I should like to have been friends with the hermit of Roche Rock, to have exchanged at intervals the amenities of my cell for his wild aerie. The disadvantage of being a saint is being a saint all the time.
>
> (*Cornish Years*, p. 363)

Edward Garnett's perceptions about Treneer's poetry also included specific reference to a woman's writing: '. . . we have had no Woman poet yet to centre her perceptions on her Body's feelings, though hundreds have spoken for the Soul, the Mind and the Heart'. (*A Stranger in the Midlands*, p. 541). Garnett's conception of what a woman might record—'the states of Virginity, of Womanhood and Motherhood'—was not the trajectory of Treneer's life. Yet she tells us a great deal about the life of a woman in the style recommended by Emily Dickinson's famous admonition to 'Tell all the truth, but tell it slant'.

One of the results of this skilfully oblique technique is to tell the story through the lives of others, thus giving us an unusual glimpse of how women, who took their independence for granted and who worked hard to gain their educational qualifications and their valued teaching positions, lived during the first half of our century. Although their lives focused on teaching, there was always space for reading, travel, writing, thought and being. When Treneer receives her Oxford B.Litt., after two years which she described as 'the freest I ever spent', she contemplates returning to teaching:

> But was I good enough to teach? I knew I was not. No one ever is good enough to teach—and everyone is too good to teach all the time.
>
> (*Cornish Years*, p. 380)

It is the persistent withdrawal and return to and from different modes of work and life that is a source of Treneer's strength. Her unpredictable departures from quite excellent jobs in order to continue her studies in various literary directions is a recurring event. Readers of the trilogy are left at the conclusion with another of these departures which also functions as a stylized narrative conclusion in the elusive, oblique Treneer style:

> I love England, and I adore Cornwall; but I dearly like to be heading away from both for a change; I like schools well enough, and I am interested in education, but how dearly I like, how very dearly I have always liked, to shake the chalk from off my fingers, and kick the blackboard into the sea.
>
> (*A Stranger in the Midlands*, p. 609)

SCHOOL HOUSE IN THE WIND
A TRILOGY BY ANNE TRENEER

From *School House in the Wind*

Mevagissey town seemed almost to hang. Its houses were ingeniously cornered together so that as many as possible were over the sea. Up the containing sides of the narrow valley they mounted skyward or stood up from rocks by the quay-side. There were strange steep alleys, courts and crooked ways which would have been wonderful for hide and seek.

Schools not too big with good masters and mistresses free to help the individual children, and not cluttered up with secretarial work, should be the English pattern. Not schools all alike but rich and varied; our education had better remain too haphazard than too straightly planned . . . schoolmasters today need to emancipate themselves from the encroachment of directors, and from the army of planners, organizers and testers.

From *Cornish Years*

The estuary of the Exe had for me no adventitious glory of association. I loved it purely for itself. It was as changeable as I. Sky and tide; wind, rain and sun; the season and time of day or night transfigured it.

No one ever is good enough to teach—and everyone is too good to teach all the time.

Camborne is an ugly town, yet I felt I would not exchange the treeless mining country in which it is set—a country so worked for tin that a house in a Redruth street might subside into an adit—I would not exchange its bareness and the stubborn, ghostly engine-houses through which the sky showed, for the green abundance of Devon.

From *A Stranger in the Midlands*

But do I dream, or is it not true, that on the motor road between Birmingham and Wolverhampton I used to come upon, somewhere, a view of almost apocalyptic magnificence.

Exeter is my true, my most beloved College, Liverpool University was a good foster mother to me; and Oxford set me free.

I love England, and I adore Cornwall; but I dearly like to be heading away from both for a change; I like schools well enough and I am interested in education, but how dearly I like, how very dearly I have always liked, to shake the chalk from off my fingers, and kick the blackboard into the sea.

Cover illustrations

The front cover shows Anne Treneer in the 1920s wearing her University of London academic gown. The photograph was kindly supplied by Arthur Gibson.

The photograph on the back cover was taken in the late 1940s, and shows Anne Treneer on the cliffs near Porth Island, Newquay: one of her favourite walks. Her god-daughter, Jennifer Harvey, says that this picture is as typical of Anne Treneer as any she has seen.

SCHOOL HOUSE
IN THE
WIND

To Cornwall

Great rocky scroll, graved by the wind,
Cut by the bright blades of sea.

Contents

1

IN THE WIND

He panted to escape but I
As he was winding thin
And narrowly was slipping by
Gasped and drew him in.
—*On Catching the Breath*

Gorran School, with a house for 'master' glued to it, stood strong and symmetrical, without beauty but not mean, triumphantly facing the wrong way. It might have looked south over the distant Gruda and the sea; but this advantage was forgone in favour of presenting a good face to the road. Master's room in school, the big room as we called it, caught the north wind while the closets at the back caught the sun. I have heard that Mr Silvanus Trevail, the architect, who designed many Cornish schools, committed suicide in the end; but whether out of remorse for his cold frontages I do not know.

The site—on top of Menagwins Hill, near Four Turnings—had been chosen so that the school might serve the children from outlying hamlets and farms as well as the children from Gorran Churchtown and Gorran Haven. It made a difference where a child came from. No one could have mistaken Rescassa for Boswinger, Treveor for Tregavarras, or Trevarrick for Highlanes or Penare; nor could the people in them have been mistaken for one another. Far in the distance one would begin to recognize some peculiarity of gait or outline, or some trick of manner. Even disabilities enriched the person. Johnny Mingo of Rescassa had a hook instead of a left hand; but it had acquired so much personality that it pretty nearly was Johnny Mingo. I should have shouted, 'Hullo, Johnny!' if I had met it out by itself; and anyone would have waved a hand in greeting to my father's walking stick or to Billy Lawry's bowler. The children were equally clear in person and trappings. 'See what a handsome great patch I got on me trowsers, Mrs 'Neer', said a tiny boy of Treveor one morning to my mother, 'can 'ee see the sewing?' Each little group of children had its own clannishness according as to whether it approached the school by Trevinick Lane, Boswinger Lane, Crooked Lane or Menagwins. As for Gorran Haven children they were like the Israelites of old—everybody else was a Gentile.

Some children came from very remote farms, and the parish itself, in Powder Hundred, in South Cornwall, was remote when I was a child. St Austell, ten miles distant, was our market town; Mevagissey and Gorran Haven were our fishing ports; Falmouth our distant romantic seaport. My father had come to Gorran as a young widower with one little girl, Ellen, whom he had left to be brought up at Poplar Farm, his own old home. On leaving college he had made village school teaching a definite choice. He had always lived in the country—my grandparents were farmers—and he loved country life and was suited to it. As he was lame he could not farm; he was the first of his family to teach. Probably his lameness had thrown him in on himself more than was customary with Treneers. When he was five, he had had what was known in his day as a low fever; it had left him with a stiff knee, and with a painful awareness of feeling. He told me once that when he was walking on crutches he had heard a servant say, 'Poor little fellah! It would be a mercy if the Lord would take 'un.' Perhaps it was this memory which gave him an intense sympathy with the young and weak; a hatred not only of illness, but of any talk about illness; a quick impulse to reassure any person who felt not perfectly wanted; and a determination that his own children should not suffer from any physical disability. He was cranky about our clothes. Our skirts were attached to bodices so that the weight should come on our shoulders, and not drag on our waist muscles. My sister soon compromised with her muscles, but I was loyal to my shoulder-bones for years.

He married as his second wife Susan Nott, of Brookvale, Gorran Churchtown. My Gran'fer Nott, one of the Notts of Trevarrick, was something of a saint from all I have heard, but handsome with it. Granny Nott was a Searle; she was clever, with a biting tongue. But on both sides of the family all I know of my grandparents is from hearsay; I was the youngest child of six and my grandparents died before I was old enough to know them. My mother, too, was a youngest daughter. She had had various admirers before the new schoolmaster arrived to cut them all out and carry her off under Johnny H.'s very nose. On our bookshelves there was an elegant copy of Goldsmith's *Poems* and a green-backed *Pickwick Papers* inscribed to Sue with love from Johnny. Apparently she was a great tease both to Johnny and Joe. My father used to laugh and say he thought he'd better have her as no one else would put up with her saucy tongue; and she used to say she thought she'd better take him, poor soul, as he needed looking after, and did not know what was good for him. He did not like roast pork.

The two were married in Gorran Church by Mr Sowel and, without a honeymoon, went straight up to the School House. It was lonely at first for my mother. Brookvale was an old cottage in the centre of the village; the School House was on the hill, alone and new. Even the furniture, though some of it had been bought at sales, was new to its place, not treasured and settled like Granny's furniture. But my mother was house proud. Miss Elizabeth Lawry said Sue's drawing-room was the prettiest in Gorran, and Miss Elizabeth was a person who knew what was fitting. Certainly the parlour, as we ourselves called it, was a delightful room even as I remember it in its shabbier days, its first glory dimmed by time and children. I can still see its olive green and gold wallpaper, its carpet in darker green and gold;

its comfortable chairs; the shining wood of piano and table, its yellow lampshade, and the books and music everywhere. It was a small room but was lucky in having four long, narrow, sash windows, two looking towards the distant sea and two towards Churchtown with its handsome grey tower just visible. The best view was from the back bedroom window. We used to say that we could see the Manacles.

At first the house seemed big to my mother after Brookvale; and her only disappointment, she once told me, was that her best tea-set was not new, but bought at Hemmingway's sale by my father, who fell in love with it and bought it without consulting her. Her heart had been given to a new tea-set she had seen in a St Austell shop. For this reason or some other she never really cherished her wedding set, though its delicate egg-shell whiteness and painted robins on sprays of bright holly would have appealed to her if it hadn't been 'Hemmingway's old trash'. Yet not one of the dozen pieces was missing when my father bought it, nor was there a crack in tea-pot, milk-jug or slop-basin. He would remind her of this when the 'birdie tea-set' as we called it began to be broken. A child would smash a saucer banging on it with a spoon; the dog would knock over a cup; Mrs Tucker would crack the tea-pot through using dishwater too hot. But my mother was unperturbed. She had, until only a couple of broken-handled bread-and-butter dishes and a cracked tea-pot remained, a kind of grudge against that tea-set.

She also disliked the exposed position of the house after the sheltered warmth of Brookvale with its orchard and gliding brook; its gay flower-beds and neat box borders; its moss-rose trees, lemon verbena and boy's-love flourishing among the vegetables and currant bushes. Granny Nott had been a famous gardener. But my father in his Gorran days had something of a Cornish farmer's impatience with gardening, and a good thing too, or the schoolhouse garden would have broken his heart. Except for snow-on-the-mountain, primroses and daffodils on the lower hedge in spring, and pinks, sweet williams and mignonette under the windows in summer, most of the so-called flower garden was in grass, bare and careless of the wind.

Except in thick mist or in high summer I hardly remember still air at Gorran. The wind either played or howled round our house; it rarely died altogether. It was a constant companion, in one's hair and in the leaves and in the telegraph poles, whirling the smoke down the chimneys, rattling the sash windows, and bringing the middle door to with a bang if front or back were suddenly opened. When I was told the story of Jacob wrestling with God I saw him struggling to open our heavy front door in the wind.

It was bare country; no trees sheltered the house. There were two stranded thorns at the foot of the garden, but they looked as though they had tried to run away and had been caught by the heels and retained the slanting attitude of those ready to race. Between the flower and vegetable gardens a long line of thorns had been planted and encouraged to grow as a fence. In some places these thorns were fairly high; in some low. We used to play the jumping game of 'higher and higher' over them, tearing our knickers, and scratching our legs, yet never feeling the scratches in the excitement. Jumping the thorns forwards and back was the recognized way of letting off steam if something really thrilling had happened to a person in the family.

The wind streamed round us straight from everywhere. From whatever direction it blew it met our house and swept on and round it like a sea-swirl over and around rocks. Winter gales were glorious. When the winds were really high, entering our house from the lanes was almost like getting into a beleaguered fortress. In the lanes we were protected by hedges. Then, tugging open our gate, we would advance a few yards in the shelter of the wall before running the gauntlet of the wind in the open garden. Sometimes we could only just manage to round the projecting corner of the house against which the wind would try to hurl us. It was called 'rounding the Cape of Good Hope'.

I played in the wind and my game was anything but elaborate. Sometimes the boys made kites, but I never aspired to a real kite. Any piece of paper tied to a string was good enough for me to go out and whirl about with. It was not with the paper and string but with the wind I played, hiding from him in a corner, encouraging him to pounce or fling or suck the breath out of my body.

The high wind was always 'he' and personal. I did not distinguish him by his different names in his quarters, but I soon knew his chancy nature, and could very early discriminate between the glorious South-West and the bitter East, though I could not have said so. The wind was associated with the Bible and Church. Going to Church every Sunday one soon knew the liturgy by heart, even creeds used rarely like the Athanasian Creed grew familiar. When the vicar said, 'The Father incomprehensible, the Son incomprehensible: and the Holy Ghost incomprehensible', I, proud of my ability to read the word, triumphantly joined in the assertion, 'And yet there are not three incomprehensibles nor three uncreated: but one incomprehensible and one uncreated.' When it came to 'proceeding' I knew it was the wind—'not made, nor created, nor begotten, but proceeding'. As I look back, Whitsun was a particularly lovely festival, not only because we wore our white dresses and summer was near, but because of the rushing mighty wind which preceded the cloven tongues as of fire. And I still think one of the best Old Testament stories is the story of Elijah angry with his God because He would not bend people to his will and make them conformably righteous. Elijah, like every reformer, had been very jealous for his Lord God of Hosts, and very anxious to liquidate everyone not ready to bow to Him. But when the Lord passed by Elijah, the Lord was not in the fire, nor in the rushing wind, but in the still small voice. When I first heard the story I knew nothing of the still small voice; but the rushing wind—yes. I was disappointed that God was not in the whirlwind. I suppose most people are. Only a handful of people in the world seem to know that God is not in the fire nor in the whirlwind but in the still small voice.

Gorran parish, though in South Cornwall, has a good deal in common with the north. It has the bareness and wide horizons of the north coast which is, after all, not very far distant. A giant could step from Dodman on to Hensbarrow and in another stride be over the Goss Moor and on to Pentire or St Agnes Beacon. Cornwall is long and narrow. 'Nature', says Carew, 'has thrust it into the sea and besieged it with ocean.' Part of the enchantment of Cornwall is the bareness. Our Dodman shares this with Bodmin Moor, North Cliffs, Goonhilly, and West Penwith. T. E. Lawrence wrote of Arabia that its bareness made green fertility seem vulgar; in the desert he was drawn out of himself and held by the vacancy, by the abstraction, and by the weakness of earth's life in comparison with the greatness of the sky. His desire to avoid what he called his sultry self was gratified, just as for many people it is gratified, in a less degree, by the naked carns of West Penwith, the country of far distances which lies between Zennor and Land's End. Parts of Gorran shared this bareness; and its heady air, too, made it easy to understand what both Doughty and Lawrence felt in the desert. Those who have walked by Trevinick through Penare, and come out on to the top of Dodman, and looked into the sparkling intoxicating space, know what Lawrence felt when he reached the last crest and could look out on the Guweira plains. Somebody told me last year that he once met my father on the Gruda and my father said, 'I've come out to drink a cupful of air, John.' We are creatures of air, so it is not strange that we are unable to live in buildings long without an irresistible craving for freshness; and it is not wonderful that people should love the very air of the place where they were born. The chief of the miseries of exile (of the world's unbidden guests) must be the sense of being cut off irretrievably from the kindred air and earth; ghosts haunt no unfamiliar places. My ghost will haunt Gorran; but I hope it won't moan about the Churchyard, or snore like a white owl. I should be loath to frighten anybody.

The School House and Highlanes were the windiest spots in Gorran. A wag once named the School House Gorran Lighthouse. The Churchtown, at the foot of Menagwins Hill, was sheltered; but Menagwins itself, where Will Richards had his forge, Agnes her shop, and Cap'n Lelean his coal-store, was pretty exposed. Will Richards was captain of the Gorran cricket team, and my brothers' hero. We had our coals from Cap'n Math; my eldest brother once said Cap'n Math watered it to make it heavy, and Will Lelean fought him for the aspersion and won. Most of the older farm-houses were sheltered, though Trelispan, Lamledra, Tregarten and Tregerrick caught the wind. Cotna was deliciously situated; so were Trewollock, Treveague, Penare, Tredinnick, Treveor and Polsue. Trevarrick was perhaps the best of all, where the earliest snowdrops grew. The Vicarage was well placed among trees, its richly cultivated garden contrasting with our wild one.

The parish was not altogether unwooded, but on the whole we merited the gibe that Cornwall has not wood enough to make her own coffins. There were trees at Tregavarras, along Old Vicarage Lane, and in the Churchyard; Trevennen Wood and Scotland were within easy reach of us. They may not be in the parish though; I am not sure of the boundaries. Trevennen may be at least partly in Caerhays parish, and Scotland Wood in Mevagissey. Caerhays, Mevagissey and St Ewe were our neighbouring parishes. Caerhays parish had no pub; a sad reflection on that sedater place. There were great clumps of trees in Caerhays Park and beautiful woods at the back of the castle. Otherwise, except for occasional oak, ash, thorn, or sycamore, and the curiously twisted elms which made in winter a delicate frieze against the sky by Bodrugan, there were few trees. Yet I connect Veryan with ash, Caerhays with sycamore, and Gorran with thorn. One oak between St Ewe turning and Highlanes was always known as Oak Tree.

The high hedges which bordered the roads and divided the fields were shelters for beasts and men. In sudden scurries of driving rain we sought a 'lew'[1] hedge. Cattle, seeking the hedges in wet windy days, would stand, their hind-quarters in comparative comfort, looking with melancholy eyes over the fields. Except for the moor-like stretches round Dodman and

[1] Lee.

the Greeb, all Gorran was field and hedge. At Hemmick the poppies and corn and a lovely blue flower—I think succory—grew to the cliff edge, so that the summer wind could be heard in the waves on the one hand and in the wheat or oats or barley on the other. Thomas Hardy has described the winter voice of the wind in holly and oak and other woodland trees; to hear it rustle the ripe oats is the luxury of summer.

There were times when we almost saw the wind. Just too late we would turn and it had passed over the waving meadow grass, or swept the upstanding ears of wheat; or printed the catspaws on the sea. I have seen the wind in light snow or swirling sand being the life of it. Snow is rare in Gorran. I always wish I had been born early enough to know the great blizzard, when the snow was heaped as high as the hedges, and the whole parish, the whole Duchy I suppose, was smoothed white and the sea looked black. My brothers remember the blizzard. My eldest brother was at Granny Nott's; in fetching him my father was up to his waist in snow, and they only reached the shelter with difficulty. There was a weird strange light in the mornings when they woke, and the dog went half off his head.

No words have been found to relate exactly the mysterious relationship of our bodies with the air—a body breathing air in and out, and surrounded by air except where the soles of our feet touch the earth. 'And he breathed into his nostrils the breath of life' comes nearest. When we walk or run or dance only an inch or so of each foot in turn touches the earth, and that only for a second. It is more wonderful to walk or run than to fly in a machine. That is ordinary in comparison. A flier in a machine is not flying; he is sitting down on something. Whereas a runner with the wind is as near being off the earth as may be. A human being cannot be completely and utterly surrounded by any element and live. In the air some tiny part of him must touch the earth, even if it is only the tip of a ballet dancer's toe. In water he must keep his head out, or his mother, like the mother of Achilles, must hold him by the heel. The less he has to do, tortoise-like, with enveloping himself in mud and mire, the better for him. He might find himself buried and know no more. Not to know anything! To be dead! It is astonishing that the idea of life should not be a conception so miraculous that for men to deliberately cause the death of a fellow would be unthinkable. I suppose Cain discovered only by chance that his brother was vulnerable to death; his horror when he knew what he had done made him a renegade. But before Cain was born Eve had stretched out her hand to possess what her eye desired. Children should be taught that only if they carry nothing in their hands can they enjoy the wind and know life from death. Then when heaven's breath smells wooingly they may sit among the sea-pinks and feel it gently lifting their hair and touching their cheeks; or when a great wind is rushing they may lean back against it and blow with it half off the earth.

2

THE FAMILY

Come out, sun and shine upon us, Ho!
Here's a boy and a baby in a wheelbarrow.

My brothers say they brought me up in the wheel-barrow, and that this accounts for certain bumps in my forehead and general scrappy appearance. When I was small they used to tell me that old Mrs Tucker brought me one winter night in a potato sack and left me on the front step; and that I squalled so loud that my father said to my mother, 'For God's sake bring the little Devil in and see if she'll stop that noise'. So in I came and stayed. And Mrs Tucker stayed too and used to stir up the boys' porridge in an iron saucepan with a wooden spoon singing the while in a cracked voice:

Ort thou weary, ort thou langueed,
Ort thou soor deestrest,
Come to me saith One, and coming
Be at rest.

Any one of my brothers meeting another after a long interval will end by a high-pitched quavering rendering in Cornish of this immortal sample of 'Ancient and Modern'. They will tell, too, of the time when Mrs Tucker put large portions of both

15

sugar and salt in their porridge; and how my mother, appealed to, made them eat it to uphold the old woman's authority. This instance used to be quoted by my brothers as an example of the discipline which prevailed in the family in their day, before my sister and I arrived and were spoilt.

Certainly I was spoilt, though I was not, like my sister, a greatly desired baby. Indeed I have a certain feeling in my bones against the advocates of birth control. In their more scientifically planned society I should never have been, and I should hate never to have been. My parents led off with four boys—Maurice, Howard, Stanley and Wilfrid. My brothers, not liking their names, refer to this as mother's romantic period. A girl was greatly desired and when at last she came, and was christened by the good family name of Susan, my parents cherished her, but decided that they now had their quiver full. They sold the pram and gave away the christening robe. So it was that when I came I had to be wheeled in the wheelbarrow and be christened in nothing much at all. I yelled at the Font.

But for an undesired baby I snuggled my way in with remarkable ease, and I am convinced that there is no position in a family like the position of youngest, and no position for a family like the position of a schoolmaster's family in a Cornish village. Everybody knew us and made much of us. I was 'my lovely', 'my beautiful' and 'my handsome', though one of the plainest little girls ever freckled by the sun. Miss Mary and Miss Ada at the Barley Sheaf even used to call me their little jam tart; and Agnes at the shop, who had so ample a bosom that I firmly believed she folded up her nighty every morning and kept it there as on a shelf, used to give me 'nicies' and 'jaw-puller', a wonderful sticky stuff, striped pink, white and chocolate. Luckily my brothers thought me a joke and hauled me about with them as soon as I was big enough. So I was always out of doors. My parents had grown too used to children to be solemn over their up-bringing. My eldest brother says he came in for all that; and indeed I have heard my mother say that when Maurice was a baby she used to prepare his food while my father stood by reading the directions from a book.

But by my time my parents no longer read directions from books, nor were nervous for the safety of their children. The others had grown and thrived, so presumably I should too if given plenty to eat and time to sleep, and space to grow, and training in telling the truth. This last training was so thorough that to this day I am verbally truthful unless given a few minutes to think.

Certainly there was plenty of space. Our nearest neighbour lived a field away. He complained that we tore down his hedges and trampled his grass. No doubt we did both. There was also plenty to eat. Although my father's salary was small we had a big garden, kept a pig and fowls and bees, and lived carelessly lavish. I always thought we were rich. Indeed compared with most of our friends we were. Most of them were farm-labourers, fishermen, blacksmiths, or workers on the Caerhays estate, bringing up large self-respecting families on small earnings. Our farmer friends were richer but made little display. Old Billy L., one of the richest men in Gorran, went about looking like a tramp, with a green felt hat on his head, and his fiery little pig's eyes looking balefully at children out of his red face. John Charles Williams was as rich as a fairy tale. But he was Squire Williams. It never occurred to me that anyone else could live in a castle with a pond in front, and with a little house near the pond called (because Noah Loten milked the cows in it) Noah's Ark. We envied the ark more than the castle, and admired Noah more than John Charles. Noah was a genius with children; so was his daughter Nellie. Dear Noah! There was I suppose something childlike in his nature which made him free of the children's world. Other men would tease him. Once they took away the ladder when Noah was last man on a rick. Noah said, 'Now how be I going to get down?' And they said, 'Walk straight on, Noah, and you'll get down all right.' Noah in his dealings with children was the direct opposite of old Isaac in the village. Isaac walked with two sticks and would shout at children or fling a stick at them. Susan would run a mile away from him, but I, to show off, would pretend not to be afraid of Isaac. He would say, 'Anne, she idn' afraid of Isaac, she idn'. He called my brother Stan 'old bumpy belly' because he stuck out in his jersey. This opprobrious term was joyfully seized on.

I cannot remember very far back into my childhood. But when I look far back, farthest of all, it is summer, and I can see two great white wild roses growing in the sun in Crooked Lane. Every Sunday two or three of us, after church at Gorran, would go to Four Turnings, down Crooked Lane, and over the pathway field to Horse Pool. There we would wait until we heard the pony trotting along by Treveor, bringing my father in the trap from Caerhays where he went twice a Sunday to play the organ. If there were too many children meeting him to get into the trap we would run behind as a kind of wild cortège. When we got home the boys would unharness the pony and my father would throw me up into the air and catch me. In the trap I liked to ride in the back seat. I can remember when I had new patent-leather strap shoes, and was riding with Howard in the back seat. We had a dust rug over our knees and when we met anyone he would say, 'Stick out . . . shoes'. Then I would shoot my feet out from under the rug to show off the glory of my patent-leathers.

The back seat in our trap was safe enough. Not so all back seats. Once, years after the time about which I am now writing, my sister Susan had a funny adventure in Sam Kitto's trap. She was riding to St Austell in her prettiest clothes, and enjoying the company of a neighbouring young man who was also riding to St Austell in the back seat of Sam Kitto's trap. Suddenly the back seat slipped from its moorings and Susan and Jack were shot together into the road, while Sam went on driving hell for leather, and did not even miss his passengers for a few minutes. Sam's was a ramshackle conveyance tied together with bits of rope. Once Susan saw me off at Highlanes in Sam's trap and wrote to me after to say that when she saw us turn the corner and vanish from her eyes she felt yea even as Elisha when he saw Elijah whirled away in the fiery chariot. She thought she saw a mantle dropping through the air.

As a child I thought my father the most wonderful person in the world. Holding his hand I would go through fields with any number of fierce-looking horned creatures. But on winter nights we liked him to be out of the house. Though sweet-tempered he was sometimes moody, and he always hated noise. So our noisy games were kept for Wednesday nights when he drove to Caerhays to the choir practice taking one or other of us with him, but not more than one. We would take turns. He hated going about with what he called a horde of children. When he was gone, especially if he took mother with him— leaving one of the boys or old Mrs Dada in charge, we played hare and hounds round the dining-room, over the chairs, and under the table and over the couch. It was the most exciting game ever I played, and reached a pitch of noise which modern children would hardly dream of. My brother Wilfrid, known throughout the parish as Cap'n because he bossed all the boys' games, was a great brewer of wine—sloe wine and blackberry wine. He once made parsnip, but the stone jars in which he put it burst before it came to the drinking. My parents say that once when they got back from Caerhays all the boys were more or less drunk on a special brew of sloe wine which Cap'n had produced. They were too overcome to take the pony out of the shafts; but this orgy I do not remember. Apparently they bribed us with a glass of blackberry to go to bed before they began the real carousal.

When Maurice was away at school Mrs Dada who cleaned the schools, or Carrie Spears, or Mrs Clarke who did my mother's washing would come to stay with us while our parents went visiting. Mrs Dada had a face like a map with wonderful wrinkles. It was she who provided the word 'niggybuggers' for the family, She told my mother one day that in the cold weather the wind blew so draughty up her open drawers that she had taken an old serge skirt and made it into what the boys do call a pair of niggybuggers. They were drawn in with elastic at the knee and kept the draught out proper. In the forefront of fashion, poor old Mrs Dada! She would have been astonished to know that. But she always wore a skirt over them.

My father cared more for music than for anything else. We had a succession of organs and pianos. He was always changing instruments to my mother's annoyance. Once we had an organ in our small 'hall' and we could hardly slide down the banisters for the pipes. But at last my father settled down with a Brinsmead piano. It had a really lovely tone and still has—for he did no further swopping once he had got something really to his liking.

He hated teaching music. Sometimes he would be persuaded to give a boy or girl lessons, but unless there was some genuine talent he would soon throw it up and offend Mrs So-and-so by saying that her son had the fingers of a sledge-hammer and no ear at all. He would not teach even his own children unless bullied into it. Howard and Susan were natural musicians and succeeded in making him set them on the way until they were old enough to go to St Austell for lessons. The rest of us would start again and again, but give up in the face of discouragement. Of Howard my father was really proud. Howard played the piano as if he were a wizard. At thirteen he became organist at St Ewe Church, a neighbouring parish. He was so excited at this appointment that he jumped our row of thorns up and down their whole length twice. He could not play the pedals at first, but began having organ lessons at St Austell. Cap'n or Stan blew for him.

In order to go to and fro to St Ewe Church, Howard was given the first bicycle which entered the family. It was a Rudge Whitworth. Howard went to St Austell to fetch it and learnt to ride on the way home; but he was so unsteady that when, calling to mother to come out and see him, he rode grandly into the garden, he fell off and tore his trousers. Often in going to and from St Ewe Howard would ride the bicycle and Stan the pony. They used to scorch down the slope between Oaktree and Highlanes. A Gorran Haven man told my father about this speeding; the two were warned, but continued to take the slope 'like a streak of light', Dart at full gallop to keep pace with the Rudge. One evening at twilight when machines and ponies go fastest and my brothers were more like a circus than usual, my father stepped out of a gateway and said, 'Stop, you boys.' The two had to dismount and walk home, one leading the pony and one pushing the bike. Moreover, the bike was impounded, and put under the stairs for days. The boys could do nothing but avenge themselves on the informant, and the only part of him they found to avenge themselves on was a pair of his trousers, hung over his garden wall by the fuchsia bush to dry. They cut off all the buttons. Nothing whatever could keep us from scorching. Later on I used to stand on the 'step' of the Rudge, balancing with my brother as we flew down the hills.

Howard was the best mimic I have ever met and, as he played at St Ewe until he went to College at eighteen, we became familiar with St Ewe personalities by hearsay and imitation. Mrs Rasleigh, the rector's wife, chiefly lived for me. She would be afraid Howard would forget at what point in certain psalms the second part of a double chant had to be played twice in order that all should fit in and come even before the Gloria. She was in the choir and would turn round and bawl in his ear, 'So foolish was I and ignorant'. Then there was Jimmy P. the choir's main bass who would say of a certain tune, 'Let's have 'un, I can do the bass of 'ee proper.' My brother was inclined to play rather fast in church, and was once furious because at a harvest festival my father, who was standing by him, was so irritated at the tempo of 'Come, ye thankful people, come' that he beat time on the youthful organist's shoulder.

Howard was nine years older than I, but he was my brother of brothers. It was partly because he did not go away to school as Maurice did, partly because he was sufficiently older than I to find me amusing. My half-sister, Ellen, I remember only as a giver of gifts. She married when I was very young, and settled in Canada. Howard would do things for me. My father would take any of us who were ready out for a run before breakfast; but we had to be properly turned out, with hair brushed and shoes clean. It was hard to get long straight hair done when mother was busy with the breakfast. But Howard could be persuaded to take a hand with the brush, tie up my seaweedy hair, help me on with my shoes, and clean them on my feet in the wash-house, while I sat on the copper top. For this I would give him two great hugs and be off with my skipping rope or hoop down Trevinick Lane.

There can have been few people with more natural magic than my brother Howard. He had and has the vitality and gaiety that make all parties go. No one could be dull with him. 'Would I were with him, whether in heaven or in hell' people might have said of him as of Falstaff. He carried laughter about; there was no barrier between him and all humanity. When he and my eldest brother, Maurice, were grown up and home for holidays, I have heard people say in the same breath: 'Good evening, Mr Treneer! Ullo, 'Oward!' He was ' 'Oward' to three parishes. Old Jimmy S. used to call him 'Owlard'. He has often laughed and said that porters will rush to carry a dispatch case for Maurice, but would see him (Howard) staggering along with a trunk on his back. His trousers get baggy; his collars ride up; his studs hide away; a back lock of hair sticks out, and a front lock stands up. He soon looks like a tramp. When we were young we made a disreputable looking pair together. Once when we were looking our worst we were in a field where was an upright granite block—not unlike a monolith, but put there within living memory for cattle to rub against. A pedantic-looking tourist brought up in the 'Hodge' tradition asked us about the block. Howard said in broad Cornish that it was called locally the Devil's Poker—it wasn't—and he made up wonderful tales about how it glowed red-hot on Midsummer night and the piskies danced round. When the person got out a note book and began to write it all down and said, 'That's most interesting, my man, I'm a collector of local yore. You seem intelligent', we were in ecstasies. He called me 'little woman'. 'And what do you know about it, little woman?' I gasped out, 'I've zeed the piskies, I 'ave.' For this piece of fantasy Howard gave me a ha'porth of Barcelona balls.

He had a quick temper and would fling anything handy at anybody when he was in one. But he usually missed; his passion would be too great for his aim. Once, much later, he was beside himself with rage when he thought I had been nearly knocked off my bicycle by an early motorist. He stood there in the road in a fury shaking his fist and shouting, 'You might have killed my sister.' The driver was a little drunk and had swayed somewhat in passing; but he had been nowhere near killing me. I hadn't even come off my bicycle.

Howard knew all the funny Cornish stories ancient and modern for miles round and would father them on our friends, using their voices and actions so that in the end we would half believe them. Local preachers were often pegs for these stories. Many local preachers were the best of men, good in their lives, and with a kind of earnestness which was better than learning. They knew the Bible in and out and round, and some of them had the Cornish gift of eloquence. Others had more desire to preach than inspiration for it; some in giving homely details when telling the Bible stories made them sound funny. One in telling the story of the Gadarene swine said, 'and then all they pigs, they took to their heels, screeching, and went slap bang over cliff. And 'twadn no good then for 'em to cry, "Chug, Chug", and rattle the handle of the bucket. They pigs never come home no more.' And there was the Hell-fire sermon which Howard fathered on a mild man we knew: 'You do know, some of 'ee, the little brook down bottom Mr Richards's garden; well turn 'un into 'ell and 'twouldn' make no difference; and you do know the little river goin' into Portluney, turn 'un into 'ell and 'twouldn' make no difference; and some of 'ee do know the great Fal because you been a little steamer trip to Truro; well turn 'un into 'ell and 'twouldn' make no difference; and some of 'ee have seen where the Fal do flow into the great Atlantic where go the ships and where is that Leviathan—well, turn 'un into 'ell and 'twould be like spittin' on a flat iron. . . . O my brethren, turn away from yer sins or 'ell will get 'ee.' I used to fancy Hell might get me when I'd thrown a stone at Susan or done some equally wicked thing.

My father reassured me. He was a Christian after the fashion of Charles Montague Doughty whose younger contemporary he was. He would, I think, like Doughty, have gone through fanatic Arabia proudly confessing himself a Christian while interpreting it in a manner which Mr Holman of Treberrick, a fundamentalist, ascribed to anti-Christ. Father's nature was attuned to every form of beauty, and particularly to the words and music of the English Bible and Liturgy. He believed, too, that children should be brought up in the traditional faith, and he founded the teaching in his own school upon it. But Hell he rationalized. I do not remember how old I was when he explained to me the irrevocable nature of words and actions and how you could become so sorry for something rash you'd done that being in a fiery torment might stand for a picture of it. T. S. Eliot has made that solemnity a new theme of poetry. I think there can have been few more understanding persons with children than my father. I ceased to shudder at Hell, feeling that he knew better than any book, but I always had a qualm when we sang 'Lo, He comes with clouds descending', a terrific Advent hymn which I nevertheless enjoyed. It was magnificently frightening. I imagined the great summons of the Trumpets, the clouds, purple with red-gold edges rolling up as at a stormy sunset, God in the midst with all the souls crowding to be judged. Hopkins can make me tremble still in 'Spelt from Sibyl's Leaves'. When I was little I had a notion that, being one of the best runners for my age in Gorran, I should be able to give God the slip and run away until His wrath was past and He was restored to His sunny Self. I was an adept at evading immediate anger.

Anger in our family was furious and soon over. Stan, my third brother, was the gentlest person, yet the most dangerous to rouse. He and Howard were great friends and never fought. But Cap'n, my youngest brother, used to fight with Stan away from the house in a corner of the boys' playground, where my mother could not see. My father, if he saw, would let them fight it out. The only time I saw them fighting Cap'n was down and Stan was kneeling on him in a fury. I knew the story of Cain and Abel and thought that this was going to be death. I don't think I was ever so frightened in my life, certainly not in any air-raid, as at that personal anger. Yet I have no memory of how it all ended.

Stan was the best of my brothers to go bird-nesting with. He had an uncanny knowledge of how and where birds would build. The boys had a collection of birds' eggs which I inherited. We kept strictly to the rule of taking only one egg from a nest and of not returning to a nest or disturbing the hen-bird when she was sitting. We feared to make her 'forsake'. In Treveor hill I can once remember Stan showing me ten or so different nests just on the great stretch of hedge and tree in the elbow-crook of the hill. We called birds by their local names— wrens were wrannies, and so on. Stan once showed me a cuckoo in a hedge-sparrow's nest. He was a bulging bird with his breast fairly bursting out of the top of the nest, and he opened his beak and gaped for food. The hedge-sparrow fed her monstrous child. Our friend the roadman used to watch the hedge-sparrow feeding that cuckoo and say she was working her poor little guts out getting worms for a great bird who was none of hers. Once in particular, I can remember going down Treveor hill and seeing a hen thrush sitting on her eggs. We saw her speckled breast and bright eyes and she must have seen our huge forms and yet she never wavered from the nest. Birds first out of the shell are amazingly ugly. I was terribly disappointed when I first saw the fledglings of robins. To think that these frog-like creatures were the children of the handsome red-breasts! Once we had a robin's nest in the rafter of the closet at the side of a part of the garden which we called 'the three-cornered piece'. We kept the door shut when the eggs were hatched for fear the cat should get in and eat the birds. There was a square open space at the top of the door for ventilation, and one Sunday the robin not only taught the birds to fly but, when we weren't looking, taught them to fly out of that hole. One little bird the cat got, a cat called Tweed. And Stan solemnly boxed Tweed's ears and explained to her fully that she was not to do it again. But a cat can't really be hit, and Tweed didn't care a tinker's curse. She still took a devilish interest in birds.

Maurice began our collection of birds' eggs and the other boys continued it. The eggs were in a large shallow box. They rested in their different kinds in little compartments made of cardboard. The box had a glass cover. To have this box of eggs to play with was a treat when I was small. The boys rarely allowed it. Those delicate shells, blue, and blue-green, and cream, and ground-colour, plain or mottled, in their different shapes and sizes, from big gull and pheasant to small sparrow and tit gave me a thrill of pleasure. By the time the box of eggs was bequeathed to me and I could look at it as often as I liked I no longer desired it. We had an ostrich's egg which somebody had sent us from South Africa; but that never seemed to me a proper egg-shell. It was thick. I saw a gull's egg bare on a rock, and the little gull pecking his way out of it. A woman at Llansallos once told me an amusing story of an egg. It was when I was grown up and was having a cycling holiday. I had bed and breakfast at a cottage where they kept cocks and hens and chickens. We were looking at them and my hostess, who was a cockney settled in Cornwall, said, 'Do you see that one with the red rag round his leg? That's our little Totty.' I asked why that one was special—it looked to me a scrubby bird. She said, 'She wouldn't come out of the egg, and the old hen left her. But we could feel life in the egg, so we put her in the hot ashes and she wouldn't come out. So we took her to bed with us, and I had her and she wouldn't come out and my husband had her and at last she came out, not out of the top where we'd peeled a bit of shell, but out of the back door as it were, and she looked beautiful, like a lovely little girl. . . .'

Wilfrid, or Cap'n, was the brother nearest me in age. There was only four years between us but, although we did some things together, we were never on terms of equality. He patronized me. He could do everything so much better than I, and he cared more for the ordinary things country boys rejoice in than my elder brothers. He had a passion for fishing, and it was he who best enjoyed rabbiting with my father. He looked after the ferrets. He was one of the best cricketers of the boys in the village and was always wanting us to come and field. I always felt extremely elevated if invited by Cap'n to do something with him alone. Sometimes we played truant for a

day together. Once in particular we took a basket to pick
blackberries so as to propitiate the powers when we got home
at night. It was always easy to purloin something from the
pantry when we were making a day of it. It must have been
September, a hot close day, with a Cornish sea-mist, and
spiders' webs on the furze bushes. We wandered and played,
and ate blackberries, and picked others for our basket, going
ever farther afield to find 'toppers' to make our peace-offering
more luscious and desirable. I know we reached Dodman, for I
remember the arms of Dodman Cross coming out of the mist.
We could hear the sea moving quietly below, but we could not
see it, and the gulls were in the mist. And then we saw a
wonderful sight. I suppose the sun was trying to come out and
that the rays were in some way refracted by the mist. We saw a
golden light, not brilliant, but mellow and suffused, yet with a
core of concentrated splendour—a sheaf of gilding. It was the
dull yet glowing gold of gilded missals. I have only once at any
other time seen anything comparable and that was off the
North Cliffs near Camborne when the sun was struggling to
disperse a similar mist. Yet the effulgence is not where the sun
is. On Dodman Point, on that day of my childhood, I thought
the splendour was God. Cap'n was not sure that it wasn't. We
stole home with no further eyes for 'toppers'. In Tewkesbury
Abbey I have recently seen a disk with wooden rays, one of the
emblems of the House of York which took as a symbol the sun
in glory:

> Now is the winter of our discontent
> Made glorious summer by this sun of York.

In the old days I suppose the wooden sun was gilded and
might have been a little like my sheaf of brightness. Mine was
living gold, yet it was a glory made by the sun in another
medium, not the sun himself in full shiningness.

From an early age Cap'n loved to shoot. He played with
catapults and guns of all kinds. I was never a shot, nor a
bowler, nor anything which acquired merit in Cap'n's eyes. I

could not even make a flat stone hop over the sea (we called this game ducks-and-drakes) whereas Cap'n could make a flat stone skim and skip up to thirteen times or so. The only shot I ever made was an unlucky one. Cap'n for a treat had made me an elder gun. I've forgotten quite how it was made. It involved hollowing out the pith of a piece of elder and begging from mother a stay-bone for a trigger. We used acorns or aglets (haws) for ammunition. Cap'n and I were seated on the garden wall, our legs dangling. We were fully armed, playing bandits. Along came a cyclist—nobody we knew—a rare occurrence in itself. 'Shoot!' shouted Cap'n. I shot wildly, and by some unlucky chance hit the cyclist in the ear. He got off and slanged us in good set terms. He said he was going on to Mevagissey and should send the policeman to carry us off to prison. Cap'n replied that he didn't care a cuss for any Pucky. (There had once been a policeman at Mevagissey called Pucky, so we called them all Puckies.) He shouted that we had a dog licence, and a gun licence, and nobody could do anything to us. I greatly admired the intrepid Cap'n for bringing in the dog and the gun.

We did a good deal of apple stealing. Once Stan was up one of the Trevesan trees and heard Billy Whetter muttering underneath: 'They damn boys been after my stubbets again.' But Billy was short sighted, and Stan was able to get away with full pockets a few minutes after Billy had passed. Our ethics in this matter were strange. We should never have dreamt of taking an orange from Agnes's shop, but apples were different. When I was about ten and we had left Gorran and were living at Caerhays, a girl called Alice decided with me to have a little store-place in the hollow of a tree for stolen apples. We would steal a nice lot at a time so as to reduce the chances of detection. But a boy called George found our store and stole all our apples. This act we thought most heinous, never considering that we had stolen first. My greed for apples once brought me to ignominy. The same Alice and I had been getting apples to eat in school. We had put them up our knicker-legs held in by elastic. But alas my elastic had grown weak with age and washing. As I went from my desk to get a book from the cupboard the elastic broke and plunk, plunk, plunk went my apples on the floor and were all confiscated.

My sister Susan was not despised by Cap'n because she never entered into competition. She quite firmly didn't like boys' games and said so. Whereas—apart from ratting and rabbit-shooting which I loathed—I longed to do all the things Cap'n did and to do them as well as he. When we added a special petition to our prayers mine was to shy straight, Susan's for curly hair. Not but that I should have liked curly hair too, but one shouldn't pray for too much, and to shy straight was the more important in my eyes. Nothing came of our petitions, but I cannot remember that our faith was shaken. We said our prayers night and morning as a matter of course, just as we went to church.

Our hair was a trial to us both—straggly, fine and long— Susan's almost fair; mine almost dark; but intractable, inclined to tangle, and requiring from our mother a great deal of brushing before it went into its nightly pig-tail.

Susan liked pretty clothes and wore them with an air. Clothes sent by our better-off aunts and adapted for the children looked better on her than on me. I was more at home in one of Cap'n's outgrown jerseys. Had shorts been in the fashion then for little girls I should have adored a pair, and I should have kept them up with a striped belt and snake fastener like Cap'n's; but we wore kilts with our jerseys, kilts which buttoned on to white calico bodices, clean on Mondays. On Sunday we wore 'best' dresses. Occasionally we had really new clothes made either by our mother or by dear Nellie Loten who was a dressmaker, and who would come to the house to sew. Our best dresses were sent us by London cousins. Once in winter we had little red suits with which we were delighted. They were miniature grown up suits—tiny tailored coats and skirts in which we both felt extremely dashing. We liked, too, green dresses made by my mother, trimmed with white fur. These had green velvet Dutch bonnets to match and edged with the same fur. But the glory of the bonnets vanished in our eyes when we went to spend a day with a certain Dorothy Onslow who was a visitor at Caerhays Rectory. We wore our bonnets, but Dorothy Onslow, a young woman of the world though only about Susan's age, laughed at them. I did not mind much, but Susan was stricken. She cried when she had to wear her bonnet again next Sunday. It was her turn to go to Caerhays Church, and she thought this Dorothy would be there to despise anew the out-moded and childish nature of her headgear.

Susan and Maurice were particular friends, just as Howard and I were. I did not get really to know and love my eldest brother until later when he was home for the long vacations from London. He was very proud of Susan and liked her to look nice. Once when he was at home for a holiday he took Susan with him to Mevagissey. In Farren's window there was a hat (a straw hat trimmed with a wreath of daisies) with which she fell in love. Maurice bought it for her and she came home proudly wearing it. Mother thought it not in very good taste but we considered it a hat of hats. Hats were not in my line and I pretended valiantly that I wouldn't have had a fellow to it if I could. But secretly I felt a pang or two of envy of Susan and her daisied vanity. Susan didn't in the least mind being thought vain. She laughed. But I liked to be thought a fellow who didn't care a button for clothes and, once I was out racing by field and cliff, or being a cowboy, it is true that I did not. But there were times when I looked at myself in the glass and wished that I had a less funny face; and it is said that I once cut off a lock of my front hair in a vain attempt at beautifying myself with a fringe.

My mother's hair was more beautiful than either of her little girls'. It was fine and straight like ours, but a rich dark brown and wonderfully abundant. As a rule she did it in a knot at the back of her neck, but was sometimes persuaded to make a queenly job of 'doing it on top'. Sometimes she would come into our room on Sunday mornings when she was dressing for early service with her hair down. It would just be out of its plait, long and wavy. We used to say, 'Go out with it like that, darling, it looks lovely like that. Don't put it up. Mr Sowel will like to see it like that.' And she would laugh and put it up with swift fingers, standing before our looking-glass while we bounced up and down in bed.

It was the kind of hair which never went grey except a little on the temples, though she lived to be seventy-six. And she kept the clear colour in her cheeks. When we were children this colour was delightful, making her look years younger than other people's mothers. Her grey eyes sparkled when she laughed. Perhaps her ready wit kept her young, for she was quick at repartee. She must have been hard pressed sometimes with a family of six and a house to keep with no help except for the washing and scrubbing. She saw to the family finances too, my father not being good with money. I know from what she told me later that there were often anxious times when bills were pressing. Looking back I see that we should have been in an awkward situation if any of us had had a serious illness, and this possibility, I believe, often worried her. But this ill-luck never happened. We all had influenza badly once, my father in particular, but in general we were so healthy a set that I personally never spent a whole day in bed until I was grown up and then I only had measles. I cannot remember that any of the boys except Stan ever had to stay in bed either. Stan when he was about twelve had an abscess in his face. I can remember it though I was very small. He was taken to Mevagissey to Dr Grier's surgery for it to be lanced, and when he came home with a great bandage round his face my father fainted. He could never bear the sight or thought of pain.

My mother was everybody's confidante. She had a deceptively sympathetic manner, and was a greatly loved person. Debonair is a word which would describe her for, although she listened to everybody's troubles, she could shake them more quickly out of mind than my father could. She was extraordinarily tolerant of human failings and, what is more rare, of human silliness. 'He couldn't help it', she would say; or, 'I suppose he was born like that.' She had, as though by nature and instinct, what the world chiefly lacks, the excellent gift of charity. She had by heart, 'Though I speak with the tongues of men and of angels', and saw to it that all her children had it by heart also. But her own charity came not in response to St Paul's admonition, but by grace, as though by luck. She was no laborious Christian or scholar, but a person with a great natural gifts whom life had softened rather than hardened. When I think of her I remember Selden, 'No man is the wiser for his learning . . . wit and wisdom are born with a man.' She had wit and wisdom and she added to these loving-kindness and an absence of hurry. In a strenuous life she kept an air of leisure, the secret of style.

3

DART

By the five-barred gate I hear him whinny,
Redder he is than the red plough-land;
But only his ghostly cob[1] I catch
With my ghostly hand.

I see him under a lew hedge,
Browner he is than the brown thorn;
But only a frisky shadow is munching
The shadowy corn.

Does he stop by muddy Rush-pool to drink,
Dredging it up through his lips so clever?
No! rushes and pool and pony and child
Have vanished for ever.

Next to the luck of being born in Gorran of likeable
parents and of having brothers and sisters was the
luck of having a pony. In the early days we had had a
donkey—Jack—but I cannot remember him. He would go very
fast when inclined, the boys said, but when disinclined nothing
but a carrot would budge him. I never knew Jack, but I did
know one or two donkeys—amongst them old Tommy

[1]Forelock

Stratton's. Tommy Stratton came round the village at regular intervals with cotton and thread and tape-measures, needles, thimbles, hooks and eyes, elastic, and lace trimmings for underclothes. Tommy was a little grey man with a scraggy grey beard, not very wise in the head. Rescassa boys, in particular, would tease Tommy. There was a tale that once while Tommy was in a house displaying his wares, Percy Mingo took the donkey out of the shafts and then put him in backwards, and that Tommy came out and looked at this amazing sight, scratched his head and said, 'Now what be I going to do now!' I can remember a baby donkey in the parish, soft and furry, a perfect creature.

But our pony, Dart, was still more perfect. I loved him next to the family; indeed he was really included with my brothers and sister, though my mother did not think it reverent to put him in my prayers to be blessed with the others. I would 'think' him. 'God bless father and mother and all my brothers and sisters and Dart' was how I put it in my mind. Dart had his name partly from Dartmoor, he was a Dartmoor pony, and partly from his speed when young and flighty. He was small with a puzzled yet tricksy expression, and with a long mane and tail which distinguished him from other people's ponies most of whom were docked. But my father said a pony's tail was meant to be worn long to keep off the flies in summer, and that a mane kept him warm in winter. So Dart with long mane and flowing tail and a 'cob' over his forehead by which we caught him and led him when he had no halter on was a kind of Samson among his fellows. When I was told the story of Samson whose strength was in his hair I saw him with a mane like Dart's. I used to plait Dart's mane for grand occasions and comb it until he looked as wild as a lion.

He was brown in colour and in winter his coat, unclipped, curled like a dog's. In summer the hair came out and he looked like a stable pony. He was kept in a field off Crooked Lane which my father rented for a small sum; later when we went to Caerhays Dart was kept on the Barns Hills above the cliffs between Pound and Portholland, a wild spot for him, though he seemed to enjoy it; he had a quarry to shelter in. I suppose having been brought up wild on the Moor he did not mind living wild when he grew up. He liked good oats though. I can see him now nuzzling his way into them and eating with a kind of surprised appreciation.

At first the boys rode bareback but by the time I remember there was a saddle. This was bought one day in Mevagissey after Dart had suddenly insisted on stopping to drink at Rush Pool and had flung Howard into the water. First I rode bareback, but passed to the saddle when my legs were long enough. Nothing in later life can quite make up to a child naturally inclined to ride for not having the opportunity— nothing at all. It seems a pity that country schools, since schools there must be, are not provided with a few ponies instead of expensive gymnasiums. Our pony could not have cost much; we were poor. But what delight he gave us: more than all the riches of the tin mines. He knew each of us personally. Susan did not ride, so I was the only girl he knew; but I fancied he liked me better than the boys because I was so light. Galloping was the fun. Galloping through the air with my knees gripping Dart's sides I knew sheer bliss. There is a kind of incorporation between child and pony, the child's delight in movement mingling with the pony's until they are more like one creature than two. Most of my riding was after we went to live at Caerhays, for by then my brothers were too grown-up for a small pony. For riding purposes he became mine. I would catch him on Barns Hills and ride over the cliff top, jumping the gorse bushes. I think I hardly knew then that the place was beautiful. I took it for granted. But it was very lovely with blue, green or slaty sea, black rocks, the rough road linking Pound with Portholland, the white Coastguard Hut, the cliffs leading to Dodman stretching out by the sea on the left and on the right the cliffs above West Portholland. Above the road were nine acres of rough riding for Dart and me. We would be together in all sorts of weather, rainy wind, or bright clear sun, with a dance and sparkle in the air which would make us both beside ourselves. No later sensation I have ever enjoyed has equalled riding Dart over the Barns Hills unless perhaps motor biking after I was grown up—motor biking to Cornwall from the Midlands. I would ride fast on a Velocette with the miles speeding underwheel. Platform after platform thundered by (as a child once wrote in a description of a railway journey), my eyes vaguely taking in the great tracts of changing English country till I came at last to Launceston gateway and so over Bodmin Moor and to my own place. Motor cycling and galloping give the maximum sensation of speed. I have had little journeys in aeroplanes but that does not compare in exhilarating hurtle. To swoop up hill on a motor bike is a literal kind of ecstasy because one feels caught out of the body and into the air; whereas in an aeroplane once in the air and moving levelly I felt almost sedate. It is true that I have never flown a 'plane and that makes a difference. I would not give a fig to ride pillion on a motor bike. But to ride or motor bike over Bodmin Moor in sun and shower when the Moor is spanned with successive rainbows! That is unforgettable. I have been over Bodmin Moor when the rainbows have been scarfed about me. I was moving so fast that the bows changed direction until I was a dancer with the world for stage and the rainbows for streamers.

But motor biking is cold transit. Wear what you will the cold will get in and catch you, whereas riding makes you warm and gay and bold. Both pony and bike sometimes threw me, particularly if I was showing off. Once at Caerhays I had been out to fetch Dart when Cap'n was home with one of his friends. I came riding bareback down the hill below the Barton, and spotted the two walking homeward under the sycamores. I clapped my heels against Dart and made the signal agreed between us for galloping. We came tearing on, Dart entering, I am sure, into the fun of showing these boys what the Wild West could do. They turned as they heard the hoofs behind them, I passed them flying, exhibiting my cowboy ease, when Dart saw a piece of white paper in the ditch and jumped from one side of the road to the other. Off I came, my pride hurt far more than my body, for there were the boys laughing at me, and

Dart, who always stood still when he had thrown anyone, looking with a mild demure sort of smile as though he couldn't jump over a straw. Except when in the saddle I was at the mercy of a very sudden jump sideways, having never had any proper instruction in riding. The only advice I remember came from Mr Sargent. He would say, 'Heels down! Head up! Heart high!' Certainly my heart was high, but my head and heels were not unacquainted with the dust.

Dart was always something of a shyer even in a trap. But he should never have been put between shafts; he felt and looked far happier being ridden. The trap took the life and grace out of him. It was, for one thing, too solid a trap for so small a pony, though quite pretty in itself with its dark blue wheels striped with gold. We never aspired to rubber bands on our wheels; ours were iron-banded. Some of our friends had rubber, and spanked along in silent elegance. Really for Dart we ought to have had something in the way of 'wheels'—two light wheels with a board between to sit on—which people used with donkeys. I used to admire just the right thing years after in Troon where there was an old woman who went with her donkey-wheels down to Camborne every day carrying hot pasties for the men's dinners. She would collect the pasties hot, and deliver them, I'm sure, not much cooler than when they came from the oven. For the donkey would go along at a terrific lick for a donkey. The old soul was known in Troon as the Galloping Major, and I believe it was she who said that if she lived and all was well she should be buried up Troon.

Dart could have gone more freely between wheels though I cannot quite imagine my father sitting on the 'board' like the Galloping Major. Ours was what was known as a proper turn-out. We even had trap lamps and a carriage umbrella. We needed both, for we were out in all weathers and often in the dark. Twice each Sunday my father, while we lived at Gorran, drove to Caerhays to the morning and evening services, and on Wednesday nights he went to choir practice. These were engagements which could not be cancelled by the weather. He would drive along the lanes by Treveor, down Treveor Hill to

Penver Gate, and along Penver Gate to the lower lodge of the castle. This lodge was quite near Portluney beach. He then had permission to use the castle drive which cut off Portluney Hill, one of the steepest hills around. The drive wound through the valley. We did not drive all the way up to the church, but put the pony in the stable at the Hovel. This was a little clearing in the woods where there were two enchanting cottages—the head gamekeeper's and the head gardener's. There was a stable, too, and a shed for carriages. Into this our trap was put and the pony went into the stable to enjoy the Squire's oats and to worship as best he might. We walked through a level pathway field and up two steep pathway fields past the Rectory to the little church. When I glance back the sun is shining, the bells ringing, and the people are going to church in their best clothes saying, "Morning, Mr Treneer, handsome morning'.

But one can choose a day to glance back into. Actually, though surely weather was much more seasonable then than now, there was as much wildness and wet as sunshine. And although in general the weather on that south coast is mild—with a great deal of mist and drizzle—it sometimes froze. Then Dart would go 'skittering' painfully on the ice in the ruts of the road; it crackled white. Once or twice we nearly upset. Coming up the steep nip from Hovel going home one winter night Dart refused to take the slippery road, and began backing sideways till we all but went over the bank. Straight rain we did not much mind, for we had a lined tarpaulin to go over our knees, and the great carriage umbrella over our heads. But in windy rain it was difficult to keep the umbrella up. If it were my turn to be my father's companion I would often drive while he held the umbrella over us with both hands. On winter nights in cloud the dark would be intense, the raindrops on the glass of the lamp would lessen the power of the light from the reflectors until the moving yellow cones hardly reached the hedges on either side. But going homewards there was no need to drive. Sometimes it was better to let the reins go slack and Dart would find his own way unerringly. He would arrive at our door steaming and curly; we would let the pools of water run off the tarpaulin, furl the umbrella with difficulty in the wildness of the night, and go into the warm parlour where the curtains were drawn and the lampshade cast a golden light, and the fire was leaping half way up the chimney. Being in is no real fun unless one has been out. Howard used to say as the wind howled round the house how wonderful the first man must have been who thought of making a great hollow space in the wind to shelter himself in; and I would feel unbelievably snug.

Longer drives were to St Austell, our nearest railway station—pretty nearly ten miles—when we were at Gorran; or to Grampound Road, eight miles or so, when we were at Caerhays. We used to drive to St Austell from Caerhays too, and occasionally to Truro, but this journey was very rare. It was too far for Dart. St Austell was too far really. He would do it manfully, but he would turn his head into every farm lane for the first few miles, hoping we were going to see some friend or other. His last possible hope from Caerhays was Bosinver farm lane near St Mewan. He would try to wheel into it; when that was passed he knew there was no hope for him until he reached the stable yard of the White Hart where we always put up.

After I was twelve or so and we had been living for some time at Caerhays I used to drive alone to St Austell to meet one or other of the boys coming home for a holiday. We called them the 'boys' long after they had grown up and had begun, early, an incredible number of love affairs. I would be jealous of each successive girl brought home, but I would pretend not to be, and that I despised all this love. I denounced 'lovish' books. But I still remember the pang I felt when I met Howard on the station with Mary, his latest chosen and, I knew at sight, the real one. She stood there in elegant town clothes trimmed with fur—it was the Christmas holiday—and a white beaver hat over dark curly hair such as Susan had prayed for. She seemed to have nothing in common with anyone as rough as I. I would not kiss her but shook hands stiffly and drove fast on the down-hills on the way home so as to try to frighten her. I would put my arm round Dart's neck on the cliffs and tell him he was more faithful than faithless brothers. It was I who had

always been going to make Howard's pasties and keep house
for him.

The best-remembered drives to St Austell are summer ones
when motors on our roads were still few. For years only Mr
Williams had cars. I would polish the harness and shine the
buckles and clean the trap and groom Dart till his coat
gleamed. Then I would set out on the leisurely drive. Sometimes until I reached Fair Cross I would not meet a thing in the
narrow lanes, so narrow in some places that a tangle of
meadowsweet and tufted vetch and loosestrife might brush
against the wheels, and all would be a-dapple from the hedge
trees over us. If I met a farm-cart or another horse and trap in
the narrow lanes one or the other of us had to back into a
gateway or into a bend in the hedge hollowed long ago for this
purpose. Dart hated to be 'backed' and most people would
back for me. Once a stranger would not back for Mr Bellamy,
our Rector, although he had the right of way. So he took out
his pipe and *The Western Morning News* and began to read and
smoke, declaring that personally he was in no hurry. In the end
his opponent 'backed'.

After Fair Cross the Caerhays Road joined the Truro main
road to St Austell and became much more populous. We drove
through Hewas Water, Sticker and St Mewan; there was a fair
amount of traffic even in those days and a good many tramps
on the road. Susan used to hate to be on the road alone. After
we had a bicycle between us, and she used to bicycle to St
Austell on Saturdays for music lessons, I used to ride the pony
up to Fair Cross to meet her. She would ride her bicycle just
ahead of Dart and me, and we would come frolicking along
behind.

I remember only two accidents in pony traps, one in our
own and one in my Uncle Dick's. In our own trap I was upset
once when Cap'n was driving. We were coming back together
from Portluney and had come Rescassa way—one could come
back from Portluney by Rescassa, Treveor or Tregavarras. We
were in the winding lane between Rescassa and Mount
Pleasant, a little farm place, when Cap'n, going at full trot,

drove too near a bulging piece of lower hedge. The step caught and we went clean over, pony, trap and all—Cap'n was quite dazed. The trap had been newly 'done up' and we thought we could hardly conceal the scratches. Dart wasn't hurt at all, luckily; nor were we.

The other accident was almost as far back as I can remember. My Uncle Dick was staying with us and he took my mother and me to St Austell. His was a smart turn-out, a high-wheeled trap and showy-stepping grey cob. Whether my Uncle Dick had been at the Barley Sheaf or not I don't know—it was his favourite haunt, and there was nothing to prevent a man from driving when he had had a peg. We met a bus, a kind of wagonette with a couple of horses. Just as we were meeting it something flapped in the on-coming vehicle. Uncle Dick's pony shied and the wheel of our trap somehow seemed to mount the axle of the near bus wheel. We tilted in a peculiarly horrible manner; I can feel the tilt still. For a moment we seemed suspended sideways, and then I was flung with my mother out of the trap and against the hedge. The other horses were rearing and plunging. It was a terrific to-do until they were held. We were shaken, but not much hurt. On this occasion, however, one of the pony's knees was cut. The family story goes that my father's reaction on this occasion was not to be anxious about my mother and me but to say, 'Well, I'm glad it was Dick's own pony'.

We had other animals at Gorran besides Dart, but no one came near him for true companionship and the sharing of fun. We had various cats, but they tended to wander and to come back with paws hurt by traps, a sight that made me weep. There were three dogs—Floss, a spaniel bitch (span'l was the local word), Shot, and Nipper. Nipper was a fox terrier and my favourite. He would share a piece of bread and butter like a Christian, taking small bites in his turn. Shot was bad-tempered (a span'l like Floss) and we sold him to a farmer living some distance from St Austell. He was taken to his new home in this farmer's cart, but in the night we heard him howling under our windows. Twice we tried to be quit of him, but he came back again, so we had to resign ourselves to him.

We had also cocks and hen and the pig, rabbits and ferrets and bees. Sometimes we had guinea-pigs, mice and bantams too. We would put out bread and milk for hedgehogs. Cap'n kept the ferrets and saw to the little bells for their necks which tinkled and guided the gunsmen when the ferrets 'laid up'. The slinky, yellow, cruel-looking animals were not disliked by me until I saw a stoat kill a rabbit. Stoat and ferret seemed related—I expect they are—and I was prejudiced against the ferret tribe ever after. When I was first enraptured by Blake's magnificent cry, 'Everything that lives is holy', I still kept somewhere at the back of my mind the thought of that stoat. I could not be quite carried away by the splendid assertion.

4

DOWN BEACH

> ... Lift a nostril, and you get
> The brown smell of a fishing net.
>
> Lift an eyelid, fishermen
> Are talking on the stick again,
>
> Talking in their guernseys blue
> Of what the government ought to do,
>
> And would do if they had their say
> Up the country London way. ...

Half our time was spent 'down beach'. I can see the cracks in the sun-baked path leading to Hemmick. Cap'n said these cracks meant earthquakes and that, if I stayed looking in, a big crack might gape so wide open that I should fall through and come out on the other side where my head would be to earth and my feet waggling in the air. This horrid picture would make me grasp his hand and trot along at a good pace.

Hemmick was a mile or so from the School House. We went up the lane to Four Turnings, up Treveor lane to the iron gate, over the stile, and through the fields to Trevesan farm. At

Trevesan we often picked up one or two of the Whetters, our friends; then down we went through the remaining fields either to Trevesan Bottoms or straight to Hemmick Beach. A longer way round was by Boswinger Lane; and a longer way still was by Penare. We usually went through Trevesan fields. One or other of the fields would be sown with wheat or oats or barley growing high on either side of a path so narrow that the barley whiskers would brush against our arms. We would rub nearly ripe wheat ears in our hands, blow away the chaff, and eat the sweet milky grains. I have nowhere else smelt the hot August weather as in Trevesan Bottoms. It was a mixture of bracken, grass, bramble and honeysuckle steeped in sun. And nowhere else have I seen such butterflies: blue, and sulphur, and rarer orange-tips, brown bryonites, peacocks and red admirals. They would wink their wings at us. Dragon flies would skim with wonderful gauze wings.

At the entrance to Hemmick was a little stream such as runs into most Cornish coves. It had a little wooden bridge over it, the water showing bright and clear here and there, but almost choked with watercress and great tangled growths of loosestrife, comfrey, mullein, agrimony, mugwort and rushes. We played with rushes, skinning them for the soft white pitch of which we tried to make flowers. The little stream with the rushes growing by it almost lost itself as it ran down the beach and into the sea. When I think of Hemmick of my childhood I think of tide out and bare feet. I suppose we had clothes to take off, but I don't remember them. The pebbles were hot against our feet; dried crackly seaweed, pixie purses and razor-bill shells pricked them. Jutting from the cliffs were lightning-veined blue and black slate rocks, with dolls' beaches in the angles between them. Each little beach had its own shoal of smooth pebble, its shells, its tangle of seaweed, its driftwood, its sea-gulls' feathers. Feathers and shells were our fortunes. There were shells with hinges, and fluted shells; shells fan-shaped and snail-shaped. Sometimes we found whelks and put them to our ears to hear the ghostly waves whispering. Scallops we treasured to use as bread-and-butter plates when we played tea-sets, or to make patterns on our sandpies. The colours in the shells were as clear as petal-colours: lemon, yellow, orange, rich brown and a delicate mauve and pearl. Most we rejoiced in shilly-billies as we called cowries. We treasured them not only because they were rare but because of their perfection, dove grey and white, exquisitely curled in like wheat-grains. There were more of these on Vault beach than on Hemmick. Vault was a beach shaped like a bow which lay between us and Gorran Haven.

Between the curving reefs of deposited treasure was hot sand loose to the toes, and then the firm sand, smooth or ribbed or wet, reflecting the sky, over which we ran at full tilt into the water; or we lurked in warm pools left in the hollows under the rocks, or we went with monkey hands and feet, toes and fingers curved like claws, up the ledges of blue rock spiked with limpets which ran down the beach on the right, and which separated Little Hemmick from Hemmick proper. I was half afraid of Little Hemmick. It was reached at low tide by an opening in the reef. When the tide came up it poured through this hole and cut off Little Hemmick except for the boys who could climb up the cliff where samphire grew. I never played alone in Little Hemmick. I was afraid the regular tide might play me an irregular trick, and the waves come feeling about their long sea-halls unexpectedly.

There was always something to play or do on Hemmick beach. We paddled or bathed off and on all day. I learnt to swim by what must have been a process of imitation, though I can remember the boys supporting me by keeping a hand under my chin. When we were not in the water we fished in the little pools, or went shrimping. Cap'n and Stan would go out to the farthest point to fish in deep water. Susan and I would make sand-castles and houses; we would design gardens set with shells and sherds and seaweed in order to play at visiting. Or we would go up the cliffs and sit on the soft tufts of sea-pinks, or on the trefoil we called boots-and-shoes; or we would pick ox-eye daisies to take home. There was a scent of rest-harrow.

When the boys had done fishing they would help to make a huge sand-castle fortified with stones and trenched round with deep trenches. We would then stand on it and hold the fort as the tide came in, a little froth first in the dikes, then lapping, lapping, until the dikes were down and the fort itself was attacked and washed away under us.

We must have eaten various foods on Hemmick beach, since we stayed there from morn till night. But the food I best remember is apple pasties. Each child had a whole apple pasty to himself with an initial cut into the pastry before it was baked. A for Anne, S for Susan, W for Wilfrid and so on. On either side of the initial a round piece of pastry was cut out, brown sugar and Cornish cream inserted, and the pieces of pastry put back. Sometimes we lifted these lids and licked the cream and sugar first, but the right way to eat a pasty was to hold it upright in both hands and begin at the top corner, biting on and on through mediocre and delicious alike to the last crumb of the bottom corner.

Years later I was amused to find that Celia Fiennes enjoyed a similar 'tart' when riding through St Austell in the seventeenth century.[1] Her journeys were made in the reign of William and Mary and were first undertaken, she tells us, to regain her health by variety and change of air and exercise.

As her bodily health improved she wished to occupy her mind, so she kept diaries of her travels, noting in them any information she gained from inns or from acquaintances and making, too, her own observations. She thought the keeping of these diaries would improve her mind and conversation, and she is earnest to persuade others, especially those of her own sex, to follow her example, and so rid themselves of the vapours. Moreover she ventures to think it would be good not only for ladies but for gentlemen to ride about England and describe it, increasing thus the glory and esteem of their

[1] *Through England on a Side-Saddle in the Time of William and Mary, being the Diary of Celia Fiennes*, ed. E. W. Griffiths.

country in men's minds and curing them of 'the evil itch of over-valuing foreign parts'. In the course of her rides she came to Plymouth and caught cold crossing by ferry into Cornwall. 'The sea and wind is always cold to be upon', as she remarks. It was at St Austell that she had apple pasty. She writes:

> Thence I came over the heath to St Austins which is a little market town where I lay, but their houses are like barnes up to the top of the house. Here was a very good dining-room and chamber within it and very neat country women. My landlady brought me one of the west country tarts—this was the first I met with though I had asked for them in many places in Somerset and Devonshire; it's an apple pie with custard all on the top, it's the most acceptable entertainment that could be made me. They scald their cream and milk in most parts of these counties and so it's a sort of clouted cream as we call it, with a little sugar and so put on the top of the apple pie. I was much pleased with my supper tho' not with the custom of the country which is a universal smoking, both men, women and children have all their pipes of tobacco in their mouths and so sit round the fire smoking which was not delightful to me. . . .

Celia suffered from smoke in Cornwall, sitting by turf fires, she said, till she smelt like bacon. But she is a grand companion to be with, undaunted by the rain driving fiercely on her. If one is longing for a taste of Cornwall and unable to get there one can do far worse than get up behind Celia Fiennes. She will soon show us things, from the little hardy horses, and the Cornish stiles, and the fires fed with turf or a great bush of furze, to the Mount, very fine in the broad day, with the sun shining on it. She had a heart for people too. At Truro her greatest pleasure was her landlady:

> . . . an ordinary plain woman but she was understanding in the best things as most, . . . indeed I was much pleased and edified by her conversation and pitch of soul resignation to the will of God and thankfulness that God enabled and owned her therein, was an attainment few reach that have greater advantages of learning and knowing the mind of God.

Sometimes on Hemmick beach we made a fire of drift-wood and scrowled[2] pilchards on a gridiron over the hot ashes. The sizzling pilchards of wonderful crispness and savour, though often scorched, were than placed on a great slice of bread and eaten as best one might. We must have looked a comic set of urchins seated round in a ring eating our pilchards. We were great hands at roasting potatoes in their jackets in wood ashes both on the beach and in garden bonfires. We cooked mush-rooms, too, occasionally; but they usually came rather too late in the year for our outdoor feasts. By September, the best time in Cornwall for mushrooms, we were usually made to come home for the midday meal.

Occasionally there were big picnics arranged by grown-ups. Two or three families of people and children would converge on Hemmick, all with baskets and hampers, for food was the great thing on these occasions. Our games were better by ourselves, but for pies and pasties, cakes and honey, cream and jellies, the grown-ups were invaluable. No picnic was perfect without jelly or tipsy-cake. On one occasion, when we were having a picnic with various friends, Cap'n pointed to the spread—it was all set out on a tablecloth with stones placed on the corners to keep it down—and said, 'I'd like a piece of that swish roll, please'. We teased him about that swish roll for years afterwards. For in addition to the mispronunciation he had broken the rule that it was unseemly to display too great an interest in the food. 'Do not poke about the dish', as an old book of etiquette had it, 'the eye should, of itself, be sufficient to select the choicest morsel.' But certainly that roll was very swish with cream enhancing the raspberry jam in luscious layers.

People took immense trouble over children's treats in those days. The treats were rare; usually we were left entirely to our own devices, but when the grown-ups did take a hand they were generous. And, possibly because they did not too often

[2]To toast on a gridiron over an open fire. Pilchards so cooked are called 'scrowlers'.

assume responsibility for children's entertainment, they were wonderfully tolerant. They knew they could not get back into being children themselves again, but they held the ring as it were. Some grown-ups were always known by their Christian names; others never. Will Richards who kept the blacksmith's shop at Menagwins was always Will Richards, whereas the blacksmith at Treveor never went by his Christian name; his wife called him 'Jorey'. We said Miss Sowel and Miss Rosa to the grown-up vicarage daughters; and Miss Ada and Miss Mary to the grown-up daughters of the Barley Sheaf; and Miss Pearce and Miss Annie to the Tregerrick daughters; and Miss Martin to dear Alice Martin of Highlanes. But how wonderfully good they all were to us! We seemed to be free of a village and yet private in ourselves.

Coming home from Hemmick after a day of endless summer hours was a great toil. I remember the immense steepness of the first field leading up from Hemmick, and myself hot and sticky with sand in my shoes. It looked as if one's short legs would never get to the top. We would go a little way and look back. Then at last one of the boys would give me a piggy-back, or two of them clasping wrists would make me a 'lady's chair'; or sometimes my father would come to meet us and carry me home riding on his shoulders. He would hold my legs one on either side of his neck and I would clasp his head.

Hemmick was our nearest beach, but the names of other near beaches, coves and havens also make music in my ears—Gorran Haven with Perhaver and Little Perhaver; Portluney; East and West Portholland; and Mevagissey in a class apart, for Mevagissey was a little town. My father went to Mevagissey at regular intervals to get his hair cut, and he would take a couple of children with him. Sometimes we caught Dart and went in the trap, but more often we walked. We walked past Menagwins and Penhall Gate, past the turning to Drowned Sheep's Lane, and came to a stile. This stile led through fields to Bodrugan Broad Lane and Bodrugan Hill. At the foot of Bodrugan Hill was Portmellon with a house or two springing up sheer from the rock, and another house or two in the valley. Sometimes it was impossible to cross by Portmellon; spring tide and storm would eat the road right up. From Portmellon we walked up and up until we crested Polkirt where the splendid panorama of harbour and coloured sea and coast was spread out before us. We would pause to look before going down Polkirt Hill into Mevagissey.

Mevagissey smelt. It was a compound of fish, cork, net, tar, seaweed and heady sea. The sea-gulls soared, swooped and screamed; they fought over fish; they swam with the water softly round their breasts; they walked on the quay (like gentle-men in tight boots as Dickens has it); they perched immobile as grey and white boolies[3] on rock or chimney or roof-ledge. The beautiful double harbour, the men in blue guernseys, the boats with coloured patched sails, the water green when the tide was high, the steps on bare, rain-washed rock, the ledges to walk dangerously on, the net-making, all the occupations of the harbour were a never-failing source of enchantment to us. We loitered and stared while my father was with Mr Crowle, the barber. Then he would join us, for he, too, liked to idle on the quays, exchanging a word with the men as they cut up bait or dexterously examined and disentangled from ore-weed great piles of nets. These nets would be hung over the quay-walls to dry. Often the harbour was brown with nets, and the air was brown with the smell of them.

Mevagissey town almost seemed to hang. Its houses were ingeniously cornered together so that as many as possible were over the sea. Up the containing sides of the narrow valley they mounted skyward or stood up from rocks by the quay-side. There were strange steep alleys, courts and crooked ways which would have been wonderful for hide-and-seek. But we did not play in Mevagissey. It was not our own place. There we were visitors and shy. All Mevagissey people seemed to live out of doors. Many houses were built over fish-cellars, up blue stone steps, and above these steps the women stood and talked in the open doorways. Doors were seldom shut in Mevagissey and no wonder; there was so much to see and hear and say.

[3]Big smooth stones.

Who would stick indoors when the fishing fleet was putting out or coming in? Little towns ruled by the tides have an electric undercurrent; and yet an air of unchangingness and leisure and indifference to the stranger. No eyes so secret, under their apparent openness, as Mevagissey eyes. We were nothing; Gorran people, and bookish people at that, for ever excluded from the profoundest knowledge.

Even in Gorran Haven one felt something of the same exclusion. Gorran Churchtown was as different from Gorran Haven (Garnouan) as prose from poetry. Impossible to explain it, but Gorran was not secret; Gorran Haven was. My heart still turns over when I go into Gorran Haven. No little church moves me in the same degree as its Chapel of Ease dedicated to Saint Just; for no other church in Cornwall seems more saturated with the age-long life of a fishing haven. Yet when I was a child the church had not so very long since been restored to decent use; fish had been stored in it, my father said, and the men who congregated on the 'stick' were half hostile. But it stands there above the beach; within a stone's-throw of high tide, with the wind around it, stone, grey-slated and weathered amidst the stone and grey-slated weathered houses. It is like a French Cathedral in that houses crowd right up to the door; it is not isolated by Close or graveyard. Gorran Haven people must come to the Churchtown to be buried. 'Then at last he up and died', as a dear old friend said to me once at the conclusion of a long tale of a man's life, his marriages and bankruptcies and renewals of fortune. He died at the very nick of time to spite his relatives most.

To get to Gorran Haven we went by Menagwins, past Will Richards's forge and Agnes's shop, to a stile on the right. Then we went through fields to Gorran Haven hill. Near the foot of this the road branched and one could enter the haven either by Cooks or Rice. The narrow village street dropped nearly perpendicular to the beach. Houses flush with the road or up stone steps rose on either side. Here and there was a bush of fuchsia; or Pride of Fowey grew from a wall; or ivy-leafed geranium and wall-flower flourished where no soil seemed to be.

One side of the haven was protected by cliffs; the other had a quay running out, to make an arm in the crook of which deep still water slept at high tide. At low tide the sea went out nearly to the pier-head. Boats for fishing were dragged up the beach; nets were drying on the quay, and crab-pots and lobster-pots gave out their lobsterish and crabish odour. It was from Gorran Haven that we went out fishing in Johnny Hurrel's boat. Sometimes we sailed, but I never sailed a boat by myself, though I could row with one of the heavy oars pretty early in life. At one time we had yachting caps of which we were immensely proud. Wits greeted us with remarks equivalent to Medical Davy's when he met James Joyce in similar headgear: 'Where's she moored, Commander?' Gorran Haven children spent their lives in and out of boats, but they did not bathe much. They washed their feet as we called paddling, but not many of our friends except the big boys 'stript'. When we bathed at Gorran Haven we went in from Perhaver, but Hemmick was our main bathing beach.

Along the cliffs to the west of Gorran Haven the coast swerved inwards to make Vault—now I believe usually called Bow—beach. The cliff-path by which we reached Vault from Gorran Haven must be I think one of the most flowery in the world. Celandines, primroses and violets crowded in spring; not little starved primroses, but moon-like beauties with strong pink stalks on which the delicate silken hairs lay. In due season came other flowers, sea-pinks and horse-daisies and bladder campion and honeysuckle. To stand between sea and sky with a floating scent of honeysuckle in the air, and the blossoms themselves 'revelling along in the wind' might tempt the gods to live in Gorran Haven.

Vault was not a sandy beach. The water runs like coloured light over shelly shingle through which the waves are sucked back in stormy weather with a wild music never rendered in words since the old English poets wrote the Storm Riddles and the sorrows of the Sea-Farer and the Wanderer. In Old English the rhythm washes through the consonants like the ground-swell through the shingle on Vault beach. Even in summer the sound of the waves below the Gruda was quite different from the sound on sandy Hemmick, or from the slap and gurgle by the quay-steps at Gorran Haven.

In soft sunny weather Vault kept its memory of storms stored in the flanks of Dodman which loomed up stark and terrible on the right. Dodman absorbs the blackness of winter in the same way as the sands at St Ives soak up and reflect the yellow summer light. We called the Dodman, Deadman. Deadman and Vault; the names were permanent reminders of shipwreck and distress through we used them lightly and thoughtlessly enough. Yet something in Dodman subdued us. We never played there. Perhaps even through our gaiety there penetrated some notion of the irremediable dependence of man on elements beyond his control; we knew enough of danger to know we were not self-sufficient.

Adding to the solemnity of Dodman Point was a granite cross mounted on three steps. The lettering at the foot read: 'In the firm hope of the second coming of our Lord Jesus Christ and for the encouragement of those who strive to serve Him this cross is erected.' The arms of the cross stood out against the sky, a powerful symbol. We were awed by it. My brothers had known well the Rev George Martin, a former Rector of Caerhays, who had had the cross set up on Dodman Point. I myself could remember picking up shells, a box full, for him to take to London when he left the secluded beauty of Caerhays to live, not as a Priest, but as a day-labourer in a London slum. He was one who took literally Christ's warning to the rich young ruler, 'Sell all that thou hast and give to the poor'. I have heard people say Mr Martin was mad; my father thought him the sanest person he had ever met. To my parents he was a cherished friend; to my brothers at an impressionable age an unforgettable influence. I remember him rather as a hand to hold than distinctly as a person; he would walk in the garden accommodating his pace to mine. He would come to all kinds of meals with us, but especially to breakfast after spending sometimes the night on Dodman. He is the only guest not staying in the house I ever remember coming to breakfast.

Chaucer's poor parson had much in common with this remarkable Christian teacher. Certainly it was true of him that:

> Christes lore and his apostles twelve
> He taught, but first he followed it himself.

On the other side of Dodman lay our beloved Hemmick and, beyond that, the Greeb, a smaller headland with great granite outcrops curiously disposed; a reminder of the days of the titans. Placid sheep now grazed where ancient energies had worn themselves out. The Greeb did not frighten us. We climbed among the piles, and nestled into corners, and ran over the springy turf. Except for a white-washed coastguard hut there was no sign of human habitation at the Greeb. It would have been a fitting place for a hermit; perhaps it had its holy man in the days when Roche Rock[4], a similar but far more impressive pile some fifteen or so miles inland, had its chapel and cell. There were no such remains at the Greeb; but if I fancied an anchorite's life, on the Greeb I would choose to live; though I should be frightened of brother Deadman in the dark nights. From the Greeb a coastguard path led over the wild indented cliff-top to the next cove, Portluney. We did not go to Portluney by the Greeb, that would have been to go round the church to look for the tower. We either walked by Tregavarras and down through the Park, or we drove by Treveor or by Rescassa.

Portluney beach was a kind of adjunct to Caerhays Castle. I imagine the Squire must always have included Portluney in any bird's-eye consideration of his admirable domain when he was absent from it. The castle cannot be criticized by me as a building. To me it is like a poem or a face known so long that it cannot be judged. I only know it has an incomparable situation. Sheltered by rising woods at the back, it is set in a fold with Portluney as a shining jewel to grace the unfolding. Much of Cornwall is most itself in wildest storm. Caerhays Castle is

[4]'It standeth upon the wilde moares farr from common societie.' — NORDEN.

loveliest in sunshine; it is civilized, almost Tennysonian, with gardens, and a drive, and woods where massed rhododendrons are at home, and azaleas and glorious white cherries. In spring there were sheets of pheasant's-eyes, narcissi and cultivated daffodils with princely trumpets. There were cyclamen under the cedar, and white violets.

In Trevennen woods, further back, wild daffodils grew. Trevennen is a smaller house which has not been lived in for years not, I think, since the days of the Dickersons; and Mrs Dickerson was a myth when I was ten. I was told she had given me a doll which I was fond of, dressed in pink silk. Trevennen is as beautifully situated as the castle; to have allowed it to fall into dilapidation is bitter proof of the general stupidity of our time. What hideous buildings have been reared in Cornwall while that lovely one went to ruin for lack of use. When I have read novels telling the tale of strong men who have sold their lives for houses, concentrating all their force into a single passion for possession, I have thought of Trevennen.

At Trevennen, as at the Castle, Portluney is a distant beauty for the eye to rejoice in, the very sea taking its place as part of a pattern or scheme of decoration, disposed and controlled. While we lived at Gorran I did not know Portluney well, though at six I had been fished out by the heels from its biggest shrimping pool. But when we went to Caerhays to live in Portluney, Port Bane (under the Barns Hills), Portholland and East Portholland became our nearest beaches. I grew to love Portluney then. I loved its clear brown river on the left, cutting off the most exciting part of the beach, where the caves and rocks were, from rare unenterprising strangers. The bladder seaweed popped under our feet as we scrambled about; long rows of waves broke on the beach—it was a wider bay than Hemmick. The only tamarisk trees in the neighbourhood, feathery tamarisk, grew on the hedge before the field leading to Portluney; sea holly grew among the bents in the dry sand above the tide-mark. Yet, as I look back, I see it all in an ordinary light, outside the enchantment of Hemmick. I had grown older.

5

FEASTS AND DIVERSIONS: UP THE YEAR

Mary listened with pride and joy,
'Why 'tis a handsome little boy
Been born out here in the cattle shed',
Shepherd after shepherd said.

But when across that poor threshold
Kings came bearing gifts of gold,
Mary turned trembling to hear
A soldier sharpening his spear.

Our feasts and diversions depended on the weather and the Church, the two being intertwined: Winter with Christmas; Spring with Easter; Summer with Whitsuntide and Trinity; Autumn with St Michael and All Angels and the Harvest Festival. There followed an interval for which there is no exact name on the calendar, and in which the Church celebrates All Saints and All Souls. Then the prelude to the birth again. 'Hark, a thrilling voice is sounding' was sung in church. Trevennen wood seemed to be waiting. Advent Sunday rather than January 1st is the beginning of the physical as of the Church's year.

I can remember when time was not measured at all; when it lay like an uncharted ocean about me. In the midst of this immersion I can hear a joint conclave of boys' voices with a murmur from Susan: 'Christmas will soon be here'. This Christmas shone as something immanent and splendid. I suppose actually it is not that first sudden Christmas I can remember, but all the early Christmases at Gorran united in one chain. The boys would write my notes to Santa Claus and set them afire. If, after the paper had caught and flamed and dulled and shrivelled and turned grey it flew, light as a ghost, up the chimney, I should get what I wanted.

Mother made the Christmas puddings, with children round, tasting this and that, and all of us having a stir. There would be a wonderful smell of cooking and baking in the house, loaves of saffron cake full of lemon peel and currants, a great ham boiled and a tongue to go with it. The goose would have arrived from Tregerrick. For a week or two beforehand Christmas extras would appear in Agnes's shop to tempt our pennies from us, especially we invested in coloured baubles for the tree, silver trinkets and sugar animals. I remember in particular a pink sugar mouse which I bought, and a wonderful little bell which was Cap'n's and which tinkled on the tree. There was a silver star which went on the top each year, and each year we had tiny coloured candles in little candlesticks, altogether smaller and more fairy-like than the candles on trees nowadays.

The tree always came from Cotna. On Christmas Eve we would take the wheelbarrow and be off to Cotna where our friends the Kendals lived. We brought home laurel and fir; box, bay and holly; trails of ivy from tree trunks, and rich ivy berries. Somebody carried the Christmas tree. It all seemed festive, even Shot who went with us would be spryer than usual and feel an extra stirring in his tail. We decorated the whole of the downstairs of the house; hung mistletoe over each doorway, and then we set up the tree in the dining-room and hung it

with our treasures. The tree was never in the parlour; that was
kept fresh and clean for Christmas Day. Christmas Eve was in
the dining-room because, before the lighting of the tree, would
come supper, for which even I stayed up.

A fire of wood and coal would be blazing, for we had our
own wood-pile at the back behind the traphouse, where we
sawed up our own Christmas fire with a cross-cut saw. I often
sat on the tree trunk to keep it steady on the 'horse'. The red
curtains would be drawn; the lamp lit; the table set. No room
cosier than ours on a winter night. The ham and the tongue, as
yet uncut, were placed before my mother who always carved.
She sat at the head of the table; my father at the foot; I next
him, Susan next my mother; the boys two on either side of the
table between us. With anticipatory glee we watched my
mother make a preliminary incision into the ham and cut the
first slice, pink and white, thin and curling. There is no such
ham nowadays; it was cured with sugar according to a recipe of
Granny Nott's. The tongue matched it. We feasted. Apples and
nuts followed and drinks. My father loved wine but could
rarely afford it; as a rule he was content with a little barrel of
beer on tap. But at Christmas time two bottles always arrived, a
bottle of port for my father, and a bottle of something for my
mother. My father had the temperament to be cherished by the
grape. He should have had wine oftener. I can see him now, his
blue eyes sparkling at the rare indulgence. We children had
something homemade, blackberry or sloe. My mother's
favourite drink was a little whisky or gin. She never cared for
wine of any kind, whereas a stray bottle of claret or sherry
would rejoice my father's blood.

After supper was over and the table cleared the great
moment of Christmas arrived for me. We let the fire die down a
little, put out the lamp, and lit the candles on the tree. I cannot
account for the intense pleasure these tiny points of light gave
me as they lit up the dark tree, the shining baubles, the silver
star at the top, and Cap'n's little bell. There were no gifts. We
did not tie presents to the tree nor place them at the foot. The
tree was simply for beauty. We let the candles burn half way

down and then snuffed them. The second lighting would be on Christmas night.

In the dining-room was a small organ. The lamp was now relit, and candles for my father to see the music. We gathered round and sang such things as, 'It came upon a midnight clear', 'Stars all bright are beaming', 'When the winter's sun was set', and 'There came three Ships'. My brothers had good voices; so had Susan and my mother. My father sang bass. I had an ear, and early knew the words and tunes so well that I have never forgotten them. But I had nothing to sing with. My notes like the house-martin's were inward.

After the singing, Susan and Cap'n and I went to bed to hang our stockings up. The elder boys sat up till later. But in what seemed to us the dead vast and middle of the night—actually, I am told it was late in the evening, before my parents had left the fireside—the carol singers came. Sometimes the ringers came, too, with handbells. My mother would come in with a candle to wake us. By its flickering light, sitting up in bed in the long-sleeved white nightdresses trimmed with embroidery which we wore both winter and summer, we would listen. I cannot describe the fascination of this music. The ringers would ring a carillon on the handbells and play a carol on them. Then the carol party would sing 'While shepherds watched their flocks by night', 'O come, all ye faithful', 'Angel hosts in bright array', 'Hark, the herald', and 'Christians awake'. Confused with sleep and with the lovely story of the shepherds and the baby of which I never wearied, it seemed to me that everything was happening at that moment. The shepherds were on the Greeb, the baby was in a nest of Trevesan hay, and in our sky was the great light with the angels singing, 'Glory to God in the highest, and on earth peace, good will towards men'.

So far our stockings would still be hanging limp from the wooden foot of our bed, but magically when we woke in the morning they were bulging. Parcels too big to go into the stockings were ranged near; we would seize our booty and go into the boys' room. The stockings were all filled alike—nuts in the toe, then an orange, a packet of dates, a packet of broad figs, and a packet of sweets. The sweets were of mixed kinds, some noble, some common. With these we played swaps—a superior sweet being swapped for two or even three of a plebeian variety. The formula went: 'Swap, sir?' 'Yes, sir.' 'How many, sir?' 'Three, sir.' 'No, sir.' 'Two, sir?' 'Yes, sir'—or according to the bidding. This was a great game. The hazel nuts we cracked with our teeth; but pasty nuts (brazils) had to wait for the crackers, though I can remember Cap'n cracking his in the hinge of the door. The scene must have been of the wildest confusion. I would pop into Howard's bed, Susan into Maurice's, and we would undo our parcels. One of the best presents I remember was a picture book which on each page had a kind of thick paper pulley at the bottom. One pulled this flap and the picture changed—a harvest field with corn-wagons and harvesters would become a Christmas scene with snowflakes falling on a woodcutter and his dog; three horses in a stall would change to a sow with piglets and a goose with goslings in a farmyard. There were more of these changing pictures. Another gift I especially remember is a humming top, and another a Noah's Ark with all kinds of animals. We would go out to show our parents the presents. I believed implicitly in Santa Claus when I was very little, but after a year or two the rumour reached even me that once upon a time Cap'n had heard my father drop a heavy copy of the *Arabian Nights* on his stockinged toe, and betray himself as all too human.

Christmas Day was joyful, but not holy and enchanted as Christmas Eve was. We went to church in the morning—Maurice and Howard with my father to Caerhays, and the rest of us with my mother to Gorran. All the other children were in the choir, but I never attained to this honour. I sat with my mother about six rows back from the pulpit, and in sermon time snuggled against her sealskin jacket (an old sealskin bequeathed her by my richer Aunt Sarah). I sang my best and was proud of being able to find all the places in the prayer book. Hymn tunes carry with them extraordinarily strong powers of association. 'Sing ye the songs of praise' or Mrs

Alexander's 'Once in royal David's city', with which Mr Sowel began the Christmas Day service because it was a favourite with my mother, fills me with nostalgia; it brings back Gorran Church in every detail, to the ivy wound round the slender poles which supported the oil-lamps. We did not then know the loveliest of the medieval carols which later my brother Howard was to help to popularize. By the time that we sang at home— 'The Holly and the Ivy'; 'Lully, lulla, Thou little tiny child'; 'Down in yon forest'; 'Green grow'th the holly'; 'As Joseph was a-walking'; 'The first good joy that Mary had'; 'Joseph dearest, Joseph mine'; 'Torches, torches, run with torches'—I was too old to feel quite that ecstatic pleasure I should have taken in them when I was six or seven. Some of the great hymns we had of course. My father would single out 'O come, all ye faithful', which, I can hear him saying, was magnificent; whereas he was scornful of Mr Sowel's choice of carols. He would imitate the old parson's bass notes in 'Carol, sweetly carol', and say that 'Like silver lamps in a distant shrine' was nothing but tinsel. But I think I connected the silver lamps with our candles on the tree, and I loved them. I loved another equally despised Christmas hymn beginning 'Last night I laid me down to sleep'.

I cannot remember Christmas Day dinner nearly as vividly as I remember Christmas Eve supper. I think when it came to the point I did not much like goose. In later years a couple of fowls were substituted for it; we never ran to turkey until I was nearly grown up. The pudding was chiefly valued by me because of the threepenny piece one might have with luck in one's helping. Otherwise I liked the almonds and raisins and sultanas and peel which were among its ingredients much better raw than cooked.

The best part of Christmas Day was the walk to Gruda with my father after the late midday dinner, and the coming in after it to tea in the parlour. Tea was in the parlour on Christmas Days. Commonly when my mother had tea in the parlour with a friend the children had it together in the kitchen—there were three doors, a passage and a room between. There is a story that once when mother was wielding her best silver teapot and enjoying Mrs Kendal's company the door was suddenly burst open and a very dirty Cap'n appeared saying, 'Mother, Howard's got tart; why can't I have tart? I want tart.' But on Christmas Day we were all exalted to the best room for tea, and it was a tea after our heart's desire. We did not stay up to supper on Christmas night. Our parents must have been glad to get rid of us. After tea we played games and sang, and ate almonds and muscatels and roasted chestnuts. Then we went into the dark dining-room and, for the second time, lit the candles on our tree. But the glory had departed; it was never quite the same the second night. We let the candles burn right down, and the splendour of Christmas was over. Though the decorations remained up, and the tree was left standing till Twelfth Night, all had grown ordinary.

On our Christmas cards would be pictures of snow, robins and holly; but we never had actual snow for any Christmas I can remember as a small child. At Caerhays I can remember a snowy Christmas. At Gorran we longed for but did not get it. More often the weather was curiously mild. The birds of calm brooded over two little girls sitting up in bed in their nightdresses listening entranced to the celestial music.

Epiphany was a favourite Sunday with us. We sang 'We three kings of orient are' and 'There came three kings at the break of day'. It is a wonderful story, the story of the wise men who followed a star, and found a baby, and worshipped the God in Man. A cold coming they had of it according to Mr Eliot; but to me whereas the shepherds were out in the freezing cold, blowing on their nails and stamping, the Kings came with warmth and colour and fragrance. I did not think they were ever cold.

After the Kings had gone with the various Sundays after Epiphany—we never relished 'Sundays after'—we began to think of the first primroses. Early snowdrops in Joe Nott's orchard at Trevarrick were winter-white and cold, almost unearthly. Lambstails and daisies, celandines and coltsfoot would appear. Then someone would find the first wild primrose. We did not count garden primroses as genuine 'firsts'. Often the first would be discovered at Pitts, the cliffs beyond Perhaver; or in Coosy Lane by Rescassa; or at Putt, between Trevarrick and Trevennen wood; or at Sentries, the steep fields behind Cotna, or in Polsue Lane; or by Galowras Mill, about midway between Cotna and Mevagissey. After the first primrose had been found it was surprising how the families of buds grew, and soon someone would bring in a tiny bunch for my mother to wear; then in the twinkling of an eye we would be 'going to pick primroses'. We took a basket and a little wool to tie up the bunches, and fairy-cakes to eat. These little cakes made of flour, ground rice, sugar, milk and eggs were as sacred to primrosing as apple pasties were to sunshine holidays on Hemmick beach. We would set out soon after midday dinner. Often it would be cold in the early spring, and we would walk far to gather very few flowers. We spotted the buds and remembered to look for them the next week. We picked half-opened darlings, and put in plenty of crinkled leaves to swell our bunches, and feathers of moss for a fairy edging. But when all the hosts of the primroses were out we hardly knew which to pick. I used to whisper to the glorious ones we missed that it was not that they weren't beautiful. I had some vague idea that their feelings were hurt if they were left. Cap'n said this was very silly; that any primrose would rather stay in the hedge or wood. But Susan and I did not think so. We imagined that the other primroses in the family (belonging to one particular root) would think the chosen one exalted. We used to imagine the other primroses telling the buds what happened to some of their relations. Sometimes we put wild violets with our primrose bunches. At one place in Trevennen wood white wild violets grew, scented, and greatly prized. We hunted for the unusual and rare; double primroses, and red ones coloured like polyanthus, and branching primroses growing cowslip-wise from a thick central stalk. Now I think single flowers lovelier than double; they are more clear and delicate in shape. But I can still see in my mind's eye a wonderful double primrose my father once found. And the

richly glowing double daffodils (we called them Lent lilies)
which grew in orchards and in the steep field below Caerhays
Rectory have to me the very essence and virtue of those who
come before the swallow dares. The little single Lent lilies
which grew in Trevennen wood did not dance; often they
shivered. The double ones had dancing hearts.

All through Lent the primroses grew stronger and more fair
and numerous. Even the earliest Easter would find us with
plenty to decorate the Church. I loved the season of Lent out
of doors. The medieval poet exactly catches what we felt,
though I did not know it then:

> Lenten is come with love to toune,
> With blosmen and with briddes roune,
> That al this blisse bryngeth,
> Dayes-eyes in this dales,
> Notes suete of nyhtegales;
> Uch foul song singeth.

We had no nightingales; the first nightingale I heard was in
Shakespeare's country by Bearley Bushes. But we shared this
sense of renewal and joy in the spring because, like the
medieval poet, we experienced unmitigated the darkness of
winter. There were only two out-door lights in Gorran and
Caerhays parishes. These were the lamps over the church
porches to guide the congregation along the path.

Lent, in church, I found fearfully gloomy. Shrove Tuesday
was a good day, nearly always fine weather. But Shrove
Tuesday was not celebrated in our house as it was in Gorran
Haven. In Gorran Haven all the children ate limpets and
winkles (we said rinkles) on Shrove Tuesday. But my mother
drew the line at cooking rinkles or limpets. She hated the smell
she said. Cap'n sometimes cooked some over a little fire out of
doors in a treacle tin, and purloined a little vinegar, salt and
pepper so that we should not be behind the rest of our world.
But perhaps our mother's disapproval damped our ardour.
Shrove Tuesday was not a great day with us once the pancakes
were eaten. My mother did rise to pancakes.

Ash Wednesday promised well. It began something. My mother went to Early Service and we went to church at night. But 'Forty days and forty nights' was a very melancholy hymn. I was sad that Christ should be wandering in the wilderness and fasting. We went once a week to the little church at Gorran Haven in Lent. I liked this because of the walk down and back with Miss Mary of the Barley Sheaf or with my godmother, Miss Sowel. But once, alas, I disgraced myself. I was next my chosen friend, Phyllis Kendal. The vicar said, 'Let us pray'. I had heard it before a thousand times. But as we prepared to kneel Phyllis whispered in my ear, 'And so we will'. This for some reason I found exquisitely funny. I shook the kneeler with my suppressed mirth and throughout the service, when my mind went back to Phyllis's words, I was subject to relapse. The only hymn which broke the mournfulness of Lent was 'Christian, dost thou see them!'

> Christian, dost thou see them
> On the Holy ground,
> How the troops of Midian
> Prowl and prowl around?
>
> Christian, up and smite them,
> Counting gain but loss;
> Smite them by the merit
> Of the holy Cross.

We all particularly relished 'prowl and prowl'. We would prowl round the kitchen table in imitation and then swoop on a bun. It was grand, too, to be invited in the midst of the passive suffering of Lent to smite the foe. I did not know who the troops of Midian were, but certainly I up and smote them with such poor voice as I had.

Palm Sunday came with its brief success, the shouting and the glory. 'Ride on, ride on, in Majesty' was one of our very favourite hymns. 'All glory, laud and honour' was second to it. We followed the events of Holy Week to the Agony in the Garden, the Crucifixion, and the placing of the Body in the sealed tomb. A child is, I think, in some sort protected from the realization of the torture of the Crucifixion. It was not until I was grown up that the most profoundly moving words ever spoken: 'My God, my God, why hast Thou forsaken me' became truly significant in my mind. As a child it was the failure of the human relationship between St Peter and Jesus which made me cry: 'And the Lord turned and looked upon Peter'. Peter is, I suppose, naturally a sympathetic character to a child; his desertion something which one longs to avert. Surely it will not be Peter who will say he never knew his friend.

As a child I never attended a three hours' service on Good Friday. On Good Friday afternoon we went to pick primroses for the Easter decorations, on Saturday we decorated, and then came Easter Sunday. One was supposed to wear something new on Easter Sunday, even if it were only a new hair-ribbon; otherwise a little bird would come and leave droppings on one's hat. I can remember my Aunt Eliza sending my mother a new hat for Easter Sunday so that this fate might be averted. We thought it a most becoming hat, and cheered my mother on to wear it; but she thought it too near the height of fashion. She didn't 'feel comfortable in it'. She loved old clothes, in this reversing the usual position between husband and wife. For my father liked a new spring suiting. The tradition at Gorran was that children should go without coats on Easter Sunday morning. There was dismay if my mother considered it too cold and refused permission to shed winter husks and show our frocks. We were sure other children's mothers would let them come without coats. And it is true that most of them did unless it actually rained. The physical warmth of childhood seemed inexhaustible. I hardly remember feeling cold. We hated coats and hats. As for gloves we never wore them except on Sundays. Elevated into wearing a pair of white cottons for Miss Rosa Sowel's wedding I am reported to have said loudly in church, 'Take off gloves, hands can't see'. There is a muffled blindness in wearing gloves, I still think. I dimly remember Miss Rosa's wedding, a great affair. Susan had a new white frock for it, and I had one of Susan's old ones hemmed up. It shows how self-centred we were. I can see our frocks but not Miss Rosa's; yet I loved Miss Rosa, who made me daisy and buttercup chains and played endless games with me on the Vicarage lawn. She would let me crawl under the net to pick and eat the old parson's red and white currants or raspberries. He would say, 'Oh, oh, oh, who is that white blackbird under my raspberry net!'.

He was a very very old man with a long white beard, and a fussy staccato manner; very absent-minded. I did not like him much, for I never knew what he would do or say when I met him. From my present mature viewpoint I can see that he was facetious with children and that I, like all small children, was wounded in my dignity by this form of condescension. With my brothers he managed better. When well over eighty he got up at half past five in the morning to wish luck to my brother Stan who was going up to London for a civil service examination. Howard was driving the examinee in the trap to St Austell station. As they were driving along Old Vicarage Lane they heard a voice shouting, 'Stop them, Billy, stop them'. Billy Tregilgas came panting through the plantation to intercept them, and behind him came the old parson with his beard in the wind to give his favourite his blessing. Stan passed his examination and was well up on the list too—although that trip to London was the first time he had been out of Cornwall, and he had been coached by no one but my father.

Easter Sunday morning was the old parson's great day. He looked magnificently pastoral. The sun would be shining and the birds singing outside the church. 'Jesus Christ is risen today', we sang. The glorious affirmation, the fine tune, the rising sap, and the jubilant birds—there was no doubt at all about it. Death and winter had been vanquished. 'The strife is o'er, the battle done; Alleluia!' There was another hymn I liked, but I have forgotten how it began. One verse of it was:

> And now the time of singing
> Is come for every bird;

>And over all the country
>The turtle dove is heard:
>
>The fig her green fruit ripens,
>The vines are in their bloom;
>Arise and smell their fragrance,
>My love, my fair one, come!

Best of all at Easter I think I liked and still like the story of Mary meeting Jesus in the garden. What other narrative approaches it?

The first day of the week cometh Mary Magdalene early, when it was yet dark, unto the sepulchre, and seeth the stone taken away from the sepulchre. Then she runneth, and cometh to Simon Peter, and to the other disciple whom Jesus loved, and saith unto them, They have taken away the Lord out of the sepulchre, and we know not where they have laid him.

'Peter therefore went forth, and that other disciple, and came to the sepulchre. So they ran both together: and the other disciple did outrun Peter, and came first to the sepulchre. And he stooping down, and looking in, saw the linen clothes lying; yet went he not in.

'Then cometh Simon Peter following him, and went into the sepulchre, and seeth the linen clothes lie, and the napkin, that was about his head, not lying with the linen clothes, but wrapped together in a place by itself. Then went in also that other disciple which came first to the sepulchre, and he saw, and believed. For as yet they knew not the scripture, that he must rise again from the dead.

'Then the disciples went away again unto their own home.

'But Mary stood without at the sepulchre weeping: and as she wept, she stooped down, and looked into the sepulchre, and seeth two angels in white sitting, the one at the head, and the other at the feet, where the body of Jesus had lain.

'And they say unto her, Woman, why weepest thou? She saith unto them, Because they have taken away my Lord, and I know not where they have laid him. And when she had thus said, she turned herself back, and saw Jesus standing, and knew not that it was Jesus.

'Jesus saith unto her, Woman, why weepest thou? Whom seekest thou? She, supposing him to be the gardener, saith unto him, Sir, if thou have borne him hence, tell me where thou hast

laid him, and I will take him away. Jesus saith unto her, Mary!
She turned herself, and saith unto him, Rabboni! which is to say,
Master!

In the week after Easter came Gorran Feast. It sounded in
anticipation better than it was. We would be running to the first
gate in Menagwins Lane to look down on the village to see if
the first 'standing' had come. In my brothers' young days
Gorran Feast had been far more important than in mine; in my
mother's day more important still. By the time I remember it, it
had dwindled to about two or three standings. I remember Mrs
Hooper, a rosy cheeked, roundabout little woman, with grey
hair in a bun. Her standing displayed long sticks of rock, huge
oranges (oranges were at their sweetest at about Gorran Feast
time), liquorice—we made liquorice-water and kept our bottles
in the dark for a short spell because we thought the liquid went
the blacker for it—gingerbreads, jaw-puller, comfits, dolly-day-
dreams, mixed nuts, and all kinds of mixed sweets. These were
grand material for the game of 'Swap, sir!' Jimmy Ivy's
standing is the other I remember. It sold toys, and strings of
beads, and beads in boxes with glass tops, and toy watches. I
bought a toy watch for which I paid threepence; but Cap'n
took it to pieces to see how it was made. Only one year did
Gorran Feast really make an impression on us and that was
when the swing-boats came. There were plenty of ordinary
swings in Gorran. We had a swing ourselves, and nearly all our
friends had swings in their gardens or barns. But these swings
were glorified beyond recognition. I had my first swing with
Howard. We sat opposite one another and crossed ropes. These
ropes looked like the ropes of church bells and had the same
red hand-grips to keep the ropes from galling the hands.
Howard pulled gently at first; and I pulled back. We swung. He
pulled a little harder, I pulled a little harder; we swung higher.
Then we warmed up to it as he saw I was not frightened. Up I
went like a bird, my head low and my feet pointing skyward;
then down, down with the bottom seeming to drop out of my
world. Down, down, and then up, my head high now and feet
earthwards. Higher and higher, the wind lifting my long hair as

I flew. I was beside myself with pleasure. When the showman ran the plank under us to stop the swing-boat I did nothing but beg for more swings—I having spent all my pennies on dolly-day-dreams (little sweets much affected by Susan and me because we got so many for the money) and a Jimmy Ivy watch. I begged swings from my brothers and shamelessly from others not my kin. I know dear Noah Loten gave me a swing. I think never, except possibly when I first heard Sammy Rowe's string band, had I been so much excited as by those swing-boats.

Our own swing was hung from a tree at the bottom of the garden. But after the swing-boats at Gorran Feast we tried to fix up a kind of swing-boat in the wash-house. Instead of cross-ropes and two people in the boat, we had one person in the boat pulling himself by a rope (with a blue sash wound round for a hand-grip in imitation of the grandeur of the swing-boat grips) fastened to a staple in the wall. The boys despised this home-made boat once they had contrived it, but Susan and I used it a great deal until the craze died down. We had at the same time a craze for what we called cork-work, though it was done not with a cork but an empty cotton reel. We would take a reel down to John Parnel who had a cobbler's shop in a little wooden house on the Plosh in Churchtown. John Parnel made and mended our shoes; he was very obliging and nice to children. He was a little bent old lame man. He would put the sprigs in our reel. We would then proceed to 'Ollie's'—Miss Olive Oliver's shop—and buy ha'porths of wool of different gay colours. Susan would then start the cork-work. I have forgotten how we did it but it involved a hairpin. We always meant to make a lamp mat of it for my mother, but never succeeded. The idea was that one of us would do a little cork-work while the other had a swing, and so on alternately. We timed it so that one had to bring a colour down through the reel before one could claim a swing. Although usually good-tempered with each other we nearly always ended in a furious quarrel over this game. We would accuse each other of not doing a fair amount of cork-work before claiming the swing-boat. In the end we would fight each other as like as not, not formally like the boys, but making for each other's hair to pull. Our anger was soon over though. However 'vexed', we could not do without each other for long; and after a fight and a separation we would soon be only too ready to 'make it up'. Soon, entwined on the old couch in the dining-room, we would forget the cork-work and the swing, and Susan would read my favourite Grimm's fairy tale, *Under the Juniper Tree* or *The Twelve Dancing Princesses*.

From Gorran Feast to Midsummer was a golden time. When the sap was rising Cap'n would make me a sycamore whistle. Sycamore was the only tree I noticed much, I suppose because of the beautiful colour of the buds and early shoots, pink and red and bronze, and the fan-like opening of the crinkled leaves. Sycamore and ferns; the curled hart's tongues with downy backs, the bracken on the Greeb which opened later. Nothing is more beautifully packed for the unfolding than bracken. How tender the tips were, curled in like babies' fingers!

Sycamore whistles could only be made when the sap was rising. I never had patience to make one for myself, but the boys made them. They would cut a length of sycamore shoot and ring two or three inches of the new skin—too delicate to be called bark—tap in with the handles of their penknives till it slipt off whole. Then they shaped the lip of the pipe, replaced the circular tube of skin, and the whistle would whistle if blown. I expect there was more to it than this, or why could I not make a whistle for myself? However, we whistled, and the birds sang—such larks there were—and the cuckoos cuckooed, and the flowers went in their great procession: from celandines to primroses and violets; from primroses and violets to bluebells and cuckoo-flowers with spotted leaves; from blackthorn to real may.

With the may came the Ascension and Whitsuntide. May was the name we gave to hawthorn. We had already nibbled the young leaves, green-cheese we called them, as they were unfolding from the buds on our thorn hedge; in autumn we should bite the haws and find them insipid. But with the flowers no fault could be found. We discovered quite soon in the game of putting flowers into families that they were akin to the rose. My mother would not have may in the house. Susan and I decorated for May Day and had junket and cream for 'lember'. We got out very early and decorated with what flowers we could find, and with fresh green boughs, before my mother was up. Although she must have heard us moving she always pretended great surprise when she came down and found the house a bower. Yes, she had completely forgotten it was May Day; no, we must have gone out like mice; never a sound had she heard; it was a lovely surprise and we were darlings.

Ascension Day came, a rather shorn festival, in spite of 'Hail the day that sees Him rise', for it was a week-day. But Whitsuntide, ten days later, was, next to Christmas Eve, my favourite day of the year. Would it be fine and warm enough for our white dresses? Otherwise there would again be trouble. Our friends would certainly wear their white dresses and straw hats unless it poured. Sometimes it was too early in the year, but Whitsuntides then were surely fine as a rule, or do I gild the weather? We sang 'Come, Holy Ghost, our souls inspire', 'Come, thou Holy Spirit, come' and 'Our blest Redeemer'. The first was our favourite, but I had been taught the alto of 'Our Blest Redeemer'. Such voice as I had was low and it was delightful to me to be able to sing something without conking out on the top notes. I liked the Whitsuntide psalm, 'There go the ships and there is that Leviathan'—Mevagissey fishing fleet and *The Queen of the Fal* being chased by something akin to Jonah's whale.

Trinity Sunday was high summer. I once had a new blue frock on Trinity Sunday, but only once. Quite new frocks were extremely rare in my experience; Susan's frocks and Cap'n's jerseys descended to me. My new blue frock is inextricably mingled with 'Holy, holy, holy, Lord God Almighty'. Mingled with it too are the blue of the sky, and the blue sea at Hemmick with its glancing plates of light. The saints were casting down their golden crowns around that glassy sea. Loitering along the lanes and fields to Horse Pool after church on Whitsunday and Trinity was very delightful. Stitchwort would be out with little seed-cases to snap; pink campion; and the first wild white roses; sweet briar roses came later. We would hear Dart trotting in the distance and then we would meet my father and whoever had been to Caerhays with him, and so home to the first gooseberry tart and cream. Cream came from Agnes's in those days, lying yellow as butter in a shallow wide glass dish.

Trinity is a festival of early June. The medieval poet wrote:

> How lovesome thou art in May,
> Thou wide, wide earth.

Even more lovesome is the earth in June—leafy June. If a person in possession of all his senses had the luck to live on earth only a single Cornish June he would, one would have thought, be thankful. What blaze of buttercups showering golden pollen on our shoes—buttercups topped with red sorrel; what waving silken grass; what dapple of light and shade through the leaves, what tangle of sweet briar in Treveor Hill. During the Sundays after Trinity, as the summer nights lengthened, my mother and Mrs Kendal would walk for a longer and longer time after church in Cotna Lane. The two had been school friends and still loved each other. The Kendal children were our friends. There were nine of them: William, Janie, Lilian, Kathleen, Sybil, Jack, Phyllis, Joan and Edward. Jack and Phyllis were nearest in age to me. My mother would walk to Cotna with Mrs Kendal, Mrs Kendal would walk back with my mother, my mother would walk back with Mrs Kendal . . . talking, talking they would go, while we disported ourselves round and about, anxious not to call attention to the fading light. Twilight is exciting even to machines; a motor bike will run with more zest as the light runs out. How much more exciting is it to children!

Hay harvest came. We went with our friends to different farms to watch and hinder rather than to help. The farmers were tolerant of children. Except for the Lawrys they all had children of their own. One or two of 'master's children' only swelled the rout. We watched the hay-cutter, played in the loose hay and round the cocks, rode in the empty wagons, and sometimes, with luck, on the top of a load. This was the greatest treat. We carried 'croust' to the workers, and had a little croust ourselves. At home we played at making hay in the garden. Our garden was by no means well kept. We let the grass get extra high in order to cut it and make hay. We raked and tossed and the scent of the sweet grass penetrated the house. 'Croust' was provided by my mother—cake and ginger pop, or herbie beer, or sherbet water. We carried our hay in the wheelbarrow, and made our rick on the three-cornered piece by the traphouse.

Hay harvest was often not in full swing until July, that is until after the longest day of the year. But it is with June I chiefly associate it; with the climax of the year's progression. In the rhythm of rise and fall which governs all things it is the rise which exhilarates. To mount, to reach the maximum height, to pause for an infinitesimal moment before the inevitable decline! I have heard that the soul can only float out of the body with the ebbing tide. The fall of the year, too, seems appropriate for a flitting. Who could die in the up-swing from January to June? In childhood one feels immortal all the year round; but even then June was, in some indefinable way, the highest pitch of the swing-boat.

6

FEASTS AND DIVERSIONS: GOING DOWN

I love my love in June for then
She wears a veil embroidered over
With sea-pink, columbine and clover.

I love my love in late September,
In the mellow sunshine when
Butterflies will illumine,

Like capitals on ancient scroll,
Her russet gown which must remember
Sobriety towards December.

I love my love in winter chill,
When the high winds hold festival
And furious the waves rise and roll.

But most I love my love in Spring,
When my bare feet upon the hill
Tread delicately the vernal squill,

And all the larks to heaven sing
This song my heart is carolling.

—*To Cornwall in all Weathers*

I cannot assign a month to Mevagissey regatta and Veryan show; they were, I think, in July or August. Other places had regattas but Mevagissey was the best as far as we were concerned—Fowey regatta was out of range for Dart. In the same way Veryan was the best of the flower shows. I remember Veryan show even more vividly than Mevagissey regatta. From Caerhays we went to the show year after year. It is connected in my mind with mazzards—little black cherries. At Caerhays we not only went to the show, but exhibited; though a third prize for sweet peas was all we ever won. Our gardening was too chancy for fatness.

A big disappointment to me in our first year at Caerhays was my failure in the children's wild flower competition. This prize I had marked down as my own. In the children's section of the printed list of desirable exhibits there was a notice which read something like this: 'A prize is offered for the best arranged bunch of wild flowers of any single variety.'

I was excited, for I fancied myself at arranging flowers. Susan who was more artistic could not compete; she was over twelve. I decided on a flower in which I greatly delighted at the time, partly because I had never noticed it growing round Gorran. The flower was centuary which grew on the Barns Hills. On stiff-looking erect stems the little flowers grew, stems very formally branched near the top, so that the petals, raying from fairy-like throats, were individually spaced and free. I thought their elegance would seduce any judge. I put only a few stems in my vase; I had an idea of displaying the separate geometry and colour of each of my chosen ones. I dreamt of that prize, and of seeing my flowers in the tent, more curiously lovely than all the others. The day arrived. My flowers had gone over with the other exhibits from Caerhays. As we were going to the show I gave the harness a special rub, and Dart a special grooming. I polished his hoofs with shoe polish. It used to be an extraordinarily lovely drive from Caerhays to Veryan. We went down the first and second hills beyond Caerhays Church, and turned left to Heras Water, where a clear stream ran across the road. Through the stream Dart had to wade; I was anxious for his polished hoofs. By the side of that stream, and all the way up the hill to Trevilveth, the most beautiful lacy ferns grew, and a delicately veined cranesbill, and a sorrel we called hare's meat. Veryan itself was a charming village much bigger than Caerhays, and more rural and leafy than Gorran. Susan and I wished we could live in one of the little round houses, each with its cross to scare the devil. There were four round houses; two and two they stood on either side of the road, guarding the entrances to Veryan. The show was held in a large field. A brass band would be playing fit to call the dead out of their graves for the dancing. Certainly such music would stir my poor scaffolding of bones. I was longing to know if I had a prize; but on the principle of 'Never seek to tell thy love', one aspect of which children understand so well, I said nothing. I wanted to go to the tent for myself and see my centuary honoured. But before we reached the tent-opening my friend, Alice Blandford, ran up and said, 'You haven't got no prize at all. Jimmy Martin's got 'un. Your bunch do look some funny'. The pang I felt at a failure in my first public examination was as nothing to the pang I felt for that centuary. I left my father and ran with Alice towards the tent. We squirmed our way through the crowd to the table where the children's exhibits were. The prize had rightly gone to Jimmy Martin's bowl of spear thistles. Thistles! I had despised them except for their silken down. Yet I have never seen any wild flowers look grander than those great fighting thistles. And far away in a corner, remote from the central splendour, was my centuary. I had never noticed that centuary closed its petals up in the absence of the sun. I had picked my bunch in bright sunlight; now it looked some funny as Alice had said. The next year in imitation of the bold democratic choice of Jimmy Martin I tried horse-daisies, but Jimmy won the prize with plumes of meadow-sweet. The year after that we were both too old to compete. Clever Jimmy Martin—his mother called him James—he became a gardener like his father, and played with flowers all his life. Very grand prizes have come his way since those days.

In addition to flowers in the tent there were fatted vegetables and fruits. We cared little for these. We made for the live stock. In their pens and hutches rabbits and puppies, and even cocks and hens had a smart strange appearance. It was like meeting well-known relatives in their best clothes at a party. We would stare in at the bulls. 'Bulls that walk the pastures in kingly-flashing coats' were fearful in our eyes. I never in my life saw a bull at large without making for the nearest hedge. 'To be horned' was our equivalent to being bombed. 'He'll horn ee', folk would say to frighten us when a bull was in the mowy. At the show we could look at the necks of the Red Devons from safe ground.

In the afternoon there was a horse-show and bicycle racing. Cart-horses, their manes and tails wonderfully tricked out, their coats sleek in the sun, would pace obediently but proudly. They seemed to restrain the power in their deliberate heavy stepping simply to indulge the little men who led them. Their submission was as though voluntary and not shameful, for they had strength to cast off any yoke if they liked to exert it. Their strength made them sure of themselves. Cart-horses never show off. They are the equivalent in horse-life to Conrad's favourite type of hero in human kind, creatures of great integrity who will do their duty in spite of the fury of the elements, and the wiles of gods and women. The high-stepping carriage horses who went round the ring looked self-conscious and flashy in comparison, but I loved them.

Best of all was the jumping. I have never had the luck to see much horse-racing, but it is an intelligible passion. There is an interesting short story by D. H. Lawrence called 'The Rocking Horse Winner', one of the little moralities he enjoyed writing. It is the story of a child living in a house which whispered, 'There must be more money, there must be more money'. His mother said luck was better than fortune. He knew that his rocking horse could take him to where there was luck (lucre) for his mother if he forced it. So he would sit on his rocking horse charging wildly until he reached Luck and a certain intuition as to which horse would win in a race. 'Sansovino' he would find at the end of his journey; Sansovino; Daffodil, Lively Spark. Sometimes he would ride and never reach Luck. He would not be sure. Then he and Basset, the young gardener enthusiast, would go lightly; but when he knew, when he was *sure*, they would go strong, they would go for all they were worth. The story ends with the child being interrupted by his mother in the ritual of the furious mad riding of the rocking horse. But he had reached Luck. He dies in a brain fever, but not until he has whispered 'Malabar' and made other people's fortunes by his own death.

There was no proper horse-racing at Veryan show, but the bicycle racing had, in its small way, the thrill which has been exploited by the flicks. Set one person or animal chasing or racing another and we are haled out of ourselves into the pursuit. I was watching John Gielgud's production of *Macbeth* in the gods of a theatre not long ago. Two small boys were near me. They stood up and watched the final mêlée. Macbeth went out left; Macduff came in right as though in hot pursuit, chasing him. 'That way, mister', the smaller boy yelled. It was the first time in the play he had been utterly caught away into the performance.

In August and September we often tended to set out with baskets and bags for picking this and that. I did not much like the picking, but I enjoyed the accessories. It has been suggested to me that in order to inculcate the virtues of steadiness and patience one might be put through a course of fruit-picking, beginning with 'urts'. There were no urts (whortleberries) near us. We picked mushrooms, blackberries, sloes and nuts. I liked mushrooming best of all, the basket filled so quickly, and the mushrooms seemed to grow like magic. They were an incentive, too, to get out early and taste the freshness of the day. The dewy twinklings and mares' tails would be like watering-cans, drenching our legs, as we made our way over fields to the good places. Rainy heat is the weather for mushrooms, soft warm rain, and enough heat to soak into fields unbroken by the plough and grazed by horses. Land need not be in good heart to produce mushrooms; indeed the more heartless the land the better the crop. 'I spy a mushroom' was the cry of the first person to strike a silken button or spreading umbrella. Sometimes we would be deceived and go haring after toadstools or puffballs. We made no experiments in cooking fungi. Mushrooms we knew and these we stuck to. We liked them with delicate pink gills, but we picked the older ones too, those with gills grown dark, almost black. Sometimes when we had miscalculated the weather, or were too early in the year, we would walk far and find nothing. But in the really fruitful season we would pile baskets high with mushrooms of all sizes; our fingers stained and smelling of mushrooms. We would try to get home in time to have fried mushrooms with our bacon for breakfast. I liked skinning them; the skin came off in fascinating strips, leaving the mushrooms soft white like shorn lambs with pink showing through the white.

Blackberrying was, as often as not, a whole day's business. In our oldest clothes we set out with a big basket or two, together with a cup or mugs or jugs for each picker. Agnes's Moors, which lay between us and Gorran Haven, grew wonderful big blackberries, for the moors were damp and reedy and the bushes big. The juiciest looking berries always seemed to be almost inaccessible, tempting us to press on regardless of scratches and rents. I never felt the scratches until afterwards, when seeing them made me feel them. In the tangled thickets would be great white woodbine cups, white even to the anthers and stigma; sprays of honeysuckle; late bramble flowers like painted ragged girls; and the green, red, and ripe blackberries. The members of the party would spread out, each trying to find a special pocket for himself, and fill his cup with big berries to make the tide in the basket mount high as the filled cups were poured into it. Sometimes we went as far as Dodman. But it was in the valleys, the 'bottoms' as we say in Cornwall, that the sensuous blackberry spell was strongest. There Pan was near. The pickers with purple-stained mouths and fingers were his subjects. So were the bullocks who sometimes went half mad in the heat, and careered wildly, forgetting all their placid cud-chewing. We would say they had the wop, and sometimes had an attack of something resembling the wop ourselves. Perhaps it was due to the hornets or the sun; I have heard the gorse-pods pop in the heat.

In September we picked sloes and bullums (bullaces) for our wine. Doughty mentions as a faery drink, 'last year's bullaces laid up in honey'; smoothly intoxicating it sounds, gliding down the gullet. We laid our bullaces up in sugar. We never managed to secure any gin. This making of sloe wine was a children's affair though my mother provided us with sugar and bottles. Sloes looked so tempting with the purple-misty bloom on them that I always tried to eat one or two and rasped my teeth. As one bites through the skin to the ungenerous green pulp, which scantily covers a stone too big for it, the watering mouth is dried up with bitterness. Thorns and the harsh fruit match one another. But how lovely the blossom is, appearing before the leaves, close to the blackthorn; life breaking in full flush from what seems winter-dead! It is the right spring blossom for the Cornish cliffs, reinforcing a contrast already existing. The virtue of all flowers, their ardent fragility, is heightened by the stubbornness from which they spring.

Nutting was the most hilarious of all our expeditions, partly because it happened only once. We went blackberrying and mushrooming many times in a season, but our store of nuts usually depended on one Saturday's picking in Scotland wood. Grown-ups went nutting with us. We carried crooked sticks and bags, and went by Menagwins, Churchtown, Cotna Lane, Cotna, Sentries and so into Scotland wood with its deep rutty lane lined with hazels. As we walked bits of stick crackled and fallen leaves rustled under foot. Rich dyes coloured the bramble and the rose. Here was the birds' harvest of berries, aglets, and scarlet rose-hips, strings of bryony, bright jack-in-the-pulpit, the luscious looking red fruits of the honeysuckle and woody-nightshade. We picked up beech nuts to string together for necklaces, and smooth acorns and oakers to play with. We climbed and swung on the trees. But most of our attention was given to the hazels on which the nuts grew in clusters, each nut in a cup with a frilled edging. When nuts slipped the cup easily they were ripe. The texture of the hazel shell takes colour smoothly; its green and fawn have given a name to one of the colours in the human eye. We have not a beech or lime or an oaken eye; only hazel. Ripe nuts were riper in colour. It is a pity we do not plant more hazel. Too many conifers are being planted in Cornwall because of their quick growth. But hazel, beech and birch; ash, oak, elm, thorn, holly and sycamore are more suitable to our Roseland. Larch plantations with their spring tufts of light green and their rose-coloured fresh cones fit the landscape better than fir and pine which are dour and Scotch. Spruce is unfitting.

Sweet chestnuts grew moderately well. We picked up our chestnuts in the castle drive and usually got a fair number. But they did not grow large and lusty like the horse chestnuts, for they were often blown down before the nuts were ripe. As they came out of their cosy lined home they looked flatish and puny, in white and brown with silky hairs at the tip, as though not properly out of their milk-teeth; whereas the horse chestnuts burst out of their more commonplace cases red-brown, plump and handsome. We valued horse-chestnuts as much if not more than the sweet ones. Of them we made dolls' furniture, particularly chairs. We stuck in four stout pins for legs and three pins for a back; the chestnut made the seat. Then we wound coloured wool round the pin-legs and wove wool through the three pins at the back. Thus in a short time a set of elegant mahogany chairs could be completed. But more valuable still were horse-chestnuts for conkers. Some conkers, polished and hardened, and preserved with care, became the real old men of the tribe, absolute king conkers; till they, after proving themselves invincible in a whole village of inferior conkers, went the way of all tyrants and were split by some young strong upstart.

By September the village was ready to praise God for the harvest. Sometimes we praised Him too soon and sang that all was safely gathered in before it was. But we knew that God would understand. No need to explain to Him that the day for the harvest festival had been fixed some weeks ago and that though Mr Kendal, Mr Nott, Mr Mitchel, Mr Lawry and Mr Lanyon had done their best, what with the weather and one thing and another, they hadn't quite managed. A few shocks still out. I have no patience with the modern scrupulous revisers of hymns who limit God's benevolent understanding of His people's little exaggerations and subterfuges. I see that in 'Hymns of Praise' the old 'All is safely gathered in' is altered to 'All be safely gathered in', and that there is some hanky-panky with Mrs Alexander's 'Rushes by the water, we gather every day'. The literal-minded were worried because we no longer gather rushes every day. Really, really! As though God would stumble over a little thing like that.

We rejoiced in the harvest in a way best expressed in Hopkins' 'Hurrahing for Harvest'. Barbarous in beauty the stooks arise. My heart leapt to it when I first read those words. Harvest festivals, though somewhat disparaged by Churchmen as upstart services with little tradition, were the most popular church festivals of the year when I was a child. Men seemed to come together with more willingness to express praise and gratitude than to bewail their sins and consider how fearful it was to fall into the hands of the living God. People went round to different parishes to harvest festivals, and chapel people went to church and church people to chapel. We did not seem to mind how often we sang 'We plough the fields and scatter', 'Now thank we all our God', 'Come, ye thankful people, come', 'For His mercies still endure, ever faithful, ever sure', and 'All people that on earth do dwell, Sing to the Lord with cheerful voice'. The first time we ever chanted a psalm in my memory in Gorran Church was at a Harvest Festival. Usually we said the psalms, the Vicar reading one verse and the congregation the next, and so on to the end when we sang a Gloria. But for one harvest festival we chanted 'O praise God in His Holiness; praise Him in the firmament of His power'. By the time we reached 'Let everything that hath breath praise the Lord', I had got the hang of it and was so loud in praise that Mr Jorey, the blacksmith who shod our pony, and who would let us blow the bellows, turned round and gave me a peppermint.

Harvest was the least liturgical, the most pagan festival of
the year. Even the decorations rioted. Dahlias would never go
to church by nature; whereas lilies might have been born in
church. Golden wheat-ears, dahlias, crimson virginia creeper,
vegetable marrows, pumpkins, apples, bunches of grapes, in
coming to church changed the church's character, not their
own. They laughed in all their expansive richness. The parish
feasted in common at Harvest Festival, but not at Christmas,
Easter, Whitsuntide, or Trinity. There was no parish tea
except at Harvest. Sitting on forms, at trestle tables, we drank
tea from thick white cups and ate buttered splits, saffron
cake, sultana cake, and jam-and-cream splits. I think kiss-in-
the-ring was seldom played except at harvest festivals.
Already when I was a child people were shy of it, whereas it
had been popular when my mother was a girl. She would tell
us how in her day, too, as it grew to twilight the games had
ceased; the bells had rung for the evening service, and church
and chapel folk had sung together, 'Let everything that hath
breath praise the Lord'. Gladness is generous and uniting.
According to Baring Gould, the Rev. Stephen Hawker was
the first to institute a harvest festival in the Cornish Church.
In 1843 he sent a notice to his parishioners at Morwenstow
saying that as in that year God had opened His hand and
filled all things living with plenteousness the people should
meet together on the first Sunday in October to offer a
sacrifice of thanksgiving. They would receive at the sacrament
bread made of the new corn. By my time the festival was less
truly religious, but hardly less joyful. Joy, however, seems to
decline as the religious motive recedes. Mere conviviality is
not life to the spirit.

With the gold of October came bonfires, and the smell of
smoke, as we burnt the garden trash and baked potatoes in the
ashes. We lit our fires in the evening as the light was falling. Fire
was the autumn God, 'bona-firies, their red beards streaming
to the heavens'. We kindled fires furtively and in the open.
Cap'n and I raced flames down dry sticks. The pointed
triangular sails of flame were our fire-ships. We could make

little fires in the coalhouse at night, for it was Cap'n's job to pick up, in readiness for the morning, wood and coal for the kitchen fire. I would go out to help him with his labour. Then on the stone floor we would burn a little paper, a few sticks, and pellets of candle-grease. Cap'n would try sprinkling a little sugar, salt, sulphur, or copper filings to change the colours. We would have green flames and yellow, edged with mauve or blue. The coalhouse was next the washhouse—both across the court from the dwelling house. Absorbed in our pleasure we would forget time stealing by until a voice would call from the back door, 'What are you children doing over there?' We would guiltily extinguish our little fires and hasten in with an armful of dry wood and our lumps of coal broken up into suitable sizes for lighting the kitchen range.

Near Guy Fawkes day we experimented with squibs and sparklers, just one or two to make sure they were not damp. Once Stan and a friend made some gunpowder, or got it from cartridges, I am not sure which. They set it in a hedge and laid a fuse. But the fuse did not go off when they thought it should. They drew near to see what was wrong and as they were about to bend over it off it went. Stan's eyebrows and hair were singed, he looked a funny sight. He had black marks in his face. He went to Howard and asked what he could do to himself so that my mother should not see. Howard suggested washing. This had a frightful heightening effect. There was nothing for it. Stan's burnt state was plain to all, but he had hurt himself too much already for parental retribution.

Our store of fireworks was always small for we had little money; but we made a guy and had a splendid bonfire. There would be a tarred faggot and driftwood with banners of flame; then as the yellow sheets furled themselves we would poke the ashes into sparks and feed our fire with furze. The consuming flowers would break fiery among the spines, swiftly ablaze, and swiftly in ashes, lighting and dying. Later from our bedroom windows we used to watch the rockets going up over Mevagissey, rockets rushing upwards, and bursting into floating flakes and spangles of light.

There is no Feast of Lights or Feast of Fires in the Church. In November came All Saints' Day. We sang 'How bright these glorious spirits shine' and 'For all the saints who from their labours rest'. But I could never love the saints nor care for Heaven. Until I was grown up, and knew Vaughan and Crashaw, Herbert and Hopkins, my joys were purely earthly. Even my delight in the great Church festivals was, I think, in looking back, more an unconscious passion for Cornwall than for the Church. When I recall Gorran Church or Caerhays Church they are always part of the weather and of the fields and the sky; rain on the roof; trees at Gorran moving their branches outside the unpainted east window; sun streaming in at the open door at Caerhays; the sound of birds chirping or singing during the quiet parts of the service; a red admiral fluttering between the pillars. At Caerhays one could even hear the bees humming over the self-heal and knapweed and clover, and the grasshoppers rattling their brackeny shanks. No doubt I forget how often as a child I was bored in church. Kneeling through the Litany I would long to be out of 'Good Lord deliver us' and into 'We beseech thee to hear us, Good Lord', a response which went on interminably. I would press my hands against my eyes so as to make violet and yellow geometrical patterns float against the blackness; or I would squint through my eyelashes at a rainbow-edged Miss Ellen Wills. She kept the post office and came into church walking on her toes. 'O Lord who at this time with one accord', Mr Sowel would say at last, and I knew I should soon stand up. 'O Lord, who at this time' and 'And now to God the Father . . .' which ended the sermon, were words I sometimes longed for to the extent of trying to conjure them out of the distance.

Yet, though not a naturally religious child, I am glad I was taken to church regularly, initiated into the Christian faith, and helped to participate in the profound poetry of the Christian year. Though inattentive I came insensibly to know the liturgy word for word, and to live in the double rhythm of the earthly seasons and of man's noblest imagining. After the fall of the year came the pause, the hush of waiting in field and church, and Advent Sunday. The Collect for Advent Sunday was the first Collect for the day I was set to learn by heart. I was very proud to be out of the Catechism and into the Collects with Susan and the boys. I determined to be word perfect. We said the Collect to my mother on Sunday mornings. It was not easy to learn and nothing was explained—excessive explanation is the wicked fairy in modern education. For me there was no tarnishing progress; the rhythmic prose swung unchipped into my mind:

> Almighty God, give us grace that we may cast away the works of darkness, and put upon us the armour of light, now in the time of this mortal life, in which Thy Son Jesus Christ came to visit us in great humility; that in the last day, when He shall come again in His glorious majesty to judge both the quick and the dead, we may rise to the life immortal. Through Him who livest and reignest with Thee and the Holy Ghost, now and ever. Amen.

I did not know how grand it was, I was only exultant that I was learning it. I shouted it to the thorns and to the wind; and my mother, when I repeated it on Sunday, said it was good.

7

VISITING

Unmoored,
Lifting,
Into the space
Drifting.

No steersman now
Save sweet delight
Dreaming with me
All night.

—*On Falling Asleep*

There were some houses which we were in and out of so often that we could not be called visitors. Of these were Cotna and Trevesan where there were children matching us in age. When I think of Gorran I feel as homesick for Cotna as for the School House. Taking the church as the centre of the village Cotna lay in the opposite direction from the School House. On leaving church we went down the granite steps under the cross by the old sun-dial, and so home. The Kendals went past the oldest old tombstones, and down the darker, romantic, shallow slate steps at the back of the churchyard into their own lane, which curved along between hedges into what we called the Oval.

I have heard my mother say that at one time the Oval used to be shaven as smooth as the Vicarage lawn. In our day it was wilder grass, and the plantations round it were wild too. Crocuses, yellow and purple, and clumps of daffodils came up unattended in the spring. In June there were scented roses called blush roses for their flushing crimson petals, velvety to touch. We used to stick petals on our foreheads, rose petals and geranium. In the orchard there were medlar trees; no other orchard had the rotten-ripe medlars. As for the house it was the house I should best like to live in in the world. It had a straight front with straight sash windows on either side of a portico with pillars. Upstairs one could get on to the portico from what was called the blue room.

Here lived Mr Kendal, known throughout the parish as Cap'n Bill to distinguish him from his brothers Freeman and Leonard who farmed Bodrugan and Trewollack. With him was Mrs Kendal whom next to my own family, and perhaps Miss Mary of the Barley Sheaf, I chiefly loved. I once read a poem about how the birds slept sweetly all night at their mother's side. Mrs Kendal might almost have had feathers. She was essentially a person to nestle against, immobile; the very antithesis of angularity and restlessness. She moved little, walking always slowly and in one; she did not turn her head about or move her arms separately from herself. She had an easy way, a softness I have never met in an equal degree in anybody else. For her to raise her voice or speak in a sharp tone would have been impossible. The babies might yell; the older children, strong and handsome, be on the rampage; the work accumulate; the meals be running feasts—she remained placid. She always came to church late, walking quietly in, sometimes during the Venite, sometimes even as late as the Second Lesson. The quickening stroke of the 'last bell' which hastened other footsteps never hastened Mrs Kendal's. Unflurried, never looking late, she would enter the church innocently; making it seem not as though she were late but as though we had all come foolishly early. Cap'n Bill would be already in place, for he was a ringer and a Churchwarden. Standing upright at the end of the Kendals' seat, and looking at his prayer-book, he would feel instinctively her approach, but would not take his eyes from his book, or interrupt his song if we were in song. He would merely step into the aisle, and she would pass by him into her place. She would then go in, kneel down for her little private prayer, stand up, look up with a slight smile at Cap'n Bill, find her place in her book and dissolve into the congregation. In all she did she was entirely herself. Perhaps her secret was that she never tried to dominate or chase anything, and so nothing resisted her or ran away from her. She had no pursuits. Her clothes were her familiars. Her plush jacket was Mrs Kendal, not Mrs Kendal's jacket; it seemed as much a part of her as her brown eyes. She was the only person who called my mother Sue. Bessie and Sue they had been to each other as schoolgirls and so remained. My father called my mother Dan'l—her full Christian name was Susan Daniel—after a character in a book called Dan'l Quorm.

Cap'n Bill Kendal was in many ways a contrast to his wife, but he was good natured too. He used to get me to say I loved him two great apples. I only once made him angry. Jack Kendal and I had ensconced ourselves in the interior of a great yew tree on the Oval. We found that if we climbed up the limbs of the tree from inside we reached a point at which our weight was too great for the limb. It swayed outwards giving us a gentle yet breath-taking swing nearly to the ground, when we dropped off, and repeated the process with another limb. Entirely wrapt in our delighted sensations we never gave a thought to the tree till Cap'n Bill was on us. He caught and cuffed Jack, and would have cuffed me too if I'd been one of my brothers. I instantaneously saw the tree through his eyes, and I fear the Judgment will be to see the effect of one's whole life with unhooded eyes as I saw that tree. Previously I had been unconscious of the tree except as an object providing us with a game. Now I saw that instead of being a tree with a great wide base and all its limbs curving up to a point, the yew had limbs which had not sprung back into place, but which were rudely wrenched outward. Cap'n Bill shouted at us how old the tree was; I forget how many years old, hundreds of years it seemed. He said it was the finest yew in Cornwall. I think it was the first time I had ever been sorry for a thing I had hurt, as apart from being sorry for myself because of what was happening to me for hurting it. Similar absorptions of mine had been vigorously interrupted when I was small, but then I had merely felt furiously angry. I can remember what must have been the one absolute and genuine artistic absorption of my life. I had got a little bit of slate—there were many sharp flat slate stones about—and I was making marks with it on the highly polished surface of a cupboard. All my self was in the point of the slate. To be caught out of the trance, and slapped, and made to realize it was a cupboard I was spoiling, was to pass from one world abruptly into another. But I was sorry for myself, not for the cupboard. Similarly, when I was making a hole in the traphouse in order to have an inner cave like Robinson Crusoe, I hadn't made it big enough for me to crawl through before I was caught; but it was a hole big enough for the Plymouth Rocks to pass through and roost (on our trap)— with nasty results to the navy blue upholstering. Other animals crept through that hole till William Smith had to come and mend it. But I was never sorry for the traphouse. I was sorry for the yew tree, which had to be put as it were in splints. Stakes were driven into the earth and rope tied round to make the yew limbs grow up once more.

Trevesan, like Cotna, was nearly a second home. We envied Gordon, Louise and Stella Whetter for living nearer Hemmick than we did, and for having flavoured treacle on their bread-and-butter for tea. Mrs Whetter—her Christian name was Petronella— let them have treacle of a raspberry or strawberry flavour and coloured red; whereas our treacle at home was ordinary. We did not count it 'going out to tea' to go to Trevesan or Cotna, or to school friends in the village. Going out to tea proper was when two or three of us went by set invitation with our parents to rather more distant friends—to the Mitchels at Penare, to the Mingos at Rescassa, to the Pearces at Tregerrick, or to our distant cousins, the Notts and

Grosses, at Trevarrick. Other Nott relations lived at Bosinver and Coyte in St Mewan parish. My favourite of all places to which to go formally to tea was Trevasgas where the Wests lived. We nearly always drove to Trevasgas; it was rather far for my mother to walk. At Trevasgas lived Mr and Mrs West, Percy, who soon farmed Trevennen on his own, Blanche, Martin, Sam and Norman. Blanche was just grown-up, and Susan and I had all the little girl's admiration for the newly-arrived young woman. Blanche West was tall with smooth chestnut hair 'done-up', and a complexion a queen might envy. On arriving at Trevasgas we were taken to the spare bedroom which was Susan's delight, so unlike was it to anything in our own house. The boards of the floor were not stained; they kept their natural colour with a satin sheen; while on either side of the bed, in front of the fireplace, and in front of the dressing-table, were snowy sheep-fleeces. Susan yearned for a sheep fleece. I gave her one in later years, but it lacked the Trevasgas white silk curliness. There the fleeces were more than the depth of one's fingers. As a farmer said to me once, when I was looking at his prize living ewe, 'Feel her fleece, Anne, feel the depth of 'un.' In addition to the fleeces Trevasgas spare bedroom had white muslin curtains tied with pink bows, and a dressing-table in skirts. It wore a shiny pink under-skirt, and a clear-muslin, full-gathered overskirt. There were more pink bows, not creased like our hair ribbons, but fresh, crisp, newly tied bows. Except for maidenhair ferns in pots I cannot remember how the downstair rooms were furnished, but there was a back as well as a front staircase, and an open fire with a chimney corner in the kitchen.

We would help to feed the animals, or hunt for eggs, or play hide-and-seek about the barn and mowy until we were called in to a resplendent tea. The Wests' dining table was long and wide, covered with starched white damask. The food was choicely dispersed here and there on dishes set with d'oyleys. Some d'oyleys had wide-dropping crocheted or knitted lace. Some d'oyleys were goffered. The flowers on the centre varied with the season, but I see them as tulips; circling round the tulips on the d'oyleys would be thin bread and butter, yeast splits for cream and jam, rocky buns, sponge cake, saffron cake or fruit cake and, as the supreme triumph, the last point to work up to—tipsy cake. Tipsy cake was home-made sponge cake soaked in sherry, covered with stiff whipped cream, and studded with blanched almonds and cherries. Sometimes sponge fingers also stuck up on the top. I don't know what the grown-ups did, but traditionally the children ate solidly from the bread and butter base through all the varied delicacies to the top of the pyramid—the tipsy cake. Had I confessed the truth I should have owned that, once the cherries, the almonds, the whipped cream, and the sponge fingers were eaten, I did not like the harsh woody-bitter taste of the winey cake. But I never did own it. Susan did; that was the difference between us. She never pretended she could see a ship through a coastguard's telescope if she could not.

In summer after tea we played again out of doors. In winter we played blind-man's-buff in the kitchen. The grown-ups then had supper in the dining-room, but Blanche got the children's supper in the kitchen. I would sit in the chimney corner and drink the hot cocoa which Blanche poured from a jug, and eat biscuits with smooth white or pink sugar on the top, or sugar in wavy designs. Once Blanche got us biscuits like animals. Then sleep would come at me. Fought from my eyes it would come stealing in from all sides through my body. The cold air, as we went out of the lighted room to drive home in the dark, would wake me thoroughly; but once in the trap, and snuggled for safety against my mother, I would surrender. I would give up protesting that it wasn't past my bed-time and float into sleep.

At Tregerrick I remember not so much the food—except the Polly apples—as the games. The Pearces were all grown up, but they played games in such a way as to make them furiously exciting. Ludo, tiddleywinks, hoop-la, snakes and ladders, snap, old maid, steeple-chasers—the Pearces had kept all the games they had had as children, and played them again with us, not in a bored way, but as if winning were the end of life. Ludo at the Pearces was utterly unlike Ludo anywhere else.

Janey and Annie Pearce, and even Mrs Pearce, would play. It was a life and death matter to throw a six and 'get out'. We yelled our disappointment when 'knocked home'. My sister-in-law has sometimes reproached me when playing with her children; she says I make them boisterous. The Pearces were like that, they made us boisterous, bless them.

The farthest distance we drove for an afternoon visit was to my Great-uncle Tommy's. He lived at a farm called Penvose, not very far from Portloe, where he would have it that the Jacka was the finest bit of cliff in Cornwall. He was a Wesleyan local preacher, with confidence in the efficacy of an ejaculated Amen. He always said a long grace before tea. He would clasp his hands, the fingers interlacing, and place them so as to make a little porch to his eyes. Then he would say:

> Be present at our table, Lord,
> Be here and everywhere adored,
> These creatures bless, and grant that we
> May rest in Paradise with Thee.

We would wait a minute with our head bowed till Uncle Tommy in his preaching voice said Amen, Amen, A-Amen. Then he would add in his brisk ordinary Cornish tones, as of one relieved that his dues to heaven were paid, 'Now, my dears, fall to.' Apple tart and cream we had at Uncle Tommy's, summer or winter. He kept apples till apples came again. The apple tart was not made in a pie dish but had pastry top and bottom. The top would be taken off, sugar and cream inserted, and the top put on again. Despising the nursery rite of the tea-table, Uncle Tommy would begin straight away with apple tart, and proceed as it were backward and downward, through saffron cake to bread and butter.

While we lived at Gorran, to go to tea with the Martins and the Sargents at the Hovel was visiting. But when we lived at Caerhays we went to the Hovel so often that it ceased to count as visiting. Mr Sargent was the head gamekeeper at Caerhays. He and Mrs Sargent were already between sixty and seventy when I first remember them. Mrs Sargent was the only person in the two parishes who wore a little lace cap and a black satin apron in the afternoons. She had, too, a little three-cornered red shawl to keep the draught from the small of her back. Their sons had gone out into the world but their daughters, Ellen and Frank (Frances), lived at home, where Ellen did dressmaking. From living long together Mr and Mrs Sargent had grown curiously alike in feature and in mind. They had a homely and accustomed goodness; it would have been impossible to connect them with any mean act or even thought. 'Cleanse the thoughts of our hearts by the inspiration of Thy Holy Spirit' they had prayed Sunday after Sunday after Sunday until there was no squalor in them. Their cottage was perfect, thatched as I first remember it, but later the thatch—the Squire had a dread of fire—was replaced by tiles. Mr Sargent was a more travelled person than most of us. Every year he went to Scotland with Mr Williams. He would tell us how once on Crewe station, where he was on guard with the dogs and the guns, a thief, not observing him, had stalked off with a gun. 'I went after him, and I said, "Why have you taken that gun?" I said. "That's my master's gun," I said . . .' We would poke the old man up to tell this story, again and again. I can see him in his fawn suit with pockets of pattern peculiar to himself, and wearing his neat gaiters, carrying his gun, and fawned on by obedient dogs. A badly trained dog would have dishonoured him. He was deeply distressed when a red setter called Mac once nipped into our kitchen and stole our Sunday joint. Mrs Sargent considered that everyone should save a little money, however small the amount coming in. She was scandalized at the improvidence of Mevagissey folk, their poverty in bad times, and their extravagance in good. She liked sober dressing. 'Ha'penny head and farthing tail', she would say of somebody wearing a fine new flower-trimmed hat, and down-at-heel shoes. When I first began to earn a salary, and came home for holidays. I always hastened down to see the Sargents on my first night at home. Mrs Sargent was much concerned that I, not being frugally inclined, and my earnings being small, was putting nothing into the savings bank. 'Now Anne, my dear, haven't 'ee put anything by yet?' she would say each time I came home. She would shake her head over my thriftlessness. Once when I told her how I had tried dividing my monthly salary into four parts and putting the four parts into four drawers of my bureau, so much for each week, and how by the end of the third week I had borrowed to such an extent from the fourth drawer that I had nothing left to live on, she laughed, but disapprovingly. When she was really amused her laughter used to begin with a quaking movement which lifted her folded hands up and down on her stomach; then it worked upwards through her heaving bosom until she wiped the tears from her eyes. Once to please her I put a pound into the Post Office Savings Bank; but Susan came to stay with me for a weekend. On the Friday evening I took ten shillings out to celebrate; on the Saturday I took the other ten shillings out to celebrate further. Mrs Sargent, when told this story, said she must give me up for lost. Anyone who would do that would never save money however much she earned. She spoke the truth.

But it was Susan who lost our very first bit of capital. I must have been about seven years old and for the first time we were going away from home to stay. We had got between us, by some manner of means, the enormous sum of five shillings. It was the summer we were wearing cream serge sailor-suits and cream yachting caps. Susan put our fortune in a purse in the pocket of her 'top'. We were tremendously excited, for I had never been anywhere by train before. Cap'n warned me not to go too near the edge of the platform; the train, he said, would seem to get me by the gizzard, and draw me towards it. And indeed it did. When the monster came rushing towards me out of St Austell rhododendron bushes, and I felt its breath on my face, and the tug which Cap'n had foretold at my middle, I clutched the person nearest me. Afterwards, when teased, I said I only clutched the person for fun; I was ashamed because it was not even an express train. We had, for my benefit, chosen a train which would stop at all the little stations—Burngullow, Grampound Road, Probus Halt and Truro. At Truro we changed into the Falmouth train and got out at Perranwell. The name of the station was growing in candytuft on one of the station flower-beds. Again Cap'n had told me what to expect, and there it was. I determined to plant ANNE in pansies, but I never did.

Several of my father's relations lived round about Perran-ar-Worthal. We were to stay at Poplar and were met at the station by one of my cousins in the Poplar trap. We were in high feather, with no thought of impending mischance, when I began to tell my cousin Tom how we had five shillings between us to spend. Susan clapt her hand to her 'top' pocket, and alas, it was empty. That purse had hopped out. From being independent persons with a fortune to spend, we found ourselves in a condition of abject poverty, for my father refused to give us another ha'penny. I was not magnanimous to Susan over our loss. I said, in bed, that if I'd had my own share of the five shillings it wouldn't have hopped out of my 'top' pocket; Susan, conscious of guilt, and so contentious, said I wasn't to be trusted with even a decent pocket-handkerchief. Where was that little hemstitched handkerchief with lace edging which Aunt Lye had sent me two Christmases ago? And who had broken her scent bottle? I had a passion for scent and, essaying to steal Susan's one day, I had broken a unique bottle of carnation which had a tiny ivory pump handle and spout at the top of it. Other old offences we threw at each other from the past; we lay in bed back to back. But we could never go to sleep 'vexed'; besides I was beginning to feel lonely. I knew that 'I'm feeling lonely' would always make Susan turn towards me however much she might be striving to nourish her anger. I said the words now, and we turned towards each other. What was five shillings!

Probably it was five shillings well lost, for the high light of our visit was Penryn regatta, where I had my first ice-cream and my first ride on the roundabouts. With thirty pennies of my own to spend I should probably have joined the angels. No ambrosia will ever taste so ambrosial as that first ha'penny ice-cream wafer bought off the ice-cream cart of an Italian, with ear-rings.

> Oh, Oh, Antonio. He's gone away.
> Left me alonio. All on my ownio.

I hardly watched the yachts at all. What with ice-cream and the roundabouts my cup of bliss was already full. The blare of the music, and those horses, so dashing in their bridles, moving in two ways at once, up and down, and round about! My cousin Tom treated me, and together we went lilting. Holding my reins, I sat side-saddle like Miss Williams at the castle who never rode astride. I think it gave me a vague notion of what I was missing through not riding Dart side-saddle, and wearing a long habit. A long-skirted riding habit, like a long, rustling party dress, must change one's nature.

I liked my cousin Alfred Harry. I sat next him in Ponsanooth chapel where we 'leaned vor' instead of kneeling down in the church way. In one of the long prayers, while the preacher was venturing to remind Almighty God of this and that, and while we were 'leaning vor' Alfred Harry, to my inexpressible apprehension and shocked delight, drew with a pin a funny face on the varnished pew. He had a funny face himself and could move his ears.

Various friends and relations returned visits to the School House, but my mother was too impatient to run to d'oyleys. She said our dishes were too good to hide. The party of ours I most vividly remember in my earliest years was a concert-party supper. Sammy Rowe of Mevagissey had brought his band to play at a concert in Gorran School, and he and the others were to have supper in our house before going home through the dark. Susan was playing a duet with Howard at the concert, so it was I who had the splendour of helping my mother with the final touches to the supper table. By the time we were ready to slip into our seats in the schoolroom the band was already under way. I shall never forget treading on air to those sounds. The fiddlers had lifted their bows, and Sammy was intoxicating himself with the cornet. He was a true musician. Once in later days, so I have heard, Sammy was playing his cornet and leading the band round Mevagissey quay, when he stepped clean over the jetty in his ecstasy; but the air refused to bear him up; he had to be pulled out of the water, dripping wet, the divine frenzy quenched. At Mevagissey Feast, St Peter's Day, there always used to be a procession to the sea.

Visiting was a favourite game with Susan and me on wet winter Saturday afternoons. We called this game 'young ladies'. Susan would have our bedroom, I would have the boys' bedroom—the boys being safely out rabbiting with my father at Beeparks. We would divide the dolls and get out our tea-sets. Then we dressed up in mother's clothes or in long dresses made of old curtains. We turned out discarded veils and jet bracelets, and carried old sunshades with deep fringes. We then took turns to visit each other, knocking at each other's doors, being admitted, being taken to the equivalent of the spare bedroom to remove our veils, and sitting down sometimes to an imaginary tea, sometimes, if mother were in a good mood, to real little bits of cake, and a mock blanc-mange made of moist sugar, pressed into an egg-cup and turned out as though from a 'shape'. I forget all the proceedings, but I do remember that we always finished by dancing Sir Roger de Coverley together, holding up our long dresses and doing all the figures, and taking all the parts of all the couples. One or other of us in these games would be Mrs Williams at the castle. How we longed for a curled fringe!

Sometimes we played churches, when Susan was always the organist and I the preacher, wearing one of the boys' cricket shirts for a surplice. We were also the entire congregation imitating the entry of all our friends into their seats. But 'young ladies' was played oftener than churches, the joys of earthly hospitality evidently touching us more nearly than the solemn rites of the church militant. Yet even Cap'n would join us in a funeral.

8

TOYS AND BOOKS

My tale is done, there runs a mouse;
Time for bed, children.
One more page to finish this story
One more page to finish this
One more page to
One more page
One more
One

—*Once Upon a Time*

We had few toys. My most treasured possession for a long time was a hanging crystal from a chandelier which had been turned out of the parlour when my mother suddenly found herself hating chandeliers. Not only did the lustrous, heavy glass please me, but when I looked through certain planes of the crystal every common object was rainbow-edged. My first icicles were even more attractive. One cold spell, we had left water out in an old cup, because someone had said that in freezing it would expand and break the cup. It had not broken the cup, but the water had turned into a cloudy lump which we were looking at when Cap'n came dashing in to say there were icicles on Cap'n Math's shed. He seized me by the hand and we tore off to see his icicles before they had time to melt. Sure enough there they were hanging from the galvanized roof—pointed, clear, stiff, brittle water. We threw up stones to break off some of these clear sticks of rock, and we sucked them, making the dark pain come at the back of our eyeballs, as it came when in summer we were as thirsty as dogs, and drank cold water too fast.

Susan used to tell me of a crystal ball she had seen when she went to tea with Mrs Morrison, wife of the Scotch cowman at Caerhays, and otherwise famous as a maker of scones which were three-cornered, whereas our 'splits' were always round. Mrs Morrison's crystal, Susan said, would show snowflakes falling if one turned it upside down. I longed to see this wonder and when, at last, I went to the Morrisons' to tea, I played with the crystal ball, and played with it, instead of going out to try and find pheasants' eggs with George Morrison. Mrs Morrison had other delightful objects such as a thimblecase made out of the two halves of a walnut. The halves were joined by a little hinge, so that one could open and shut the walnut. A coach and six might have driven out of it at any minute.

My next favourite object was a little pair of scales which Maurice gave me for one of my birthdays. They were almost an exact replica of the scales in Agnes's shop. The stand was black, the shaft and the beam were of brass and one did the weighing in little brass pans suspended by three chains from either end of the beam. There were real weights. I can feel my hands stripping the pennyworts of their 'rice', weighing it up, and twisting paper packets in Agnes's professional way for anyone who would buy of me. The golden maize grains which we gave the fowls were stock-in-trade when I played shops. I sold maize on ivy-leaves, and maize on pennyworts, or, for large orders, a whole handful of maize wrapped up in a dock-leaf.

Susan and I had dolls, dolls that would open and shut their eyes, and dolls that would squeak 'Mama' if pressed; nevertheless our favourite doll was a wooden stool dressed in various discarded baby-clothes, and christened in our wash-hand basin as a member of the Church of England. We baptized her Gwendoline. This doll with her bland-looking wooden forehead made me cast longing eyes at an advertisement of a very large doll which was appearing in various papers at the time. A picture of the doll, elegant and smiling, bore the legend beneath: 'Baby's clothes will now fit dolly.' No money was required for the doll; all one had to do was to send for some samples of cloths for cleaning silver, sell the cloths to obliging friends, send the money to the address stated and the doll would be the reward. All alone, for Susan despised it, I set about this commercial undertaking. I received the cloths, and in some confusion, sold them to my friends' parents. I sent the money up and, with eager expectation, watched for Jabez Gross, our postman. At last Jabez brought the reward, but I could not believe my eyes. It came in an envelope; it was nothing but a rag doll, a picture of a doll printed on calico to be cut out and stuffed. That doll, folded up like a tea-cloth, cost me a great deal of chaffing. Everybody knew.

I am not sure that the dolls we liked best of all were not the dolls Aunt Sarah showed us how to make out of poppies, single, scarlet, wild poppies. We would take a poppy on a stalk, bend back its lovely petals to make a skirt, tie a wisp of grass round to make a waist, stick a grass stalk through for arms, and let the black head of the poppy form the head of the doll. These dolls were like dancers standing gaily on one leg—fairy creatures. I do not know how we had the heart thus to spoil the poppy petals for we knew the poppies were alive. We would keep watch on the bursting buds to try to catch a poppy in the act of opening. We knew how the petals showed first crushed and crumpled from their packing in the bud; we knew how the sun ironed them out smooth and perfect; and yet we could spoil them without a pang. We tried to make scarlet dye from their petals, just as we tried to make scent from rose-petals, and from violets, just as we would bite the bottoms of the honeysuckle florets to taste the infinitesimal drop of nectar, or roughly uncurl the coppery-fringed bracken fingers, or hart's-tongue tips. One day I tore a whole sunlit host of honeysuckle growing on the bottom hedge of Furzy Brake. I jumped and climbed until I had pulled down the sprays that floated highest;

I wanted them for my mother. But that day, when I had picked my great bunch, I knew I had spoilt something. Sometimes we would join in a passing craze for pressing flowers, or in a hunt for skeleton leaves; or we would press tutsan leaves, or boy's-love, or lemon verbena to keep between the leaves of our Bibles.

Not many of the things we played with were bought for us. I do not remember this as a hardship; Maurice does. He says he once eyed a little sailing boat in Sammy Warne's shop at St Austell. He wanted it, and wanted it, and wanted it. Each time he went to St Austell he went to gloat until, one day, it was gone. Some luckier boy than he had had it. He remembers quite distinctly saying to himself that he would give his children everything they asked for when he was grown up. Susan and I certainly wanted a doll's pram and were not given it; but then Ellen Sargent made us an incomparable doll's bed. Muslin curtains it had hanging from a circular canopy; and it had a real mattress and bedding, even to a bolster cloth and pillow-cases.

A sailing boat or a doll's pram might be withheld; but books never. Mr Frederick Warne of St Austell was our bookseller. His rather dark shop had shelves nearly to the ceiling; and I can see him standing on a ladder, his pencil stuck behind his ear, handing down to my father two little books bound in dark blue leather, the books were *Tom Brown's School Days* and Lamb's *Tales from Shakespeare*. Why the appearance of these books made so strong an impression on me I do not know. They were pocket editions on thin paper, seeming to be born for the parlour; yet they were to be on our own bedroom shelves. Schoolmasters had the seemly privilege of a good discount on books in those days and, in addition, there were children's windfalls in the shape of specimen copies.

Usually I cared little for the outsides of books. Like all my family I dived straight into the print. Reading came as naturally to us as eating; I believe if Nip and Tweed and Dart could have been provided with print suitable to their minds they would have learned to read by contagion. Our range was wide. The other day I was in a lending library when a small boy arrived with three books to change for his mother. The librarian said, 'What does your mother want, sonny, two loves and a murder, or two murders and a love?' Our reading at the School House was not so lush, though it tended to be gory. My mother liked her gore tinged with history; I have seen her take a lurid cover from the back of a book and put on something more sober, so as to avoid being teased by my father. Her favourite books were romances, memoirs, and domestic novels. She read her favourites by Trollope about once a year. I have never seen anyone else read with such complete absorption, the tears cruising unnoticed down her cheeks in tales of disaster. She was tender-hearted, and pity runneth soon in gentle heart as Chaucer knew.

Although my father cared for books—he liked to buy, not borrow them—I would not call him a reader in the sense that my mother was a reader. He read with critical detachment; my mother with headlong abandon. He would leave any book to go out rabbiting in winter, or to enjoy the summer sun. My mother would be glued to the page until the climax was reached and passed. I have seen her with a great pile of mending by her side take a book as though drawn by an irresistible magnet. 'I'll just read a page or two first', she would murmur and in a moment she would be lost to the needle. There was time for reading when the lamp was lit, and the curtains were drawn, and the winter nights grew longer and longer. We played, too, but reading was the greatest resource. Only Susan liked making things. She did not like neat sewing any better than I, but she was wonderful at making pretty things with a light stitch here and there on this and that. She liked reading too. I learnt to read, I imagine, by watching the words as Susan read aloud to me. Looking back it seems as though, at one minute I was being teased for not being able to read at all, and the next minute I could read anything in print.

Apart from nursery rhymes and picture books with such stories as Cinderella, Puss-in-Boots, and Red Riding Hood, the first story I vividly remember is 'So-fat and Mew-mew'. Susan would read me this little tale and we both adored it. It began: 'So-fat and Mew-mew were a little dog and cat. One day they made up their minds to run away.' The naughty creatures went through a pitiful series of adventures, but always brave, clever So-fat comforted and supported Mew-mew, and licked her paws when they were sore. At last, when our souls had been harrowed by the suffering of the pair, there came a turn in the story comparable to the moment when the Ancient Mariner sees again his church and hill and lighthouse top. Mew-mew suddenly recognized a gate or a hay-rick, or a friendly cock; and magically they were at home. 'They made up their minds never to run away again.'

Next came fairy tales. My father was generous in provision of these both in his family and school. One serious-minded Bible Christian remonstrated with him, saying that he was filling up the children's little noddles with what wasn' true and couldn' be true. Better f'it the children read their Bibles than old lies. My father read him the Old Testament story of the trees who wanted a king; how they asked the olive and the olive said, 'Should I leave my fatness, wherewith by me they honour God and man, and go to be promoted over the trees?' My father said, 'Did the vine and the olive and the bramble really speak?' Mr H. said it was different if it was in the Bible; but he did not complain any more.

We had a rich collection of fairy tales, but we tended to read the same ones over and over again. Generally speaking I liked Grimm better than Andersen, but there were a few of Andersen's I liked better than any Grimm. Andersen was in dark blue covers with gold on the back; Grimm was light blue and had plain covers. When I was tired of dominoes, or five-stones, or of making card pagodas, there was Andersen, ready to fall open at some well-worn page—*Little Claus and Big Claus*, *The Snow Queen*, *The Little Mermaid*, *Eliza and the Eleven Swans*, or *The Red Shoes*. I fancy Little Claus was my equivalent to Charlie Chaplin, the little funny poor chap getting the better of the rich, serious, bad big fellow. And Little Claus had a horse. He would shout when he had borrowed all

Big Claus's beasts, 'Gee up, all my six horses! Gee up, all my six horses!' Gold was measured by the bushel; great blows were struck, and cunning tricks planned. Little Claus's horse was cracked on the head with a hatchet; Little Claus's old dead grandmother was cracked on the head with a hatchet. Little Claus made pretended magic by treading on his sack and making it squeak. It was fun to be in the loft watching with Little Claus while the farmer's wife gave roast meat and wine to the Sexton; more fun still when one heard the farmer arriving on his horse, and he and Little Claus went into the house and Little Claus conjured the hidden good things out of the oven, and the hidden Sexton out of the chest. 'What does your sack say now?' asked the farmer. Best fun of all was when Little Claus turned the tables entirely on Big Claus, enticed him into the sack, and flung him into the river to seek for shadow-cattle. No punishment of a villain was too vindictive for us.

The Little Mermaid with her red sun-garden under the sea, and her statue of the Prince, was likely to induce that curious feeling, impossible to explain and unpredictable, which we called feeling lonely. It was not fear, but a mood of desolateness. Fear stalked us in the wicked Marshes through which the Mermaid had to pass in order to reach the dwelling of the witch who gave her the burning drops to sprinkle on her fish's tail. But it was the end of the story which was likely to make one feel lonely. The elder sisters, their white arms linked, their hair shorn as a gift to the witch, brought a sharp knife that the Little Mermaid might plunge it into the heart of the Prince. He had not loved her and given her a human soul. If she killed the Prince she would return to her father's palace under the sea; otherwise she must become sea-foam. She went to look at the sleeping Prince, and she threw the knife far out to sea as the sun rose. I read this story so often and so intently that I seemed to swim in and out among the Sea King's treasures, and to ride the crests of the waves with the Little Mermaid as they lifted her high so that she could look into the ship in the storm and watch the Prince. When Johnny Hurrel took us out in his boat in summer, and we rowed near rocks rooted deep in purple water, and peered down into the depths at huge weeds swaying, and creatures gliding, the story of the Little Mermaid was not fabulous.

The places we knew provided settings for our stories. In the story of 'Eliza and the Eleven Swans' the little rock which the swans had to reach before sundown, when they were carrying Eliza over the sea, was a rock 'down Hemmick', with the sea all round it, and only just room for the brothers to stand on when they were changed into human form. The agony of suspense— would they reach the little rock in time—was renewed with each reading. In the same story the churchyard to which Eliza went to gather nettles to spin into flax, and make shirts for her brothers, was Gorran Churchyard. It was the dark, gloomy part, towards Cotna Lane. Ghouls seated on the railed-in tombstones might well have stretched out horrible hands.

The Red Shoes was a story with a moral, but we never noticed that. 'Karen thought only of her red shoes', of those red shoes which she had secured by tricking the short-sighted old lady who had adopted her, and who would not have approved of red morocco shoes for church at all. It is when the old soldier says, 'But they are dancing shoes' that the horrible part of the story begins. For Karen is forced to go dancing over the world; through thorns and briars she danced; she danced until she was utterly weary and still the shoes would not let her rest. So she found the hangman's house and she said, 'Cut off my feet, cut off my feet.' And he cut them off and the little feet in red shoes went dancing over the world by themselves. That hangman and the little dancing feet were more horrible than anything else I read.

We liked stories with detail. Part of the enchantment of *The Snow Queen* was the neighbourliness of the rooms in which Kay and Gerda lived, so close to each other that they could step out on to a common parapet and sit under the rose trees in the window-boxes. Those roses were as real to us as the roses in Cotna garden. And the snowflakes in the storied winter surpassed the real. No flakes in Gorran danced and veered and flew as thick and fast as the flakes in *The Snow Queen*. These were a poet's snowflakes and could be as large and as many as he chose. And the window panes could be as beautifully patterned by frost as he chose. And what a device it was of Kay and Gerda's to heat a copper ha'penny on the stove and press it against the pane to make a splendid peep-hole! I could feel my right eye squinting in readiness to look through that clear round hole in the frostiness. All the properties in the story were good. Kay's sled for example. If we could have had enough snow to go flying down hill on a sled we should have burst with exhilaration. All the other properties and people were endeared to us: the old woman's cottage and garden; the little robber maiden with her reindeer whose neck she tickled with her sharp knife; the Lapland woman and the Finland woman; the solemn cold palace of ice where Gerda kissed Kay and melted his frozen heart until he wept the little distorting bit of glass out of his eye. 'And they lived happy ever after.' 'Once upon a time.' Even the beginnings and endings of the tales were to a cherished pattern as my sister and I read them in the tree we called 'the wagon', or entwined together on a couch that had been Granfer's, and which we always called 'Granfer's couch'. The poetic essence of the Grimms' tales we read is in a lyric in George Peele's 'The Old Wives' Tale'. No other few words evoke so potently the stories in which ripe apple trees cry, 'Shake me! shake me!' and magic is natural:

> Gently dip, but not too deep,
> For fear thou make the golden beard to weep.
> Fair maiden, white and red,
> Comb me smooth, and stroke my head,
> And thou shalt have some cockell-bread.
> Gently dip, but not too deep,
> For fear thou make the golden beard to weep.
> Fair maid, white and red,
> Comb me smooth, and stroke my head,
> And every hair a sheaf shall be
> And every sheaf a golden tree.

Cap'n had a large, heavy copy of the *Arabian Nights* bound in red which he would lend at a price. His too was a little green-backed book called *Froggy's Little Brother*. He would say, 'Very well, if you won't field you shan't have my Froggy tonight. Now see the mighty J.A.' And he would straddle with his bat like J. A. Cumberlidge, a friend of my father's, and a famous cricketer at Mount Charles. I cannot explain our attachment to Froggy. Froggy lived in a garret, swept a crossing, and brought up his little brother Benny on penny meat pies. He was very good and courageous, and I fancy Benny must have died, for it was a 'sad' book. So was *Little Meg's Children*. Perhaps she lived in a garret too. We wept over her; but garrets were romantic.

Oddly enough we did not weep over *Uncle Tom's Cabin*. We chiefly read about Aunt Chloe's Cabin—as desirable as a garret—the escape of Eliza with little Harry over the ice-floes; and the Topsy episodes. The escape of Eliza's husband, George, was a part we incorporated into various games. The slaver would chase George and the Quaker up our pile of sticks where there was one great tree-trunk leaning against the closet. George would say 'Are your pistols in order?' and he and the Quaker would get up to the topmost point of the tree-trunk. The slaver would shin up after them and the Quaker would say, 'Thee ist not wanted here, friend', and push him down. I thought for a long time that a Quaker was a fierce fighting chap, good for shoving.

When I was about nine Howard read me the first part of *The Swiss Family Robinson*. I would have given anything to be out in a storm on the sea, and in one of those lashed tubs with all the useful things which were to serve the family on the island. When the cattle and dogs were let loose from the wreck, and given a chance to swim behind the tubs, or rest paw or legs on them, it seemed to me better than Noah's Ark. For in addition to the animals and the tools there was Mamma's enchanted bag. Noah's wife had not thought of such a thing. It never occurred to me to jeer at the bag, nor indeed at the Robinson children. I fear I accepted Fritz, James, Ernest and little Francis in all good faith. I enjoyed the book up to the point where the boa constrictor swallowed the donkey. That did for me. I can see those waves of crushed donkey progressing through the inside of the boa constrictor yet; I used to read the book to myself until it neared that point, and stop. I turned over to the end, but never got the hang of it. I've an idea that my son Fritz—he was the hunter and sportsman of the family—found a girl called Jenny in a tree. I had no use for strange girls coming in to disrupt families. This disruption happened too often. Edward Beverley in *The Children of the New Forest* fell in love with a girl called Patience and the story went to pieces. What a good story it was when the Beverley children were still young—proud Edward and resourceful Humphry, and Alice and little Edith. I liked stalking deer with Edward, but even better I liked bringing in domestic creatures with Humphry. He got hold of ponies, and a heifer, and made a regular farm of it. A delightful life those children lived in that forest. Forest! The very word in the title ensured the success of the book.

The Swiss Family Robinson and *The Children of the New Forest* were in the boys' book-case. Here were stores of books which my brothers were now discarding and which I seized upon. Susan did not like adventures, but when we grew out of fairy-tales I read little else for some years. *Alice in Wonderland* I had at just the wrong age. I was too old and yet not old enough. I had looked forward to it enormously, for it was to come by post as a birthday present. It was coming from Warne's, and I was told what a lovely book it was. It came; I stayed away from school to read it, and I was sick with disappointment. I thought it silly. Not until I was grown up did I realize what my elders meant by praising the book to the skies as they did. 'How dreadfully savage!' said Alice, when told of the head-severing propensities of the queen. But I liked something really dreadfully savage. I could not appreciate 'It's a fine day, your majesty, quavered the Duchess', which was current as a saying in the family circle; and I did not see through the puns. The only thing I liked was the Cheshire Cat.

When I should have been delighting in Alice I was absorbed in such stories as *Cast up by the Sea*, *The Three Midshipmen*, *Through Fire and Through Water*, and *Snow Shoes and Canoes*. I

cannot say how often I read these books. *Cast up by the Sea* had
a Cornish setting, but it had a little of everything in it—
smuggling, press-gang, shipwreck, desert island, a black boy,
and savages. I cannot remember the course of the story at all,
but I do remember a wicked old hag called Mother Lee who
would mutter 'Luck comes from the south-west.' When she lit
fires on the headlands to guide the smugglers in they would
say, 'Mother Lee is trimming her lamps.' There was a fearful
picture of her on the cover of the book all going up in flames. I
fancy she caught herself afire in a storm when she was kindling
false lights.

The Three Midshipmen were boys in the navy at the time of
the Napoleonic wars. I enjoyed their story so much that
Maurice sent me for one birthday *The Three Lieutenants*, *The
Three Captains* and *The Three Admirals* all bound up in one
volume. But alas! my three daredevils grew less interesting as
they advanced in their profession. An admiral's scope is more
limited than a midshipman's for purposes of dashing narrative.
The lower the rank the greater the flair for danger. In *Through
Fire and Through Water* the boy was not even a midshipman; he
was a powder monkey. Jack was his suitable name. He was
nearly shot by highwaymen before he went to sea at all. He was
driving over Salisbury Plain with Mr Box the coxswain and
others when a horseman galloped out of the night and shouted,
'Your money or your life.' Jack lunged at him with a carriage
umbrella, but not before he felt his scalp creep. The shots went
through his cap, but did not touch his head. Mr Box said to
him that night when they went to bed in a Portsmouth tavern,
'Say prayers, boy, don't mind me.' His other saying was, 'Hold
tongue, boy, no sauce.' Once they got aboard the frigate—I had
to have frigates in my stories—the narrative was a succession of
fights. Then Jack rescued his Captain's daughter on a runaway
horse at Valetta, and he was shipwrecked with Mr Box and the
surgeon in desert Africa. I remember the mirage. There was
also a mirage in *The White Kangaroo*. Jack and Mr Box and the
Surgeon were made slaves in Algiers. But Lord Exmouth
bombarded Algiers and the slaves were released. I remember

bits of Lord Exmouth's letter beginning, 'Lord Exmouth to the Dey of Algiers'. I was thrilled when someone told me Lord Exmouth was a Cornishman.

Marryat I liked, especially *Midshipman Easy*, *Peter Simple* and *Poor Jack*. Q.'s *Black Rock* was a prime favourite. Henty I never greatly cared for, though I read him. Ballantyne was better: 'A heavy hand was laid upon my shoulder; it was Bloody Bill.' There were few school stories, but one called *Tom, Dick, and Harry* I remember vividly. It came out either in *Chums* or the *Boy's Own Paper*, both of which journals we took. It began 'A shot! A bang! Silence!' and it had a rhymed letter in it. It had never occurred to me up to that moment that a letter could rhyme. The hero or rather the buffoon of the story—for he was always doing foolish things—was nicknamed Sara. On one occasion after he had got himself burnt in a fire, his mother had a tea-party for his friends to enliven his convalescence. One of them replied to the invitation in this astonishingly witty way:

> Dear Mrs. Jones I'll come to tea,
> At three o'clock you shall me see,
> I'm sorry Sara's been laid up
> And drinks his physic from a cup.
> And now, farewell, as great John Knox said
> Yours truly Samuel Wilberforce Coxhead.

Memory is a strange, fickle, undiscriminating jade. There is much lovely poetry I would gladly be able to recall; instead I have irretrievably fixed in my mind this idiotic fragment.

I read no girls' school stories. *Little Women* I did not read till much later. I could not be induced to begin a book with such a title as *Little Women*. I despised it. A girls' book I desired was a story of which the synopsis was given among the advertisements on the back of *From Fag to Monitor*. I read this synopsis again and again. I savoured the title—*For the Sake of a Friend*. When I asked for the book the others teased me so much that I hid my desire with shame; but I am sure that one reason why my first published books consisted of four girls' school stories was *For the Sake of a Friend*. I wrote in my age what I was unable to read in my youth.

I did not read much poetry—none to myself. Susan used to say 'Over hill, over dale', to me in bed. The only other poem I remember liking is 'Mazeppa':

> Bring forth the horse, the horse was brought;
> In truth he was a noble steed,
> A Tartar of the Ukraine breed
> Who looked as though the speed of thought
> Were in his limbs, but he was wild . . .

Dart was my Tartar of the Ukraine breed; if I could have met a few other wild horses and dashed in among them I should have been happy. But the only herd we ever chanced to meet was Barton cows.

Of all writers the one who held me entirely spellbound was Scott. My brother Maurice introduced me to him when I was twelve or so. Maurice was home from London for a long vacation; he was working for an examination and did most of his reading on the cliffs above Portluney. We would bathe together. I, as though from Mamma's enchanted bag, would produce a piece of cake or an apple; then we would go up on the cliffs among the kidney vetches and the bladder campions and read. No doubt Maurice told me a little about *Anne of Geierstein*, and gave me the book to keep my busy tongue still. I have forgotten most of the story, but I shall never forget the beginning—the mountains, and the mists, the two travellers, and Anne saving the younger traveller after he had crawled along the face of a terrific wall of mountain with a raging torrent beneath. I think Anne came skipping lightly from rock to rock and standing poised against the sky just after a mass of rock had slowly detached itself from under the young man and fallen with reverberating echoes into the abyss leaving him cold at heart but clinging to a tree. It went something like that. Grand stuff. I know after reading it that in all our balancing feats in the village—we were always balancing on top bars of gates or the school railing or tree branches—I was that young man with an abyss not only on one side, but on both; my progress a simple bee-line through space.

After *Anne of Geierstein* I read *Quentin Durward*. I chose it because Howard told me that Charles of Burgundy came into that too. He told me about Louis XI praying to the little figures on his hat, and about the astrologer who tricked Louis and saved his own life. I enjoyed reading that incident in the story. I cannot remember the order in which I read the rest of Scott, but I think I read all except *The Pirate*, *Tales of a Grandfather*, the poems, and the short stories. I liked my stories long, the longer the better. I would look regretfully at the thin number of pages remaining to be read in a grand book. *Tales of a Grandfather* had a title that repelled me; yet I was not put off by such titles as *The Antiquary* and *The Heart of Midlothian*. If any reader could, by an exercise of will, have made a character in a book obey his dictates I should have made Jeannie Deans tell a lie for Effie. I pretty nearly pushed her into it. But no, she would not. No doubt I skipped a great deal in the stories, especially the beginnings; and the Scotch words annoyed me. But I always gathered enough to follow the divagations of the unknown horseman or disguised maiden to the moment when expectation was generously satisfied. The Knight of the Leopard stood revealed as Kenneth of Scotland; the Black Knight was no other than the Lion-heart himself. Di Vernon's strange gallopings were made clear and Mary Seaton and her twin brother ceased to plague Roland Graham by their dual identity. I lived the story I happened to be reading pretty nearly as intensely as I lived my own life. 'What doest thou here in Helen Macgregor's country?' I would shout to the sea-gulls from what I considered some inaccessible crag. I would be any character from the bow-legged Smith to Fenella; from Alice Lee to Meg Merrilies; from the Gaberlunzie to the Earl of Montrose. It was nothing to me to be a flaming Highland torch one minute and the Earl of Leicester the next. What trap-doors I went down! What rusty locks turned in their hinges behind me! What panels slid open! What pictures moved in their frames! Could the fleeing Prince Charles only have had Dart and me in his service, he would soon have put his foot on Cromwell's neck. What gallops I had on secret missions! I wish I still needed only a deserted chapel, a winding path, a friar in a cell, a flagon of wine and a venison pasty to set me wandering in the enchanted forests of romance. But alas! Edith Plantagenet will no longer drop a rose at my feet, and Saladin's scimitar is blunted.

Scott never frightened me; whereas I did not read Dickens for years because of my early fear of Quilp's malignancy. Part of the *Pickwick Papers*, which Howard read aloud, was the only Dickens given the chance to make me laugh when I was young. I suppose such characters as Andrew Fairservice were more within my humorous comprehension than the funny characters in Dickens. I remember a remark of Fairservice's about the weather and gardeners—that if there chanced to be a fine day Sunday would come along and lick it up. This struck me as most amusing. Sundays were always licking up our fine days. But Scott's necromancy left me free of fear; yet at the time when I was reading Scott I would play with fears. At Caerhays my father continued to take *The Western Morning News*, but Mr Bellamy, our Rector, took *The Times*. The two papers were interchanged at night by the obliging medium of Anne. On winter evenings, running down the dark drive under the trees, I would play at shying at shadows, like Dart, for I was not really frightened. Sometimes the winds would be holding carnival in and out the great branches of the trees which moved in the darkness. If I put my arms round the trunk of a tree I could feel the life of the wind stirring even in it and in me. My evening world could be turbulent and eerie, but there were no fears such as must have haunted Mr De la Mare's childhood. The occasion when my blood ran coldest was when William Smith went mad for love of Miss Blacket, and he came up to the School House, and he lifted my father clean off his feet.

9

VILLAGE SCHOOL

Walled in an hour,
Then with a shout
Out, out again,
To field and lane.

Unlike my elder brothers I did not want to go to school. Maurice and Howard, at four and three respectively, had embarrassed master by appearing in his big room as smutty as tinkers, one riding the poker and the other the fire-shovel. The two eluded my mother and invaded the school premises so often that at last they were formally placed on the register. Susan went to school when her time came, but left as early as possible and, except for music, for which she went to St Austell, finished her education at home. The result was lovely—I have met only a few other people so little injured by formal education.

I could not be induced go to school at all as an 'infant'. I learned to read at home by no method; most of the methods are more complicated than the end they serve. I also learned to cook; I dearly loved the kitchen. My world did not seem furnished until somebody had lighted the kitchen fire—it was Cap'n's job for a good many years. No wonder the hearth-fire has become a symbol. The dead ashes would be taken away and, all bright and clean, the flames would shoot up the chimney, while Cap'n watched with a smut on his nose. We had an old-fashioned Cornish stove. The fire could be either 'open' or 'turned down' to heat the oven. In the early morning it was open. We had breakfast in the kitchen.

When the others had all gone off to school I entered into my kingdom of garden, lane, thorn tree, trap-house, wood-pile, wash-house and kitchen. The kitchen was not a little modern cooking laboratory with every inch of space utilized, and everything having to be in its place because there is no room for it anywhere else. It was the sunniest room in the house; it was biggish; it had a fire, a hearth-rug, an armchair, other chairs, a settle, a solid table with drawers, pretty window-curtains, a picture of Ellen Terry on the wall, and a blue stone floor. It was the hub of the house as the kitchen of a little house should be. Above all it was warm. No woman would want to hurry out of it.

My mother would first make herself a fresh cup of tea and look at *The Western Morning News* which my father had monopolized during breakfast. She never read a book in the morning. Even when we were grown up and able to provide an easier life for her, she told me she never read in the mornings without a guilty feeling. She could reprove me in those later days for the way I skipped through the house-work and say my only merit was dispatch. She did not aim at dispatch. She had the inestimable gift of conferring grace and comfort on a house. We would call to her to be reassured she was there— 'mother'—almost before we opened the door.

Each day had a different routine and a different smell. Monday was washing day with the copper fire burning in the wash-house. Various people washed for us in my childhood. Mrs Clarke is my chief memory, an oldish woman with a little bun of silvery hair at the back, and hands crinkled with washing. There would be three heavy wooden trays mounted on stocks in the wash-house, one for the first water, one for the second water and one for the blue. White clothes would go through the second water into the copper and out of the copper into the blue. In the copper which was filled from the wash-house pump the water would be bubbling and steaming. The wash-house was soon full of steam. Mrs Clarke could usually be persuaded to give me some water and soap and even, when in a good humour, some blue and some starch. I did my washing in the dipper, and when weary of washing I blew bubbles. Like most Cornish women Mrs Clarke enjoyed having children about. I dearly liked hanging up the clothes. The skirts and the knickers and the pillow-cases would billow out and dance in the wind. Wet Mondays were calamities. The modern airing cupboard in little houses is an enormous boon. We had no airing cupboard, and we all hated the business of drying off in the wash-house and kitchen. It must be remembered that there was no laundry service at all. We were ten miles from the nearest laundry. Even the sheets and blankets were washed at home. I am all for modern laundries. But the clothes we washed at home and dried on the line hoisted high above the three-cornered piece were wonderfully fresh and sweet. Tuesday was ironing and mangling day. No form of labour is more immediately rewarding than ironing, the rough becomes smooth as though with pleasure, and it is delightful to put on clean freshly ironed clothes. In those days to be entrusted with the handkerchiefs to iron was a treat. Now I haven't patience to iron anything. The secret of a happy life is to do the right things at the right age. Very little girls usually like helping to keep house. It is a form of play. A very small niece of mine enveloped in an apron, and washing up the tea-things while I dried them, sprinkled some Vim into her sink when the job was completed and said gravely, 'I always like to vim me sink.' In a few years' time to vim the sink will be merely a tiresome necessity instead of a delightful promotion to grown-up responsibility.

Wednesday and Thursday were ordinary days—bedrooms were cleaned on Wednesdays, the downstair rooms on Thursdays. I never did like the smell of furniture polish; I made myself scarce on these days and early made up my mind I did not want a house of my own. But on Friday mornings I knelt on the settle with my elbows on the table alert and eager. Baking day! Mr Hicks the baker brought our bread from Mevagissey, but my mother made the yeasty buns and cake. Cooking as an occupation does not pall. As we were a big family my mother could play with really satisfying quantities of flour, white flour in a deep earthenware pan, yellow without and white within. Flour is a particularly well-named substance. To plunge one's arms into flour right up to the elbow—how much better than the finest sand or the most rich smooth mud! Then there would be a little salt, the fat to rub in, currants or sultanas to clean, lemon peel to cut up, sugar to add to the mixture, and a little crater dug in the floury mountain to put the yeast in. The yeast in milk, with a lump of sugar, would have been in a basin working overnight. Sometimes there was saffron rich in colour. When all the ingredients were in, the cake was wetted up, kneaded, and left to rise in a pan with a piece of clean blanket over it by the warm hearth. The rising always seemed miraculous, as indeed it was. The solid dough would rise and rise until it was ready to overflow the pan. When it was really plumb, or plimb—the spongy mass would be divided into the greased cake tins and in addition there would be a sheet of buns (knubbies) new for tea. Cake was not cut new, though sometimes when it came out of the tins, cleft, browned and crisp, I was given a hot crusty bit. Sometimes too I had a special bun which I had patted into shape myself; or if 'we' were making pasties—a little pasty. I could crimp a pasty with anyone when I was seven, and I have never lost the art. Another thing we made was yeasty splits. Yeasty splits with jam and cream! How foolish man is so to behave as to reduce his eating to bread-and-marge. My mother would have been horrified at the idea of margarine. We had butter from Agnes's, a half-pound at a time, yellow, rich and flaky, printed with a cow. Different farms had different prints. These prints ensured a standard of excellence. A good farmer's wife would be ashamed of bad butter under her ensign. One print which I liked very much, I think it was Tregerrick print, had a device in ears of wheat. A half-pound of butter, neat, upstanding, printed and placed on a lordly dish was common. 'There is enough for all', as Mrs Ramsay might have said. But we did not, as children, have butter and jam; butter or jam was the rule. We could, however, have a piece of each at the same time and make a sandwich.

I was very loath to quit my homely pleasures for school, but at last I 'stood in lines' with the others in the playground. Of the first day I remember nothing; the picture in my mind of early school days is composite. I know I was small for my age, wiry and untiring; and that I wore a kilt and top, with an anchor worked in red on the sleeve, and a pinny to preserve my kilt from ill usage. My straight hair was parted at the side and tied on top with a ribbon, or it was combed back and worn with a ribbon like Alice.

The bell and the whistle were fun. Often we would play as far away from the school as possible; bell made us run towards school, whistle made us tear. I liked to play with May Gross and Francie Spears down Crooked Lane on a stile leading to Nicholls' Fields, or on a stone-heap down the same lane. This stone heap was perfect for playing 'mothers', as it afforded us material to build a fireplace in the sort of little house we made. The playground could just be reached if we waited for the bell at Nicholls' stile. In the girls' playground we stood in lines according to 'standards' or, on wet days, we played 'more sacks' in the lobby, until authority intervened. Then, to a tune on the piano, we marched, the girls by their door, and the boys by theirs, into the big room. On the boarded floor the boys in their hobnails made a sound like the trump of doom.

In the mornings we began with prayers and a well-sung hymn. I don't think any of us were in any doubt as to what we were supposed to be engaged in; whereas a little boy I know who went to a village school recently, and whose mind had been kept by his parents unprejudiced in the matter of the gods, reported on the first day that they had begun school with a funny game called 'Shut eye'. The same child re-told the story of Adam and Eve to his little sister. 'And Dod said, "Now don't you touch that apple tree". And', very dramatically, 'they did. And Dod tame into the garden, and they hided away, and Dod said, "You tum out of that". And they tame out. And Dod said, "Now you do out of this". And they went out and'—long pause—'they had ice-cream each'.

We had scripture every day immediately after prayers and I enjoyed it. For a child to be early absorbed in figurative writing seems to me an enormous advantage; and then there were the puzzles of conduct. 'Was Balaam a good man?' my father asked once after we had read the story. I said no in decided tones. Had he not beaten his donkey? But Balaam, it seemed, was a good man. It was years before I realized that he was a man of vision. Jacob, again, whom I detested, whereas I was ready to weep for Esau when he said, 'Bless me, even me also, O my father'. Why was Jacob chosen and Esau rejected? Apart from the quality of the stories the discussions which arose made us think. We were engaged, in a simple way, on the proper study of mankind. And the drama was of the violent kind which children will have in some form or other. I can see in my mind's eye two boys in Caerhays School enacting impromptu Elijah and Ahab. 'Art thou he that troubleth Israel?' 'I have not troubled Israel; but thou, and thy father's house, in that ye have forsaken the commandments of the Lord, and thou hast followed Baalim.'

I enjoyed scripture, but sums were another matter. I did not like sums. I could see through the problems, but made mistakes in working out. Quick and inaccurate was the verdict. And whereas my friends' sums would look beautifully neat mine, try as I might, would be smudged and blotted. The ink-pot had a devil. It was the same with writing. How glorious it was to have a new exercise book, and how careful one would be on the first page! Then the inevitable 'crossing out' and the quick deterioration in the spidery hand. Some of my friends never made a mistake. All was fair, and a delight to the eye. My father was not severe over my tattered script but he was severe with my flowers of speech. I still remember my mortification when I, having written about the lambs 'frisking in the verdant pasture lands', was told, 'playing in the green fields, Anne, playing in the green fields'. An excellent lesson in English. But though mortified in spirit I continued my floral tributes; I never could resist a word. The pleasure in using it was keener than the pang of the snub.

The subject I liked best of all was history—beginning with the stories I read before I went to school, with reprehensible instruction in partisanship from my brother. In the book I had at home was a picture of the Roman soldier of 55 B.C. or was it 54 B.C. dashing into the water with his Eagle, and calling the others to follow him. I showed this hero of my heart to Cap'n so that he too might admire. Cap'n said, 'But he isn't on our side', and pointing to the Britons on the cliffs, poor uncouth heathen with great rocks ready to heave at the handsome invaders, he said, 'Those are our chaps.' I was dumbfounded. I said I didn't want to belong to that lot, and I wasn't going to believe it. Cap'n said to my father, 'Aren't we Celts?' My father, who was reading, said absently, 'Yes, the Cornish are more or less Celtic.' Cap'n said, 'There you are, Anne, so are those Britons Celts. It's all the same. That one (pointing to the most ferocious-looking Briton) might have been your great, great, great, great, great grand-father. I dare say he was.' It was most disturbing. I knew all about sticking up for my own side, and I fancy I really tried to transfer my affection to those Britons. So my historical sense was perverted by false patriotism at the very start! I wonder what little girls make nowadays of their scientific and pasteurized Histories. I expect their big brothers defeat the authors' laudable intents somehow.

In my first history books I merely enjoyed the drama of the various stories and, when I had got over the shock at the primitive appearance of my earliest forebears, the grandeur of being English. But the books had the advantage of initiating a permanent taste for history. And after all one advances. One does not remain a gazer at bad pictures of Britons on the cliffs and of Becket being hewn down at the altar. 'Will no man rid me of this turbulent priest?' What! I do hope it isn't all omitted from the new history books.

Geography I liked chiefly for the names. Other people made lovely maps which I wistfully envied. 'And don't 'ee make the coast-line too thick or you'll make smudges.' My father heard one of his pupil-teachers giving a class this advice in good broad Cornish. My coast-lines were always too thick, I suppose, for there were always smudges. Nevertheless hope sprang eternal. I could see the perfect map which I should one day draw. In the meantime I browned the mountains, greened the valleys, blacked the rivers, put a hint of blue round my coastline with a fish or two for fun, and printed in the names with a mapping pen. For some reason this fine pen-nib seemed immensely grand. I did not only maps I was supposed to do, but other maps from the boys' atlas. India and South America were my favourites. I liked Tierra del Fuego, and the river Bramaputra.

I think we worked harder in school than children do now. But the hours were short. My father did not like long hours himself. The tell-tale bell would often reveal to the village that he was giving the children a good long play-time. 'Master is reading the cricket news I s'pose.' But once in school he worked hard and so did the children. There was no idea that a pupil with a slow mind and disinclination for books could be allowed to do the practical work he excelled in and grow up illiterate. My father did not profess to teach boys to farm or give their work a 'rural bias'; but he did teach them so that they could keep their accounts when they had become successful farmers, have some enjoyment from reading, know something of the world and its history, and write a decent letter. A contemporary of mine at Gorran School, now one of the most knowledgeable men with sheep in the west country, told me that he'd been a dunce at 'problems', and hated to try until my father played a game of draughts with him and said, 'The same faculties that make you play a good game of draughts, John, could make you work out problems on paper.' John set to work with fresh heart. My father acted constantly on the assumption that a child's power of growth is in himself; he nurtured the germinal spirit; once a child 'had a mind to it' he knew that half the battle was won.

He was pretty free to teach as he liked by the time I went to school. This freedom is a necessity. Schools not too big with good masters and mistresses free to help the individual children, and not cluttered up with secretarial work, should be the English pattern. Not schools all alike but rich and varied; our education had better remain too haphazard than too straightly planned. The schoolmasters of my father's day emancipated themselves from the Code and the grand parade of the annual examination; schoolmasters today need to emancipate themselves from the encroachment of directors, and from the army of planners, organizers and testers. A child is more than the sum of his analysed parts. He is a spirit and incalculable. He needs someone with faith in him. Surprise visits from His Majesty's Inspectors were paid in my day. Relations between Inspectors and inspected (the relation is that of Capital and small letters still) have become increasingly cordial as the 'I spy' attitude has declined, and it is of some benefit to the schools to be in contact with an outside mind. But inspect is a difficult word for a difficult art. I doubt whether inspection serves any very great purpose. Lazy teachers use their wits and dodge, and in any case a lazy schoolmaster does less harm than a ruthlessly ambitious and competitive one. He may even by some chance raise up a demon of endeavour in a boy. It would be better to spend the money on sabbatical years for teachers, sending them hither and thither round the world looking at things—not necessarily schools. The trouble with all schools is the stuffiness which tends upon their state. All teachers teach too long. The best schools in appearance can be the deadest. Life has a way of being inimical to that neat organization which appeals to inspectors. Plans! Records! Schemes! All so much easier to inspect than the living, growing Tommy and Alice, playing noughts and crosses under the desks. Children must indeed, like seeds, develop in the dark. How little count is taken of the individual force of soul working unseen to make each child into its utterly original unique self, enjoying its own felicity. Children are too often conceived of as passive, something to be manipulated, a danger accentuated in our age of frenzied planning. I hate the words 'creaming' and 'streams' and 'intelligence quotient'.

The swiftest improvement in elementary education would result from a determined effort to be rid of under-staffing. 'It will drain him dry as hay' I sometimes murmur when I see young teachers with their vitality being sapped by impossibly large classes and multitudinous duties. Given a really well-staffed school much work with 'youth' now being done by unattached youth-leaders and W.E.A. lecturers could be undertaken, and the whole venture co-ordinated. The germ of such an idea was in the old village school. In his younger days my father, in addition to teaching the older children in his school, taught two or three pupil-teachers to what was the equivalent of the school certificate examination. He had a large night school for grown-ups. The first string band I ever heard, and it fiddled me off my head, was Sammy Rowe's at a night-school concert. Much that a W.E.A. lecturer now does my father did. He also ran the cricket club and so forth. He worked too hard. But his work was varied and interesting and kept his own reading alive. Above all it was voluntary. The school was vital to the whole village and not merely to the young children. With a full-time and visiting adequate staff the work would not be too hard and the village school would regain significance in the community. A first-class schoolmaster living in a village is very different from a W.E.A. lecturer visiting it. The trouble has always been the effort made to staff cheaply.

The worst features of Gorran School were that the fires were covered up in great ugly black stoves, and that the windows were too high to look out of. There was only the sky to be seen. The best feature was that we were soon out of school, and that once out we had absolute liberty, with no supervision, no homework, and no meddling with what we chose to do with our own darling time. Lessons over, we played, with intoxicated zest, the game which happened to be in season. We had a grand succession of games, a ritual recurrence. Why a certain game should begin at a certain time I do not know, but some fine day conkers would be out and marbles would be in, or skipping-ropes and hoops would make an appearance, and hippety-beds be deserted. While a certain game was in season we played it with passion; then, for no apparent reason, we were all playing something else. Not all games corresponded to the weather. Marbles, for example, was not, as one would have expected, a warm weather game. No; boys blue with the cold would be playing knuckle under, and fingering their glass alleys. I never had skill in marbles, but I dearly loved Cap'n's glass alleys, and even his coloured ordinary marbles which he carried in a little bag tied with a running noose. Boys swopped marbles and won them from each other with a Shylockian air.

Girls would watch the boys play marbles, and back their champions, and sometimes play themselves. But it was not a girls' game. There was considerable distinction between boys' and girls' games. Boys never had skipping ropes; whereas we girls played 'All in together this frosty weather' for hours. Our hoops were different. Girls had wooden hoops and sticks; boys had iron hoops with iron crooks. Cap'n (if in a good temper) would lend me his iron hoop. Iron was associated with boys. In a sense they were shod with iron, for most of them wore hob-nails in their boots, and could strike fire from the road flints as Dart could. I was ambitious for a pair of hob-nailed boots, and tried to persuade John Parnel to put some hobs in when my shoes were mended. The nearest he would come to it was 'boot protectors'—little iron lozenges cunningly shaped. I can remember, as if it were yesterday, my joy in these protectors. When old John Parnel handed my shoes with the protectors in he said, 'There, my handsome, now you'll make the stones bled.' Both boys and girls played 'Horses'. Boys would not often join in ring games, but in summer the girls played a great variety of these, and a few like 'The wind and the wind and the wind blows high' were played in winter. Other ring games I remember are, 'Walking round the Village', 'Poor Sally sits a-weeping', 'Twos and Threes'. A good many guessing games had a formula. 'Here come I Lady Queen Anne' was one. In summer I wonder how much time we spent with meadow grasses playing 'Tinker, Tailor', or in the lanes idling the hours with 'Even ash in my hand'?

There were little game-cycles within the big cycles, and some games like Edie Mop and Tig and Puss in the Corner were, like gorse-flowers, in season all the year round. A game called 'Old Man Smack' which my mother told me should properly be, 'Home Last, Smack!' could be counted on at any old time of the year to be the rage for two or three days at a time. In this one person as old man stood in the middle of the playground, and all the other people were in two 'Homes' on each side of the playground. The game was to run across from one home to the other and not be caught. If caught one joined the old man in the middle. All the caught people joined hands until to get through these rovers without being caught was a desperate venture. One had to be not merely touched, but absolutely captured; so one could tear along leaving any loose pieces of clothing in the hands of the enemy. It was a regular berserk game for the last two or three in the homes. The last person to be caught became 'old man' in the next game. A game similar to 'Old Man Smack' was 'Fire the Blazes'. We played a variety of this game after school over the fields when, as Fire, I used to chase the Gorran Haven children down to Rice or Cooks.

We spoke broad Cornish in the playground. Long may it continue. I can still speak it—not the Cornish language but the Cornish dialect—with anybody; and the only way to acquire it perfectly is in childhood. As far as I can hear in Cornwall the children seem to be keeping it going in spite of the attacks of the pedantic, and the zeal of the standardizers, and the anxieties of the too-class-conscious. I was with a friend the other day whose little boy is at a village school in Cornwall. As we were passing the playground she said to another boy, who sat on the wall, 'Denzil, will you tell Martin his mother wants him?' The shout went ringing across the playground, 'Curly, ye ma is holl'in.'

The only piece of apparatus we had for games was a stand with holes in the sides drilled by my father with a red-hot poker. Into these holes we stuck pegs. We then stretched a rope across resting on the pegs and played 'higher and higher'. I delighted in jumping. Jumping, sliding and riding induced a kind of physical beatitude. I wish I could have learned to skate as a child. We never had ice enough. But for brief periods we would be able to make excellent slides in the playground. We watered them to make them freeze on light snow. Then we played 'Keep the kettle boiling'. When I first read of Mr Pickwick on the ice I knew he was a friend of mine, and that impression has continued.

In looking back at the play with which we sped the hours at Gorran I notice its freedom from anxiety. It was fun to jump highest in 'higher and higher', but it did not matter. Next day someone else might jump highest. No one kept a score; no game was competitive beyond the moment; play is no longer play if it serves some end other than that contained in itself. We did not play for our school, or our team, we just played; there was no responsibility except that demanded by the game itself; and so no dividing of the energies, no splitting of the person. The game demanded a kind of integrity; we were intent.

And these games were in some sort creative, never taught except by other children, and little interfered with or encouraged. Encouragement kills play. Hockey, which I greatly enjoyed in after years, is not play in the sense that our games at Gorran School were play. In *Family Reunion* T. S. Eliot makes a character say, 'We never had time to invent our own enjoyments.' It seemed to me to throw a flood of light on the characters he was depicting. I was interested to find when reading a life of Sir Humphry Davy, that Cornish education in his day left as much freedom for wandering by cliff and field as in my own. Sir Humphry said he enjoyed much idleness and he praised it. He said he believed he owed more to it than to the formal education he received at Penzance and Truro. He wrote, 'I consider it fortunate I was left much to myself as a child and put upon no particular plan of study. What I am, I made myself.' He left a hundred pounds, the interest of which was to be given to the pupils of his old school at Penzance, not on condition that they were meritorious and hard-working, but on condition that they were given a whole holiday on Sir Humphry's birthday. Do Penzance children get that holiday? Are holidays becoming suspect in that 'smooth and asphalt land' to which so many of our country children—even our babies—are now 'conveyed' by bus?

10

CAERHAYS

Silver and gold and jewels bright
Here are spread for your delight;

The raindrops on the birch your gems,
Your red-gold in the bracken stems;

Your silver in the festival
Shining of the sudden pool;

Poor as naked worm you fare
Who are to such vast riches heir,

A millioneth part you could not hold
Should you seek to grasp your gold.

Open heart and open eye
And all are yours for passing by.

—Bend in the Road

WE went to live at Caerhays when I was ten. As the distance from Gorran to Caerhays was only three miles our furniture was taken over in Caerhays Barton wagons. It was a wet and windy day; the tarpaulins flapped and the horses smoked; the beds got soaked and my mother said she would never change houses again. A saying we kept up for many years was spoken by one of our helpers, as our furniture, top-heavy and perilous, swayed on a wagon: 'Howard, is there room up there for the commoade?'

The School House at Caerhays was not joined to the school. It stood alone not far from the church, neat and new and too near the road for its height, like a top-heavy rick. Its situation was less windy than the Gorran house, but no one could call it sheltered. The red and pink roses which the Squire had had planted to climb up it never had quiet to climb. They would get a little way and the wind would take them; they flowered, but they flowered low.

Although it was a smaller house than School House Gorran, it had four bedrooms; and as even my youngest brother was now to be away from home except on Sundays, Susan and I moved into a bedroom each, Susan with rejoicing, I with reluctance. Our pink knotted nightdress-cases, lined with silk, no longer rested companionably on the same white counterpane. If one of us forgot to say her prayers we no longer lay in the bed's growing snugth discussing whether God wouldn't be just as pleased with our prayers if we said them where we lay as if we got out and knelt down in the cold to say them. At first I merely pretended to like the idea of separate rooms, but soon I came to value a sanctum all my own more than anything else in the house. I set up a bookcase with all the boys' discarded books in it.

We moved to Caerhays in the stormy beginning of Holy Week. By Good Friday the weather had changed to fine. After church we saw the various Caerhays men in their gardens teeling their taties, an established Caerhays custom. There they were—old Alfred Snell, crippled with rheumatism, but still gardening; Jim Beard, whom I always see in my mind's eye sitting on the shaft of his cart in the rain with a bag over his shoulders. Once we took his horse out of the harrow and he went right across the field without noticing. He would shout to me, meeting me wet through on a wild day, 'Good grawin' weather!' John Blandford was a gamekeeper; but he was also one of the most assured and tidy gardeners in the place. His garden would all be 'in' before anybody else's, and his onions would come up in the most orderly rows. No lettuce, carrot, parsnip or shallot ventured out of line with John Blandford. In the right season the begonias and chrysanthemums in his front garden were a splendid spectacle—bronze chrysanthemums with gold-backed petals; and curled beauties of a colour between dandelion and furze. His double daisies were doubly double; his stocks extra-scented; his pansies pansier than ours. He had a growing family of children who became my friends. Mrs Blandford always made tartlets on Saturdays for Sunday tea, and sheets of 'nubbies' which stuck together in the baking as they expanded in their lightness. She would break a bun off the regiment for us. Dorset people, the Blandfords were originally, but well worthy of their adoption in Cornwall.

Gardens were more thought on at Caerhays than at Gorran. The Sargents and the Martins at the Hovel had gardens never without bloom. A monthly rose bush in the Sargents' garden was one I particularly loved Garden scents rather than wild scents lingered round Caerhays—lilies of the valley by the Martins' gate; moss-roses by the Sargents' gooseberry bushes; sweet violets or heliotrope under the Blandfords' wall; mignonette on either side of our own path; great tea roses over the Rectory veranda. All the land was more intensively cultivated than at Gorran; garden flowers grew even outside the gardens, but they were almost wild garden flowers, fragrant. The roses were not composed, scentless images, but full of nature, having the virtue of roses. Trees were heavier with leaves, birds' song riper—the coo of pigeons at the Hovel, the evening sermons of rooks as one went up Portluney hill from the beach. No Gorran birds cooed or preached. Lark was the Gorran bird.

I knew on the first Good Friday that Caerhays was all right—though not quite as good as Gorran. We walked to Portholland in sunshine. Celandines were sparkling. We went down through the sycamore avenue, half way up Barton Hill, over a stile on the right, and through a field called House

Close. Then we went down a steep field called Furzy Brake. Furzy Brake led to Stony Hill, from the top of which we could look down on Portholland, with its sea brimming full and bright. I knew I should be happy. We went along Barns Hills to see Dart. He was happy too, happier than he had been in Will Richards's field down Crooked Lane.

Caerhays was a hamlet rather than a village. A Church, seven cottages, a school, school house, a village Institute and the Rectory gate made up the whole of it. The Rectory itself was out of sight down a weedy drive, a rectory more beautifully situated than any other rectory I have seen; and most rectories and vicarages were built before houses defaced the sky-line. Mr Bellamy lived in it, a bachelor parson very different from the saintly Mr Martin, and quite different from old Mr Sowel. Old Mr Sowel was Cornish himself, and the only one who was ever called the passun. There was no passun's wife either at Gorran or Caerhays in my up-growing. Perhaps that is why relations between school house and rectory were so cordial. We loved Mr Bellamy, a courtly person, not unworldly, an excellent preacher and Churchman. But he introduced a new element. It was from him I first heard the word protestant as a term of contempt. He disliked the Jubilate and would not have it. He called it 'that Protestant thing'. The Rectory was two fields away from the Hovel where the Sargents and Martins lived. In addition there were three houses at Pound, and a big old home-farm called the Barton where the Kneebones lived, and where I have shared so many delectable meals that it amazes me my body does not show the better for it. I always think of Mr Kneebone as the modern equivalent to Chaucer's Franklyn, and who can say better than that? Down the drive was the Castle itself, and there were a few outlying farms—Polgrain, Little Polgrain, Polmenna, Tubsmill, Trelucky, Treberrick and Polsue. Trevilveth must have been in Veryan parish, I think. In Caerhays itself there was no chapel. The little chapels were in Portholland and West Portholland. Harsh words have been said about the personal appearance of the Cornish chapels. Some of the pretentious ones are ugly. But some of the plain little ones in the hamlets, and especially those on remote carns, have something of the same appeal as beehive huts among the furze and the bracken and giant outcrops of granite. They touch us by their humanity. 'Where you do worship 'tis your life almost' an elderly women said to me when Pentewan chapel was bombed. Now the chapels are losing their strength; but the study of the Bible which they encouraged provided Cornish people with dignity of speech, and a preoccupation with questions not paltry. ' 'Tis a bitter cup she've got to drink out of' I have heard of a person in grief; or 'It was a high dawn' of a red sunrise, as though the rising of the sun were a splendid ritual. It is easy to poke fun at dressing up in Sunday clo'. I once perpetrated some verses which I called The Land of Sunday Clo':

> We never see the piskies,
> In mowy or in barn;
> We never catch the spriggans guarding
> Gold upon the Carn;
> But one enchanted land we know,
> It is the Land of Sunday Clo'.
>
> We wake up in the morning,
> And wash and brush our hair,
> We put on nice clean underthings
> That have been put to air.
> Then out of our rare front door we go
> Into the Land of Sunday Clo'.
>
> And soon a man may see us
> Walking in the street;
> With Sunday hats upon our heads
> And Sunday shoes on feet;
> We go to serve the God we know:
> Lord of the Land of Sunday Clo'.

Luckily He was not Lord only of the black suit and the best hat. I have often wondered what Cornwall would have been like if we had become predominantly Quaker instead of predominantly Wesleyan. One would have thought that with our make up we should have chosen either symbol and ritual at their richest, or extreme plainness. Instead we chose the communal halleluia! I believe it was because we liked singing hymns; or because we are emotional and inventive rather than artistic; we liked to give Billy Bray a chance to say his say in the pulpit as well as the Passun. Had we been Quakers our Meeting houses might have been the fit complement in appearance to our churches. I shall never forget coming upon the little Friends' Meeting House called 'Come to Good'. It was in spring, recently, when I was bicycling in Cornwall. Between Feock and Falmouth I came upon a building of extreme simplicity, with thick whitewashed walls, three inset latticed windows, and a roof with projecting eaves in brown rich thatch. At one end was a thatched lean-to supported by posts. The lean-to had straw on the floor. This straw and the ivy-grown mounting-block made me feel that a seventeenth-century group of Quakers might arrive at any moment and take exception to so carnally minded a sister as I. The trees were not in leaf; only budding. There were deep-rooted clusters of primroses with long stems in the hedges; hart's-tongue and lacy ferns were unfolding from the dead; late celandines glittered; cuckoo pints and blue speedwell. Bluebell leaves everywhere gave promise of the next flowery session. The window shutters were grey, and inside the Meeting house were benches of plain wood. There was a single seat where the altar would be in a church. Nothing was faked or concealed or decorated. I had come right across Cornwall from Perranporth, where the sound of gun-practice was heard, and soldiers were standing to be moved like draughts on a draught-board. Here on the contrary was quiet; half dissolved in air and light, one might come to know the practice of the presence of God, and reach that Peace which passeth all understanding.

Our Wesleyan and Bible Christian chapels have not the quiet of 'Come to Good', but they have for their members the human friendliness of communion and singing. The Quakers valued silence; Cornish people eloquence. 'Did a preach 'un or did a read 'un?' will still be asked of a sermon. 'And if a didn' preach 'un, with no note in his hand mind you, he idn' up to much though he may be nice chap enough and know the Word.'

Both Portholland and West Portholland had chapels; but sad to say I never once went to a service in either. To me Portholland suggests Mrs Johns's shop, place of my frequent pilgrimage while we lived at Caerhays. Caerhays and Gorran people ordered their fundamental stores from Mr Box at St Austell. He sent a clerk round for orders once a month; and the goods ordered were delivered once a month by a horse van driven by an old wizened chap called Isaac. One Christmas Eve at Caerhays, when we were expecting Isaac to deliver the Christmas goods, he did not come. We were in consternation. Wherever is that old Isaac got to? Evening fell; the lamps were lit, and still no Isaac. Eleven o'clock and we went to bed; and no Isaac. At about one o'clock the village was awakened, and Isaac stumbled in at the various doors with the customary wooden boxful of goods. So many people had 'treated' Isaac in their kitchens, it being Christmas Eve, that he had been overtaken by darkness, gone to sleep, and lost his way coming up the drive. He had got down to Noah's Ark, where his horse began to enter the water of the pond, and only saved himself and Isaac by his good horse-sense. Howard, who was home for the Christmas holiday, began composing with me a story about this adventure of Isaac's. It began 'It was snowing heavily. An old man ploughed his way . . . '

When my mother forgot to order anything from Box, Anne had to 'run down to Portholland for it'. In summer I could both shop and bathe. Portholland was a good safe bathing beach— too safe. Unless the tide was right for diving in from the side rocks, it meant a long wade through shallow water. Because of the sea-wall, and a kind of bastion behind which ran the public road, spring tides and rough seas were spectacular at Portholland. I have seen waves attack the wall like demons, recoiling and flinging themselves anew into the assault however often they were repulsed and broken into clouds of spray. One

would think they must master the wall and bridge. Then the
tide would assert itself and, in the fearfullest storm, make the
waves recede. I was more aware of the rhythm of the tides at
Portholland than anywhere else. The most deliberately dangerous thing I have ever done was to walk along the wall which
separated the gardens of several cottages from the road across
the beach, when the tide was high on one side and the gardens
flooded on the other. I was dared to it. We—the village children
of Caerhays and Portholland—were always daring each other.
There were particular tests; bicycling down certain hills
without brakes was included. We ought to have broken our
necks.

Mrs Johns's shop was on the right as we entered
Portholland. We called it Mrs Johns's for in it Mrs Johns, or
Carline as her husband, Tommy, called her, reigned supreme.
Tommy had his boat, but Carline had the shop. When I knew
her Mrs Johns was already old, with beautiful silvery hair worn
in a fashion all her own. It was parted in the middle, brought
smoothly down over the ears, and fastened in a bunch of
sausage curls at the back. I hardly remember seeing her out of
doors; she was a stay-at-home. She once said to me when I
offered her my piece of smoked glass to look at an eclipse of
the sun, 'No, Anne, I do never like to gaze upon the heavenly
bodies.' In the shop everything was sold from lard to lace.
Biscuit tins fitted into their pigeon holes on the left, and at the
back, facing the counter, were ranged the glass bottles of sweets
which stuck together at times, and had to be stirred up with the
yard measure before they could be induced to go into the little
paper packets and be weighed up. We would scan the red and
yellow pear-drops, the green translucent acid-drops, the pink
and white peppermints, and the Barcelona balls bulging with
nuts, and falter in our choice. Chocolate was in wooden boxes;
sheets of chocolate-coloured paper and crinkled pink paper
were revealed when the lids were lifted. Fry's chocolate was the
only kind, cakes of chocolate cream, or flat squares of plain
chocolate. Mrs Johns would say, 'Now which will 'ee have,

clane or crame?'[1] Neat drawers which slid silkily in and out contained such things as currants and lemon peel, citron, tea, saffron, sultanas and rice. We envied Mrs Johns these drawers. Nothing we could devise in playing shops could rival them, whereas the line for drapery on the right could easily be imitated. Red cotton handkerchiefs had pride of place on the line and, at Christmas-time, handkerchiefs having 'A Merry Christmas' worked in the corner in pink and blue, with a wonderful flourish issuing from the final S and rioting in prodigal amplitude about the whole design.

Tommy, sleeping partner to Carline in the shop, was master in his own boat. My brother Howard went out with him constantly when he was home for holidays, and I would go too. We took an oar each, and rowed for Tommy when he went out to see to his crab-pots. He would swear under his breath with an admirable diversity of expression at the spider crabs— damned old gavers. When we asked him questions as to the why or wherefore of the strange shapes and forms we peered down at in the clear deep water about the rocks, he would say 'I s'pose it was ordained so for to be.' His other reply was 'Aw, 'iss, 'iss.' We liked the early morning rows best of all. I still think the grey turning of waves on a beach just before dawn is the spectacle which catches one furthest away from those trivial occupations of living woven over and concealing the strangeness of being alive on the earth at all. One catches a glimpse of a world before time was and more lasting than life. The comfort and elation of sunrise after the greyness is expressed in 'O be joyful in the Lord, all ye lands'. My brother and I were silenced by the variety of sunrise from sullenness to splendour. Tommy's voice would be heard in the stillness, 'Pull right, pull left, pull left—aw my dear boys you've missed 'em both' as, sometimes mischievously, we made him miss the bobbing corks of the crab-pots. Tommy always included me in the masculine generic; he warned Howard against the girls. Once when he and Howard were looking over some nets

[1]Plain or cream.

together in the shed at West Portholland a number of girls drove down to bathe. Howard was watching them when Tommy said, 'Come in, my son, and veil yer eyes. They'm too many guns for you.'

The boat was kept at West Portholland where the cove was narrow and the sea deep in shore; there was no quay. The two coves were connected by a cliff road and, when the tide was out, by shoals of rocks at the cliff-foot, left bare and shining by the receding tide. To go from one Portholland to another, leaping at speed from rock to rock, was a sign that a boy or girl was no longer one of the little ones, but one of the big children. I completed this test almost immediately after my arrival in Caerhays, determined as I was to sustain the honour of Gorran in the eyes of new companions.

Perched on the cliff above West Portholland was the cottage of Miss Lucinda Hill. Blake's saying, 'Energy is eternal delight' was justified in her. She was always on the go with her tongue or her hand or her feet. She kept a cow, the pride of her eyes; a pig and fowls. To have a cow like Miss Hill's, and a boat like Tommy Johns's were my ambitions. Miss Hill's cow was no ordinary anonymous cow, but a personal friend, as indeed was the pig. A saying of Miss Hill's always remained with us. She often offered us a glass of skim-milk to drink after we had bathed, and she would say, 'Drink 'un up; pig don't want 'un.' Sometimes she gave us a bun which my brother did not like; he would hide his in his pocket while Lucinda was absent driving out the chickens who had a habit of intrusiveness. Once my brother forgot he had put his bun in his pocket and after Lucinda's return, in the course of conversation, he drew out his handkerchief and the bun with it. It fell on the floor in full sight, and for a moment we were speechlessly caught out. Then the one shining moment in my life of social aplomb occurred. 'He do keep his bun to eat going up Stony Hill', I said. 'Bless the chield', said Lucinda, 'eat 'un up; he shall have another to eat going up Stony Hill.' Crumb by crumb under Lucinda's gaze my brother ate his bun and was given another to put in his pocket to eat going up the Hill. Lucinda had a wonderful head of short grey curly hair, and her wrinkles were so deep and numerous as to be a glory. I can still hear her saying, 'Goodbye, my handsomes; and if mother do want a little chicken for Sunday, tell her I got a proper little one she can have.' She had a great fancy for my brother Howard. She would say to me when he was away, 'Bless his blue eyes. When is 'a coming home again?'

Susan never went to school at Caerhays. I had to face Caerhays children alone and felt very uneasy. It was not only a question of whether they would like me, but whether they would like my father. A schoolmaster's daughter can find life difficult. Naturally she is one with the children, but home affection butts in and prevents her from being happily agin the government when the popular tide is setting that way. Luckily for me relations between governor and governed were generally cordial both at Gorran and Caerhays. When they were not, with the fatal Cornish adaptability, I took the protective colour of my contemporaries. I came to love Caerhays School. It was a charming school, set back from the main road in a grass playground, and having great rounded windows to let in the sun, and open fireplaces to show the fire. The average attendance at the school ranged in my day from about twenty to thirty children. There were two rooms, a small room for the children under seven who were taught by a mistress, and the big room where all the other children were taught by my father. He had come to Caerhays because he had thought the work would be lighter. Actually he found it hard because of the age-range of the children. He worked out a scheme which was very like what is now known as the Dalton plan. Work was arranged for us and at certain times my father came round to the different groups to cope with difficulties. I certainly flourished under this method and liked it. For one thing I escaped the bugbear of reading aloud. For a quick, glancing, skimming reader this is always very tiresome, and detrimental. My father bought a large number of Stead's penny books—'Books for the Bairns'—and when we had finished the task in hand we could read to ourselves. Also we could garden. The knowledge that there was something pleasant to do when we had finished a job encouraged us to work quickly. It is better to consider reading as a reward than as an examination subject.

I soon came to like Caerhays children, but I missed my Gorran friends and dearly liked to go back there. I used to say I was going over to have a little Gorran air. The air round Gorran really is different, more exhilarating and freer than the softer air of Caerhays. My father would often forget to post his weekly 'returns' to the District Clerk, and I would have an afternoon off sauntering over to Gorran to post them. Our post at Caerhays went out at eleven o'clock in the morning. Eleven o'clock at the pillar box by the Rectory gate, or else there was nothing for it but to go to Gorran. I did not mind how often the family forgot to post; I enjoyed the journey so much. I have discovered since that my father sometimes forgot on purpose to oblige me.

Caerhays was a church school built by Squire Williams, and maintained by him, until it was handed over to the Education Authority. My father had been promised complete freedom in the school; except for the rare and friendly visits of Inspectors, he obtained it. The Squire's attitude to the school was an amusing example of the very English habit of divergence between theory and practice. At Gorran the school was run by an education authority which was, in theory, committed heart and soul to the education of the people; in practice there was a certain niggardliness and cheese-paring; a neglect of warmth and sanitation.[2] At Caerhays I have heard my father say that theoretically the Squire was very cold towards bookish education, perhaps because, like us, he had known so many people of high integrity, good sense and religious feeling who had little of it. In theory he was less enthusiastic than a committee. In practice he provided a clean sunny school with blazing wood and coal fires in winter, and plenty of space

[2]But Mr F. R. Pascoe, Secretary for Education, was an enthusiast. His delightfully vivid account of Cornish schools in the *Cornwall Education Week Handbook*, 1927, p. 37, is always worth re-reading.

everywhere. I think he never refused my father anything for the school from a field to a daffodil bulb.

Looking back it seems to me that the Squire's limitation was that he was rather a person who did his duty than one who enjoyed himself. He never sang in church. When he died bottles and bottles and bottles and bottles of wine had to have their necks broken and their lives lost because they had never been taken care of, much less drunk. I have been told that old Charlie H., who helped to cart the debris out to the Barns Hills, turned a somersault clean head-over-heels with his horse and his cart for joy of the mere smell of it. The Squire was incurably sober. He would give us a brace of pheasants but not the right bottle to go with them. Probably he would have been happier as a very private gentleman than as a man with great possessions which he felt he held as a trust. He was Lord Lieutenant of the Duchy, yet had no more taste for ceremony than for wine; he would rather look at a rhododendron bush than preside at a banquet. I can see him striding along on his great feet in big boots in a field ahead of us. He once stopped to spud up a thistle with his stick; it came up all of a sudden and over he went 'like a tab'. His word was law in Caerhays; perhaps that was why Gorran was different. There nobody's word was law however benevolent. 'I shall tell 'Ee about this', I can remember old Simon Rickard of the Lower Lodge saying to my father as he hobbled out rather late to open the gate for our pony-trap. Perhaps no human person should be Ee. Yet Ee kept his and our lovely Caerhays as lovely as when he inherited it. How else could it have been preserved from the jerry-builder and those who 'develop' Estates. Dodman Point, I think I am right in saying, was one of the very earliest of the National Trust properties. It was given by Squire Williams. To name the Trust in the same breath as the jerry-builders is wrong. Usually, I am glad to hear that places have come under the ownership of the Trust, and Ferguson's gang has seemed romantic to me. But I sometimes fear that even Cliffs will not bear embalming; and books like *Britain and the Beast: A Survey by Twenty-Six*

Authors[3] infuriate me because I hate sermons by people like Mr C. E. M. Joad. He makes me feel contrary. If he inveighs against orange peel I want to flip a piece at him. He has all the new cant. The old cant of the Churches has been forgotten so long that all its phrases begin to wake up and take life again, fresh and endearing. But Mr Joad uses, 'develop our latent potentialities'; 'newly enfranchised citizens of leisure' (this was before the war took away leisure from everybody); 'education in the appreciation of beauty'. He divides his sermon into three parts with sub-headings. Oh, oh, *oh*, Mr Joad!

Squire Williams knew no cant. I have heard my father say no man was freer from the tyranny of words; I believe his advice was sought after in affairs. But I have never met people who were associated with him in public work. My memories of him are childish and with children he was probably at his best. He did not change his manner for them, but treated them with his accustomed gravity. If I met him out I knew he would shake hands with me as well as with my father, and that I should not have that awkward moment one had with most grown ups wondering whether one would shake hands or experience some equivalent to being patted on the head. Perhaps ceremony is freedom. I never remember his coming into school. Mrs Williams came to give away the prizes. We had had no prizes at Gorran. On the whole I think it better for a school to be without prizes. Children are happy doing a thing for its own sake as long as no other motive is introduced. I sometimes think of Dr Johnson's dictum when I consider the fiercely competitive nature of the system today: 'By exciting emulation and comparisons of superiority, you lay the foundations of lasting mischief; you make brothers and sisters hate each other.'

One thing prizes had encouraged at Caerhays was sewing. My eyes opened wide when I saw how the girls could sew. They were—the girls of my age and upwards—really beautiful needle-women. Their hands seemed cool and witty while mine

[3]Ed. Clough Williams Ellis, 1937.

were sticky and stupid. I can still see their clean cotton and delicate stitches contrasting with my dirty cotton, uneven tackings and drops of blood from my pricked fingers. The way they gathered and tucked and feather-stitched left me gaping with admiration. They cut just what was required whereas I, asked to snip an inch, would saw an ell. I never mastered the art of needlework.

It was after we had been at Caerhays three years or so that the question arose, 'What do you want to be?' I did not want to be anything. Susan seemed to be getting along quite nicely being nothing. But my parents said I must be something. Unlike my sister I had no taste, apart from cooking, for domesticity. Even when I cooked I made more litter than a cook should and was inclined to shirk the saucepans. On one celebrated occasion I hid all the dirty dishes in the copper, a notion so entirely foreign to the tradition in which I had been brought up that I think I must have possessed original genius which failed to develop. I was always ready to flee the house. Like Mistress Anne Killigrew, whose poems I read in later years, I could have said:

> Arise, my Dove, from midst of Pots arise,
>   Thy sully'd habitation leave,
>   To dust no longer cleave,
> Unworthy they of Heaven that will not view the skies.

There seemed nothing for it but for me to have a profession, for since I was not pretty I was not like to find an Earl of Leicester to install me in a bower of bliss above the pots and pans. If I did I might end down a trap-door.

My father was not anxious for me to teach. But what could I do? Nursing? I had a horror of it! Clerking? My figures would never add up! A shop-girl? I had a fancy I might like the grocery business, but Carline, when consulted by me, did not need a 'prentice. Somebody—a school-inspector, I think—said I had better try a Minor Scholarship for St Austell. I was not displeased at this. It would not be as bad as a boarding school. I should have to live in St Austell, but I should come home for week-ends. The idea of the examination did not worry me at all. My brothers had tossed off examination successes without losing any sleep, why should not I?

The day of trial drew near. I polished up Dart's hoofs for it and we drove in to St Austell. I felt forlorn among the other candidates until I saw a girl with brown eyes and almost yellow curls. I conceived a romantic attachment to her on the spot, though I did not dream of speaking to her. She was laughing and careless and at ease. To my admiration she said in clear casual grown-up tones during the examination, 'May we have a window open, please?' May we have a window open, please!— with no shyness, just in ordinary tones. I hadn't even perceived what was wrong with the room, though I was stifling. As for boldly asking to have a window open, I should as soon have thought of playing bo-peep with the aged and bearded invigilator. I can remember only one question in the whole of the examination and that was 'Who wrote *Troy Town*?' I put an enormous Q., and informed my examiner that in my opinion *Dead Man's Rock* was the better book. By the time the examination was over I did not think I'd done so badly though my fingers were covered with ink, a good deal of which had conveyed itself in smears and smudges on the paper, and my handwriting looked no better than usual though I had taken pains. I did not wish to fail, though neither did I wish to go to St Austell to school.

But I did fail. Some weeks afterwards I was sitting on the table in the kitchen shelling peas when my father came in and said, 'Well, Anne hasn't passed, so that's that!' My heart leapt up, although there was no rainbow in the sky. I said, 'So I shan't have to go to St Austell, after all.' My father said, 'Not this year, any way.' Then he said, 'Mabel Teague has passed.' All my complacence slipped away. Mabel was my friend and contemporary at Gorran School, and I had thought we were about equal. My pride was distinctly hurt. I wished I had passed, even if it meant going away.

My family took my failure philosophically. My father laughed and said examiners threw all the papers against a sticky wall, and those that stuck passed, and those that dropped failed. I was never reproached. But I began to work at home. My father said I could try another scholarship, this time for intending teachers, next year; and that I'd better do some work so as not to be behind the others. We did together the first three books of Euclid and a good deal of Algebra; I began Latin, and I read as much history from as many different books as I could lay hold of. As a result, when I passed the examination a year later I was behind my contemporaries only in having no foreign languages. I remember nothing at all about the second examination.

The July and August before I went to St Austell were halcyon days. I was free of one school and not in another. Howard was home for all August, and Maurice for part of it. Stan and Cap'n came for a fortnight in July. I drove up to meet them in turn at St Austell and we came home to find the others watching for us by the gate below the church. This gate commanded a view of the road almost to Treberrick. It was a golden summer. Certain themes and airs of Chopin, Beethoven and Schubert bring it back with irresistible force. We were out all day and played and sang all the evening. I can hear Cap'n, a good baritone, singing 'Trumpeter, what are you sounding now?' with unconsciously prophetic feeling; or Maurice trolling out music-hall ditties; or Mr Bellamy's one and only song, 'So we went strolling, over the rolling, over the rolling sea'. The hours seemed made for sunshine, or moonlight, or music, or making love. Everybody was falling in and out of love with the ease of early Shakespearean comedy. I remember the dust in the lanes through which the wheels of the trap went softly as I drove to St Austell to meet this one or that; the clean leaves when the rain washed them; the swallows quartering the fields, skimming and turning with a speed that took one's breath away; the warm slow evening; the dumble dores blundering about with a scaly rattle. I would spend idle hours on the cliffs, watching grasshoppers like stiff-jointed bits of animated bracken, ladybirds with varnished spotted cases into which to fold their gauze wings. 'Ladybird, ladybird, fly away home.' I used to wish I could be compact and complete like the lady-bird, secure against the weather, yet unburdened; able to fly.

There was one excursion we always made when one or two of my brothers and their friends or current lady-loves were at home. We would have Johnny Johns's wagonette, and get up very early in the morning, and drive first to Portscatho, then on to Percuil where we got a steamer. We went by steamer to Falmouth where we stayed an hour or so, then we boarded *The Queen of the Fal* for the trip to Truro and back.

I did not care particularly for Falmouth in those days. But some years after, when I was camping at St Antony in Roseland, I bicycled in the cool of the evening to the Lighthouse by Zoze Point, and realized for the first time in my life the splendour of Falmouth harbour. In my arrogance I had thought of Falmouth (God forgive me) as a place for 'visitors' and to be avoided. But when towards sunset I stood on the rocks below the lighthouse, facing the harbour, I knew that everything that had ever been written or said about the beauty of Falmouth harbour was true. The sun made a broad road of gold between me and the Castle; crossing this road the sails of the boats turned gold. The sea was merry with a gently-ruffling breeze. The estuary had an aspect of glorious spaciousness; and from it the tide ran up into land, up the creeky Fal, running up to Penryn, running up to Malpas and Truro, run-ning up to Percuil; it used ages ago even to run up to Tregony. Facing me the outline of the Promontory was sharp and clear with the sun at its back hiding Falmouth town. The docks lay to the right with big ships hinting of the busy sea-traffic of bygone Falmouth. I watched the hills at the back and the far-distant smooth lines of a carn. To the left the coast stretched in a long line in shadow to the Manacles. I saw the sun set, and at the moment of its setting the lighthouse light—and I suppose all other lighthouse lights in Cornwall—came on. No wonder that to the Cornish the lighthouse lights seem as punctual and natural as the heavenly bodies. I have always liked the late Charles Henderson's story of the old man at the Lizard who wanted the parson to read him a passage from the Bible and asked for the passage about Lizard Lights. The parson was puzzled till it was explained to him that the passage was 'The sun, the moon and all the lesser (Lezzard) lights'.

In the old days of our visits to Falmouth I cared more for Jacob's Ladder than the Lighthouse or the Castle, though the harbour was always a source of pleasure and anxiety. People would be grumbling at the iniquity of having to give a penny to go through the turnstile on to Princes Pier; and once on the pier the crowd seeking *The Queen of the Fal* would surge towards a set of steps. After we had been there some time an old man in a peaked cap would shout with malicious joy, 'This way for *The Queen of the Fal*', and the crowd would surge in his direction, the last persons now becoming first, and all elbowing and jostling till one was nearly shoved into the water. It seemed as though there would never be room for us all; but soon the last person was handed aboard and there we were, up-country people, and Cornish folk, and haughty persons in full yachtsman's rig, looking so much more nautical than any *nauta* I have ever seen.

A churning and a hooting, and we would move off through the dancing water of the bay into the smooth heavy river water, the scene ever shifting and changing as we advanced; the prospect now opening up, now closing in on us, till it seemed we were land-locked and could progress no further; then we would round a bend into fresh reaches, with banks wooded to the water's edge, dwarf oak and rose and thorn. I used to think I would like to live at Pill Creek; or one could perhaps become ferryman at King Harry Passage, with the ferryman's money to live on and a little house thrown in. There are dear little houses on the banks of the Fal.

And so we would come to Malpas and to Truro which looks its best from the river, once you have passed municipal ugliness and come to the wharfs. The Cathedral was the first Protestant Cathedral, with the exception of St Paul's, to be built in England after the Reformation. The site is the old St Mary's Church; and as that in its turn stood in the old High Cross, the place has had Christian associations for many centuries, though it is only just over fifty years ago that the choir and part of the nave of the Cathedral were consecrated, and the lovely Western towers were not finished until 1910. Those learned in cathedral architecture have always found it difficult to judge Truro Cathedral for what it is in itself. Knowing that it is imitation Early English, they have looked at it and, expecting it to be lifeless, have found it so. They have not seen its freshness nor its suitability for Truro as Truro is— the market city, not of the wilder parts of Cornwall, but of the tilled and cultivated Roseland district, a land of little woods and cornfields, a southern and sunny place. To appreciate Truro Cathedral one must come towards it in *The Queen of the Fal* past the sheltered creeks and orchards. Then the spires are necessary and right.

Mabe granite went to the making of the outside of Truro Cathedral and, although much Bath stone is used inside, china-claystone from St Stephen's has its place, grey polyphant from east Cornwall, and Lizard serpentine. The clock tower is roofed with Cornish copper, and the colour adds a note of fantasy, as though some jinnee with a sense of the ridiculous had come and clapped this green cap on in the night while the builders slept . . .

I was confirmed in the Cathedral the summer of the year I passed the scholarship examination. Alas, just as Karen thought of her red shoes, I thought of my new white frock.

I tried to make time go slowly that summer, and enjoyed everything with the sharpened pleasure of one about to go into captivity. Lodgings had been found for me at St Austell in a little crooked house full of cats. Grant's Walk was the alley, and through it in addition to the cats of my hostess, Miss Susan V—, walked all the cats of St Austell, black and tabby, white and marmalade, short-tailed and long. The alley was jewelled with eyes. I was not anxious about my lodgings. I knew I should like them; but about the school I was filled with anxiety. How should I fare among all these youths and maidens and what should I do without the sea and Dart? I began to pity myself; I envied Susan.

My mother talked of clothes. The only clothes I had were made up of such odd bits of bright coloured stuff as had come my mother's way from various aunts. I loved bright colours. But my aunt assured my mother that a navy blue suit was what I needed, and though my mother said doubtfully she'd never fancied me in navy blue my wordly-wise aunt's advice prevailed. Navy blue it was; and when it came fresh from a Truro tailor's I put it on and felt like a snuffed candle. I suppose I had other clothes; but in that navy blue I changed from being a poppy into something sober like pennywort. I wished with all my heart I'd had the sense to fail the examination a second time.

Term began on a Tuesday. On the Saturday I drove my own luggage in to Grant's Walk, pretending to myself in the gloomiest fashion that the trunk was my coffin. I told Dart I should die young; and at Faircross I nearly ran into Mr Bellamy's dog-cart while shedding imaginary tears at my own funeral. Mr Bellamy was returning from Grampound. He stopped and cheered me up and, if it hadn't been awkward with the two ponies and traps, would have turned back and accompanied me into St Austell himself to console me with tea and buns. As it was we agreed it wouldn't be very companionable to drive six miles together in separate traps, so he went off home to his nice Rectory. I've had a hankering to be ordained ever since, and a fancy for the title of Rural Dean.

At first it was said that my father would drive me in for the first school day on Monday evening so that I should be all shining and ready for Tuesday morning. But I pleaded so hard to stay until Tuesday morning that my parents allowed it. It meant my mother's driving me in, and she hated the lonely roads. However, she did it. We started at about 7.30 and she drove me as far as St Mewan from which I was to walk. I tried to drive slowly but Dart was lively, tossing his head, and full of early morning tricks. We reached St Mewan hill in no time. I turned the trap for my mother, kissed her and kissed Dart. He took no notice. He was too full of joy at being turned for home at St Mewan instead of having to go in to St Austell. He frisked off in high spirits, and soon he and the trap and my mother in her old brown golf cape with its plaid hood were lost to view. I knew I should be late. I walked slowly to make myself later. I meditated on schemes by which I might take to the woods from Monday to Friday nights, and yet make it appear to my parents that I had been to school all the time. If only I could become a Palmer or a Gaberlunzie. Slower and slower I walked, but at last I came to the door of the disused chapel in which the school was being held while its new quarters were a-building. I opened the door and went in.

CORNISH
YEARS

To Susan

Contents

Acknowledgements

Of the poems used as epigraphs to the chapters of this book 'Winter Pride' and 'To the Giver of Breath' are reprinted by permission of the Editor of the *Observer*; 'History on Viewing a Collection of Weapons' by permission of the Editor of the *New Statesman and Nation*; 'Belinda's Garden' by permission of the Editor of the *West Country Magazine*; 'Beech Tree in October' by permission of the Editor of the *Spectator*. The others have either been taken from *This World's Bliss* or have not been previously published.

1

TWO PARISHES

An open primrose
And an exquisite feather;
What wing and what star
Have brushed earth together!

—*February in Trevennen Wood*

hen I was a child I did not know that Gorran in
South Cornwall where I was born was beautiful, nor
St Michael Caerhays, the neighbouring parish to
which we moved when I was ten.[1] It was my sister Susan who
whispered to me that we need not mind if the Cody-Coats, a
family of boys who came to stay at Gorran Haven in summer,
and whom we called Cody-Coats because they wore Eton
jackets to church on Sundays—we need not mind if the Cody-
Coats stole our saucepan and our frying-pan from the cave at
Hemmick. They would go away with August, she said, but we
should live in Gorran and Caerhays for ever and ever.

We always seemed to belong to the two parishes because,
while my father was head master of Gorran School, he used to
drive our pony, Dart, to Caerhays on Sundays, and play the
little organ there. And when he left Gorran School for

[1] I have described our lucky childhood in *School House in the Wind*.

157

Caerhays, and we transferred ourselves from the school-house on high ground near Menagwins, to the schoolhouse on high ground between Sentries Lane and St Michael Caerhays Church, we still felt like Gorran people and were interested in Gorran news. News travelled like lightning in Gorran. It used to be said that if you cut your finger in Gorran Haven it was hanging at Cooks, and cut off clean as a whistle in Gorran Churchtown. Our letters at Caerhays were brought from Gorran by Jabez Grose, and we always had a little chat with Jabez. Mevagissey news was carried by Thomas Hicks as he dealt out from his van his golden-brown loaves, and saffron cakes crowded with currants and lemon peel. Nicky Liddicoat, the fish-jouster, often went through St Ewe and Veryan before he reached Caerhays; by then his news was ripe for the telling. Johnny Johns from Portholland went to St Austell once a week, on Fridays, market day. We had St Austell news from Johnny or from anyone he took up and back in his wagonette. When Mr and Mrs Kneebone at the Barton went to Truro market on Wednesdays, they kept us in touch with that region of the outside world. Having heard all the local news by word of mouth we liked to read it confirmed in print in the local papers. I loved the Cornish local papers and love them still. Wherever I am I can read the *St Austell Guardian*, the *West Briton* or the *Cornishman* with pleasure. They are the only papers I ever read right through from Births, Deaths and Marriages to the projected movements of the Stud Bull. I like the story of the lady rider to hounds who, when asked at a Hunt Ball if she had read *Gone with the Wind* replied, 'No; is it in the *West Briton*?'

Southward, Gorran and Caerhays parishes were bounded by the sea. To the west Veryan and Cuby bordered Caerhays; to the east Mevagissey bordered Gorran. The large pastoral parish of St Ewe, and St Austell which gave its name to our market town, lay between us and Cornwall's ridgy backbone. There in the distance, hazy on hot summer days, or clearly outlined when rain threatened, we could see the Arch Beacon, Hensbarrow, a thousand feet up. Sharp-eyed folk standing on the Dodman, or gazing through a five-barred gate, or mounted on a hedge or up a tree would say they could spy Roche Rock. I have said I could spy Roche Rock when in truth I was not sure even in which direction to look. The rock was only sixteen or so miles away and yet it seemed to me immensely distant. To us the whole upland region was fabulous, with its camp of great white tents, not tents really but dumped china-clay waste fashioned into constant shape by wind and weather. I have seen these glistering pyramids in summer seeming to sail between earth and air. In the distance the sides of the pyramids appear smooth; nearby they are seen to be grooved, furrowed and channelled, patched with gorse and more grey than white.

From our bedroom windows at Caerhays we could look across the valley to Gorran or more correctly, St Goran Church tower; and Gorran cricket team was still our cricket team. My father often went over to umpire for it on Saturdays. Caerhays, though the boys and girls played cricket in the field behind the school, and the men came to play in the evenings and to criticize us, was too small to support a regular eleven like its neighbours Veryan, on the one side, or its Gorran neighbour on the other. Gorran and Veryan were special rivals. Gorran would do anything to beat Veryan. It was better to beat Veryan than to beat town teams like St Austell, and Truro, or good school teams like Probus, though Gorran had fixtures with them. 'We'm playing Vuryan. We'm going lick 'em this time sure as taties. We could ate Vuryan this year.' Parishes like St Ewe and Mevagissey hardly counted in cricket. But Gorran counted and still counts. My elder brothers, Maurice, Howard, Stanley and Wilfrid (known as Cap'n) all played for Gorran in their day. Maurice played less than the others for he went early away from home to school. Cap'n was the best all-round cricketer, Stan the best bowler and Howard, my father used to say, was erratic. He would make a fine score one week and be out for a duck the next. When the little demon within him concurred he could hit out with impunity. He still thinks that his proudest moment was when on one of his good days he made so many runs for Gorran that he was chaired, and old

Parson Sowell said, 'Take off your cap, my boy; take off your cap.' And my father, who always hummed a snatch of Anglican chant or hymn tune when he was agitated, came towards him over the grass humming, 'Lord I am not high-minded', and said, 'You did well, boy.'

And Will Richards praised him. Will Richards, who died two years ago at the age of seventy-six, was a man whose word of praise meant much to my brothers. His photograph always takes my eye on my brother Howard's desk. He stands as he used to stand by the forge near the elder bush at Menagwins, his arms folded, the neck-band of his shirt unbuttoned, his sleeves rolled up, his cap on his head. His father had been blacksmith at Menagwins before him, and his grandfather before that. Later his son Lowry, at school with me, was to join him in a perfect partnership. The forge was stone-built. It had a window of small over-lapping panes, and a door in two separate parts, so that on occasion the bottom could be closed and the top open and Will could lean out. In the yard, where an old harrow rusted, grew the elder tree. The yard wall curved with the curving road. As we began to round it we heard the champ of a bit or the jingle of iron traces. Some great cart-horses were so big that the yard would hardly contain them; we might see a brown tail jutting out of the gap, or a shining rump as we approached; and we heard Will shouting, 'Woa-up!' or 'Woa-back!' People not working themselves like to watch other people working. Nearly always there was someone at the forge watching Will and Lowry, and waiting to blow the bellows. Then from the blackness fire would wake and sparks would sparkle. Will would take out glowing iron, beat it into shape, and quench it sizzling in black water. The smell of quenched iron filled the forge; the air was thick with it. Between jobs, Will and Lowry would always be ready to talk, Will wrinkling up his forehead which ran back into corrugated lines like the sand at Hemmick as the tide went out. Proverbial sayings in Gorran contained metaphors from shoeing. When in recent years I was giving my opinion as to how a difficult evacuee child should be treated Polly Burley observed, 'Everybody do know what to do with a kicking horse except he that got 'un.' And when I thought of borrowing money to buy a house in Mevagissey Nellie Watty said, 'A big horse, you know, Anne, do need big shoes.'

Will was genial in dealing with people, but not so tactful as to be tame or smooth. His feelings showed, and he could be hot-hearted; but there was something in him immensely reassuring and kind. He was at once human and God-fearing without a trace of cant. His personality made things go. When he arranged cricket teams people quarrelled but played; while he was captain of ringers the bells rang merrily; while he was church warden the church seemed established for good. Children felt safe and not silly with Will. 'Hullo! my dear!' he would say. 'Hullo!' We were reassured and knew we were welcome. He used to whistle hymn tunes; not a few confined favourites, but dozens of different hymns. With them he carried his Sunday into his weekdays, but he never carried his weekdays into Sundays. He would no more have thought of carrying corn on a Sunday than of mending a plough. Not the finest hot dry Sunday in a cold wet week could tempt him. He might regret the day; he might complain of the weather; but he kept his rhythmical period of repose. He was philosophical about climate. Like the local preacher he would have said, 'Tidn' no good for 'ee to pray for fine weather with the wind where 'tis.' His wife, Ellen Kate, happily still living at Menagwins, had a laugh tilting upwards and upwards till it drew you out to laugh too. It was ha-ha-ha-ha on an ascending scale. What she thought at the moment she said; every sentence was full of pith.

Will Richards has a son in Gorran. My parents have no son living in Gorran, and no daughter either. Yet we still belong. We belong because we remember every detail. We remember the ice splintering white under our heels in the wheel-rutted farm-lanes in winter as well as the honeysuckle scenting the summer hedges; the great hoof-prints filled with water in the churned February mud by the mowhay gates as well as the primroses and violets; the rabbit-droppings on the Greeb as well as the wild thyme. We know the stinging-nettles in the ditches with the soothing dock-leaves hard by; the penny-worts in the patterned stone hedges flanking the stiles; the veined ivies and the oak-leaf ferns. August makes us see again the cracks in the parched, hard path leading down to Hemmick. We were there when Walter Ford, cutting the trash in the hedges, chose one or two favourites among the thorns on top, and spared them each year, and tended them, and let them grow into trees bearing the leaves we called green-cheese in early spring, then pearly buds, then flowers with watch-like, open, innocent faces, then the polished, dark red berries we called aglets. We know the lanes. If two of us meet as we did recently in Indiana where my eldest brother lives, we can walk together in memory the deep hidden lanes, almost like leafy caverns, that link Streets, Treninnick, Tregerrick, Polsue (the Gorran Polsue), Bennets, Metherose, Galowras and Lancallen. The primroses in Polsue Lane are moons in beauty. We saunter down Cotna Lane and by the field path to Sentries; and through Scotland Wood, and turn right to Portmellon, or left over the uplands to Penwarne and Mevagissey, coming out by what used to be Mr Howard Dunn's house, and taking the coloured harbour full into our eyes.

All my brothers belong more to Gorran than to Caerhays. By the time we went to Caerhays to live they had all left home and only came back for holidays. But to my sister Susan and me Caerhays lanes and fields and cliffs are as dear as Gorran, and as familiar. Caerhays is a compact, secluded parish, all owned, except the rectory, by Mr John Charles Williams when I was young, and by his son, Mr Charles Williams of Caerhays Castle now. Caerhays Castle! A good sound it has, much better than Caerhays House would be. And Mr Williams's house is a castle. Not an ancient castle; it was built by the last of the Trevanions at the beginning of the nineteenth century; the ruin above the battery walk was placed there to suit the fashion of the time. But I would rather hear the rooks caw about that fanciful ivy-mantled tower than about all the true old ivy-mantleds in the world. I have an image in my mind of the castle itself as I write. I imagine I am standing in the park which leads to Tregavarras. I look down at the pond with its grey-green rushes and its water-lilies. I see the bullocks feeding on the level pasture as though all time was theirs; I see the grey walls and the symmetrical towers, and the battlements, and the woods enfolding secret fairy-lands of flowering trees and shrubs. And there, right by the castle—so near that I suppose Mr Williams could walk out of his bed and into the sea in five minutes, if he wanted to—is Portluney, which has its name from the fishfull, brown, little river Luney.

Many farms have passed to families with new names. More than any other family now gone from Caerhays I miss the Rhoddas at Polsue. (There is a Polsue Farm in Gorran parish too.) At Polsue, beyond Treberrick on the road to Fair Cross, Ruth Rhodda used to have her friends to tea on Sundays, and entertain them in a room quite independently of her parents and of her sisters, who dispensed tea and smiles to their young men in other rooms still. Ruth, Alice Blandford and I, as though we were grown-ups visiting one another, would feast alone on spiced cake, and rice cakes, and jam tarts with a crust of yellow cream daintily deposited on the jam. Ruth was a dainty person. She laid the tea grandly with doilies starched and goffered on the dishes, and flowers in a red glass vase with fluted trimmings round a stem rising from a shallow stand. The window looked on to the mowhay. I rarely see hens jutting their heads without thinking of Polsue. I liked to feel the maize grains slide through my fingers in the bowl as I played with them before I scattered them wide to the cocks and hens. Polsue fowls were active, stringy birds who laid their eggs in all sorts of wild places. There were never such hens for stealing their nests; in soft spring sunshine I can see the primroses in Polsue Lane and a hen coming down with a whole brood of unexpected chickens. Animals did more as they liked at Polsue than at other farms; the ducks brought themselves up. Even the calves were very independent. We fed them after tea, and helped to milk. I learnt to milk at Polsue. Then we used to walk to church for evensong, hurrying up the last two hills as the bells were being rung down. If we were in church early we used to hear Mr Charlie Dustow shout 'Stand' between the peals; and sometimes the six ringers would take so long turning down their sleeves and putting on their coats that, before they had reached the north aisle, Mr Bellamy would be waiting to begin, 'When the wicked man turneth away from the wickedness which he hath committed, and doeth that which is lawful and right, he shall save his soul alive.' Bert Paddy, a well-knit, square-shouldered figure, used to lurch as he turned into the narrow space between the front seat of the nave and the pulpit. On festival days our hearts would beat for the safety of our decorations.

Lanes and paths led to the church. Polgrain Lane was one of my favourites. On hot August days I used to go up Sentries Lane, just at the back of our house to the left of the pump, and go down through Sentries[2] fields to Polgrain Valley and sit on the little bridge over the river with my feet in the brown water round the rushes, and weave myself hats of meadowsweet and ferns. Susan was by this time too big for such occupations, and I was too big really. So I made and wore my hats secretly. It was easy to be secret at Caerhays in the lanes and the woods, or on the cliffs, or in the fields through which ran the church paths linking scattered souls. Caerhays Church and Gorran Church held and hold the parishes in their keeping. Wherever you walk the church towers may rise suddenly into the distant view. Gorran, in particular, is a noble tower; whether you are walking by Scotland Wood to Mevagissey, or back to Gorran by Penare from the Dodman, the pinnacles of the tower are a recurring theme. Caerhays tower, less elegant, is solid and sound against the weather. What it lacks in height it makes up for in situation. It is like a wayside chapel to which a knight might come in Arthurian romance.

My brothers used to drive over to Caerhays with my father when we lived at Gorran. But they did not go to Caerhays

---

[2]There are Sentries [Sanctuaries] Fields in both Gorran and Caerhays parishes.

Church as Susan and I did in their late teens. Not one of my four brothers found work near home, although my youngest brother used to say he was going to be a farmer like old Mr Lanyon, and my brother Stan used to say he would be a carpenter like George Martin and make Cap'n's gates and wheels for nothing. That was when we used to go over to Highlanes to watch George Martin making wheels; and to play with the curly shavings, and sniff the woody smell; and when we used to see Mr Lanyon driving Dinah into market from Lamledra.

Susan and I used to think that the most perfect way of life would be for two of our brothers to have farms near enough for visiting and we would keep house for them; I for Howard and she for Maurice; or I for Cap'n and she for Stan. This neat arrangement for pure content was actually exemplified for us in Gorran by the Lawrys. Mr Billy farmed Treveor with his sister, Miss Elizabeth; and Mr John farmed Tregarten with his sister Miss Susan. But neither my sister nor I could ever have emulated Miss Elizabeth and Miss Susan, most notable housekeepers. There is a strong tradition of good housekeeping and good cookery in Gorran parish. Not that Miss Elizabeth and Miss Susan were extravagant. I have heard that when a pig was killed at Treveor Miss Elizabeth would gather up every eye of fat to run down for lard, so that when the table and utensils came to be washed the dish-water was hardly greasy. It was said that Miss Susan disliked to 'tap' a fresh half-pound of butter for the family. If there were not sufficient left over for home use after the last half-pound had been patted, she preferred to wait till the next butter-making. And this frugality was admired. It was felt that the sisters were not 'near' but orderly; warriors in the grand style against waste and dirt. Husbands held them up as patterns to their wives. Certainly things minded them. I best remember Miss Elizabeth, as upstanding as the monkey-puzzle on her lawn. Treveor was trim; its iron gate painted white as snow; its lawn with hardly a daisy showing—a dandelion would never dare. Miss Elizabeth was the opposite of the sun-drinking dandelions. Her wide flower border, to the right of the lawn and of the white gate as we looked in from the road, had all the flowers in their season—all the garden not the common flowers. Her marguerites did not look like horse-daisies; they were elegant, elongated, slender, growing white and gold and green in a beautiful colony near the house. What delighted us in Treveor lawn was that it spread smoothly to the veranda from an unfenced bank; all its green surface open to view. Treveor was a good farm or rather (according to Mr Kneebone of Caerhays Barton) Treveor was made good by Mr Billy Lawry. He put good things into it. A farm, says Mr Kneebone, can be filled up, and plumped, and rounded like a good stomach; and contrariwise, by another type of farmer, the goodness can be taken out of it, and taken out of it, until there is nothing left but an old wrinkled skin. Mr Billy left his land in far better heart and stomach than he found it. So did his neighbour Mr Thomas Grose of Trevarrick where our pony, Dart, had been a colt.

Many friends of mine and Susan's married farmers or men who, like Lowry Richards, had fields in addition to some other such job as blacksmithing. I like to think of Ella Richards standing by a window that looks out into a network of sky and blade and branch above a green bank. When she makes a special little sound all the feathered creatures come gobbling, and quacking, and clucking—the turkeys, and the ducks, the ducklings, the hens and the handsome cocks. If I had turkeys and ducks and hens and handsome cocks I should probably forget to feed them; and the milking of cows is not my favourite occupation. When I did have a garden I let more weeds grow than garden flowers, and I never planted rows of peas and beans and a gooseberry bush, or red and white currants. Yet my fancy has always been for a few acres with creatures and apple trees; and a house with jars of jam in the pantry, and sections of honey; with a cool place for primrose and cowslip wine, and cherry brandy, and sloe gin. I wish that all my brothers had been farmers and had farms at Gorran; then I need have owned nothing. I could have visited them all in turn, milking an occasional cow, and picking the blackberries for the jam, and the mushrooms for the ketchup, and the sloes for the sloe gin. But none of us stayed at Gorran or Caerhays. All my brothers went away on this pursuit or that. By the time I was fourteen Maurice, the most intellectual of us, was chasing chemistry in London; he was to settle in America, though he came joyfully home as often as he could afford it, and never seemed really apart from us. Howard, the most artistic of my brothers, and the most ready to help people, had become an organist and schoolmaster in Exeter. He earned his living by doing work which he both enjoyed and knew to be worth while, an enviable thing. But then he, like my parents, was religious. Stan, the most philosophical of my brothers, and the most modern in his outlook, considered and still considers that the best thing, in a machine age, is for everyone to do his measure of dull work and keep his darling leisure for himself and his affectionate family. In a properly run world no one need do dull work to the point of becoming dull himself he says. But the world is naturally slow to change; and it is no use to shoot people in order to make it change quicker. Men must live. That it is better to live in a muddle than die in an orderly fashion my brother has steadily perceived. If I were God I should design a little corner of heaven where my father and his third son might meet and go to a cricket match together, and then light their pipes and walk in one another's gardens, considering one another's early broccoli, spring onions or sweet peas. There should be no children for my father to teach, and no post offices for my brother to go and look at—Stan went into the post office. My father and my third brother were perfect characters to enjoy leisure and ease. But so, indeed, was my youngest brother also. He, the most sporting of us was, by this time, dreaming in a London warehouse of getting rich quickly and coming home to buy Beeparks, so as to spend his time shooting over Dodman and fishing off Long Rock. Stan, too, had a hankering for Beeparks; but Beeparks belongs to John Grose who had the sense to stay in Gorran and keep his eye on what he wanted. We, who were all considered so clever when we were young, have no land.

But land often causes disruption in families. Perhaps because he had nothing to leave, my father, if there were that sunny spot in heaven, would enjoy meeting all his four sons, a not so common thing in families. I have said what pleasures he would enjoy with Stan; with Howard he would listen to the heavenly harmony; with Cap'n he would cap St Peter's fishing stories; with Maurice he would argue. Maurice used to say that before coming home on one of his visits from America he used to give himself more than ordinarily to current affairs so to have ammunition for the endless talks and arguments in which he and my father indulged. My mother would be there to keep an eye on them. She was one for loving and giving and not for changeful opinion. Almost any sunny heaven would do for her if my father were there; indeed if my father were there I am not sure that she would even mind if the nook faced north. Whereas my father, whoever was with him, would be conscious of the absence of the sun. He always thought he would like to live at Little Polgrain where he would be facing due south.

My brothers all had an idea of what they wanted to do. Susan and I were more elusive; secretly we merely wanted to stay where and as we were. But soon, even Susan was going to St Austell on Saturdays for music lessons, and I had to do something. I did not, like my brother Howard, choose teaching because I wanted to teach. It seems to me, on looking back, that I chose a life which involved telling other people what to do because I did not know what to do myself. In as far as I can be said to have chosen teaching at all it was the thought of the long holidays that prompted me, and the absence of any alternative. Tommy Johns, whose shop at Portholland I have described in *School House in the Wind*, held me in derision when I suggested that I might do well in the grocery business. I should not put the sweet-bottles back in their proper places, he said. The lemon-drops would get mixed up with the Barcelona-balls, and the scales, true as the Day of Judgment in the right hands, yes, true as the Day of Judgment, would not be used to a nicety by me. 'You'd never have the patience for it, my dear maid, never have the patience for it,' said Tommy. 'And'—he began nearly every sentence with *and*, balancing on the word a second or two before venturing on the further stepping-stones of his speech—'And . . . you'd better follow in yer feyther's footsteps; tha's what you'd better do; follow in yer feyther's footsteps. You cean't do better'n that; no, you cean't do better'n that. And . . . you'd never knaw; there may be something in 'ee; 'iss, there may be something in 'ee . . . Now.' The word *now* pronounced some little time after the conclusion of a sentence always signified that Tommy had finished his say as for that time; no more was to be hoped from him.

So I drifted towards teaching. These things are managed better now. One of the most promising of recent developments in education is the provision made for mature persons with experience in other walks of life to receive training as teachers. I was inexperienced, but I had some true knowledge. I do not know at what period I saw the primrose and the feather recalled at the beginning of this chapter. I saw a primrose newly opened, the first of the year, and a feather lying on the moss beside it, a feather not bedraggled but perfect. I saw them as complete in themselves, magical, different from the primroses among whose cold stalks I had insinuated my fingers as a child, and different from the feathers I had picked up and drawn softly along my cheek to try and make the sprung barbs lock into the web again. I recognized their glory with a sudden transporting delight, such as at odd moments I had experienced before; seeing two wild white roses one Whitsunday morning full out in Crooked Lane, or a great bush of honeysuckle on the lower hedge in Furzy Brake. These unpredictable enchantments were mine while I still lived in the two parishes; before I set out one fine morning in our pony-trap for St Austell, where there was an improvised secondary school to which I had won, at second go, an Intending Teacher's Scholarship.

2

ANOTHER DAY

In my neat body,
Smooth as a rush,
Pliant as willow,
See how I fare
Over the earth,
Through the clear air,
A-top the green billow,
In my neat body,
Smooth as a rush,
Pliant as willow.

Mr W.D. Raynor, tall in his black scholar's gown, prayed every morning in a detached voice: 'O Lord, our Heavenly Father, almighty and everlasting God, who has brought us safely to the beginning of another day . . .' *Another* day, not *this* day, as I had always heard it in church. For three years I heard this prayer and for three years I tried to imitate Mr Raynor's scholarly stoop. I was away from home. I could imitate anyone I liked; for here nobody knew how I ought to look. The only person I had ever tried to imitate before was Janey Yelland. I had heard my brother Maurice say that she had an attractive scowl. I thought I would have an attractive scowl too; but had quickly been told by my mother, 'Stop making up faces, Anne.'

At St Austell County School, nobody said, 'Stop making up faces, Anne.' I could try out anything. Home and school did not know one another. They were ten miles apart, a long way measured in foot-lengths or pony-foot-lengths. And, mercifully, there were no parents' meetings and no terminal reports. 'You don't like being talked about behind your back, does one?' as a parent once put it to me in later years; yet the only time I saw Mr Raynor and my father have much talk together I burned to know what had been said about me. It was after a Saturday cricket match between St Austell and Gorran on Gorran ground in which my father had been umpire, and in which Mr Raynor had played as a substitute for a member of the St Austell eleven. I had been as astonished when he entered the field in his white flannels, and carrying a bat, as if Achilles in shining armour had presented himself for combat. That Mr Raynor should come to Gorran! That he should slightly lift his hand in recognition as he passed me near the scoring-board! I hoped with all my heart that, when the tea interval came, the tea would be smoking-hot, and Thomas Hicks's saffron cake be new and crisp and full of fruit. I fancied myself pouring out a steaming cup for a Mr Raynor who had knocked up fifty runs or so. I did not care if Gorran was licked. But alas! alas! My brother Stan, who happened to be home for a holiday, and was playing for Gorran, bowled my chosen clean for two. And in the tea-interval I replenished other cups but could not for the life of me venture on Mr Raynor's. Instead I pretended I did not see him. I avoided his cup and through the tail of my eye watched, in mortification, its being filled by Mrs Drew. She was wife to tall Mr Drew who always licked his finger while he awaited the bowling. The action was automatic. The bowler took his hop, skip and jump and delivered the ball, and Mr Drew licked his finger and smote.

I had not spoken to Mr Raynor, but my father and the hero had certainly had considerable chat together. Walking back to Caerhays with my father after the match, I hoped to have some report of this conversation, but my father said nothing, and I did not like to inquire. At last going up Portluney Hill I could bear it no longer. 'Did Mr Raynor say anything about me?' I asked.

'About you?' said my father absently—he generally forgot to answer our questions for a quarter of a mile or so. At last he remembered to reply. 'About you? No; we didn't say anything about you. I told him that Stan's bowling was very simple really. Raynor is a poor bat. But he's seen a lot of good cricket. At Lords he saw . . .' When I asked Susan what she thought of Mr Raynor she said he hadn't pressed his flannels. Stan at supper remarked that Raynor seemed a nice enough fellow, but that St Austell must have been hard up for a man to play him. My Mr Raynor a nice enough fellow! After that I kept my admiration to myself and practised my scholarly stoop only when walking through St Austell Fore Street.

There was no need for me to walk through Fore Street to school. I made a circuit so as to come into that street and fall in behind Mr Raynor. With stooping shoulders and eyes bent he hunched along in the middle of the street and I, with stooping shoulders and eyes more bent, hunched along on the near pavement. I lodged in a little house in Grant's Walk. There was no boarding house attached to the school; those of us who lived too far away to go home every night became independent lodgers in St Austell during the week, and went home for weekends. I lodged with Miss Susan Varcoe and her father, old Mr Varcoe, who made and mended shoes in a wooden shop in the back garden. The house was shared by two tremendous cats, much pampered by Miss Varcoe. She was a grand woman. Open-hearted as charity, she turned out her toes, praised the Lord, and salted the food. Every dish she salted with equal generosity. 'It's a little salt, isn't it, Miss Varcoe?' I sometimes ventured, eyeing the steak and kidney pie remaining on my plate. 'Food is nothing without a bit of savour, my dear,' Miss Varcoe would reply, adding another pinch of salt to her greens, and vigorously shaking the pepper-pot. Either the salt or a good disposition gave her a wonderful vitality. She could mimic half St Austell, and was a great stand-by at Pleasant Evenings in connection with the chapel. To me she was a surprise. I had never before lived with a person so ready to give herself to everything human. The talk was always of people and their doings; never of any idea under the sun as in my father's house. There we all argued for arguing's sake my mother said. I have seen my father and my brother Howard push one another from the music-stool in order to illustrate a vindication of some cherished theory. My mother had principles; she was a conservative and a churchwoman in grain, and would never take another side for fun. 'You don't mean what you are saying, my dear,' she would admonish my father if she considered he was going too far in trying to shock some visitor's funda-mentalism. Or, 'You have talked enough, Maurice,' to my eldest brother if he was pressing my father too hotly with the foils.

Miss Varcoe did not argue at all. She was content to be, and to observe other people as they were. She lived a life of kindness. Her recreations were going out to visit an uncle— Uncle Penrose she called him—and to various chapel func-tions. When she was out I had the house to myself, for the old man, Mr Varcoe, preferred his shop to the house. Like my Great-Uncle Tommy, he had a fringe of whisker around the smooth table-land of his chin, but, unlike Uncle Tommy, he talked very little. However, I made a silent conquest of him, and he sometimes brought me tribute of sweet apples.

I had a fire of my own and a little room to work in at night if I wanted to work. But there was no planned home-work at St Austell when I was there. We did as much or as little as we liked. The school when I first went to it was in process of being converted from a pupil-teachers' centre into a secondary school. All of us, except a few 'Minor Scholars' who came in at an earlier age, were intending teachers. We were housed on West Hill in a disused Methodist chapel, as bad for its purpose, I imagine, from the point of view of the staff, as could be conceived; but to us more fun than an ordinary school building. There were three main rooms—the old chapel itself with the pews still there; a middle room which had been made partly into a laboratory, and partly into a lecture room; and an upstairs room reached by strange routes. There were one or two little rooms into which we did not penetrate often. No doubt Mr Raynor robed himself in what had been the vestry and the mistresses may have had the organ loft. Certainly they were invisible to the student eyes when in retreat.

Until we moved into our new building, when additional masters were appointed, three mistresses made up Mr Raynor's staff, as excellent a three as ever taught under difficulties. Miss Passmore was small in stature, but with more energy to the square inch than anybody else I have ever encountered. She had an idiosyncrasy in speech, more individual than a lisp; her words were faintly explosive on the lips. She wore pince-nez, and when she placed them in position she could have subdued a herd of buffalo with her indomitable eye. No one ever ragged Miss Passmore. The only time I encountered her in the career of her displeasure was for jumping the pew-backs from the front door to the rostrum. This sport was a favourite one with the boys and I, who had been used to flying over the rocks at Portholland, found it easy to imitate them, though I could not, like one of the Mevagissey girls, ride a bicycle round the gallery. Jumping the pews was my one distinction and I made the most of it. But one day there was a sudden silence in the applause that greeted my turn, and when I reached the rostrum, and looked round, it was to see Miss Passmore at the back of the room. She was lightning in attack and I did not again jump the pews when she could possibly be expected. As a teacher she was lucid and convinced, driving always eagerly to the point; whereas Miss Flamank, more romantic, was diffuse and filled with enthusiasm. She taught history, and her first lesson on the ancient inhabitants of these islands has something to do with my interest in bee-hive huts and erected stones to this day. I did not try to imitate either Miss Passmore or Miss Flamank, while Miss Gough, whom gladly I would have imitated, was, I knew, beyond my range. I could never hope for auburn hair, a tall figure, and a blouse that never slipped from its moorings at the back. Her leather belt sat her figure so well that all was comely. Her safety-pin, if safety-pin she used, did not, like mine, work its way forward to the common gaze. Miss Passmore also was a model of neatness at the waist, whereas Miss Flamank's blouse had been known to work loose in moments of generous historic gesture. Miss Flamank had all the human frailties. It was even said that she had a young man, and enterprising boys, when asked to compose a sentence containing an adjectival clause, would try to make her blush with some such sentence as, 'The lady who was engaged to Mr Brown of Aberdeen . . .' It was rumoured that he was indeed a Mr Brown, but of a city nearer home than Aberdeen.

I had been more used to boys than girls and at first I eyed the girls with some timidity. At Caerhays village school there had only been two girls of my age; here there were several, and to me they looked wonderful. Their hair was elaborately done whereas mine was still tied in a childish way. The older girls wore frames and puffed their hair at the front and sides, tying the remainder at the nape of the neck with an enormous black ribbon bow. This was the most fashionable mode. Milly Turner was an exception. She wore her golden-brown hair short and curled; and Vicky Stauffer wore her long brown hair in two unfashionable but, to her, becoming pigtails. Gladys Pawline had naturally wavy hair and her black bow, uncreased and crisp, stood out like wings. Winnie Salmon alone did her hair like mine, but it reached nearly to her waist as did Winnie Evans's tawny pony's mane. Doris Furze outbid her name in a bush of fox-red hair, a veritable burning bush almost too thick and curly to tie. It seemed to have a life of its own and to strive perpetually against its bond. I remember heads more clearly than faces though faces, too, were very individual. No one attempted make-up so that faces did not all seem to be impressionist copies of one intended face. I made friends with Vic, Gladys, the two Winnies and Milly, but especially and particularly with Vic. For the first time I experienced the pleasure of having a very close friend outside the family and of being a member of a club—the Âne Club we called it, our crest being a donkey. Like all secret societies its exclusiveness was its attraction and the donkey club, though there was no initiation ceremony and we had no rules and no set meetings, served its turn. Interest in it waxed and waned. Sometimes it seemed entirely extinct, and then it would flicker up again like a picnic fire. Its freedom to die down or brighten up was its merit. Attempts to make these natural and amusing adolescent groupings rigid and lasting, above all the effort to make them serve some useful social purpose seems to me quite a perversion of the instinct, like trying to make poetry do a person good. If a club needs an outsider leader it is not a club.

Another pleasure I had at St Austell which I had not known at Caerhays was team games. In my first summer, while we were still in the chapel, though we had been up to the site of the proposed new school to see the foundation stones laid, we formed a girls' cricket club. The boys played in a field near the new site, we girls decided to play too and have a team of our own. In one or two preliminary games my training under my youngest brother, by whom as a cricketer I had been rightly despised, stood me in such stead that I made one or two catches and found the bowling so simple after the bowling of 'the boys' that I even scored runs. To my intense rapture and glorification I was elected captain of the budding club. Milly was secretary, and I made a bloomer by writing to ask Mrs Raynor to play for us in our first match against the boys. To me was addressed the reply in which Mrs Raynor promised to play and hoped we should give the boys a good beating—to me, not to the secretary. She was my 'sincerely, Alice Raynor' not Milly's. For this indiscretion I was reprimanded by the secretary and told to mind the business of my own office. It wasn't for the captain to write and receive notes. However, our friendship rode this wilful misconception of duty on my part. The Hon. Sec. henceforward ran the business of the cricket club and of pretty well every other society started at the school. She was even then, in embryo, the chairman of an urban district council, which she was later destined to become. No other intending teacher had quite that charm and ease, that air of being at home in her clothes, that sparkle in the eye, that ready wit with which to discomfit an opponent in debate.

Among us she was the least introspective, the readiest to give herself without reserve to some cause or interest. She took people to heart. The first time I ever heard her speak she asked to have the windows open in an examination room. She has been asking for windows to be opened ever since, and has ventilated many a stuffy corner. I can see her now turn upon a disputant with, 'Well, really, Mr Hobba,' or, pushing back the curls from an emotional forehead, merely take a breath and, as though words were beyond the reach of her exasperation, look at the person.

After cricket—when we had moved into our fine new granite building on the hill, with its view over the distant sea[1]—came hockey and tennis. My passion for hockey now seems to me unaccountable. But when I first had a stick in my hand and dribbled a ball up the field and whacked at it for a goal I was as one possessed. That first season I had no real notion of team play at all. Other people had to hit the ball at times of course, but Anne was the mainspring of the action, and ready to sneak the rolling treasure from under any stick and usurp any place as she ranged the field. I had always loved running; now I had something to run for. The first time I played I got the ball in front of my stick, raced madly up the field never yielding it to friend or foe, and shot a goal before the other twenty-one had well recovered from their surprise at my velocity. I shall never forget my mortification when told this was not hockey. What were a ball and stick for, I thought, what were the goal posts for? I had shot a goal, hadn't I? My only previous experience had been in a family game we called 'pallets' in which with a bent stick from the hedge, and a cricket ball, each member of the party had fought madly for himself and the opportunity to smack at the leather. I think really the old Cornish game of 'hurling' would be the ideal game for me. I never read the

---

[1]The school at a later stage is memorably described in Mr A. L. Rowse's book, *A Cornish Childhood*; but by then, under an authoritarian head master, all was changed. Mr Raynor had tried to run a free school.

description of it in Carew's *Survey of Cornwall* without longing to be up and at it for myself and for my parish.

In time I learnt to play hockey in accordance with rules and even enjoyed the science of passing and outwitting the disposition of the opposing team. But, although I became captain of the eleven, and sometimes played centre-forward, my chosen place was left wing; I was a born loose skirmisher. At work, too, I skirmished; though I skirmished hard I was a picker and chooser. Science under Mr Lodge was not my forte. Nothing I ever weighed or measured weighed or measured the same the second time. At my lodgings in Grant's Walk it was easy to follow my own pursuits; I was an independent lodger, not a boarding-school miss. My first discovery at St Austell was the pleasure of verse. When I first opened a paper-backed copy of Scott's *Marmion* and Miss Gough directed Winnie Evans to begin reading it aloud I thought how foolish! When she might have chosen *Quentin Durward*, when I might have displayed my intimate knowledge of *Anne of Geierstein*, to be set to read a thing cut up into lines with rhymes and twisted sentences. I began to scribble a note to Winnie Evans and to tweak Vic's plaits. I was in a thoroughly idle mood when it came to my turn to read aloud and I had suddenly the experience of floating on a tide of words. I looked forward to my turn to read again so that I could again feel something inside me flowing into something without. That evening in my lodgings, when the old man was safe in his garden shop, and Miss Varcoe was at her Uncle Penrose's, I shut the door and surprised the black cat and the tabby by standing up and shouting out *Marmion*. From bobbing on the short lines I swung into the main of the story. Constance Beverley! The grim consistory court in which, to the distant and fearful roar of the waves on a rocky northern coast, she was sentenced to be immured for vows broke and convent fled! I could not lose myself in Constance's rhetorical denunciation of her judges and her threat of Lord Marmion's vengeance now, but I could then. Priest, palmer and paladin; knights and bowmen; port-cullised castle and savage battle-field; denunciation, defiance and defeat—these were my

opportunity. Lord Marmion turned . . . In class I always hoped
with all my heart that certain passages would fall to my share. I
would even, as we proceeded, make calculations of pages and
lines and be bitterly disappointed if a passage I wanted fell to
one of the boys, to Nancarrow or Edwards; or if Jules Stauffer,
Vic's brother, forded his way through. We were taught nothing
of elocution; Miss Gough had far too much sense. The only
time I ever heard anyone 'put in the expression' in poetry was
Lizzie George in reciting *Napoleon*. We had all chosen
something to say by heart from an anthology. I had chosen
Waterloo. 'There was a sound of revelry by night.' Lizzie had
learnt, 'Farewell to thee, France'. We said it to Miss Gough in
the usual way, Lizzie being as circumspect as the rest of us. But
one day a Mr Cherril, an inspector, came in and asked to hear
our poems. Most of us muffed them. The mere presence of the
irascible Cherril drove our lines from our heads. He was
complaining that we mumbled when Lizzie arose as a Mother
in Israel. 'Farewell to thee, France,' she shouted, standing
dramatically like Napoleon himself on deck, 'When thy diadem
crowned me, I made thee the gem and the wonder of earth.' We
looked, we listened. Lizzie went on, growing every moment
more intense and more falsetto. Mr Cherril was stunned. Then
suddenly it began to seem funny. Vic and I gave a preliminary
heave and in a moment were struggling with great gusts of
suppressed laughter. They rose in the abdomen, convulsed our
side walls, and issued forth in water at the eyes. The agony of
keeping some sort of still surface above the quakes was rending
us when Mr Cherril fixed us with his gold-rimmed glasses. The
poem ended, he said to Vic, 'What have you been reading
lately, Victoria?'

'*King Solomon's Mines*,' said Vic in a kind of volcanic burst.

'And what can you remember of it?'

'He had . . . he had . . . a glass eye,' said she.

'And what have you been reading?' snapped the inspector
at me.

'*King Solomon's Mines*,' I said.

'And what do you remember?'

'He . . . he . . . had false teeth.'

Mine was the shot which sent the stopper out of the bottle. We were helpless to the growing blasts of laughter in us. We gave ourselves up for lost. Mr Cherril with a glare which included us all, even the undefeated Lizzie George, went out of the room.

From Scott we passed to Shakespeare. My first experience of Shakespeare was disappointing. I had already read Lamb's Tales and cherished most the stories of the least successful plays. *Cymbeline* was my favourite of all. The *Winter's Tale* came next and *Timon of Athens* next. The plays themselves I had neither seen nor read. I had sometimes looked into a complete Shakespeare when hard up for something to read, but had never got beyond, ' 'Tis bitter cold and I am sick at heart' or 'When shall we three meet again?' The absence of narrative repelled me. Now we were to read a whole play taking parts, but I doubt if *As You Like It* is a good choice of play for the unsophisticated. I did not find it funny; I was untouched by the poetry of the greenwood. And then all this talk of love! I made it loudly known that Shakespeare was, in my high opinion, vastly over-rated.

But when it came to *Richard II* it was another matter. Nothing I had ever read before in my life could compare with it. I mouthed John of Gaunt. With prophetic and awful hand outstretched I thundered out the Bishop of Carlisle. But although as John of Gaunt I fiercely admonished Richard, Richard was, even in his petulant, unscrupulous youth, my darling. Every time I re-read the play I trembled for him. Success would never be his, but Bolingbroke's. Not for him was hateful Northumberland thrusting on. I think I glimpsed what has seemed to me since a central theme of Shakespearean tragedy—that a man who glitters as a god, and imposes his single will as though heaven and earth were at his beck, must come to know and confess his mere humanity. It is not that the terms of mortal state are so fickle that 'life is loss, and death felicity'. It is not the fickleness of life, but in the discovery of its significance that pity and comprehension are born. When Richard says,

I live with bread like you, feel want, taste grief,
Need friends . . .

he has discovered what Cleopatra was to discover when she
said at last—she who had been royal Egypt, she whose hand
kings had lipped trembling:

No more, but e'en a woman, and commanded
By such poor passion as the maid that milks
And does the meanest chares

Lear, the strongest of them all, so strong that he could not
break, was driven mad by the intolerable wrongs of men, and
the fury of earth and sky, before pity for all men was born in
his heart, as he realized that he too was one with poor
houseless wretches and came to his tremendous words, 'take
pity, pomp'.

I feel that I can never be sufficiently grateful to Miss
Passmore for having shown me Shakespeare. Not to have felt
his glory when I was young would have been to grow up an
altogether poorer creature. We read plays and we acted at least
some scenes from them. When we acted *Richard II* to me was
assigned the role of the well-meaning, loyal, two-minded neuter
the Duke of York. I might have learnt much from him. He is the
prototype of many a later one among our elder statesmen—
men with a more earnest and loyal desire to play fair and do
right than intellect to discover what is right to be done or will
to do it. But I knew nothing of that. I despised my role and
envied others theirs as, clothed mainly in one of our blue
dining-room curtains, but bearing in my unarmed state a shield
in silver on which I had painted a cross of St George, I strove
to endow the Duke with more significance than Shakespeare
had assigned to him. In my bedroom at home I played all the
parts I wished were mine. The number of pieces of glass I
shattered while enacting in private every single part in the
deposition scene would have re-glazed a house.

It was not until we came to do *Macbeth* that I had a grand
part. When I heard that I was to play Macbeth to Betty

Atkinson's Lady Macbeth my heart danced for joy. But being by that time a bewildering person even to myself, I pretended I was not. I pretended to be afraid of my life to try, and nearly got turned out of rehearsals for mumbling. I had a confused notion that I should shine more bright at last by seeming smirched at the start. I would be poor at rehearsals but on the night I would dizzy them. As a result I nearly lost the chance of playing on the night at all. Yet this narrow shave did not teach me a lesson.

As a child at home I never posed. No child could very well pose in Gorran or Caerhays; criticism would have been too familiar and deflating. I always like a story of Gorran Haven criticism told me by my friend May Grose. She was at a concert held in Gorran School. A Sticker man was singing. May's neighbour poked her head so as to place her mouth on a level with May's ear and said,

'Wake, idn' a?'

They listened again.

'Wake as watter!' said May's neighbour. The song went on.

'Waker'n watter!' she said. Still the song went on.

Then May's neighbour said:

'I wish I was home with me knetten!'

And that was the end of that.

Some such graded and final disapproval would certainly have been applied to any poor performer or affected person in Gorran. As a result we were very cautious of trying anything on. But in St Austell I was always trying something on. Perhaps it was my age, or perhaps it was contrariness. It seemed to be almost impossible for me not to say no when I meant yes, and yes when I meant no, not to refuse what I wanted and want what I refused; not to pretend to despise good looks and pretty clothes when I secretly wished as much as anyone else to be admired; not to mock at love and yet fall into it. The discovery of Eve in herself lay heavily on the girls of my generation. Modern girls are lucky. For us, nurtured almost exclusively in a masculine tradition in reaction from the too feminine culture of the women of the Victorian age, to pass from childhood to womanhood was to tread a devious and doubtful way. All our games, reading and endeavour directed us to be straightforward reasonable men, governed by our minds and will; yet we found ourselves in spite of all our endeavour subject to the unreasonable moon, set to dance a rhythm to which our mothers had given themselves up joyfully though fearfully, but against which we struggled. Now balance has returned again. Or has it? Are present-day girls under their more composed and delightful surfaces as uncertain as we were?

The more I read the more puzzled I grew. Milton's music conquered me even while I was being furiously angry at his treatment of Eve, dear Eve! I now hated Bible stories which as a child had enthralled me. And I shall never forget my impotently mixed feelings when I first read the ninth book of *Paradise Lost*—the beauty and the knot. And the Greeks were no better. When I came to read translations of the Classics there in the centre of the intricacy was Helen.

Perhaps women should not read. But how much I enjoyed it all! How much I enjoyed all the free pathways to knowledge opened up for me at St Austell. We went up the several fields under separate guides and no single prospect was ever hinted at to which the paths might lead. Up to the age of fifteen my education had been broadly but religiously Christian; after that age, apart from my own family and some of my friends, no one I met whom I greatly admired ever spoke of these things. Had it not been that I went home every weekend, and that Cornwall was a naturally religious place, I might have come to consider the most profound mysteries childish. We were on the threshold of what might be called the cocky period of the human spirit; the period of H.G. Wells. It was fashionable to be irreverent and to reduce the subtle religion which had lighted generations of noble minds to the level of the derided Lord of H.G.'s poor old mother. Not that this was the spirit at St Austell. Looking back I think that our unexpressed ideal was an Anarchy in which, while not seeking to love our neighbour, we were prepared to let him live in accordance with his own ideas as we would live in accordance with ours. It was an open-minded education which made us try to see both sides of every question. Its merit was that it would never turn young people into fanatics or persecutors; its demerit that it left us without conviction, we who were moving towards an age of positiveness. Yeats was to write in his later years:

> The best lack all conviction and the worst
> Are full of passionate intensity.

How that tragedy could have been avoided I cannot tell. But if I have any conviction about what is known as higher education it is that St Austell was right in according freedom. That in adolescence and maturity the mind and spirit must be free to explore and express is, with me, a matter of more profound faith than what is known as Faith. But it is in the Faith that I would have young children nurtured; in the Faith and at home. And in secondary schools it is mad to have divinity positively handicapped as at present. Thomas Traherne's sentence may be pondered by us all:

Nevertheless some things were defective too [in Oxford under the Commonwealth]. There was never a Tutor that did professedly teach Felicity, though that be the mistress of all other sciences. Nor did any of us study those things but as aliens, which we ought to have studied as our own enjoyments. We studied to inform our knowledge, but knew not for what we studied. And for lack of aiming at a certain end, we erred in the manner.

3

MONDAY MORNING AND FRIDAY NIGHT

> You spools that wind
> The glittering light,
> Turn slowly, slowly
> In my sight.
> Your various offering
> Gradual bring,
> No hastening!
>
> No hastening,
> But smooth and slow!
> While stepping I
> As softly go,
> Thorough the white
> To golden light,
> And so to night.
>
> —*To a Holiday: That its hours may pass slowly*

While I was at St Austell County School I went home for every weekend except once in the depth of winter. One other weekend I was supposed to spend at St Austell, but at the last moment my father felt this to be impossible, and drove up for me. I can fling my heart up again at the memory of the sight of him in the trap waiting for me at the foot of West Hill. And I can fling my heels up too for, overcome with excitement at his unexpected and glorious appearance, I began to run full tilt, tripped and fell headlong, to the amusement of two of the boys who helped me up. I could have killed them.

In my first two terms it meant real hardship to my mother for me to come home weekends. I had to be driven back in the pony-trap each Monday morning, and on Fridays I was either fetched in the trap or I went home in Johnny Johns's bus. That my mother should thus have driven the pony in all weathers on Monday mornings in order that I might be at home for weekends fills me now with compunction. For my mother was not one who loved the wind and the rain. On the contrary, her devotion was to the house and hearth, to be dry and warm with everything handsome about her. Nor did she like driving Dart; for, although now growing old and sober, he could still be frisky on occasion, and my mother had a real fear with which in those days I could not sympathize, of the lonely roads between Fair Cross and Caerhays. She was afraid a tramp might jump out of the hedge and ask for a ride. During my first September and October it was to me a joy to be out so early, to watch the sun rise and pour glory over the stubble fields. The deadest straw shines in the sun. But as the term drew on towards November and December the mornings grew darker and darker; Susan would get up early and light the kitchen fire, making the room warm and cosy for our breakfast. Then I would harness the pony, and my mother would come out wearing the old warm golf cape my Aunt Eliza had given her, a cape of horse-back brown with a plaid hood. Then, with the trap lamps chasing the shadows under the hedges, we would set off, I driving, and my mother, if it were a wet morning, holding the trap umbrella over us both. All kinds of weather I remember on those mornings, but soft, grey, misty weather predominates; or the fine Cornish rain which is one of the most wetting of rains, a rain which is never malicious but which seeps through all clothing with gentle persistence, and with a lulling soft sound which is not a pattering on the umbrella. On other mornings the wind might be up, blowing in the trees, and blowing my hair, and tossing Dart's mane; or it might be a frosty morning when the sun rose red and the cold numbed our fingers. My mother had the kind of fingers which went white and dead in the cold however warm the gloves she wore. I cannot imagine how she endured what I so thoughtlessly enjoyed. Every kind of weather was right for me as long as I was out in it.

My mother used to drive me to the foot of St Mewan Hill from which I walked in to school. One morning as I was on the way a dog-cart which had gone spanking by me on previous Monday mornings drew up. The driver asked if I would like a lift. I mounted joyfully. A rubber-tyred dog-cart and a chestnut mare were to me the height of elegance and tone. I took a sidelong glance at the sanguine, ginger person on the box and approved. I regretted as we drew up opposite the school that there was no one about to see me descend; I loved Dart's curly coat, but he was not in winter an impressive pony to look at, whereas here was stabled gloss. However, no one was about to be astounded at my grandeur. Everyone except my tardy self was at work; and on no subsequent Monday morning was I ever able to show off. Yet on each Monday morning now, until I began to ride a bicycle to school, it was from the dog-cart that I descended to the chapel on West Hill. Mr Thomson's road ran into ours near Fair Cross. We arranged to meet him there; I transferred myself regularly from our trap to his, and my mother was saved many miles of road. I immensely enjoyed those drives and the explosive conversation of Mr Thomson. After a preliminary rumble his words would issue from his lips with a pop as of a cork from a wine bottle. Once the stopper was out the vintage flowed freely. I learnt a good deal about the price of corn and cattle and the points of a bull. I contracted the habit of half-closing one eye in a professional, farmerly, auctioneerish way when I encountered bullocks, and I always wished I could go on to some auction or fair with Mr Thomson instead of proceeding to a French lesson with Miss Gough. But Mr Thomson never invited me to michie.[1]

In my first two terms I often went home on Friday nights in Johnny Johns's bus. It was really a one-horse wagonette. When we hired it privately, as we did on rare occasions of financial flourish, in order to drive to Portscatho and Percuil, we called it a wagonette; but on Fridays it was Johnny's bus. Four o'clock! And I would come racing from school to assemble with other Caerhays people who had come up to shop and were laden with parcels outside the White Hart yard. Often we were so many that Johnny would say, 'I don't know where I'm going to put 'ee all to, I'm sure. Anne, my handsome, you'll have to ride on me knee again I b'lieve.' This manner of locomotion was even grander to me than driving with Mr Thomson. Mr Thomson never gave me the reins. Johnny did, and off I would go, flourishing the whip, and chaffing the passengers, or exchanging backchat with the drivers of familiar traps. At Pentewan Hill we were all turned out to walk up. We all knew one another and enjoyed details of purchasings and glimpses of the purchased. Old Mrs Beard was once embarrassed by an 'article' which she had bought and which refused to conceal its form in the wrappings—a nice little article with roses round. Contrary to promise, Mr Beard never came to meet and support her. She kept on saying, 'Where's feyther to? I cean't think why feyther idn' 'ere,' a saying we kept up in the family for years. Whenever any arrangement went awry we would say, 'Where's feyther to?' Exciting stories were told. Once I remember there had been a fire at Trevarrick at Charlie Coombe's. Charlie had a son David of whom Miss Oliver at the shop in Gorran Churchtown used to say she didn't like to see him coming in too well, his trousers looked so temporary. He tied them round with binder twine. It was Miss Oliver who used to say in precise tones, 'And what will you have with the farthing?' Well, Charlie Coombe's wife, Mary, had made a kind of ceiling under the rafters of the bedroom by sewing together

---

[1] The Cornish word for playing truant.

white flour-bags. One night a candle caught the curtains afire and the flames leapt up and caught the flimsy flour-bags. Out ran David Coombe to the Notts and Groses of Trevarrick shouting, 'Our house is a ball o' fire; our house is a ball o'fire!' Mr Grose and Mr Nott and all the Grose boys dashed to the rescue and with buckets of water put the fire out. But it was a near thing. I could listen all night now to John or May Grose or Tom or Elam telling the saga of Trevarrick, as it used to be at about the time when I drove home, on Friday nights, in Johnny Johns's bus.

When spring came I began to ride my bicycle to St Austell on Monday mornings and back on Friday nights. It was less fun than driving with Mr Thomson and coming home in the bus; but those early mornings, when I bicycled so silently that other creatures were not disturbed by me, provided a different pleasure. Birds live in an ecstasy of freedom in the morning; flowers are breathing—blackthorn and celandine; primroses and violets; then bluebells on the tops of the hedges deep in ferns. I did not take Johnny's route to St Austell. He went Pentewan way; we usually drove or bicycled Fair Cross way. Down the two hills below the church I would skim; up to Treberrick; by Washaway to Fair Cross; on through Hewas Water, Sticker and St Mewan until, flying down a hill, I would be carried by the impetus almost up the next hill to the chapel gates. As far as Hewas Water the way was solitary and solitude, says De Quincey 'though it may be silent as light is, like light, the mightiest of agencies; for solitude is essential to man.'

Quietness in communion I felt in the eight o'clock services to which now, having been confirmed, I went with my parents and Susan in St Michael Caerhays Church on Sunday mornings. The little church, sanctified for centuries, stills the mind in a way peculiar to itself. It is a little wayside church overlooking the fields. Some churches seem to imprison the air, but at Caerhays the air wandered sweetly in and out through the open door. I wonder sometimes what might have been the history of ecclesiastical religion if all the churches had been sunny. At night with the dim lamps lit, it was very solemn.

Sometimes, though, I laughed. Once during a Lenten service when only Howard and my mother and I were in church, a little mouse came out and played round Mr Bellamy's feet and made as though to run up his trousers. We were reading the psalms, saying alternate verses with the Rector, and when we came to the versicle, 'Then stood up Phineas and prayed and behold the plague ceased', the plague did cease, for the little mouse whisked off. Howard's voice quavered in his reading; mine quavered. My mother whispered under her breath: 'Be quiet, Howard; be quiet Anne,' and quavered herself. It was an intolerable moment. How we longed to be outside and able to tell Mr Bellamy about the mouse, instead of being there with God between us and him, he unconscious and religious, we profane and full of uncontrollable laughter because of a mouse.

As soon as I began to ride a bicycle to St Austell my weekends depended on myself. I never missed one. On very rough, wild Friday nights I was supposed to stay up in my lodgings; but I always used to say it wasn't raining at St Austell. 'No rain; not a bit of wind,' became a joke. The long school holidays reinforced the weekends in keeping me closely in touch with home. During these holidays my sister and I spent some of the choicest times of our lives. For our brothers, too, came home for holidays. We liked it best when they came alone. But, alas! All my brothers very early in life began to go a-roving by the light of the moon. They began to bring girls home and soon, with one accord, they began to get married. Stan led the way; he married Kate. Then in course of the next few years Howard married Mary, Maurice married Helen, Cap'n married Edith, and Susan and I became aunts. I must say that all my brothers were fortunate, very fortunate. The pretty girls they married made them good wives; for all four, though they were so different from one another, had quality which matured well. Not one of my brothers married a Cornish girl. Kate was Wiltshire; Mary a Devonian; Edith a Londoner; Helen a Scot. My mother was a little sad, a little wistful that her sons married quite so early; it is not an easy time in a woman's life when her sons marry. It is a hurt which no philosophy can quite heal, a hurt repeated in successive generations. It could be the theme of a novel, a theme in which irony is inherent—if such a novel could be written with tenderness. Instead, it is the vulgar humour of the mother-in-law theme which has pervaded English writing and cartoons. My mother was easily wounded. For my part, although I admired and came to love my sisters-in-law, I was wildly jealous of them at first and a little jealous for years; indeed I have only recently become entirely free of jealousy. I expect the whole thing is summed up in a couplet May Grose's wise old Granny Nott used to quote:

> It takes more grace than I can tell
> To play the second fiddle well.

But I did not spend all my time being jealous; the feeling came and went in gusts. The holidays were wonderfully enjoyable and, long after my brothers had homes of their own, the tie with Caerhays remained very strong. Even my eldest brother whose work took him to New York—in those days he bought a ticket to America for £12 10s. 0d. and there were no more formalities than if he had taken a ticket to Looe—he came home at stated intervals for a holiday. I shall never forget his first homecoming, waiting by the gate to the left of the second hill below the church, and hearing Johnny Johns's Gipsy—there was too much luggage for our trap—trotting from as far distant as Treberrick, bringing the travellers home on a quiet summer evening—home from America.

One afternoon of a summer holiday occurred the affair of the asters, which for some reason we have always remembered. My father hated to have the flowers in the garden picked. Even sweet peas which, he was assured on all sides, and especially by Susan who loved flowers in the house, flowered the more if constantly picked, he mourned over. Roses drank the dew till they were old, old roses in our garden. If Susan picked some for the house my father would say reproachfully, 'Susan has been picking my little roses again.' Asters escaped Susan, for Susan did not care for asters, though my father cherished them in special. One day there was to be a partial eclipse of the sun and we had all armed ourselves with little bits of smoked glass to gaze through. My parents were in the garden seated with their pieces of glass in their hands waiting for the eclipse when Howard looked down on them from a bedroom window and had the bright idea of dropping a wet towel on them, in hope to knock their glass out of their hands. The towel missed the target and, instead, broke the necks of two beautiful asters, a purple and a red. My father had been tremendously proud of his asters; for once they were better than gardener Martin's at the Hovel. 'If you must play such silly, childish tricks you'd better go back to Exeter and play them there,' said my father. Consternation. My father hardly every lost his temper and we were completely out of countenance. But nobody could ever maintain any anger in our family. After a bit we heard my father humming a few notes. He called up, 'I'm going to the Barton, boy. Are you coming?' They made it up.

Holidays and work, mid-week at St Austell and weekends at home, made a most agreeable mixture of hours for me. Then the Cambridge Senior Examination loomed. It was an examination which corresponded roughly to the present School Certificate; only names change in education. I cannot remember much of my preparation for it; I remember much more vividly Susan's examination pieces which she was practising at the time on the piano. She always practised a long time on Saturday nights when my father was often out, and when her lesson was fresh in her mind. She went for lessons to St Austell to Mr English the organist of the parish church. She rode to St Austell on the bicycle; we had only one between us. In the afternoon I would ride Dart up to Fair Cross to meet her. My week's work was over and her ordeal with Mr English was over and we would give ourselves up to glory, she skimming on ahead, I on Dart determined to keep up. When Susan got off to walk a hill Dart and I would flourish grandly by for a few steps, then stop and walk with her, and talk of the mood Mr English had been in, or of how Miss Gough had a new coat.

With the Cambridge Senior Examination my stay at St Austell as a full-time pupil ended. Of the examination I remember my fearful flurry day after day; the little jump in my heart as I turned over the question papers; and the appalling minutes during which my mind jibbed and refused the start. What I needed, but had no power to command, was a warm feeling during which I poured out, hot, everything I knew; writing wildly until the very second when we were called upon to stop and give in our papers. I was never one to revise any effort of the little demon who was working for life within me once I had set him going. I gave him his fling and he saw me through.

It was early September when the result came; I was staying with my father's cousin Johnny Kemp, at Reskivers Farm near Tregony. They had a wonderful stove in their long, low kitchen, a furnace which, blackleaded every Saturday, shone like a black boy. On the slab the pans of milk were scalded. there was always a pan with the yellow cream beginning to crinkle on the top. Lyly, Johnny's daughter, used to go out blackberrying with me, and Mrs Kemp made a tremendous succession of blackberry tarts for the men when they came in from the fields. Blackberry tart and cream. I can almost taste the rich, red juice, still. I connect it with *Bibby's Annual*, a journal I never saw except at Reskivers.

One morning Lyly and I were going out on our usual round of the blackberry bushes when my brother Howard, who was at home for a holiday, came driving Dart along the road to Reskivers. He was waving the whip and shouting, 'Hey, ho! We Treneers are the Ones!'—my brothers had all been good at examinations. 'You've passed with a distinction in history. Examiner must have been drunk.' I did not stay to collect my nighty which reposed in its case on Lyly's bed, nor my brush and comb from her dressing-table. My toothbrush was forgotten. Into the trap I jumped in my old blackberrying rig and took the reins. Dart, who was always excited when I was excited, made for home like mad. The distinction in history nearly made me pop with pride. Even my father, so sparing in praise, said as he came humming 'Onward, Christian Soldiers' down the garden path, 'Good girl, Anne.' Miss Passmore sent me a postcard of congratulation and Mr Raynor a telegram. I treasured both like love-letters.

4

THE STUDENT TEACHER

Come, wind, and rustle my silk leaves,
A leafy pleasure is mine in June,
Wearing silk, a worm's cocoon.

Such joy of summer my heart receives
As ever lady under the moon;
Come, wind, and rustle my silk leaves,
A leafy pleasure is mine in June.

Of mulberry the worm weaves
My silken robe, an airy tune,
Melodious as a summer noon.
Come, wind, and rustle my silk leaves,
A leafy pleasure is mine in June,
Wearing silk, a worm's cocoon.

—*Wearing Silk*

It is a genuine difficulty to know what preliminary training in the elementary school—the word 'primary' is happily ousting the word 'elementary'—should be given to a young person before going to college. By the time I was eighteen the old pupil-teacher system was dead. Various other devices had been tried and discarded. In Cornwall the plan in vogue was that, after passing one of the qualifying examinations, the intending teacher should spend a year alternately teaching and being taught. One week he was teaching in an elementary school, and the next he was continuing his own studies in his secondary school. It was hoped that during this time he would discover whether he was fitted for teaching or not. That some such trial is desirable before a person is committed to an expensive and somewhat irrevocable training is, I am sure, a good thing; though the alternate-week system was found unsatisfactory and quickly abandoned. However, for a year that was the scheme under which I worked.

My first difficulty was the choice of my elementary school. Permission for me to teach in my father's school at Caerhays was refused. Although father and daughter would have suited one another admirably such family conclaves were not encouraged. St Austell Central School was suggested or Gorran, where my father had been head master before we moved to Caerhays. I chose my beloved Gorran, and to Gorran School I went alternately with St Austell County School for a year. I knew immediately that I was one who would more gladly learn than teach; I doubt whether I have ever had a genuine impulse to teach anyone anything. However, my teaching difficulties at Gorran were few, so pleasantly were things arranged for me.

Mr Britton was head master, and with him worked Miss Janey Pearce, Miss Alice Martin, and Miss Louie Lelean. My family had been friends with the Pearces of Tregerrick and the Martins of Highlanes from long before the time that I was born. I remembered Miss Pearce from the days when I was very small, from the days when Mr Sim Stevens, who courted all and married none, would ride his fine horse past her classroom window, and Miss Pearce would look out and they would talk together while we played. Miss Pearce had a succession of beautiful bicycles which she kept clean and shining; every year or so she had a new one to replace the old. One Rudge-Whitworth, enamelled green, with neat gold lines traced against the green, was immensely admired by us all.

Miss Pearce was both dashing and spruce. She wore a navy-blue bicycling skirt which she kept well over her knees by a patent device. A stretch of elastic clasped the inside of the skirt to an elastic band worn round the leg. When other people's skirts were ballooning and their owners were endeavouring, with one hand on the handlebars, to preserve their modesty with the other, Miss Pearce went bicycling decorously on. With the skirt went a smart, striped, shirt-blouse, a starched collar and tie, and a tricky sailor hat. I never saw Miss Pearce in a blouse that did not look freshly ironed. Over its sleeves, to keep them clean in school, she drew gay, cotton sleeves which were kept up with elastic just above the elbow and caught in at the wrist. Miss Pearce never looked chalky, and she was never late.

Miss Alice Martin, on the contrary, was endeared to me because she never left her delightful house at Highlanes until the last minute, when she took to the lanes like me, with a piece of bread and butter in one hand, and tucking in her refractory blouse with the other. She was roundabout where Miss Pearce was rectilinear, late where Miss Pearce was early, free-hearted, bountiful, and as richly nurturing to the young as good leaf-mould. I loved Miss Alice and admired Miss Pearce who had a sharp tongue. She could put a person down. Miss Alice was kind; children played her up, but they never played up Miss Pearce. Yet there was jubilation if Miss Pearce went out to play as she sometimes would; joining in the skipping, playing marbles to beat the boys. Looking back I see that she had in a strong degree that mysterious thing known as personality. Her mood coloured other people's days for them; when she was gay others were gay; when she was gloomy or sarcastic she withered other people's leaves. With Miss Alice children displayed themselves as they chose in their every varying dispositions, provoking or engaging. Nothing could ever be easily found in Miss Alice's room; reels of cotton, needles, chalk, thimbles, dusters, pencils, exercise books, pens—all the things that obeyed Miss Pearce, disobeyed Miss Alice. In Miss Pearce's room things stayed in their places until she said, 'Percy Mingo, you may give out the books,' or, 'Janey Teague, you are sitting up nicely, you may give out the pencils.' In Miss Alice's room things spread themselves on the floor, and on the window-sills, and on the stove. In this room Hans Andersen could have told endless stories of the conversations between dusters and scissors and tape in strange proximity. Whereas in Miss Pearce's room all things were silent, segregated, and subdued.

Miss Louie Lelean was quite different from either Miss Pearce or Miss Martin. She was not much older than I and could be called Louie. 'My senses!' Mr Britton would say, finding us laughing together in the sunny end classroom, from the windows of which we could watch the distant ships go by. 'Don't you girls know it is time to ring the bell? Too long a play-time! These children do nothing but play unless I am about. 'My senses!' And he would try to look fierce under his drooping, mild moustache. 'My senses!' was his favourite expression. 'My senses! You children know nothing. What can you have been doing all your lives? Not know the capital of Australia? Do you really mean to tell me that no one in this class knows the capital of Australia? My senses! I'll have your heads off.' I soon got to know that Mr Britton's fierceness was chiefly verbal, though when he said, 'My senses! I'll trim your sides,' some unlucky boy was likely to be beaten. His eyes were brown. I never knew him more angry than when a boy said that Shakespeare wrote the Acts of the Apostles. To me as a beginner he was kind, inspecting my notes of lessons, listening to my efforts in class with a fatalistic expression as who should say, 'Raw raw! My senses! How raw these students are!' As all the Gorran children knew me well by my Christian name it was of no earthly use for me to try to stand on my dignity. We joggled along together; sometimes they were good, and sometimes they were naughty; and if they were inclined to be naughty I told them a story. I invented all kinds of tiny rewards or distinctions to make them work. My idea of teaching was to have my class looking good. I did not have many lessons to teach. Often I watched other people and often my time was my own to do what I liked with. I kept a long novel always handy. *Westward*

Ho! I remember reading at that time. When Amyas Leigh climbed up and up a tree in Panama, and looked out on the Pacific, I was at his elbow; and I shrieked with the poor English sailor who was taking his ease with his dusky wife in lovely lotus land as the tiger sprang on him. An awful warning to all who neglected their duty, said Salvation Yeo. The first time I had a class hanging on my words—a gratifying experience to an ageing teacher let alone a young one—was when I told the story of the Armada, with details—facts and fictions were all one to me—taken from *Westward Ho!* An audience of children is a spur to the invention of the novice. History will always be pleasantly coloured and dramatic while there are young teachers.

Best of all while I was a student-teacher at Gorran I liked the dinner-hour. Nearly all the children went home to dinner so the break had to be long enough to allow them to walk the distance home and back. The gang spirit was cooled by the spell, and the children became themselves again, separate creatures with separate mothers. We were all renewed by being apart, and I never remember a stale, afternoonish feeling. Children from very long distances brought pasties or sandwiches and ate them out of doors if it was fine, or in a classroom if it was wet. Miss Pearce, Miss Alice, Louie and I used to meet in the end classroom in winter and display our dainties. A favourite luncheon with Miss Pearce was a cold wing of chicken and a slice off the breast, with jelly adhering. We brewed endless, companionable cups of tea; for all three of my colleagues were connoisseurs in tea. Miss Pearce, in a good mood, would entertain us all in dinner-hour. All the Pearces were good conversationalists and could tell a story well. On November days the rain would be washing down the window panes and we would be snug within, seated round the ugly stove. Sometimes one of us would go out to pay a visit to the children lively round their stove in another classroom. Miss Alice might prepare needlework if it were a sewing afternoon; Louie might mark her books. But always for the first part of the dinner-hour we talked and I, proud to be considered so grown-up, was included friendly-wise.

But fine dinner-hours in summer were the best of all. I remember fine, hot dinner-hours in July, just before Walter Ford trimmed the hedges. We used to call it cutting the trash. A poor, despised word like trash was ill-applied to the lovely flowers that fell beneath the hook. In July, before the cutting, when the hedges were royal with flowers, I used to persuade Louie to bicycle with me out to the Greeb to eat our dinner on Clickers Rock. We said 'Clickers' which was probably a corruption of 'Clitters'. Clitters Field is mentioned in Gorran Parish Books which name the farm fields, and 'Clitter' is also a Dartmoor word for stones. I cannot think that there is a lovelier place for wild flowers than along the lanes from Gorran schoolhouse to the Greeb by Boswinger. Purple and gold were July colours. The flowers grew in great patches; stiff betany; picris, orange-gold; mauve scabious; toadflax, orange and lemon; festoons of purple tufted-vetch; honey-suckle rioting skywards, and falling in flowery cascades, pink-folded buds and gleaming, satiny lips; blue devil's-bit scabious which we called devil's-buttons; cream bed-straw; rest-harrow; knap-weed, self-heal, and strong, coarse yarrow, with its pungent tang, and feathery leaves. Sometimes we left our bicycles by Trevesson town-gate, and walked through the town-place to fields above Hemmick, to smell the camomile in the top field, and see the scarlet poppies and white feverfew about the rick. But for the most part, on sunny days, we sat in nooks of the grey rock piled up on the Greeb, breathing the sparkling air, and looking out over the shift and change of the sea; letting our eyes slide westward to the Gull Rock, to Nare Head, to the Manacles; or eastward to dark Dodman. It was on these summer days that I wore an old silk frock, and felt the wind fluttering my leaves. We could time ourselves by the birds. As soon as the children began to go into school the birds swooped down on the playground to eat up the pieces of pasty, or bread, or saffron cake left about. White wings over Mevagissey Harbour when the fishing-boats came in; and black wings over Gorran School play-ground after dinner.

I enjoyed, too, my bicycle ride to and fro to Gorran School from Caerhays, a distance of three miles each way. I could never make up my mind to start early except on some mornings, when I allowed time for a bathe on Portluney Beach on my way. Ordinarily I pedalled under the sycamores and up Barton Hill, eating my breakfast as I went, and with only time to wave my hand to Mrs Kneebone at the Barton and Noah Loten in the Yard. Skimming down Pound Hill I would think to catch up with time; but Portluney Hill, cut through the rock, needed caution at the bends. On winter mornings, hoar frost sparkled in the field before the castle and along the level way to Penver Gate. In spring it was a ferny way; there is a deep nook to the right above Tregavarras filled to its cool depth with ferns. I never like to go to a place and come back the same way. So usually I went to Gorran by Tregavarras, skirting Boswinger and reaching the school by Four Turnings. Going home after school I went by Crooked Lane, past Old Vicarage Gate to the foot of Alms House Hill. I turned right and wriggled past Mount Pleasant Farm to Rescassa and so to Penver Gate. Thus going I subscribed a little arc with Penver Gate as the pivot. I chose to come home Rescassa way because the bend in that hill came near the top and after rounding it I could let myself go floating, flying down the hill. My father when he drove to Gorran from Caerhays chose Treveor way, but Treveor Hill was too sudden to make a good bicycling track. Every inch of the way was familiar to me from early childhood, every stile and stretch of hedge had associations either with my family or the families of my friends. In the road by Mount Pleasant my brother Cap'n and I had upset in our pony-trap. In Old Vicarage Lane the Mingos had had a more spectacular adventure. William, John, Leonard and small Percy Mingo were driving their black pony when he ran away, galloping like a mad thing. Percy was singing out as they whirled down Old Vicarage Lane, 'This is the way to travel, me boys.' But his exultation turned to crying. At Treninnick Gate William tried to keep the pony straight ahead for Highlanes instead of attempting the bend sharp left by the familiar Mount Pleasant

way to Rescassa. The pony, however, was not to be balked of
the short cut, and, by Murder Ground, over they all went as the
trap struck the hedge. Upsets were not infrequent in pony-
traps. On Polmassick Hill old Mr Lanyon was upset when he
was over ninety. He was driving in a little four-wheel turnout
when he met a motor car and his pony turned clean round and
the whole thing upset. But Mr Lanyon slipped out somehow
between the shafts.

'Are 'ee hurt, Mr Lanyon?' said the owner of the car, beside
himself with anxiety. 'Are 'ee hurt?' 'No,' said Mr Lanyon, 'but
if I hadn't been a nimble sort of chap you would have killed
me, killed me you would have.'

Sometimes for a longer ride home I went up past Highlanes
and Oak Tree, turned left through St Ewe, went through
Polmassick and home by Treberrick. Polmassick is the most
sheltered of hamlets, deep down in a valley where the little river
Luney flows from its source in the china-clay country. Oak
Tree is still a handsome tree. An old woman used to sit in it
knitting at midnight people said, and some ponies would not
pass without shying; the old woman knitting in Oak Tree was of
one kind with the headless woman in Bodrugan Broad Lane.
That lane has hedgerows so overgrown as to form green
cloisters. One night John Grose was walking home from
Portmellon when it came to a stinging hail shower. The white
grains hissed and rebounded on the road as John took shelter in
the dusk under the deep hedgerow. It grew darker and the
white hailstones made everything look strange and fearsome.
There was a whirling wild wind blowing. John began thinking
about the headless woman when all at once he heard a voice
and jumped nearly out of his skin.

'The shower is over now I think, my boy.'

John had taken shelter all unbeknownst close to a fellow-
shelterer. People liked to try and frighten the timid. Mrs
Grose told me that when she was a girl the whole parish
avoided Murder Ground at night. It was said to be haunted.
Once when she was walking with Miss Kitto in the lane by
Murder Ground they saw in the moonlight something which

seemed to be gliding along behind the top brushwood of the hedge.

'Do you see anything funny, Mrs Grose?' said Miss Kitto beginning to tremble.

'Don't take any notice. Walk right on as if we hadn't seen anything. Perhaps someone is trying to frighten us,' quavered Mrs Grose. And a well-known friend was trying to frighten them. He had heard their voices, had set his hat up on his walking-stick clothed in his lank overcoat, and so engineered a ghostly glide as he walked softly in the field on one side of the hedge and the girls walked in the lane on the other side of it.

I enjoyed my weeks at Gorran, and my journeys; but my thoughts were always preoccupied with St Austell. For those who planned our work it must have seemed a hopeless scheme to have one set of sixth form students one week and a different set the next. But for myself I liked the week's breathing space which gave me time to read whatever I chose. Had Mr Britton worked me hard at Gorran it would have been a different story; but Mr Britton neither worked his students hard nor made them over-anxious. The irregular St Austell instruction suited me better than a scheme which implied too strict a supervision of my studies. We were not driven in blinkers. And then at St Austell there was the pleasure of Vic's company and sometimes Milly's. My parents had changed my St Austell lodgings to a house in Mount Charles, a house owned by a Mr and Mrs Bunt who had no children of their own, and who decided it would be pleasant to have two or three young people about. It was extremely pleasant for the young people. Vic and Milly were already there and I joined them. We shared a room at the top of the house as a study-bedroom and we had meals and were otherwise sociable with Mr and Mrs Bunt. My father was inclined to poke fun at Geo. P. Bunt who was the District Education Clerk. 'Geo. P. Bunt!' he would say with a snort. Truth to tell my father would never have been fair to any Education Officer to whom he was always forgetting to post his returns. 'Utter nonsense!' he would say; 'Utter nonsense all these forms! What child was ever the better for them?' English education according to my father was being delivered over bound and gagged to a set of file-keepers who hardly knew a boy from a girl! Geo. P. Bunt was a nervous man. He had a habit of stretching his neck up out of his collar; he never crossed my father. He was a local preacher but he never tried to convert his three guests. To us, both he and Mrs Bunt were kindness itself. The only gesture of authority Geo. P. ever tried was to make Vic sew a button on her coat. She would not. It became a matter of principle that she should not sew on the button. No Hampden over his Ship Money was more obstinate. We dimly saw that the whole question of the Bunts being *in loco parentis* was involved; we were determined to be independent lodgers. Vic openly won her case and no attack was ever made again on any sin of omission or commission on her part. Feminine and gentle-looking, Vic has never in her life done anything against her will. Even tailors do her bidding. If she says she wants a heavy lining with a heavy tweed coat—she likes her coats built like houses—she has her way; and she always did have her way as a girl—with the Bunts and Mr Raynor and Miss Passmore and whoever else attempted to guide her steps. She had three brothers—Jules, Ted and Byron—to contend with; they must have strengthened her will to withstand all aggression. She stood firm for her own course, whereas I got my way by seeming to yield. Mrs Bunt thought I spent too much time alone at Porthpean, Trenarren and the Blackhead. I appeared to go less often but in truth I went oftener. It added to the fun to creep downstairs with my shoes in my hand of an early summer morning and, before the Bunts were waking, take my joy of one or other of my chosen spots and be back before breakfast time. Early study had made me hungry Mrs Bunt would say as I demolished porridge, bacon and eggs and cast a hungry eye on little beef pasties which were always kept handy against the fiercest onslaughts of our appetites. Growing girls needed food, Mrs Bunt said, equably. She liked us in a quiet, aloof way; and we liked her. My favourite time at Trenarren was by morning moonlight, with a clear sky and stars going out as morning dawned. I did not often go quite so early. Yet I think, on looking back, I would rather have missed everything else at St Austell than those heaven-revealing mornings; the apartness in suffusion of fresh day.

5

TRYING TO GROW UP

How strange are trees that lift their leaves in air,
While their roots rout amidst the worms and dark;
How strange are wild flowers that with fragrance rare
Invite winged creatures, and with delicate mark
Direct. The sea is strange, filled with strange fish,
Coloured like sun-rise, or striped waves at dawn;
The sky is strange, with clouds now dragonish,
Now to the blue ethereal height up drawn.
Birds fly, grasshoppers hop, hares hunted run,
The thrushes sing, and housed snails silent creep.
Nothing remains at rest beneath the sun
Of things that dance and dive, or walk and weep.
How strange is earth! And, ah! How strange am I,
Appointed here to live and here to die.

Vic and I had made up our minds that if we were to teach, and if we must go to college, we would go to Truro. It was near home. We received a good deal of advice as to why we should go elsewhere. We might take the Cambridge Senior Examination again, obtain exemption from Matriculation, and go to a university. We were not inclined to any such mad risk. With luck, we thought, we had got through the examination once; but luck was tricky. A history examiner would never be drunk twice. What fools we should feel if we tried again and this time we not only failed to get Matriculation but failed altogether. To nothing that demanded a second trial of our mental strength in the slippery fields would we give any consideration at all. Then why not go to a London training college, Mr Raynor said. London would broaden our minds. But in the secrecy of our attic we decided that we did not care for breadth. Truro or nowhere we said to all our advisers, and for Victoria this was a heroic decision. She had never learnt the catechism; I had.

Truro was a diocesan training college, and an old one as training colleges count age. The work of training had been carried on first in Fairmantle Street. There is a record of a grant of £200 made to the Truro Training School by the National Society in 1822; and there, for thirty years, pupil-teachers were trained for the Exeter Diocese, which then included Cornwall with Devon. From 1857 to 1859 the school in Fairmantle Street was recognized as a temporary training college and ten Queen's scholars were admitted. These numbers, after a residential college and a practising school had been built on Mitchell Hill, were gradually increased to sixty. The college was still, wisely as I think, confined to sixty or so students when Vic and I were at Truro. Long before that, Cornwall had become again as in ancient days a separate diocese, and the Principal of the college was the Suffragan Bishop of St Germans, with Miss Mary Gee as Vice-Principal.

Vic and I, having written to obtain particulars of admission, found that we must take the Archbishop's Examination in the Book of Common Prayer and in certain specified books of the Old and New Testaments. To me this prospect was not particularly alarming as I had been religiously brought up. But Vic had not, like me, been taken to church Sunday after Sunday until the Liturgy was as familiar in her ear as the sound of her own name. And she had no one to prepare her, whereas my father thoroughly enjoyed preparing me. Such teaching was his favourite work. I passed on to Vic as much as she would permit—very little of St Paul who was not a sympathetic saint to either of us, and a good deal of King David whose prowess in the various walks of coloured life served instead of London to broaden our minds. Mr Raynor and Miss Passmore took no note at all of our adventure in religious knowledge. We were a couple of privateers.

The day of the examination arrived and we went to Truro for it. My father drove me to Grampound Road Station in the pony-trap, and we joined Vic on the train. Probus Halt, and then the clustered grey Truro houses brimming the hollow; the towers of the cathedral rising in the midst; the head of the creek beyond and, on Mitchell Hill, a queer high and low building which was the college. I should remember nothing of the examination if it were not for a question on one of the papers which startled me into comprehension. The question was, 'Discuss David's foreign policy'. For the first time I stumbled on the realization that people were always the same; that time was one; that only the dresses and manners were different. David had had a foreign policy just as George III had had a foreign policy and just as His Majesty's Government were putting into operation a foreign policy at that instant. I don't suppose I saw the implications as clearly as this, but I know that my old childish notion of the Bible stories dropped off, and I saw David and the Queen of Sheba as an adult student would see them. David's foreign policy was the only examination question I have ever enjoyed answering, and it won me a prize which I did not know was offered. I remember the lunch that my father gave us after the examination. I can hear him humming as he looked through the papers, and his declaration that they were well set questions. If we hadn't been able to do David's foreign policy we were very silly little girls. It was what he had been driving at all along but differently worded. Had we illustrated with a sketch-map to show the favourable position of Palestine in relation to . . .? Anne, he supposed, would have made a poor effort with a map; careless little girl! But he ordered me a second ice when he perceived that I was a little cast down at this aspersion. He had a rooted conviction of my invincible carelessness, but never liked to see me daunted.

Not so very long afterwards Vic and I paid a second visit to Truro—this time to be interviewed by the Vice-Principal, Miss Gee. Nobody remembered that I had nothing to wear for an interview until the day was upon us. Then it was seen that my school suit was short and shabby, my best one shabbier and shorter still, and that my hair was done in a manner ill-beseeming a prospective student. My mother and Susan went into consultation and Susan reluctantly and with many injunctions not to spoil it—did I remember that nice white blouse which Maurice had given her and which I had inked?—lent me a green skirt and a new blouse. I did my hair in a plait and tied it with one of Susan's wide black ribbons; I wore one of her hats and a coat of my own. Susan's skirt came well down towards my ankles and, masquerading thus as a budding young woman, I went off in Johnny Johns's wagonette to Truro. It was Truro market day.

Vic's interview was earlier in the day than mine as she was 'S' and I was 'T'. Her ordeals always ended just as mine were beginning. I walked up to the college feeling vain of Susan's skirt and my black bow. I swished a little from side to side to make the skirt swing. Johnny Johns put up somewhere at the back of Lemon Street, and I walked over the bridge and up Mitchell Hill. At the college door I adjusted my hat and, feeling that a suspender was working loose, was in the act of giving my stocking a tug when a maid opened the door. She showed me into a little room on the left, where I sat all alone; I was the last of the candidates to be interviewed that day. I wished with all my heart I was 'down Hemmick' instead of accompanying this would-be teacher who was sitting on the chair in my place, and with whom I have never been able to feel identical. Yet when Vic came in, her own interview over, and looked at my usurper and said, with a spontaneous burst of laughter, 'Oh, Anne, you do look a freak!' I was mortified. I said to Vic without conviction, 'Freak yourself,' and at that moment the maid came back and said, 'Miss Treneer,' and stood there holding the door. Vic, quick to divine, said, 'I was only teasing; you look grand really,' and in I went. Miss Gee was sitting at a desk, but everything about her was soft, billowy and feminine. She wore, perched on dark hair, a hat decorated with roses under veiling. She had good grey eyes. My rawness met her civility and was quenched. Perhaps I divined that she enjoyed handling souls, for I immediately sheathed mine. Quite irrationally I disliked her then and always; it was not until long after I had left the college that I gained through other people's judgments a juster estimate of a remarkable Edwardian, whose mind wore the boned, lace neck-band of the period. As it was I felt myself beginning to glower in a little corner behind the young woman who was putting up my façade.

'You look very young, dear,' purred Miss Gee; 'too young, I am afraid, to come up to college in September.' I replied that I was of the common age and was, indeed, a day older than my friend Victoria Stauffer. I cannot remember anything else of the interview except that I feared Miss Gee might kiss me on parting, and whither should I plunge? The doubt as to whether or not I should be accepted for the coming September allayed with some cold drops my skipping spirits. Vic had been pretty well promised a place; if I could not go with her, I thought, I would not go at all. However, the door was opened to me; its hinges oiled by my prowess in the field of David's foreign policy. My prize was ten pounds to spend on books, and when I received it I thought the heavens had opened, and that I sat in a circular glory like a saint.

Vic and I left St Austell County School that July with reluctance. We had been remarkably free there, chasing up the various paths of learning, nothing closed to us, nothing forced on us. We had been even with the boys; our attic had been a beloved refuge; going home for weekends a recurrent refreshment. Now we were to live in a community of women. At about this time three evils befell. My brother Howard caught pneumonia and nearly died in Exeter. Susan went up to help nurse him, but I stayed at home locked in with fear for the first time in my life. Up to then I had felt like Coleridge, that no one whom I entirely loved could die. Happily, my brother recovered and we laughed together again, but a certain fear of insubstantiation remained. The other evil was that one wet day my father slipped and broke his leg. When the leg was set and he was in bed, the rigidity of the plaster-of-paris case seemed terrible under the bed-clothes, and the knowledge that he could not curl his leg under him if he wished. Books which I read aloud to him come back to me intensely heightened by this demand on my sympathy for someone I loved. We had had little pain in our family. I have never re-read *Dr Jeykll and Mr Hyde* since that time; but the horror of Hyde's trampling the child mingles with the colour of the down quilt as I sat by the bed and read aloud; and with the smell of antiseptics. I hate a hospital smell. The third evil and one which by no means I could get round was the perception, which I could no longer blink, that Dart was growing very old. The fire had gone from him and he looked at me in a mournful, plodding way. I did not ride any more. We drove shorter and shorter distances; but even in the sunny quarry on the Barns Hill he seemed dejected. He was often still and no longer wanted to jump the hedges. Only in passing the tannery at the foot of Grampound Hill fear still made him shy.

Susan at this time was concerned about my clothes. I see my father beginning to get about on crutches and Susan groaning over my unhappy state in relation to the fashion of the times. I was born out of due season. The fashion of 1926 would have suited me in 1909; whereas the 1909 fashions, the long skirts, the waists, the frilly blouses, the hair puffed out over a frame, made me look, if ever I forlornly attempted them, confoundedly odd. Susan would poke and pull; she would try on the thing herself and look elegant; try it on to me, and lament aloud. What was the matter with me that I could not look like anybody else! Then I would turn on her in a fury and tell her I didn't care what I went to Truro in. I would walk up to Miss Gee with nothing on at all. That would shake her out of the morass of her softness.

My parents went off to Boscastle in order that my father might recuperate in the stronger air, and Susan and I were left alone. It was a wonderful mushroom season. We would go out to the Barns Hills, or to the fields between the Hovel and Trevennen, and pick basketfuls. They were a kind of solace; picking them we were children again. We forgot our impending separation, and our exasperation with each other. In the evenings I would watch Susan doing her utmost to send me to college with the things she thought I ought to have, embroidering my linen bag, making me pretty nightdresses, sewing name-tapes on towels and pillowcases; then I would burst out that I did not want any of my old things, that she needn't bother herself, that I wasn't going to any old college with any old Miss Gee. A less patient sister would have boxed my ears; instead we would make it up and go, wildly happy, on the beaches and on the cliffs, rejoicing in being alone, in skipping all the normal mealtimes, in turning the routine of the house upside down. When my new trunk came with my initials on I kicked it; when I opened parcels all containing new clothes I flung them about. Most of all I had a spite against a new suit and against a new frock for evenings. I became suddenly devoted to my old school sailor hat and packed it secretly in the bottom of the trunk, together with a faithful old green pleated skirt. I suppose I felt a need to cling to something.

I forget how I and my trunk reached Truro, I can only remember the hopeless despair when I said goodbye to Susan, and my grief that I had been behaving so intolerably. Then I remember the quadrangle at Truro and some young woman telling me that I was to be in dormitory 7, and another that we must unpack our possessions downstairs and carry them up on trays, and another that there would be high tea. My senior, Jessie Greenwood, introduced herself, small, dark, merry and so kind that I remember with thankfulness the beam in her eye after all these years. Vic was in dormitory 3, far removed, and we were not at the same table for meals. Over that high tea, which turned out to be a hard boiled egg, I mournfully beheld her from afar.

6

TRURO TRAINING COLLEGE

I dreamt I skipt from skin and bones,
Into the starry mansions;

Yet knew I'd give my soul to be
Once more of the old earth earthy;

To hear a blackbird singing clear
With a gross unpurged ear;

And with an uncelestial nose
Savour the sweetness of a rose;

Run with the wind; my Holy Ghost
Has never known the Angelic Host;

My daily bread and rarer wine,
Small traffic have with the divine.

Oh, who would, for immortal ichor
Change his warm blood and earthly liquor?

And, dear my Lord, what I love is,
Not other but this worldës bliss.

—*This World's Bliss*

213

I always associate Truro College with Tennyson. There was a deodar on the lawn and, although we were not sweet girl graduates, we were certainly in our golden hair; Dorothy Purchas quite literally, the rest of us in our various degrees of black, brown and mousy. No one wore her hair short or her skirt. Every night was heard the sound of rhythmic brushing in the dormitories.

With Tennyson went a pinch of the modern, a strong dash of the medieval and a tincture, very faintly perceptible, of Lowood Institution. The college had been built and was largely maintained by the subscriptions of church people; but the subscriptions were supplemented by a government grant and by our own small fees. I did not realize then as I do now that Miss Gee was doing her utmost to modernize the college and had succeeded in a way that would have astonished the Founders. In the early days the students had been meek indeed. They had been made aware of benefaction. They had gone two and two to church and had worn bonnets when nobody else wore bonnets. Hardy gives a harsh picture of them—in a different church college—in *Jude the Obscure*. But Truro can never at any time of its history have been harsh or crude. It was, for one thing, blessedly small and had avoided that metallic quality which seems inseparable from large institutions. Its tradition was gentle. All its old students bore witness to it particularly, I think, its oldest students; those who, in 1909, women of fifty or sixty, with many years of teaching experience, came back to see us at Whitsuntide reunions. In the general ordering of our lives the medieval predominated. We might have been serving a novitiate, our very cubicles were austere, narrow and cell-like. In dormitory 7 we called ourselves the celestials and were nearest to the sky, being up six flights. There slept eight people, each in her curtained space, four juniors and four seniors. Each cubicle contained a bed, a chest of drawers, a bookcase and a chair. We might decorate our walls as we would. I did not decorate mine; all I put out on the chest of drawers was a picture of my brother Howard playing the organ. I used to imagine how he would laugh if he could see me at Truro. I would sit by my window looking out on to the garden, listening to the wind in the deodar and holding imaginary conversation with him. It was in Truro that I grew to find the night sky friendly. My cubicle was in a corner and I was profoundly glad of this, for it meant that I did not have students on both sides of me. I cherished the wall which made me feel a little private. Sometimes, I could hear Miss Cooper, lecturer in botany, poking her fire; but in general there was silence behind the wall. We were all under Miss Cooper's wing. Shelley was her nickname because she quoted the poet with such warmth in her lectures. We waited for 'as the poet Shelley says', and would smile at one another; but Miss Cooper was an enthusiast, and even while we smiled we respected. She was a little like a Cranford storybook lady, with delicate, pink cheeks and fluffy, greying hair, a faint opaqueness and drooping in one eye, and a gentle voice. She was very easily hurt, quick to take offence, and prone to emotional forgiveness. I never went through a forgiveness but I heard of them. It was Miss Cooper's duty to put out the dormitory gas-light at ten o'clock; then she would say, 'Good night, girls,' as though we were still at school, and we replied, 'Good night, Miss Cooper,' after which presumably we slept. Instead we often flitted about. I remember the comic shadow of my dangling feet as I sat on the curtain pole in dormitory 5 and listened unseen to Miss Peat rebuking the dormitory for unseemly mirth. I might have been Donald Duck. We were often extremely childish, the result of being treated as children. A friend of mine once scrowled a pilchard over the fire in the part of the building we called the cottage, and the smell of pilchard permeated all things; Miss Peat arrived, lifted up a nostril, and was told it must be the jam boiling over in the jam factory down by the wharf. I hated the smell of strawberry jam for years. Truro reeked of jam in July.

In the morning at seven o'clock we were awakened by a dreadful bell. No time has even seemed to me more precious than the warm minutes I spent in bed after this imperious summons to a life of duty. Surely, surely, slumber is more sweet than toil! Our time was apportioned. When we had wrested ourselves from our drowsiness, we sped in various stages of undress, but always with the decent blouse and skirt covering all, to the classroom for early study. I believe if one got out early enough, one could get a cup of tea before study, but I never rose in time for this. It was a supervised study; we sat at our desks, the lecturer on duty sat at hers. Only Miss Gee, I suppose, was in bed. How cosy she must have felt! After early study came breakfast, and then various 'charges'. Our charges varied week by week. On dormitory charge, we swept out the room and cleaned the bath; on dining-room charge we helped lay the meals and to clear them. This charge was greatly liked as, after clearing, we usually managed to make ourselves toast over the dining-room fires at night, and sometimes a Welsh rabbit with cheese secreted during supper. Library charge was less popular; the librarian had too keen an eye for dust. My favourite charge was lab. charge. The lab. never seemed to look different whether we dusted it or not, so Jessie Greenwood and I volunteered for this charge whenever we could. It was while on lab. duty, while presumably we were dusting all the little bottles and replacing them clean, that she taught me the military two-step, and the valeta, and improved my waltzing. Singing the tunes and waving our dusters, we danced. 'Heel, toe! One, two, three! Heel, toe! One, two three!' we sang; or, whistling the tune of the Blue Danube, we waltzed about the benches.

Charges done, it was time for chapel. We went to St Paul's Church at the foot of Mitchell Hill every morning. I constituted myself organ blower at as early a date as possible so that in my secure position behind the curtain, I could read in peace. I always chose a not too exciting book so that I should not go right off into the story and forget to come back to blow in time for the hymn; but once when I had chosen *Pendennis* and had read it safely for days and days on end, I did go right off at the death of Mrs Penn. The organist waited for wind and no wind came; the students waited for the organ and no organ played; Miss Gee and Canon Kerr waited for the students and no students sang. Then somebody came and shook me by the shoulder; I began to pump frantically, but the gaff was blown. I was deposed from my office. After chapel came lectures until one o'clock with a mid-morning break for physical training on the terrace. In the afternoons we might, in theory, play games or walk; but this precious time was frequently encroached upon. After tea, lectures and studies were renewed, until supper time. We then had chapel again, this time in the senior classroom where there was no organ to blow. Any little darling minutes that remained, were, I am half inclined to believe, our own; but I may err! It sounds extravagant. Trying to stuff too much into the hastening moments that poor mortals can command is a vice which has always dogged and still dogs training colleges.

The Victorianism of Truro was marked in our deportment, and in authority's attitude towards young men. These creatures were supposed not to exist. Very few students invited even a brother to college. I did not invite one of mine. I used to think sometimes that if even one, let alone all four of them, arrived and looked at our doings and began chaffing or teasing us, that the whole college would vanish like an illusion. I used to imagine Cap'n jesting with Miss Peat, or Howard telling Miss Cooper a funny story, or Maurice singing 'Mrs Henry Hawkins' to his own accompaniment with variations on the common-room piano, or Stan just standing and looking at us quizzically without saying a word; but none of my brothers ever saw me at Truro. They would never have believed it was I drawing margins. As for my sister Susan, I cannot remember that she was ever induced to enter the college doors. If she had she would have transformed the life there within a month. She was once vaguely interested when I spoke of dances on Saturday nights; but when she asked who we danced with and I said that we danced with each other, Susan said, 'Oh!'

We began drawing margins in our first week and continued to the end. 'Back to your margins, girls,' Miss Bevan would say as she delivered excellent lectures on Method. We drew the margins and wrote our notes in beautiful notebooks, notebooks which were given out during the first few days of term and lasted us our Truro lives. They were sumptuous books; their like do not exist today. They were the very idea of notebooks. The paper in them was superfine, thick and glossy. The pen fairly slid over it. The covers were stiff-boarded, dark-green; inscribed on them in a flourish of gold was 'Truro Diocesan Training College. My deeds will speak'. Our deeds threatened to speak for us everywhere, hateful little things! The most handsome of all the notebooks was for nature study. Extra thick it was, with dark-red covers, and interleaved with drawing-paper. I beheld it with a reverent eye, a savage might have worshipped it. In its pages Vic and I were to record in the process of time our observations on the behaviour of the elm over the space of a year. Shall I ever forget the elm, the wych and the common? Our blasted elm it became within a month. It refused to alter its appearance with sufficient speed for our weekly record. Were the winter buds any bigger? Indeed they were not. If ever I wish to smile at the past I can picture myself with Vic blinking at the elm or caudling away with water and paint and words at our records. From being stately creatures all the trees became jokes. I can hear Dorothy Purchas on the slow activities of the beech, or Hilda Pears in caustic comment on the lime. I envied her her coral buds and honey-coloured flowers. I think Maggie Kemp espoused the thorn. But our trees were a glorious excuse for extending the limits of our walks. 'May we go as far as Tresillian Woods, Miss Cooper? Our wych-elm there . . .' or, 'There is a most interesting elm at Pencalenick, Miss Cooper; we thought, perhaps . . .' If our trees failed us there were all Nature's startling devices at our beck. I went far afield in search of dodder and sundew. In the holidays I reached Bodmin Moor in pursuit of cotton-grass. A murmured reference to enchanters' nightshade was sufficient excuse when we were caught by the outgoing tide and stranded in the polished mud on a creek of the Fal.

Church, too, was an excuse for walks; for summer evening walks through the fields about Truro. Truro is a city in the fields; cows are almost numbered among the citizens. I remember the scented fields of June; the sheen of summer glancing from the waves of grasses as they bent to the breeze; or this same sheen catching the gloss of a horse's flank, or of Dorrie Hicks's splendid hair. In summer we chose to say our prayers at the most distant churches within range. St Michael Penkivel was my furthest record. I had my bicycle at Truro by then, but even so St Michael Penkivel, approached by intersecting lanes, green-banked and high-wooded, so that one seemed to be cycling towards the sleeping beauty, took me so long to reach that I was too late to go to church at all. I looked at the church, wished Lord Falmouth was a family friend, and pedalled back to college again, with the heavy dumble-dores blundering against me. Nearer churches were Kenwyn with its tree-lined church path and shadowy churchyard; Kea, and Sweet St Clements. For walks in Truro itself—the city was out of bounds except on Saturday afternoons—I was mainly indebted to the fact that in my senior year it was my duty to buy and arrange flowers for the senior classroom; and in my junior year Jessie Greenwood bought and paid for the cream for table five. We contributed 1d. a week towards cream to eat with our apple pie on Sundays—'Tell the juniors there's plenty more.' With flowers to pay for and cream to order for Jessie, I rarely lacked an excuse if I wanted to wander where the little brown rivers flowed through Truro or by the old wharfs. I dearly liked the little bridges. I hardly noticed the light and gracious cathedral when I was at Truro, except when Canon Sampson preached. He always tried to convince us of sin, and I could imitate him in the holidays, waving my arms to amuse one or two of my brothers from the pulpit-like look-out on the Dodman when, as always in a summer holiday, we walked out to that purple-dark headland. Sometimes in Truro I whisked up to the cattle market to see if I could spot any of Mr J. C. Williams's cattle, or a Barton wagon, or Noah Loten, or Jim Strout; but my deeds always threatened to speak for me in the cattle market, and to take off my hat would have been to make myself the more conspicuous. Even children wore hats in Truro, and on Sundays every hand was gloved. I never heard of anyone encountering Miss Gee without her gloves on.

My happiest memory of lectures at Truro is of the courses in English and history given by Miss Goode. Miss Goode was a remarkable tutor. Of average height, pale, with luminous eyes, and dark hair turning grey, she presented a subject and held together the people in her audience without confounding the individuals into a mass or allowing the subject to grow flaccid. She had a candid mind. Between the taught and the subject taught she held a delicate balance. Few achieve this. The authors read in English, though the plan was too circumscribed, were well chosen for our age. Tennyson to me is entwined with gardens; and Truro was the market town of a land of gardens, of cottage gardens and the stately gardens of great houses. It is on the borders of Roseland, amidst cultivated land in good heart, with woods through which the sea comes creeping up by way of the tidal Fal; bringing the smell of the sea; bringing the smell of mud drying on the lower branches of the trees; bringing the cry of curlews melancholy at night. *The Dying Swan* is a poem which fits the Fal by Tresillian; and 'Heavily hangs the broad sun flower' the Bishop's garden at Lis Escop. A child said to me once that she liked poetry because she liked the taste of the nice words in her mouth. Tennyson's poetry gave me that voluptuous pleasure. The voice lies sweetly along the words in Tennyson's poetry.

Browning flung me into the rapids of meaning. In the frail canoe of my mind, I went swirling past the rocks and into quiet pools, keeping my craft afloat as I could. I can remember one holiday at home, during which I was exploring Browning. My father and I had driven by Tubbs Mill and Trevennen to Rush Pool, and so to the top of Tregony Hill above Dr Grier's house in Mevagissey. Now that Dart was old we did not drive down the hill. We wished to spare him; so I waited in the trap at the top of the hill while my father walked down to Mevagissey to get his hair cut. As I waited I read *Fra Lippo Lippi*. At first it was words, words, words, with snatches of tune; and then I discovered what it was all about. It exploded as Hopkins would say. I could see the old Monk and hear him talking, and looking; and seeing a face for Judas. I saw his life and his art in a flash, heard him lending his mind out, and knew that he knew as I knew and as the poet who evoked him knew:

> The Beauty and the wonder and the power,
> The shapes of things, their colours, lights and shades,
> Changes, surprises . . .

I relished the glow of existence in Browning, the earthly-based rapture to which he could attain in such things as:

> Oh, good gigantic smile o' the brown old earth,
> This autumn morning! How he sets his bones
> To bask i' the sun, and thrusts out knees and feet
> For the ripple to run over in its mirth; . . .

And as a poet he seemed and seems to me incomparably dramatic. What an influence he has had! Would Mr Eliot ever have written that most dramatic of lyrics *The Game of Chess* if Browning had not written?

In Matthew Arnold we tasted the rhythm of our own melancholy and the melancholy of the moon-blanched beaches, a melancholy which, as a child, I did not know, but which seized on me all the more strongly at Truro. In a part of the garden we called the wilderness, fearful lest anyone should hear me, I would say aloud, *Thyrsis* and *The Scholar Gipsy*. They provided an objective outlet for that passion of regret that invades the soul as it feels itself becoming entangled. This melancholy in its profound and tragic import is experienced in *Hamlet*, the play selected for our detailed study:

> There's something in his soul,
> O'er which his melancholy sits on brood . . .

The poets Tennyson, Browning and Arnold, and I think the tragedy of *Hamlet* too, are for the young; not for children, but for young people growing towards the world. That is why they fare ill at the hands of mature critics who have a sort of spite against them, punishing in them their own inability to respond to them in all their recesses any longer.

Truro College was earnest. In prose, George Eliot reinforced Robert Browning in trying to persuade us that life's business was to make a terrible choice. But I used to let my mind flit away from the serious import of the fables themselves to the bar of the Rainbow or to Mrs Poyser's kitchen. I read many Victorian novels at Truro; but I read none of them with that profound and trembling interest with which I had read Scott at home as a child. I suppose I shall never in this world of fiction journey again with anyone as I journeyed in those early days with Jeanie Deans. Scott was not Victorian; but at Truro we were Victorian in essence, even in the authors we chiefly studied. In one respect, though, we were modern. Maggie Tulliver never did physical training, whereas in our skippings, and jumpings, and games we were looking well forward. Truro was in that respect more modern than many a college today. Miss Fountain in my first year, and Miss McDowell in my second, were recognizably experts in their profession. We liked to look at Miss Fountain and to watch her move. She wore a short, dark-green tunic in the morning, and a long grey-green dress at night over a cream blouse with bishop sleeves. We wore short black tunics over white blouses. It was a wonderful relief to slip out of our lady-likeness into this practical habit and prance about the terrace. 'Deeply breathe in!' We breathed in and stretched ourselves within our cage of bones. 'Deeply breathe out! control it!' and out our breaths fluttered. Even in my first year I was as earnest as a savage about my physical training; in my second year, under Miss McDowell, I was fanatical. I fitted up some apparatus in the wash-house at home so as to keep up the business in the holidays. I hung from curtain poles, I vaulted over the mangle. I remember when Franklyn Davis and his men came to paint our house at Caerhays and white-wash the wash-house how they teased me about what they called my Jimmy Aisem. Both Miss Fountain and Miss McDowell knew what they wanted and how to teach. Gone was the tentativeness of education; here was something positive and graduated. With a physical training 'table' I knew what I was at. Miss McDowell's lectures on anatomy and hygiene were as clear as daylight. I see her standing by our skeleton—the Lady Bones of many a practical joke—recapitulating with precision. I left Truro with the feeling that I could at least help children to have nice, straight, lithe bodies. My own scholarly stoop had received swift attention. The back of my neck now sought my coat collar; heads up and chins in was the watchword. I laugh still as I think of myself trying to draw in my chin. How could one draw in a chin? And there was Susan as straight as a lath with a chin neither in nor out; yet Susan had thought of none of these things. She had neither cultivated a stoop with Mr Raynor nor uprightness with Miss McDowell.

I enjoyed games at Truro. Badminton on a sheltered terrace out of doors was the best of all, partly because the game was new to me, partly because the courts were in the garden and we could play in odd half-hours, partly because it is a light and leaping game. The rackets are half the weight of tennis rackets and the shuttle-cocks are feathered. Any wind spoils out-door badminton; that was why I was bathed in anger when the court on the lower terrace, which we called the wilderness, was taken as the site of the proposed new college chapel. I grudged this site to God. Although I liked the idea of a college chapel, a windy site I felt would meet the need, whereas the shuttle-cocks needed a dead calm. Once when two of us were running down to the wilderness, waving our rackets for a game between lectures, we nearly knocked down the Bishop as he entered by a side door. A set of steps which I was jumping brought me up against him with some abruptness. He showed Episcopal equanimity. We liked the Bishop; but our favourite cathedral dignitary was the Precentor, who was also the college chaplain. Canon Corfe was not a good lecturer, I imagine, for we used his divinity hour to read or paint or write at leisure. No one can ever have lectured to a more abstracted audience. Near the end of the time, taking off and readjusting his pince-nez, he would say, 'Is your clock right by any chance?' 'A little slow, Precentor,' we would reply, and he would thankfully escape from us. When he took the whole college for choral singing on Saturday evenings, it was quite a different matter. This was my favourite hour at Truro. We learnt an infinite variety of songs and sang them with all our hearts. We sang them with all our hearts until Miss Cooper, who took choral practice when the Precentor was absent, entered us for one of the Cornish Musical Festivals. I have a notion the festival was at Chacewater but this is impossible. There was no hall at Chacewater and we did not sing to the sky. I suppose it was at Redruth. I remember we filed on to the platform in such numbers in our sailor hats with the black and white hat bands and 'My deeds will speak' emblazoned on our fronts that Sir Hugh Allen was transfixed. But our deeds spake not; we were cold. There came from us a thin trickle of polite sound, very different from the warm music in the senior classroom. Words failed Sir Hugh to describe his disappointment in us. So many, and so lamentably incapable of any attack! The absence of colour in our voices! The! ... He wore himself out in denouncing us, and then he worked himself in again conducting the combined men's choirs. He took off his coat to it, 'Sing like the devil, men, sing like the devil!' he was yelling at them before the performance ended. The men went ramping off, but we dwindled away. There was no spirit left in us.

For some students art and handiwork were more favourite recreations than music and games. But not for me. How I hated making baskets of wet canes! How I loathed the very sight of raffia work! How Vic and I giggled over two little pairs of knickers on which we had sewn throughout our days at St Austell County School, and on which we continued to draw thread throughout a series of Lenten missionary meetings at Truro! These modest but ill-made little garments went at last in a parcel to those whom Vic and I blithely called the Heathen Chinee. They would have amused a set of Dervishes. I should have adored to see a little Chinee arrayed in those knickers. Miss Gee, I remember, read to us while we stitched. A history of the place of the philanthropic parcel in the comity of nations during the first half of the nineteenth century could make a pretty thesis. Vic and I never thought in those days that we should ever be the recipients of parcels ourselves. We did not know with what joy we should open them. I have eaten royal cake out of a parcel sent by her American brother Byron, and have gone clad in fine raiment sent by my American brother Maurice. But blessings on both our American brothers. Their parcels were better than fine gold; they were fun.

Miss Peat taught handicrafts and art at Truro. 'Don't be afraid of a little colour, girls; don't be afraid of a little colour,' she would say. I certainly got a notion of thick paint. Good teachers lend themselves to caricature. Miss Peat was our constant joy. She was a majestic figure with decided, handsome features, and she was unassailed by any doubts, except as to the physical strength of young women. It was very dangerous to our delicate systems for us to carry anything heavy. I would place myself in position to shoulder something, a little stand or chair or platform, just to hear her say, 'Don't move that alone, dear; don't move that alone. Get six strong girls to help you, dear.' She hated noise; she did not like young women to be robustious. She shushed us in the corridors. At certain periods of the day there was a recurrent murmur of Sh! sh! sh! about the halls of Truro. I can hear it with the wind in the trees, and the pigeons cooing, and the sound of Penhaligan's mower on the sunny lawn. Once when the Bishop was lecturing in the junior classroom Penhaligan mowed too near. The Bishop moved towards the window and shouted in a voice that had roused congregations to righteousness, 'Penhaligan!' Penhaligan went on mowing. The Bishop turned to us with, 'The man doesn't hear me.' I, perceiving the pleasant sunshine outside, suggested that I should go out and tell Penhaligan to withdraw a little. I had a delicious slow saunter, and I did not repeat to the Bishop what Penhaligan said when I invited him, with the Bishop's compliments, to move a little further off. Penhaligan was exactly like Jerry Cruncher in *A Tale of Two Cities*. His face was red, his hair bristled, his fingers stuck out. 'If the students wean't put their hockey buts in the basket, I cean't clean 'em, Miss Treneer; tha's all 'tis; I cean't clean 'em.' Or, 'Miss Treneer, it tidn' no good telling me the hockey buts is still wet. Tidn' my fault; 'tis that dratted apparatus. 'Tis things tha's wrong with this college; things! That there apparatus and me lawn mower, miss; bought in the year one.' I once was late for a hockey match through listening to Penhaligan on 'things' and when I got to the field Miss McDowell told me I didn't take things seriously.

Miss Holloway was the only person who could manage Penhaligan. Miss Holloway managed us all. 'A nice warm vest, dear! That's the cure for chilblains; a nice, long, warm, woollen vest. Nice combinations would be even better than a nice vest; but you girls won't wear them, I know, dear, any more than you'll eat your nice suet pud . . .'

In my junior year Ethel Morrison, one of the seniors, used to make us laugh over all the little day-to-day happenings at Truro. She fitted her commentaries into the framework of the Baconian essay. After supper, standing on a chair, she would deliver the compositions to an accompaniment of laughter and the beating of spoons upon the board. They perished like all the best things with the moment; but if they were as funny as I seem to remember they were, they were very funny indeed. They struck straight home at any grievance, foolishness, or inflationary sentiment. If relations were never strained between seniors and juniors when I was a junior I think it was largely due to Ethel Morrison. We had no Ethel Morrison in our year and we missed her when, in our turn, we became seniors. We said our juniors were uppish and sent them to Coventry. This was extremely awkward for me as my junior was Dorrie Hicks. She came from Pengruglar, not far from my home. She had been to St Austell County School, and her aunts knew my parents. She was not a junior but a friend. She had glorious red hair and was half as tall again as I, and twice as sensible. I forget how the fire and smoke affected us at the time; we grinned at one another from the opposed ranks, I think. The whole affair was typical of what happens when too much segregation is attempted; it was not much more foolish than the class war.

The best day of the year at Truro was Ascension Day. It was a holiday with no organized festivity. We went to the early

Eucharist and after that we were given a pasty, a banana, a bar of chocolate, and freedom. In our junior year Vic and I walked to Perranporth and then to St Agnes on the cliffs. By nine o'clock in the morning, on top of Truro brim, we had freed ourselves from the burden of our paper bags by eating the whole day's provisions. After that we travelled light as air. Perhaps it was partly emptiness that uplifted us; certainly I nearly floated off on the gusts of furzy scent that ravished us on the cliffs between Perranporth and St Agnes. When we got back at night and sang, 'Hail the day that sees him rise', I knew exactly what levitation was like.

Another wonderful day was entirely unexpected. It had never occurred to me not to honour the King, and I had a pang of regret when King Edward VII died; but my spirits rose with a bound when I found that his death cancelled all arrangements at Truro for an Old Students' weekend, at which the juniors would have made themselves useful. The juniors, it seemed, were free. I coaxed my senior, Jessie Greenwood, to catch Miss Gee in the throes of indecision. Could the juniors who lived near at hand go home for the weekend? I stood at the college gate waiting; Jessie came spinning towards me and I was off within a second of the permission. I was afraid Miss Gee might change her mind. I walked home from Grampound Road Station in a state of hilarity, ill-suited to the preparation of black gloves, black hats, and black shoes incipient at college as I left it. The last mile's walking of an unexpected visit home is royal; and then the opening of the garden gate and the door; the cry of, 'It's Anne'; the warmth and the blessing. I knew by my mother's face that she thought for a moment that I'd carried out a threat that I had often laughingly made, and walked out of Truro for good. I was glad I hadn't, she would have thought it wrong. 'With Mary's permission,' I sang as, with my arm round my mother's waist, I waltzed her round the kitchen.

The worst times at Truro were the weeks of school practice, and the occasional giving of criticism lessons. If in hell I lift up my eyes being in torment I shall know I have lost my

Illustrations, and that Miss Bevan is making a note of my blank face. I once gave a lesson to little children on the Epiphany in which I never even reached my Illustration. Miss Gee was listening to me and I talked so much about the Kings and their possible doings in the East that I had only dimly approached the point of my lesson when the bell rang. Miss Gee, going over the lesson with me in her room, gently remarked on this failure. 'And where, dear, were your illustrations?' said she. 'Had you no illustrations?' 'Yes, Miss Gee; I had a star,' I said; and I had made a star, a lovely gilded star, and this I had meant to draw forth like a conjurer at the dramatic moment; but the star never rose in my lesson, the Kings were still in their possible pasts. Another criticism lesson I gave was to older children on my dearly beloved Henry Trengrouse of Helston. For this I made a handsome little model of the breeches-buoy. I had a little china doll and pulled her from the wreck to the shore. The children and I were alike enthralled. Again and again I saved our doll from a watery grave, and my supervisor never came in to see that illustration. School practice—I think we did a fortnight or three weeks at a stretch, three times during the two years—kept me awake at nights. I taught at Bosvigo School, Truro, under Mr Shakespeare; and Trewirgie School, Redruth, under Miss Harris. I liked Trewirgie. We went up Carn Brea on the last Friday afternoon by permission of Miss Harris the head mistress who was a darling, and who gave her novices comfort. She said you could never tell whether or not you liked teaching from school practice. It was all quite different when you knew the children and had a class of your own. I have found this to be true. And the set lesson except as an occasional stimulus is over-valued. Plan the work and let the children get on with it. Sufficient space, the right books in plenty, music and pictures, enough material to stimulate ingenuity, no illustrations, and friendliness—it is almost as simple as that, but not quite. I have heard many head mistresses say that they prefer to have young teachers untrained; and certainly I have met many good teachers who have never been through any set course in education. But one would not venture to doctor the body without a strenuous course of training, and minds and souls are not less delicate. The trouble is that a broken spirit does not show so easily as a broken arm. And the relief is, as Sara Coleridge's old nurse said, 'Bless you, ma'am, it is very hard to *kill* a baby.' Children are blessedly resilient. If they were not they would all have died under our tender dread of complexes in the last twenty years. But they are still alive and shouting, and ready to try out the powers of the new students as they tried out mine. Looking back now at much over which I was impatient when I was young, I see that Truro College had one tremendous asset. It put first things first. At Truro the purpose of education was seen to be—for all the fun I have made of gilded stars—to guide children towards a way of living. Our tutors themselves were un-self-seeking and disinterested. They were, in short, good women. There are still saints among teachers, of whom, alas, I am not one; but I have met them. Their devotion keeps the spirit alive. Colleges like Truro helped to produce them. If the supply should run short the teaching profession will grow dingy.

7

TREVERBYN

Let's michie, boys, make mocks and play;
She's new! Hey nonny, nonny, nonny ney!

When first I went to live in a community at Truro, I found the confinement intolerably irksome; but at the end of two years I was half loath to leave. The narrowness of physical being made the mind turn inwards. In the garden that summer I used to think I should like to stay for ever and not go into the world, or build any scaffolding for myself. Instead of seeking far and wide I would contract and contract to a pin's point, and yet all the world would be mine, because all the world was in me.

From this contemplation I was roused by the business of finding a school and earning my living. The more the mind tries to pitch and settle on a head of clover or spray of meadow vetchling the more some vexatious duty intervenes and bids it fly off. There is always something to be done which one does not want to do. I have never been able to be entirely abandoned. I can be neglectful but not utterly neglectful; I can take little thought but not no thought. 'Take no thought for the morrow.' At Truro they used to say it meant, 'Be not over anxious'. I hate these hedgings. 'Consider the lilies of the field, how they grow.' I was ever ready to consider the lilies—only I preferred roses—how they grew and toiled not. But, alas! I was not a rose or a lily. I had not their useful roots, but only feet and hands and a restless head. A root and leaves must be an exquisite form of economy. However, as roots and leaves were not mine, I decided to earn some money. I wanted to earn money to give it to my mother whose naturally serene mind had sometimes been fretted by the lack of means in bringing up a family. I thought what fun it would be to change my first cheque. I could teach during the week and have weekends to myself, weekends at home. For I was determined on one thing, I would find a school near enough to Caerhays for me to go home every weekend.

The school I found was Treverbyn Council Mixed. Council Mixed was one of the most comic of all our comic attempts at naming schools. The historic names, British, National, Voluntary, Board, Council, were all bound up in some way with financial administration or with warring religious sects and secular bodies. We sought compromise and often named to hide; whereas Miss Pinkerton's academy was at least Miss Pinkerton's. Of the old names 'board' persisted longest; it persists still as an opprobrious term, though it ceased to be official forty years ago. Our bitterly ugly names have corresponded to something ugly in the essence. There is, to my mind, much in a name. A rose would not smell quite so sweet to me if it were called tab. However, I did not give much thought to Council Mixed when I was twenty. I was more concerned with the name Treverbyn, beautiful in my ears. In the pleasant Cornish manner of those days, even the word Council was entirely relegated to official correspondence. In the parish the school was plain Treverbyn school and, since there was no other, all the girls and boys in the neighbourhood went to it, at least until they were eleven, and the majority until they were fourteen. A few girls chose to stay an extra year; and these big girls were both helpful to the school and helped by it.

I first set foot in Treverbyn on a scorching hot July day. At Truro all through the final certificate examination heat had melted the marrow in our bones and made us sweat our thoughts on to the paper. The blinds, pulled down to keep out the sun from the senior classroom windows, never flapped. Air was still and dead and so, by the end of June, were the examination candidates. In July the sun was flamy. I had decided to work for the month of July as an uncertified teacher at Treverbyn, so as to read myself in. On the first Saturday I went up to reconnoitre, bicycling the distance from home. Treverbyn, up among the clay dumps, is not very far from Bugle. The landscape is not quite earthly, more like a scene from the mountains in the moon. Here are glistening sky-pointed pyramids, deep pools like cloudy turquoises, and white streams. I was half surprised that the cows in the small, bare-hedged fields gave ordinary milk. Yet this district had been familiar to my eye in a distant view from childhood. We used to look at it from the Dodman and tell the weather from the clarity which outlined or the haze which veiled it. I remembered going over a clay pit once with my cousins from Bosinver. I remembered the sky-tips aloft; the concentric level ledges of the great pits on which we walked; and the opaque, strange water below us. The colour, the unclothedness, and the violent shadows might please the eye of a modern artist. Anything more unlike the leafy Polgrain valley which I loved can hardly be conceived. Polgrain is at sea level. Treverbyn is high up towards Hensbarrow. To a cyclist the way from St Austell up to Treverbyn provides collar work. I was hot. I thought of the local preacher who arrived late in the pulpit one Sunday, his bald head steaming like a crock on the fire. He said, 'I'm sorry I'm late, brothers, but I came up that hill some coose.' I went up the hills between St Austell and Treverbyn going some coose, heat or no heat. I was to meet the head master in the school at 3 o'clock, and I was never one to leave home for an appointment with an amplitude of time. With little trickles of sweat on my forehead, and my black shoes dusty, I opened the door of the main room of the school at half-past three. I found the head master inside practising strange contortions. He swung towards me with a mighty, imaginary stroke as I stood in the doorway. If I had been a ball I should have gone whizzing through the walls to Newquay. As I was merely the new assistant mistress, I stood and looked, and the head master went adroitly on. I could only think he was practising shooting goals with an airy hockey stick. 'Practising hockey?' I ventured at last. 'Golf,' he said; and went on lunging. I have never watched a more heating performance on a summer's day; in addition I was piqued at not being taken more notice of. So with a Gorran flink I said, 'Well! as I have seen you, I'll go now,' and prepared to slope. That made him rest his arms at his sides at last. I was quite relieved to see him quiet. It was strange that I should first have come upon him practising a game, if golf can be called a game, for he was far from being a gamesome man. He was one of those people who seem born grown up, born old indeed. I could never fancy Mr Boxhall as other than he was at that time, not much more than fifty I suppose, but to my twenty years that seemed very old. He was good-looking, with a sombre and dominating personality, and a face like an etching. He was used to having his own way; other people looked to him, he did not look to other people. As we talked of the school, of the class I should teach and of the lodgings suggested for me at Penwithick, I had a sinking of heart. Perhaps all young teachers' hearts sink; but few can have sunk deeper than mine. I had a feeling that I should never be able to do the work. 'Needlework,' said Mr Boxhall. 'Of course, you will be responsible for the girls' needlework. It has always been considered very good here. In my wife's time . . .' He was a widower; his wife had taught in the school. Well! I wasn't his wife, I assured myself. I could leave, I could even leave before I began if I wanted to. I did want to. Needlework would not remain very good under my dispensation I was sure.

I dreaded Monday morning; but the reality was worse than I could ever have imagined. A class of forty or so—they seemed to be all the children in the world—forty or so nicely behaved little girls and boys fastened their bright eyes on me as Mr Boxhall introduced me to my classroom. With the uncanny instinct of ten-year-olds they realized that I was delivered into their hands; that I was not a disciplinarian; that I was as uncertain of myself and my surroundings as a Jenny Wren. In calling the register, I mispronounced a name. All the children shouted with laughter. After the register came scripture. Two little boys, a cheeky red-haired one with pale face in which millions of freckles had almost joined into one, and a dark little boy, innocent-looking and rotund as the infant St John the Baptist, fought to give out Bibles; another boy joined in the scuffle; then another. The little girls looked on with expectant, self-righteous enjoyment as the disturbance spread. Mr Coad, an assistant master from the next classroom, appeared at the door, smiled at me and glared at them. They resumed the mien of willing cherubs. All through the morning, through arithmetic and reading and geography, this little comedy repeated itself; eager co-operation, pushes and shoves, disorder spreading, pandemonium, Mr Coad; eager co-operation, a pinch and a fight, disorder spreading, pandemonium, Mr Coad. In geography lesson Mr Boxhall arrived and beat Freckles and St John the Baptist. In the last lesson, history, I told the story of Drake's voyage in the *Golden Hind* and my end was peace. All the little boys and girls looking as though they could never do a naughty deed or say a naughty word, went sailing westwards with me. I had my illustrations. In the best Truro tradition I scored a success. Most interested and most intelligent with questions were Freckles and St John the Baptist, who appeared to bear no scrap of malice for their beating.

For four July weeks I struggled. My first cheque was hardly earned, and I sped to the bank with it. I forget the exact amount. It was something like four pounds, nineteen shillings and elevenpence. I remember the golden sovereigns sliding towards me on the little shovel. I immediately laid out my All. I bought Three Nuns tobacco for my father, a white blouse for my mother, a pair of suède gloves for Susan, a handsome Byron for myself, a pipe for Howard. It never occurred to me that the money should be used to live on, so accustomed was I, during my twenty years of life, to being provided for. It was old Mrs Sargent, when I skipped down through the Rectory fields to the Hovel with my tale of gold y-spent, and a packet of her favourite peppermints, extra strongs, who put me in mind of this prosaic usage. She said, 'Anne, my handsome, what have 'ee got left to live on until next pay day?' and her whole person quaked with laughter under the folded hands. She would sit by the window in a low chair, her hands folded on her stomach, except when she used them to push her spectacles up to her forehead, so as to bring the naked eye to bear on her guest before delivering a potent word. No head mistress has been able to dislodge me from an airy perch with such a bump as old Mrs Sargent; but this time nothing mattered. The blessed blessed holidays had come. The month of August. I have always enjoyed the harvest holiday but this one was celestial. I told my troubles to my brother Howard and the sea, and then I forgot all about standards three and four, and Mr Boxhall, and the needlework cupboard into which I had shoved everything and locked the door before a tangle of knitting and sewing could fall out.

But in September I had to return to the charge and I found myself no more effective for having, in the meantime, received news that I had passed the Teachers' Certificate Examination, and was, in the eyes of the Board of Education and the Cornwall Education Committee a fully qualified teacher. In fact I was about as fully qualified as a blackbird. Perhaps I was exceptionally unable; perhaps I had not a glittering eye. I know that many of my friends in my year at college did not have my troubles; but I know, too, that many had; and I know that it was purely a matter of large numbers in a class. If I were any god of power in English education I would not care what other reforms waited, I would not rest until I had reduced the number of children in charge of any one teacher in any one class. Adults can look after their own education. It is a matter of religion and music; of making and showing excellent films and plays; of beautiful pictures; of noble and comic literature; of building houses and cities satisfying to the imagination as well as to the body; of travel and freedom of intercourse. But in schools large numbers involve all the wrong methods from the start. Since the number was large the only means I had at my command was to interest the whole group by giving set lessons;

whereas what the children needed was to be working for themselves. The wicked ones were good as long as they had enough to do, but how fast they worked and how fast they read! I was always wondering what the adventurous could do next. I almost wished the children were slower. Somebody once remarked that very few people can teach, but any firm female can make children learn. It seemed to me that I did not even have to be firm to make children learn; they would learn of themselves if they had opportunity. But there was so little room to move; there were too few books of insufficient variety. Materials were scanty. That children should sit in desks for most of the morning was still the rule. I have never taught children more full of energy or more intelligent. The naughty ones seemed to be bursting out of their suits with ingenuity and invention, their pockets bulged with marvels. But we always seemed to be veering towards the noisy instead of towards the quiet, which I, at that time, thought fitting.

My friend Vic working at Mount Charles found life easier but not too easy. We used to meet after school and consider each other's woes. I did not envy her for having girls only; to me the big girls at Treverbyn were the most terrifying of all my pupils. They sewed; and to my poor ignorance their sewing was entrusted. How we got along at all I do not know. The worst thing I did was when a charming, dark-haired, polite girl said she wanted a front opening cut in the nightdress she was making. 'Has anyone else reached the same stage?' said I. Three others had. 'Bring the nightdresses,' I said. Thinking to save time by cutting four front openings at once, I laid the garments on the table flat on one another, seized the scissors to wield which, in the Treverbyn tradition, was the mistress's prerogative, and cut. 'There you are, Milly!' I said, presenting the pretty girl with the top garment. And even as I said the words I knew what I had done. I had sawn through eight thicknesses. All four nightdresses now had back openings as well as front. They looked very funny as the girls held them up. 'We shall have to run and fell up the back openings,' said Milly. 'Yes, run and fell them up for your lives,' I said. We were like conspirators until those four nightdresses were finished and hustled out of school. I never heard what the parents said about them. Milly's sense of artistry had been dared by the disaster. She had prevailed on me to cut two other slits in the back and had embroidered little patterns on the three joins. The other three girls had been content to 'run and fell'.

When I first began teaching I was much troubled by what people would think and what they would say. How would my class be looking and behaving if anyone should come in? This weakness was partly the result of our system of training. During periods of school practice one never felt safe; the classroom door was always being opened by head mistress, class mistress or supervisor. Criticism—we even gave 'criticism lessons'—was the essence of the system of training. I doubt whether the plan was good. It made us think outwardly of the class as a whole rather than inwardly of the separate children. I knew my class was often doing its best work when all the children were buzzing like bees and not being to a stranger's eye 'good'; but how I liked to see them being good, how I liked them all to be sitting up listening to me, intolerable creature that I was! Once when I was giving a scripture lesson on the Lord's Prayer Mr Boxhall walked in and found Freckles, St John the Baptist and a few others playing instead of listening. He said the whole class must stay and have the lesson after school. I have never felt more furiously unforgiving than as I stood at four o'clock talking about, 'And forgive us our trespasses as we forgive them that trespass against us'. I nearly told my head master that he was my ghostly enemy. He was certainly the enemy of my peace of mind though he supported me strenuously. Singing lessons were a fearful ordeal for me because during that lesson, which I took with the whole upper school, Mr Boxhall stood grimly by. I could not go a-maying with any zest while he was there, and most of our songs were about Going A-maying. Once we had a 'Round' which Mr Boxhall chose. It was about poor Thomas Day:

Here lies poor Thom-as-Day
Dead; and turned to clay.

I used to give a rendering of this ditty to amuse my brother in
the holidays. The sound of Thomas Day still brings back to my
mind's eye Treverbyn school, even to the beans I set to
germinate between damp blotting-paper and the sides of a
glass jar. Poor beans! Di-cotyledons! Did I use the word di-
cotyledons to the children I wonder? I expect I did, being
foolish enough for anything. I was foolish enough and also
eager enough. 'Anne tries' could have been written of me in a
terminal report. But if I had not been able to go home for
weekends I think I should have fallen beside my five wits. It was
very lonely. As the autumn passed over to the winter the
evenings were long in my little sitting-room at Penwithick. Mrs
Benjie Bassett, my landlady, was kindness itself; but I felt I was
attempting work for which I was not man enough, or rather
woman enough, to do well. In the old Gorran phrase I was like
a flannel patch on a calico shimmy. Miss Hilda McDowell was
the only person who put any heart into me. She had been tutor
in physical training during my second year at Truro; for her
occasional encouraging word and for her faith in education, I
shall always be grateful. Myself, I was always losing faith. It
seemed to me that almost anything would be better for children
than the class-system I was struggling to maintain.

It must be remembered that many young teachers are still
wrestling with large numbers in classes, although we have had
thirty years—years interrupted by two wars, I admit—in which
to carry out reform. To my father I did not talk much of school,
for the simple reason that, during weekends, I wanted to forget
it. Besides, my father hated large numbers himself, and had
quietly taken a school in which there was no problem of the
kind. But, rain or shine, while I worked at Treverbyn I never
missed a weekend at home, although it was a wild enough
bicycle journey some nights. Much of the way between
Treverbyn and St Austell lay in the very fang of the wind. As,
on dark winter evenings, I cycled home, a smelly acetylene

lamp lit my bicycle, making a glow-worm glimmer of light. But the dimness of illumination was not dangerous; after Hewas Water I rarely met other travellers. Near Treberrick I began to look out for my father and Susan who always walked a mile or so to meet me. The pleasure of hearing their voices, the glow of their companionship as we walked home together will always be with me, and my mother's welcome at the door when she heard our footsteps. She would come out wearing something pretty, seeming so unlike Treverbyn. Everything at Caerhays was unlike Treverbyn, although the places were only fifteen miles apart. Treverbyn was an unsheltered district; when it was raining the rain possessed earth and air. Some Monday mornings I was so soaked with rain that I slipped out of my wet things in Mrs Benjie's passage, and ran upstairs with nothing on, a proceeding which Mrs B. considered not quite nice, but which was appreciated because it saved the stair-carpet. Treverbyn hedges did not give the shelter of Caerhays hedges. Caerhays hedges were full of comfort. Long may the hedges last! Stretches of hedge along the alternative route from St Austell to Caerhays—the way by Pentewan, Pengruglar and Highlanes—have been replaced by ugly, barren, cement walls. When I see them I think of what Charlie Nicholls said to May Grose when he was building her house at Milfords by Trevesson Gate in Gorran parish. She thought she would like a wall round her garden. 'A wall's cold, my handsome,' said Charlie. 'Have a hedge! The wind do blow against a wall, and rebound, and shoot up over 'un like a kite. But a hedge do soak the wind in.'

Christmas came and went. In January, on my twenty-first birthday, my brother Howard sent me a complete Shakespeare, and in his letter he said he had heard there was to be a new assistant mistress in a school at Exmouth, only ten miles away from Exeter where he was teaching. I began to sing. Then I stopped. It would mean farewell to my weekends at Caerhays, farewell to Susan, and farewell to Cornwall except in the holidays. However, I said I would apply and told Mr Boxhall I might leave Treverbyn at Easter. He was kind; he even praised me, and I have a weakness for praise. I can drink it in foaming glasses. From then onwards Treverbyn began to improve; garments were made, children grew accustomed to me. February skies are lovely over Treverbyn, clear-washed, delicate, shimmering. The larks began to sing and of all the places in which I have lived larks are most jubilant over Treverbyn, Stenalees, Bugle and Roche. They toss themselves up in an ecstasy of aspiration, higher, higher, singing with all their might between the bare uplands and the sky. I began to feel that wooded country would stifle me after this free, scented air. The furze flowered in March, spicy, nutty, with a firm texture in the clear wing-petals. Hooded, the furze flowers laughed at the rain. I liked to walk out at sunset, and see the sky-green colour lying in lakes between the streaked clouds, purple or fiery on the horizon. From the top of Hensbarrow or of Roche Rock I could survey my domain, looking far out over different levels and plains of dissolving beauty to the coast north and the coast south. Near at hand the fields and hedges with their duns and browns and greys were a foil to the glory of the sky. Then all the small delicate flowers began to come out. I suppose the hermit of Roche Rock, whose chapel is there to remind us of him, watched the flowers in his day. I left Treverbyn at Easter just as the celandines, the sorrel and the strawberry flowers below the rock were giving place to primroses, wood anemones and bluebells. I did not spend a summer at Roche, or taste the great juicy blackberries that grow on the moors until years later when Harold Harvey, who married my friend Marjorie Pascoe, became head master of Roche school, and I went to stay with them in the new white schoolhouse which was built for them near the hermitage on the rock.

8

DEVONSHIRE INTERLUDE: EXMOUTH

Red you are, and rich you are,
And wild you are, and broad you are,
And loved you be; but ah! to me
Cornwall is lovelier far, said she.

—*To Devon*

Although I was twenty-one, I had only once been out of Cornwall and that for the space of three weeks only. Now I was to be interviewed for a job in what to me was one of the foreign parts—Exmouth, in Devonshire; and I was to spend the weekend with the family of my brother's beloved Mary. Her father was an inspector of schools, and I feared he might be disposed to look upon me with a gimlet eye. He would know the points of a likely candidate for the post of assistant mistress in a girls' school as well as my friend John Grose knew the points of a sheep.

But Mr Bicknell not only had a reassuring manner, he had a reassuring person. He was a man with the most purely jocund appearance I have ever seen, and he had a soul to match. No one could have been a greater contrast to Mr Boxhall! Whereas

Mr Boxhall was spare and saturnine, Mr Bicknell was sanguine and round. His name was Samuel. Mr Boxhall's Christian name I never knew; in all probability he never had one unless, perhaps, he was named William. Mr Bicknell seemed all Christian name. I was to discover later that he was learned as well as wise; that he had faith in children; that he loved the world and was religious in it. On this first meeting I could only be thankful for him; he looked his best carving a leg of lamb for his large family, and twinkling at me over his napkin which he tucked in somewhere between his chin and his Falstaffian waist.

Unwittingly he put me on my mettle for the interview. I heard him tell Howard he was afraid the Managers would think I looked too young. Would they indeed? thought I. I placed my new hat firmly on my head and made up my mind I would look older than a retired schoolmistress I knew. I remembered the look of her, and how she never laughed, how to indicate amusement she gave a little breathe out, and said, 'ha, ha, ha,' and took a little breathe in and said, 'he!' Howard and I practised this dainty mirth going down in the train to Exmouth until the entire coach must have heard our laughter.

Of the interview I remember little except that the Rev. Thomas McClelland, a parson exactly like his name, who was in the chair, asked me if I was the candidate engaged to a Mr Pye; and that I had an almost irresistible impulse to say, 'Do you mean Mr Pigeon, or Mr Lick-and-Taty?' I refrained and concentrated on trying to decide whether the Rev. Thomas wanted his candidate to be engaged to Mr Pye or not. I decided that he did and responded with a modest blush that I was. Soon after this they told me I was appointed, and I said goodbye and tried to go out through a cupboard door. I have never been good at distinguishing the right door in moments of elation. I need no rum to make me drunk. Howard was delighted at my news as we wanted to be near each other; but he was concerned about my engagement to Mr Pye. He asked me whatever made me say yes when I could so easily and truthfully have said no. I told him I had no idea, and we went down on the Maer—the sandhills beyond the coastguard station, where, in those days, there was no sea-wall and no promenade. There grew by the shore, blue-green sea holly and sparse bents; and yellow-horned poppies on the cliff. We made up all sorts of stories about Mr Pye and me, and of how his heart would fail him when he learnt that our engagement was broken off. I never heard anything more of this fabulous man; nor did I ever find out to which candidate he was really engaged.

My brother and I went to tea with Miss Harborough, gentlest of women, who was to be my new head mistress. While dispensing deliciously thin bread-and-butter and fairy-cakes she broke the thread of a sentence to say, 'Mr Treneer, would you like an egg?' I told Howard it was because of his lean and hungry look and the glitter in his blue eyes. 'Mr Treneer, would you like an egg?' became, for some unfathomable reason that no family can ever explain, a joke.

I went back to Treverbyn till the end of the spring term. Then I exchanged the quick, bright air of the Cornish uplands for the softness of South Devon. I felt at first like an old lady I knew who came back to Cornwall from an up-the-country visit. She said, ''Iss, 'twas all right up there, my handsome; but I couldn' breathey.' I felt the same in Exmouth. Often I couldn't breathey. But it was late spring when I arrived, breaking quickly that year into summer. As I walked and bicycled about the countryside I felt in some way luxurious in my new blue, terra-cotta, green and blossomy land. The first time I walked up the Otter Valley from Budleigh Salterton to Otterton, and saw the cows knee deep in the river under the trees I thought that summer had come to stay for good, so settled and content it seemed with the mingled coolth and sunny heat. I loved the Otter for itself, but also because Coleridge had been a child at Ottery.

The estuary of the Exe had for me no adventitious glory of association. I loved it purely for itself. It was as changeable as I. Sky and tide; wind, rain and sun; the season and the time of day or night transfigured it. I would walk to Lympstone by the railway path when the water was still as satin with a grey shot light beneath the blue; the wind might freshen, and fleets of tiny wavelets charm my ear; great clouds might come up, their dark masses casting indigo shadows on the estuary and the long rhythmic lines of the hills behind Starcross. When the tide was out I walked by the mud; but even the wet mud-banks reflected splendours. The splendour was most dramatic nearer the sea at sunset in October and November. But at all months of the year it is grand to walk from Budleigh Salterton along the cliffs westward to Exmouth and see the estuary spread out to take the eye. For this view one should keep up on the high cliffs and descend to the level only when forced at the end. But for walking close to the sea one can go down at low tide to Littleham Cove and walk bare foot on sand right down to Exmouth Pier. I used to like to walk west along the sands with a distorted sun reflected in the wet sand, keeping always in advance of me so that I should never be so impious as to walk on his face.

Another favourite walk was by the narrow uphill lanes— there was hardly a house beyond Hulham Road in those days— to Black Hill and Woodbury Common, from which there was a view of the coast so wide that red sandstone gave way to the glittering cliffs about Lyme Regis. Some of my walks with friends were far afield. I remember in particular a walk to Branscombe and back by the cliffs; and often we went to Sir Walter Raleigh's birthplace at Hayes Barton. Sometimes we went by boat to the Warren to be saturated with air and sun all day; or we took Susan's favourite walk along the sea-wall to Dawlish, turned inland for a mile or two and then down Smugglers Lane to the second sea-wall which led to Teignmouth. We liked to take a boat to Shaldon and walk up Fuzzy Dee. In another direction, after taking the launch to Starcross all sorts of pleasures were open to us. A favourite excursion was to take our bicycles to Starcross and go by devious ways and villages to the top of Haldon to see the world, and spy out the distant cathedral riding Exeter.

In Exeter were Howard and Mary, married now, and set up in a little house of their own. I envied them their little house and the fun they had together; but I was no longer very jealous. Mary was a sister-in-law one could not help loving, and when Friday night came I often went dashing up to Exeter to spend the weekend with them. And I, in my turn, could have visitors in my lodgings at Rill Terrace where I lived with Miss Emily Salter. She was the eldest daughter of a famous Exmouth schoolmaster, Mr Charles Salter, an old man over seventy-five, but still teaching, still wearing knickerbockers and bicycling stockings, mascot of the Exmouth football team whose play he watched every Saturday, a splendid shrimper, and one who used to boast, as he waggled his beard at me, and gave me advice about teaching, that he had caned all the substantial tradesmen in Exmouth. Only the tradesmen in the poorer little shops had not been caned by him. That was why they were poor. He used to call in and see us every morning and share our bacon and eggs. As he opened the door Em would say, 'Fath-er' on a downward note, and in he would come. I had a little bed-sitting-room with the only really nice bureau I have ever written at; but I had all meals with Em and breakfast with Em and 'father'. Em had the clearest brown eyes. If you can imagine a chapel-going sparrow Em would be that sparrow. She was a Plymouth Brother; but she did not try to convert me. I thought it strange when I had been there some little time and she had really grown quite fond of me that she should not bat an eyelid at the idea that since I was not one of the Elect I should go to hell. Quite cheerfully she would see me going off to a dance believing that I should howl for it some day.

Susan came to stay, and my father arranged his summer holiday so that he could spend a week with me. After school we used to go for evening trips on the *Duke* or *Duchess*. My father loved trips. On Saturday we went by train to Camelford, and by a brake with four horses to Tintagel. On a dizzy crag high above the sea I knew that I was Cornish, not a Devonian. Miss Salter admired my father; he had such charming manners she said. I always thought that this compliment was a little hit at my two abominable brothers, Mr Howard and Mr Stanley as she called them; for I am sure she never knew what they would do or say next; nor, alas! did I. They found Miss Salter irresistibly guileless. They would tell frightful stories, taller and taller lies every minute, while she, gazing at them with bright brown eyes, had a naughty feeling that she was hearing more about life than a nice Plymouth Brother should. She never asked Stan to say Grace, but she used to ask Howard. 'Mr Howard, would you ask the blessing?' Em had texts even in the lavatory.

At school I was still as uncertain as the weather, yet as fanatical as a dervish. I taught the girls in the top group, girls of about twelve to fourteen years of age. I liked them; but I liked the idea of physical training even more. I suppose I had the instincts of a dictator, for I loved to see them all in the playground moving rhythmically at my command. This was the 'hips-firm' period of physical training. Rain or shine we danced and skipped, and marched, and deeply-breathed-in. Other mistresses might think the weather inclement; but not me. Out we must go. Some children must have loathed it, but they put on a cheerful countenance. In other lessons though less fanatical I was no less dogmatic. Only in painting would I let them work their own will, not knowing how to induce them to work mine. I may have half-killed them with physical training, but I spared them the worst horrors of Art. Much of the art lesson having been taken up with the operation of giving out paint-boxes, drawing-books, water and paint-rags, I used to say, giggling to myself at the memory of Truro and Miss Peat, 'Don't be afraid of a little colour girls,' and they would go splashing to it. Some of the children merely made a mess and I sympathized with them; but some occasionally produced what seemed to me startling revelations. I had a passing insight into what education could really mean. Some little Tooze or some little Smerdon or some little Pigeon would show me that she had something within her to unfold at which I had not remotely guessed. But the bell would ring; we collected the paint-boxes, the drawing-books, the paint-rags and such water as had not been spilt and I would wrap myself round again with the false ideas I had of my function. I must make my pupils learn. Even in poetry I would not let direct and lovely things have their own way with the children. I had to be pointing out beauty. How I taught in those years! With what idiot assumption that I was doing right! If a child would not work I kept her in. Once when I had kept a child in, her mother bounced into my room. She could not fix me with her eye because she had a squint which glanced off the blackboard to the right of me. She shouted: 'Who dew 'ee think you be, keeping the children in? You b'aint nort but a gert girl yourself.'

When it came to needlework it was too true that I was nort but a gert girl. Here, as at Treverbyn, all my confidence forsook me. Sewing and knitting prevented my happiness and changed the whole course of my life. At Exmouth, not only had we to make things, but we had to order the materials—the blue, and green, and yellow zephyr for blouses and dresses; the nainsook for nightdresses; the calico for knickers. Bales of stuff came. We had to make it into clothes and sell the finished garments for the price we had paid for the material. No scheme could have been devised more likely to plunge me into despair. Ranks of figures have always made me shudder; yards of green zephyr have never made me say to myself, 'That would make a pretty dress.' Now I had to face both figures and stuff.

If I could have done as I did in painting, if I could have allowed the girls cheerfully to experiment, I might have survived. Yet I think not. A technical business like dress-making needs first-class technical teaching. This is realized in schools now where the unskilled no longer wield the scissors. As it was I relied, in cutting out, on Miss Peat's diagrams; it was not for a couple of years that I bethought me of buying some paper patterns. I managed better with the patterns. But I loathed the cheap cotton stuff we used. When I tore it into lengths it made a hideous rending noise, and it smoked. I have the smell of that smoke in my nostrils yet and if, as I have been told, it is a china-clay product which stiffens cheap cottons, so much the worse for china-clay. I see myself standing by a yellow varnished table, surrounded by girls anxious to help. But they all wanted to go too quick for me. Cut out and laid flat knickers look like a map. I could never see which edge should join which so as to make anything so recognizable as legs. Clever girls would seize the maps and make the whole thing come right in the twinkling of an eye. Slow girls would get the different joins inside out. I have never seen anything to equal the confusion and griminess of some of the knickers. Yet even under my poor direction some girls, naturally dainty-fingered and constructive, made for themselves clothes—blouses and nightdresses. We even made a frock or two.

I can never look back to these days without remembering a shy, dark-haired girl called Ruth Gibbs—one of the most able, yet modest, unassuming children it has ever been my lot to teach. She was earnest in everything, not playful. Some souls seem to be born older than others. Ruth did things quietly, deftly; she had a mind which instantly perceived. She would show me how things went in a way that might not wound my vanity. At thirteen she was more mature than her mistress at twenty-one. I longed for her to take a scholarship which she could have done with ease; but for some reason she would not enter. She worked as a clerk later, and did not live to marry or grow old. She liked to sit in a certain corner of the classroom, a little remote except from a fair-haired friend named Florence.

It was Ruth who taught the whole class to make gloves. I had embarked on gloves thinking that thumbs and fingers would be less difficult to do than heels and toes. We had a peaceful lesson during which the girls knitted their cuffs and I read a story aloud. Then Ruth reached the point at which a thumb must sprout. We pored over the directions in the book, I quite bemused, Ruth clear as daylight. 'Shall I take the book and try, and you go on reading?' she asked. She retired to her place under the window and knitted a thumb, then she knitted five fingers. As all the other girls reached the danger points they went to Ruth. Pretty nearly everybody in the class completed a nice pair of gloves and someone made a pair for me, though I have no idea to this day how a thumb becomes a thumb.

Just as the gloves were nearing completion we had a visit from a woman inspector, a Miss Castelle. Miss Castelle used to arrive enveloped in a golf cape which seemed to give an air of immense authority. She was a large woman, dark and ruddy. I always quite undeservedly won her praise. For though I never kept my record book up to date, and Miss Castelle was scrupulous about record books, the school was so built that she could never reach my classroom without warning. My colleagues teaching nearer the front door always bore the first brunt and sportingly sent me news of the Approach. Then, under cover of the lid of my desk, and aided by my ready fancy, I would hastily fill in the little daily spaces in the book. By the time Miss Castelle appeared I would be busily teaching.

'May I see your record book?' she said on one occasion.

'Yes, Miss Castell,' I replied, and produced the tome.

'Ah! you keep it up to date, I see.'

Without a blush of shame I took this tribute to my faculty of speed under pressure, and she turned to the class with whom I felt firmly in league.

'Gloves. Oh. yes! I see they are knitting gloves. What method have you used?'

Speed under pressure will enable me to bring a record book up to date, but will not bring a ready or convincing lie to my lips. Verbally I am very truthful. 'Father, I cannot tell a lie', has often made me laugh as I have made desperate and damaging admissions. I told Miss Castell exactly how the gloves had grown into existence.

'Excellent,' she said to my extreme surprise. 'Excellent! The girls should work out things for themselves. Most teachers teach too much.'

I made great game with the other mistresses on the staff over this story. Even gentle Miss Harborough, the head mistress, who was delicately fastidious as to personal honour—she did not like the tale of my doings with the record book—was amused by the story of the gloves.

But although I had come off successfully with this piece of bluff, needlework continued to worry me. I could not be happy over it nor over the sums in the arithmetic book about how to read a gas meter and an electric meter. I suppose if one had to read a gas meter or die one would do it; but in normal living why not rely on the gas-man who calls obligingly for the purpose? I hated that arithmetic book. It filled the mind with dark suspicions that a person would always be cheated unless she worked out everything to the nearest penny. I determined to free myself of both needlework and arithmetic for life.

Miss Passmore, when I, in consternation at Treverbyn, had consulted her about giving up teaching, had advised me to change from elementary to secondary school work. I could then, she said, choose to teach the subjects I liked best. She did not remind me that this advice was the same she had given two years before when I had obstinately, in choosing Truro, made the course impracticable. She now patiently tried to show how I could yet free myself of needlework. I had wanted to teach in a village school if I taught at all; but I could see now that for this work I was not gifted in the right directions. I have never felt much urge to do my neighbours good, and a village schoolmistress should be sociably-minded. It is not enough for her to run with the wind shouting poems. Miss Passmore, who knew I liked learning, advised me to be systematic and read for a London external degree. When I went to live at Exmouth she said I had better attend classes at Exeter University College. For months I did not trouble; I have never liked having my reading directed. Besides, although school was hard, games were good. And there was every kind of game to be played at Exmouth. But in September 1913, after one particularly unlikeable day at school, I went up to Exeter, found the ugly building of the University College tucked into Gandy Street and, in a great flutter, approached the office of the Registrar. Mr Woodbridge smiled at me. He made it seem a perfectly natural thing to do—to come to inquire about classes and read for a degree. In his friendly absence of officialdom, in his easy way of removing real and imaginary difficulties, he typified something in the young and struggling University College which fostered it, so that it grew well. There were comparatively few students doing university work in 1913. Today, 1947, with Principal Murray at its head, the college has become the University College of the South-West, with immediate hope of a charter and independence, with a splendid estate, halls of residence, the nucleus of worthy buildings, and such a staff that university studies are available in every branch of learning. Exeter has peculiar claim to become a university city. Within the crumbled outline of its walls, not far from the ghost of the ruined castle on the Red Mound, stands the living Cathedral Church of St Peter, its massive, almost squat outward strength enclosing the rhythm of its pointed arches. Exeter soars within proportions of enduring symmetry; and with this symmetrical endurance goes an evanescent music of floating bells, and flowers and trees. Exeter is dappled in June. In moonlight it is serene. I remember hearing Bach's St Matthew Passion in Holy Week in the cathedral and, after the Bishop's blessing—'the Lord lift up the light of His countenance and shine upon you and give you peace'—I bicycled to Exmouth, and saw the moonlight lying on the estuary as I looked down on it from the top of Exton Hill. The situation of Exeter is gracious for students. Its river, which rises in Exmoor, broadens into a distant pattern of water visible from the top of the Norman towers of the cathedral. Up the river the Danes swept. King Alfred still seems royally steadfast in Exeter. To learn Old English there, to read the Anglo-Saxon *Chronicle*, is to read and learn in a city where the Danes are present in place-names as well as in the laconic prose of the *Chronicle*. Among the cathedral treasures is the Exeter Book, a collection of Old English poems. The spirit of poetry is preserved in the enduring vellum and handsome script of a thousand years ago. Historic buildings of all periods, but particularly of that period when the wool trade most flourished, composed the city when I was a student. And even today, in spite of the depredations of the German terror, and of our own more persistent and insidious vandalism, much remains. What is lost is the old cohesion of glory and squalor in the labyrinth of twisted alley, and mounting step, and inserted church; of Georgian curving spaciousness and squeezed Elizabethan daring. A wall would take a leap. We lack all daring now. Council houses are anything but daring. We never take a tiny allowed space and see how cleverly we can build a good little suitable house in it. No; we encroach and sprawl on the fields. Nothing girds us in, no little sonnet-plot.

I was glad to go to Exeter. For me, freely to learn at night became a wonderful mitigation of having to teach by day. I invested Mr Fletcher, Mr Schopp, Mr Harte and Mr Sager with haloes of glory, and arrived at Mr Sager's first botany class armed with a rusty razor which Miss Salter had lent me. She kept it to cut her corns with. Mr Sager shouted with laughter at the sight of it. He made the laboratory resound, while my confusion urged him on to fresh excesses. He pretended that I had come to cut his head off; he cowered. I began to wish I could cut off his head before he had finished. He was a facetious man; but most lucid in instruction. Under him even I—once provided with a bright razor—became neat-fingered in cutting and staining sections, and quick-eyed in perceiving what was revealed by the microscope. I even drew; I became patient of classification; I paid attention not only to the sound but to the sense of the words as Mr Sager talked of the 'reducing division of the chromosomes' or discoursed on 'the mutating evening primrose discovered by Hugo De Fries in a de-serted po-ta-to field near Amsterdam'.

Latin and French I enjoyed more, and Mr Schopp and Mr Fletcher gave me hours of extra time. I have never been generous with time myself and I am still amazed in looking back at the allowance made me. In Latin I outlived a succession of evening students who would begin and then drop off. Yet Mr Fletcher not only continued the class for my sole benefit, but doubled the length of it. My pleasure in Latin was intense. To pass from desperate dealings with my stock book—I had a stock book for needlework—in which nothing would come right, to the study of a language in which, with attention, everything would come not only right, but often exquisitely right, was as good as a plunge in a limpid stream when one was hot. My work in Exeter made me see my school duties in better proportion; I withdrew a little, to my own advantage and, I am sure, to the benefit of the children. No notion has been more pernicious in the schools than that which supposes that teachers merely teach. The apprenticing of youth to a master of an art, trade or profession was far sounder; it discouraged dabbling on the part of pupils and preserved the master alive.

I began to find school more tolerable; but not so tolerable but that I was always glad to leave it to catch the Exeter train at 4.30. Miss Milford and I used to put the clock on a little so as to make sure of catching our train. Collins, the caretaker, would say, 'That dratted clock, that dratted clock! Fast again! Yew dew never know where yewm tew with that clock.' But soon he began to guess where he was tew. He began to mutter, 'That clock dew go under more than his own steam that clock dew.' And then, one term, we came back to find that Collins had defeated us. He had skied the clock. So high up on the wall had he placed it that none of us could reach up to add steam to time. 'Show his feace up there that clock dew,' said Collins to me. Miss Milford was furious. She was tall, with an elegant figure, a clear colour, dark hair and grey eyes which could be very scornful. 'That man Collins,' she said, 'runs this school.' She had a way of saying, 'that man Collins'; or 'that child Endicott' in a tone which annihilated the very idea of Man or Child. She dressed well. Her beautiful colouring in winter against a fox fur is one of my pleasantest memories of Exmouth Church Girls' School.

Not quite. My pleasantest memories of all the schools in which I have taught are memories of breaking up. It is almost worth while being a teacher to share with children the joyous sense of end of term. Old scores are cancelled. There is a giving of gifts, a shaking of hands, a relaxation of rule, a bustle and a chatter, and a benevolent glow of goodwill between teachers and taught which will drive away care. There were forms to be filled in though. Miss Leyman, Miss Milford, Miss Carter and I would sit round Miss Harborough and perform the frightful feat known as 'doing up the registers and filling in Form 9'. How I ground my teeth over forms; it is a wonder I have a tooth left. By the time we had concluded our operation with the registers and the forms it was always too late to catch a Cornish train. I used to go up to Exeter, spend a convivial evening with Howard and Mary and catch the mail train two or three hours after midnight. Bicycling through the Exeter streets in the quiet of the night was an experience I always enjoyed, together with the grand sense of triumph and freedom when I and my bicycle were safely aboard and the train went gliding out. Beautiful journeys I have had. One in particular I remember at a Whitsuntide, with all the country from Plymouth to St Austell bathed in an early summer radiance. Light shone translucent through the early leaves of beech and oak as we looked down on the woods from the train; shadows of trees lay cool on the fields; deep-rooted bluebells and cock-robins were dewy in the ferns. At St Austell Station Susan was waiting and came dancing along the platform in a pink frock. She had bicycled up from Caerhays to meet me and we rode home together down the Pentewan valley with all the birds singing to us as if we were queens; up Pentewan Hill, out to Highlanes, down Rescassa Hill, a few minutes to wonder afresh at the magic of Portluney; then up Portluney Hill, past Pound and Barton to see my father coming along under the sycamores by the lodge to meet us; and so home to my mother and breakfast in the kitchen. My father was always a little remote when subjected to demonstrativeness; but my mother warmly returned kiss for kiss. She would laugh for joy to have us home.

9

EXETER INTERLUDE:
WAR-TIME

Long quest to kill the delicate body;
Shot with cannon or culverin,
Stabbed with bayonet, pierced with pike,
Pounded with iron and hoof; yet thin,
So thin, so thin the delicate tissue,
Delicate tissue guarded with skin,
Touched to the quick with a prickle or pin.

—*History: On Viewing A Collection of
Historical Weapons: Edinburgh*

It was when I was going home for a summer holiday that the
fear of war first struck at me. I had always heard of war. My
father, keenly interested in European affairs, had dreaded
it, and had talked to idle minds of how to avoid it. He, who was
religious, knew too well that, although many desired peace, so
few cared for the things that made for true peace, that strong
defence was essential. I had lightly dismissed my father's
concern as one of his little oddnesses; he was in many ways
unlike other people I knew. But when Mr Kneebone, with
whom I was driving home one day from St Austell in July
1914, said as we passed St Mewan, 'What about the murder of
this Arch-Duke, Anne? Do 'ee think it will lead to war?' I

suddenly knew with an awful pang that this war would come. I said, 'Don't 'ee be so silly, Mr Kneebone. All you men d'think about is war. I believe you d'want war.' But I was talking to hearten myself. I have talked much nonsense to hearten myself in war-time since then.

Caerhays was looking lovelier than ever; Susan and I had never been more up in the air. We were expecting Howard and Mary; we were expecting Cap'n and Edith; there was rumour that Stan and Kate might come. But it was the war that came. I was standing by the kitchen table one morning in August when my mother opened a letter from Cap'n; she began reading it aloud, stopped suddenly, and finished reading it to herself. She said, 'He has volunteered,' and went into the garden. Then Stan volunteered and was gone; Howard was rejected on medical grounds; Maurice manufactured chemicals in America. Boys we knew in the village and round the farms volunteered and were gone; the four Castle boys were gone; Charley Rosling was gone from the rectory. All went away and were gone, all the young men we had grown up with.

Then rumours came and grew. There was no wireless in that war. Jabez brought rumours; the papers printed rumours. For Susan it was worse than for me; I have never been so tender-hearted as Susan, nor was my heart so much engaged. I was ashamed of my hard heart for I threw myself into study with a frenzied desire to forget. I deliberately and selfishly tried to shut my imagination up; to build up walls of history and English, botany, Latin and French round the sensitive centre of my mind so as to keep misery out. News of the death of my friends; unavoidable knowledge of what was happening in Flanders—'With man's blood paint the ground, gules, gules':— I read the line in *Timon of Athens* and cried for a day not for the actuality, but for the piercing bitterness of recognition the words forced on me. I never talked of the war; I never helped; I never nursed. When I reproached myself I also told myself passionately that if everyone were as selfish as I there could never be a war. Each living soul would love life too well to dare to try to kill another. I did not then know Coleridge's *Fears in Solitude:*

> Therefore evil days
> Are coming to us, O my countrymen!
> And what if all-avenging Providence,
> Strong and retributive, should make us know
> The meaning of our words, force us to feel
> The desolation and the agony
> Of our fierce doings?

I did not then know this poet's prophetic warning. But I was beginning to have an inkling; I was slowly learning to distinguish poetry from rhetoric; I was beginning to see how poetry could bring home to the soul the horror of certain deeds, but how rhetoric might spawn them. What did those who mouthed speeches care that a man might die for it? One man? Millions of men! But death is obscured by numbers. Our hearts are so small they can only mourn for one.

The only practical bit of work I did was on the land. In the holidays I became a workman at Caerhays Barton and, in August 1915, Mr Kneebone set me to cut 'dishels'—'milky dishels'—as we called the mauve-coloured thistles with silky, downy fruits which infested the fields. I had a hook and I first attacked the dishels in the field by the church. I cut with such furious, freshman's energy that Willie Rundle, a boy I had been at school with at Caerhays, and who was cutting dishels in another field, was moved with compassion. He waved to me to come his way, and he came towards me. We met in the churchyard, and sat down on the granite kerb of Mr Bellamy's grave. Willie said: 'You mustn't work like that, Anne. You'm working too hard. You must stop a bit every now and then and take a titch-pipe, and whet yer hook.' He took out his whetstone and whetted my hook, and we lingered in the sun. My father considered Willie Rundle a naturally intellectual boy, and had hoped he might have opportunity of learning. But further schooling was not possible for him. He worked at the

Barton; but he had not the right kind of intelligence for farming, and was too delicate for war. He died quite young and people used to say his ghost haunted Caerhays churchyard.

Like me, Howard worked at the Barton during his wartime holidays—he was refused for the Army until the last war year. At the farm he did more varied work than I. Old Jim Strout, who did not speak very plain, used to call him 'Howlard', or 'Howlard, Sir', when he remembered to pay tribute to what he considered Howlard's superior erudition. One day Jim and Howlard were driving bullocks when one bullock put down his head and threatened Jim in a surly fashion. Jim, who had his stick in his hand, turned on the bullock and said, 'Horn me, would 'ee? Horn me, would 'ee?' and added a few expletives.

Howard, who saw Mr Kneebone coming, said, 'Steady on, Jim, here's the Boss coming.'

Jim said, 'I don't care bloody hell for the Boss. Horn me, would 'ee?'

By this time Mr Kneebone was within hearing. He said, 'Now then, Jim; now then!'

Jim said, 'Oh, Boss, I didn't know you was so near. Run along in front Howlard, Sir, will 'ee? Run along and head 'em off.'

But one of Howard's best times was when he went to Truro market with Mr Kneebone to buy some pigs for the Squire. Mr Kneebone bid for the pigs; they were knocked down to him, and he and Howard went down to Tregoning's for some lunch, and to do some other business. When they came to take the pigs home they weren't there.

'Where be my pigs?' said Mr Kneebone.

'Your pigs?' said an attendant. 'Your pigs? I didn't know they was your pigs. Chap with one leg just been and took 'em off in his cart.'

'After 'un, Howard; after 'un, my son!' said Mr Kneebone, who had a game leg. 'We shall lose they pigs.'

Howard hopped on to somebody's bicycle, received directions, and was off on the chase. Pretty soon he came up with the man who had the pigs netted in his cart.

'Hi,' he said, 'stop. They'm Mr Kneebone's pigs. He bought 'em for Squire Williams, C'raze Castle.'

'Squire Williams and C'raze Castle be damned!' said the man. 'These pigs was knocked down to me.'

'Come on back to the auctioneer and prove it then,' said my brother. 'Mr Kneebone d' think he bought the pigs.'

Back they went, and the auctioneer was found. He consulted his book.

''Iss,' he said, 'they'm Mr Kneebone's pigs. Bought for Mr Williams, Caerhays Castle.'

The pigs were transferred to the Barton wagon, and Howard and Mr Kneebone began the fifteen miles drive home. Both smoked peaceably, with Mr Kneebone saying at intervals:

'He meant to have they pigs you know, Howard. Another hour and he'd have got clean off with they pigs.'

'If you hadn' been pretty spry you know, Howard, he'd have had they pigs. He meant to get clean off with they pigs you know, Howard.'

Mr Kneebone had no opinion of women doing farmwork. It was clean outside the tradition in which he had been brought up. He kept me on outlying light work, not mingling much with the men. Once, though, I was employed helping Howard and Nicky Hennah to put a wooden paling round a rick which the cattle were getting at. I can see Nicky now and hear him saying as he screwed up one eye and squinted along a shaft of wood, 'A little bit more this way, Howard, will 'ee? Aw! Just a little bit more t'other way, Anne. Tha's av ut. No need to be too particular. 'Tis only a temporary job.' After that everything in the family was a temporary job.

It was during one of these summer holidays that I had news that I had passed the London Intermediate Examination. My father was pleased. He liked any academic success that came to any of his children. We used to say we had to pass examinations in order to get a letter from him. He wrote in formal, compact and precise English, and once sent back a careless letter of mine corrected. I had now to consider which studies I should drop and which continue. I found I wanted to continue all five;

all had their allurement. Had I any Greek I should have chosen classics. History I had always enjoyed. In the end I chose French and English—these two languages could then be taken in combination for the London Honours Degree. I chose them partly because Mr Schopp wrote and suggested them, but more because of Chénier's poem, *La Jeune Captive* and Molière's *L'Avare*.

I had read *La Jeune Captive* at school and had not been particularly moved by it. But that first year of the war I learnt it by heart while cutting dishels. I used to say it aloud, putting into the saying of it all the pity for people in the world of which I could never speak to anyone; pouring into it the energy of spirit which should have gone into the practical work of alleviating distress; of being, like my mother, a consolation. But I could not be like my mother. Instead I would be out in Church-close in the sun, now swinging my hook, now pausing to say:

> Je ne suis qu'au printemps, je veux voir la moisson
> Et comme le soleil, du saison en saison
>   Je veux achever mon année.
> Brillante sur ma tige, et l'honneur du jardin,
> Je n'ai vu luire encore que les feux du matin,
>   Je veux achever ma journée.
>
> O Mort! Tu peux attendre; éloigne, éloigne-toi . . .

Contrasting with this poetry was Molière. I cannot help loving comedy, all kinds of comedy. I have not fine eyes like Elizabeth Bennet but, like her, I dearly love a laugh. I had not read Ben Jonson then, so Molière was to me something entirely new. Out in the fields with no other person near, I would be chanting *La Jeune Captive* at one moment, and at the next I would enact Harpagon. Outside Shakespeare I had never come across any speech so truly dramatic, so comprehensive of poor, pitiful, human passion, and of corrosive evil, as Harpagon's when he literally beside himself because he has lost his darling money. Most drama is so thin. But Harpagon! How ridiculous, how pitiful, how tremendous he is, snatching a whole audience into his life:

> De grâce si l'on sait des nouvelles de mon voleur, je supplie
> qu'on m'en dise. N'est-il point caché là parmi vous?

I would put down my hook, catch myself by the arm, shake myself and say:

> Qui est-ce? Arrête. Rends-moi mon argent, coquin . . .
> Ah! c'est moi. Mon esprit est troublé, et j'ignore où
> je suis, qui je suis, et ce que je fais.

With what tenderness I would murmur to myself, with a pleasure I still cannot begin to explain, 'Mon pauvre argent; mon cher ami!' Perhaps it is that Molière is nearest Shakespeare in his ability to catch in his net of words the up-rising suggestions which spring from the quick of the mind when some passion makes it go faster and faster until, like a child being run off his feet, he leaves the earth. Molière keeps his feet; he is not a poet exactly. Or is he? What speed he has, not through two, three or four layers of fleeting and pictorial suggestion like Shakespeare, but in sequence. 'Je me meurs, je suis mort, je suis enterré.' The lean, spare words shoot the mind forwards.

I never regretted choosing French. French literature clears up the fuzziness of young minds. Claritas! I love a sparkling wine. At first, apart from attendance at Miss Major's lectures in Old English, I gave nearly all my time to French literature. Mr Schopp invited me to his house, and he and his wife and little daugher, Bérénice, became my friends. The work we did had little relation to the college courses. It became private and, alas for Mr Schopp, unpaid tuition. We read in the garden, in the study, and on the beach at Exmouth by Orcombe Point, where the Schopps had a beach hut. When I felt guilty at taking so much of another person's free time Mr Schopp would smile under his drooping moustache and say, in the slightly guttural tones which he had never lost—he was a German by birth though he had lived in England since the age of eighteen or so, and had married a Yorkshire wife—that he prepared his lectures with me. He would arrive on the Maer of a summer evening burdened with tomes and dictionaries. I never caught his enthusiasm for philology; but the poetry to which our studies in words gave me the key was the purest pleasure. Not to have read the *Song of Roland*, and the *Poems* of Villon; not to have lingered over Du Bellay and Ronsard would have been to have missed some of the choicest old excellent vintages. Much has faded from my memory but much remains. When I say to myself the sonnet beginning: 'Heureux qui, comme Ulysse, a fait un beau voyage', the poetry is mingled with the sound of bees in the flowers in the Schopps' garden; with Mrs Schopp's voice calling us to tea on the table by the window overlooking an apple tree bearing huge red apples. In spring Mr Schopp used to go round helping the bees; he would stand on a ladder, his head among the flowering boughs, pollinating his fruit trees with a paintbrush. I hear the sound of Exmouth waves as I re-read the *Song of Roland*, recall the gritty sand that sometimes blew in our eyes and into the midriff of the books. I can hear the disgusted tones of my three little nieces—Dorothy, Joan and Betty—with whom I was sometimes playing when Mr Schopp's figure wavered into view: 'Here's that horrid old man Schopp coming to take away our Anne. We'll stick pins in him; we'll fill him with red-hot needles. Horrid old man Schopp!'

At about this time my father retired from teaching. He had been schoolmaster at Gorran and Caerhays for nearly forty years, and when he retired he did not wish to live where associations were so strong. Perhaps my mother did; I am not sure. My father had always liked being in places where he was not known. In his summer holidays he had been used to go off alone; usually staying with relatives, but making their houses a convenience as sleeping-quarters, while shamelessly giving everybody the slip by day; going off by himself, seeing cathedrals, hearing music, watching the Australians at the Oval or at Lords; or county cricket with Stan in Bristol. The two shared this passion; I used to tease them and say they grew alike watching cricket.

My father had a fancy to live somewhere near Exeter when he retired. Part of his own college days had been spent there and he cared, I think, for nothing else quite so much as for cathedral music. Then, too, there was a very strong bond between him and my brother Howard who was at that time organist of St Michael's Church, Exeter. My father used to criticize the music, for he was naturally one to bestow more criticism than praise. 'The accompaniment was a little loud today, boy, I thought. No need to have it all organ.' Or, 'Too fast, boy; you take the psalms too fast; you never did have much sense of time. I remember at St Ewe once . . .' Or, 'I don't know about your basses, boy. No balance! What you want is another good tenor. Boys good of course . . . but I noticed in the Te Deum . . .' He would argue with my brother who, he considered, played Bach too often. He loved Handel himself; and my brother would tease him by disparaging Handel. Susan would join in the teasing. She would sing, 'All we like sheep have gone astray' in joyful staccato tones. 'All. . . we . . . like . . . sheep . . . have . . . gone . . . a . . . stray. All we like sheep have go-o-o-o-o-o-o-one a-stray.' Why be so merry over it? she would ask. Surely we ought to be sorry for our sins instead of shouting out our joy in them so blatantly in God's ear. Susan thought Handel was of the devil's party without knowing it, as Blake said of Milton. On rare occasions my father praised the music and then my brother was elated; but it was very touching that my father's most unqualified praise of any service of my brother's was on the Easter Day before he died. The music had been exceptionally lovely on Easter Day, and when we came in my father said, 'I must congratulate you on the music, boy. It was very good. Beautiful I should say,' and he went away humming, 'I know that my Redeemer liveth'. My brother laughed and said he felt he had nothing left to live for after such a compliment. But it was my father who did not live to hear another festival service. This was, happily, many many years later than the time at which I am writing. He who had been wont to say he would never live to take up a pension, lived to enjoy a pension for twenty-five years. I only hope for so good an innings myself.

After long discussions Exmouth was chosen as the place of retirement. My father loved trees, and Exmouth and the country round were wooded then. It was near enough to Exeter for frequent visits, but easy too for the fields and the sea; and I was there. Unluckily my father and I chose the little house, and our only idea of a house was somewhere to put his piano and my books. Neither of us cared to be in a house for long at a time; but my mother and Susan did. They did not like our choice of a roof. We could only say that we had hunted up and down and found nothing better; houses were scarce and dear. And they, because it was their nature to take the unpromising and transform it, resigned themselves. With beech leaves, or lilac, or bronze and red chrysanthemums Susan adorned the rooms we had; while I consoled my mother with airy pictures of the cottage and the garden we were never to have.

With my parents and Susan at Exmouth I found it not so bad to be teaching even needlework, and my intention of changing to secondary teaching receded. I continued classes in Exeter. Reading French books and English books was all my joy; but when I considered taking an advanced examination in what I had read I quailed; for nothing can be conceived more unsystematic than my English reading. I followed my own sweet will among the books. I went light-heartedly from author to author, leaping the periods and confounding the persons. If I decided, when I sampled an author, that I did not like him, I put him out of my sight. If I liked him I read everything of his I could lay hands on. I imagine I should still be working in this casual fashion and putting off the examination until another year if Miss Wright had not come as English lecturer to Exeter. She doubled my pleasure in poetry by sharing it; and it was she who suggested that I should abandon teaching for a time and give myself entirely to learning. But how was I to live? My brothers who at one time could have helped me were now impoverished by the war, and faced with many responsibilities. Miss Wright said that I could borrow from the Central Bureau for the Employment of Women. Darling bureau! What other people feel for some benevolent great aunt, I feel for that bureau. It lent me fifty pounds. And strange to tell, the secretary who wrote to me about the business was a Miss Kathleen Passmore, sister to Miss Mary Passmore of St Austell school. No shower of rain has ever watered the earth more gently than that fifty pounds watered me. College awarded me a free studentship; I had fifty pounds in my pocket; I resigned my job. The children in my class gave me little private presents as well as an official one, and I felt sorry to be losing precious affection; but I was out of school, out of school! I went round Hoopern fields on the first day of freedom—there were few houses up there then—saying to myself:

> Colin he liveth careless,
> He leaps among the leaves!

I was hardly able to keep my heels on the earth.

And then as though the gods were jealous of such light-heeledness as mine, Susan fell ill. The cold finger which I had been keeping out of the front door of my heart, closed tight against the war, came in at the back and touched me with a worse chill. For Susan was the dearest thing I had. Yet I had not really bothered when she had decided to go and make munitions in Exeter. My mother, she said, would no longer be lonely without her as she would have been at Caerhays. Susan's idea is always, if anything detestable has to be done, to help with all her might, and get it over. She hated the war as much as I did, but it was clear enough to her that we had to fight and win, or lose and die, and she would be directly helping to win, said Mr Lloyd George, if she would make munitions. She began at first going to Exeter by day and coming home to sleep at night; then one day, when she had had to get up so early and was so sleepy that she put on one green stocking and one red one, and never noticed it till she happened to glance down upon her wicked legs walking along past Buller's statue, she decided to stay in Exeter all the time and live with Howard and Mary. It was lucky that she did. Mary has twice the eye for illness that we have, and three times the promptitude in action in an emergency. When

Susan suddenly had an intolerable pain Mary got Dr Andrew quickly enough for her to be taken to hospital and operated on for acute appendicitis in time. Only just. I knew how little poetry counts compared with a life while I waited.

Susan recovered; she made munitions again, working for victory. And Sister Léontia, Sister Augustine and Sister Célestine, to whom in return for French conversation I was giving English lessons at the Convent of the Holy Family at Exmouth, prayed for victory. I neither worked nor prayed. As soon as Susan was better I forgot all the vows I had made about being a more responsible woman and went tippling at my pleasures again. Now that there was no school to go to, I used to bicycle slowly into Exeter, going generally by Woodbury Castle, Clyst St Mary and Clyst St George for the sake of the birch trees and the wide space; and coming home by Topsham so as to go down Salmon-Pool Lane to sit among the twisted tree roots by the river, for the secrecy. I read among the roots, using them as armchairs.

Sometimes, now, a friend went down to the river with me. This was Muriel Price whom we called Cyrano because of her chivalrous nature and distinctive nose. She had a nose which made other noses seem half-hearted, and a mind unshaken by winds of false doctrine. She and I became special friends partly because we were both older than the average run of students, partly because we were opposites. She was endlessly surprising to me because she was methodical with time, and she could say what she meant. She knew what she meant before she said it, whereas I never seemed to know what I meant until it was out, when it often astonished me as much as her. Without Muriel I should have wasted all the good money of the Central Bureau for the Employment of Women. For to my infinite surprise as soon as I had all my time to do university work I found I did not want to do it. I fear that what becomes a duty is no longer a perfect pleasure. What pleasure is there in paying taxes? Whereas giving away anything is the greatest fun. Now I wanted to write poetry. This was partly Miss Wright's fault for she offered a poetry prize.

I would take out books as of old to study among the tree-roots and instead, with a delicious sense of slipping out of Time, I made up verse. I found I had the knack. When I was not making it up I was running French ideas into it. I had to do an essay on La Fontaine for Mr Schopp. Instead I set dozens of fables into English. One of them was a warning to myself:

> A grasshopper, a merry mummer
> All the summer,
> Found that he had but little clo'
> When in the winter fell the snow,
> Nothing to wear and nothing to eat,
> No wing of fly, no wormës meat.
> He went to the ant and said, 'Ah, me!
> I've nothing to put in my belly,
> Perhaps you could lend me a bite, dear thing,
> To keep me going until the Spring,
> Then, on my jump, if I'm not gone West
> I'll pay you back with interest.'
> But the ant is far from the vice of lending
> To those who go their thriftless ways;
> She said, 'And in the warmer days
> What kind of service were you tending?'
> 'Night and day to all who came
> I sang.' 'You sang? You sang? That's cool!
> My dear good insect, you're a fool!
> You sang! Well now, dance to the same.'

As I detested La Fontaine's ant, I embodied my own philosophy in an adaption of *The Labourer and his Children* which I ran into Cornish dialect:

> A Cornishman, who felt his end draw near,
> Called to his children and said, 'Aw, my dear,
> I tell 'ee I d'feel most terrible queer.
> But there's a thing or two I'd like to say.
> 'Fore you d'carry me up Bethel Way.
> The first is this, Don't 'ee go working hard,
> You wean't have time to think upon the Lord;
> The second is, 'Don't 'ee go working late,
> The Lord won't love 'ee for yer big estate;
> 'Tis best I b'live not to be working 't all
> Then you can look 'ee 'bout and praise it all.'

I made dozens of French verse translations and I also wrote some verse which I entered for the poetry prize; it was a dash of Shelley, who was my angel then, diluted with my own variations on the abstract notions of truth and beauty; the whole mixed with the moonlight over the sea from Barns Hills. I had forgotten all about faith, hope and charity by that time. I signed myself 'Heligan', not with any ill-spelt reference to the sacred spring, but after Colonel Tremayne's house between London Apprentice and Mevagissey. One day Miss Truscott, a St Austell student, came into the common room to say that it was on the notice board that Heligan had won the prize and she was sure it must be me. Who else would have thought of using the name Heligan?

I had the fun of choosing books for my prize. I went in for quantity rather than for fine bindings. I chose Coleridge's Poems, a Herrick in two volumes, and two volumes of Andrew Marvell; and because I still loved my brother Howard better than anybody else I bought him a delectable little copy of *Lorna Doone* out of my prize money; it was fun to have him associated with my triumph and we both liked to read about Jan Ridd and Jan Fry going out in the snow of that bitter winter and bringing in the sheep. As I read and re-read my prizes, one sentence of Marvell's prose lodged in my mind for ever. He said, 'I think the Cause was too good to have fought for.' When I have nothing else to do I still take this idea out and ponder it. Andrew Marvell has been among the enduring of my fitful loves. I cannot imagine a time when I shall cease to find refreshment in *Thoughts in a Garden*. No actual ripe apple, no nectarine or curious peach has touched my mouth so voluptuously as those worded ones; nowhere else has fair quiet seemed so desirable. Spenser would never make me a Puritan; Andrew Marvell might. But if Charles II intervened I should forsake my dear Andrew for him no doubt.

Going up to London for the final examination was an adventure; I had only once been to London before. Now I went under Muriel's wing and we established ourselves in Harrington Gardens. I did everything foolish I could. I lugged up dozens of books which I hadn't time to open much less read; I never knew where I was going in London, but stuck to Muriel like a shadow; after the first paper I decided I'd failed and might as well go home, away from this nightmare of a city. Only the fact that I did not know how to get there by myself prevented me from seeking Paddington Station. The influenza epidemic was beginning and candidates on either side of me reeked of eucalyptus until I thought I should become metamorphosed into that hateful Australian tree for ever. I fancied I felt my sprouting leaves and branches when I ought to have been concentrating on Grimm's law. When the examination was over, if it had not been for Muriel, I should have been in a strange fix; for when we came to pay our bill at our boarding house my money had gone—clean gone. We ransacked my case; had I put the money between the leaves of a book? We shook the books, but no notes crying, 'Spend me! spend me!' dropped out. We poked, we prodded, we unpacked and packed again. Then Muriel who had a blank cheque filled it in to pay both her bill and mine, and as her family had stayed at Harrington Gardens the cheque was accepted without trouble. I did not find my money until about a fortnight after when, hunting for a pair of clean stockings, I unwound a tightly folded pair, a pair I had taken to London. There neatly concealed and coy was my money. In good country fashion, I had done my best to protect my all from 'they thieves up London'.

Now that my fifty pounds were all spent I had to consider getting some fresh money. The Reverend Mother at the Convent of the Holy Family at Exmouth suggested that I should come there and teach for a time. I taught the Nuns— Sister Augustine and Sister Célestine were preparing to take London external degrees in English and French—and I taught the children of the school. My duties were strictly confined to teaching certain subjects, the community preferring to keep all matters concerning the general policy and discipline of the school in their own hands. For me there were no duties and no registers. If anyone had been away the Rev. Mother came round in person to make inquiries. Once when I was giving a nature lesson to the little ones, and had drawn a squirrel eating a nut on the blackboard, the Rev. Mother came in to inquire for a child who had had influenza. Then she turned to the blackboard and exclaimed, clasping her hands, 'Ah childrens! What a beautiful caat!'

They all shouted indignantly, 'Ma mère! It's a squirrel!' She was not discomfited, she said smiling, 'Ah! I am stupeed! I see now it ees a squirrel. I see his nuut.' I remembered that at Truro the inspector's comment on my blackboard nature drawing had been, 'Knowledge of the subject good; but execution . . .' and he had passed on. He was a thin drooping man with a mouth a little twisted away from the centre towards his right ear. His hobby was purple shadows. 'You take an orange and what do you see? A purple shadow. You take a top-hat and what does it cast likewise? A purple shadow! You take a . . .' He was almost too easy to imitate. Poor Purple Shadows! He considerably cheered our innocent lives at Truro.

I enjoyed working at the convent; it was a small school—most of the tiresomeness of school-life comes when the school is so big that masses of moving children have to be regulated. When fifty 'units' of the same age take the place of Veronica and Mary the game is up; to confuse bigness with goodness is one of the vulgar errors of our time. The Sisters had an immense advantage in knowing what they were aiming at. Their desire was to train the children not only in knowledge and feeling, but in virtue. They had no doubt at all that the soul of a child was the battleground of good and evil forces, and that it was their duty to incline hearts towards good and fortify them against evil in the drama of existence. They had the advantage of a great tradition, a profound poetry, a symbol. That children are imaginative before they are reasonable Christian education has understood. I have never had a vocation, but I can feel the beauty of it; the Nuns were tranquil—at least to the outward eye. I was seeing the school, of course, with the eye of an adult. Certain children saw it differently. Some years later when my brother Maurice's children, who had been brought up in America, were spending some months in England and making Exmouth their head-quarters, it was suggested that they should go to the convent school for a time. There were three of them, Roberta aged about ten, Marjorie aged about eight and Bill aged five. We thought, I fear, of saving not Bill's small soul, but his small pants. He used to slide down the Exmouth sea-wall until the seats of these were torn to shreds, and he walked with bottom exposed. Fully clothed, the three children set out for the school, Roberta looking rather like the sleeping beauty; Marjorie artistic and compact, thinking it would be grand to have a school hat-band; Bill, hands in pockets, walking with a pioneering air, alone. 'We men!' he sometimes said to my brother. Girls and man came back with a distinctly pugnacious air. They weren't going again. Nothing would induce them to go again. Bill said he didn't like those old black crows; and Roberta and Marjorie said the girls were proud. For the rest of their stay in England their education was on the beaches; and perhaps this pleasant alternative rather than any real objection to the convent was at the root of their obstinate refusal to attend. I murmured to the Rev. Mother something about the children's going back to America rather earlier than we anticipated. But I never went out with one or other of them hanging on my arm without meeting one of the Nuns: 'The children have not gone back to America? No!' And I would reply, as the children scowled, something about the uncertainty of boats nowadays.

The war came to an end while I was at the convent. I was reading *The Ancient Mariner* aloud to the assembled Nuns, to whom it was part of my duty to give a lecture on some English poet each week, when suddenly everything that would hoot, or ring, or clang in Exmouth hooted and rang and clanged. I danced about the room, and the Sisters momentarily forgot their habit of reticence and devotion. They laughed; their eyes woke up and sparkled. We were lucky as a family in that war. All my brothers came home. Cap'n was very ill; but he was alive.

Some time before, I had had news that I had been placed in the second class in the London examination. I should teach needlework no more. Instead I went back to Cornwall to teach English and French. At about this time Susan, too, decided to become a teacher, and this decision brought us, if that were possible, even closer together. Unlike me she did not fumble. Her imaginative sympathy with children made her immediately successful; and she has played her part with hundreds of others who have striven to transform our infant schools into places of natural growth and gaiety.

10

NORTH CLIFFS AND GODREVY

Pendarves Street, Roseworthy Hill,
By lanes and hedges winding still,
Up the hot brambled path, and there
The cliff-top, clean and scented fair

With the warm scent of summer; thyme,
And heath bells drowsy with their chime,
And low furze offering to the skies
All its painted butterflies.

I am one with the earth whose child am I,
On the warm scented earth I lie,
Elbows in heather, knees pressed to earth,
One with the mother who gave me birth.

And there before me the sheer cliff edge.
I wriggle nearer, the extreme ledge
My elbows touch, and chin in hand,
Half in air and half on land,

I drink of the great grail of God;
No more am I one with the lifeless clod;
God's chalice is filled with the foaming sea,
The wine of beauty, O God, for me

This wonder, this passion of delight;
Come pain, come sorrow, come death the night
Of life, by this draught I can
Give thanks I am not earth but man.

—*North Cliffs*

I have missed much of all I might have seen of the loveliness of the world through an irresistible craving for Cornwall. To think that if I had spent every fresh second of my days looking at a fresh glory I could not have exhausted all glories, and that I have hardly looked beyond the first I knew, coming back again and again to what was familiar! Sometimes I am sorry; and sometimes I wish I had been narrower still, desiring not all Cornwall, but merely all Penwith or all Roseland, merely all St Austell Deanery, merely all Gorran parish, merely our own garden, merely one foot of hedge in it. I sometimes think I could have spent all my life looking at one violet.

When I came back to Cornwall it was not to the St Austell district where I was born, nor to Truro where I was at college; I went further west. I went to live in Camborne in Penwith, and came to know country governed by fresh heights. My new landmarks were St Agnes Beacon; Carn Brea that held Redruth in its keeping; Trencrom confronting me as I sped through Hayle; and the smooth-running progression of Godolphin and Tregonning. I am not sure that I did not pray to Godolphin and Tregonning as the sun came up. But that was later. I came to Camborne to work in the Camborne County School for Girls, helping first with French and English, and later teaching English throughout the school. As soon as I got back to Cornwall and sniffed the air I knew that I was twice as fully alive there as in Devon. My very eyes seemed wider open. Camborne is an ugly town, yet I felt I would not exchange the treeless mining country in which it is set—a country so worked for tin that a house in a Redruth street might subside into an adit—I would not exchange its bareness and the stubborn, ghostly engine-houses through which the sky showed, for the green abundance of Devon. Devon breeds poets; but Cornwall is a poem.

I was met at the station by Gertrude Woodthorpe, another new member of the school staff, a young woman of about my own age, with tawny, shining eyes. She said to me in anguished tones that lodgings were so hard to get in Camborne, that we were sharing a sitting-room although, she thanked heaven, we had separate bedrooms. I said with equal anguish that our fate was hard, and together we went up Mount Pleasant road in the mist. During the course of our first evening together she said gloomily that she wanted a sitting-room to herself because she meant to write. I immediately said that that was why I wanted a separate sitting-room too, though I had never thought of writing until that minute. My versing had been mere play with words written anywhere. Our sitting-room fire would not burn; we tried to make it draw up the chimney by holding in front of it a copy of an old *Observer*. The *Observer* was a big paper in those days; it caught fire and blazed and blazed. If either of us had had a sitting-room to herself I feel it might have been blazing yet. Our combined beatings and smotherings put it out and we began to regard one another more amicably. We were hungry too; we were always hungry. That first year after the 1914 war was a hard time for food; and the air round about Camborne, which we breathed on long tramps while we hunted for separate sitting-rooms, made us so sharp set that once we came in at tea-time and ate the whole of a large saffron cake. Shame at what we felt our landlady must consider our greediness brought us still closer together. We would debate whether we could bear to leave just a crust of cake so that we should not seem to have entirely swept the boards.

It was on one of our early walks together that I first saw the sea shining away beyond North Cliffs. What that piece of coastline between Godrevy and Chapel Porth came to mean to me I should find it hard to exaggerate. At first in Camborne I had only my legs to carry me, and I tended to walk again and again the country near at hand, with this piece of coastline as my first love in every weather; my perfect joy; better than any book or any person, more sublime to me than any church or cathedral. I delighted to leave the drabness of Camborne, to walk by the Mining School down the street to Rosewarne, to pass along a ferny lane and fields to Reskadinnick; to go along by the red tin stream in which the little wooden traps flipped up and down; to reach the bridge where a willow was the first to burst into golden palm in spring; to run for a minute into a little wood where primroses were out by the end of January, primroses growing safe from the weather in little bracken houses, the dead stems forming pillars, the crispy crumpled fronds an airy roofing. Then I would go up the last steep fields and on to the cliffs and drink the frothing cup of space.

But I also had to go to school—teaching has always been a great interruption to my way of life—and to find a separate sitting-room. By the time I had found it in the house of Mrs Curnow, Gertrude and I were enjoying our joint ménage though neither of us would admit it. My new sitting-room was at the back of a little house in Vean Terrace off Beacon Street, a sunless room which looked on a mound with one tree. On that tree a blackbird would whistle a tune and repeat it. I have never heard any other blackbird so much in command of himself. He seemed deliberately to practise a phrase which also he taught me. As I whistle it I can see the linoleum on the floor and the hearthrug turned upside down to keep the colours clean. Not till Susan arrived to spend a weekend with me, and promptly turned the mat the right way up, did I have the wit to know it had colours. I thought it had been born drab. It suited the harmonium and the little leather-covered sofa, the leather armchair and the four upright chairs. The paper was pale green with yellow roses ever-ready to burst into colossal bloom. On the wall was an enlarged photograph of Mrs Curnow's son Leonard who died in a decline. My bedroom, which was in the front of the house, was delightful, sunny and white.

Mrs Curnow—her old mother called her Weeza, short for Louisa—was a widow. We took to one another, and soon I was no longer hungry. I grew fat on basins of broth, Cornish pasties, under-roast, saffron buns, jam tart, and cream. On Saturdays Weeza would make me a hot pasty, wrap it up in a napkin, and I would take it 'out North Cliffs' to eat. It was on one of those Saturdays that I saw one of the most beautiful sights I had ever seen since I was six.[1] It was between Deadman's Cove and Hell's Mouth where the cliffs are more than ordinarily high, and where the waves wash round rocks haunted by shags and cut into fantastic shapes by the sea and weather. But on this particular day nothing could be seen. A white mist, the dull drowsy mist of Hakluyt's northern explorers, filled the cup of space. No motion of the waves could be distinguished; only their sound reached my ear and the cry of the sea-gulls. Then the sun began to drink up the mist and the wind freshened. No revelation of all the kingdoms of the world and the glory of them could have been more enchanting. The shoulders of the great rocks became visible through draperies of floating white. The grey waters were seen to tumble at their feet. Then in a moment the further sea showed a deep, heart-stirring blue; but stranger than all, at a point where the mist still lingered, there gleamed a concentrated, irised light, like a rainbow contracted into a saint's aureole, or that truth-compelling light in the old tale which the child touched and the radiance remained on her finger. It seemed as though it could not fade. But even with the thought it grew thinner, phantom-like; its rose and pale gold rarefying into sightless substance. Soon only the fluttering sash of mist remained half way between the cliffs and the horizon. All else was the purest, the most joyous blue, with great dark shadows where the giant cliffs still slumbered. Spray danced over the sunken reefs; the gulls flashed their wings against the sun; the bracken on the cliffs glowed gold and brown. As at the Creation a new world had arisen, steeped in the first dazzling and radiant light.

[1] I have described the earlier experience in *School House in the Wind*.

This experience was in autumn and I had gone to Camborne in January. By this time Gertrude had definitely decided to change over from teaching to writing and the other close friend I made on the Camborne staff—Marjorie Pascoe—used to go home to Truro for weekends, so that I was free to walk alone. I hate eating alone—unless it is a pasty on the cliffs—but in walking the way is sufficient company. In recollecting the country round Godrevy—later I lived near it in a winter cottage as well as in a summer tent—slide hustles slide on the screen of my memory, and I tend to confound the seasons. I no sooner remember the white roses with their delicate petals, and smell the fragrance entangled in their grove of anthers, than I see and smell a great patch of maize-coloured furze, a spicery with greenness in it. I have seen furze so dazzling-thick with blossom that I have had to shade my eyes. Then instantly I see furze after swaling, with twisted black arms against the blue of the sky; or I see cowslips above Fisherman's Cove; or sheets of vernal squill; or I see blackthorn trees in blossom and find them crossed by the bare thorns of winter-time with dun-coloured sparrows flitting round them like pieces of the inanimate turf given power to fly. I have walked the cliffs in cold and wet when the sparrows and the gulls seemed the only things alive—the sparrows live earth, the gulls live sky. I used to wonder what I was.

I liked to walk from Godrevy by Hell's Mouth to Reskajeage in winter and have tea at a farmhouse there, tea with hot heavy cake, and splits with cream and jam or honey. Going in out of the wild and taking the first sip of steaming tea was wonderful. Hell's Mouth is not a wide inviting mouth, but like a trap and dark; the sun never shines into its caverns and there is no path down the cliffs. Gulls whirl round screaming. I used to like to choose a day of cloud and sunshine, for then the masses of cloud would help the masses of the cliff and the whole appear terrifically sombre yet exhilarating. It is a high excitement to stand on the little natural platform to the right of Hell's Mouth in a wind. The wind seems to have no relation to the normal air which we take in little sips sedately. It has a living quality and rushes us out of ourselves and into itself in a literal ecstasy. The view landward is a reminder of that 'windy sea of land' of which Milton writes. It is almost bare of trees with long, low, sweeping waves and tumbling hollows; the outline of the carns sharp and clear; never fuddled. The eye passes from the slow curve on curve of the hills of Penwith, by Carn Brea and Carn Marth to St Agnes Beacon; on the other side is Navax, with its line running smooth almost as water down the snout to its broken, ragged edge in the sea.

From Hell's Mouth I used to go by a path that dips into the cliff, so that the sea rolls below a green slope. But now and then the path sweeps upward and the open country comes into view on the right again. Carn Brea is the king; the active dominating carn. He seems to be playing tricks he is so active, now in this quarter, now in that, now showing his great shoulders, now wholly hidden, now poking up his crest again. The gully above Deadman's Cove leads to the top of North Cliffs, after which in those days the downs became wilder and gloomier—some parts are ploughed now. These Downs are at their most characteristic in winter. They should be walked on a November afternoon when a young moon will rise early and the wind is chasing clouds, and the waves are pitching in. Landward there are no colours but browns and the rusted red of heath, and greens, and ashen greys blended with the slate of the cliffs and the madder of the sea-weed; but at sea the brightest colours may be out, sapphire and the most dazzling white; deep purple by the rocks and, in certain lights, as the waves arch their necks, a lovely luminous green. In some places the track is bare, in others springy with turf and obstinate moss which is trampled but persists, and is thicker and warmer for having to curb its feathers. Seawards as we near Reskajeage are two rocks which seem to be streaming out to sea, so that the Old English epithet 'utfus' might be applied to them. Their dark hard bases, ringed by the tide-line, are of a leaden colour shading to a reddish purple where the sea-weed clings; and the texture of the rock is streaked with white lines like cross lightning.

Reskajeage is forbidding, with a steep, shaded slope on one side and a sunny slope on the other. Robert Bridges might say of these as of another cliff that no June could stir them to vanity; yet June white roses grow most freely here. In November all is harsh and bare, and in the ear is the sea's winter music. From the cliff top all the sea noises are blended roundly into a satisfying harmony. Nearer the base, as the path descends to the narrow beach, is heard the grinding of stone against stone, and the boom as a wave breaks into a hollow rock—the drum of this wild music; the swish and hiss of the froth and, in the lulls, the liquid gurgle of unbroken water in the crevices, and the slap and swill between the great crescendos. Nothing here is human. The goats with their primitive yellow eyes—the sea-gulls have yellow eyes too—are the only living ones. They go about the cliffs, warm in their goat-hair, on their poor thin-looking legs which are yet so sure. I used to envy them their security against the weather.

Weeza's bright fire was pleasant when I got back to Camborne. And she would come in and talk of clothes; something new she had bought at Humphry Williams's in Redruth. She had all the Cornish instinct for dressing up; she told me once she just 'couldn' go chapel if she hadn' got a coat with a nice bit of silk-lining to put up, and a little hat cocked one side'. I can see her trying on a new hat and preening in the looking-glass that capped the harmonium.

My sister Susan astonished Weeza whenever she came to stay. If ever I ventured to bring in flowers and leaves Weeza made oblique remarks about the beastly old mess as she swept away the petals and laid my cloth with a firm hand; but Susan could have planted a whole horse-chestnut in the sofa and Weeza would have uttered no protest. From the moment Susan arrived, turned the mat the right side up, and remarked firmly that she didn't like and couldn't eat cabbagy broth, Weeza recognized a master spirit. She was impressed by my friend Marjorie Pascoe, too. Weeza kept a wonderful front-room into which we never penetrated for the profane purposes of living, although keeping the front-room clean was an arduous weekly ritual. When Marjorie, who had recently become engaged to Harold Harvey, told Weeza the news, Weeza said, 'You'll find, Miss Pasca, that anybody ought to be made of wood instead of flesh and blood to look after a house as well as a husband and a family of children.' Marjorie replied that she hadn't the slightest intention of making herself a slave to a set of cushions. The answer struck Weeza. She fairly began to wonder whether she wasn't wasting her energies. But within a week she was saying as she smacked the furniture about, 'Miss Pasca do say she wean't be a slave to a set a cushions. Leave she wait!'

It was with Susan that I had a particularly memorable summer walk to Godrevy; part pure enjoyment and part sheer endurance of heat. Susan said I nearly killed her. It was partly that she had on elegant shoes and was anxious for their shape. She cannot bear sensible shoes; she hates the sight of her feet in them. She will look at a stout pair and what she calls a nice pair before taking a walk; and insensibly her feet will stray into the nice pair. Then, when we get to rough places, she will look down and caress her favourites, saying the poor darlings are being ruined as usual by one of Anne's short cuts.

We went early by Treswithian and Kehelland and Menadarva. Menadarva is one of the loveliest of the lovely names in the Camborne district. 'I went to Menadarva' is a little poem in itself. We went from Menadarva along the red river to Godrevy, taking with us pasties which Weeza had got up early to make. She would do anything for Susan,—Susan who wore a white piqué frock and bright jacket. Weeza pretty nearly bought herself a white piqué, but decided in the end she'd never play tennis. Godrevy is exquisite on an early summer morning when Trencrom steps out of the robe of mist and the whole wide bay lies dreaming between the arms of Clodgy and Godrevy Point. St Ives, Carbis Bay, Lelant and Hayle are included in its sweep. But nothing can be seen of Hayle town. The houses spattered about Carbis Bay are baptized by distance, and St Ives is nestled in the curve of the island as in the crook of an arm. Around St Ives and Lelant the girdling beaches are smooth bright gold, but near at hand the breasts of the Towans are knobbly.

We lay on the warm turf; the best of the sea-pinks were over, but all the promontory was sown with little flowers, with thyme and trefoil and centuary and tormentilla. I think every sense is pleased as a body reclines on a bank of thyme on a summer morning at Godrevy. We ought to have stayed there all day. Instead I wanted to show Susan the young gulls at Navax, so we went along a path which I liked because one could hear the wind frothing through a field of oats on the right and playing its deeper sea-note on the left. On the grey ledges of Navax it was easy, earlier in the season, to observe the nesting birds. Young gulls are brought up hard; no feathers, no moss. In the corner of a rock which can only be called nest by courtesy, they are hatched in the open and learn to fly into space. It is a half painful pleasure to watch the young birds fly. They are mottled grey and brown and almost indistinguishable from the rock; it is best to spot 'nests' on the ledges and watch selected families until they reach the age for flight. They sit and appear to ponder; and the parents wheel round and soar, and do trick flights, and fish and quarrel. Then the young ones stretch their wings, and nearly take off, and settle again; and stretch again; and then, they select a moment when I have shifted my eyes and miraculously they fly. Some are a little drunken at first, but they attain a swift strange proficiency, and seem to show off, and whirl about, and then come back and have a tremendous scream with the old birds.

We watched the gulls; and we ought either to have gone back the way we came or to have cut across the promontory and so reached the North Cliffs stile easily. Instead, I pretended it was just as near to keep to the edge of the cliff. I have walked that cliff path hundreds of times. It dips into the face of the cliff so that the traveller has cliff above and cliff below and seems to be walking between sea and sky, caught enchanted in 'that mortal and right lined circle that must conclude and shut up all'. The pure curve of dark blue sea against the fainter blue of the sky is so lucky a marvel. A shade more in the sky, a shade less in the sea, and we can imagine all confounded, the magical line erased. Nothing is more astonishing about the universe than the luck of it, and our luck to be in it, and provided with two such look-outs as eyes, and a nose for the fragrance. We came to a royal stretch of mingled heath and fern and honeysuckle, and I lost the path; and Susan, like the children of Israel, murmured. Her nice shoes! Of course there had been a short way across the top. In vain I told her to sniff the thyme and watch the bees. Bees could fly up out of it, she said; but how should we get up out of it through all that furze and fern, and bramble. She didn't care about Osmond the waterman or whatever else they called the Osmunda Fern Royal. Yes, Aunt Lye had hunted for one everywhere when we were small; and promised us half a crown if we found one and we never did; but here now was a boggy place to make our plight worse; and we wanted a path; it seemed as though we were lost for ever between the blues. The sun began to scorch us. It was a grand moment when we at length pushed through entangling thickets and climbed up to a path that led between the sea-cliff and a field of clover with tall picris and tinker-tailors to the open world again. Fisherman's Cove was ahead, a cove to which one may descend by a winding ferny path, beautiful, but less beautiful than the path to the cove immediately adjoining it which some folk call St Martin's Cove and some say it has no name at all. We kept above it, through ox-eye daisies, I never venturing to suggest a descent. I tried to keep Susan's thoughts on the flowers ahead; but she stopped and turned and looked back exactly at the point where it was clearest to see that we had walked right round a peninsula instead of across the neck. Above its hump the sea at Gwithian and Godrevy, so near though we had walked so far, showed like a land-locked pool. Susan has always used this summer day as a classic instance of my obstinacy in always choosing the hardest, longest way— except in the matter of washing up dishes when I hustle the plates I have washed on to the rack without streaming them under the cold tap.

We spent the rest of the day by Hell's Mouth, Susan refusing to be seduced into a little wood near by. I always think it a pity she missed the wood which may not be there now; it was unexpected then. It was reached by a grey and broken gate in the hedge opposite Hell's Mouth and was a complete wood with oaks and sycamores and ashes; but its glory was its ferns, harts' tongues and lacy ferns, and a whole fernery of ferns royal sweeping up with a curve that had the force of motion. Honeysuckles grew there, flinging out their arms joyously above, embracing anything, and bursting into a bacchanalian riot of blossoms. There are no other such tipsy flowers as honeysuckles. Wantons! I used to think it was like a Grimm's fairy-tale, for I would come to a place where the path lost itself under dark privet; and stooping through I entered a neglected orchard with three or four apples on crooked trees; and down the path came hens, not fluttering and inconsequent, but jutting their heads and walking with quick determined steps in a phalanx towards me, then falling in and moving with me like a guard of honour. Here were two cottages where Hans was probably in his cage putting out his bone every day instead of his finger to show the witch he was still too thin to make good eating. By the path to the left was a hollow where bog-plants grew, ragged-robin, and money-wort, and bog pimpernel, and white little starry woodruff. Skirting the thick black ooze I used to pass into a second wood. This was at first more stately and spacious with horse-chestnuts and beeches and tall oaks that looked like elms in the distance. And here were laurels, and hollies and a great flowering elder. Then the path went through trees that dwindled, and through ranks of guardian nettles, over a gap by a rocky outcrop into the open sunshine of a meadow. To the left was a marsh with green-grey willows and yellow flags, and one heard the sound of running water. In front was the smooth hump of a field blocking the further view.

Susan would never have forgiven me if I had brought her face to face with that hump after our cliffy explorations earlier in the day. Instead we reclined on the cliffs until the cool of the evening, and then walked back through the fields to Camborne by way of Reskadinnick. It was the short way home.

11

YES, MISS PRATT

Snowflakes lightly are borne hither and thither
In the grey air reluctant; they care not whence
Silent they come; they care not feckless whither
They go in the wide vessel of winter space.

Ever hesitating, yet without murmur at last softly
Wavering they alight fluttering by a resting place;
And like birds on slender feet by the wind driven
Skim, then drop to their nests and quiet lie.

But you, the seagulls, snowflakes of summer, swirling
And flashing between the blue sea and blue sky
Are never silent, the cliffs with your cries are riven,
Never restful, on your wide wings, whirling, whirling.

—To Seagulls disturbed at Navax Point

It was not only the proximity of the cliffs and the sea-gulls which made me happy at Camborne. I was happy in school. Camborne children became and have remained my favourite pupils. It was exhilarating to teach a subject I enjoyed to children who enjoyed it. Whether my exhilaration was good for my pupils' English is another matter. Children are fearfully exposed to teachers, and I unloaded my enthusiasms on them. I would come in from the cliffs murmuring Keats:[1]

[1] *Keast*, which looks like a form of *Keats*, was a Camborne surname.

> It keeps eternal whisperings
> Round desolate shores, and with its mighty swell
> Gluts twice ten thousand Caverns, till the spell
> Of Hecate leaves them their old shadowy sound.

Soon a class would be murmuring these lines too. I used to dilate on words. *Gluts* I would say to children who hardly knew what a verb was, 'throw all the weight of the sentence into the verb'. Or I would dwell on the exquisite rightness of the epithet *shadowy*. Verbs and epithets! I hardly minded what the subject was. Always I had poems in my head.

Every morning the whole school assembled in the hall—there were about three hundred children, ranging in age from the kindergarten, who might be three, to a few sixth-form girls of eighteen. The school stood in lines, not horizontally, but each form like a long tail drawn up behind its 'Captain'; so that Miss Pratt, when she appeared on the platform, saw the school not in tiers with the little ones in front and the school rising by different stages to the tall sixth at the back, but as a sort of low cliff sloping upwards to her left from the shingle of the kindergarten. I liked to stand by the kindergarten. They would be saying in their small, separate voices all down their line, 'Good morning, Miss Pwatt,' long after the rest of the school had finished their brisk, unanimous salutation and opened their hymn-books. Miss Pratt smiled at the kindergarten with her faintly crooked smile. I think she liked them best of the school. She was a dignified figure on the platform, firmly planted in country boots, and with hair drawn off her forehead in an intellectual Girton way. She used pince-nez, and she wore a black velvet band around her neck. As she read the prayers I said poems to myself. My favourite for a long time was:

> Upon a sabbath-day it fell;
> Twice holy was the Sabbath-bell
> That called the folk to evening prayer;
> The city streets were clean and fair
> From wholesome drench of April rains;

And, on the western window-panes,
The chilly sunset faintly told
Of unmatured, green valleys cold,
Of the green thorny bloomless hedge,
Of rivers new with spring-tide sedge,
Of primroses by sheltered rills,
And daisies on the aguish hills.

I would spend several days on end with Keats and then change
to Blake—to the Mad Song or to 'Hear the voice of the bard',
or to, 'Oh, sunflower, weary of time!' I did not say all the
poems I myself learnt to my classes. I had some notion of the
suitable. But I am bound to say that I thought very little of the
children in comparison with poems. If I was shivering on the
aguish hills they had to shiver too. I was hardly conscious of
whether my pupils were bored or not. On the whole, I have
gathered since, they were not. Camborne children were like
me, only too responsive to words. It was therefore a real shock
to me when a girl good at science, and with a genuine
appreciation of English prose, confided to her mother, with
whom I was friendly that she would like poetry if Miss Treneer
would not spout for hours about some favourite word or other.
This remark gave me my first inkling of how not to teach
English poetry. The final revelation came many years later
when in another school another head mistress came up to my
form-room to hear me teach. I am not tongue-tied with classes;
far from it; my tongue is all too glib. But if any grown-up
enters my form-room suddenly, I feel numb and dumb. The
poem I had meant to teach flew clean out of my head; I could
not catch hold of a single syllable of it. Then I remembered that
the children had poetry books. They took them out of the
desks; I borrowed a copy and turned to the first poem in the
book. 'Will you begin, Julia?' I said. Julia was delighted as I
should have been when I was small. She pushed back her
straight hair and read out clear and bold. I said, 'Mary,' to the
next child, and 'Helen,' to the next, and so on round the class.
We read the entire poetry syllabus for a term in that one lesson.

I have more frequently failed through zeal than not. Although I always profess not to be zealous I feel a rising zeal as I teach—pure auto-intoxication, no doubt; teachers, like preachers, have something of the actor in them. I suspect that when a teacher goes away from a class feeling warm and delighted, the class is often stiff and cold. Then, too, I was fiercely critical when I first went to Camborne. I fell upon the children's compositions like a whirlwind. I shall never forget when a large girl wept. I had forgotten how easily I, although brought up in a critical family and surrounded by critical friends, was daunted and downcast by criticism myself. I felt like crying to think of the hurt I had done and, for a time, I was more careful of youthful feelings; but the sight of slovenly English makes me forget my kinder intentions. Now, as an experienced teacher of English, I think that criticism of their immature work is bad for children. It gives them a kind of mental stammer in writing; they pause in the act, and wonder what Miss So-and-so will think; and that is death to all live expression. Where would Pet Marjorie have been if she had had an English mistress like me instead of a wise old friend like Scott?

Luckily, both Miss Pratt and the Secretary for Education were wiser and more tolerant than I. Miss Pratt's great virtue was that she did not care a button what anybody thought. We need put up no show. The school had originally been a private school, and in its new County Council building it retained a spirit of independence. It avoided the worst features which girls' high schools have tended to take over from the boys' public schools. We evaded those moribund functions—Speech Days—for years. Miss Pratt was never doctrinaire; she was as free of red tape as my own father, and as incapable of being manipulated. She saw questions in a broad human light, not through the narrow beam of scholarship. She never let any method harden round her; in an emergency she would turn her hand to teaching any subject, and expected us to do the same. My friend Marjorie used to say she herself taught nearly everything under the sun at Camborne, and to all ages, before she finally reached the kindergarten for which she had been trained. Miss Pratt was convinced that it was fatal to settle down. Just as I was preening myself on my English she said to me, 'Dear, I want you to take some senior Latin.' 'My Latin prose has never been good, Miss Pratt,' said I. 'Brush it up, dear, brush it up,' said she. And, with the aid of some private lessons from a classical scholar at Penzance, I did brush it up. However much our withers were wrung we always said, 'Yes, Miss Pratt,' in the end. We would laugh ruefully in the staff-room over, 'This little phrase which comes so pat, is, Yes, Miss Pratt':

> One day I'll find myself near Hell,
> And see the flames a-dancing well,
> And there will come a little devil
> To say, 'Now won't you join our revel?'
> I shan't be able to reply
> 'No, thank you, Sir, I don't like fry,'
> But I shall answer with a sigh,
> Wiping my feet upon the mat,
> And hanging up my only hat,
> 'Yes, Miss Pratt.'

Miss Pratt smiled at this ditty with the rest of us. And if we said 'Yes' to her she reciprocated with 'Yes' to us. 'Sir Frank Benson's company is playing at Plymouth, Miss Pratt, do you think we could arrange to take the Fifth Form up to see *The Tempest*?' 'Yes, Anne dear; and you had better have Marjorie to help with so big a party.' The fun of it—instead of going to school! My impression is that Sir Frank, as a hairy Caliban, went swinging from knotty oak to cloven pine by his tail. But I don't suppose he did.

Sixth-form work in the necessary variety of subjects is bound to be a difficulty in country grammar schools sparely staffed; yet sixth-form work, both general and academic, is absolutely essential to the health and well-being of such a school. Travelling specialist teachers in some subjects might be a solution. I would rather have some travelling teachers than have some schools truncated of their sixth forms and other schools with big sixths. A school must have a head and a tail like every other living organism, even if it is a little head and a little tail. I think Camborne had a great advantage in its tail— the kindergarten. Surely big girls verging on womanhood, whose main function in life must, generally speaking, be with children, ought to have some little children under the same roof with them while they are being educated. The kindergarten at Camborne meant that there was a flourishing Froebel class for older girls who were attracted to that work. Big girls separated too far and too long from small children tend to become faintly monstrous. Camborne had an advantage, too, in not being rigidly academic. Children more interested in dairy work than French verbs managed to get in. And a good thing too. Could any scheme be more idiotic than the present idea of rigidly separating the academic and the practical? People learn by mixing with others unlike themselves, not by being tied up in similar bundles. It is good for a very bookish little girl to make friends at school with someone who will carry her off to stroke the horses and feed the calves. 'With eager feeding food doth choke the feeder'—if only we could get away from the idea that our intellectual children need intellectual stimulus. They need to go slow; they need to live. A flame which is to burn steadily through life must not be fanned to too great a brilliance at the start.

A book which made me think at this time was *How to Lengthen Your Ears*, which Mr Pascoe handed to me with an ironical comment during the first of the many weekends I spent at hospitable 5 Clifton Gardens, Truro. Mr Pascoe, who had been schoolmaster, school inspector, and then Secretary for Education in Cornwall, recognized, for he himself had strongly felt, the profound influence of place and family in education. He had been born and brought up in Bugle, and his best stories were prefaced with, 'There was a man up Bugle once'. I liked the man who wrongly guessed the weight of a pig in a weight-guessing competition. He said, 'There now! Wha's d'a think o' that? I knaw'd that pig was heavier than I thought he was.' And the man who thought he had been deafened by a mine explosion

to whom a neighbour said, 'Cean't 'ee hear what I'm saying of?'
And the deaf one replied, 'Not wan word.' Mr Pascoe used to
tell me stories of when he first went round inspecting schools in
Cornwall; I liked a tale of how he went into one country school
and found the master brewing beer; he said he didn't think
school the place for brewing beer. The schoolmaster said it was
the best place he had; and when Mr Pascoe called again beer
was still brewing. I suppose this occupation might be regularized
under the heading of 'Vocational Training' now.

How to Lengthen Your Ears was a diatribe against compulsory
education; whether well-written or not I do not know. It
certainly impressed me very much. The argument was that
only the rich could now save their children from being turned
into asses by being compulsorily sent to school, and having
their senses atrophied and their minds smothered with print.
The only other book in which I have heard the common
school education inveighed against so roundly is in R. G.
Collingwood's *The New Leviathan*. Parents should teach
their children themselves according to the late Professor
Collingwood; and teachers should merely be kept as pets, to be
called in when both grown-ups and children need instruction
in any particular specialist branch of knowledge. An enjoyable
life for a teacher, I think, sitting in some sort of pleasant
equivalent to a kennel, getting on with research in his own
subject, and waiting to be called in. Whether I myself should
have enjoyed instructing Professor Collingwood, together with
his child or children, in the art of poetry, I am not sure. I
cannot fancy myself saying, 'Whence come ye, merry maidens,
whence come ye!' to Professor Collingwood. But I suppose no
English pet would have been kept by the Professor. He would
have instructed his children in English himself, and I should
have retired to my fastness to shake my lengthened ears for joy.
I suppose I should have shaken my ass's ears until somebody
came along, took one look at me, and turned me out of the
commonwealth. There is a perpetual spice of danger about the
artistic or intellectual life; we have a way of looking enviable, as
though we deserved a bash on the head.

It was an enviable life I led at Camborne with friends and books and a subject to teach which was my own chief source of pleasure. Marjorie Pascoe and I became firmer and firmer friends the longer I stayed at Camborne, and after. She was of a Cornish type supposed to be predominant, but which is not. There are as many fair as dark children in Cornwall; in the kindergarten were always some children with silvery-soft, straight hair. But Marjorie looked Spanish with hair blue-black, a creamy complexion without colour, and eyebrows arched over greenish eyes. Sudden sparkles of wit pleased her a second before she uttered them, so that she smiled in advance; I have known no more inward, yet free and illuminative smile. But it is impossible to re-create in a book a witty woman; wit dies on the pen. Even Meredith could not succeed in it. Marjorie's wit was born of the moment and was gone with it. Yet wit serves a woman well, not withering with her beauty. My sister Susan has it, my friend Marjorie has it; so that living with either of them is never dull; the unexpectedness of their replies is the only factor I can see in common between them and my mother, who also had a happy wit. She would look up with a flush at my father and say something compounded of the instant, herself and his last sentence. He was the more wise, and she the more witty without being sharp, so they fitted together.

Marjorie was no actress; she was too consistently herself, too little Protean. But I made her act in all sorts of plays. Of only one element in the teaching of English have I never had any doubt, and that is of the value of plays—of play-reading and play-acting. To mix staff and children is a benefit sometimes, and when I had a play in which both staff and children acted, I hounded Marjorie into a part. As for me, I was always ready to produce, to stage-manage and to enact the best part. I was a female Bottom when I was young. The only thing I would not do was to learn my lines. I can see Marjorie and myself sitting on a gate by Penponds conning our parts the night before we played *Comus* in the vicarage garden. She was the Lady; I was Comus; the children were delighted to be animals. The brothers were even more stiff in our performance than in Milton's verse. *Comus* in the vicarage garden was not a real success, though I thought it was at the time. I would not risk it now; one becomes more of a poltroon as one grows older. I could not now caper about exclaiming, 'What has night to do with sleep?' to an astonished congregation; but I did then and felt exhilarated by it. Even more than *Comus* at Penponds I enjoyed scenes from *As You Like It* which I did with Troon players in the vicarage garden at Treslothan; and *Mr Sampson* in which the senior French mistress, Miss Laity, was inimitably Cornish. We had our giddy heights and dizzy downfalls. One year the chairman of the Governors, Mr C.V. Thomas, was so pleased with a performance of *Michael* that he gave each member of the cast a book of her own choosing. And the following year, when we tried *Riders to the Sea*, he is reported to have whispered to Mr Pascoe, as a dripping body was brought in on a blackboard, 'What on earth made her choose this?' Mr Pascoe is said to have replied, 'God knows.' But Miss Pratt cheered up the English mistress that night over a special crab supper. 'They've no taste, Anne. It was a splendid thing to try. I'm surprised at Mr C.V. and Mr F.R.'

We were always so eager and so rough and ready in our performances that we generally had some slight contretemps which we weathered, coming up to the surface after being downed by a falling chair or bit of scaffolding. We had a very tiny platform which was temporarily enlarged for each show by Mr Laity, the school caretaker. Mr Laity had far too musical a disposition to be a safe carpenter. Once when we did *She Stoops to Conquer*, Zoë Parr, the gym mistress, who was enacting Tony Lumpkin with immense verve, cracked her whip and fell off the platform altogether; but she was immediately up again, cheering and whooping, and persuading the audience that falling off the platform was exactly what Tony Lumpkin had been meant to do at that point. Nellie Nobbs was a delightful Miss Hardcastle in that play, and Freda Westlake, her foil, a delicious Miss Neville. We did all kinds of plays; but Shakespeare was always my true love. We acted play after play of Shakespeare. It is nonsense to say that Shakespeare is spoilt by being read and acted at school; he is the only thing worth going to school for. I have seen most beautiful and moving school performances. The full pathos of Viola's—

> I am all the daughters of my father's house,
> And all the brothers too . . .

Of Cordelia's—

> So young, my Lord, and true . . .

Of Miranda's—

> Oh, I have suffered
> With those that I saw suffer . . .

can only be heard on the lips of earnest children, unconscious in their hearts of what their voices carry. Grown women adulterate poetry with personal feeling.

One of the bugbears in the life of a teacher of English is marking; it is, alas, true that effective English teaching demands correction of exercises. A parent once suggested to me that her daughter's written work would improve if I gave more time to correcting it. I could not resist saying, 'Oh, Mrs X, it is quite gone out of fashion to mark books; didn't you know? I put everything the children write straight into the waste-paper basket, it's so much better for them.' I only wish it were. We probably over-do 'composition'; it is cruel to make children write on themes about which they have nothing natural to say. Not all children are inventive. Written work in connection with history and geography—particularly geography—is likely to be more fruitful. A child once told me she hated writing 'English', yet admitted that she loved writing when it came to geography essays, the simple reason being that she was no longer searching in her poor empty mind and stomach for words. Yet pupils must write if they are to learn to use English properly;

and I sometimes think that nothing is more important in education. 'Further,' as Doughty wrote at the close of *The Dawn in Britain*, 'it is the prerogative of every lover of his country to use the instrument of his thought, which is the Mother-tongue, with propriety and distinction; to keep that reverently clean and bright, which lies at the root of his mental life, and so, by extension, of the life of the Community: putting away all impotent and disloyal vility of speech, which is no uncertain token of a people's decadence.' Doughty's Arabs learnt to use their language in a pithy manner by talking; and I think children learn best by talk. I am not sure that I would encourage any child who did not ache to write, to use pen at all until she was twelve or so. Children are delightful in informal debate and discussion; they will consider eagerly all kinds of questions, and often express themselves with a pointedness entirely lacking in their written words. Once, when with a class of twelve-year-old children I reached, by what strange route I have forgotten, a consideration of whether things were actually existent or only existing in the eyes of the beholder, a little girl called Rosemary stood up and said to me with great earnestness, 'Do you mean, Miss Treneer, that this desk might be a solid thought?' A metaphysician could hardly have put it better.

I think indirect methods are better than direct in the teaching of English writing. Why did the Elizabethans, who were not directly taught English at school, write with so much more colour, verve, and glow of wit than we? Why are their rhythms so warm and curling, while ours are so thin; why are their words so physical and ours so lacking in substance? Would frequent practice in translation be more beneficial than 'composition'? We need to call up such Tudor schoolmasters as Ascham and Mulcaster to inform us. We might summon Alfred the Great, the first teacher of English on record, a noble and heartening ancestor. He translated for his people. I cannot but think that Arthur Waley's translations from the Chinese and Japanese are among the most beautiful and enduring English writings of our own time. Perhaps the matter of China and Russia will be to our own age what the matter of France was to our medieval writers, and the great classical texts to the Elizabethans.

At this time I was still reading with enormous pleasure myself. I joined the London Library. Cutting the string of their beautifully tied up parcels, taking off the outer layer of brown paper, unwrapping the inner sheets of printed packing paper, and seeing which of my ordered books had come, and which 'with the Librarian's compliments, were not available at present, but would be reserved for Miss Treneer'—this was one of my major pleasures at Vean Terrace. On winter nights my fire would blaze, my lamp give a soft light, and I, hunched up on a chair with my elbows on the table, or reclining on my sofa although this position was too far from the lamp and made me squint, forgot all about the difficulty of teaching English in the pleasure of my own reading. I bolted books, or perhaps bolted is the wrong word; for at this time I was becoming very fastidious, not to say precious in my tastes. I was under the spell of Pater, Santayana and Max Beerbohm. Shall I ever forget discovering Lord George Hell and Zuleika Dobson in one and the same London Library parcel? It seemed too much. My emotions overflowed at the magnanimous generosity of Dr Hagbert Wright. I believe I thought he tied up the parcels himself, selecting books personally from treasures piled up in underground caverns, treasures which ranged from *The Dynasts* to *The Watsons*; from *Marius the Epicurean* to *Peacock Pie*.

12

WINTER PRIDE

> I saw the hillside
> Of Autumn's sowing,
> Too green a-growing
> Wounded for winter pride.
>
> The lumpish cattle walk;
> And bruised and broken
> Lies April's token,
> Till the triumphing stalk,
>
> Pride's penance done,
> Out of the dead
> A gold head
> Lifts to the August sun.
>
> —*Winter Pride*

Everybody laughs at theses now. And everybody thinks reading for degrees a waste of time. What lured me on to write a thesis I can hardly say. I suppose most of us fancy our names with decorations, and Anne has had some pretty ones in its day: Queen Anne; the Grand Duchess Anne; Lady Anne. I cannot think why we have made the word 'Dame' a title of honour; its associations are all dull. Dame Anne is worse than

Miss Anne; but Anne Treneer, M.A., I thought this would look classical. The only book I had written before was a story for children; but I had far too wholesome a dread of the taste of the children I taught myself to attach my own name to that. All very well for me to criticize them, I thought in my cowardly way; but what about their criticizing me? I enjoyed the remarks incognito. Nothing can be more amusing, or more illuminating for a teacher of English, than to hear her pupils' comments on her own work. That I remained in hiding was, I think, base; there is an element of Jekyll and Hyde in it—writing poor stuff with one hand and trouncing it with the other. But hide I did; and I checked my facility with the pen by launching myself upon a thesis on George Meredith whose work I read in full after making the acquaintance of *The Victory of Aphasia Gibberish*.[1] Max Beerbohm's other parodies were so good that I had to read Meredith in order to enjoy the 'Victory' as much as I enjoyed the other parodies in the same volume of writers whose art I knew well. I still think this parody a better glance at Meredith's foibles than all the voluminous comment and laborious wit to which his prose has been subjected. The very title, *The Victory of Aphasia Gibberish*, touches the victim, recalling Meredith's pleasure in the naming of his girls and his preference for names ending in 'a' from Clare Doria Forey to Carinthia. The description of Gibberish Park is good; but it is in the dialogue that the parody is supreme, and in the little side notes on gesture which Meredith loved to make, in the mock aphorisms, the substitute phrases, the witty metaphors, compressions and leaps. I liked the parody especially where Sir Rhombus, the lover, is talking to Aphasia about the advisability of following the rest of the family to church:

'You have prayer Book?' he queried.
She nodded. Juno catches the connubial trick.
'Hymns?'
'Ancient and Modern.'

[1] *The Chap-Book* (Chicago), Dec. 15th 1896. A revised version, *Euphemia Clash-thought*, was printed in *A Christmas Garland*, 1912.

'I may share with you?'

'I know them by heart. Parrots sing.'

'Philomel carols.' He bent to her. 'Complaints spoil a festival.'

She turned aside. There was a silence as of virgin Dundee or Madeira susceptible of the knify incision.

'Time speeds,' said Sir Rhombus, with a jerk at the clock.

'We may dodge the scythe.'

'To be choked with the sands?'

She flashed a smile.

'Lady! Your father has started.'

'He knows the aphorism. Copy-books instil it.'

'It would not be well that my Aphasia should enter after the Absolution,' he pursued.

She cast her eyes to the carpet. He caught them at the rebound.

'It snows,' she said, swimming to the window.

'A flake. Not more. The season claims it.'

'I have thin boots.'

'Another pair! . . .'

'My maid buttons. She is at Church.'

'My fingers?'

'Twelve on each!'

'Five,' he corrected.

'Buttons . . .'

'I beg your pardon.'

She saw opportunity. She swam to the bell-rope and grasped it for a tinkle. The action spread feminine curves to her lover's eye. He was a man.

Obsequiousness loomed in the doorway. Its mistress flashed an order for port—two glasses.

Sir Rhombus sprang a pair of eyebrows on her. Suspicion slid down the banisters of his mind, trailing a blue ribbon.

Inebriates were one of his studies. For a second she was sunset.

'Medicinal,' she murmured.

'Forgive me, Madam! . . . A glass. Certainly. 'Twill warm us for worshipping.'

Meredith's novels and poems were my familiar companions for three years; after which I did not read them for twenty. But I feel that I could, with justice, send to Meredith's shade the message which his own Lyra gave to her Uncle Homeware for her husband, Pluriel,[2] 'Tell him I ran away to get a sense of

[2] *The Sentimentalists.*

freshness in seeing him again.' What amused and attracted me in him then—his cleverness and play with words—repels me now. He should have written for the living stage; it is the only thing that would have clarified his language. As it is, he himself has become a subject for the slim feasting smile of his own comic muse. But he can stand aloof and smile serenely back; for in each of his chosen modes, lyric and comedy, he achieved something absolute. *Love in a Valley* can never grow stale; and *The Egoist* retains its power to penetrate our thick hides. Yet Meredith rarely makes a reader laugh out loud as Dickens does; his comedy is arranged for a purpose. His natural, spontaneous genius was lyrical and passionate. I cannot help wishing he had never tried to do mankind good. When I used to go round the Camborne lanes saying *The Woods of Westermain* to myself it was not its didactic middle which made me toss my heart up with the lark. I never learnt that part. Nor, in *The Ordeal of Richard Feverel* was it the hard work which had gone into the moulding of the Baronet which made me admire. It was 'Golden lie the meadows; golden run the streams; red-gold is on the pine-stems; the sun is coming down to earth and walks the fields and waters'. I used to like to blow with Meredith over the earth and hear his trees wrestling with the wind: 'The bull-voiced oak is battling now,' I would shout, as I whirled about Pendarves Woods.

For the smoky, forked flame of Meredith's more sombre writing I cared less, admiring often without delight. I disliked in some of his work the presence of little gentleman Georgie. He was called little gentle Georgie when he was a boy by the unkind. His acquaintance with disaster in the failure of his first marriage gave tragic import to the series of poems to which he gave the title *Modern Love. Modern Love* has a fascinating form. It is a tragedy of manners to be enacted on the stage of the mind, with all its entrances and exits complete, and every gesture; comment, chorus, décor and dance all folded within itself The masqued figures of the husband, the lover, Madam, and the lady advance and retire, conjoin and separate. I wonder that no one has made a ballet out of *Modern Love.* The stepping is accurate, the passion explosive yet stylized, and the whole conception searingly satirical. One theme is powerful in Meredith's tragic writing. He had a feeling that past days were like eager ghosts alive to haunt the present. 'The waves,' he wrote, 'wash long and wan off one disastrous impulse.' His most grandly conceived, though not his most successfully executed work on this theme is the magnificent, unequal *Odes in Contribution to the Song of French History.* What a noble artist Meredith would have been if he could more constantly have wedded word and idea in the inevitable and terrifying union of:

> The Gods alone
> Remember everlastingly. They strike
> Remorselessly and ever like for like,
> By their great memories the Gods are known.

We who can cast our glance over a still longer period since Napoleon may well shudder at the long memories of the gods. I sometimes think if Meredith had not been vain he might have saved the world—if art could save the world. But he tried preaching. Preaching will never save anybody, however good the text. And I think Meredith had a good text. 'More brain, O Lord, more brain.' But I don't know. Perhaps we need more feeling, not more brain, we who seem as unimpressionable as rhinoceroses. Preaching hardens. What an amount of lay-preaching our young people are subjected to nowadays! People have never been so be-preached at and be-thumped with words since the days of Praise-God Barebones.

I did not enjoy Meredith when he preached and formul-ated his faith in the clear-eyed, courageous rejection of the faith in which I had been brought up; and yet in my contradictory way I did continue to read him partly in the hope of finding a religion. I could respond to earth as the bacchante mother; I knew her revelry of ripeness, her kind smile; I tried not to be afraid in the woods of Westermain. And yet my heart would not let me accept what to my reason seemed so feasible, that the individual must die, and live only in his offspring; that all that would be left of my friends after death should be a quintessenced memory going to build up some great dream of good. I did not care for any dream of good once the effect of Meredith's eloquence on me had cooled. I have said that I did not take Meredith to my heart when he tried to formulate a creed. Yet his faith in earth did act upon me in such a way that I tried to make a religion of it for myself. If I had not gone home so often I might have succeeded in becoming an apostle of Meredith. But my former faith retained its hold because of my affection for my parents and family, stronger-rooted than any mere ideas could be. I still went to church because they went to church. The wonder of God made incarnate in the mystery of human birth at Christmas; the impulse to repentance and penance in Lent, corresponding to how deep-seated a need in poor humanity; the awakening of life even in death on Easter Day—these were a more profound and permanent poetry than Meredith's reasonable faith could ever be. I still could not accept the symbol of a cross; I still did not feel the sacraments; I wanted the Holy Ghost, the Lord and Giver of Life, too cheaply; but I knew that my mother in her Christian faith and hope had an inspiration at once more human and more divine than any I had drawn from Meredith.

I did not read Meredith to my pupils; I preferred to keep him to myself. Reading him led me to all kinds of pastures, green and otherwise, in this period. In addition, he himself had been much written about, and I enjoyed reading other people's opinions of him.[3] I am of those who like reading books about books. I even chased Meredith through the periodicals, and once I literally undid the out-porter at Camborne Station. One Saturday afternoon he came staggering up to Vean Terrace with a huge, heavy, flat, thick parcel for me.

'Whatever have 'ee got there?' he said, panting through the passage, and casting his burden on my sitting-room floor. 'Whatever es a? Need a horse and cart he do. Scat me braces I have lugging of un up.'

[3]Of these books, G. M. Trevelyan's was a revelation to me.

His braces had been scat by a bound volume of *The Times*, in which the London Library had obligingly marked one short article for my delectation. After that, when making my London Library list, I used to add the proviso, 'If not too heavy.' Whether I was being cautious over the contents of the books or their physical weight I left it to the library to decide.

It was about this time that I went to Paris and was startled there to find the moon almost put out by artifical light. I used to look up at her and wonder if she could also possibly be shining on the sea by Gurnard's Head. I went to France with my brother Howard and we stayed first in Paris and then just outside it with the parents of two girls who had previously come to England as pupils in my brother's house. All was novel to me. I had never stayed in a flat before; I had only drunk wine at rare parties. The volubility of Madame, the bow of Monsieur, the elegance of Marie, and the sulkiness of Robert were alike strange and foreign. I adjusted myself first to the wine—its colour; its sparkle inside me; and then its body. I had peaches in wine; peaches smelling of summer. Madame was like a damson. She looked at me after a day or two and said, 'I do not like her hairr; it is ugliee. She will not get a maan!' Then a day or two later she eyed me again and said, 'It shall be wafed,' and wafed it was. When I caught sight of the back of my head in a mirror I did not at first realize whose it was; I must admit that I was more than pleased when I recognized this nice-looking head as mine. But my brother did not like my curls; they looked unnatural he said. And when we went for a day's excursion and rode water-bicycles on a river I was quite glad to fall in and be ducked and come up with curls all washed out. I cared more to please my brother than Madame.

We went to see half the church organs in Paris; and sometimes my brother tried the organs and we shook hands with organists. I did not like the churches. The Madeleine made me smell a kind of stale penitence until I gasped for air. There is much in religion that repels me. We went to Notre Dame on the Feast of the Assumption. I was shaken by the glory of the Mozart Mass; but when the Cardinal in his scarlet passed close to us, and worshippers pressed forward to kneel and kiss his ring, I was restrained from following their example by I know not what hint of Puritanism within my Pagan bones. What moved me most during my visit was a performance of *Andromaque* at the Comédie Française. Previously, in my ignorant way, I had without a moment's hesitation preferred our English manner of tragedy to the French. Racine as I read his plays seemed to me not for an instant to compare with Shakespeare. What, I had thought to myself, was the value of all these long speeches which merely described action? But when I heard French spoken by an actress in such a way that it vibrated my bones I knew that in drama, no less than in lyric and epic, the spoken word is of the essence; I have never forgotten that low, intense, rapid poetry.

On our way back through London we went to the Queen's Hall to my first Promenade Concert and heard Myra Hess play. My brother declares that when she had finished I said to him, 'And I thought you could play.' I cannot believe that I could have been so rude; but he says it shook his conceit. I do remember that we spent our last few shillings on the most English supper we could contrive in London and that, having no money left for an hotel, we dashed into the midnight train at Paddington to have a night's lodging and a journey in one. I got out sleepily at Exeter soon after three in the morning; my brother went on to St Austell to join Mary who was staying at Caerhays Barton. He had been looking after our money; I forgot to ask him for any, and there I was in a drizzly rain without a farthing. I did not like to wake up any of my friends in Exeter; so, as it was a Sunday morning, I bethought me of sheltering in church. I went to St Michael's and there fell sound asleep in the porch. Suddenly I heard footsteps so I got up and pretended I had come to Early Service. Then, as I knelt during the commandments, I thought of the early bus to Exmouth and, trying to look faint, I tip-toed out of church and fled from a verger bearing sal volatile into a bus which took me to Exmouth. It waited near my home while I dashed in to fetch my fare.

Next time I went to London it was in the wake of my thesis. My fluster as that examination hour drew near was extreme. I had done a vast quantity of reading, but I could not persuade myself into continuous writing until Time's hounds were not merely barking at my heels but leaping up my back. It was in vain that my friends warned me that I was being foolish; that my examiner would judge not by what was in my head but by what I had conveyed to paper. I was like a person in a nightmare whose will cannot make his feet move; or like a car in the snow when the wheels spin. I took a perverse pleasure in doing everything except the thesis. Even work I was much less interested in took precedence. When at last I had finished the writing, I found that I had allowed too little time to get the thing typed; that it was far too long; that I had lost my list of authorities; that the footnotes were confused. I slashed out whole chapters; I played cards with references. The thesis came back from a typist in the nick of time to be hurled into the post before the closing date of the London examination. Once I had posted it I decided that everything was all right. When any piece of writing of mine is finished and posted, however wretched it may be, I feel like a lily of the field, unspotted.

In this complacent mood I went up to town and stayed this time at Sutton with my youngest brother Cap'n and his wife Edith. They took me to see Pavlova dance. Nothing in my life before had ever given me such celestial pleasure. In addition, Cap'n, who liked a little revelry, feasted me, and was amused at my new pleasure in wine. I am not sure that I did not reel into the examination room; but no doubt a little Gothic and Old English cooled me. There were papers in both subjects. Then, still exalted by Cap'n's pleasant ways of entertaining me in town, I went for a *viva* on the subject of my thesis. I have never been regarded by a more disapproving eye than Professor Edith Morley's. She sat facing me, thesis in hand. I know faintly what the Day of Judgment is like. By her side sat Professor Allen Mawer holding my indiscretions in Gothic. All the bubbles of Cap'n's champagne went out of me, leaving me flatter than the flattest beer. Professor Allen Mawer, whom I was to meet again in pleasanter circumstances, looked like a good-natured lion. Professor Edith Morley was large, dark red, and full of nature—like a glass of stout. Sickert might have drawn her leaning against a mantelpiece smoking a pipe. She began by telling me that I had an untidy mind, and then took me unerringly and unfalteringly through my subsidiary failings. I disowned myself; I set myself fairly up as a guy and looked on. I hadn't a word; and I felt cold as a fish. I was asked which Fletcher wrote *The Purple Island*. I had read *The Purple Island* but the name 'Joseph' eluded me. I said with a ghastly attempt at lightness 'not Beaumont'. I got out, and met Cap'n with a friend and told them the worst. I shall never forget the balm of their jeers at Professor Morley. They said I was a fool to be wasting my time on M.A.'s. What did I want with an M.A. at all? I did not admit that I thought the letters would look nice after my name.

I failed. My chagrin was extreme; and I was further mortified because I knew I had ridden for a fall and obtained it. I stamped on my thesis. I said I would never look at it again and I suppose if I had not been afraid of setting Weeza's chimney a-fire—she had a mortal dread of fire—I should have roasted it on the coals. Instead I forgot it in other adventures; I took my first little cottage and moved out of Weeza's into my new abode.

13

ON THE TOWANS

A clear sea-pool in rock;
And one foot stretched to the shock
Of the green water.

Sun-cascades over me
Divide, where at the knee
Closes cool water.

Not with rude plunge and stir
Would I your crystal blur,
Pellucid water,

Yet fain from foot to chin
Would stand garmented in
Gown of green water.

Round fringed anemones
And uncouth weeds of seas
Glide, clearest water,

So, up my body trim
Let slip your liquid rim,
Water, water,

Till, closing over me,
Half in pale fear I see
You snake-like water.

Resist, incline, consent
To the coiled element
Water, green water.

—Preparing to swim in Godrevy Pool

The cottage was at Venton League on the outskirts of Hayle. It was one of two cottages joined together, thatched and white-washed; it had a good-sized sitting-room with a casement opening on to the prettiest of gardens, a back kitchen, two bedrooms and fleas. The bedroom windows were so low, and the front garden was built up so high, that on Saturday mornings the postman used to stand on the bank and hand me my letters in bed. I can still see the envelopes edging their way in between the roses. Eva, my new landlady, who lived in the second cottage with her lodger, Mr Pippin, was an original, an ex-music-hall actress, still bursting with vigour, good-nature and song. She made light of the fleas. 'Fleas, dear?' she said, when I showed her my pyjamas all be-spotted, and asked what could be done. 'Fleas! Harmless little things, dear. When I had a poultry farm they used to be hop-ping about.' Impossible to describe the joyous lilt of her voice as it ran up, 'hop' and danced off 'ping'. However, she brought me some Keatings, though we never really got rid of the pest, one or two always survived to keep up the stock. Eva said I brought them in from the Towans; but these were no rabbits' fleas. Besides, I have often lived among rabbits; I like to keep so still on a warren that they come out to play regardless of me; and stamp with their hind legs to warn their fellows when I move. Yet only at Venton League have I ever suffered from fleas.

The Towans or sand-hills at Hayle seem monotonous to the casual eye; they stretch from Gwithian to Hayle River, and reappear on the other side of the estuary between Lelant and Carbis Bay. The two churches on the Towans, the Church of St

Uny at Lelant, and the Church of St Felicitas at Phillack, are peculiarly fit for Cornish worship. In the mist, and amidst the sand, they symbolize I know not what of mystery and permanence in the shifting blindness of our days. The Towans can look most desolate; the sea appear a waste of waters; but wide. Coarse bents have been planted in the sands to bind them. The wind streams through this green hair blowing it back; and the sun sends white light like fireflies glancing along the blades. The wind is caught alive, even in pictures, even in photographs of the Towans. And one is exposed or not exposed to this element at one's pleasure. There is generally one lew[1] side to a sand-hill from whatever quarter the wind blows. I have cheated much wind and caught much sunshine on the Towans. I used to snuggle into a hollow and laugh at the wind which could not catch me. The levels behind the sand-hills are covered with turf, sown in summer with flowers; self-heal and thyme, and trefoil so low and thick that the whole is resilient underfoot and aromatic. Not all the plants on the Towans are low. Beds of alkanet flower in the loose wilderness. Alkanet is a borage, hairy and vigorous, with flowers more than sky-blue; I have stood amidst alkanet taller than myself, and extending so far round me that I seemed in a jungle of alkanet. The colour as one approaches on a summer day is startling. In the meadows behind the Towans feverfew spreads its flowers as though offering them to the sky; here, too, poppies and white campion grow. I have never seen so many white campions as at Hayle. As for the scarlet poppies with their black centres, all July is in poppy petals.

I grew to like the Towans so well that I did not want to come in from them at night. And here I found the value of being a schoolmistress. Parents! How useful they are! The parents of a pupil of mine named Alice Bastion had a summer hut on Gwithian Towans—there were only a half-dozen or so huts at Gwithian then. They asked me to tea and helped me to buy my first tent. We scanned the advertisement columns of the *Daily*

---

[1]Lee.

Mail. I was for something very small; but I must have a tent I could stand up in said Mr Bastion; man wasn't made to crawl. I thought the whole thing must be light. 'Blow away with a summer puff,' said Mr Bastion. 'We don't want to have to come out and catch 'ee by the leg to stop 'ee from being carried up aloft.' In the end I bought a cottage tent, for 37s. 6d. with ropes and pegs and poles complete, 'the whole enclosed in a stout canvas bag'. That tag in the advertisement still amuses me; for the bag was so very stout when it arrived that my idea of tying it on the back of my bicycle was ludicrous. It was so stout that it took Mr Bastion all his time to lift it. However, we got it to Gwithian—men are so handy—in Mr Bastion's car. Then Mr Bastion, Mrs Bastion, Alice and I put up the tent under the managerial direction of Mr Bastion. Two poles in three parts fitting into little brass sockets; ends soaped under Mr Bastion's orders so that they should come out of the sockets easily when we came to strike camp. We grew more technical in our terms every second. Alice and I each held a pole upright at a suitable distance apart; Mr Bastion, hidden in the voluminous folds of my green cotton cottage slipped first one little button-holed eyelet over the sharpened top of Alice's pole, then the other little eyelet over the point of my pole. Mrs Bastion shook out the guy ropes; Mr Bastion shouted that we mustn't lose any pegs. Then to a volley of, 'Keep her straight, Alice; drive her home, Anne; there's a fold in the canvas there, Mary; suant, now, suant!' the tent went up and the pegs went in. They were wooden pegs which one could hit plumb on the head with a mallet.

I went inside to enjoy for the first time my enclosed space of greenish light. But Mr Bastion wasn't satisfied. We did a good deal of adjusting; we trenched the tent round. By the time all was finished to his satisfaction and we had eaten one of Mrs Bastion's marvellous suppers—the tent was pitched quite near their hut—it was bedtime. I spread my ground sheet; I shook out my hessian bag of straw; I lay down under my blankets. But not to sleep. I listened to the sea; I heard the sound of a horse moving, the steps coming to my ear through the earth. Then I saw a flash of lightning. My tent was open towards the sea, the flaps tied back with tapes. I tried to sleep again. But now the tent began billowing and struggling like a wild thing; thunder roared; lightning flashed. Mr Bastion appeared with a lantern. 'Hadn't 'ee better come into the hut?' he said. But no: I was as frightened as a sheep, but I wasn't leaving my tent. Then the rain came, venomous rain it seemed, determined to get at me through the cotton. I felt a dewy, misty spattering on my face from the force of the pelting drops outside. But no drops of rain came in; I began to enjoy my dry, warm position in the midst of such a tumult. It is wonderful to be so near the weather and yet out of it. And when the storm subsided I looked out and saw the great torn masses of cloud and a gibbous moon reeling.

And then morning came, and I went to bathe in a tidal strait called Sheep's Pool. In Sheep's Pool the tide rushed up the narrows between the long sets of rock. Perfectly safe on an incoming tide; but boisterous and warming. Mrs Bastion fried us bacon and eggs and made coffee. Coffee on the Towans at half-past seven on a sunny morning after a storm! Mrs Bastion made grand coffee. And, ah! her 'yeasty splits' with plastered butter and honey!

My sister Susan and I had always wanted a tent when we were small; but we had never had one. My mother was glad to feel that she had her brood safely under her feathers at least at night. We used to play tents on our bed, one kneeling up in the midst as a living tent-prop with a sheet hung over her; the other pretending to do the work of a camper within the folds. Sometimes we tried to dress in tents. Susan came to stay with me at Venton League but she preferred the cottage to the tent. She loved the cottage garden and Mr Pippin's ducks which quacked and waddled. She filled the sitting-room with roses.

I had to get up early when I was staying at Hayle or at Gwithian in order to get to school at Camborne by nine o'clock in the morning. Usually I bicycled. From Hayle it was quickest to go by Roseworthy Hill, a slow climb for a cyclist. But in those days it was not dangerous, the traffic on the roads being so much lighter than it is now, for a cyclist to keep his right hand on his own handlebar, hang on to a lorry with his left and go up the hill as though riding on straight-forward-moving roundabouts. A lorry belonging to Messrs Hoskin, Trewithick and Polkinghorne regularly gave me a tow in this way. When I bicycled in from Gwithian I usually went by Gwinear Road and Barripper, always trying to fall in with a Mr Hoskins who brought his children in to school in his car. I used to hold on to the back of that and be conveyed to school in a most sociable manner. The children longed to see me fall off. They used to shout, 'Drive crooked, Daddy; shake her off, Daddy; whip behind!

Very occasionally on extra fine mornings I got up early enough to walk by North Cliffs to Camborne; or I would go up the Red river valley by Mendarva and Kehellend to school. I remember one June morning a transparency in the air, a coolness and fragrance indescribable. The sun was shining through the dew-drops on the mares'-tails till they were alight like fairy chandeliers. I believe if I had lingered I might have remained enchanted in that valley for ever; but we shatter our own crystals. I often wonder what the world would be like if no one had a sense of Duty. Wordsworth's Ode to the stern daughter of the voice of God is not my favourite among his poems.

Catering in the cottage was not too difficult when friends came for a weekend. Marjorie and her young man, Harold Harvey, were the easiest guests, for Marjorie was the best hand at frying eggs I ever met with. Instead of chivying one egg at a time about the pan as I did, she would in a nonchalant manner, chattering the while, break half a dozen into the pan and fry them together and take them all up whole. Oranges, and eggs, and lettuces, with all the adjuncts for a salad, were easy to get and nothing is simpler to make than junket. Junket and cream and raspberries! Mr Pippin used to give me raspberries. A fish-jouster used to come round with fish, but he went at such a lick in his cart shouting: 'Pilchards, fresh pilchards; six a penny, pilchards, fresh pilchards,' that by the time Eva and I had pulled ourselves together, seized a plate, and hunted for our purses he was half way up to Connor Downs. We caught him sometimes. Once when he said he had hake I said absently that I'd have one. He said, 'How many children have yer mother got, my dear?' I said there was only me. He said, 'What you do want, my handsome, is four pennard.'

People motoring through Hayle malign it; a dull, curving street they say, with a nasty bend left, a level crossing, and a higgle-piggle of houses and shops. A few nice square houses overlooking the Pool they say. They miss the old wharf and the ferry boat to Lelant; and all it has meant to seafarers to find this opening in the cliffy, northern coast, this mouth with the sea-tide running up the river which flows from Clowance. The Irish saints found shelter here hundreds of years ago. From the Lelant side in particular the estuary is dear to me. The cry of the birds, the smell of mud round the reeds at low tide, the vivid green of the weed, the river Hayle silting up, but still running; the brimming stillness of high tide on a quiet evening or morning. I have seen the whole estuary liquid gold at sunrise, and I have heard the birds calling across the water as St Uny must have heard them. Time has left its marks on Hayle—evidence of days when it was the port of the mining district, when ships were built and repaired and re-equipped there. Ships plied between Hayle and Bristol three times a week regularly when the Vicar of Bodmin compiled his Register in 1847. During the recent war Hayle woke up again; ships were built and factories were busy. But inland from Hayle, up the valleys and on the uplands, with the lines of Godolphin and Tregonning running clear, it is a timeless, unchanging area, separating the Channel and the Atlantic. Marazion to Hayle is only four miles. To see the lie of the whole district a splendid vantage ground is the top of Trencrom, the carn which lifts itself up two miles or so from Lelant. I used to walk up to the top of Trencrom and spend all day there with all my beauties spread out round me like a map. You can see the advantages of Hayle estuary from the top of Trencrom; you can turn from the sea that creams up towards the Towans, to the running carns behind, or to the sea in which rides the fairy castle of St Michael's Mount.

I was as happy as a king at Hayle, and I cannot understand why I did not stay quietly there doing as I liked. Some nagging suggestion within myself that I had failed, some desire to show Professor Edith Morley that my mind was not as littered as she thought, impelled me one spring to take my thesis out again. I fell upon it with energy and spite. I cut and scraped, and polished, and white-washed. I ruined it with white-wash. I hid its joints, I modified its forthrightness, and I attached a list of authorities to its tail. I employed a careful typist. I re-read the Old English poets and the works of H.C. Wylde, and off I went to London again.

This time my reception was so different from my former one that I sometimes think I dreamt the whole thing. I was re-examined by Professor Allen Mawer, but, as his companion, Professor George Gordon replaced Professor Morley. I am told it is quite impossible that he should have conducted a *viva* in shirt sleeves; but that was my impression, and that Professor Mawer, looking more like a good-natured lion than ever, had his feet on the table. We discussed the Old English Riddles. Professor Gordon asked me no questions at all. He said he rarely enjoyed reading theses, but he had enjoyed reading mine. We shook hands. I was free, and I had obviously passed. I went out closing the door quietly, and began to waltz in the passage. Suddenly Professor Gordon looked out, evidently expecting another candidate. Our eyes met; he half raised a thumb. I hope there is a second life if only that I may take a turn with Professor Gordon to the strains of the celestial orchestra.

In due time my thesis came back to me nicely packed in superlative brown paper with gummed label. That day I chanced, in the staff common room at Camborne, to look at the advertisements in *The Times Literary Supplement*. The advertisements in this journal allure teachers and at the same time they keep us steady: 'A Senior English Mistress is required at _____ Grammar School for Girls. Ability to help with Boy Scouts a recommendation. Apply by letter stating other out of school activities and special qualifications.' This last clause makes one pause. Has one any special qualifications? And those Boy Scouts! As likely as not we stay where we are. But this advertisement I looked at was different. The William Noble Fellowship, Liverpool University, it was headed. No testimonials, no activities. Candidates were invited to submit a piece of work to the Adjudicators. All the winner of the fellowship would have to do was to write a book. My lethargic nature was stirred. I went out in a free period; I bought a gummed label from Smith's; I stuck it over the existing label on the already so beautifully tied-up parcel in which Meredith reposed; I directed it to Liverpool University, named my references in a letter-card, and was back teaching Lower VC within half an hour. After this piece of concentrated activity the whole matter went out of my mind.

I was awarded that fellowship. I went back to Hayle one Friday night to find a letter awaiting me from Professor Oliver Elton. He said that I had been elected to the William Noble Fellowship for the coming session, that he himself had liked my study of Meredith, and that he would be glad to have me working in the English School at Liverpool. I went tearing back to Camborne to tell Miss Pratt, nearly breaking my neck on the way by hanging on to a fast butcher's cart and not noticing a lorry approaching from the east. I had supper with Miss Pratt who was as pleased as I was. She said she was sure she could get the Governors' consent to a year's leave of absence for me, so that I need not say farewell to the cliffs and the Mount for ever. I could come back when I had written my book.

Then in the night a hundred doubts and fears assailed me. Could I write a book? Did I want to read the works of George Meredith once more? I did not. I was reading Conrad just then; I was far out on eastern waters with Tom Lingard and the mysterious Edith Travers. Then next morning, skipping along the sands and chasing the waves between Gwithian and Hayle, I had what I thought was a blinding flash of inspiration. I would write a book on 'The Sea in English Literature', beginning with the Seafarer and the Storm Riddles; including

Spenser's horror, and Smart's shout of glory; Smollet's types, and Swinburne's surges, Marryat's straight tales and Conrad's exciting psychology. In that book St Michael's Mount could be set fleeting anew. Cornwall would have a splendid place: smuggling . . . the Falmouth Packets . . . Devon . . . Raleigh . . . Sir Humphrey Gilbert . . . Drake, Westward Ho! I hurried into my cottage and wrote Professor Elton saying I was tired of Meredith and wanted instead to write a book on 'The Sea in English Literature'. Liverpool was on the sea, I said, so that would be very convenient to me. In his gravely courteous reply, without a trace of a smile—we did not smile together over *The Sea in English Literature* until years later—he said he sympathized with me over Meredith, but considered 'The Sea in English Literature' a less good subject for a book. A little vast perhaps. But he was all for people choosing their own subjects and having their own way with them. Liverpool—on the Mersey—would no doubt be as suitable a place as any in which to write the book if, after reflection, I still wished to do so. I was faintly dashed; I wished I had remembered about the Mersey; but I was not to be put off my large designs.

As I was not due to go to Liverpool until October, and the school broke up at the end of July, I had an extra long summer holiday. I went to Austria for it, to Vienna and Salzburg, travelling with a group of people for the most part academic, who wished to polish up their German at the university in Vienna. A course had been arranged. I, who had no German to polish, had the more opportunity of seeing people and places. I remember my confusion of mind; my alternating moods of delight, and of shame and misery. It was the summer of 1923. Austrian students met us on our arrival with nosegays of flowers. I lodged with another student of our party, Nannie MacCullum, in the house of an ex-colonel and his wife. They said they had never meant to fight us; we said we had never meant to fight them. We had vast bundles of paper money; they had lost all their savings. They gave us beer—a drink which I detested—but did not afford beer for themselves. I never ventured to try to persuade them to drink what would have been a pleasure to them, and was a pain to me. I was shy. Once I poured my beer into a plant while our landlady was out of the room. She came back with little cries of pleasure and said, 'Ah, you like the gut beer; yes!' and refilled my glass—tall glasses with waists they used. Nannie and I peered at one another over the brims. Nannie was a delightful companion, a Scot; a good German scholar, and speaking English with what was to me a novel accent; she trilled her r's. When I mocked her she said the only good English spoken in the world was Scotch. She once heard a man say of a woman who spoke good English that she must be either a Scot or a very well-educated Englishwoman. I maintained that the purest English was spoken in Cornwall round about Truro. We liked each other; she was a lilting, gay person.

Of the excursions we made, those which took us on the Danube or up the mountains exhilarated me beyond all telling; but when we went to see museums, galleries and palaces I sought the word *Ausgang*. I liked getting out, and away from these things. I have never been able to enjoy collections, any more than I can enjoy the whole programme in a long concert. The collector's instinct is one of the stupidest of the stupid instincts of man. I pitied King's treasures, no longer cherished in their separate beauty, and pictures hung in gangs; just as I pity flowers bunched by the head in florists' windows. Mass! I hate mass. Men in ranks look like wood toys. Women in ranks are still more frightening because it is more foreign to women's natures to be merged and rigid and commanded. Men have been broken to it for generations, but with us it is just beginning. We seem to be following men down the road to perdition, doing what we are told, thinking what is expected, and perceiving what others perceive. We shall soon be blessed fellows to whom the sun looks like a guinea. We are forgetting Blake. He said:

> 'What,' it will be question'd, 'when the sun rises, do you not see a round disc of fire somewhat like a Guinea?' O no, no, no, I see an Innumerable company of the Heavenly host crying, 'Holy, Holy, Holy is the Lord God Almighty.'

In Vienna in 1923 hatred of the Jews was freely expressed, and, since it was the first time I had met with this hatred, it struck me dumb with fear. Compressed hatred explodes. It is a bitter and humiliating thing to realize for the first time that in our incapacity, our ignorance and malice, we must always in some form or other shift the burden of guilt from ourselves to 'them' or 'it'. Being abstract-minded I had blamed a personification of war; I had blamed It. The Austrians were blaming Them for all the ills that ever they suffered. Their hate was stirring towards action. The first grown-up short story I tried to write was of a hunted Jew. I made him hide in the ice-caves to which we had climbed on one of our excursions. I made him escape into Germany. I did not know that in Germany he was being hunted too; that he would be hounded through the world. Ernst Toller and Adolf Hitler were young then. I had never heard of either.

14

LIVERPOOL
INTERLUDE

In the morning of summer what glory
What worship! The sun is up-rising,
With gold and with crimson surprising
The fields that lie grey with dew hoary.
In the morning of summer what glory
What worship!

In the noontide of summer what benison
Falleth of fruit and of flower!
Man's festival innocent hour;
Bread and wine which the Carpenter's Son
Took with thanks. In the noontide of Summer
What benison falleth!

In the evening of summer what Breath,
What Holy Breath moves in the leaves!
'Tis coolness, coolness He weaves,
And comfort, comfort He bringeth.
In the evening of summer what Holy Breath
Moves in the leaves!

—For a Summer Festival

When, one rainy October evening, I got out at Lime Street, Liverpool, and looked about me, I thought I had perhaps died and reached purgatory without knowing it. Then I decided that this was hell itself. I reached University Hall—to which I had chosen to go rather than find lodgings—wondering which Circle I was in. But the Hall was light and cheerful. Miss Chapman, the Warden, spoke a rarely musical English; the young women next door to me, Margaret Stoyle who was studying Modern Languages, and Kathleen Shedlock, preparing to become a veterinary surgeon, were friendly and welcoming. I had a room of my own and a coal fire.

But I never learnt the geography of Liverpool. All my time there I felt like a waif. Every street played tricks on me, even the street I lived in. One day University Hall seemed to be on one side of it; and the next day on the other. I have never known stationary objects so malevolent. It was some time before I even had the wit to realize that all the tram-lines converged on Pier Head. The first time I went to Birkenhead I insinuated myself on a cattle ferry instead of on a passenger one. Then, perceiving my error, I pretended I had sheep aboard, and became fearfully involved when I was unable to drive off my imaginary flock. In Liverpool all things were in motion without order. Only the procession of lighted trams, which I watched from the steps of the Picton Library, had order. Except for these moving galleons of light, the sunset splendour of Pier Head, the choppy grey waves of the Mersey, the sea-gulls which could fly to Godrevy, and the ceremony of ships, I remember no more of Liverpool than if I had been a snowflake. One angry altercation I remember which conjures up a whole scene of cloth caps, and shawls, and shouting, and derision, and two angry faces, and faces turned to laugh. A taxi-driver yelled to an old woman who did not jump nimbly out of his way, 'Hey! Ma! D'ye think you're home in bed?' And she yelled back, 'Not so much of yer *Ma*. When you've bashed yer head in by the Grace of God 'tisn't I'll nurse yer.'

I went to the university buildings to call on Professor Elton and wished, not for the first time, that I was tall. I have to look

up. Professor Elton when I first knew him was like a lofty crag,
rocky. He was the least soft of critics, and had a way of making
the washy look washier. As he walked up and down the room
he turned now and again and, focusing me with his eye,
volleyed a couple of sentences in my direction. I tried to return
the ball upwards and outwards. But it is hard to hit a moving
object; our interchange grew slower and slower and at length
ceased altogether. A steady silence settled in. It was then that,
with a sudden lightening of his aspect, as though a good
thought had occurred to him, he said, 'But you will like to meet
our Miss Trenery; she too is Cornish.' And I found Grace.
Grace Trenery was lecturer in the English school at Liverpool
University. Her father had been a captain in the Merchant
Navy; he came from Hayle; she knew Hayle; her uncle knew
Hayle; her mother knew Portloe; and would I like to come to
tea on Sunday? I went to tea pretty nearly every Sunday while I
lived in Liverpool.

It is impossible to describe the comfort of these Sundays.
Mrs Trenery with her kind person, her love of poetry—like my
father she knew much by heart—had the lovely politeness of
the Cornish women of her generation; there was warmth in her
courtesy which was inherited by her two daughters. Hospitality
is the queen of virtues. However cold and cloudy the day
outside, however ugly the Liverpool congeries of warehouses,
shops and dwellings, I opened the door of the flat into
humanity and laughter. I remember a ship in a glass bottle; the
sound of the kettle singing; Mrs Trenery's welcoming smile;
and Miss L.K. Barrie, head mistress of Wallasey High School
at that time, and later of King Edward's, Birmingham, sitting
on a divan in front of the fire and saying very little. She was like
an island; a piece of silence surrounded by conversation. But
when she did talk she made me see parts of Scotland in my
mind's eye as vividly as I could see Cornwall. She had a great
gift for delineating wide tracts of country and making the
colours glow. Next to walking myself over open country I liked
to hear her describing it. Her words were springy as heather.
And she had an apt way of recalling to Grace their various

encounters with strange people. *Casual Encounters* is the title of a book which Grace must write some day. The encounters arose partly because Grace has no sense of direction anywhere, not merely, like me, no sense of direction in Liverpool. She could lose herself in a hazelnut, and time has little meaning to her or to anyone in her company. I was invited to spend an evening with her once at Professor Case's. She said we might walk; the distance was not great. We walked up and down streets and other streets and round corners, I taking no count of the way. Grace herself is a territory sufficient; when I enter in I feel folded warmly round, and unwilling to come out into the cold. I remained snug; but with an uneasy consciousness that the Cases expected us at eight. 'Oughtn't we to be nearly there?' I said at last. We stood still and gazed about; Liverpool has few features. I recognized nothing; Grace recognized nothing. Luckily she did remember the address and we managed to find a taxi which took us, late and apologetic, to the door. Professor Case looked Elizabethan with a trim pointed beard. Grace had worked with him on her fine edition of *Much Ado*, one of the volumes of the Arden Shakespeare of which Professor Case was editor-in-chief. He was an exact and exacting scholar.

I was not exact but I was swift. Within a fortnight I had sketched out my entire book down to modern times. No doubt if I had had the gift of prophecy I should have garnered in the future. A wide sweep with quotations from all my favourite authors through the ages: that was my idea. I submitted my sweep to Professor Elton. He took my sheaves as he called them, invited me to meet him again, and I passed a most illuminating and appalling half-hour. Whatever kind of writer I was to become in future it was not a sweeping one. I grew cautious in thirty minutes—only I have a little devil of incaution in me who will always up and out again. Professor Elton's method of giving a writer a sense of responsibility towards his subject matter was quite simple, and depended for its effect on the impact of his personality, and the respect one felt for his own work. He would say, pointing to a poor specimen of my perishing sentences, 'Did you really mean this?' Or, in reply to a doubtfully hazarded remark, of which I immediately perceived the futility once it was out, 'Would you repeat that?' He went through my 'sheaves' and annotated them. Often I perused his annotations with hot ears and speechless fury. But an occasional marginal hieroglyph, which he said was to be interpreted as a compliment, kept me wrestling with expression, though jibbing at the labour like a refractory horse. I am not one who likes emendations and third thoughts. As for my subject I never really regretted choosing it. It taught me more than a more sensible pursuit might have done, since it carried me through many periods and kinds of literature and left me lingering in many a splendid place. Released from the onus of examinations I read with a delicious sense of freedom in the English Library—an ugly room, but with books all easy of access on the shelves. I dearly love to go exploring among books, taking them out and sampling them at my pleasure. The well-chosen English Library was a paradise of convenience and temptation. In addition there was the Picton Library, and the University Library under the guardianship of Dr Sampson. This library was the reverse of free and easy. I spent considerable time in University Hall heartening students who were due to be interviewed by Dr Sampson for some lapse in the entering or returning of a book. Strong women wept on my hearthrug at the mere anticipation of the dread moment. It was in vain that I told them they couldn't be hanged, and that nothing else was irremediable; they passionately bewailed their carelessness. I must say I have never been so careful myself in any other library to fulfil every jot and tittle of the law. I once took, quite unintentionally, a valuable book out of the Bodleian with my own books; I knew what it was to feel that the hounds of hell were on my traces as I raced back with it. The library was closing, but I prevailed on a sandy man with thin hair to allow me through the exhibition room and so into the English reading-room where I insinuated the book among the others under my reserve slip. How appalled Joseph's brethren must have felt when their sacks were opened and the golden cup disclosed! I felt extreme guilt while that Bodleian book was in my unlawful possession. I suppose hardly any other Bodleian book has ever been out in the fresh air almost to the door of Lady Margaret Hall. I committed no such offence at Liverpool and I never saw Dr Sampson angry. The only time I encountered him he was very peaceable though pungent. He came into an inner room of the library where I was reading a copy of Saewulf's *Pilgrimage*, the story of the journey of an English merchant in which there is a grand description of a storm off Joppa. The pilgrimage, originally in medieval Latin, had been translated by T. Wright and included in his compilation *Early Travels in Palestine*. Dr Sampson came and looked over my shoulder, making me jump. Except that he was better looking, he was a little like one might have expected Dr Johnson to be, in an untidy coat. He said, 'Do you know anything about the Saewulf manuscript?' I said that there was only one manuscript which was in the library of Corpus Christi College, Cambridge. He said, 'Don't you want to see it?' I said no. He said, 'Don't you want to study old manuscripts?' I said no. He said, 'Don't you want to learn paleography?' I said no. 'Do you trust that editor?' Yes, I said, I did. 'And that translator?' 'Yes'. 'Who is T. Wright?' I said I didn't know. He said, 'You'll always be happy; you have faith,' and he never took any interest in me again. But I took a great interest in him and in his gipsy poems. I happened to be staying in Oxford with the Eltons many years later and heard Professor Elton's account of Dr Sampson's funeral with full gipsy ceremonial in Wales. It is the only account of a funeral by which I have been profoundly impressed.

I did not study paleography nor prepare myself for a scholarly interest in manuscripts. But I became more and more interested in reading Old English literature. I went to Professor Allen Mawer's lectures and I made attempt after attempt to translate Old English verse into modern verse. Professor Elton had tried his hand, but said he was not proud of his results. But he showed me the manuscript of Lascelles Abercrombie's Nightingale Riddle which was so good that I was convinced that translation of Old English into a modern idiom could be not merely adequate but beautiful. I tried *The Seafarer* and the Storm Riddles and the fine sea poetry of *Beowulf*. But I never succeeded in pleasing myself. As an instrument for expressing the wintry sound of the sea the form of verse used by the Old English writers is unequalled. The peculiarity of the music of a breaking wave is that it starts from many points, not from one fixed point. This peculiarity is echoed in the Old English line. The three combined stresses and alliterations are like the curled lips of the wave, from which the music is variously poured; and these breaking points shift in every line. There is no monotony and there is no rest. As the wave withdraws, the rough shingle of the consonants prolongs the roar. I knew exactly what I wanted to get. I could hear it in the holidays when I was walking on Vault Beach, near Gorran Haven, but I never encompassed what I sought. I never managed to enmesh either the pebbly dispersed sound, nor the sound of the crowding of the storm, nor the hiss of hail, 'coldest of grains', nor the laughter of the iceberg as she dug into the sides of ships. Nor could I recreate the forelands and the nesses and the windy walls. A few lines of H.C. Wylde's prose achieved more than anything I managed for the cliffs—'steep rocky slopes, toilsome upward tracks, narrow paths where only one can go, ways hard to find, towering headlands, and many a place where goblins dwell'.

Apart from Old English the sea poetry which gave me most unfading pleasure was Spenser's. He did not, like the Riddle-makers, let his spirits fly out into the storm and go heaving and smashing and exulting with it; he shuddered at the deep, gaping mouths of the waves. The interest is transferred from the furious glory of the elements to the man at their mercy. Spenser expresses fear. But it was not Colin Clout's horror of the Irish Channel to which I returned; it was to the magic of the sea fantasy in *The Faerie Queene*, renewable as morning and summer. How lovely I thought the wavering story of Florimell's love for Marinell, when first I gazed through the clear pool of Spenser's music at its intricacies. It spreads itself out like the

tree sea-weeds which as children we used to watch floating
with other treasures in the sea-pools of the rocks. If the story is
taken out of its element it collapses into a damp mass, like
those same sea-weeds if taken out of the pool. Poetry can never
be transferred.

But in its proper place this poetry is a spell which enchants
us as direct natural representation could never enchant. Even
physical sensation is heightened by it. It is impossible to
express in a direct way the sensations of a human body being
lipped by the waves and borne up by them. But Spenser
achieved it indirectly once for all when Florimell casts herself
into the sea and Proteus takes her in his arms:

> Her up betwixt his rugged hands he reard,
> And with his frory lips full softly kist,
> Whiles the cold ysickles from his rough beard,
> Dropped adowne upon her yvorie brest.

I can read the story of Marinell and Florimell and its
consummation in the marriage feast of the Thames and
Medway over and over and over again. In Spenser the English
waves on a summer strand are changed before our eyes to sea
maidens:

> Their watchet mantles fringed with silver round.

I sometimes think that Spenser alone among the poets has
vivified, in a truly poetic form, England's sea and rivers. His
liquid words are the dappled surfaces of water. I have never
seen the Medway except in the bridal dress Spenser made for
her, a vesture:

> That seemed like silver, sprinckled here and theare
> With glittering spangs that did like starres appeare,
> And wau'd upon, like water chamelot:

Spenser saved my senses in Liverpool; his poetry is an
incomparable solace to those who are away from where they

long to be. Perhaps he made it so faerily tangible because he was away from where he wanted to be himself.

Liverpool that winter seemed to me, when I could penetrate beyond its dead-dragon-like bulk, to be surrounded by flat fields, with last year's birds' nests frozen in the thorns. When I went to Exmouth at Christmas I was in such a whirl of excitement that I nearly seized and kissed the wrong man for my father on the crowded Exeter platform to my father's annoyance, for he never liked to feel shame at the foolishness of any of his family burn in his own bosom. He was humming a hymn tune hard by the time I reached him. But nothing mattered as long as I was home. He had felt, too, that I was a long way away in Liverpool. He thought his sons had better brains, but he missed his daughters more. Whenever Susan went away he was inconsolable till she came back, and I had my impregnable place. We used to go to Black Hill together to fish in the reservoir. He looked exactly like a fairy on Black Hill. It was his unwrinkled fresh-coloured face, his little pointed white beard, his bright blue eyes and something timeless in his figure. No one ever enjoyed his retirement more I think. He could fish, staying out nearly motionless all day, watching the water but not catching anything. He used to say he would like to live in a wood; but he never did. I hope there are beech trees in heaven, or meadows with buttercups, or something resembling Dartmoor with bees humming in the heather. He loved to be out of doors as much as my mother loved to be within, reading by the window, her lips moving as she read the most absorbing parts. All my excursions beyond my home merely warmed up my heart afresh to come back to it. The more I was away, and the more I got to know a great variety of people, the more I realized how enormously lucky I was to have been born into a family I not only loved but liked. I had thought this affection was usual; I began to perceive it was quite rare. Susan and I slipped down to Caerhays Barton for a few days in January, but it was too early for primroses. That year in Liverpool is the only year of my life in which I have not found wild primroses towards the end of January or the beginning of February. Susan sent me primroses and violets in a great biscuit tin, enough for me and all my friends, but she could not send me Trevennen Wood or the Woodbury lanes.

The flowers I remember vividly round about Liverpool came out after the Easter holidays. There were bluebells and buttercups, buttercups that made the flat fields shine with summer. I used to set them glowing in a basket among grasses and take them to surprise Mrs Elton. Mrs Elton had come to be, with Grace Trenery, my compensation for Liverpool. She was a Highland Scot, the person most compact of poetry in its changingness and its unchangingness I ever met. Her nature responded to every breath and reflection, yet stayed clear, and retained a morning, fleeting quality. I suppose it was a quality of truthfulness to itself, an entire absence of falsification or of coating. It was not that she was easy to know; but whereas most people protect themselves by a hardening and thickening shell, she protected herself by an increasing delicacy, and tenderness, and fineness of touch which, though it made her the more vulnerable, made also for more instant withdrawal. I remember her first note inviting me to lunch and to spend the afternoon; I remember my absurdly early start so as not to be late; changing buses would take time I thought! I remember loitering about in the searching cold for the right moment to ring the bell, and the pleasure of being shown into a room of which an image still lives for me in the fire-light colours. Mrs Elton could never live in an ugly room. It was as natural for her to make her surroundings harmonious as it is for me not to have any surroundings at all or heterogeneous ones. With her the useful and necessary had just sufficient of order, seemliness and ceremony to redeem daily life from flat familiarity. I always think the most beautiful moment in the story of the two disciples on the way to Emmaus is when their Companion by the way is made known to them in the breaking of bread. It amazes me when I look back to consider how unselfishly Professor and Mrs Elton extended their hospitality to the raw and shy. Mrs Elton had been shy herself. When I knew her better I used to love to hear of her girlhood, of her friendship with the Burne-Joneses and others whose names and work I knew. Instead of mere integuments linking the generations here were connections still vital, still feeling. And Yeats, my favourite of poets, Mrs Elton had known him well and his sister, Miss Lily Yeats. J.B. Yeats, the poet's father, had been a close friend of the family; he had called Professor Elton the Englishman, which was a good soubriquet. Yet this quintessential Irishman and this Englishman had been able to make allowances for and appreciate one another. It was perhaps because Professor Elton, though he was the Englishman, had no trace of the provincial or of the sectarian in his mind; nor was his perception contained by any particular period or century. Literary fashion and the criticism which depended on it he despised; and he could examine with interest manifestation of the human spirit foreign to his own temper. Nothing, I think, could be more alien to him than the various manifestations of religious enthusiasm—in his massive adherence to reason his mind was eighteenth century in tone—yet his essay on Enthusiasm is an acute and even a sympathetic study. He had a truly critical mind; his instinct was to examine and judge; but he did not pre-judge—except perhaps the 'odd'. To the odd he was not indulgent. He was equipped to judge by the immense range of his accurate knowledge; but his criticism has also the vitality which comes from force of feeling. He did not pretend to a feeling for poetry in order to make pronouncement; he made pronouncements because his feeling for poetry was profound, and extended to the literature of many nations up and down the thread of time.

He had a stately sense of metre and rhythm and proportion. His reading aloud, for combined meaning and music, was the best I have ever listened to. I only heard him once in Liverpool; but later in Oxford, when I was a frequent guest in the house, he could be persuaded to read aloud after coffee at night. One could even make requests. One request of mine was for Byron's *Vision of Judgment*. I had it that night—the wit, the mockery, the gale of laughter, the tremendous swell of indignation, the mastery of the thing. Other renderings of which the echoes linger in my ear are of Spenser's *Mutabilitie* Cantos, Smart's great *Hymn to Creation*. Marvell's *Upon Appleton House* and Skelton's *Philip Sparrow*. When I first knew him Professor Elton's main interest was already beginning to swing from English criticism to translation. The Slavonic languages—Russian, Polish, Czech, Serbian—he learnt them all in succession and translated their poetry into English. Listening to some of these translations read aloud—some short versions of modern Serbian poetry in particular had great power—I tasted a communion with strange peoples which no political oratory has ever produced in me. Nations are linked most closely by their poetry; more poetry and fewer pamphlets; and a council of translators perhaps! Fine translations are too few and those which exist are not disseminated.

Mrs Elton's poetry was more lyrical; her pity nearer home. She had pity especially on all prisoners and captives. She was singular I think among those in whom pity is strong in that for her those whom she pitied retained their humanity. 'Objects of pity' is a perilous phrase, terrifying because of depersonalization. Objects have no rights. But for Mrs Elton people in prison were still people to be connected with the world outside and with their own past. She had known women prisoners in Liverpool. Her recent book *Locks, Bolts and Bars*, a study of prison conditions during the Napoleonic wars, with stories of the escapes of English and French prisoners, emphasizes the abiding humanity of the fugitives. A hundred little touches, matters of choice, mark the book as hers. But she can be contained in no book or poem. Her meaning was in herself; her appreciation of the absurd; her richly-stored memory; her voice—she spoke on up breaths as well as down breaths; her manner so utterly her own; a certain felicity inseparable from her; her occasional, rare Scottish stories; her elegance.

As soon as summer came I no longer felt like a prisoner in Liverpool. I could get out of it on my bicycle. The longest trip I took was to the Lakes, setting out suddenly one day, merely because after a visit to the bank I had money in my pocket. It was one of those early June days which come as rare gifts, and which convey the impression that it will never rain again. After leaving the bank I had bicycled so far through grimy ways in order to get out of Liverpool and its worse satellites that it seemed a pity to come back. I had a thin mackintosh in my saddlebag; I added to it a toothbrush and a cotton nightdress which I bought for 1s. 11d. I wired Miss Chapman at the Hostel, and I reached Lancaster in time for bed and breakfast at a C.T.C. house. Those lodgings sponsored by the Cyclists' Touring Club I have always found satisfactory and in those days they were cheap. The sun next morning was as splendid as the day before. I bicycled through the air grinning with pleasure; I remember chiefly wild roses, the pink ones; and I remember coming to the level lake of Windermere and feeling so sharp set with hunger that I felt I could eat a Hansel and Gretel's cottage, roof and all. I remember the beauty in evening light of a little polished lake, and I remember the lodging I found at Grasmere, my bathe in the lake, the supper of cold boiled beef and pickles and going up Dunmail-Raise in the sparkle of morning. Sometimes I left my bicycle and climbed. I climbed Helvellyn. I remember the glory of Thirlmere as the mist, lifting, revealed it in its primal clarity; how at the top my pleasure was spoiled by the chill which struck through the cotton frock and the short woollen jacket I was wearing. Unpreparedness is not the watchword for mountaineering. This truism I did not fully appreciate until, after bicycling and climbing for a week, I went round the lake on which Keswick stands and turned my wheels for Windermere. It began to rain. I knew Cornish rain, but not rain like this, relentless rain without a rift anywhere in any region of the sky. A lowering sky and malicious, sending forth rain which took pleasure in smiting at me, in running down my neck and into my shoes. The drops pelted and spun. Mud splashed my cotton garment until I had the appearance of a crustacean; my hands grew so cold that when I stopped at a pub for a hot drink my fingers could not undo a button. I made for Lancaster pedalling hard. The wild roses did not smile at me now; they were, like me, in eclipse. I began, not for the first time, to perceive I was no true tramp; I discovered how, as soon as wet rain soaked me, I began to think of comfort, of a hot bath, of a fire, of steaming coffee. I began to think how pleasant University Hall was and pictured Kathleen and Margaret brewing coffee. I smelt hot buttered toast. By evening I reached Preston and took refuge in the despised train, my bicycle going into the luggage van with other bicycles, and I going into a third-class carriage with other third-class women who did not like the look of me. On few occasions, I must say, have I presented a less pleasing appearance. I was too well watered for society. One old lady gave me advice. She said, 'My dear, do you know you are saving up for yourself a future of misery and dependence, misery and dependence? Rheumatism!' I thought I felt a premonitory twinge in my wrists. I began to steam. I tried to take my mind of rheumatism by thinking of lying in a bath right up to the neck in hot water; I could feel the ring of water slipping round my neck; I could feel the water as I played with it; I could feel the weight of it as I tried to lift my stretched out legs. 'Bath salts!' I said to myself. 'Kathleen's best bath salts!' And with that I went to sleep, and the old lady who had threatened me wih rheumatism woke me up at Liverpool. I slipped unseen into the Hall just before midnight, stripped off my garments into one hot bath, and insinuated my person into another. It was better than roses. I sometimes fear that of the two strange constituents of which we are compounded there is more body to me than soul. Yet I am slight in figure. My soul must be the merest shadow of shadows.

The next journey I made was after I had bidden farewell to the University of Liverpool and my status of William Noble Fellow. I had had a good year. And I would busily have prayed for the soul of him 'who gave me wherewith to scoleye' if I could have thought he would have liked it. On the whole, from what I could gather of the late Mr Noble, it seemed to me that he would have condemned the practice as Popish. I had heard that he handled his beautifully bound books in gloves, and that he provided clean pairs for any guests he took into his library. His soul was probably in a better state of grace than my own.

Still I thought of him as I made my way out of Liverpool. The kindest benefaction, the freest, the most gracious any rich man can bestow is, I think, to give a young man or a young woman, or an old man or an old woman if it comes to that, time to write a book, entirely unregulated time to write a book in a place where he is likely to make some friends. I was not sorry to say goodbye to Liverpool. I was extremely sorry to say goodbye to friends I had made there.

The best of friends is that they abide and can be found again. I was leaving friends in Liverpool, but I was going towards friends I had made earlier. Bertha Wright and her friend Catherine Maclean were at Caerphilly near Cardiff, and my idea was to bicycle slowly down through Wales, stay a couple of nights with them, go on to South Devon to my family, and then into Cornwall to Truro to be a guest at my friend Marjorie Pascoe's wedding. I posted my wedding garments and my wedding present; I made arrangements to borrow a hat on the spot; and, free of care, I set out again on my travels unencumbered with goods; this time my improvident trusting was not punished. It seems to me now incredible that I should have started without a map, trusting only to fitful memories of odd words dropped here and there which had made me want to see certain places. I skirted the north coast to Conway, and then zigzagged south through the midst of Wales, going sometimes by directing posts, sometimes by what people said; staying in cottages some nights, sleeping out some nights and hearing frogs croaking. I forget where I heard the chorus of frogs. Time was all my own. Nobody was expecting me at any particular moment. I felt a participation, an outgoing of myself, with Wales, which I never experienced in the Lakes. The people seemed akin to me. They told me funny stories before I went to bed, and made me practise pronouncing with a proper Welsh accent the enormous long names of places. Nearly all my hosts were chapel-goers, but some denounced the Bible-punchers. There was a man, I was told, and he made the collection indeed at the chapel. And he was asked one Sunday how much it was. And he said, 'It is in my own pocket with my own money, whatever. I will tell you of it next week. And to market he went, and a little heifer calf he bought. And it was Charity they called her when she grew into a cow indeed. A fine cow she was.'

The weather was hot in Wales. I remember going up a turfy mountain because it was in my way, and my gratitude for the solid shade of a rare rock under which I rested, moving myself round with the shade as the sun moved in the sky. It is idle to tell me that the chariot of the sun is not driven across the sky every day. He flamed in Wales. I went by green ways and heard the music of falling water; once by Festiniog I found myself among the slates; one night I knocked at a door and was told by a woman who was not Welsh, and who minced her words, that she was sure her boarding house would be too expensive for me. I said I hoped all her sheep would die. But I don't suppose she owned any sheep. Parts of Wales smelt of them. I can remember the outline of Cader Idris against an orange and lemon sky as I turned away from that prim house and the mincing woman. Three weeks or so of July I idled in Wales and I do not remember that it rained at all. I became summer's tanling in the Black Mountains. And I came to Brecon, and so down to where I began to look for precise directions to my friends' house near Caerphilly. It seemed miraculous to me that the roads they had indicated on their little plan should be there; that those roads had remained still and quiet while I had come down from Liverpool; that the house should be just where my friends had told me it would be, and that I should go in and find them both, and be welcomed, and delight to listen to their voices, so different from the voices of my companions by the way. Catherine gave me unguents for my burnt face; cooling and fragrant appliances. And I went into a bath, head and all. I remember the fruit we ate; and the talk at night. I remember a new volume of Mr De la Mare's poems, and how I cut the pages open with my forefinger, not thinking of its being Catherine's book until I perceived the jagged edges; I remember going to bed; the coolness of sheets; a bedside light; and making up verses:

In your spare room lies abed
My body clean and comforted
With nightgown smooth and linen sheet
And fleecy fall of fine blanket . . .

And then I fell asleep.

UP TROON

No whisper of wave, yet caressingly, curve on curve,
Smooth lines open and swerve
Around me. In the still air,
Wide arms and quiet breast
Woo me that I may rest
Lovingly there.

I would not seek for home or human fellow
In this silence the carns hallow;
Silent the sky is spread
Without rift or fold descending
From the high arches bending
Over my head.

Then in the silence was it the mist's white finger
That warned me not to linger,
Or was it the hoofs of Pan
Heard far away in the hollow
And seeming to follow, follow
Me as I ran?

—*On Bodmin Moor*

From Cardiff, taking my bicycle with me, I crossed by steamer to Weston-super-Mare and thence, by easy stages, now skirting rivers, now hidden in lanes, now flying down the moorland hills and now crawling up them, I came to Truro, to my friend Marjorie Pascoe's wedding. As I went I chanted sometimes snatches from Spenser's *Epithalamion*:

> Open the temple gates unto my love,
> Open them wide that she may enter in.

It was a fine thing to be married I thought; but better to be drinking the air before me as I rode.

The wedding impressed me very much; I tried to pray. I remember the arch of light illuminating Marjorie as she entered the church with her father; and how the sunshine received her and Harold together as they left the darkness of the aisle when the service was over. I drank champagne and was wild to be off again, free of my wedding garments, and feeling the air opening and closing behind me in the lanes of light. I wanted to reach Bolventor on Bodmin Moor that evening, and soon I had left the Goss Moor behind me and entered on the wilder waste. On a summer evening the moor is still; there are no trees with leaves to rustle. In winter when a wind blows it hisses and froths through the wiry vegetation with a timeless, desolating sound that links us with what is most ancient in man's history. As I bicycled over the moor that evening on the main Bodmin-Launceston road it was absolutely quiet; only near the occasional pools—Doughty's 'like liquid flint' best describes them—were birds flying low and calling. At Bolventor I put up in the little post-office on the opposite side of the road to Jamaica Inn, had supper and went walking on the moor. All the heath seemed soaked in summer, the earth warmer than the sky. Swallows which lilt even in their downward motion—I can imagine lilting up but not down if I were a bird—darted round me as I reached the summit of a tor. I began to wish I had never arranged to sleep cooped up in a room like a lidded box when I might have inherited a moor and an entire sky for my sleeping chamber. The enchantment of the moor is in the suggestion of fluidity fixed, the long, sweeping lines that flow and yet are motionless, smooth-backed waves that will never break. By the sea there is always a murmur even on the calmest night; in farm lands the wind is in the oats and the wheat and the barley; it whistles through thorns in the hedges. In the woods it has a thousand instruments to play on. But on this summer night on the moor, within four miles or so of Bolventor, all was incredibly silent, as silent as snow. And tranced in the silence was all time past. I was not frightened. Then, almost without my perceiving it, the summer haze became a mist. I did not mind; I still loitered; there was plenty of time. It was only when I began to make my way back that I knew the deceptiveness of distance; the confounding of space; the bewilderment as direction is lost; the cattle-tracks that lead only to other cattle-tracks; the silken cotton grass that gave warning of the sucking sound of quagmires. I remembered stories of cows and horses caught in quagmires, victims too terrified to help those who were trying to get them out with ropes. I wished for a friendly tree with life in it. Here were only ling and furze and bedstraw white with devil's spit; peat; stone outcrops orange with lichen; and brown pools like fathomless eyes. If I had been a witch I could not have felt further removed from the human events of the morning. I began to run, I fell down, I should be caught. I got up again. And as suddenly as I became frightened I ceased to be frightened; I was free of fear. I was only walking in the mist on the moor not very deep in from Bolventor. I should get back quite easily. I did get back but not until well after midnight, just in time to prevent the old lady with whom I had arranged to lodge from rousing a couple of men to make a search. No will-o'-the-wisp mis-light thee! If I had seen a will-o'-the wisp I should have felt reassured. It was the nothingness of everything which unstrung me. I have often felt the shadowyness of existence. 'Let me never be confounded!' I sing the canticle with a double intention. Identity? What is it? I can puzzle myself stupid over that. 'I am; say that I AM hath sent thee.'

When the holidays were over and I went back to Camborne to school I was not as sorry as I thought I should be. Teaching has compensations. Camborne children are not undemonstrative and I felt welcomed home. Poor children! They little knew. For now, refreshed by my long spell, I was like a whirlwind in the school. The course I chose for the upper school was enthusiastically wide. Instead of 'set-books' I chose a syllabus known as 'Outlines of English Literature'. We made a chart to show how the great English writers and their works fitted into time, and then we read what we liked—which often meant, I sadly fear, what I liked. We trusted that something in the English paper of the Cambridge Senior Examination—there was a 'general' paper in those days—would suit us. Some girls, who no doubt would have cared for literature anyway, grew to read with attention and delight under this scheme. But for some I think on looking back it must have been burdensome. It demanded more than a fair share of time from girls with a scientific or mathematical bent. Yet a narrow course of set books can be deadly; no single book suits thirty different girls. More than any other subject the teaching of English needs leisure. Given time every child in the land could enter into some corner of his birthright. One has only to watch small children listening to stories, or girls of eleven acting them. I especially like to watch girls of twelve or thirteen when they perceive that a story is funny. The reactions of children to literature, children not brought up to feel that there are some things they ought and some they ought not to like, are very downright. 'Aren't we going to read anything but these old stories of Gods and Heroes?' a black-haired gnome of a child asked me once. 'I hate these old Gods and Heroes.' I asked her what she had been reading under the desk. Children never realize how completely their faces give them away when they are reading under the desk. When told she could read her book openly—it was *Jane Eyre*—something was lost to her. There is a stolen, breathless enchantment in reading under the desk which open reading lacks. From eleven to fifteen or so most girls are in the ravenous stage for reading. They need enough;

good and bad alike; they take plenty of roughage. We need to lay in large provision and give ample opportunity for sampling. It grieves me to the heart in the present time of shortage (1947), that educational publishers should be producing, instead of good reading books in abundance, idiotic 'Courses in English' and 'Comprehension Tests'—all the dull paraphernalia for the study of language; as though language and literature can ever be separated alive.

But often I have had my doubts about the teaching of literature, especially when I have been preparing candidates for entrance to Oxford or Cambridge. Papers seem to be set to test maturity of taste in immature persons. Taste cannot be assessed. It is a matter of experience and personal idiosyncrasy. I remember my hot rush of shame when first I read Mr Somerset Maugham's *Christmas Holiday*. Was I, in teaching, like that frightful mother? This satire of Maugham's is an awful parable for all those of us who are engaged not in producing poetry and pictures and music and sculpture, but in peddling them. We talk. We can hardly escape damnation. When I think of Venetia showing her children what to feel in the picture galleries of Paris; when I see her in her dining-room with its pictures in the most modish taste, and its electric fire simulating flames, I always decide to resign from teaching. To trade in feeling is the worst of trades. In these periods of doubt I shun literature, I elicit groans from all the upper school because, instead of reading poetry or acting stories, we practise diligently analysis into clauses and written exercises which I mark with furious attention to 'correctness'. 'Alice's spelling still needs great care,' I write in the terminal reports.

Evangelists are busy with the arts, busier than ever. As an army of caterpillars I sometimes see us, preying on the fairest flowers and fruit. 'From all who are interested in the arts, from all teachers, lecturers, regenerators . . .' do we need some such new clause in the Litany?

The fear of being a cicerone made me begin to scheme, as soon as I got back to teaching, to get away from it again. Two years of freedom I aimed at this time. I began casting about for money to live on during the two years and decided that I must save up; I, who had never saved a ha'penny in my life, now adopted this unlikely expedient. Thoreau's *Walden* gave me an idea, but I did not resort to the woods; I took an unfurnished cottage in Troon, my landlord being the Mr Bastion who had helped me to erect my tent at Gwithian. The Bastions lived in Troon where they kept a shoe shop, and where Mr Bastion made and mended shoes. My cottage was one of four standing in a row in Troon Square. On my left was Mr Percy Rowe's shop; on my right a farmhouse owned by Mr Jewell stood at right angles to the cottages. At night I could hear a rat making his way from Mr Jewell's outhouses to Mr Percy Rowe's sacks of barley-meal. I never saw him; I heard his pilgrimages, and the pilgrimages of his kind. My cottage was too lean for his visits compared with Mr Percy Rowe's; but through my walls he danced his gallop galliards on the way to the feasting. I had three bedrooms in two of which I placed beds, and in the third a tin bath. I had a kitchen and a sitting-room which I furnished with Miss Pratt's kitchen table and five pounds' worth of remarkable antiques. I surprised Troon with Susan's taste in blue curtains. Susan came to stay and thought both Troon and the cottage ugly. It is true that when she arrived I had lost the key so that she had to get in through the window; that I could not find the matches for some time and that, showing her round with a bicycle lamp, I let her trip down the unexpected step into the kitchen. She has never forgotten the fine casserole of chicken I provided for her supper though.

Food flowed in Troon. I had had the notion of combining with a saving in rent—I only paid four shillings a week for my cottage—a saving in food. Beans had been Thoreau's main dish. I bought beans. But even when at long last I succeeded in cooking them so that they were soft I felt a strong distaste for them. Beans are not a human food. I would as soon not eat as eat the unaccompanied bean. Instead of attempting it I went to see Mrs Lovelock in her shop and Mrs Percy Rowe in hers. With these shops at my door and Mrs Bastion near, it would have been the merest affectation in me to subsist on beans.

Instead I ate everything that was nice. Although times were hard in Troon, and unemployment throughout the district brought despair to many an honourable man, although the railway station was the frequent scene of farewells as men from the old Cornish mines went out to use their skill in the new mines of other lands, food was abundant and sound, various and cheap. We received the tribute of the world. Yet it was the food produced near at hand which I enjoyed most. I stepped about two dozen paces for cream and rich butter, chickens and eggs. Troon wives were good cooks. How I should like a Troon split with cream and honey, a saffron cake, or a hot pasty now. The Galloping Major (an old lady riding on the shaft of a donkey-wheels) used to take pasties hot from the home-ovens, down to the men at Holman's Foundry. I was always being given something either to warm my nattlings or the cockles of my heart. Some home-made elderberry wine did make me feel that it had reached and set aglow these mysterious organs. When Mrs Bastion baked splits she put some through the window for me. A casual acquaintance in Beacon—not even a parent—remarked to me once as I was on my way through the village to school that he'd heard I had no leeks for winter. 'What, no licks? You must have licks. Licky broth and licky pasty are the thing for your vitals in this bitter weather, my dear maid.' When I got back to Troon that night licks were sprouting like young palm trees on either side of my door. My fecklessness provoked compassion and some scorn. I hate the look of a naked rabbit. Skin one I could not. Mrs Lovelock said to me, 'What! a great maid like you cean't skin a rabbit? You ought to be 'sheamed.'

The Bastions had had my cottage distempered cream. Alice darkened my sitting-room floor with some such stuff as oaker-line. The bedroom floors I did not even darken; they retained their boardiness. Mrs Bastion said she thought Troon would think it funny if I didn't have a bit of carpet or canvas on the stairs, seeing the stairs were the first object that met the eye when the front door was opened. I don't remember whether I succumbed to a bit of canvas or not. I rather think I did. It is always foolish to be thought 'funny' in a village. Once a handsome toad found his way into my front passage; I got him to hop on the fire-shovel and was bearing him to the door when the postman opened it. I nearly precipitated the toad against his middle button. 'Why didn' 'ee take un up in your hands?' said he. Why indeed? Why shouldn't I touch a toad or a bat? Perhaps it was memories of Grimm and Andersen. Wicked step-mothers and witches placed toads in their bosoms and exchanged malice with them. Perhaps my fire-shovel scared all the other toads away. I daresay my toad told the other toads of the great terror, how upon the platform of an engine he had been lifted up. I never had another toad in.

Water was a difficulty at Troon; we all had to fetch it from the spout in buckets or pitchers. I was lucky in that Mr Percy Rowe fetched his with a pony-contrivance drawing a barrelful at a time; and I was welcome to use from his store while it lasted. I only drew water with my pitcher when the barrel was empty. I had my own rain-water barrel at the back. So had we all. I used to hear one of my neighbours washing outside in the mornings. He would sing a hymn, often trying a four-line hymn to a six-line tune or vice versa, and fitting the words in as best he could between the gurglings he made as his hand passed over his mouth in washing. 'There is a green . . . gurgle-gurgle-gurgle . . . hill far a-a-way without . . . gurgle, gurgle, gurgle . . . a city wall.' When I heard, 'There is a green hill', or 'Oh, where is my wandering boy tonight?' or 'When the roll is called up yon . . . gurgle, gurgle, gurgle . . . der . . .' I knew it was time for me to wash myself and get ready for school. 'Rimmington' was at that time a tune which had suddenly taken hold of Troon. Boys whistled it; the Galloping Major sped her donkey on with it; men added grace notes to the main. We all sang Rimmington, though Miss Eustace's aunt declared that there was no more tune in it than a stick of rhubarb.

My daily bicycle ride from Troon to school was largely through built-up ways; down through Beacon I would speed, down Beacon Hill to the school by Camborne Railway Station.

But before I began the descent I could look over the low stone hedges to a landscape opening under the eyelids of the morn with a radiance that set me singing. Tregonning and Godolphin lift themselves clear of the darkness or the mist. Even in rainy weather or cold, even in furious gales or hopeless drizzle through which the derelict engine-houses gloomed, I never reached school without feeling my heart glad. I quaffed the air; and it enlivened my ghost. As I reached the school gates girls would be streaming in from Redruth and Portreath; from Lanner and Carnkie; girls from as far afield as St Day and St Agnes. Girls from Hayle, Gwithian and Conner Downs; girls on bicycles from Praze. From the familiar Camborne streets they came walking, and from the near farms and hamlets, through Treslothan woods or Knave-go-by fields. I felt especially drawn to the country children, children who, on Saturdays and Sundays, were living almost unchanged such a life as I myself had lived at Gorran and Caerhays. Lilian Blair and her sister from the schoolhouse at Praze especially used to remind me of myself and my sister. They would come sometimes, on nipping days, with little hot bottles of water in their pockets to warm their hands. Bicycling is cold work in winter for the first mile or two.

On Saturdays and Sundays I enjoyed bicycling to the villages from which the children came; I liked to know their journeys. I particularly recall Crowan as I saw it one Sunday afternoon, a Crowan drenched in sunlight, a Crowan given over entirely to sleepy cats and a sheep-dog stretched out on the crown of the road too happy to raise his head as I passed. Sunday-dinner seemed to have overwhelmed the world. Once when Susan was staying with me we went out beyond Praze to Clowance, and explored the deserted gardens. We wished the empty house were ours; we would not have left it desolate, we said, like those St Aubyns. The river Hayle rises in the Clowance woods. Susan has not my passion for trespassing, but when she does trespass she trespasses in the grand manner. I once gave my name as Fanny Price, Mansfield Park, Hertfordshire, to a gamekeeper who asked it of me in some wood I had reached from Liverpool. But Susan one day assumed without ostentation the air of a Pendarves. She was taking her ease in a private part of Pendarves Wood when fellow trespassers approached her, wavered, and said, 'We hope we are not intruding.' 'No', said Susan, a Jane Austenish idiom springing naturally to her lips with the pride of possessions. 'Pray, go anywhere you wish.'

During winter evenings in my cottage I continued to struggle by fits and starts with *The Sea in English Literature*. By this time my enthusiasm had frosted over. To prepare a subject is a pleasure; but to set out one's findings in order on paper is a sore task. Words are small units. If the Liverpool Adjudicators had not approved my first draft and given me a grant in aid of publication, and if Professor Elton had not periodically suggested that I should send him my 'sheaves' I should have kicked the whole thing into the waste-paper basket. I did kick it there frequently, but never in that final manner which ends in a bit of shrivelled ash. After much pain of writing and re-writing, my manuscript was ready. I had meant to write a kind of Introduction to Conrad; instead I had reached to within three hundred years of him and laid down my pen. The Liverpool University Press published the book. When I returned from blowing about on the cliffs one dark November afternoon to find my six presentation copies awaiting me in a neat parcel I was elate. But when I opened the book almost the first quotation which caught my eye was a comic misprint. I had quoted J. C. Squire's poem:

> There was an Indian who had known no change.

The line read, in my book:

> There was an Indian who had no change.

I was hot with shame and confusion. But when the reviews came in, and reviews were long and laudatory in those days, no one had noticed my error. Only Professor Elton and I exchanged, when I next went to Oxford, our final smile in relation to *The Sea in English Literature*.

The next thing I did was to buy a motor bicycle. I was walking in Exeter High Street with Susan during the Christmas holidays when I saw displayed in a shop window an elegant little motor bicycle, a two-stroke, a Velocette, the latest model. I kept on returning to eye its blackness, its sheen, and its slim mile-devouring look. I asked the price; forty-odd pounds; and I had forty-odd pounds saved up towards my two free years. I compared the distant pleasure of two free years and the immediate satisfaction of the Velocette. Distant prospects have a cold appeal; the immediate is enticing and warm; I should save railway-fares I said to the reluctant side of myself, and the Velocette became mine. I bought it that day and went up to take delivery two days later. As in bottom gear I chugged up and down a lane, and strained my ears to catch the instructions of a beery voice, I wished with all my heart I had kept my eyes fixed on distant hopes instead of setting myself astride a snorting little dragon. By the time I got into second gear my spirits lightened; in top they rocketed. My instructor whirled me out of Exeter on the pillion; at the top of Exton Hill he left me and off I went to Exmouth. Had there been any traffic to speak of on the road I should have broken my neck. As it was I arrived triumphant and hooting, but unable to stop, outside our dwelling. I had to go down the street and up another before I found wit to stop and get off.

A week later I set out on my new possession for Camborne. A motor bicycle likes to eat up the miles fast, but I was ill-prepared to digest them. I had no overalls, and it was a sparkling, frosty, January day. My luggage was not well adjusted. I had tied it on with a bit of string. Round about Okehampton the air seemed to crackle with cold, and my hands were no longer my obedient servants. An R.A.C. scout gave chase. He warned me that my luggage was falling off. 'Vibrations, you know,' he said. 'You new to it? Nice little machine you've got.' I glowed. Yes, I was quite willing to subscribe to the association which maintained such very helpful persons; for while talking he had made my luggage so secure that it cost me an effort to dislodge it at last. I went through Launceston Gate into Cornwall; over Bodmin Moor to Bodmin; over the Goss Moor to Indian Queens; from Indian Queens to Redruth. The terror of Redruth steep high street! It was a Saturday afternoon and Redruth inhabitants, thronging their own legitimate highways, challenged me to kill them if I dared. There is nothing in the world like Redruth's bodily resistance to traffic on a Saturday afternoon. And in those days there was no more skiddy track than the three miles, complete with tram-lines, between Redruth and Camborne. When at last I pulled up in Troon Square I felt as though I had been through the difficulties and dangers of an Arctic expedition and a jungle exploration combined. Redruth is not even a still jungle; all the teeming vegetation is on the move, unforeseeably in motion. How glad I was that the Bastions were always ready to make and share tea as I sat by their fire and recounted my adventures. My clutch was a bit fierce, Mr Bastion said as he examined and tested my machine. I knew well how fierce it was. Had I not nearly sprung like a tiger at the chest of the policeman on point duty at the foot of Redruth High Street?

When I began going to school on the Velocette I missed my old silent swoop to Camborne. In compensation, instead of pushing a bicycle up hill when my work was over, I went flying up faster and faster to Troon and as far beyond it as I wished.

In Mr Bastion's opinion I gained my education as a motor cyclist cheaply. Showing off was a temptation to me as it had been when I had ridden Dart as a child. In those days when I was showing off the pony always shied and threw me; the Velocette seemed to have the same talent. One Sunday night, when fools' corner by Camborne Church was well lined with idlers, ironical eyes watched me take the bend too fast and nearly precipitate myself through the plate glass of the Co-op; only the Society's prudent erections of railings kept me and the Velocette out of the premises. A remark of Bob Lovelock's taught me sense. We were discussing freewill and predestination in the shop one night. Bob, or perhaps it was Jim

Lovelock, said that during the war the thought that comforted him most when he went over the top was 'what is to be will be'. I said I didn't believe in this. Supposing I went full tilt down Beacon Hill, I said, and discovered too late to pull up that the gates across the level crossing were closed, and I smashed right into them. I should be dead, but I should have chosen; it wouldn't have been a case of 'what is to be will be'. Jim Lovelock replied: 'I was always supposing you wasn't being a damn fool.'

I learnt not to be a damn fool with my Velocette and soon I felt as safe on my two wheels as on my two feet. I could worm my way at snail's pace through the congregation of Redruth citizens, or fleet the miles carelessly over Bodmin Moor. For long-distance travel on main roads a motor bicycle is perfect; the rider does not notice his own noise or his own smell, and the speed exhilarates. A friend of mine used to say that when he'd had a couple of pints at the Ring of Bells he went home of a Saturday night feeling full of rhythm. That was exactly as I felt after a journey on the Velocette; I felt full of rhythm. Time after time I made the journey between Exmouth and Camborne, entering Cornwall sometimes by way of the ferry to Torpoint, sometimes by way of Tavistock and Gunnislake; more often by the Launceston Gate. Once I did it in the very early morning, reaching Camborne in time for school at nine o'clock. Speed kills reflection and induces a cheap beatitude. I who was horrified that men should kill one another in a passion, or for greed, or to maintain the right, or because they were commanded, never considered the more revolting chance that they might kill one another because they were in a hurry, or drunk with speed. Sheer luck and some skill, not caution or any sense of responsibility towards others, saved me from collision. I felt as safe on the roads as if I were in God's pocket. I became the motor cyclist complete; I read the *Motor Cycle*; I quoted Ixion; I followed the races and, in fancy, cheered on the Velocettes. I even felt that my Velocette ought to be at my distant beck. When I had ridden to Land's End, left my Velocette and walked along the cliffs to Porth Curnow, I used to feel that I ought to be able to whisper a magic phrase and call my steed of steel to where I was from where it was. I began to put faith in the twirling of a pin. I frequently used the Velocette to bring me within walking and finding distance of some old quoit, some stone-circle, or cross, or holy well. For this new interest I was indebted to Carwinnen Cromlech which stands in one of the Pendarves fields near Camborne; and to Mr C.V. Thomas, chairman at that time of the school governors, who gave me the run of his library in which there was a good collection of Cornish books. Previously I had passed stone circles and cromlechs time and again in different parts of Cornwall, and thought of them only as landmarks and familiars or, with conventional flippancy, called them devil's frying pans. They need the dusk and mist, or a storm, or a lowering overcast sky to make themselves felt; or to be seen in wide, treeless wastes which have themselves a savage grandeur. But Carwinnen Cromlech is only about one and a half miles from Camborne. To reach it from Camborne I used to go up Pendarves Street, through Pendarves woods, round Treslothan Church, up Lovers' Lane and over the hedge into a field. Because it is in a field Carwinnen, notwithstanding its powerful uprights and grand coping stone, is a little subdued, a little domesticated, a little as though put in a cage to be a specimen, patronized by Pendarves. I used to wonder whether, in a home field, it felt like a Red Indian in an urban villa. But although on one side are the grasslands, woods and park of Pendarves, and even a house—Pendarves House—on the other side the furzy brakes which flank the field lead up to the wild moors about Troon, Nine Maidens and Wendron. I liked to wander about the moorland above Troon. On the moor, or standing under the great coping stone of Carwinnen, personality was dwarfed and petty problems melted away. I used to think to myself that the moor and the stones remained, but the men who had lived were gone, and had left nothing but the grey stones set up here and there not as memorials of themselves, but as reminders that the moor had continued in rain and shine while man, so alien to earth, had wandered on it beset with his other fancies.

What does the moor know of continuity? What does it know of the succession of flowers and fruits? Yet it remains while man with his passion for continuity dies, and only leaves the stones which he has set up, stones which moved him because they were, unlike himself, independent, without the pangs and uncertainty of blood and sap.

16

WEST PENWITH

I am fire of the fiery sun whose ray
Kindles my clay;

Of one substance with earth, her wine and wheat
Quick in my feet;

My dancing blood follows the motion
Of moon and ocean;

And I am the word, to weave and wear
The living air;

Lapt, lapt in Thy livery,
And breathing Thee.

—To the Giver of Breath

While I had my Velocette all Cornwall was open to me at weekends. One Saturday I could stand on Pentire Rumps and Point, the next on Dodman. I had become like one of the old giants, taking giant strides. It almost seemed to me as though I could have one foot on Rough Tor and the other on St Agnes Beacon or Carn Brea; one on Trink and the other on Carn Kenidjack. I surveyed my land; only the coast between Padstow and Hartland was a little beyond me.

That stretch I haunted later. From Troon I got to know Gweek and Constantine and Manaccan; Cadgwith and Coverack; Kynance, Mullion, Poldu and Gunwalloe. From Fowey to Lizard was mine, and from Lizard to Land's End, with all the creeks and windings, the bottoms and the downses. But most familiarly of all I got to know West Penwith, that extreme western tip of Cornwall which is a little Cornwall in itself. Just as the Tamar makes Cornwall almost an island, so Hayle River makes almost an island of West Penwith. I came to know it by heart as I know Gorran and St Michael Caerhays.

St Michael had his footing in my new territory as in my old. In West Penwith his splendid mount is lifted up. The mount was my place of pilgrimage, not to go on to, but to look at from all quarters and heights, in all seasons, and at all times. If I live to be a thousand years old I shall not weary of looking at the mount. In my thousand and first year I shall crawl up past Sancreed Church by Sancreed Beacon to look on it from there; or I shall totter down from Mr Green's farm at Busullow till I reach the field-stile to Madron; or I shall pant my way to the top of Castle-an-Dinas and see the mount from there. If I am too feeble for that in my thousand and second year I shall manage to get into the train at Hayle when the columbines are out, all the purple columbines that take the eye on the railway banks, and see the mount beyond the ugly railway litter and the bulrushes of Marazion Swamp. In a bath chair I shall be wheeled along the Promenade and see the mount anchored in lead and silver, or floating in the blue:

> It seemed amid the surges for to fleet.

That line of Spenser's is the most visible thing ever written about the mount.

Penwith is wild; the flow of the land is wild, for all the tillage and civility, for all the growth of Penzance and the gardens up the Gulval Valley; for all the sheltered plots of early 'taties', jonquils, violets and anemones which snuggle into the very cliffs themselves. The rock is near. Between Penberth and Porth Curnow the path may lead you through garden nooks where the dark earth is so tilled that it looks sifted fine as flour. But close at hand, starting out to sea, rearing its gigantic crests is Treryn Dinas, naked and impregnable. More soaring is Tol-pedn Penwith to which my favourite approach was along the cliffs from Land's End. Land's End, compared with Tol-pedn and Treryn Dinas is disappointing. On the landward side it has come to look like a shabby old fur, worn, dingy. But the trodden paths cannot spoil its seaward strength; its piled cubes, its space of unused air, its sea navy-blue with a heady sparkle, or grey, or lucent green. Out to sea are the Longships. To the right is the smooth line which slips into the neck and runs over the head of Cape Cornwall. Nearer, between Land's End and Sennen Cove, the cliffs have the storied, sculptured formation that Sir Humphry Davy loved. He knew the broken arches of the cathedral caverns, just as he knew the beauty of the moonlight lying on Mount's Bay. Davy, to me, is very present in Penwith; I thought I saw him once before it was fully light on a midsummer morning. I had ridden over from Godrevy to see the sun rise. But it was a cold grey misty morning, and the sun never rose at all. I was cold and hungry, and I thought I saw Davy in a coat with capes.

Planned occasions rarely turn out well; beauty is always a lovely chance. It is given every chance between Land's End and Tol-pedn. I used to go along close to where the Armed Knight rears himself out of the sea, past Enys Dodnan, with his soft head and fine carved claws and caverns. The cliff path at first winds along by a hedge of great stones roughly built, and hoary with lichen; then the hedge breaks off and the path is open—a path to race along, with air on both sides to buoy a person up, and make him feel like Mercury with winged sandals. The coast here shows some sign of crumbling. In places the cliff is earthy and, when the tide is out, there are fleets of smooth boulders upon the shore, and rocks round which in calm weather the sea lies in green lagoons. There is a first funnel-like creek, Zawn Wells, but no sand as yet only huge stones with shingle at the head of the creek into which the water churns at high tide. I used to look back from the next cliff at the great natural archway through Enys Dodnan, and at the crests of the Armed Knight, and then speed onward to Pordenack.

Pordenack is like a good poem, never disappointing to return to, grander than I remembered, with always some fresh aspect to show. It is formed of cubicle rocks, pressing and flattening one another, in massive pillars. The deep groovings lend to individual rocks a peculiar expressiveness. Some have grand expressions such as are graved by time on noble faces; and some are comical or peevish like cracked old shoes. In decoration wind and time play odd tricks. Here are rocks with the flat foreheads and long muzzles of monkeys; rocks like coquettish tam-o'-shanters; rocks nuzzling one another like little fond animals; rocks like grim old men or angry duchesses. Some stones balance themselves impossibly all along the coast. They laugh out in the wrong place. They are ridiculous because we feel we must contradict them and tell them they cannot possibly remain like that. The rocks between Pordenack and Carn Boel help us to appreciate sculpture. Here again is felt the thrill of related shapes, the tenderness, the strength or the impudence which can be implicit in poised masses.

Among books which describe this coast my favourite is Blight's *A Week at the Land's End*, published in 1861. If Blight does not know the name of a place he makes one up. I once asked a man who was ploughing the dark earth with a cloud of gulls in his wake, the name of a creek. He said, 'I doan' knaw; he abn' got no name, b'lieve. He's only a little small wan.' Blight will have none of that. From him we know when we are passing the Lion's Den and the twin crests of Carn Evall; from him we recognize Moz-rang and The Horse's Back and Zawn Reeth on the way to Nanjizel, or Mill Bay as some call it. Nanjizel has beauty landward and seaward. To the east the rock with its slim opening through which the light shines is unforgettable. Someone called this cove the Song of the Sea; perhaps because of the combined music of a brown, sweet, tumbling brook with the sea's resounding bass; but I think he was not Cornish. We are a people shy of being so openly poetical. We are much more likely to grunt something about the old wind blowing of 'ee inside out on the old cliffs.

It certainly can blow 'ee inside out on Carn les Boel, with its hooded forms retreating from the sea. Above, the turf is close shaven, with great outcrops of grey stone. The path winds by rocks which seem like the burying places of giants, with squat turrets for watch and ward.

Down to the sea and up into the air one goes by gully and cliff until Tol-pedn is neared. It is a mighty promontory, with its back humped, and with great claws set in the sea. As one approaches, the sea at Porth Gwarra shows behind the neck of the promontory. All the claws are nobly set, but Tol-pedn itself is the grandest. By the chair ladder, where the granite soars sheer upward, the cliff-climber most hardened against giddiness may find his heart turning to water within him. Here is the place to feel the thrill of the perpendicular and the perilous forward slant. The actual funnel from which Tol-pedn gets its name, 'the holed headland' is disappointing compared with the seaward cliffs. The cliffs have a purposeful air in their strength, whereas this great rent is a jagged accident. But the whole headland impresses itself on the wayfarer, in summer or in winter, but most of all in winter. Then, towards evening, the sea is black about it except where it boils in foam; and the wind sweeps over the treeless downs behind. Here Lear might have wandered; for here 'the bleak winds do sorely ruffle; and for many miles about there's scarce a bush'.

Fierce storms can lay a land bare of all but the most closely fitting vegetation, but it is below the tide-line that the enduring grain of the rock can best be felt. Here the sea works delicately into the bone itself. Where it washes on granite no hint of softness can remain, no lichen as on the upper rocks, no crannies filled with sea-pinks, hardly a roughness for seaweeds and limpets to cling to. All smooth and clean. Every excrescence swilled away. It is from such rocks with their purpled roots in the depths that the great cliffs rise between the crags of Land's End and the promontory of Tol-pedn. One remembers them not least for their infinite variety. Now the cliffs are in soaring exultation, abrupt, with broken uprights, turrets and sharpened spires; now starting backwards, now heavily projecting; here huddled from the storm, here poised in stupendous masses; now showing a wild energy of fantastic outline, now depressed, frightened, stunted, beaten. The whole is grand but grotesque, enduring yet changing, defeated yet for ever triumphant. A history of storms is in the grooved and haggard face of Tol-pedn, with its crossed conflicting seams, the great rending of its base, the inconsequent perching of its wild decoration. It is worth days and nights of travelling to come once more within sight of this promontory, and to continue by the cliff path to Porth Gwarra and St Levan. I like to go when new celandines are sparkling under the old bracken fronds, and the blackthorn is snowy; and out at sea are waves turned back by the wind.

Corresponding with Treryn Dinas on the north coast of Penwith is Gurnard's Head; corresponding with Tol-pedn is Bosigran or, perhaps, Botallack. I used to leave my Velocette at St Ives when I wanted to go to Gurnard's Head. I used to walk the path through the fields from St Ives to Zennor, pay my respects to the Mermaid and to St Senara herself, most delightfully named of saints; I used to read once again that sad remembrancer engraved on the sundial: 'The glory of the world passeth', and so on to Gurnard's Head. Sometimes the season's successive flowers trod on one another's heels. Once in May I picked honeysuckles on the cliffs, and a fisherman said they must have cheated the wind and caught the sun. On certain days when sky and tide are just right the sea round Gurnard's Head is unsurpassed in the range and depth of its colour. The sea is deep inshore; and this liquid, coloured light varies in hue through peacock and clear green to purple. I have seen pools of peacock floating in the green. I have sat among the opening bracken and bluebells, or on tufts of sea-pinks, caressing the throats of their red buds, and watching the colours change out at sea.

Inland the four parishes, Zennor, Morvah, Madron and Gulval, which meet at Four Parishes Rock behind the Galvers, are an amalgam of wildness and fertility. The flowery Gulval Valley leads from the south up to the moors, and the ancient mines, and the tremendous cliffs about Bosigran, Pendeen Watch and Botallack. Inland the lines of the carns flow into one another like a melody. They stretch, they run, or they lie still without fuss. The pattern of the fields within their granite stone hedges does not obscure the shape of the treeless land wide open to the face of the sky. If the fields could fly away they would fly in patterns like the starlings that wheel over them. The sun is all alive there, chasing the shadows; and the present is all alive in the shadows of the past, shadows that seem to go back almost to beginning of time. You cannot walk across country north, south, east or west from Mr Green's farm on the Bosullow Downs without stumbling upon some ancient memorial to the human spirit, or some ruined monument of human labour, or some high place, or inaccessible cliff castle to which people were chased; or some hut in which they lived at home; or some quiet holy well or cross for worship.

It is the ruined monuments to tin and copper that take the eye first, though only Geevor Mine of those about Pendeen was working when last I was there. The masonry of the engine houses and of the walls on the cliffs between Pendeen Watch and Botallack has a strength that crumbles very slowly. One is reminded of the old work of the Giants in *The Ruin*. The Brisons out at sea are hardly more savage and desolate than the granite walls and towers with their arches, and their empty window-sockets through which the sky looks and the wind howls. The figures named in the books, or quoted traditionally, of the depths of some mines and their tunnellings under the sea make the imagination reel. I have never been down a mine; I should always think to myself, 'Suppose the top closes in before I can get out!' To peer down a disused shaft, or to hear a stone strike the distant water is enough for me. The only remains of mining I take comfort in are the shallow scratchings, scooped holes now filled to the brim with ferns and flowers. These tiny miniature valleys make green hiding-places. It is a curious sensation to lie in one of them in a secret green world, made almost to fit one's body, and consider the luminous sky unfathomable overhead. The bal tracks over the downs lead from town and hamlet and solitary house—we Cornish like solitary houses—to the mines. Men used to walk along the bal tracks from as far as St Ives to the Levant Mine or up to Ding Dong.

Old engine houses like Ding Dong, said to be the most ancient mine in Cornwall, are landmarks for circles of miles; I used to quarter Penwith by landmarks, going across country from area to area dominated by its familiar. At different times I have walked from Trencrom to Trink, and from Trink to Castle-an-Dinas, and from Castle-an-Dinas to Ding Dong. I have been from Ding Dong to Chûn Castle, and from Chûn to Carn Kenidjack, and from Carn Kenidjack, now lost, now found, to Chapel Carn Brea. Rhythmically the heights change about one; it is a tremendous harmonic progression. There are days of intense clarity. Penwith is light. The atmosphere can be so pellucid that one's very body seems to be without density and to thin itself into the air.

On dull winter days light that has soaked into bracken gives back its radiance. I have seen dead bracken on the slopes of Castle-an-Dinas burning with colour in November; and yet not exactly burning. It is a deep quiet glow. And yet not exactly a glow. It is saturation. November violets are similarly drenched and steeped in colour. Moist grey days bring out the tones of green, and dun and russet while, in the distance, the Galvers darken to purple. Carn Galver is like a great, modern battleship heading for the sea. From all directions this carn is a shapely sight. All Penwith is shapely. It has wiry outlines. The enduring beauty of St Ives is in its form, which no building has quite been able to spoil; and in its everchanging colour. The sands about St Ives and Carbis Bay and Lelant are yellow with the stored sunshine. And then, too, St Ives has its harbour. Who could be dull watching the boats, and the nets, and the seagulls, and the water rocking the light, and the fishermen working or lounging. But St Ives has become a resort, and resorts are exposed to insidious dangers; they are kept women. And artists kill the thing they love. Fishermen are safer custodians.

Resorts always seem to have cut themselves off from the ancestors and to have no future. They are sprouts. But it would be difficult for any place in Penwith to cut itself off from the ancestors. The dead have an equal share with the living in Penwith. I think no one could come suddenly upon Chûn Cromlech without a strange feeling. It is about four miles from Penzance, some distance in to the left of the main Penzance-Morvah road. A turning to the left leads to Great Busullow. Where the road ends a cart-track circles gradually to the right. Just when you think you will never find Chûn you see it, like a great stone mushroom, the uprights seeming to be giants ossified while bending their might to support the coping stone. Chûn Cromlech and Chûn Castle keep the solemn downs about them. Lanyon Cromlech, on the right of the Penzance-Morvah by Lanyon Farm, is too near the main road to have any but a landmark's power; and the antiquaries point a finger of derision at it because it has been restored. Men-an-tol has been altered, too, they say. But that does not spoil it for me. Men-an-tol, the holed stone. The holed stone is a thick, strong block of granite rooted in the earth. It has a round hole through which a person may creep, or his body be passed; on either side of the holed stone are single upright posts. The whole suggests some rite to be practised, some rite which men might perform protesting against it in their souls yet fearing to omit because, though law is not to be cajoled, chance is capricious, and therefore vain, cruel, revengeful, sudden, open to blandishment. In this place where Men-an-tol stands, where all seems savage, where there are no trees, no refuge except the rocks, human fear might readily master human reason and lead to frenzies. Or perhaps as cooler heads would have us believe all this is lurid fancy, and it is best to laugh and creep through the hole to insure ourselves against the rickets.

Men Scryfa, the written stone, is not more than about a quarter of a mile from Men-an-tol. It is a single upright shaft of granite and on it is written 'RIALOBRAN CUNOVAL FIL'. Men Scryfa seems less old than the other stones; perhaps because it is written on. The Nine Maidens give an impression of great age, though they are not now considered to be so old as was once thought. Like others I have been seduced to study the stones. I like to read the antiquaries. But as one walks on the moors, the stones are not interesting antiquities to speculate upon; but part of the personality of Cornwall—things we accept as we accept the features and characters of our friends. Chûn and Men-an-tol, even if you do not choose to go out of your way to visit them, are there; with Carn Galver, and Ding Dong, and the bracken, and the brown pools, and the pink stone crop in its season on the tops of the grey hedges with their huge, untooled granite boulders, and the half sharp air which anyone who has tasted must always long for. They are part of Penwith.

In its essential aspect no country could be more pagan than the country round Ding Dong, the Galvers and Zennor. Its aspect is not humane, not civil; but savage, desolate, splendid and, above all things, unchangeable. To know how our ancestors felt we have only to go into one of the huts which cluster here amidst brambles and bracken. Then we not only know how they felt but we know that we are they; that time is only a figure; that all life exists concurrently. I suppose most people have from time to time the feeling that they live, ordinarily, in a particular channel of time, but that sometimes they slip out of it into a sea of other time. Then the idea of time as a cord on which separate existences are strung reasserts itself; and we wonder at this gift which has come through to us and understand what the ancients meant by piety. Reverence and dutifulness towards those who have been before us cannot but be felt in this place strewn with memorials. Antiquaries are divided in opinion as to the ancient purposes of the stones, but it seems natural to believe that they were first memorials to the dead, then, altars to whatever power presides over death; then, since men have relations not only with the dead and with God and the Devil but with each other, solemn meeting-places to discuss human affairs. This does not preclude the idea that the stones were set with due regard to the movements of the heavenly bodies. The feeling that the same spirit is in the round ocean and the living air and the heart of man and the ancient heavens did not find expression first in Wordsworth. Antiquaries are like editors, a little apt to bury the poem beneath the comment. And the erected stones are Cornwall's poem. They are in keeping with the natural stone fantasies of coast and carn and, harmonizing thus with the character of the land itself, they express it as it has never been expressed in words. Ireland has an ancient literature, and Wales, but not Cornwall. There is, in the ultimate sense of the word, no Cornish poem. We have romance. We still hear Jenefer's weeping in the waves off Boskenna, and Iseult is the Cornish queen. But we cannot read her story or Guinevere's story in old Cornish. And apart from Arthurian romance such legends as persist do not probe deep. There is a strange obscurity, a sense of withdrawal about this land which has been peopled so long by men whose fitting memorial is the grey silent stones. They speak to us in a way which Truro Cathedral cannot speak. Tender associations and memories gather round the cathedral for those of us who have been confirmed in it, and educated to reverence it. But the old stone circles and cromlechs appeal to a side of our nature which Christianity has never touched and which is nevertheless our virtual selves. On wild evenings when all is bare and the wind rises and the moon races on her back now dipping behind masses of cloud now swinging into the open sky—then the little people awake, not in their own quaint persons as the old folk have told us, but alive and in ourselves—in these strange living castles where alone with us they have their dwelling-place and their immortality.

It is not strange that Cornwall should have been preoccupied with religion. The Cornishman is bound to feel his dependence. In a country narrow, difficult to cultivate, and open to sea and sky, it would be hard so to ring him round with comfort and security that he should grow to forget the slenderness of the thread of his life. On the cliffs and moors man is involuntarily humble and involuntarily yearning. He does not want to be quite alone. He seeks communion with something which is not in the earth but which, since it is in himself, must also be somewhere else; but stronger, more perfect, more admirable than in himself, worshipful and to be thanked. This land fosters us in an atmosphere of mystery and grandeur, exposes us to sudden dangers, and makes us conscious of the forces working behind appearances. The glory revealed when the clouds are swung open at sunset, the sweeping winds, the majestic obedience of the sea—these transcend common acceptances, the habit of taking all for granted, and so people have sought a God. Every period of Cornish history has produced its seekers.

What were the older expressions of the religious feeling in Cornwall we can only dimly divine. I imagine that we were a people more prone to terror than pity; to unite with the storm in exultation rather than with the victim in mercy and pity. But Christianity came to Cornwall early and hermits and saints made it their dwelling. Some stories of these are boisterous enough. Many saints had as good times as giants. With Christianity, as with the older religions of Cornwall, it is not the word or legend which reveals, but the things that remain—holy well, and stone, and cross, and towered churches, and meeting-houses built with devotion.

I liked particularly to visit the holy well at St Levan with its worn granite steps leading down to the water, and its ivy-covered coping above. But most frequently I went to the holy well near Madron Village. There is a stile on the right beyond Madron Church which leads through fields to Bosworthan Lane. A little way down the lane is a gate, and a path through a sheltered brake, and by a wooded hedge where birds sing. Ash, elder and thorn give way to a marshy place which makes a fastness for the well. The walls of the baptistry are still standing, and there is a doorway; but here, as with the stone circles, the sky itself is roof. All round everything is green; within, it is still and hallowed. The well is a well of quietness, and the altar a stone which could not be profaned without a wrench to natural piety. Some say that St Madron was a woman, and it is a sanctuary a woman might have chosen; though it was probably a man, for men as a rule have more time to be saints. Had I been Madron I should like to have been friends with the hermit of Roche Rock, to have exchanged at intervals the amenities of my cell for his wild aerie. The disadvantage of being a saint is being a saint all the time.

Holy wells were wells of healing. The water of a holy well might purge away more than physical stain by its cool repose, its cleanness, and because it is so deep that it has no need to hurry away from itself for fear of stagnation. To me, too, the grey crosses which the wayfarer comes upon casually in every part of Cornwall are symbols of endurance and comfort rather than of suffering. They are not tortured signs. I have said, and I think it is true, that no country could be more pagan in aspect than some parts of Penwith—saints have liked to neighbour the wilderness. But everywhere in Penwith is the cross; sometimes a stone of an older time signed with the new sign, the symbol of hope, the new, potent talisman against the evil and death. There are crosses by the wayside, and on the moors, and in the church-towns; spaces sealed with this sign are known as the Cross. We always spoke of the enclosed space outside Gorran Church as the Cross. John Lloyd Warden Page in his book, *The North Coast of Cornwall* has happily quoted from the fifteenth-century *Dives et Pauper* in this connection.

> For this reason ben Croysses set by ye waye, that when folke passynge see ye croysses they may thynke on Him that deyed on ye croysse, and worshippe Hym above althyng.

At the time I was exploring West Penwith I was reading Charles Doughty. Here was a writer who had manifested in words the vast tract of Arabia as I could never hope to manifest my little Cornwall. Or could I gain at least some inkling of the way? Often in his poetry Doughty brought home some springing English scene as vividly to my senses as, in his prose, the wide desert. I saw in his sky and sea-scapes the work of a master. But there was something beyond. These pictures were painted in the execution of some large design and took their sheen from it. Doughty created occasions for his lyric flights; he ventured, and yet was steadfast. The poems were objective and yet I felt in them, as in *Arabia Deserta*, the spirit of Doughty himself, his courage, his truthfulness, his freedom from vanity. There was a dual quality in Meredith, the presence of something showy in his mind of which there was no trace in Doughty. What the two had in common to attract me was command of image and scene. Doughty had known both the splendour and the gentleness of the sun. He could write:

> Sun cometh forth horned, and bearded be his looks
> In token of fervent heat.

Or he could fit words to a desert shower:

> In that there fell an April shower that shone about us like golden hairs in the sun; and the desert earth gave up to our sense a teeming grassy sweetness.

I found many a gibe in Doughty at the glibness of Victorian English; he had sought and found his telling words in the earlier reaches of our language. But were his changes in the accepted order of words justified in an analytic language? Had he done anything more than forge an idiom suited to his own genius? I wanted to study his words and their origin as I read not only *Arabia Deserta* but *The Dawn in Britain, Adam Cast Forth, The Titans, The Cliffs* and *The Clouds*. I decided to give up teaching again for a time in order to read and think. I went to Oxford. I had only enough money for a year. My father said I was foolish. What about my pension? But I did not care for pensions. I started up my Velocette and away I went out of my dear Cornwall. The Prefects at Camborne gave me, as a parting gift, the one poem of Doughty which I did not possess—*Mansoul*.

17

OXFORD INTERLUDE

Michaelmas daisy and dahlia
Put off their full regalia,
Each crown
Is ragged grown.
But the beech-tree tall,
More lovely in her fall
Than in her prime,
Puts on the splendour of time:
Her proffered gold
Resumes all glories that her growth foretold.

—*Beech Tree in October: New College Garden*
(To the Memory of Mrs Oliver Elton)

I had been admitted as an advanced student to Lady Margaret Hall; but this was not my first visit to Oxford. I had frequently spent time there, reading in the Bodleian and drifting on the Cherwell. The Cherwell and the Bodleian were Oxford to me. In the Bodleian I felt all ghost and no body, and on the Cherwell all body and no ghost. There is no pleasure in which the body feels more fully 'poured out in looseness' than floating under the willows of the Cherwell. But it needs some preliminary effort to be lazy on a river. I saw the Cherwell first with Professor and Mrs Elton on an August afternoon. Professor Elton, when he could be induced, was a wonderful guide. He had taken me to see various colleges including his own, Corpus; then we walked in Christ Church Meadows by the river and, as we stood, a swan came and took my shoe-toe in his beak, and held it for a second before moving on. I kept still because I did not have the sense to do anything else, and I was surprised that Professor Elton thought my stillness a form of courage. His fancy pleased me very much, though I knew it to be without foundation. It takes courage for me to touch a bat, but not to stand still when a swan gobbles at my shoe.

That summer afternoon we watched girls and young men glide along the river. Punting looked very easy to me. I got up early next morning and wandered among the willows until a representative of Mr Timms was ready to oblige me with a punt and a pole. I stood on the punt where the girls and young men had stood and, saying nothing of my lack of skill, found myself adrift upon the Cherwell. Mr Timms's young man had the fun and I had the fury for at whatever angle I inserted my pole, and however I shoved with my ungoverned strength, the punt swung round instead of moving forward. There was I, the focus of a revolving punt and of the derisive eyes of the youth who, shouting instructions at me, made me first confused and then angry. When guided from afar by shouts my hands and arms and legs turn into a lot of independent devils, spiting me. At last I secured sufficient equilibrium to shout at my instructor in my turn to go and get his blasted breakfast and leave me to it. He said, 'Well, if you fall in and drown don't blame me.' I said I had not the faintest intention of falling in and drowning. With that I plunged my pole into the water again, slung all my weight on to it and the punt, instead of going round, shot forward at last—but without me. I could not part company with the pole. For a second I must have been exactly like a monkey on a stick, and then I was in the Cherwell. A slow-motion film of this performance would, I think, be exquisite. The young man found it exquisite enough in quick motion. His was the kind of laughter you only get in Dickens; it had shaken him nearly into an apoplexy by the time

I had swum on to the landing-stage leaving punt and pole separate and at large on the river. I was hastening off without a word when he said, 'Ere, you 'aven't paid.' There were demonstrations with thunderbolts which must have been enormously gratifying to Jove; but I don't suppose even he ever delivered a bolt when wet. It is extraordinarily de-thunder-bolting to be wet. I do not imagine that anyone, wet, has ever got the upper hand of anyone dry. Beowulf and his nicors were all wet together.

I did not next morning get my punt from Mr Timms. I went further up the Cherwell. I went several mornings and, during the days, I primed myself with hints on how to punt. Whoever I happened to be talking with the conversation tended to veer towards the art of propulsion. Some spoke with clarity and some were as cloudy as cabinet ministers when, though determined to reveal no meaning, they use words. I could, of course, have asked a friend to come and teach me, but that would not have been the same thing. I wanted the skill to come to me when I was alone one morning. And it did. It came suddenly with pleasure and ease like a tune. And I went up the Cherwell, under the trees and over the trees' wavering reflections; and out between the meadow banks where the cows were grazing; and past the reeds and the meadow-sweet; and I tied up for the first time for a whole summer day near a swan's nest by Water Eaton; and I came slowly drifting back at night, trailing my pole in a way I never permitted myself after I became a member of Lady Margaret Hall.

Once a member I was rapidly taught 'L.M.H. form' on the river, and have never dared depart from it. I can hardly bring canoe, punt or sculler into the bank or to a landing-stage without feeling the critical gaze of Trixie Jackson or Charis Waddy upon me. I thought I had learnt all there was to be learnt about boats from Tommy Johns. Not so. I had never done a trick on bow or turned a canoe in the minimum number of strokes. Tommy had never told me to keep my elbows in. I loved the early mornings on the river. If anyone says L.M.H. to me I see the thatched boathouse and the ladies' lace which grew so luxuriantly up the creek in June. I hear the notes of cuckoos and pigeons. Or, in autumn, I see the yellowing leaves afloat on the water and smell the breakfast sausages as we return to the hall sharp-set.

Apart from rigorous supervision of my form on the river, my two years in Oxford were the freest I ever spent. Professor Elton, who had retired from Liverpool, and was living in Oxford, was again my supervisor. He and Mrs Elton were living in the Woodstock Road and their house bade me welcome. Mrs Elton's room, opening on to a garden beyond which the air was free to Wytham Woods, had a charm for me which I can never hope to recapture in words. From the delicate water-colours on the walls, from the books on the white shelves, from the colours a-tuned to a quiet harmony on the hearth-rug, there emanated a peculiar inducement to be happy now. I loved that room, and the time I spent in it, from the moment I eagerly entered to the moment when I reluctantly went away. Mrs Elton has died now; we shall never see again her smile with its hint of glee, or hear the sound of her voice, as delicate as wind-stirred leaves. She was more purely a theme for poetry than any other woman I have ever met, and to be with her was a solace. She was framed for laughter too. She made me laugh, and I made her laugh. Her memory was stored; but she enjoyed any little fresh experiences too. She slept in a punt, a covered punt which I had on the Cherwell, during my last Oxford vacation; and her pleasure when she awoke early to the scent of the meadow-sweet and the swaying of the water-flags, and the birds singing, and the cows munching, gilded the morning.

She went with me to hear the May Morning Carol from Magdalen Tower; we heard much music together. But she did not, like me, go to Christ Church, or New College, or Magdalen College Chapel to hear chant, and fugue, and anthem. I liked to go on Sunday morning to Christ Church for the exquisite singing of the Litany. The ears are charmed in Oxford with the sound of bells and with singing. One need not make arrangements in advance. These services are eternal at the appointed hour and season. At Whitsuntide one is not defrauded of 'Come, Holy Ghost, our souls inspire'. There is a lovely and safe recurrence as of the sunshine on Magdalen as one walks down the High.

While I was at Oxford I was *in statu pupilari*, but not irksomely so. Members of the Junior Common Room might not, I discovered, ride motor bicycles, but Miss Grier quickly arranged that I might ride mine. I liked Miss Grier. She was large; adequate both physically and intellectually for the work she had chosen. She was just the opposite of the aunt in one of Mr Joyce Cary's novels, an aunt who had become merely a sense of strain. The Principal of a women's college needs to rule without seeming to; no flock is more difficult to manage than a flock of young women. They will not be driven; but neither will they respect ineffectiveness. Miss Grier was effective because of the person she was; it was impossible to imagine her ducking or sidling. I had not much talk with her; but I knew that she was one with whom, if need arose, I could talk without reservations. She had not those little closed territories in her mind which some administrators acquire and which have to be skirted; but she had nevertheless, I imagined, a firm hold on what Jane Austen called principles. 'What are her principles?' Miss Grier, I think, would not have been in doubt. I still was. Perhaps that was the secret of her attraction for me. Or perhaps it was a certain humorous comprehension at which one guessed; a tolerance both of the solemnities and the flippancy of young people. She did not exalt minor incidents into crises. I liked her lack of hurry. I move fast. Miss Grier's was the rhythm of a larger nature; and she gave the impression of having plenty of time; even when one knew she hadn't. I wish I could see her again in academic cap and long black gown bicycling, upright and stately, down the Banbury Road; bowing, from the waist up, in recognition of acquaintance. I should like again to see her stand and deliver a sermon; or walk, in barbaric splendour that far outshone the wealth of Ormuz or of Ind, to her place at the High Table. She was a very complete person, loving learning, but not sequestered; able in all affairs, aiding education far beyond the limits of Lady Margaret Hall. I have often tried to picture her in China, a country to which, as Representative of the British Council, she has gone since she retired. She would be rather like Doughty in Arabia or Professor Elton among the Irish. It is well not to be too adaptable.

I found it very difficult to adapt myself to a flat and civil countryside. I found myself seeking Boars Hill and Shotover for a breath of air. But even on Boars Hill civility was present. I wrote an angry verse:

> How I hate the unassuming
> Houses on Boars Hill!
> How I loathe the humble pretence; be presuming
> You poor half-timbereds, and lord it;
> Get up, for Heaven's sake, and crow over it;
> Don't be deprecating still!
> Your cultured unobtrusiveness labels you;
> You didn't mean to spoil it, did you?
> You're preserving it from the herd, aren't you?
> You're preserving it dead, pretending you haven't killed it,
> Damn you!

Of places to which I bicycled from Oxford, Upper and Lower Slaughter touched me most memorably with their beauty. I shall never forget seeing them in summer when the lime trees were in flower so that the air was perfumed, and the ear was filled with the murmur of insects. I remember the honey-yellow sunshine, and the trees above their shadows, and the clear brown of the little tributary of the Windrush; and larkspurs blue against a Cotswold stone house.

I used my motor bike; but not so very often. In Oxford I forsook my habit of hurrying away from where I lived. I drew in. I found that in Oxford the very heart of the place was best. I drew the Bodleian round me. During several holidays I had spent some of my time in the Bodleian library. It was blissful when I first became a reader and was able to sit, small, compact and unknown, in the midst of time and books. Other people in the Bodleian never seem real to me, and I imagine myself entirely disembodied to them. It is strange that one should come to feel so much alive by being so be-spirited and de-personalized. I loved to order books and see them mount round my desk in ramparts; books some of which had, perhaps, not been handled since Doughty had handled them sitting, possibly, where I sat, and dreaming of the poem he would some day write and which he did write in thirty-six years' time. *The Dawn in Britain* was long in the imagining. Sometimes I read books which had little to do with Doughty. The magic words, 'For purposes of study', would bring me any book. I commanded Genii. I could intoxicate myself with books; and then dance down the wooden steps of the Bodleian, making little patterns of sound to please myself as I skipped round the corners, and out into the quad.

Who can describe the gravity of the Bodleian Quad, a gravity courteous by day, remote and harmonious as a dream in moonlight? It takes the heart with its beauty. I used to let my eyes run up the lines of its solemn walls, then drop to the worn stones under the several doorways to the medieval schools. They are hollowed by the tread of a multitude of scholars' feet. They are humble. The Bodleian Quad has an indwelling spirit, some quality of the medieval mind, God-fearingness perhaps and absence of brag. I admire too with all my heart the large design of the Renaissance Cardinal. But I feel it to be different. I liked to pass through the portals of Christ Church, pausing under the lovely staircase roof, and go out into the Meadows, to feel the wind with freshness and vigour blowing the elms; or the cattle might be feeding in quiet, while the trees held in their branches the blue haze of Oxfordshire. Oxford air is coloured. I liked to pass under the walls of Merton and Corpus, to nod at the flowers that looked over the wall. But the most beautiful thing I ever saw in Christ Church Meadows was the reflected sunset sky in flood-water, and the astonishing appearance of buildings which one thought could not possibly be reflected at such a distance. How could Tom's Dome, and the flutings of St Mary's, and the Cornish strength of Magdalen Tower, find place together there? And yet in my dreaming memory they did; in the cold twilight, in the leaden yet rosy depths, a city was inverted in a watery world, liquefied. The walls could be made to waver by a pebble, yet they were imperishably pictured.

Once I walked in snow round Addison's Walk and Christ Church Meadows accompanied by a student from Johannesburg. She was as excited as a puppy by the snow. She cupped in her hands the ivies filled with snow; she laughed with joy at the birds' foot-prints; among the tree trunks, all striped on one side with the long snow mark, she stood enchanted.

One of the pleasures of Oxford was to know intimately other students from various parts of the world. Among those doing research who became my friends was Elizabeth Handasyde, an elegant Scot. When I first met her, immaculate from head to toe, at dinner with Miss Janet Spens, I was conscious that I had caught back my hair with a paper-fastener, and crushed my long skirt into motor-bike overalls. I was crumpled; she was shining. But we liked one another. She had a lucid mind, cool, but open to poetry and to humour. It was she in recent years who lent me John Aubrey, and Arthur Waley's translation of *Monkey*. Dear Monkey! Elizabeth had been ordered wine. She could not, she said risk becoming a secret drinker. When we knew one another well how delightful it was that my busy mind could present me, among other reasons for not settling down to write, with the suggestion that it was time to dash along to find Elizabeth and save her from the vice of drinking alone. She commanded her clothes and they obeyed. Her summer dresses, after a day on the river, would look as though freshly taken from the laundry parcel and donned that minute. But she was not inordinately vain of this good gift. She recognized thankfully that it was from heaven.

Hilda Prescott was another friend who idled with me on the river. She was a senior student of L.M.H. who had returned to work at the book which afterwards became *The Spanish Tudor*. We referred to it, less felicitously, as *Bloody Mary*. Lying back among the cushions of a punt Hilda, with her tall person, her distinguished narrow face, her marked features, her dark complexion, her dark straight hair cut in a bang, her eyes with their secret fires, her strong religious sense and fanatical spirit, looked more like a Norman lady than any actual Norman lady ever probably looked. She had strayed out of time and could, as she talked, draw her friends back with her into imagined epochs which she peopled with creatures partly of her own fashioning and partly historical. Together we read Traherne. I knew *Centuries of Meditation*; she introduced me to Traherne's poems.

Olga Bickley was different again. She had come from Italy where already she had done admired work. Born of an Italian mother and an English father, she had inherited the precious qualities of two countries. A sun more potent than ours had given her her dark rich colouring, and added strength to her abundant hair. In everything she was the opposite to the scrimped and niggardly. Brought up in Italy, moving with ease in literatures I knew only in translation, she was, nevertheless, passionately of the present. She gave herself to her innumerable friends with prodigal devotion. She would strain all her resources for a friend; but for herself she was the least calculating of women. She was a cordial. When with her one felt that it was jam today.

Others among us were Christine Burleson, an American, lively and Jamesian; Catherine Lamont, a Canadian who warmed my heart to all Canadians; and Mrs Barnes, a Swiss student, learned in the intricacies of language, but not proud. All gave the lie to the popular conception implied in the name 'blue-stocking'.

We worked; but I found, as always, that I worked less well now that I had plenty of time than when I had to wring time out of nothing. I doubt whether I ever feel any urge to write until somebody asks me to wash the dishes. In Oxford there was no equivalent to washing the dishes so I read. If reading maketh a full man I was brimming over. I never wearied of reading; but writing was another matter. Absorbed in a book I was dead to the earth and my friends; but when I was preparing to write all sorts of little devils danced about and tempted me into the sunshine. They turned themselves into water-lilies, white and yellow, and floated before my eyes until I went to find Catherine Lamont so as to paddle with her in our favourite canoe, the *Windrush*, to Islip. I would hear the dry, old man's cough of a swan in my mind's ear, and never rest until I had persuaded Elizabeth to take the double sculler to Water Eaton to see papa in state, leading in procession the orderly cygnets, while mamma, bringing up the rear, her leg stuck out amidship in *dégagée* fashion, floated on the keel of her own inverted breast, her stately neck a prow undulated by every ripple. In Doughty's poetry I found the essence of summer days by English river banks. It was one of the never-to-be-exhausted pleasures which kept me faithful to him. In vain Professor Elton told me that, while admitting the splendid prose, he could not away with much of Doughty's verse. It was, he said, to his ear like a stick drawn along railings. Greatly daring I blamed his ear and, in my writing, quoted passages which occasionally wrung from him an endorsement, and an assent. In the meantime, I could enjoy without needing company, poetry which so well suited my private pleasures:

> I stayed, where pleasant grassy holms depart;
> Those streaming water-brooks, bordered all along;
> With daphne and willow-herb, loose-strife, laughing robin;
> With woodbind garlanded and sweet eglantine,
> And azure-hewed in creeky shallows still,
> Forget-me-nots left our frail thoughts to heaven.
>   Broods o'er those thymy eyots drowsy hum;
> Bourdon of glistering bees, in mails of gold,
> Labouring from sweet to sweet, in the long hours
> Of sunny heat; they sound their shrill small clarions.
>   And hurl by booming dors, gross bee-fly kin;
> Broad-girdled, diverse hewed, in their long pelts:
> That solitary, while eve's light endureth,
> In Summer skies, each becking clover-tuft haunt.

Even when, as sometimes happened, I grew tired of cultivated Oxford, it was Doughty who transported me to the austere delicacy of desert, or to the northern seas. I liked to read of the voyage of Joseph of Arimathea to Britain, and listen to the tales which old Adherbal, the pilot, told:

> The pilot old, tells, how his ship-feres cast
> Away, far in the sides were of the North,
> Where hanged the steadfast star, above their mast;
> Nor this, that we know, day, nor night, is there,
> But each, by long returns of half the year;
> Their year one day: men plough, at dawn, and sow,
> Harvest at noon; and gather fruits, at eve.
> Yet in their long night, is clear flickering gleam,
> Of frosty stars. Cold cliffs, of that sea-deep,
> Are blue-ribbed ice; whence oft strange lofty sounds
> Are heard, as lute strings knapped, of the ice-god.

I came to know Doughty well through his prose and verse—which is as he would have had it; but I had never thought of him as having lived in part contemporaneously with me. Not that I agreed with those who said he was an Elizabethan strayed out of his century; Doughty, in all his thought, belongs to the scientific age. I knew very well as a fact, that he had been born in 1843 and had died in 1926. Therefore it was clear that he had breathed the air of this world, gone to sleep, wakened up, heard the birds sing for thirty-five years during which I, too, was breathing the air, going to sleep, waking up, hearing the birds sing and seeing, in a very narrow compass, the world he had seen at large. I knew from Hogarth's biography that Doughty had married Caroline, daughter of General Sir William Montagu Scott McMurdo, by whom he had had two daughters. But it had never occurred to me to think of them as alive. I would as soon have thought of seeing Milton's 'late espoused saint' as Mrs Doughty. Mr Cockerell (now Sir Sydney Cockerell) changed all that. Doughty's Scribble Books, the notes he had made and carried on his person throughout the hardships and perils of the Arabian Journey, the notes from which he had composed *Arabia Deserta*, were in the Fitzwilliam Museum. So I kicked up my Velocette and off I went to Cambridge to see them. Cambridge was not coldly official; it was kind. I examined the Scribble Books at leisure. Mr Cockerell took me home to tea and showed me other treasures including the black-letter Chaucer which Doughty had had with him in the desert. Mr Cockerell had known Doughty; he had letters in his handwriting; he gave me one. He asked me if I had met Mrs Doughty and he promised to give me a letter of introduction.

And so it came about that I was soon kicking up my Velocette once more and, this time, heading for Kent; for Merriecroft, near Cranbrook. Merriecroft seemed to me the very name for a house and garden in which blackbirds would have a ripe and merry note, sheen-winged insects would hum, and the coloured flowers be like some silent music of earth's field. I hardly thought of Mrs Doughty though, as I neared the place, I fingered her letter and read again her directions for the way. The directions were clarity itself, but I nevertheless shot up the drive of the wrong house. I therefore arrived at Merriecroft in the guise of one who had made an initial error, and I have never lived it down. The name bestowed upon me by Mrs Doughty, and which has clung, is not complimentary.

I felt that I knew the house and garden in advance. But I had not remotely imagined Mrs Doughty.

She was an artist; she lent out her eyes. Through them I saw many things as freshly as a painter sees them, and she talked with that perfection of idiom and liveliness of phrase which our generation has lost. Every word was individualized on her lips without forethought. Whereas Mrs Elton was imaginative and witty, Mrs Doughty was quick and downright. One risked precipices; nothing was sloped to ease a perilous moment. Slap! bang! down I went! But I could recover. I could get up and tilt for a fall again. No small mercies were offered. I have rarely felt more exhilarated than when talking with Mrs Doughty; the danger of it, and the gaiety, and the pleasure I had in her spoken English. Listening to her I agreed with what I had somewhere read—that great ladies are, in the naturalness of their speech, the custodians of language. Even before I met Mrs Doughty I knew how mistaken were the critics who said that Doughty had lived only in Arabia; he only lived fully when he got back. His poem *Adam Cast Forth* resumes *Arabia Deserta* in a more complete fable of human existence. It makes Adam's acceptance of the human condition the climax towards which the poem moves. Doughty was no mere bookish poet.

But he had adored his masters, Chaucer and Spenser. I had the privilege of working in his study which remained then much as he left it. His notes were there. I could see how he worked; what books he had constantly by him; what methods he had used in his practice with words. I knew Blake's 'Without Unceasing Practice nothing can be done. Practice is Art. If you leave off you are Lost'. Doughty never gave up practice. He delighted in words as a painter delights in paint. He sought and tasted them, admiring those of high lineage, words which had endured through centuries of work and thought; words which were exact; words which preserved nice distinctions. He hated the confounding of substance in a general term. His scorn of 'costermongery' flashed out; here was no costermonger but a poet who was determined in his making, like a medieval mason, to use the best stone. From the time when I first read it I have always been moved by the figure at the close of *Mansoul* in which Doughty likens the work of a poet to the building of a cathedral; Mrs Doughty told me how he liked to sit alone and meditate in Ely Cathedral. Something of its sublimity passes into the work of the man who was big enough to admire it creatively. Doughty's own thought was that of a man trained in a branch of exact science, and trusting in science. It is to me a great moment when, in his myth, he makes his seeker-after-truth pass under the arch of humility into the temple of adoration; frustrated, yet filled with awe and praise.

Doughty moved to an unhurried, deliberate rhythm; in the desert he was the opposite of the bird-witted Arabs. His portrait, painted by his daughter, Dorothy, shows him as the genius rather of the radiant, than of the burning sun; as the genius of that 'mere humanity', by virtue of which, he said, there is no land so dangerous through which a man might not pass. Like Chaucer his poetry has an April quality; birds' notes are in it.

Both Doughty's daughters had received from their parents a creative gift; Dorothy had her father's boldness in conception and his large-hearted valiancy; Freda his delicate perception. Both were distinguished ceramists. The fancy which had set earth-born elves and great-bearded little wights leaping over the clods on Claybourne Cliffs was active still, though with other materials. Dorothy and Freda disclaimed any gift with words; yet I have never heard the difference between a gull's manner of flight and a rook's expressed so graphically as by Freda Doughty. Both sisters had been given something better than formal schooling; they had been helped by their parents to look at things. They had not their mother's quick, piercing, indomitable virtue with words. I loved to hear Mrs Doughty tell some story of the day-to-day happenings at Merriecroft; or to hear her laugh if I managed, in my turn, to tell some Cornish story to please her. 'Delicious!' she would say, 'delicious!' and turn away to the garden, to the scented plants near the house which were her favourites. When I think of Merriecroft I smell roses and mignonette, lavender, rosemary and geranium leaf; I see a sweet-chestnut tree and hear the quacking of ducks; and I have a sudden perception in the house of Arabian scenes; the Eastern sunshine of Mrs Doughty's pictures on the walls. I am one that sees things suddenly after passing them a hundred times without noticing.

Through Mrs Doughty I met the first critic who had written a full-length study of her husband's work. Professor Barker Fairley, now of the University of Toronto, and a much praised authority on Goethe, was at that time Professor of German Literature at Manchester University. He lived at Buxton and to stay with him I rode my Velocette to Ashbourne and walked, for the first time, the Valley of the Dove. As I held in my heart both Isaac Walton himself, and Doughty's presentation of the scene in which that honest, civil lover of the chub had fished, I immensely enjoyed my walk up the dale until, indulging in what Susan calls one of my long, short cuts, I got entangled in the surrounding hills, and saw no less than seven donkeys together, mournfully and without irony beholding me, their slatey coats hardly distinguishable from the dun background. I asked them the way and one hee-hawed. There is nothing like, for enjoyableness, hospitality received after a day of scrambling. Margaret and Barker Fairley and their children, when I finally reached Buxton, were a glorious contrast to the seven donkeys. I was stimulated and heartened to talk of Doughty with friends who cared for his work as much as I did myself. I received immense help from Barker Fairley, most generous of minds, and also from Margaret who, when my book on Doughty came to be published, corrected the proofs, a heavy task; for printers hate to print Doughty's punctuation. He intended it to mark pauses for the voice, not to point the grammar. Doughty, like any other sensible poet, meant his verse to be read aloud—though not in an organ voice a-tremble with anticipated emotion. That voice reminds me of a stop in church organs. My father would walk out of church if anyone used it. 'Do you hear that, Anne?' he would say in an agitated tone meant to be a whisper. 'Give me my hat, my dear.'

It was Barker Fairley, at that time preparing a book of selections from *The Dawn in Britain*, who encouraged me to bring my book to the point of publication. His own fine book on Doughty, now alas! out of print, had been published by Jonathan Cape; he advised me when at last my manuscript, after much pulling, and poking, and burning, and a dip in the Cherwell was ready, to send it to the same firm. Edward Garnett praised it; I was electrified. The thing became a book; how trim compared with the bruised and battered typescript. Printed books seem stand-offish and aloof to their poor parents. My father, Professor Elton, and Mrs Doughty praised it. My brother kept it at his bëddes head—it was a splendid soporific he said. Susan murmured. She said she had never liked patchwork, and a page studded with quotations looked patched. But ah! the pleasure of confounding them! Of waving the *Spectator*—my family has always been respectful to the *Spectator*—before their eyes, and rolling on my tongue the praises of my fellow-admirer, my co-efficient in Doughty, Dr Herbert Read, a poet himself. A poet, too, was Hugh

Macdiarmid, who had always acclaimed Doughty, and who now took occasion to sound the trumpets for him afresh. These champions I set up on high with Mr David Garnett. As for Doughty's denigrators, those Haddocks' eyes, I worked them into waistcoat buttons in the silent night.

My book was most unworthy of its great subject; but I think the pursuit was a grand way of completing an apprenticeship. My name was by this time chastely embellished, for I had been awarded the Oxford degree of B.Litt. I was ready to start teaching again. But was I good enough to teach? I knew I was not. No one ever is good enough to teach—and everyone is too good to teach all the time.

18

TWO PARISHES AGAIN

Where Belinda's garden slow
Falleth to the Cornish sea;
Where the tall white daisies blow,
And bright poppies stand a-row
Round a path whose pebble and shell
Washed clean by the ocean swell
Are the sole paving, even thou
May'st find peace now.

May'st find peace now;
Nor wait for thy rigidity
When, in thy pale perfection,
The warm flesh shall forsake the bone,
And the Breath shudder and win free.
Whilst thou art in thy fine body
Seek quiet where the hollyhocks grow,
And the marigold's a-glow
Where Belinda's garden slow
Falleth to the Cornish sea.

—*Belinda's Garden*

I was still as poor as when I had borrowed fifty pounds from the Central Bureau for the Employment of Women. I should never, I began to feel, write one of those letters I fondly imagined, letters of a wealthy woman, letters running something like this: 'Dear Miss Passmore, I wonder if you remember me? I am enclosing a cheque for a thousand pounds in slight recognition of the benefit I received in the year . . . ' Or, 'Dear Miss Grier, I am enclosing a cheque for a thousand pounds in slight recognition of the Bursary you awarded me when I was on my beam ends in the year . . .' Or, 'Dearest Susan, A thousand pounds, darling, in slight recognition of all . . . ' In these imaginative flights I always sent a thousand pounds. I love the rounded simplicity, the pure beam of a thousand pounds. But I never gained even enough to buy the cottage I promised my mother, and which we walked about in the firelight. This cottage was to be in a sheltered place like Trevarrick; it would have a garden with flower-beds and box-borders; there would be lemon verbena and a moss-rose bush by the porch. At the foot of a little orchard full of Lent lilies would run a brook set with watercress, and ferns, and having a single plank to cross by. Susan, too, fancied such a cottage with shells on the window-sills. But my father habitually scoffed at it. Damp! Crippled with rheumatism we should be. Think of old Alfred Snell hobbling about on two sticks! My father's denunciations of the cottage were more real than the cottage itself. They almost brought it into existence. Outside sanitation! He knew all about that; a closet down the garden path hidden with lilac! How long was lilac in flower? Cosy? Nonsense! A sitting-room like old Mrs Sargent's, stuffy with the door closed and draughty with it open. If he was going to own anything he wanted something spacious, something in which he could have a little organ.

Alas! we never had either the cottage or the space. My mother died in 1932 at the age of seventy-five, after an illness during which she was most tenderly cared for by my sister. It was incredible that she should die; she looked young still, and her face had in death an appearance of serenity, of expectation utterly fulfilled, almost as though the riddle of a breath had been solved. A great stillness replaced the instantly-changing expressiveness which had been her grace in life:

> She could curl up in sleep, awake could range
> The wide world over, now a bitter change;
> So straight and still, nor any room to turn,
> A rigid discipline is this to learn.

My father missed her hourly when he was indoors; no other loss could have been so grievous to him. Most happily, however, he had resources out of doors, pleasures in which my mother had not shared. He could still go fishing, watch cricket matches, and garden in his allotment. Instead of the rather cold-hearted, windy gardens which had been his in Cornwall he was now co-partner with Mr Baker, a retired schoolmaster from Bradninch, in a plot which sloped south-west to the estuary of the Exe. I liked to sit with my father there in the sunshine, praising his green peas, and maintaining stoutly that they were better than Mr Baker's, though Mr Baker grew the most astounding, plump marrow-fats. His pods cracked with peas like the pictures on the seed-packets. This richness was due to bone-manure my father used to say. It was my job to fetch the bone-manure. 'Go down on your bicycle, Anne, my dear,' my father would say almost as soon as I got home for a holiday. 'Go down to Pratt's and bring me up a little bone-manure. Susan, you know, draws the line at bone-manure. Says it smells. But it's what Mr Baker uses.' My father's fish, too, had to vie with Mr Baker's. 'Only one today,' he would admit, opening the fishing basket he wore with a leather strap slung over his shoulder; 'only one; but it's a fine mullet! Baker has five or six wretched little pollock.'

He loved the summer and the light; and he hated the winter and darkness. Indoors his wireless was his greatest solace. I can hardly imagine anyone who has more enjoyed the miracle of music over the air, or who has been more annoyed by indiscriminate applause. 'If they think that well played,' he would say testily after a prolonged claque, 'they have no more sense of music than this cat'—pointing a finger at Tweedle, purring unconscious on the hearth-rug. But he often overflowed with applause himself and when, as sometimes happened, my brother Howard suddenly appeared, pretending to conduct the whole orchestra, sharing in my father's enjoyment, his cup of pleasure was full. The two pairs of blue eyes, so alike, and so alive, would sparkle in unison.

My father lived to be ninety-one, moving more and more stiffly, but with his senses unimpaired and his mind unclouded. He died in the midst of war, in 1943. Like many another Cornishman of his generation he was one of the innumerable frail links binding England and America. Of his grandsons, one, Capn's second son, Victor, fought in the Royal Navy; another, Maurice's son, Bill, once the little boy who had worn out his pants sliding down the Exmouth sea wall, fought with the American Marines. Only a short hour before his death my father was listening to a speech by Mr Churchill. He was utterly confident in him. But in the old days he had been wont to inveigh against 'young Churchill' and call him rash and a hot-head. It was not until 1940 that my father entirely forgave Mr Churchill for changing his party in 1902. His admired man had been Mr Balfour. Both my parents were Conservative to the marrow. My mother was shaken once, and that by her favourite, Mr Baldwin. We had been wont to tease her about her dear Stanley; but he made, with my mother, the tactical error of publicly recommending a book, *Precious Bane*, by Mary Webb. She hastened to get it, looked at the end as was her habit, and then began to read at her quick usual rate. I happened to be in the room when she had finished it. She said, 'Well!' Then she took off her glasses and gazed thoughtfully at me. 'I begin to wonder, my dear, whether we can trust Mr Baldwin's judgment,' she said. But she voted Conservative again in the next election. After all Mr Baldwin was not the Party.

On leaving Oxford I looked about for a job in Cornwall and, finding none, I went to teach English in King Edward's High School, Birmingham, while waiting for something in the west to turn up. I was attracted partly because Miss L.K. Barrie was head mistress of the school and I felt that we shared ideas about schooling; but even more because, in the excellent, free, old high school tradition there was no regular afternoon school at King Edward's. I spied leisure, and a fresh region of England to explore. Out of my first month's salary I put down a deposit on a new Velocette, took delivery, and heigh ho, for the Malverns! I came to them, saw their melodious line, set my Velocette to a rubbly path, fell off, grazed my knuckles, abandoned the bike, walked to the top of the Beacon and took a breath. Ever since, exploring all that Malvern country has been to me a main delight.

But the Malverns never ousted Cornwall. Cornwall was still my chosen of all destinations.

I did not know when, on my Velocette, I went speeding to Oxford, that I should not return to Cornwall to work again; that Cornwall would become my holiday land, but not the land in which I taught. Instead of being my settled home it became a destination. Three months is the longest stretch I have ever spent without seeking it; but visiting a place, however frequent the visits, is not like living there. Yet the visits have lent to Cornwall for me the glow of holiday-light. I have come speeding on through the counties in hoar-frost to Tintagel. That was on my new Velocette. I have come, how many times, by the night train, turning out at Bristol to join the dim nocturnal life between eleven-thirty and one, reaching St Erth in the morning, and walking over the Towans and through the nut grove, to St Ives, having breakfast with Florence Drew, walking by the lower path or over the hills to Zennor, down to Gurnard's Head, up to Mrs Green's on the Bosullow Downs, across to Land's End and Tol-pedn Penwith, or to Mrs Bailey's at Lamorna, and back through Sunday night on the night train from Penzance. These weekends, little breathless sips of Cornwall, renewed the life in me. Short holidays are sweet.

But long holidays are sweeter. We have spent them in farmhouses, in cottages and tents, often returning to the two parishes, Gorran and Caerhays. Latterly, since my parents died, my sister and I have preferred our summer holiday in tents. In the wet we lie low and read until it is fine again; we have sometimes lain low a long time it must be owned. We have clung to our ropes in order to prevent ourselves from being carried up on high. In 1946 storms raged as though in winter. The waves hurled themselves up the beach at Hemmick, forced a way up the little river, blighted the water-cress beds, hurtled stones as though they were sticks, and churned the froth to spume. At Vault the backwash withdrew screeching through the shingle. One morning after the wildest of nights Mr Bunny rose, hastened to the window, looked out upon our patch, and said to his wife, 'My Gor, Mary! they tents is still there; they maidens must have pegged they down proper.'

But this summer (August 1947), we have come into the golden sunshine, that sunshine which always has its turn to transfigure the earth if one goes on living and hoping. As I write the last pages of this book Susan and I are encamped once more in our three little tents—one each and one for the saucepans—on the same patch as during the rainy August. It is a triangular patch, part of our friend Thomas Grose's farm of Trevesson; it lies between the hedge of his last steep field and the road that leads from Boswinger to Penare. By the side a little brook runs, bordered by loosestrife and water-mint, bramble and the great white cups of bindweed. Hemp agrimony grows tall. Janey Ashton, once Janey Kendall of Cotna who, like her mother, cherishes flowers and babies, told us when she came to tea that the name was Virgin Mary and that the flowers picked in their prime, and dried and steeped in water were good for gatherings. The plant had virtue she said. We watch the butterflies—cabbage-whites and painted ladies; red-admirals; the shyer flitting blues and saffrons; the rare orange-tips. Two dragon-flies with a blue-black rattle of exquisite wings chase one another. Ahead long tranquil waves gather darkness in the early morning and sun-sparkles at noon before they turn lazily to foam. Behind is a cornfield in all the beauty of sheaves set up in shocks. The patterned lines are lovely, for the field is not flat. It slips over a curve at the top and lies in dips and folds. The harvesters are Tom Grose and his brother John, and their Uncle Will Nott, eighty but still able to bicycle from Trevarrick to Trevesson and do a day's harvesting. In the next field—Mrs Edward Michell's of Boswinger—the corn is being carried by his sons and their helpers, while he stands at the top of the lane to warn cars not to come down the winding, steep way when the wagons are mounting. I regret the absence of horses in the wagons; but Jane is glad that they need no longer strain themselves in the heat and be stung by the flies. At Cotna in the old days she said her mother hated most to see the horses draw the threshing-machine. 'Is Darling between the shafts?' she would say. 'Shut up the door, my dear, so that I can't see.'

The hum of the machines in the fields joins with the hum of insects. Grasshoppers whirr; great prosperous handsome drones buzz; worker-bees look too busy and meagre to enjoy themselves. They have achieved a utility cut. Our work in the tents is little and that little is enjoyable. We pick sticks to light the fire and fry the mackerel and red mullet which we get from the Fishermen's Co-operative shop in Gorran Haven. All is spruce in the Fishermen's Co-operative. But Jack Patton doesn't think much of us for being so helpless as to buy fish. He could show us how to set a spilter so that we should never be without a bass at Hemmick. But we are no fishermen; a few mackerel when we went out in a boat from Mevagissey is all we have caught. They were coloured like an early morning sky— pink, and pearl, and bluish under their dark top-markings as they lay in the basket. In the sea they were slim lords of themselves and life, with the water fitting round them everywhere. As they slid through the lanes, water closed behind them as air closes behind us—strange phantoms of the water as we are strange phantoms of the air.

'People change; but the place don't change much,' Mr Uglow said, when we met him going up through the park to see his sheep, just as he had been to see them thirty years before. We met Mr Allen, too, carpenter at the castle for double that number of years; Mr Allen is getting on for ninety if not quite ninety. He was walking home to Tregavarras from work. It will take him ten years he told us to get the castle into order after the various things it went through during the war, including twenty or thirty evacuee boys. 'And Mrs Williams was sorry to see 'em go,' says he. We looked down at the castle from the top of the park. 'People change; but the place don't change.' Was that it? Was that why we felt instantly at home in the two parishes? 'They can't be in their camp yet,' says Lowry Richards, church warden in his father's place, 'they haven't been to church. They would have been to church; they're a couple of Gorran girls.' We walk to Caerhays Barton and, as of old, I go with Mr Kneebone, from field to field, counting up the livestock, making sure that all creatures are present before nightfall. Then we get back go the house, to Mrs Kneebone who has done so many more kindnesses than the ordinary run of folks. She does them while protesting that she never never will. She is the main exemplar in my life of the son in the parable who said to his father, 'I go not,' but he went. Just the opposite from me. I am all too eager to say, 'I go, Sir,' but I go not . We walk to Gorran. Perhaps my brother Howard arrives and looks at the spot where he and Maurice spilt the tar. They had wheeled the tin of tar in the wheelbarrow all the way up from Gorran Haven. As they neared the home gate Howard, playing 'Burn bumps', pinched Maurice's bottom, made him wince, and the tar was upset. My father sent them all the way back again to fetch some more.

We take other familiar walks. At Portholland Johnny Johns is in his shop; but the shelves are sadly depleted. 'Woodbines, boy, Woodbines!' he admonishes a would-be customer, 'you'm living in a dream of the past, a dream of the past. Me and Howard Treneer, here,' pointing to my brother who is sitting sideways on the counter, 'me and Howard can mind when Ogden's Guinea Gold was threepence a packet, threepence a packet.' He is as derisive as his father was at the idea of my keeping a shop. 'You'd never have the patience for it, my dear maid, never have the patience for it.' Perhaps we walk to Trevarrick and hear Elam (William) Grose recalling the days when, as a boy, he used to go rabbiting with my father who, if he missed the first shot might say, 'I shan't do anything today, Elam, my boy; I might as well be home in bed.' How well all we Treneers know those days which we inherit from our parent! From Trevarrick, perhaps, we walk back by way of Almshouse Hill to the Milfords and call to see Mrs Grose and her daughter May. Mrs Grose says, 'I enjoyed your book, Anne, my love; but arn't 'ee ever going to write a book with a bit of love in it? What I like is a little bit of love.' On our way down to Hemmick we may call to see Tom and Ida with whom we went to school. When it rained too heavily on our camp Tom came down through the soaking fields to persuade us to come up to the house. 'When you'm tired of it down here just say, "Well, we'm going home now, and come up Trevesson." ' We have no house in Gorran or Caerhays; and yet we have, in the two parishes, that for lack of which so many millions are in sore distress—a natural home, our proper place.

A STRANGER
IN THE
MIDLANDS

To Helen and Maurice

Contents

1

AN INTERVIEW AT
KING EDWARD'S

O ne summer morning, in the year 1931, I got out at
Snow Hill station, walked down through the Arcades,
and stood in New Street outside King Edward's High
School for Girls, Birmingham. It was a tall building squeezed
in between the intricate façade of the Boys' School and the
Hen and Chickens. The building was tall and narrow, and
Twist, who had his office just inside the front door, was narrow
and tall, though his shoulders were broad. He had been in the
army, and still looked a soldier, every inch. He greeted me. I
was the young lady—I was no longer young, but this
condoning of the past was part of Twist's success—I was the
young lady who had come to see the Headmistress—time of
half-past eleven. I said I was, and Twist conducted me in; he
never merely took a person. As on parade, square-shouldered,
we went into a silent corridor, up the silent stairs, to a silent
landing where, to the silently expressed command 'SQUAD
HALT', I halted. From a door on the left Gumery appeared.

I have often wondered what early pressures, or absence of
pressure, acting on a strain of original virtue, produced
Gumery, with her serenity, her patience, her appearance of
contentment, and the quiet of her service. I suppose there is
not a soul who ever was at King Edward's in Gumery's day

who does not think affectionately of her. By the time I arrived she had already served the school thirty years. There she stood, her features a little blurred, her hair smooth; she was wearing a dark stuff dress, with a little white at the throat; and the dress was protected by a large, white, nurse-like apron, an apron with a bib in which were inserted three rows of open-work trimming. Her hands were ready. I was to find that Gumery's hands were always ready; her entire self was ready, whether to bandage a child's arm, mend a ladder in an ill-starred stocking, comfort, with a cup of coffee, some mistress who had sped to school without breakfast or, with her talk of the past, make some old girl feel at home again, someone who, perhaps, had wandered in and, finding nearly every other face the face of a stranger, had been feeling all forlorn.

From Gumery I passed to Miss Piper. Miss Piper was the headmistress's secretary. She had brown hair, not quite straight but not fuzzy, that happy hair which keeps in place, and which is almost essential to a good secretary; there was also a light of irresistible drollery in her rather full, dark blue eyes; it was as though a comedian had dressed up in an elegantly ironed silk shirt, and was enacting the part of the perfect secretary. She took me to Miss Barrie.

I knew Miss Barrie. I had last seen her floating like a cork off Carbis Bay. She had a wonderful gift of being able to cross her ankles, clasp her knees with her arms, and float. When I tried to do it I always toppled sideways. I had first met her when I was a research Fellow at Liverpool University, and she was headmistress of Wallasey High School. A common friend had introduced us, and had kept us in occasional contact with each other through the intervening years by short, glorious spells of holiday in Cornwall. So we knew each other well, but only in holiday moods, not in work-a-day circumstances. Yet, after the manner of teachers because, however lightly you make take it, teaching is an incomparably interesting profession, we had talked a certain amount of shop while haunting the Hayle Towans, with their windy tufts of marram grass, or the wide shadow-haunted downs of West Penwith. Walking these airy places in desultory communication, because we were both framed to enjoy places more than ideas, and because Miss Barrie had that rare distinction among men and women of not talking too much, we had, nevertheless, got to know each other's minds on the subject of schooling. We were agreed that most children were over-taught, and given too little time to learn; and that it was not hard work but anxiety which caused strain. We were also agreed that the secret with difficult children was to find something in which they could absorb themselves; that happiness for them was in absorption; and that young people could feel invigorated and renewed by mastering even the instruments of learning if given time to feel the thrill of conquest at the right age. I always remember her telling me of a little girl who found for the first time this satisfaction when she mastered long division. For a time she sent not letters to her parents but elegantly set out long division sums. Miss Barrie had taken the Mathematical Tripos at Newnham. She was always interesting when she talked of teaching mathematics; but she cared about the teaching of English too, particularly as it affected the child unready with words, the mathematical child faced with a fanciful 'essay subject' or stupidly asked to state why she liked a poem. So we had talked every now and then, and, while walking over the downs or up the carns, by the cliff-paths or along the towans, I had caught many a glimpse of King Edward's School, to which Miss Barrie had moved from Wallasey. I had never thought to see her at her desk being a headmistress; she had never thought to see me applying for the post of a teacher of English.

'I warned the English department to expect you in motor-biking overalls,' she said.

I smiled in the assurance of my borrowed hat, and looked complacently at my borrowed hand-bag, a crowning touch bestowed on me by a friend at Lady Margaret Hall where I had been working as an advanced student.

Miss Macdonald and Miss McDermott came into the room, Miss Macdonald, Irish, and head of the English side, Miss McDermott a Scot, also teaching English, and Senior Mistress of the school. To the girls, I discovered later, they were affectionately known as Sandy Mac and Little Mac. Still preening myself on the clothes which had so startled Miss Barrie, I shook hands with both, and they bore me off to show me the school, and to tell me what work I should have to do if I fell victim to them. As I listened I forgot my hat, I forgot my handbag, I began to deflate. I could feel the bounce going out of me. I knew at once that they were wonderful English mistresses, very different from me. It was not that they were conceited or boastful; they were friendly and amusing. But the schemes! The way the whole thing was planned! I have never been much of a planner. And then, the questions they asked me, questions nicely calculated to test my weak points. Should I be prepared to help with the Admission Examination? I gulped. I knew that I should be either indifferent about a paper or ready, if my interest was roused, to haggle over half a mark. There is something about beta minus plus plus, which satisfies the requirements of my wavering disposition. In thinking of all this I was unable to make any reply at all. And Miss Macdonald laughed. Irish met Cornish. Miss McDermott remained judicial for a moment and then laughed too. So I laughed. It seemed, for one thing, very comic that an Irishwoman and a Scot should be engaged in the act of appointing a Cornishwoman to teach English in the heart of Saxondom! We waived the question of the entrance examination. What tempted me was an offer of a very generous share in sixth form and University Scholarship work combined with junior work. I need not, unless I wished, do any School Certificate work at all. I happen to detest the School Certificate, the dullest examination every devised by dull souls; to postpone it to the age of sixteen is mental cruelty to able minds.

I was then handed over to Miss Sayers, while Miss Macdonald, Miss McDermott and Miss Barrie fell to balancing my qualities and deficiencies in Miss Barrie's room. Miss Sayers talked to me. She was a mathematician and a golfer; tall, blithe and debonair, with the nose of a duchess. It is probably this nose which has led her to the castle where now she reigns as headmistress. Her Christian name was Isabel. She had been a student during Miss Major's term as mistress of Girton, and she told me much of interest about a personality of whom I was to hear more and more at King Edward's. Miss Major had been headmistress of the school before her translation to Girton. Miss Sayers also talked of beds. She was an enthusiast for comfortable mattresses, arguing thus: We spend an average of seven out of twenty-four hours in bed. By arithmetical progression this tots up to a simply enormous sum in a lifetime. I forget the figure now, but I was staggered at the time. One avenue to a happy life was obviously by way of the Slumberland mattress. Miss Sayers was lyrical, and how right she was I only knew when in later life I stayed in her flat. It was bonfire night; she gave a party with fireworks, and bushels of roast chestnuts; and I slept in one of the beds. Like Christopher Sly I dreamed I was a Lord.

Miss Sayers's talk did much to make me think I should like King Edward's. Work, she said, could generally be arranged if one wanted to play a really important golf match. A few afternoon lessons were creeping in, but the bulk of the hard work, apart from practical work in the laboratories, was over by one o'clock; and on Fridays the 1.5 train could sometimes be caught to Town. Fares were low. Edwardians could be in London by three o'clock except on their games day. Theatres! I have no golf but I dearly love a play. I began to see great possibilities in teaching English at King Edward's; so when I was escorted back to Miss Barrie's room, and was offered the post, I said yes, without apparent hesitation. Yes, I'd come, I said.

In the train going back to Oxford where, after teaching for some years in elementary and secondary schools, I had been indulging, at Lady Margaret Hall, in that private and delightful reading sometimes called Research, I began to repent. As soon as I have said yes, I always wish I had said no. I began to wish it with all my heart and soul. Birmingham! Whatever could have induced me? But when I reached Oxford I found that my friends had prepared a celebration; plainly I must rejoice. I could not help flaunting my acceptance. It was a hilarious party. Most of my friends were research students like myself; but I had also found friends among undergraduates years and years younger than I. It was one of these undergraduates, staying up late in the term because of a viva, who had prepared the feast in a room in Park Town. She was recovering from measles, and had lain in bed counting the thirty-five reproductions of Italian masterpieces with which her cultured landlady—landladies were crowded with culture in the L.M.H. area—had vexed her walls. She and the others were glad of an occasion to be gay. They teased me. What had I always said? That I should go back to teach in Cornwall near the sea? I let myself go at the party, but in the night all my hesitations returned. How happy are those diamond natures who not only cut instantly through the jungle of mixed desires to a decision but who, having reached such a point, do not try to turn round. I turned and turned in bed, trying at least to go to sleep.

Such a night for me follows a regular pattern. I lie still and try repeating to myself:

> Out in the dark, over the snow,
> The fallow fawns invisible go . . .

Then my thoughts begin to leap about in my head. I turn over and lie still. Then I try saying:

> He there does now enjoy eternal rest,
> And happy ease which thou dost want and crave . . .

The thoughts are leaping about in my head again, even when I have reached:

> Sleep after toil, port after stormy seas,
> Ease after war, death after life, does greatly please.

So I turn and lie flat on my back and keep still again. I start saying:

> The curfew tolls the knell of parting day,
> The lowing herd winds slowly o'er the lea.

The Elegy is, as it were, a hereditary poem in the Treneer family; my father always puts himself to sleep with it. It usually suffices for me. But on this night nothing would suffice until I had determined against committing myself to any school however good, and to any headmistress however much I liked her, in the vicinity of New Street Station, Birmingham, and of Snow Hill—so lovely a name, so unlovely a place. I would send a telegram to Miss Barrie next day and revoke.

When I got down late to breakfast I found a letter from Miss Barrie herself, written as soon as I had left her. She said that she was sure that by the time her note reached me I should be in the act of composing a wire to rescind my ready decision. But she wanted me to consider. Birmingham, although one would not imagine it, was set in beautiful country; I should find varied pleasures on my Velocette. I need not stay at the school a term longer than I wished; but she felt I had a contribution to make to King Edward's if I finally decided to come. Oh balm! Oh blessed praise! And after Cornwall had taken no account of me. It would be a curious study to consider how far our lives tend to be directed by pique and praise. To be influenced by pique is very humiliating; one should, I am sure, resist it, or try to. But praise! How can one help being influenced by praise? If it comes from the lips of one we ourselves admire, it is a heady wine, a triumphing air; it is like the air over Dodman Point, to be breathed with rapture. How can one resist praise? And then, too, after celebrating with such a zest the night before, it seemed damp and chilly to tell Helen, Mary, Elizabeth and the others that I was not after all, going to Birmingham-on-sea. So I sent no wire to King Edward's. Instead I confirmed my acceptance and, elated by the certainty of salary to come, I celebrated again with money borrowed on my prospects. Then I went to Timms's with further borrowings and hired a covered punt so as to camp for three weeks on the Cherwell when term should finally have ended, and I no longer be *in statu pupillari*.

I had enjoyed being *in statu pupillari* at Oxford. Exeter is my true, my most beloved College; Liverpool University was a good foster mother to me; and Oxford set me free. It is a pity not to go to Oxford, however late in life, because of its beauty. And, for a teacher, research in her own subject is an absolute essential if she is to retain freshness. Yet 'research', when applied to work done by students of the arts, is a misleading term, borrowed from the sciences, and doing infinite harm to English studies. I use it for convenience sake. 'Reading' or 'meditation' are better words than 'research' to describe what I was given leisure to do at Liverpool and Oxford, and for which I shall always bless both places, and the scholars in them. Such readings cannot be done when one is an undergraduate. Then there is a sense of urgency; it is hard to be young; I wanted to take all lovely poetry and all fine prose as my province when I was at Exeter. In Liverpool and Oxford I learnt a kind of delicate patience.

But quite apart from learning and meditation it is good for a teacher to go back to College. I have heard some advanced students complain of the indignity of being, in their dotage, once again pupils, and members of a Junior Common Room. But in practice, at Lady Margaret Hall, research students were in all essentials free persons; and for a teacher to become, after some years in the schools, a member of a Junior Common Room is the most illuminating of experiences as far as her methods and practice of teaching as an art are concerned. Illumination to me was often painful. Meeting as I did, on free and easy terms, young women fresh from the sixth forms of schools of every type, day and boarding, public and private, old-fashioned, progressive and stationary, schools in the United Kingdom and schools abroad, I found that they had one thing in common. They shared it with young women brought up in convents and with young women who had been subject to governesses at home. They were, with some exceptions, fiercely critical of their upbringing, and of their teachers. Gratitude in the early 'thirties of this century was altogether out of fashion. Only ridicule was smart. I have heard people who were enjoying the fruits of good scholarships, largely as the result of their schoolmistresses's efforts, rend these poor souls lately in charge of them to tatters, and vaunt their own maltutored genius. For some time after I came to L.M.H. I did not reveal myself as one of the despised species; but after some months I found myself one day hotly defending some unknown English mistress who was being attacked, and in the course of the argument I gave myself away. My youthful friends were delighted; they said what a clever fox I had been to lie low for so long. It is almost impossible to be huffed with the high-spirited young. There is joy in them; they are nearer the Kingdom of Heaven than the old and just.

I felt regretful at leaving these friends for school. School relationships must, of necessity, be different. I do not think it wise for teachers and taught to stand on their heads together. Any theory which involves an attempt at being a child with the children is anathema to me, and so is any intrusion on children in their dear, unguarded exhibition of themselves in art and speech and gesture. Children need the secret dark, and teachers have to restrict their thoughts and speculations in schools. In fact they have to edit their minds for the young and that is, at bottom, why teaching becomes irksome. One acts a part and one cannot act a part for long without becoming that part. I left Lady Margaret Hall—where I could say what I liked without pausing to consider—with reluctance. I did not really want to go to King Edward's. And yet I thought of the school with a certain pleasure; it had, I imagined, something in it of silence and recollection amid the turmoil of New Street. Perhaps the mind was its own place; but I knew, as I idled among the water-lilies of the Cherwell, that the mind had never been its own place for the likes of me.

2

A NEW COAT AND SKIRT

It was my father who said to me when I reached Exmouth after a delicious three weeks on the Cherwell, 'I should have a new suit, Anne, if you're going up there among all those women.'

'I have no money,' I said.

'You can hang it up at my tailor's. Matthews never sends in the bill till after three months.'

It was typical of him, who had been poor all his life, that he should go to the best tailor in Exmouth. A Matthews suit, he said, lasted and looked well to the end. Only once had he been seduced by the cheap. My brother Howard, who makes any suit look baggy in a week, came down from Exeter to see him, wearing a new masterpiece.

'Not a bad bit of suiting that, boy,' said my father cautiously. He would not commit himself to real praise until he knew where the suit came from. When my brother announced with glee the number of shillings he had paid for it my father at first pooh-poohed the whole set up, coat, waistcoat and trousers. But after a time he returned to the original theme. He did like the stripe and it seemed to him quite a decent bit of cloth.

Soon afterwards he startled my sister Susan and me by saying he was going to have a suit like Howard's. In vain we hold him he was more difficult to fit. Up to Exeter he went and, accompanied by my brother, ordered a suit. I shall never forget his disappointment when the resulting garments arrived and he put them on. He came down the stairs humming, 'The Saints of God! their conflict past', and said to me,

'What do you think of it, Anne? Not a bad little suit?' He was talking to persuade himself.

'It looks splendid,' I said.

'H'm! "And life's long battle won at last, No more they . . ." ' (No words, only the hummed tune.) 'Coat a little bit long do you think?'

'Oh, no; it seems just right to me.'

' "They cast them down before the Lord!" Trousers a bit wide in the leg?'

'I suppose it's that style of suit,' I said.

' "O happy Saints! for ever blest, In that . . ." Not like a Matthews suit, is it?'

'No; but you can get two like that for one of Matthews's.'

' "Calm haven of your rest!" . . . I don't want two.'

He did not wear the suit many times. One day I heard him coming downstairs humming, 'Now the day is over'.

'Anne', he said, 'I've decided to send this suit up to little Stan.' He nearly always placed the epithet *little* before the name of my third brother, Stanley, although my brother had grown from a skinny little boy into a very sizable man. 'I shall send the suit up to Bristol to little Stan. It will do for him to wear in his garden. A good gardener, Stan! He always was the only one of the boys to know the difference between a potato and an artichoke . . . "Shadows of the evening, Steal across . . .". If I gave the suit to the boy Howard, he would be wearing it in the cathedral.'

But now my father was all agog to choose a Matthews suit for me. 'Don't have patterns, Anne,' he said, 'tell them to send up a bolt or two of cloth. You want to see the broad effect. And just fray the end a little to make sure that it's a pure woollen cloth, and not half cotton, adding weight without warmth. And see to the texture, Anne. A nice Matthews suit will last till you get back to the west. A wretched climate, Birmingham! But Lichfield cathedral is well worth a visit; you can easily reach Worcester and Hereford; and have another look at Gloucester Cathedral and Tewkesbury Abbey on the way up.'

There were not many such buildings my father had not visited in his day, and he had an extraordinary memory for detail. The first thing I was to do when I reached Birmingham was to go to Warwick . . . The Beauchamp Chapel! . . . Warwick Castle!

When a suiting was finally chosen, and what was termed a classic made for me, I tried it on and stood before the critical eyes of my father and my sister Susan. My father greatly approved; my sister Susan said the suit gave me an air, but that unless I had just the right blouse the colour would make me look as blameless as a serpent. My father had chosen a sober colouring to match what we imagined to be the sobriety of King Edward's school. When I disclosed to Susan that I had added to my outfit two tussore blouses of neutral shade, and warranted to wash and wear for ever, she despaired of her once gay companion. She had been to the little shop she patronized and had on approval a fly-away frock; but this treasure she nobly abandoned in order to provide me with the right blouse and handsome gloves. Thus equipped I was said to look very well; one friend shouted to me across the Strand, 'Sal, I hardly knew you!'

The suit, as my father had prophesied, wore to eternity. I gave it away finally to a strange old soul who 'did for me' in a cottage I had at Bearley. She wore it to the end of her life on better occasions. She always called me 'Miss Treenix, Mum', on the strength of that long-lived suit. 'Cloth like iron, Miss Treenix.'

Having considered my clothes my father next gave his mind to my journey. He did not like my Velocette; he pictured me cold in a ditch, or devoured by lorries; but he dearly liked to plan a journey for me, and to tell me what I must be sure not to miss. We arranged that I should spend a night with my ever hospitable brother Stan and his wife Kate, in Bristol, so as to give myself plenty of time next day to view Gloucester Cathedral, Tewkesbury Abbey and, if I had time for a little détour, Malvern Priory Church. I was to report to him how they were all bearing up. I was also to make sure that Kate had not given away his Exeter suit to the little old beggar-man to whom, he said, she was constantly giving good clothes which he, the little old man, pawned, and then appeared as ragged as ever to touch Kate's heart anew. If Stan did not want the suit perhaps Cap'n . . . or even Maurice . . . clothes were dear in America. But of course, if Stan was making use of the suit . . . So I committed my new clothes to a goods' train, and myself set out on my Velocette for Bristol. Over Woodbury Common with its heathy stretches and glorious views of the Exe Estuary I sped, dipped into Ottery St Mary, went too fast up Honiton's wide street, and so I came at a more leisurely pace by the autumnal flats and the strange surveying humps of Somerset, to Bristol and its gorge. I saw the faery bridge leaping across it. In modern times we have been engineers not architects. Our only thrilling works are bridges and battleships, floating castles from which the mechanical birds take wing, and return to rest. But I did not come to rest on a battleship, I came to rest in my brother's comfortable house. It takes a wanderer really to appreciate a home, a wanderer by the way, who anticipates his welcome, and finds it never fails.

Next morning I set out early for Gloucester. I meant to pay merely a perfunctory visit to the cathedral; I meant merely to see just enough to write a letter home. As I rode I recalled one or two stories I knew. I remembered the story of the judge and the witch. Someone has said to me once, in my father's hearing, that I could probably ride a broomstick. My father said there was no law against it, and told the story of the Gloucester judge before whom a witch was brought to be judged in the days when fear of witchcraft was strong and punishments barbarous. Judge Powell tried Jane Whenham for witchcraft in the King's Bench. Her prosecutors swore she could fly.

'Prisoner, can you fly?' asked the judge.

'Yes, my Lord'

'Well then, you may; there is no law against flying.'

She was not convicted, even although she confessed. This story has always lingered in the recesses of my memory. What made Jane say she could fly? Could any vanity be so strong as to maintain its assertions in the courts of pain and death? I should have said, 'No, no, I've never dreamed of flying.' I should have said this at the sight of a match, or a puddle, let alone a bonfire and a pond. Could Jane, perhaps, fly after all? Or was she mad? When she was dismissed, was her vanity more mortified than her terror assuaged, or was she perhaps not sensitive to pain? Perhaps it did not course like lightning through her body to possess its fibres.

I meant, as I have said, to take merely a tripper's glance at Gloucester Cathedral. I have not the prevailing distaste for tripping. We are, after all, merely trippers, every one of us, on this wonderful earth, with only casual glances available to bestow except on that to which we were originally rooted. We should be giddy if we tried really to look at everything, and cathedrals are not my dear darlings. But I knelt humbly in Gloucester Cathedral; I felt its tremendous affirmation. Seas of doubt could swirl about these piers but they would stand. I have often returned as a pilgrim to Gloucester. From the fluidity-in-massiveness of its crypt, to its piercing tower, this great building is a fortress of strength, and a song of praise. The curves of arches in the crypt sweep up and over like ferns; the circular columns stand fast; the great east window of the choir might draw the most insolently temerous mind, the most churlish imagination, to take some part in the crowning of the Virgin. I like to wander in Gloucester Cathedral, to stand in its Lady Chapel; or in one of the little recesses or carols in the south cloister. Looking up the word 'carol' in the Oxford English dictionary, I found the following quotation. It referred to Durham, but no doubt the Gloucester carols served the same purpose: 'In every window three pews or carrells, where everyone of the old monks had his carrell, several by himself, that when they had dined they did resort to that place of Cloister, and there studied upon their books, every one in his carrell all the afternoon.' The cathedral carries the mind irresistibly back to the monastery, to the service by day and night, to the life dedicated to worship and study. Because they are, for all their glory, in the strictest sense functional buildings, because their every detail recalls human life, though human life transcended, the ancient cathedrals have a beauty denied to all modern imitations. I was profoundly shocked, for some reason which I could not analyse, by the unfinished cathedral of St John the Divine when I went into it in New York. It seemed like some great dead thing.

Effigies do no usually affect me, but two effigies in Gloucester haunt the imagination once they are seen: the effigy of Robert of Normandy, lying on a mortuary chest before the High Altar, and the effigy of Edward II, best seen in the North Ambulatory. Robert's effigy is oaken; he is not lying flat, but one knee is raised, and his arm seeks his sword as if he would get up and fight again even now. Edward's figure is in alabaster. One longs to be able to see the face more clearly, a face with its suffering resolved and sealed in peace. Marlowe's Edward II has usurped for me the place of the historic prince. I thought of his royal state and the contrast with his misery and terror in Berkeley Castle where he was imprisoned and murdered. I remembered Marlowe's line, 'They give me bread and water being a king.'

I was moving out of Cornwall, where the only queen I ever dreamed of was La Beale Isoud, into a land where Norman, Plantagenet and Tudor kings and queens had been immediately present, and were present still. I cannot imagine a Shakespeare play about the story of Tristan and La Beale Isoud; that is another poetry. Hotspur mocked it. In England it is Shakespeare's poetry which peoples places, beginning with Gloucester, which leads to a land quickened to the imagination by the history plays. I know where I should like to see the first part of *Henry IV* staged: in the courtyard of the New Inn at Gloucester. Better than anywhere else I can imagine, in that court, the coming of a troupe of players, and a play being watched from the galleries and windows.

At Tewkesbury my mind was still running on the history plays. I admired, as the most casual visitor must, the glorious arch which marks the west front of the abbey, but I did not go into it. Instead I walked by the river for half an hour and, although I did not inquire for the actual site of the Bloody Meadow, I thought of Queen Margaret on the 'plains near Tewkesbury' cheering her followers with nautical phrases; and of her son, Prince Edward, a captive taunting his captors, stabbed in turn by King Edward, by 'misshapen Dick', and by Clarence. It is easy, by the river at Tewkesbury, to imagine the ghost of the Prince greeting Clarence, when he in his turn dreamed of death, with words which have become the standard epithets for a perfidious man: false, fleeting, perjured.

Tewkesbury does not feel far inland; there is hardly a more watery town than Tewkesbury. Even as I rode in the plain with the Cotswold region on one side, and the Malvern chain on the other, and saw Bredon lifting his great shoulder, I still felt in no way Midlandish. It was after I left Worcester, as I rode towards Droitwich and then to Bromsgrove, that I began to remember that I was going to work in a place almost as far away from the sea as I could get. And yet that way is not depressing. There is a hint of forest left in the occasional great trees; there are wide sweeping curves, and spurs of hill from which extend fine prospects. I did not go over the Lickey Hills, those hills which help to make Birmingham endurable. I kept to the plain main road and I found that, even when I reached the city boundary, I had not left the trees entirely. The trees which divide the lanes of traffic do much for this side of Birmingham. Then ugliness closed in. I had been told to guide myself by the Campanile of the University but at first I hardly distinguished it from a chimney. I did not guess as I turned up the Edgbaston Park Road, that I should come to find the University buildings very good by moonlight. I rode cautiously on until I crossed the Hagley Road, and came to a street, whose name I forget, and to the house where I was to lodge. It smelt of gas. It had a long garden at the back, but there were only dahlias in it, and I have never felt that dahlias were exactly flowers. In the house was a fellow lodger, a new master at the Boys' School. He said to me mournfully, 'So you, too, have come to New Street', as though it had only needed that to complete his dejection.

Mrs Whipse, so to call my landlady, had no features; she was so wraith-like she hardly seemed to divide the air. At supper my semi-colleague, whom we will call Mr Probert, said wearily, 'She always forgets something. Tonight it's the salt. No, don't move. I'll do it. Mrs Whipse!'

'Yes, Mr Somebody!' said Mrs Whipse, materializing in a misty way.

'No salt, Mrs Whipse.'

'Well, now, Mr Somebody; I could have sworn I'd put the salt. But, what's salt? Nothing, is it, Miss Somebody? As my poor husband said just before he passed away, "Nellie," he said—I was christened Nellie, Miss Somebody; my mother never held with Ellen if you meant Nellie—"Nellie," he said, "what's anything, anyway?" And that's what I say, too, Miss Somebody, what's anything, anyway? But here's your salt.'

Mr Probert helped himself to it with what the novelists call a hollow groan.

3

IN MISS CREAK'S DAY

When I woke next morning I certainly agreed with poor defunct Mr Whipse that nothing was anything anyway. I felt as lethargic as a bun, and decided that the gas leak must be in my bed-sitting-room. I confided this fear to Mr Probert when I met him at breakfast—we had a bed-sitting-room each, but took meals together in the dining-room. He instantly went into my room and said he wondered I hadn't been gassed in my bed. He then ran a match along the gas-fittings in so reckless a way that I began to fear I had escaped being gassed only to be blown to the moon. However there was no explosion, only a tiny lick of blue flame which went out and in like a devil's tongue. Mr Probert called Mrs Whipse, and she said she'd never known gas to leak in any house of hers before, from childhood upward, no never. And Mr Whipse had always said, ' "You stick to gas, Nellie," he said; don't you have any truck with being electrocuted," he said.' 'And if he was alive now, Miss Somebody, I shouldn't have to take guests into my nice house any way, but life is hard for the fatherless widow.' I said I was sure it was, and agreed with her with all my heart. I have never thought 'guests' desirable in any house, and could have told her that I'd rather have a shack of my own than eat off gold plate in the house of the Lord; only I thought it was irrelevant to grow biblical; and Mr Probert said we must catch a bus.

He had looked up buses to New Street in the most thorough manner possible, so we got on one of the right ones, an extraordinary thing to me. When I see so many buses running along, I tend to get on the first which obligingly stops, and by indirection find direction out. With Mr Probert I got on a direct bus and reached school at an earlier hour than I was ever to reach it again. He disappeared with a wave of the hand into the dignified and decorative Boys' Building; I was greeted by Twist at the entrance of the vertical Girls' School. Twist was dealing out, to girls dressed in black and white, so that they had a faintly magpie appearance, dinner tickets. To me he gave a great brass ticket big enough for a coffin-plate.

Girls were an afterthought of several centuries on the King Edward's Foundation; they had, I believe, only crept in through a liberal interpretation of the word 'youths', and were still, after fifty years, considered novelties of a shady kind. One sorely tried bachelor master, in the early days when girls began encroaching on the Foundation, said that he wished all the girls in Birmingham had one neck, and that that had a rope round it. I had made myself familiar with the history of King Edward's by reading a little book which Miss Barrie had given me on the day of my appointment: *King Edward VI High School for Girls, 1883–1925*, compiled by Winifred I. Vardy.[1] I, who have always been attracted by anything which concerns Richard II and cold towards Edward VI, was pleased to learn that the original licence went back to the days of the more artistic king. Miss Vardy tells the story so well that I cannot do better than quote her words:

'In the year 1392, at the request of the Bailiffs and Commonalty of Bermyngeham, a licence was granted by King Richard II for the establishment of a Gild. This was called the Gild of the Holy Cross, and was of a remarkable character. It was neither a trade Gild, of which there were so many in the Middle Ages, nor a Gild Merchant, like the Merchant

---

[1] My most warm and grateful acknowledgements are due to the author of this book.

Adventurers of Bristol, nor yet one of the town Gilds, managing municipal affairs, the forerunners of present day City Councils. It was founded for charitable and religious purposes and for public social service. Women as well as men were admitted to be members. The gild maintained two chaplains for service in St Martin's, an organist and bellman; it also supported a midwife and had two Gild Almshouses. The rest of the income of the Gild, which came from grants made by three Burgesses, was devoted to keeping roads and bridges in repair, and to making gifts to the poor. The payment made to the King for licence to establish the Gild was fifty pounds, a large sum in those days and the generosity of the three Burgesses who gave the land—John Coleshulle, John Goldsmithe and William atte Stowe—ought to be kept in remembrance.

'For a century and a half the Gild continued, and then Henry VIII confiscated its land and rents and annulled its Charter, but in the reign of Edward VI two-thirds of the Gild lands of the rental value of £21 were restored, and a Charter was granted for the endowment of a school consequent on a commission of inquiry which reported that "The said towne of Birmingham is a very meete place, and it is very meete and necessarie that theare be a ffree School erecte theare to bring uppe the youths." This Charter now hangs in the Governors' room. It provided that there should be one Master or pedagogue . . . one sub-pedagogue or Usher, and twenty governors who were to make fit and wholesome statutes for the Government of the School.'

With the subsequent history of the Boys' School I am not here concerned, though it is a fascinating history, and the school records alone have provided material for four volumes issued by the Dugdale Society. Nor am I concerned with the many distinguished men brought up to 'godliness and good learning' on the Foundation. I confess my two favourites are Canon Dixon, the friend of Gerard Manley Hopkins, and General Slim who once came to the school and gave us, boys and girls alike, a half-holiday. He first asked for a holiday for the boys; but the fallen faces of the girls, and a faint moan coming from the direction of those who, equally with the boys, had lined his route and lustily if somewhat shrilly cheered, recalled him to himself and to his normal wisdom. He turned to the headmistress and begged of her also the boon of half-holiday. I have not studied General Slim's campaigns in such detail as I have read the works of Canon Dixon. His poems are dearly loved by me. So delicate a poet and critic, so understanding a friend, so diligent a priest and historian would, of his mere self I think, be a notable return to the succession of discreet and trusty inhabitants of Birmingham who have organized and maintained the school in growing prosperity from the days of King Edward VI to the present reign of King George. And Canon Dixon, of course, is not alone. A host, more famous in a worldly way, are with him; and during the last sixty years they have been joined by many women.

Miss Creak—Miss Edith Elizabeth Maria Creak—was the first headmistress of the Girls' School when such a school, named King Edward VI High School for Girls, was opened in 1883. It was separate from the Boys' School; but it was grafted on to the original Foundation, and had part in its dignity and honour. Miss Creak must have been a most remarkable woman. As soon as I read Miss Vardy's book about the High School I began to take an interest in Miss Creak, an interest which has deepened with time, with the conversation of old girls, and with being engaged daily in the act of prayer under her pictured, enigmatic eyes and mouth. It is not a good portrait as portraits go; Miss Major's picture by Orpen is on an altogether different plane as a work of art; and Miss Barrie's as a likeness. But even in a mediocre picture Miss Creak's eyes scrutinize the school. They see; they mean; and yet Miss Creak looks detached and even humorous. She must have governed. Her head sits her figure like a well-balanced rider on a horse; and her figure, in its turn, is felt to be firmly established in the saddle of life. That a very ordinary painter should have made so ample-bosomed a woman as Miss Creak, with her hands lightly crossed in her lap, a heavy woman growing old, look as though she is riding side-saddle, and has a perfect seat, is a remarkable achievement. How well she must have known people by the time she had finished with being a headmistress; and what an extraordinary thing is personality! I know a very ordinary dog who has acquired it. Once, no one would have distinguished Kim, particularly, from other dogs of his kind. But because he has lived in a choristers' school, and has gone to prayers regularly except on his nights out, he now has the appearance of a Dean's Chaplain. He has never taken notice of any school bell during the day, but some mysterious faculty helps him to distinguish the nightly prayer bell. A master may say, 'I must go to prayers; Kim has already gone in.' And in his proper place Kim will be found, sitting with an air of grave decorum. The faintest movement of his tail will be made when the headmaster comes in, the austere and uneffusive recognition of one Dignitary by another. In the touching act of nightly prayer, when youthful voices recognize the purpose of the day, and commit themselves to night and God with recollection, it always surprises me that Kim does not join in the responses.

From all one hears of her one knows that Miss Creak, like Kim, had acquired personality. But Miss Creak was no ordinary person to begin with. At twenty-one she was a headmistress. Making decisions early and firmly stamps a definite character on the features. She was already sealed by the time she came to Birmingham at the age of twenty-seven to be first headmistress of the newly established Girls' High School on the King Edward's Foundation. It always amuses me when the present generation is called the age of youth. Youth, now, seems to be forty. Miss Creak was twenty-seven when she came to Birmingham, and consider what she had done by that time! She had had a flying start in that teaching was in her at least an inherited tendency. Her father was Albert Creak (M.A. Lond.). That M.A. Lond. has significance perhaps. Those who were not churchmen tended to go to London rather than to one of the older universities and Miss Creak, we learn later, was a member of Dr Dale's congregation, at Carr's Lane Chapel, while she was in Birmingham. Mr Creak, who kept a boarding-school for boys at Hove, where his pupils lived in his house from the age of eight or so to seventeen or eighteen, must have had a pretty thorough knowledge of them by the time they came to be directed towards the world. There was no need for him to turn his boys over to a psychologist to consider for a couple of hours, or to test their intelligence in forty minutes. He must have become very familiar with their intelligence, perhaps too familiar. That is where an unknown psychologist may score. No one can truly assess a boy or girl, because no one can assess a spirit; but Mr Creak must have been in as strong a position as is humanly possible to divine a youth's potentialities. He was not in charge of a thousand boys. He did not count heads. The word *unit* to him was not part of the jargon of school and army education; *unit* then, ugly little word that it is, was merely 'the least whole number' in arithmetic. It should have remained an abstraction and not have been intruded into the world of living souls, young living souls. I feel sure Mr Creak was not one of the damned who think of people as numbers; and I don't suppose he had a printed form in his school. His reports on boys would be confidential letters to their parents, written on paper on which there were no little ruled spaces to confine him if he needed to say a great deal, or to be filled out with windy words if he had nothing much to add that Half. And yet! Just suppose one were doomed to live in Mr Creak's house for ten years if one didn't like him, and didn't like Mrs Creak, and thought Edith Maria a prig.

Not that I think Miss Creak was a prig. She was educated with her brother and the other boys in this school at Hove; and then, when she was sixteen, she was one of four girls who went up to Cambridge. Under Miss Clough, these four were the first students in what afterwards grew into Newnham College. Lectures were available to them only by courtesy and, although they took examinations, they might not be awarded a Cambridge degree. That privilege took another seventy years, pretty nearly, to achieve, so devilish an innovation was the teaching of women in Universities thought to be. I suppose it was feared we should grow uppish, and so we have. I often wonder what Queen Elizabeth, Emily Brontë, Christina Rossetti and Jane Austen would have been like if they had gone up to Cambridge, and whether there is any significance in the fact that both Virginia Woolf and Dr Edith Sitwell were privately educated. Miss Creak herself, one notes, was not the product of the girls' school system which she did so much to inaugurate; but she did go to Cambridge. She took the Classical and Mathematical Triposes, went to the High School for Girls at Plymouth for a couple of terms as assistant mistress, and then became headmistress of the new school of the Girls' Public Day School Trust to be opened at Brighton. Her brother writes of her: 'My sister organized the school, engaged the staff, opened in January 1887, and in the following July kept her twenty-first birthday.'

Young Miss Creak of Brighton must have been an extraordinarily interesting person to know. High School time-tables were not overburdened in those days, so she found time to study as well as to teach. She went to University Extension Courses in Constitutional History and Political Economy, and she read for a London B.A. Degree which she passed with First Class Honours. The reason given by her brother for the move from Brighton to Birmingham is typical of Miss Creak, and of the school she was to build up. 'The keen, hard-working atmosphere of Birmingham was very welcome after the distinctly less strenuous Brighton ways and outlook on life.'

'Strenuous' is the word. When I think of Miss Creak I think of *The Pilgrim's Progress*, not of Christiana but of Christian himself. Her way, when she came to the foot of the hill Difficulty, was his. How I admire them for choosing the path which led straight from the gate, by the spring, into the narrow way which lay right up the hill! Miss Creak kept what she conceived to be the purpose and end of life plainly in view. But her progress, as one reads of it in Miss Vardy's book, with its hint of misunderstandings at the close, has pathos. Again Bunyan is most expressive: 'I looked then after Christian, to see him go up the hill, where I perceived he fell from running to going, and from going to clambering upon his hands and knees, because of the steepness of the place.'

She established, between 1883 and the year of her retirement, 1910, during a reign of twenty-seven years, a very distinctive school, broadly, but essentially puritan, I should say, in religion; inculcating a strong sense of duty; perhaps tending to make naturally delicate consciences too delicate. It was a school for the strong. Intellectually rigorous, with a tilt towards the sciences, and a further list in the direction of Cambridge; saved from stridency and egoism by genuine hard social work; a contentedly local school, though a school placed to serve every district of Birmingham; a day school of the best kind, allowing leisure for home duties to girls drawn from homes where good nurture was available and availing. For the King Edward's of Miss Creak's day was a very homogeneous school. The girls were drawn largely from educated homes; where exceptions were made it was on behalf of those who showed not merely good average intelligence, but promise of an unusual kind in academic studies. There grew up, therefore, in the very centre of Birmingham, an exclusive school, but exclusive intellectually, not socially. It offered the delight and discipline of good teaching to the most able minds in a great city. It went at the right pace for the quick—the cruelty of making the quick go slow is slurred over in our present-day system. On the other hand there must have been humiliation and great harm done to any slow or woolly-minded child who managed to get into King Edward's. I should myself have been intimidated by Miss Davison's traditional war on the 'vague', and her dislike of the word '*it*': 'Friend, what is that *it*?' she would thunder.

But for the girls able to stand up to it the school in its most rigorous days must have been immensely stimulating. Children do not enjoy the *soft* either intellectually or morally. The lawless then must have found it as exciting to break a little rule of Miss Creak's as, in these more lenient times, to do a little amateur house-breaking. Children will have drama in their lives. It must have made the high-spirited heart beat faster to encounter Miss Creak.

One art which has been of great importance to King Edward's High School for Girls throughout the sixty years or so of its history is music. I am with the Greeks, and with medieval and Tudor teachers, in considering Music the most quickening and formative of the arts, the most generally enjoyable, the art most capable of inducing enlivening memories, to pupils taught at school. Schools are very dangerous. Nearly everything would be better taught in very small groups, or even to individual children than in large classes. Most able children could, in a single year, if undistracted and well directed, learn as much as they learn in four years of chopped-up time at school. But singing is a joyous bond; it gives lightness to the mass, and can nourish the spirit in company. Even its most ordinary terms fall pleasantly on the ear: singing in unison; singing in harmony. Only a shallow and unimaginative generation would have mocked at the idea of a heaven figuratively described in terms of music; but then, our Gradgrinds, and our seekers after titbits of fact, have no rudimentary conception of any art at all. Allegory and image are foreigners to their blank intelligences. Generations of King Edward's children have learnt first under Mr Gaul and later, as I shall hope to show in the course of this narrative, under Miss Denne Parker, and now under Miss Holmes that music is not just one more 'subject' but, in its essence, festival. Mr Gaul wrote in his letter of resignation which illness had made necessary, 'I assure you that it upset me very much taking a step which meant saying goodbye to one of the joys of my life; going to King Edward's did not mean going to school but to an afternoon party twice a week.' The word *party* gives the clue to much voluntary music at King Edward's. And with this word *party* which at once makes me think of the many 'musicals' I enjoyed at King Edward's, I take my leave of the school as it was in Miss Creak's day, only noting further that her established tradition was: plenty of free hours for reading untrammelled in the library; not too much teaching; not too many distracting activities; hard concentrated work and true leisure, that is, time in which a child is free to do what she chooses, not what some organizing fiend chooses.

4

THE FIRST MORNING

I have been for a long time standing in the vestibule, my brass dinner-ticket clasped in my hand, talking of the school as it was up to 1910, the year in which Miss Creak retired. Yet I still do not feel justified in mounting the staircase. Miss Major had succeeded Miss Creak. She had been headmistress until 1925, when Miss Barrie had come to Birmingham. So on that September morning, when I clutched my great ticket, and wondered whether Twist had been in the yeomanry or the infantry, Miss Barrie had been headmistress for six years. At the risk of being tedious I must say something of the school as it was between 1910 and 1931.

Miss Creak was English, Miss Major Irish, Miss Barrie a Scot and Dr Smith is English. This variety in the mixture has made for a good succession. Miss Creak gave the school rule, earnestness, absence of pretence, intellectual zeal and endurance; an independent spirit, but a spirit imbued with the sense of the eternal. It is very clear, as one talks with old students of that early period, that it was a Christian's faith in the soul's destiny which made each girl feel responsible; and reliance on the gift of grace through prayer which gave the weak courage. Belief in 'the power of an endless life' removed the daily from the trivial. After all, nothing is trivial when the daily issue is of such tremendous import to the continuing and evolving soul. But, as we know through the endless series of

421

spiritual dramas, allegories, exhortations, poems and novels, as well as through the lives of the saints, the Way is never simple. The strong soul can be gulled by itself, the tender and delicate overwhelmed; and there are the involuted and cunning wiles with which we deceive our hearts. While having no doubt of the teaching of Christ and Saint Francis, I have often wondered unhappily about the effect of a strong inculcation of a moral sense, through theological dogma in education. For myself, I only know that I cannot be serious for long. I must laugh or die.

Miss Major, from all that one hears of her, made the school laugh. She was an Irishwoman with a vivid identity, a quick wit, a perception of the dramatic in human history which made her an enthralling teacher, and charm of manner for young and old. Her reign was a period of brilliant intellectual achievement by Edwardians; the atmosphere was gayer, and, while building solidly on the original structure, Miss Major added grace. She kept firmly to the principle of leisure to learn rather than haste to teach. I have been told over and over again how stimulating it was to be a teacher with Miss Major. There was no tension, my friends of that period say. But I always think that for myself I might, with Miss Major, have tried to be clever. To my mind it was Miss Barrie who gave the school ease. With Miss Barrie I was to find that, oh, so blessedly, neither girls nor staff had to try to be anything but what they quite naturally were. Miss Barrie had a kind of large carelessness; an unsearching, not anxiously moral humanity; and a sailor-like directness. I don't think either Miss Creak or Miss Major sailed a boat. If Miss Barrie felt grumpy she showed grumpy; if I felt flippant I could say silly things without fearing that my reputation as teacher and churchwoman was blasted for ever.

Conducted by Twist, and greeted by Gumery, I went up the stairs and was delivered to Miss Sybil Ravenhill, one of the four old Edwardians on the staff of the High School when I joined it. When, as occasionally happens, I pause to think about school education, and about teachers, and of how terribly influential for good or evil these are; and when I say to myself I am unable, and must resign, I find it salutary to let my mind dwell on these four: on Miss Sybil Ravenhill, Miss B. K. Rattey, Miss Margaret Orton and Mrs Hopkins, all Edwardians of varying period, all so utterly different from one another, all so entirely and inevitably themselves. Then I am reassured. I say to myself these four would have been like they were if they had gone to school in Colorado, or not at all. No pressures, no leniencies, I say to myself, alter the essential being; and with this helpful generalization—which mentally I contradict next day—I can go and call my register feeling as irresponsible as a dish-washer. Every teacher must know a few sophistries to keep her heart up.

Miss Sybil Ravenhill went with me to the third form room to help me with form business on my first morning. She warned me that when I called the names the girls would answer, 'Present, yes, no,' or 'Present, no, no,' or 'Present, yes, yes,' (or 'Absent ha! ha!' thought I). But I did not breathe this thought aloud. Instead I listened to the explanation of the formula. 'Present, yes, no,' meant 'Present, I am here; yes, I have changed my shoes; no, I have no conduct mark or order mark against me.' The variations are obvious. The whole thing was very speedy, and, to the uninitiated, quite enigmatic. Miss Ravenhill then guided me to hear the scripture verse; to see that everybody's clothes were marked; to allow the Form to choose monitors and form-captains—to see that each girl's desk fitted her, that each girl who sat on the right last term should sit on the left this—I forget what happened to the ones in the middle—she then left me to make friends with the form. But before she left the room I felt I had made friends with her. Dear Sybil Ravenhill! How gracious she was! How delicate! How fine in all her perceptions! It has always grieved me to the heart that she died so shortly after her retirement. I once saw her take what I took to be a dying bird into her hand and hold it for warmth against her body. It had been stunned and the warmth revived it, for as we walked along the lane towards Sybil's home—I was going out to tea with her—the bird stirred and fluttered. She held it out in her hands and it flew lilting off.

I was only on the staff of King Edward's for one term with Miss B. K. Rattey before she retired. She was utterly different from Miss Ravenhill, being strong, dogmatic, and confident, where Miss Ravenhill was gentle and full of hesitancies. Miss Rattey would have agreed with Chesterton, 'A teacher who is not dogmatic is a teacher who is not teaching.' She had been one of the first women to obtain the Lambeth Diploma in Theology, with Licence to teach it. The policy at King Edward's has been to have a specialist in Divinity as in other branches of learning; Miss Rattey took these classes, as also classes in German. I always found myself becoming faintly sycophantic when, as occasionally happened, I had a free period with Miss Rattey. It seemed easier not to disagree with this formidable mind; with these determined and unshakable opinions. I had in common with her and Miss Orton a keen delight in the actual words of the liturgy and of the Bible; I tended to let what we shared in common bridge the vast gulf which opened between us in our theories of education. I knew that we seemed to get on together better than we did because we had been brought up to speak the same language; I never quite let her know how much my mind had, as it were, gone a-whoring after Bertrand Russell in the matter of educational theory; or how much I agreed with Blake about the danger of unacted desires and impulses. With Miss Rattey I was always, as it were, the fellow who smiled first in order to try and make the other fellow smile. I, in some sort, played up.

Miss Rattey was one of those people about whom good stories are told. Such characters grow rarer like rare birds. In the old days, one gathers from memoirs, every staff common-room boasted one or two. They are characters having a quality of fearlessness, conforming to their own principles and foibles, but heedless of other people's. My story of Miss Rattey is not typical and may be apocryphal. It is merely a story which would not have been funny if it were about anybody else. Miss Piper told it me, one evening on Clent Hill, where I was camping; she told it me after a supper of bacon and eggs as the shadows lengthened over Keeper's Cottage. Once upon a time,

Miss Piper said, soon after Miss Barrie came to King
Edward's, there were two old mackintoshes, one belonging to
Miss Rattey, the other to a mistress whose name I have
forgotten. These mackintoshes hung permanently in the staff
cloakroom, so that, in the event of sudden rain, Miss Rattey
and Miss Y. should not be found unprovided. Miss Y. was
young, not established like Miss Rattey; but the mackintoshes
were of equally scandalous age and dingy hue. One Friday
afternoon in winter it began to snow. Miss Rattey had departed
at one o'clock, before the weather darkened, leaving her old
mack on the peg. Miss Y., who had to go to London for a
meeting, remembered at the last moment that the shoes she
had on were not snow-tight. So she conceived the notion of
cutting out of her old mack a pair of socks to put inside her
shoes. She got the scissors from Gumery, spread her mack,
placed her shoes on a nice waterproof-looking portion in the
centre of the back, and hacked out what we in Cornwall would
call a very keenly pair of socks. She put them into her shoes,
and off she went to town; her feet dry and warm through this
exercise of her mother wit.

But on Monday morning, when the staff were all assembled
for the daily meeting, there was a sudden abrupt and wrathful
entrance on the part of Miss Rattey, holding up a mack in the
back of which were two large wavy holes, like feet. 'Who', she
said, 'has done this? Who has destroyed my waterproof?' There
was a hush. Nobody laughed, although the foot-holes looked
absolutely stunning. At last Miss Y., who had been dumb for a
second or two through consternation, began, 'I'm afraid, Miss
Rattey, I'm very much afraid, I'm terribly afraid . . . London
. . . shoes . . . snow . . . idea of socks . . . scissors . . . darkness of
staff-cloakroom . . . proximity of pegs . . . twin-like
resemblance of sister-macks . . . very very sorry . . . new mack
. . . next cheque . . .'

'Your ancient garment like my Faithful Friend?' began Miss
Rattey; but at this point Miss Barrie began the staff meeting
and the incident was closed. Miss Rattey would never accept a
new mack; only at intervals she murmured something about

people who could not distinguish between worn-out frippery and a sound waterproof.

Mrs Hopkins, my third Edwardian on the staff, was unlike either artistic Miss Ravenhill or dogmatic Miss Rattey. I have never met anyone else more utterly self-forgetful, more entirely lacking in self-esteem, yet unyielding when it came to evangelical principle. I doubt whether King Edward's had ever been the right school for her. I expect it had increased her natural diffidence. Her talents, precious in themselves, were not those of most account in an academic atmosphere. Perhaps the fact that she had not been in quite the right niche herself as a girl helped to make her the sympathetic and imaginative teacher she was. She cared intensely that children, especially timorous children, should be given courage; she helped girls through the difficult fears of adolescence. Domestic Science was her subject; but I expect her teaching in what an old Cornish friend of mine calls 'the ways of life' was more essentially valuable than her instruction in the rule and practice of making light cakes and roasting joints. But I must add that the juniors always went off to cooking as to a treat. Those theorists who argue that academic-minded children should be given a bookish education, and practical children be instructed in the arts and crafts, should see the little academics joyously don their long-sleeved white overalls and skip off to cook.

Miss Margaret (Biddy) Orton is the most difficult of my four Edwardians to give any impression of. I should prefer merely to print an old photograph of her as a little girl, with her dolls' tea-set, pouring out tea. It has that intense absorption in what she is doing which marked one who was my colleague at King Edward's for seventeen years. Figuratively she lowered her head, and butted into her objective. Like Miss Rattey, whose pupil she had been, she had obtained the Lambeth Diploma in Theology, in addition to the History Tripos. When I first came to King Edward's she was only serving for part of her time in school; with the other part she kept her father's house—he was a doctor and a widower—and brought up her brothers. She was a scholarly historian, accurate, with a forthright manner. One was never in any doubt as to what Orton thought of things. We became *Orton* and *Treneer* in our frequent brushes with one another on the subject of the respective duties of history and English mistresses; but, like good political opposites, we fraternized, and were *Anne* and *Biddy* in the more comforting associations of common life. When she had lost her temper and then come round, Biddy was especially delightful. I can see her looking up in exasperation from a pile of history essays. 'Treneer,' she would say, laying down her pencil, 'I don't know *how* to correct this! At what *stage* do you teach them to paragraph?' Or . . . 'Treneer, are you doing *anything* about Katherine Dee's spelling?' Or . . . 'Treneer, the utter lack of *Grammar* in the Lower Fourth!' But I shall never forget my inward rapture when, after reading my book *Schoolhouse in the Wind*, Biddy Orton said to me, 'But, Anne, it's so well *written!*'

I have done my four Edwardians scant justice in presenting this shadowy outline of their idiosyncrasies. I must add that beneath their differences and variations they had something in common—they all rang true. I think there was not a fibre of shoddiness or affectation in any of the four. And they all cared to teach. Mrs Hopkins equally cared to farm. At first I thought it a pity that, partly through self-distrust, she diverted her fostering powers from children to lambs. But she was very tired. After the early death of her husband she had brought up two sons; she taught; she provided school meals. I am not sure that she did not find the provision of lunch for the staff the most temper-trying of her duties. Some of us would lose our dinner-tickets. I lost mine the first day. She had been a land girl during the first World War, had greatly liked the life, and always had looked forward to returning to the country when her sons were grown up and independent. She has carried out her plan and is happy. I like to picture her among the creatures; for Mrs Hopkins still provides.

As one becomes experienced as a teacher it is much easier to make friends with the children in a new post than with the staff. I must confess that I found the assembled staff at King

Edward's extremely daunting, not only on my first morning, but for several terms. When I was first taken into the common-room I found I liked the room, but that I was less responsive to the moving and talking bodies who all seemed to know what to do except me. I did not perceive at first glance that there were two other orphans as much at a loss as I was. To me, all seemed equally knowledgeable. They were consulting two strips of paper. I had had two strips of paper posted to me, but I did not understand the hieroglyphics on them. Miss Macdonald introduced me to various people. There was a blazing fire in the room which had rather the air of an old untidy library.

'Staff-meeting in Miss Barrie's room,' said a voice in my ear. Each morning, before prayers, there was a staff-meeting at King Edward's. As we stood round in various attitudes that first morning I thought I had seldom seen a more interesting collection of faces and heads; I suppose it is the daily repetition of the scene which has stamped it on my memory as vividly as if I were recalling the faces and figures in a painted throng; or as if I looked, one after the other, at single portraits in a gallery. I see Edna Hobbes, physicist, standing in the recess of the oriel window. She might have been half gipsy and half medieval lady of high degree; a face with clear contours and the rich dark colouring Augustus John might have chosen to paint; a head with dark plaits wound round it. Standing near her, always punctual, with a face of quite different shape, broader, and with lips which curled up in a rejoicing way when she smiled, was May Udall, biologist. Joyce Field, historian, was also of the brown-haired group. Her face attracted me at first sight more than any other in the room, although I was never to get to know her well; she left King Edward's to become a headmistress early on in our acquaintanceship. Another very memorable head was Jean Davidson's. She had short hair of horse-chestnut colour which caught a vivid light where it waved. Nancy Dickenson (French mistress) had a fairness of the delicate golden kind; Lorna Macdonald was almost buttercup; Joan Holland black-haired with puckish active eye-brows; Alexandrina Makin rather like a hazel tree, with a gleam in her green eye. Sybil Ravenhill's blue and silver grace would, I think, have made any artist pause and consider. There were many others. I describe at random as points of colour flash before me. It was a memorable staff. I should be hard put to it to think of any other closely associated group of women more personally distinct, and with minds and imaginations better lit.

The meeting went swiftly. People knew what they wanted to say and spoke to the point. Miss Barrie in the chair, large and sunburnt, her short, greyish hair rather wingy, reminded me more of wind and sea than of school. She never wasted a syllable. 'We'll push the business on; we'll push the business on!' I sang. But not out loud. I never sang in a staff-meeting in my life. It was hard enough to have to speak. I never mastered the art of lucid statement in staff-meeting. I always seemed like a poor soul crossing a stream on stepping-stones when I had to speak. I dashed, as it were, in; stood on one leg in the midst of my sentence; looked in agony at the shore I had left and at the shore I had to reach; wavered, stuttered, fell in, and reached my objective gasping like a fish. However, for many weeks I managed not to speak at all. I got into the way of confiding to Ailsa Jaques, a gymnast, but also the most charming and easy of speakers, any little point I wanted to make about my form. Ailsa Jaques should become an Announcer. There are few voices which never irritate; hers is one.

Miss Barrie's is another. When the meeting was over, and we went down to the Hall, where the school had assembled for Prayers, and I heard her read Prayers for the first time, I knew I was safe from the damnable fury which sweeps over me when some people address the Deity. There was nothing of, 'Hear, Lord, for thy servant speaketh,' nor of, 'Paradoxical as it may seem to Thee, O God!'; she was not falsetto; she did not put in too much expression. The Founder's Prayer and the General Thanksgiving were repeated daily. I am in favour of repetition; it is good to have some words and rhythms set in your mind for ever if they are good words and rhythms. The Founder's Prayer is:

'We give Thee most humble and hearty thanks, O most merciful Father, for our pious Founder, King Edward the Sixth, and for all our Governors and Benefactors, by whose benefit this whole school is brought up to godliness and good learning; and we humbly beseech Thee to give us grace and to use these Thy blessings to the glory of Thy holy Name, that we may answer the good intent of our religious Founder, and become profitable members of the Church and Commonwealth, and at last be partakers of Thy Heavenly Kingdom, through our Lord and Saviour Jesus Christ.'

I think it is more important for a headmistress to have a voice which does not irritate her staff than for her to have good organizing ability. Miss Barrie was a good organizer; if she had not been the staff could have made a shift to do without her. But to be daily irritated by a voice must be terribly wearing. Heaven has always mercifully preserved me from that. Prayers at King Edward's have always been quieting; I love the words of the Lord's Prayer and of the General Thanksgiving murmured by young voices; and, although some hymns are pestilent others lift up the heart, and to sing together is a good beginning for the day. Not so to march together. The marches that used to be played on the piano in New Street as Form after Form went out of the hall by different doors, all the girls moving at once, and all reaching at last the great central staircase and going up it, round on round—those marches nearly killed me. The tunes used to grind through my head as if my head were a barrel organ and I not in control of the handle. Nowadays other music has been substituted for the march as the girls assemble for prayers, a blessed innovation.

Before the end of my first morning at King Edward's I had discovered my two fellow new members of the staff, Cecil Waterfield and Joan Holland. Joan, who had been at Girton with Isabel Sayers, seemed not so new as Cecil and me. Cecil told me in a free period that she was the new mistress of German; that her assistant in the teaching of this language was Miss Rattey; and that Miss Rattey had said she hoped the tail wouldn't wag the dog. I said I didn't know where to go, or what to teach, and that I'd lost my paper-strips of information. Cecil said I needn't worry; that I looked as efficient as all the rest as long as I lay low. She'd been on the point, she said, of asking me a question; I looked such an old hand. I felt as I do in London, if anybody asks me the way. I felt cosmopolitan, proud, a woman able to deal with life, and turnings, and time-tables. I told Cecil I knew all about 'Present, Yes, No.' I also told her I felt as though I couldn't breathe; she said we'd go to the Lickey Hills one afternoon that week.

So we went to the Lickey Hills, where I did breathe great draughts of air, and where we walked on high bare places, and through woody glades which made me feel miles from Birmingham. And another evening we went to Clent Hill, walking to it through the fields from Halesowen. I still remember vividly standing in a field at the foot of the hill, and listening to the music of the evening wind in a line of poplar trees.

5

DENNE AND MARTIN

It was Cecil who got me out of Mrs Whipse's lodgings. But for her I feel I might have been lingering yet with the shade of Mr Whipse, the ghostly hearts of cooked cabbages, and the faint voice of Mr Probert saying, 'She's forgotten the mustard; no; don't move; I'll get it . . . Mrs Whipse!' I confided to Cecil that, although the gas-man had mended the leak, and Mr Probert's lighted match no longer produced a little devil's tongue in the region of my gas-bracket, my room still smelt to me somewhat gaseous. Cecil came to tea. She took one swift glance round, produced a piece of paper and a pencil, and wrote in large printed letters: WANTED. We concocted an advertisement which we inserted in the *Birmingham Mail: Wanted by professional woman* . . . The office of the *Birmingham Mail*, obligingly situated almost opposite King Edward's, then became our lair. We lay in wait for replies, bore them into the neighbouring Pattison's and, over tea and toast, enjoyed our answers. I only wish I had kept a few of them; human documents, presenting the people to the people; Mrs Whipse multiplied and multiplied.

We scampered about in Cecil's car seeking lodgings. Each fresh lodging-house looked worse than the one before. And then I had a stroke of luck. Miss McDermott introduced me to the owner of her flat, an able, full-natured woman, whose profession it was to make habitable rooms and arrangements for precisely such people as I. She let me a delightful bed-sitting-room in her house in Montague Road. There was a nice little shed for the Velocette and I liked my new bed-sitting-room. The advantage of a bed-sitting-room is the pleasure of undressing by fire-light and in the warmth; and of having all one's books around if one wakes up in the night. The disadvantage is—in a genteel bed-sitter such as I now had—the tiresome business of the morning and evening transformation of a bed into a divan, and of a divan back into a bed. Having been brought up in the days, and in a place, where flats were unheard of, and bungalows considered South African, I have an obstinate prejudice in favour of going upstairs at night, and of getting into a bed which has been through the full country ritual of being turned, aired and made. I dearly love smooth sheets. Old mother Holle, in the fairy tale! How sound was her method of discovering whether a girl was a good wench or a slut by the test of shaking the feather bed! Was it not a shower of gold which rewarded the faithful shaker, and a drenching with dirty water which paid out the slut? I fear I should have received the drenching if old mother Holle had tried me out; but it would have been because of the frailty of my nature; my principles are not sluttish; I abhor sluttishness. And yet there is a persistent rumour that in a room I once had, I swept up lupin petals in November. My room in Montague Road was kept clean for me.

Nearly all the established members of King Edward's staff had flats or houses. Cecil, too, had secured a flat. She has always had uncanny ability in finding herself happy places to live in; she always argued that where one lived one was. I argued that from where one lived one radiated; that a house was merely a place to get out of. Her first Birmingham flat was one of her most remarkable ventures. It was a ground-floor flat in one of the noisiest quarters of Birmingham, but its sitting-room opened upon a garden leading to a forest. Those few pines really felt like a forest. I have stood on the pine needles, breathing, when the sun shone warm, in an oasis of scented air; and I have felt as remote in time and space as later I was to feel under the oaks or beeches of Arden or Malvern Chase. That confined grove even contrived a hint of blue distance; it went on round the corner, so that it appeared unhedged by Birmingham matter, though ringed by Birmingham sounds. Only after midnight, when the clank of the trams and the grinding of brakes and the vile hootings ceased, I have stolen out in the moonlight, and found that the wind had resumed, with its sea-like music, its empire in the pines. On occasions when I have slept in that flat I have felt like an urbanized usurper in what might be called a pocket of wildness. I have felt as closely united with pre-industrial time as once, on the footholds of the Tatra Mountains when, having drunk too thirstily of the local wine in a kind of youth hostel hut, and resumed walking, I was overcome by drowsiness. I lay down and slept under some scented conifers, and surely, when I awakened, it was none of I.

Another house which I began to visit later in my first term at King Edward's was also a bower of bliss in an unlikely place. It belonged to the visiting music mistress at the school, Miss Denne Parker, as the girls called her, using her professional name. She was a singer first; the fact that she was also a teacher was the incidental in her life, though not in the life of the school. Silence and real music, voluntary for the most part, seemed to me, when I went to King Edward's, its characteristics; the silence was due to the long established rule of no talking in the corridors, and to the thickness of the form-room walls. The beauty of the singing was due to the fact that it was taught by one who really sang herself, and who was also a human person of the widest range of understanding. She was never afraid to make her classes laugh; and the children in their turn knew that she would not be offended if they tried a joke. I remember a Clerihew which a girl named Elizabeth Ryder made when the *Phoenix* offered a prize for a verse of the kind. Elizabeth's clerihew ran:

> Miss Denne Parker
> Sings like a lark, her
> Resemblance dies,
> When it comes to size.

Denne was the most amused of us all at this production; I can see her now as she laughed. She had a singer's figure, a singer's way of breathing and standing, a singer's poise, and a singer's vitality as though, obliged by her art to pay more attention to breathing than shallower creatures, she had learned the secret of quaffing deep without cup habitually. She quaffed in a Shakespearean way. I can imagine her meeting Shakespeare, jesting with him, singing, 'Come away, come away death' to his satisfaction, and acting either Queen Hermione or Mistress Overdene to pleasure him. Her range made her generally availing. Very few people have sounded so many of the notes of their own compass, or been able to atune themselves to so many different types of people. I have known her bring richness into a room which seemed, before she entered it, as meagre as a Lenten fast.

She had married Martin Gilkes, eldest son of Dr Gilkes, Master of Dulwich. Martin had been classical master at Shrewsbury; but at the time of which I am writing he was Extra Mural Tutor in English of Birmingham University. I first went to tea with Denne and Martin on a November day. They had left their house at Knightwick and were living in a late regency house in the Hagley Road. It is noticeable in Birmingham that dwelling houses fairly near the centre of the city are often sound, compact, plain and roomy, with good gardens at the back. As you go out, the architecture becomes progressively worse. I have always had an affection for the house where I first shared a meal with Denne and Martin. The weather was foggy. My Velocette wound her course impatiently between looming buses and cars on a filthy road. Birmingham can be exciting on a wet winter evening when the lights are all a-flash, for muddy water will take clean reflections of colour; and it can look mysterious in fine twilight just before the artificial lights come on. But this was Birmingham in a November fog, the kind of fog that clots in the throat, and makes you feel that the air above Dodman Point must belong to another planet. The dark, gathering in on a foggy day, seemed to reduce living on earth from a lyrical glory to something gloomier than a dirge, for dirges are music. Here were only noise and disorder. I defy anyone to imagine stones obeying Orpheus, and singing a way into their places in the topless towers of Ilium, amidst the soggy dirt of Birmingham towards nightfall in winter.

Wearing dripping overalls, I stood outside the Hagley Road house in the murk. It seemed impossible that the barrier should ever fall and I be taken in out of the ugliness. When the door did open it disclosed in a pool of yellow light, Martin, whom I saw then for the first time, standing very tall, and wearing a red cloth cloak with capes. Looking like a cardinal he welcomed me in. Many have tried to describe the special courteous quality of Martin Gilkes. I think it was the result of being in no way an assumed manner. It was a pure emanation from the most searching spirit it has ever been my luck to encounter. All people were his demesne; he knew them through himself. It was impossible to surprise in him the note of bleak and bitter condemnation. His comprehension was such that it exercised not pardon, but a faculty of seeing the creature, as it were, pre-guilty. It saw before, not after the event. With him, understanding was due to contemplation never to be turned aside by disgust. It was more than compassion; it was too kind, too un-contemptuous, too un-aloof for pity. I suppose it was charity. He had reached, by the study of psychology and philosophy, a position not unlike that which my own mother had reached by intuition and grace.

Denne was in the kitchen baking scones for tea. Denne is at home in a kitchen, in a studio, on a platform, in a fishing-boat or making hay. She is even at home in a school. The scones lent to the kitchen the good smell of baking. A small boy whom we will call M.J. was sticking transfers of birds on the wall, and talking with incredible articulateness to Bridie who, at that time, helped Denne and taught M.J. I never heard Bridie's second name; she was always Bridie. She fitted into the scene— Irish eyes, a face that looked used to rain, and hair like russet leaves. Denne's hair was dark, and she had sea-blue, change-able eyes on either side of a nose with the bridge of her Scottish ancestors, a very decided, handsome nose.

We had tea and then went into Martin's room. Peat was cheap and obtainable that year, and Denne had tons of it; we might have been hundreds of miles away from Birmingham. I saw, for the first time a room which, wherever it was placed in the world, would be unchangeably Martin's—his books, his reproduction of The Birth of Venus, his pipes, a hint of philosophy in the air, a fire and a fug. Martin hated open windows. He loathed picnics. If Denne and I, in later years, went for a picnic on the Cherwell, Martin sought the Mitre; he was at home in bars, both for the old beer, and the conversation there. On my first visit to the Hagley Road, and on subsequent visits, there was music and talk; we went into Denne's room to hear, say, Brahms, and back to Martin's room to resume the conversation. It was towards midnight that Martin was most Coleridgean; but always he would be ready to put down his pen and turn from T.S. Eliot or Ezra Pound and talk. He liked, of Pound, the things I liked least. He loved to discourse on the earlier *Cantos*. I have always cared for, and still cherish, Pound's easier poems, one or two of which have an exquisite, medieval, thin, brook-like music: and it seemed to me that, in 'The Return', Pound has written a poem which was poignant. I did not know then what poignancy it would yet gather from the course of Pound's disastrous unawareness.

Extravagant praise was not Martin's classical way. Often he thought me extravagant, and my lack of critical caution amused him. But it was an extraordinary pleasure to me to be made free of so catholic a mind. He was constantly occupied, during the ten years which followed my first visit, with the poetry then being produced, and with the poetry of the immediate past. His *Key to Modern Poetry* remains a useful introduction to poetry between the two wars. His short stories which appeared in the *Cornhill* and the *Adelphi* can be re-read with pleasure; particularly the story entitled 'Peter', a story perfectly planned, and told in quiet lucid prose. But Martin's most enduring work was with people; he was in the fullest sense of the word an educationist; for, although he was revolted by the dull business which commonly passes under the name of education, he had the only gift which makes teaching worthwhile. He could open minds.

To those who were trying to write, and who sent him their work—and these were many—he was ever generous. His criticism was direct and straight. Whereas Denne and I might compromise, seeking to say the thing that would not hurt, Martin said just what he intended; but in such a way as not to offend susceptibilities; his gentleness went with his criticism; his gentleness and his humour. He regarded his own ill-health, a legacy of the war, in which he had won the M.C., in a detached, half-humorous way, as though his body were not himself. His interest in people, their feelings and their conduct was infinite. For me, I am like Horace Walpole; I have a disposition not to care at all for people I do not absolutely like. It was a happy circumstance that in Birmingham I met a greater variety of people than in all my life before. After my first visit, I consorted frequently with Denne and Martin, with M.J. and Bridie, and with the innumerable company who sought the friendliness of the house. It was a nourishing place for body and soul. To the end of his life Martin was a seeker, whereas I cannot study to understand the self. The self remains, indestructable, un-analysable, living, laughing, contradictious entity that it is. The self is that which is prior to being, according to Hopkins and the Fathers. How can we hope to get at it? Why should we if we could? I used to ask Martin that. But with him anything human could be contemplated. Good and evil were the opposites which were the life of one another; and all diversity was in the One. And the One? Of the One he talked into the small hours while the peat smouldered.

6

I BUY A NEW VELOCETTE

Cecil Waterfield and I quickly came to the conclusion that Denne was one of US as well as one of THEM, THEM being the staff of King Edward's as a close corporation. Joan Holland, too, making comic sallies on either side of the border, was of both US and THEM. As for the rest of THEM Cecil and I reconnoitred cautiously, comparing notes as to which of THEM had asked which of US to tea, or supper, or to the Rep. I made slow progress with THEM partly because I was always out of Birmingham for the week-ends.

As soon as the happy Fridays arrived in their glorious succession, and my required bodily presence—and my spirit, too, that is the worst of teaching—in school was over for the week, I was over the hills and far away. Having secured a nice little shed for my old Velocette, I conceived the notion of buying a new one. In a shop near the Bull Ring, I saw a very handsome little two-stroke, a Velocette, like my old machine, but with every latest improvement, and with that slim, feasting, speedy, greyhound look of the species brought to the highest pitch of perfection. Yes; the obliging shopman would take my old bike in part payment; yes, a deposit of ten pounds would be quite sufficient if—there was a hint that some indication of my financial stability would be welcome. I murmured something about being a mistress at King Edward's, and, for the first time, perceived the advantage of teaching in a school generously admired by Birmingham citizens, and with a parentage spread over the whole city. King Edward's High School! Well! Of course! No need for any formalities about the instalments. His manner, pleasantly business-like before, was now warm. Was I one of the new teachers? Had I come across his daughter in Lower VIb—brown eyes and hair, exactly like her mother—but whose brains? Nobody quite knew where they came from. Physics! Top for physics! Always top for physics! English? No; Dolores always found English the hardest thing. She could never make anything up. So off I went with my new Velocette, and with a lively personal interest awakened in Dolores and her defective powers of invention when it came to writing English essays. Yet I had told Cecil that the Science people were the devil to teach; that with some of them it was like reading Herrick to the Rollright stones. Parents see everything so differently from subject-mistresses. I always stand up for parents when they are being downed by the teaching profession. 'Stupid and obstinate; will make a good parent,' as one exasperated master reported on a boy. I think it is better for a child to have a parent who thinks too much of her than a teacher who thinks too little. The happy relationship between staff and parents at King Edward's was one of the school's pleasantest achievements.

With my new Velocette, almost as obedient as the horse of brass at which the people wondered, at my command, I enjoyed a series of grand week-ends. I was free, every other Friday, at one o'clock; and even on the alternate Fridays, when I coached hockey in the afternoons, I was nearly always free by five. On my best Fridays, the one o'clock Fridays, I never waited for lunch. Mrs Hopkins would make me up a lunch packet, if I asked in time. If I did not ask in time, Twist would sally forth to a little place he knew of and buy sandwiches. Mrs Hopkin's packets were best—ham and tongue sandwiches, with mustard; a couple of bananas and a few chocolate biscuits; or hard boiled eggs, and lettuce, and apples. Food was easy to come by in those days. During the autumn and spring terms, while I had the room in Montague Road, my way out of Birmingham was generally by the Hagley Road, often turning right by the New Road, and so out by way of Wolverhampton. The journey from Birmingham to Wolverhampton by train is so hideous as to make the heart contract. But do I dream, or is it not true, that on the motor road between Birmingham and Wolverhampton I used to come upon, somewhere, a view of almost apocalyptic magnificence. I remember it under a stormy sunset sky when I was heading for a little village in Wales to spend the week-end with my friend Grace Trenery. There they gave us so much Welsh mutton to eat that I thought I might become a sheep and baa; I remember that I left Grace, who had a day longer than I, with the knuckle bone.

Most often I went out by way of Quinton, Halesowen, Hagley, Kidderminster and Bewdley; for I fell immediately in love with Shropshire. This was due to Ailsa Jaques, the gymnast mentioned before, who had acquired neither a gymnast's voice nor mind. She was a mountaineer, and her real idea of a good week-end was clinging to some crag of Snowdon. It was then, as with Meredith, that the merry little hopes sprang up in her. But she knew also the nearer at hand, more moderate, open country. She recommended Wenlock Edge to me in one free period when we were chatting; she gave me an address at Much Wenlock where I could comfortably stay, and she gave me also directions about the minor exhilaration of riding or walking on the Edge.

So I came, one Friday night, to the place where St Milburga's bones were laid. Unworldly saints have much enriched the world. Some wholesome spirit remains at Much Wenlock, which is not to be visited merely for its buildings and its ruins. If I were asked to prescribe for a disturbed person I would send her to Much Wenlock. Then I would send her motor-bicycling along Wenlock Edge. I would let her taste of Little Stretton and, finally, I would let her discover, alone, the nature of the Long Mynd, whose stubborn strength seems to have existed from time everlasting. I came often to the Long Mynd while I lived in the Midlands, and there I felt no stranger; for there is something in the Long Mynd akin to the stones of West Penwith.

I liked the Long Mynd for wildness and Ludlow for civility. I went many times in my first year to Ludlow. But my most vivid impression of it was when I went, three or four years later, with Joan Holland and her brother Jack, to the pageant at Ludlow Castle, in the course of which *Comus* was played. It must have been high summer. I was living at Bearley then, as I shall tell later, a little village near Stratford-on-Avon. Joan and Jack were living at Leamington; they arrived to fetch me in their car, and we drove by enchanted ways, and stopped to eat ham rolls, and long crisp leaves of lettuce; and there was coffee, really a memorable coffee, so rare at a picnic. Ludlow is one of those places which pleases the more the better it is known. Its church, the church of St Lawrence, is sunny; it has huge lights, and yet there are withdrawals and recedings and distances; and a grand organ. The houses are not mummified; The Feathers is not a black and white sham. This little town on the Teme, and in a pass of the hills, has a way of making the visitor feel that it has long been established as a meeting ground, a place of concourse. The castle is on a rock; but the town is on the ground with a big proportion of its houses half-timbered.

Comus always seems to me one of the most woody of poems, a Masque of forest and river. I do not recall very vividly the pageant at Ludlow Castle as a whole—the year must have been 1934, because it was the tercentenary of the original performance of *Comus*, made by Milton and Henry Lawes to celebrate the appointment of John Egerton, Earl of Bridgewater, as Lord President of the Council in the Marches of Wales. I do remember the music which accompanied the vision of Saint Milburga. I knew Much Wenlock, so I was interested in the translation of the sainted bones; and I remember a boyish Sir Philip Sidney being seen off to Shrewsbury School. But *Comus* was the memorable part of the pageant, particularly if one knew it well enough to follow the words without actually hearing them very distinctly, and if one was fairly familiar with 'All this tract which fronts the falling sun.' To me that tract belonged, indeed, to the blue haired deities, for I saw it oftenest as azure distance. But the leafy labyrinth in which the lady was lost I too had wandered in; Corvedale meadows might still harbour flowery-kirtled Naiades; I might have said with Comus:

> I know each lane, and every alley green,
> Dingle, or bushy dell of this wild wood,
> Any every bosky bourn from side to side,
> My daily walks and ancient neighbourhood.

The performance of *Comus* at Ludlow needed a smaller audience, a more confined space; the words are too exquisite for a straining voice. The voice must flow so as to fill the words exactly; no more. They must be heard in such a way as Comus himself heard Alice Egerton's song, when she appealed to Echo, living within her airy shell. Comus said of that song:

> Can any mortal mixture of earth's mould
> Breathe such divine enchanting ravishment?
> Sure something holy lodges in that breast,
> And with these raptures moves the vocal air
> To testify his hidden residence:
> How sweetly do they float upon the wings
> Of silence, through the empty-vaulted night,
> At every fall smoothing the raven down
> Of darkness till it smiled!

Of all water music—and English poetry is murmurous with water, and rustling with leaves, it embodies the turn of waves, and the smooth sliding of rivers—I think the liquid tones of the Spirit's call to Sabrina, she who oft at eve

> Visits the herds along the twilight meadows,

is the most, to use Milton's own word, adjuring:

> Sabrina fair,
>   Listen where thou art sitting
> Under the glassy, cool, translucent wave,
>   In twisted braids of lilies knitting
> The loose train of thy amber-dropping hair;
>   Listen for dear honour's sake,
> Goddess of the silver lake,
>   Listen and save . . .

And then the reply of the Goddess of the river Severn as she rises:

> By the rushy fringed bank,
> Where grows the willow and the osier dank,
>   My sliding chariot stays
> Thick set with agate, and the azure sheen
>   Of turkis blue, and emerald green,
>   That in the channel strays;
> Whilst from off the waters fleet
> Thus I set my printless feet
> O'er the cowslip's velvet head;
>   That bends not as I tread;
> Gentle swain, at they request
>   I am here.

I wish Milton has more often experienced the pleasures he named contemptuously in *Areopagitica*: 'There be delights, there be recreations and jolly pastimes that will fetch the day about from sun to sun, and rock the tedious year as in a delightful dream.'

How utterly different even the youthful Milton is from Shakespeare! When I used to pass through Shrewsbury, and haunt the Welsh Marches, my mind was as often occupied with Falstaff as with Comus. Shakespeare, too, must have known Severn's crisp head and sedgy bank. For the drama of personal relationships, and for the natural use of heroic verse, matter-of-factness meeting and damping exaltation, I know nothing better than the scene in the first part of *Henry IV* in which Hotspur rants about Mortimer, and finally says to the Earl of Worcester, 'Good uncle, tell your tale; for I have done' and Worcester replies,

Nay, if you have not, to't again;
We'll stay your leisure.

I do not commonly occupy my mind by picturing battle-fields, but the Battle of Shrewsbury is an exception. I can laugh and laugh again when Sir John, seemingly a corpse, interrupts Henry's casual dismissal of his valued life by jumping up and disclaiming all connection with deadness. This action, combined with the speeches on honour, on the evil of cold-bloodedness in Prince John, and on the virtue of sack, provides that most rare conjunction, the irresistibly comic with the profound. How hard I tried to get my sixth form to compre-hend and appreciate Falstaff! I felt that if I could get a little Falstaff into these girls I should not have taught in vain. I see now that this was a comic situation in itself. Appreciation of Falstaff comes late in life. I myself had been too fastidious, too heroic and too lyrical to appreciate Falstaff when I was their age. But teachers will be meddling.

I only once went up the Wrekin, and that day the weather closed in. It rained. I knew I should have no view from the top, yet I could not make up my mind to abandon my project. A stupid adherence to purpose made me go up and up, getting wetter and wetter, to gaze out over an obliterated world. In the greyness I stood, a mark for the penetrating drops. The mind is not its own place to me; my mind will never be of that absolute quality that my body can be indifferent to cold and wet, let alone pain. I remained for a very brief while, the only sentient being in the desolation, but when I began the descent, I came upon a tramp by a fire, making tea in a tin can. I looked so wistfully at his embers—the flames had died down—that he invited me to warm myself. So I steamed a while, and he gave me a black draught from the tin. It is extraordinary what damage one is prepared to do to so precious a part of one's being as one's inside in the name of good fellowship. My tramp was taciturn. When I left him he was gazing at the wood ashes. There he was with that bit of stubbly growth on his chin which tramps have. They never seem to grow beards, and yet they cannot be called shaven. And he was sitting as only tramps sit, his bundle beside him. I never went up the Wrekin again during all the years I spent in the Midlands. I viewed him, I took my bearings from him, I spied him in all weathers in all seasons; but I left him alone.

For week-ends not too far away from Birmingham I often chose the borders of Worcestershire and Shropshire. I used to leave my Velocette in a garage at Bewdley—the name means 'beautiful place', but I never gave Bewdley a chance to engrave itself on my memory. I used to go immediately to Severn bank, and walk the path past the bungalows and shacks to Upper Arley. From Arley I used to be able, I have forgotten by what route, or how far it was, to penetrate into Wyre Forest. There I could find recesses which were never surprised by other footsteps; and twisted oaks which reminded me of the oaks on the banks of the Fal, by King Harry Passage. I do not remember royal trees of mature growth, but little oaks and birch . . . It was often very silent in the forest; but down by a stream there was a life of growth and creatures, and I was the intruder; there birds were at home. I like to hear birds uttering small companionable speech when they are settling for the night, but are not quite stilled. The notes cannot be called song. They are minor expressions of satisfaction with the day and acceptance of the night. I suppose their wings are weary, and their eyes tired of the restless warding of their owners from danger. They give themselves up; they have to trust the dark against what can no longer be fended off. I have often wondered whether a bird's freedom is worth what he pays in fear; all wild things are fearful.

I made no systematic survey of northern Worcestershire and Shropshire. I depended more on hearsay in the staff-room than on books; and often I seemed merely to let my Velocette choose. My wheels took me to the foot of the Clee Hills; or they arranged for me a walk on the Long Mynd. Once they took me to Clun and Newcastle, where I had one of the best long week-ends I ever spent. I stayed in a place which provided chiefly for the Cyclists' Touring Club. I poured tea for a varied assembly to whom only Chaucer could have done justice; their talk was not so much of the pleasures of the way as of the number of miles traversed in the given number of hours. One old man bicycled each week-end from somewhere in the Black Country to Clun; he only had an hour or two in his beloved place. As for the youths, they seemed hardly to care whether they had any time in a place or not. Bent over their sporting handle-bars, and loaded with what seemed enough equipment for a week, they pushed the air before them.

I remember vividly a week-end spent at Hopton Wafers, somewhere in the neighbourhood of Cleobury Mortimer. I came upon woods with wonderfully blended colours, and felt a great desire to dawdle. I went to a little lodge, and asked if I could, perhaps, be put up for the night. I was invited to stay. It was a place of rest. There is a religious history attached to Hopton Wafers; but there is no real need to inquire into it. The peace abides. My landlady told me that a former owner, who had planted that part of the wood which I so much admired, had deliberately aimed at variety and harmony of distant colour when his trees should be full grown.

Often I came back to the staff common-room on Mondays with tales of places discovered which made the historians smile. I always have a kind of notion, if I come upon some wonderful thing unsought, that nobody has seen it on earth until I arrived with eyes a-gape. I should have been splendid company for Adam. I realized, after a few minutes, when I had begun expatiating on Stokesay Castle one Monday morning that, to the History staff, I was doing the equivalent of their coming to me and saying, all aglow, that they had discovered a lovely thing in Shakespeare beginning, 'I know a bank whereon the wild thyme grows'. Stokesay Castle, a fortified manor, looming up not very far along the road from Craven Arms, is an amazing sight to come upon suddenly, and to explore; but even now, after sixteen years or so, I hardly dare say so. It is in all the history books ever written, and in all the topographical books; every history mistress has a plan of it, and parties of girls are taken to Stokesay for educational purposes.

7

A TENT ON
CLENT HILL

My pleasure in Shropshire made me want to live out in that direction. When the summer term came, and the sun increased in strength and seductiveness, I found it impossible to spend the long evenings in Birmingham, or to sleep away the nights in the Montague Road. One Friday afternoon I saw a little tent rolled neatly into a small compass in a shop window in New Street. It looked as though it would just fit on my carrier; so I bought it and a blanket, and off I went to a pub called Gipsy's Tent, between Halesowen and Hagley. There I left my Velocette.

I then went through the meadows and by the wood to the top of Clent Hill. It was Trust Property, I knew; I should not be able to pitch my little tent wherever I chose. But I had made friends, when on one of my many visits to the Clents, with the people who lived in Keeper's Cottage, a cottage standing alone among some trees. Belonging to the cottage, but at a considerable distance from it, was a wire-fenced vegetable garden with a wide grassy verge. On this wide border, I thought, I might be allowed to set up house; just as, in Cecil's wood, I was in a nest of wildness in tame Birmingham, here I should be on a strip of tameness with the wild all round me. And so it came about. I had not found an ideal place to pitch, but better than nothing. It left me with the Clents to roam in, and Walton Hill opposite, together with the deep lanes; and yet it was near enough to Birmingham for me to ride my Velocette in to King Edward's every day.

So, although I was living in the Midlands, and not in Cornwall, I was able to live independently in a tent again. Every night I sped out to my little fastness, and every morning I went from it to school, leaving the country behind me, dodging the other whizzing objects in the Hagley Road, and slowing down as I approached the density of New Street. I did not mind the traffic. I was the captain of a little machine as obedient as legs; but no motor bicycle likes going slow, and being pulled up and manœuvred in and out between obstacles, enormous obstacles such as buses and lorries, which make motor bicycles feel small. A Velocette prefers to fleet the miles carelessly, far away from its mechanized kind. And it seemed a pity that my early morning journey should end in a school which, for all the good words I have spoken of it, was very dark inside.

It was dark; but one could be seen. Clothes became a major difficulty, clothes and books. You cannot house a library or city clothes in a tent; and on Clent Hill there was not, as formerly at Gwithian, the sea for me to bath in. I needed some sort of foothold under a roof, and an available bath-room; and here Denne and Martin came to my rescue. They let me keep my books and few possessions in their house, and they let me have their garden room. This was a sleeping shed in the back garden; a very beautiful and superior sleeping shed, painted green, with green blinds to pull down against the wet. Here, when it was not practicable to go out to my tent, I could abide, where the form of wild life was not rabbits and hares, hedgehogs and badgers and birds, but a tortoise and one small boy who brought others of his tribe to play. Tortie! I see him creeping along with his convenient house on his back. His dragonish head and opaque eye, with scaly lids, could be withdrawn into the very centre of his being. Motionless as death he could be. The small boy and his companions were not of the motionless kind; they played and climbed like monkeys, and would gather round to share with me only when I fried sausages. M.J. had a courteous instinct rare in little boys; on one occasion when he and his friends had settled like crows around my frying pan, he seemed to feel that to partake of my hospitality, and then disappear with the gang, making no further acknowledgement of my presence, was not quite the thing. He leaned over from the shed roof, where he and the others had ensconced themselves, and said to me as I read in solitude below, 'Come up on the roof, and play if you like, Anne.'

He called his parents always Denne and Martin, and he must, I think, have argued in his first articulate sentence. He prefixed his lucid speech with, 'But, Martin . . .' or 'Denne, I think . . .' He was no fonder than I of school when the time came for him to go. Sometimes in the mornings we chanted in unison, 'We don't *want* to go to school.' He had the kind of laughter which might move a Dictator to forget his stupid assumptions and join with him. I took him to the Botanical Gardens once and, as we paused before the bear's cage, the bear began a stream like Niagara. M.J. was entranced by this spectacle. While other folk, with eyes discreetly turned away, passed on, he stood before the cage in exquisite glee, legs wide apart, hands in pockets, transfixed by this extraordinary abundance, this huge plenty. He laughed so much that to me, too, it began to seem funny. Even when the performance was over, and we were far from the scene, the memory of it would convulse my companion at intervals. Walking home down the Hagley Road he suddenly stopped and said, 'Anne, that bear!' and nearly magicked the Hagley Road out of its frightening every-day-ness with cascades of laughter.

I only once ran upon the rocks with M.J. and that was on one birthday in his early life, when I had given him five shillings. We set off for the town together to spend it. On the way down he told me he'd seen some puppies in the market, and that it was a puppy he would like. Never thinking of Martin's devotion to cats, and of the cats and kittens in the

Hagley Road, I said that would be fine. We went to the market and we bought a minute puppy, actually for the five shillings, and M.J. carried it off in a paper bag, with its head protruding. 'Is it a dawg?' said a man on the mushroom-stall to me, as I stopped to buy some mushrooms. I said I hadn't thought of that. 'Give it 'ere,' said he. 'No, it ain't a dawg.' 'Never mind, Anne,' said M.J., 'I'm glad it's a bitch, we shall have a litter of fresh puppies in time.' And still I was not warned. We went into Corporation Street, where M.J. gave me the pup to hold, while he went to spend, at Smith's, a half-crown someone else had given him. I stood with the pup in my hands, while the entire sixth form of King Edward's seemed to pass by. And then the pup was sick. 'She's been sick,' I said to M.J. when at last he re-appeared. 'We shall have to throw away the paper bag,' he said. I dived into Smith's and demanded a paper bag with such urgency that the startled young man handed me one without a protest; but we had no sooner transferred our little dog from one bag to the other than M.J. said, 'Anne, I'm afraid I'm going to be sick, too.'

'No, M.J.,' said I, 'you just can't be sick in Corporation Street; New Street is only just round the corner, TWIST might see.' This diverted his attention. I got him safely on the bus, and thought no more of the matter until the next time Denne came to King Edward's. 'Martin,' she said, 'was livid.' 'What about?', said I. 'That puppy!' 'What puppy?' 'My DEAR Anne!' 'Not the puppy I gave M.J.?' It had never occurred to me until that moment that the little dog might cause any trouble; it had a gentle face.

Denne went on to tell me the whole story. Martin disliked dogs anyway. And SUCH a dog. Martin liked cats. Denne had reached home to find Martin in wrath, M.J. in tears, the puppy misbehaving, Bridie threatening to resign, the supper spoiling. The puppy had eyes, ears, nose, head, tail, body, legs all of different breed; never before had there been such a mongrel born. It had yelped all night; Martin had had to go down to see to it half a dozen times. They had, in the morning, persuaded their good friend the cobbler to take it off their hands, and I'd better keep out of the way for a bit. I did. But soon I was asked to supper and reconciliation. Martin seemed his usual self; he said not a word of the incident until supper was over and he was making for his own room. Then he turned and said, 'Anne, that o-dious dog!'

I camped for two summers on Clent Hill, and always enjoyed it. Clent and Walton Hills, haunted by picnic parties as they were, retained their stubborn original virtue. Even by day they were not forthcoming to people; at nightfall, and in the early morning, they reverted entirely to themselves. When we animadvert against people in open spaces, we always mean the other fellow, never ourselves and our friends. I had many a supper party near my tent; the one thing I cook really well is ham and eggs, and I can make coffee. But when we were in the height of hilarity we never considered we might be destroying the hill for some lover of the quiet moonlight; it was only when some other revellers destroyed MY moonlight that I was vexed. One thing I always intensely admired about many of the poorest Birmingham mothers was the way they struggled to bring their children out on the hills; I reflected, when I heard of the long queues for the Lickey Hills on Sundays, that had I been a mother, and poor, I might have left my children in the streets, rather than face the morning travel and the peevish return at night. Clent village was much thronged on Sundays, and the lower slopes of the hill; but Saint Kenelm's retained its country Sunday quiet. I liked Saint Kenelm's Church partly for itself, and partly because of the link with Chaucer. The patron saint is that Saint Kenelm whose legend and whose dream Chauntecleer wished his wife Pertelot had read, so that she should not treat his (Chauntecleer's) evil dream of the beast, whose colour was between yellow and red, so common-sensically, not to say medicinally.

After my first summer on Clent Hill, and after spending a long summer holiday with my father and my sister Susan in a cottage at Lelant, it seemed impossible to settle down in Birmingham for a winter. So I found two rooms in a house near the water tower at Romsley, not five minutes' walk from the scented pine woods. The house was owned by Mr and Mrs Holloway. Mr Holloway was a most ingenious inventor, and through him I understand the lives of Trevithick and Trengrouse. He was self-forgetful and unregarding of all but his contrivances; Mrs Holloway was younger than he, practical, pretty and exerting herself to the utmost to keep them both afloat. They suited me. From my sitting-room window I looked over a bluish plane to the Clee Hills and the far Wrekin. On the left was the melodious line of the Malverns coming into focus or hidden, according as the weather decreed. All the winds of heaven blew round that house; an east wind was said to blow straight from the Urals. 'Nothing between us and the Ural Mountains,' Mr Holloway would say; and I could well believe it, so bitter was that wind. From Romsley I could get to Cornwall without going through Birmingham; there were lanes direct to Bromsgrove.

Mr Holloway went into Birmingham to a small factory he owned. Daily he manœuvred and coaxed forward, as though by will-power, an ancient car. I went on my Velocette, down the steep hill past the Rising Sun and the toffee factory to Halesowen; uphill to Quinton, and so by the Hagley Road to Broad Street. At the foot of Broad Street I swung left past the Town Hall, and then right to the junction of Corporation Street with New Street. At this junction I was nearly always held up for valuable minutes while I calculated how far on my colleagues must be with the staff-meeting.

Those staff-meetings! As I worked at King Edward's for seventeen years, and daily staff-meeting gradually lengthened from the original three minutes, through five and ten, to pretty nearly fifteen, I reckon I have passed thus heavily through something like one thousand five hundred hours of dear life. Perhaps such hours are somewhere chalked up to me for righteousness' sake. I can only hope so. Perhaps some time I shall enjoy the usufruct. That idea enchants me. To enjoy at one and the same time the usufruct of my duteous hours and my Post War Credits. Time and Money! What a combination! I can never understood the fashionable disapproval of unearned incomes—the only delightful money, I should have thought:

> Shake, shake, hazel tree,
> Gold and silver, over me!

Mud and slush were more often my portion, wet mud sluiced from the wheels of buses in a spattering swirl. I wore overalls and a leather coat over breeches and leggings and as many sweaters as I possessed. I kept my head warm with a leather helmet pufiled, as the medieval poets expressed it, with fur; my eyes I guarded with goggles. Thus accoutred, I knew the comfort of Tortie. The trouble was getting all my clothes off. It was hardly suitable wear to teach in. So under the sweaters I wore a clean blouse; and in the staff cloakroom I kept a neat skirt and cardigan into which I rapidly changed on arrival. Only once was I in a quandary. I had taken home my skirt meaning to replace it with another of different hue; but I forgot it. There I was in nothing but breeches. But Ailsa Jaques came to my rescue. She kept in the staff cloakroom a kilt, a genuine Scotch kilt—or are kilts Scottish?—a kilt of many colours and innumerable pleats. The material in that kilt would make ten skirts; no wonder Scots keep sheep. I have never felt so skirted as when, having missed staff-meeting, and caused Ailsa pretty nearly to miss it, I went down the wide staircase to prayers, swishing my kilt. The yellow-skirted fays weren't to be compared with me for lustre in mine own esteem.

I was not always so lucky. One morning, frosty after thaw, I skidded in the Hagley Road. I came off and lay for a second or so, broad-wheel-on, in the jaws of an on-coming bus. the Velocette was saved, and I was saved, but the righting of machine and woman took time. That was the morning when Miss Hobbes remarked that I came to school as though riding an obstacle race. Sometimes, in the worst weather, I journeyed to school in Mr Holloway's car. One morning, half way to Birmingham, we decided that one of the wheels was coming off. Mr Holloway was so universally cheerful and inventive that, no doubt, if the wheel had come off, we should have run along through the lanes of the air. As it was we wobbled, we stopped, he tinkered, and we drove on again. Mr Holloway was a man of amazing equanimity. When difficulties accumulated round him his rosy cheeks remained rosy, he went on breathing easily; I have always suspected that he was a Taoist without knowing it. It was in vain that I urged him on when we had started late. 'You know, Mr Holloway, I shall be late for staff-meeting again.' 'Only a woman,' Mr Holloway would reply, slowing down rather than speeding up, 'only a woman would worry about being late for a staff-meeting. That's why,' he continued after a long interval, 'women are not inventors. They are always buzzing ahead towards their next engagement. An inventor . . .' and here the words died away on his lips, and I nearly died away into the air, for we were far from being alone in our meditative world. 'An inventor needs time . . . oceans of time . . . oceans and oceans of time . . .But I can always make time. I . . feel . . . time . . . all . . . round . . . me even . . . in this . . . tra . . .'

When Miss Hobbes wondered how I managed to over-leap my obstacles, and get to school, even she did not know Mr Holloway's tendency to create Time all round him while driving down Broad Street in a motor car with wheels that wobbled.

8

A ROAD ACCIDENT

The following summer an event happened which cured me of any propensity I myself had towards manufacturing Time all round me while driving a motor car. In the Easter holiday of that year my father said he thought it would be a fine thing if I exchanged my motor bike for a small car. He always felt nervous when I went off on the bike, he said. There were more people killed on motor bikes than on any other type of vehicle. Besides, if I had a little car, he could go and see a few cathedrals with me. I did not want a car in the least. Even in an open car the air is checked in its flow round the driver by a wind-screen. What I liked was to move along fast with the air flowing not only down my throat but round every part of me.

However, it happened just as that time that one friend of mine wanted to sell her Austin 7, a good enough little Austin 7, with a pale yellow body. Another friend, a youth, passionately desired a Velocette. By a slight adjustment of money I could therefore change from motor bicycle to motor car with ease. 'So much safer, it would be,' said my father, 'so much drier.' 'You wouldn't look so rough and wild either,' said Susan. 'I can't imagine how Miss Barrie puts up with the way you arrive at school.' I said an Austin 7 was tame after a Velocette. But in the end I was persuaded. Reluctantly I gave up my Velocette to the youth, and bought my friend's car. It was in excellent condition. She was a good driver and a careful woman.

I never liked the change from the start. I had grown used to a steed which responded to every movement of my body. I resented it when the Austin stayed square on her four wheels instead of swaying as I swayed when going round a corner. I had two or three lessons in driving, and then took my father out for a spin. We went to Bradninch. Once there, I forgot how to turn. However, I turned at last; we did get home. When I told my coach next day that I had taken my father out he said, 'Your father is a 'ero.'

My father's extreme pleasure in the little car was the one good point in its favour; but before I could treat him to many little rides, or take him up to view York Minster, it was time for me to go back to Birmingham. I drove sedately through the counties until I pulled up outside Denne's house in the Hagley Road. Here I packed my camping equipment and began, as usual, my summer life, sometimes sleeping in my tent, which again I pitched on Clent Hill, and sometimes in Denne's garden room.

That term we were doing scenes from *The Merchant of Venice* as a form play. I have always enjoyed form plays and all informal acting, scenes quickly arranged and played with other children only as audience. Birmingham children were nearly as clever as Cornish children at transforming themselves in the twinkling of an eye into other persons and other creatures. The classrooms in New Street were perfect for impromptu acting. The walls were very thick, we could laugh as loudly as we liked without disturbing the lesson going on next door, and in the form-rooms, each child kept a white overall to put on when she went to cookery, and a green overall for science. Impossible to describe to any grown-up person how children can disguise themselves, given five minutes and a white and a green overall. Their ingenuity was endless, and their radiant faces, when they had achieved something fresh, entirely justified time taken from more serious work. We used to break up into four troupes, so that every child had a chance of acting, or presenting a scene from any book we happened to be reading.

This particular summer we were reading, among other things, *The Merchant of Venice* in one of the lower fourths, and our idea was to enact the trial scene at the end of the term before the two parallel forms. There were three parallel forms in each age group at King Edward's, but A, B and C did not mean that the A's were supposed to be brilliant, the B's moderate and the C's mediocre—a detestable plan, I think. the forms were intended to be equal. The quick and the slower learnt together, so some helped all. 'Every man shift for all the rest, and let no man take care for himself', as Stephano put it. It is astonishing what two or three very able children in English will do for the entire batch.

I was accustomed to taking big parties of girls both to the Birmingham Repertory Theatre and to Stratford. On one occasion, two or three of us took a group to London to see John Gielgud act Richard II; as far as I remember we were able, by making party arrangements, to enjoy the whole day, return ticket to London, theatre ticket, and tea, for less than ten shillings a head; it was an unforgettable performance. To watch Richard near madness in the last scene, to hear the churning of thoughts in his mind, was a revelation of the delicate equilibrium of mind, soul and body; the thoughts mounted like waves and broke, like spray, against the control of the will. It was a machine 'racing' its engine. But it was not *Richard II* which we were reading in the Lower IVs; it was *The Merchant of Venice*. I decided not to take a formal party, but to take Portia, Shylock and Antonio down with me in the Austin on a Saturday afternoon to see their counterparts act.

The day seemed auspicious enough when I left Clent. The weather was fine; there was plenty of time. One girl did not turn up at the appointed place, so I went off with only two, Portia and Shylock. I chose the route by the Alcester Road, through Ullenhall, a route I greatly like. At one point I mistook the road. That meant turning back. I think the superstition that turning back is unlucky has something in it; most superstitions have. It is unlucky not to curtsy to the new moon because the person who does not curtsy to the new moon must be more absorbed in something less beautiful than the heavenly bodies; it is unlucky to turn back because that person must be prone to inattention. I certainly was not consciously inattentive. I was driving, as I thought, with care; not unduly fast. The way was not wide; but not twisty or as narrow as some Cornish lanes are. I was nearly opposite a pub when, from a side turning, a car came across the main road dead in front of me. I had been screened from the driver of the car by a large stationary dray full of beer-barrels. I braked, but it was too late; the head of my car went into the other car's body; my windscreen was shattered. Portia, the child sitting next to me, was cut by the glass; Shylock, the child at the back, was unhurt. So were the people in the other car. A doctor came quickly from Henley-in-Arden; he rendered first-aid to the child who had been cut; an ambulance came, and I went in it with the child to a hospital. It seemed an age; the driver was not sure of the way through the maze of Birmingham streets; if anyone ever desired passion-ately to recall three minutes, I did. If only I had not made a mistake in the way I should have passed the danger spot a few minutes before that car emerged from the secondary road on to my main road. We reached the hospital. The relief of that arrival; the speed, the smoothness of all the arrangement, will always be with me: the feeling of having the child at last in safe hands. I vowed always to give half my income to hospitals in future; a vow I did not keep. The child's parents came. I got back to the Hagley Road—I do not remember how. Then I was violently sick. I was in bed when I heard Denne say: 'Just an ordinary little nose, Doctor Dain.' He was trying to decide what my nose had been like to start with, and whether it was broken. It had come so violently into contact with the windscreen that my face was a plain convex from ear to ear; and my ribs, which had banged against the steering wheel, were bruised. I had horrible dreams. All I longed to know was whether the cut in the child's cheek would leave a mark.

One piece of thoughtfulness I shall always remember; the Henley-in-Arden doctor, a busy man who did not know me personally, took the trouble to write me a note saying he hoped the accident would not prevent me from taking children to the theatre in future. He thought taking children to a real theatre, so that they should not be confined to picture shows, was a valuable duty. He said the collision was a pure accident, not my fault, and advised me to drive again as soon as ever I was able. I might have done this. The child recovered. Insurance was paid me for my car. There was no real reason, I suppose, why I should not have driven again. But I never did. I who had been so light-hearted, so unimaginative, in relation to speed on roads, could never be unimaginative again. I bought, at Halesowen, a second-hand Raleigh, a pedal bicycle. I had not taken any fear of being killed; I had taken fear of killing. At a maximum speed of three miles an hour I was not likely to endanger any child's life.

I tried hard to take the Henley-in-Arden doctor's advice, and not to shirk the responsibility of taking children to the theatre or for picnics. But I never again enjoyed these excursions as I had done before. I found that, instead of eagerly planning parties, I tried to avoid them. Now that roads have become so dangerous, grown-ups cannot so gaily assume responsibility for children as they did when I was a child, and this I think is greatly to the children's loss. Grown-up people in Gorrran and Caerhays, and even 'big girls', often gave my sister Susan and me delightful times when we were small by taking us hither and thither. Now I think there is a strong feeling that the safest treat for children is to take them to the Pictures. I feel saddened when I see queues of children for the picture houses on gloriously fine Saturday mornings. They see only shadow shows instead of the living breathing world; and instead of wandering, escorted by their senses amidst wonders, they are in a mock world, often a hideous one, and breathing staled breath.

I seemed just at that time to be purely unlucky in taking children out. I began to feel a painful inadequacy, an inability to cope with time and time tables, space and children. It was the custom at King Edward's for each form to go with its form-mistress for a picnic towards the end of the summer term. I had hitherto enjoyed these functions. My chosen age for a form has always been children of about eleven or twelve years old. Girls of this age are delightfully fresh, imaginative, full of energy, and ready to explore. For two or three years I had taken my form by bus to Gipsy's Tent. Then we had walked by the fields and the wood to the top of Clent, where there was splendid space for play, and my tent to make tea in. How different these children were on the Hill from their town selves! They left school wearing clean cotton dresses, white socks, black shoes or sandals, panama hats with black and white bands—as trim a set as could be met. They looked pretty too. I remember one year when about four different coloured cottons for summer uniform might be chosen: blue, or yellow, or green, or a printed pink cotton. Looking down on the school assembled in Hall from the gallery was rather like viewing a garden of gay flowers. In clean dresses, then, my form queued for their bus, got out at Gipsy's Tent, and began soberly to walk, carrying various packages with good things for tea. They started soberly, and gradually became excited like colts; they began to run and shout. I usually had one or two sixth form girls with me. When we reached the bare hill these older girls organized all sorts of games for some of the children, while some wandered to the groves, and some ran down to Clent for ice-cream, and one, named Judy I remember, once caught one of the Clent ponies and arranged rides for the more daring. Then tea. What an unpacking of good things! By the time I had tasted of the various dainties the mothers had provided I had always eaten too much. My treat was generally fruit—cherries or strawberries. I see the baskets of cherries which the prefects and I carted; and hear the chanted sharing-out. Pony rides and cherries are disastrous to summer frocks. In the various games hair-slides were lost, hair blew wild, socks were greened, shoes made earthy. On the way back to Gipsy's Tent we looked more like a gang of toughs than a form. Then we would begin the tidying up—hair smoothed back, hats on. And so into the bus and home.

A picnic on Clent Hill was easy to arrange. But one year my form was very anxious to go further afield, and one of the

Prefects, a girl named Betty, a girl good at games, with auburn hair and an eager face, suggested to me that we should go to a summer hut her family had by the river, seven or eight miles from Warwick. It seemed a good idea to me. Betty was a born organizer. She did all the work. We went by train to Warwick, caught a bus to the chosen site, and had a perfect picnic. It was an open field full of buttercups and sorrel and hard-heads. Willows shaded the river. There was safe bathing, and I think I remember a boat. Time sped. Ah! time sped! Neither Betty nor I remembered soon enough that there was an early last bus from that pleasant countryside back the seven miles to Warwick. We missed it, and there we were, twenty-three children, seven miles from Warwick, Warwick twenty miles from Birmingham, and many children with a considerable journey after that. I cursed myself. To walk the seven miles and catch a train early enough to take the children home without anxiety to the parents was out of question.

Luckily Betty knew the farmer on whose land her parents' summer quarters were built. She went to consult him. And soon she came back radiant. He would take us all to Warwick station in the cattle truck. To the children this was the triumphant end of a triumphant day. We went through the field to a lane; the good-natured farmer arrived with a big covered truck with slats for breathing spaces. He let down the steps and the girls ran shouting up them into the body of the truck. One little girl named Tessie climbed up next the farmer's seat in front. Betty and I went in with the 'cattle'. We stood; the farmer started up; the truck moved off; we swayed together. At every abrupt lurch or change of speed we locked arms for support. There were shrieks of laughter. When we reached Warwick station and the boards were put down and my form ran out of the truck I said to the farmer:

'I'm afraid you've never had a noisier lot of cattle.'

He said: 'I've never had such a handy lot for going up and down the steps.'

9

SNAPSHOTS OF SCHOOL

The girls, especially the child named Tessie who had had the seat by the driver, agreed that the ride in the truck was the best part of the best of all possible picnics. That particular lower fourth year was the liveliest form I ever had as my adopted family for a year.

A form closely resembles a family in that the form-mistress, like a mother, sticks up for her own against too much hostile criticism. A tiresome child never seems so tiresome to her form-mistress, who has come to know her very well, as to the various subject-mistresses who see her only in a given set of circumstances. Even in official talk, even in staff-meetings, Miss Barrie might say, 'Chloe Price? Yours, isn't she, Miss Camous?' Or, 'Chloe is yours now, Miss Mielke, what about her?' And it was amazing how Chloe's character seemed to change in a few weeks when she had changed form-mistresses, and become 'My Chloe Price' to someone who had formerly denounced her as an idle young monkey.

Towards the close of each term there was generally an odd hour in which form-mistress and form made merry together. My form sometimes seized this chance to make known to me any little grievance of theirs. On one occasion they had evidently been telling one another that if they weren't allowed with impunity to borrow a book when they had forgotten their own, I oughtn't to borrow, either. The last English lesson of a term was usually given over to charades. My form decided to enact me on this occasion. I have forgotten the word chosen to be represented, but one scene was in a classroom. A small class was standing ready to receive the mistress, just as classes are supposed to stand at King Edward's. 'I' came dashing in a little late, said good-morning before I was well inside, and began the lesson before I reached the desk. Soon the class was asked to get out a certain book and Tessie put up a hand.

'Please, Miss Treneer,' she said, to the figure representing me, 'I've forgotten my book, may I share with Mary, please?'

'Yes, Tessie, but it will be an order mark I'm afraid.' And in the same breath, 'Will someone lend me a book, please?' The form greeted this request with shouts of laughter and, 'Order mark, Miss Treneer, order mark.'

For some years after I went to King Edward's there was in force a system of order and conduct marks, a system devised, I suspect, by Miss Creak. An order mark was given for breaking any rule framed to prevent confusion and noise among large numbers in a little space—for running on stairs and in corridors, or for talking when and where silence was enjoined. Order marks were also given for forgetting books. Conduct marks were given for more serious crimes. The advantage was that an order or conduct mark could be given and no words of admonition mouthed; the disadvantage was that the unco' guid tended to be a little smug when, at the end of the term, no mark was discovered to be entered against them. I found it awkward to be half encouraging some meek child to acquire an order mark or two. With the bold, blithe spirits there was the difficulty of deciding whether the frequent order mark was deserved. What really constituted running? That was often a difficult point to decide.

'Running in the corridor, Veronica?'

'Oh, Miss Treneer, that was a quick walk.'

When I asked one lower fourth form to suggest a motion for a five minute debate, Veronica suggested, 'That a slow run is a quick walk'.

Exhortation is, I think, the worst way of dealing with the young. Small, known penalties like order marks, always provided they are not kept from term to term as permanent records—each term should start fresh and fair—are of service to those who, because of some past circumstances of which the school is probably unaware, need to feel big by being unlawful. Such children should be allowed to feel big to their heart's content without being driven to commit too desperate an act. Modern methods, which ignore a good deal in order not to focus attention on behaviour, tend to drive some children to extremes in order to obtain the notice they crave. Some girls will always seek the excitement of law-breaking. I have heard the most exciting-sounding conversations going on amongst girls about the smallest matters. Probably all Jane did was to flick a note to Mary, and all the mistress said was 'Give me that', but in the reporting it all sounded most sensational.

The modern idea of Record Cards, following a child from year to year, and even from school to school, is monstrous in its utter disregard of a child's nature. It is absolutely essential that a child should be able to feel, after a bad term, that she is starting to try again, with a new untarnished future. The old phrases, 'turning over a new leaf', 'starting a clean sheet', show more understanding of psychology than the keeping of elaborate continuous records. Let us, for heaven's sake, forget a little. When we abolished conduct and order marks at King Edward's I was glad to see them go; I disliked the business of counting them up each term, and they tended to make small matters seem important. But while we retained their use life was notably free of wear and tear for the staff. The staff common-room was down a long corridor into which pupils might not stray. Any message from a pupil was conveyed by Twist or Gumery. This withdrawal, making for peace and quiet, helped towards the maintenance of good humour which is essential for fruitful school relationships. Good humour is the product of unfretted nerves. Friction arises when the high-spirited young encounter the tired mature. It is not only humane, but politic, so to provide for the lives of teachers that they come freshly to their work. Freshness is all. Children have no mercy on the weary. They are not merciful creatures. Dr Johnson knew they had no mercy on oddness either.

In a day school the form is the natural unit. Inter-form affairs were enormously popular at King Edward's. The school was also divided into Houses: Bordeaux, Beaufort, Tudor and Seymour, so that girls of varied ages should unite in social function and games. But the artificially created House in a day school has not the vitality of the natural House in a boarding-school. Apart from games, the most enjoyable inter-House event during the year was the music competition. Each House chose a conductor and a choir. Denne selected two songs, a part song and a song in unison, which all choirs must learn; in addition each choir might choose a song to sing. The accompanist had to be a member of the House. When the time was ripe, the whole school assembled in the hall, on chairs on either side of a wide central gangway; Denne with Alex Makin, vice-president of the musical society, sat at a table in this gangway. Denne had clean sheets of paper before her, and a little bell at her right hand. She tinkled it. The first choir, wearing House colours—the colours of the four Houses were red, yellow, green, blue—came on to the platform. The accompanist went to the piano; the conductor took her stand. She concentrated the attention of her group, glanced back at Denne for a nod, raised her baton and began.

I have listened entranced to much sweet singing by House choirs. In addition there was the interest of seeing how the several conductors would acquit themselves. Some girl, perhaps, whom one had judged to have no ear for poetry, was here seen to reveal something quite different from what one had considered her stolid self. The music competition offered opportunity to succeed or fail; one could see a nervous girl taking courage, summoning her personal pluck and innate power to the ordeal.

Denne radiated confidence to the choirs while the test was on; then she teased them all. The singing over, the choirs filed into the hall and sat in front and Denne, after some minutes spent over her notes and marks, went on to the platform, and surveyed the school as they clapped her. Her speech of adjudication followed a known pattern. She made grand play with the art of suspense, managing to give the maximum amount of criticism, praise and advice, while keeping back the results. Even in announcing her final decision there was a recognized and expected pattern of play; there were pauses, interpolations, a pretence of having muddled her notes, or counted up the marks wrongly. 'And now,' she would say, at last, having shuffled her papers, turned them upside down, and re-shuffled them, 'and now for the marks. Bordeaux!' (Here the newest members of Bordeaux who had never been to house-singing before prepared to clap.) 'Bordeaux! I forgot to say that the diction of this choir . . . whereas Tudor . . . one minute, dears . . . Tudor's rhythm . . . but Seymour, so well served by both conductor and accompanist . . . and Beaufort' (a sigh of supreme satisfaction from the Beaufortians), 'Beaufort's tone and blend . . . I have therefore given . . .'.

All through the adjudication and announcement Denne managed to keep every girl eagerly attentive; now it was as though the lid were off the pot. The school let itself go entirely and was only brought back to quietude when all the choirs filed back together on to the platform to be conducted by Miss Denne Parker herself. How they sang then! Singing is, I think, one of man's most glorious gifts, and woman's too, and child's.

Other cherished House events were the history party and the swimming gala. I think always of Miss Thompson and Miss Orton in relation to the history party; of Miss Jaques and Mrs Field at the swimming gala—Miss Jaques with a megaphone directing events. I wish I could draw or paint. It needs colour to show the clear, greenish-blue water of the swimming bath, the girls in swimming suits and bathing caps which so changed the characteristic look of faces that I was often puzzled to recognize a child. I see mistresses with towels over their dresses to protect themselves from splashes; I watch the dives; I watch the long slender bodies going a little askew as, after the dive, in one of the races, they keep under the water for as long as possible, while the length traversed under water by each competitor is marked. Each head at last emerges to shake off water and gasp in air. I watch those strenuous contests, the relay races; I laugh at the comic, final obstacle race. By the time I reached King Edward's my enthusiasm for hockey and netball had waned; I rarely watched House matches; but the swimming gala and the gymnastic competitions always revived my former pleasure in sports and pastimes.

There were various House parties; and all Houses united once a year for the Social. Miss Macdonald disliked and derided the word Social. It seemed to her the essence of all that was to be detested in the mis-use of words. 'Party, party, *party!*' she would say. But year after year the school obstinately adhered to the word Social. To Miss Macdonald this usage was even worse than pronouncing *hurrah, hurray*. I have heard the school begin to shout *hurray* and be carried into *hurrah* before the third cheer by the operation of Macdonald's vehement spirit. I loved to tease Macdonald. 'Why not let them say Social?' I asked. She looked at me as at one of whom she had once entertained hopes, but whom she now mourned among the lost for ever. 'Social, Treneer, social—how can you bear ut? Social in that context is utterly unbearable.' As though innocently, I used to flout her shibboleths; 'serviette', I would say, for the fun of seeing the word 'napkin' gather almost irresistibly to breaking point on her lips. The right English word in the right context nestled at Miss Macdonald's very heart. And yet she was the wildest creature. She had more in common with the March Hare than with decorum. She was passionate for beauty, for the simple word, and for the seemly grammatical usage. If I could return to the staff common-room in New Street I should best like to enter it and find an argument in progress between Miss Macdonald and Miss Makin, on what, to the lay person, might seem some minor point of language. The minds of the opponents came alongside, engaged and grappled. With what examples from the classics, Old English and Middle English they bombarded each other; with what mounting passion they dragged out English,

Latin and Greek dictionaries for fresh munitions; how they
would appeal to supporters in the ring which gradually formed
round them as principal contestants; in what a huff they would
quit the scene by different doors; with what a laugh find
themselves washing hands in neighbouring basins in the
cloakroom, and renew their glancing, accustomed amity!

I see myself marking Entrance Papers with Miss Macdonald.
At the Entrance Examination we set, in English, a Comprehension Test, questions in English grammar, and a composition. If
a child chanced to do well in all three sections it was plain
sailing for us; equally so if she chanced to be stupid in all three.
No troubles would arise over these candidates until we met
those members of the staff who had marked the mathematics
and the intelligence tests. But our own border-lines; shall I ever
forget those who were on the border line in our subject? The
chances were that a girl would do a good piece of composition,
and know no grammar; or she would reveal to us by her
dealings with the Comprehension Test that she understood
what she read, and convince us by her essay that she would
never master the English sentence in writing, or have a notion
of her own.

'What do you make of No. 207y8, Treneer?' Macdonald
might say, glinting at me over the bundle of her papers. She
had the bluest of blue eyes, often blazing blue eyes they were.

'No. 207y8!' I would reply, searching madly through my pile.
'Just a minute, Macdonald. No. 207y8 you said? I've given her
thirteen out of twenty. She's fairly good.'

'But she has NO imagination,' Macdonald might say, gazing
at me through her forest of buttercup hair, by this time almost
standing on end. 'She hasn't a spark; not a spark; no life; no
imagination; no ideas. We might as well admit a wooden bread-
board into the school as 207y8. Listen to what she says about
Fire Fairies! LISTEN, TRENEER!'

There were always children who had no soul piling up marks
for grammar.

'Grammar merely tests how a child has been taught,'
Macdonald said. 'Ability in grammar is the result of clear

teaching; the most ordinary mind can score marks in grammar.'

'Then why do we set grammar questions,' I asked, 'if they merely test the teacher?'

'Ah!' said Macdonald darkly. 'But grammar must be taught, Treneer. It's only our grammar questions which stand between Birmingham and illiteracy. Once we give up examining in grammar the preparatory schools will give up teaching ut.' Not only by a certain richness in the pronunciation of the indefinite article, and by the colour of the syllables as she read, so feelingly that they glowed with life, the traditional ballads, did Macdonald remind me of her Irishness. There was vehemence in her. With what wrath would she read advertisements for English mistresses in *The Times Educational Supplement* which said, 'Oxford or Cambridge preferred'. When she became a headmistress, she said, she should put, 'Dublin and Edinburgh preferred'.

She did become a headmistress. She became headmistress of the Abbey School, Reading, where she numbered Jane Austin among the old girls. Almost immediately afterwards, Miss McDermott was appointed headmistress of Pontefract High School. I was left forlorn, the surviving member of the English side at King Edward's.

Miss Barrie sent for me one morning while I was enjoying a free period in the staff common-room. She said she would like me to take over the English department; but that there were, of course, various responsibilities. I opened my mouth to refuse. Miss Barrie said she was giving me time to think it over, and back I went to the common-room, where Miss Hoggan, head of the Classics side, was marking books. I did not, at that time, know Miss Hoggan very well. She was extraordinarily able. She had a mind which never seemed to refuse and jib. It operated distinctly and decidedly on any material which presented itself, and she was a women of fine taste. Her house, her pictures, her garden, the flowers on her desk, were such as to give pleasure to the beholder. Pasque flowers in a clear glass jar are still in my eye. If she recommended a book I was pretty certain to enjoy it.

I told her of the decision I had to make.

'Well, you'll accept it, won't you?' she said.

'No, I don't think so.'

'I think you're very foolish.'

I looked at her smooth fringe. She was anything but a smooth person, but she had a finished appearance.

'You may dislike any new person who may be appointed, and you won't be able to say that you'd prefer to be head after all. You'd like choosing the books for the various sets, and making syllabuses; you'd like to do what you chose with the Sixth.'

'I enjoy being light trellis,' I said, 'I'm not a bit anxious to be one of the props.'

However, Miss Hoggan made me realize that the existence of light trellis depended entirely on the nature of the props. Should I find other props as much to my taste as Miss Macdonald and Miss McDermott had been? If I became a prop I should help to choose the new trellis. Miss Barrie always gave the department a say in appointing.

I did not wish to be a long time in making up my mind. Miss Hoggan clinched the matter by saying,

'If you try it for six months, and find you don't like it, you can quietly give it up; whereas if you go on being trellis and don't like your new props, you won't be able to do anything about that.'

I went in to Miss Barrie straight away and told her I had decided to be a prop.

I never regretted the decision, chiefly because the people appointed to the department were not only very congenial, but also exceedingly good at their chosen work—Miss Baker, Miss Bull, and later on Miss Stevens, now headmistresses, one and all.

10

MISTLETOE COTTAGE, LOXLEY

I was in the staff common-room one Friday morning awaiting the gong for lunch. Twist beat a gong instead of ringing a bell in the old New Street days. I was idly looking at the advertisements in the *Birmingham Post*, when I saw a cottage advertised at Loxley. It was called Mistletoe Cottage, and it was to be let at reduced terms during the autumn and winter months. I hastened to Miss Piper's room and found from her time-table that there was a train to Stratford at 2.10. I cut lunch and hurried to Snow Hill station, and called at the Inquiry Office. Yes, it was possible to get a three months' season ticket between Stratford and Snow Hill. Yes, there was a train which would bring me in from Stratford before nine o'clock in the morning. I could leave Stratford at 7.55 and reach Snow Hill at 8.50. I caught the 2.10 full of anticipation, reached Stratford, and inquired for Loxley.

'Loxley! You'll have to have a taxi.'

'I want to find out how far it is.'

'Loxley is two and a half miles isn't it, Bill?'

'Loxley? Three miles at least. She'll have to have a taxi,' said Bill.

'I want to find out how far it feels.'

Both Bill and his mate looked at me dubiously.

Another porter joined us. 'Loxley,' he said, 'is a good four miles. She'd better have a taxi.'

'Which way is it?' I asked.

'Oh, it's along the Loxley Road, four and a half miles or so,' he said. 'You go down Bridge Street, over Clopton Bridge, turn left, and then right; and keep on till you get there. No, never heard of Mistletoe Cottage, but you'll find it easy enough. Hardly any houses there. Better have a taxi.'

But I didn't want a taxi. You can only learn how far off a place feels by walking it. If I was to do the journey every day I must find out that.

I went down through Bridge Street. It was a Friday. Stratford had reverted, as it always does on a Friday, to being not a theatrical Stratford, but the market town of a farming district. Open booths, displaying all kinds of fruit and vegetables, gay and useful clothes, hardware, glittering toys and trifles, were set up in the broad main street. I seemed transported back to the time before Shakespeare's birthplace was made so deadly respectable; back to the days when it sported the sign of the Swan and Maidenhead. Or further back still, when Shakespeare himself was alive and young, when he met Autolycus, the spiv, crying up his 'lawn as white as driven snow'; when he overheard the country clown telling over what he had to buy for the sheep-shearing feast. I did not know how alive that clown was until years and years later when I saw Paul Schofield enact him in the Memorial Theatre. He made this clown, of whom I had always thought as a rustic stuffed with straw, as natural as daylight, and funnier than the rascal pedlar. When I see or read the sheep-shearing feast scenes in *The Winter's Tale*, I feel certain that Aubrey was right about Shakespeare: 'that he was a handsome well-shaped man, verie good companie, and of a very ready, and pleasant smooth wit'.

The yellow October sunshine warmed Stratford as I went over Clopton Bridge, turned left, then right, spurned the villas and reached the lanes. I saw the scattered fantastic elms, and the low pleached hedges over which the eye swings to so wide a horizon that the sky is a fitted dome. I met no one. The only sounds were here a bird note, there a stick breaking under my feet, and a soft sound of wind in the thorns; the leaves were mostly green still, but with hints of yellow and red. I went on till the sky moved in to meet me, as the road rose a little; on my left I passed an old farmhouse with thatched, wavy roof, and an open barn raised on wooden pillars. Then I came to a steep green on the right. There were a few cottages; there was a smell of wood fires; and there were snow-berries and elderberries on a tall hedge. I looked at a cottage and said to myself, 'I wish that was Mistletoe Cottage.' It was.

I opened the gate, walked down the path, and knocked at the door. There was no answer. I have rarely felt more disappointed. Through the window on the left, I could see a fire blazing in an open brick fireplace. There were apple trees and pear trees in the garden, together with a few late dahlias, michaelmas daisies and straggling roses. I wanted the cottage.

'I'm Miss Manifold.'

The owner had come upon me from the rear, while I was geaking in at the window.

I explained my errand, and Miss Manifold invited me to tea. We came to terms. I could have the cottage for ten shillings a week until the next Easter. During the summer months Miss Manifold had a much higher rent for the cottage. What she wanted was a tenant for the winter who would keep the cottage warm and dry. There was a girl in the village who would come in daily to clean for, I think, five or six shillings a week.

'When can I come?' I asked.

Miss Manifold was leaving the cottage next morning for another house she possessed in the south. I might move in in the afternoon if I liked. I walked back to Stratford singing, 'O Lord, how manifold, how manifold are thy works'. There actually was mistletoe on an apple tree at Mistletoe Cottage.

I took possession on Saturday afternoon. The cottage was furnished; so, apart from my books and a few clothes, there were no arrangements to make. I seemed hundreds of miles away from Birmingham when I went out to pick sticks with which to build a splendid fire on the open hearth. It was one of those hearths which need never be cleaned up. From the ashes of one fire new flames leapt up. I hate to touch coal cinders, but I love to touch wood ash, soft and flaky, white and grey. I cannot remember at all how the cottage was furnished, nor how many rooms there were. I think there were four rooms and a room which had been made into a bathroom. Down the garden path was what M. J., who came to stay in the cottage, later, with Denne and Martin, always referred to as the Nelson. I do remember that the beams were so low that Martin was always banging his head. Men must have grown taller surely since the old cottages were built.

I lived in the cottage for two terms, until the following Easter, when two people from the theatre, who always rented it for the season, took it over from me. I had grown to know the village well. It was hardly a village, a hamlet rather. The church was apart, in an elbow to the left, on the road to Wellesbourne. It had a fifteenth-century tower, but I think the church itself had been restored in Queen Anne's day. It made me think of Addison. There was a nave with no aisles, and a clear glass east window with curiously disposed leaded panes at the top. I watched the trees through them. The parson had a splendid view from his raised, box-like pulpit, which he reached by a little door. He could look right across the plain to Stratford. It was a cold church. Coughing often drowned the parson's saw, and my nose felt as red as Marion's—not due, I may say, to imbibing Flower's Ale, though this beverage was advertised at Loxley under the sign of the Fox.

The week-ends were, of course, the most beautiful time for the cottage. Time is best when it appears to stand still, and worst when one feels as though one is passing through it. I passed through it on week-day mornings. It took me twenty-five minutes to bicycle with ease to the station. What I tended to do was to cut it fine and, instead of being able to linger a minute or two on Clopton Bridge, have to pedal hard up through Stratford. Stations should never be on inclines, even slight inclines. Yet, in spite of my difficulties with time, autumn and winter mornings on Clopton Bridge are among my most treasured memories. The bridge itself is a beautiful structure; the Avon has not been entirely ruined by the machinations of the Improvers; and the Memorial Theatre is impressive in early light, just before the sun gets up, when one perceives masses but not detail. The Avon frontage was not glassed-in in those days. I like well enough to dine behind that glass frontage, but I think it has made the theatre more hideous than it naturally is. Bridge, river, tree and church, and some mellowed houses make the beauty of Stratford. A rising sun and Holy Trinity Church spire, above the soft Avon, flowing yellow-gold with its complement of swans, offered a feast of beauty sufficient to last through a Birmingham day. It is lucky that the sun does not rise at the same time every day, or, as it were, in the same place. It is as though God knew that his creatures would like variety when he ordained the seasons, and day and night, and twilight, and the varying moon, and the wheeling stars. I shall never grow weary of being out in all times at all seasons and in all weathers—except in a black east wind. Yet I am not one who, once in bed, readily rises. It was King Edward's School that got me up early and out. Direful duty drove me through sweet pleasures. One needs an initial prick: then, once out of bed, rain or shine, there is always something to see between six forty-five and nine o'clock.

Often, when there were late functions at school, or if I went to the theatre, or stayed in Birmingham for an orchestral concert, I slept in a friend's flat or a friend's house. Good friends are part of life's feast of variousness. It was joyful, at the close of a party, not to be turned out with the other guests, but to be spending the night with the hostess because Loxley was so far off. Sometimes I was unexpectedly invited to stay and, as I was smaller than most of my friends on the staff, I slept in pyjamas or nightdresses several sizes too large for me. This roomy comfort came to seem desirable as it did to Confucius, who wore his night-garment half-a-length too long. I like this intimate detail of the habits of the sage, just as I like the story of Montaigne—that he sometimes arranged to be awakened in the night by a pulley attached to his toe, so as to become conscious of the bliss of being in bed.

But some late nights I refused hospitality. I caught the last train to Stratford so as to walk back to my cottage, through moonlight, or starlight or the black rain. One does not like to be thought mad even by oneself, and it seems always a little mad to go out from the fireside to walk deliberately in the night. But to have to walk back from Stratford to Loxley, because there was no other way of getting there, was not mad, merely a necessity; and before I reached my goal I had always warmed up to enjoyment. I remember one night of light snow on sparkling, moonlit frost; and I remember one night so black that I thought, perhaps, I had died and was in the world of perpetual night 'and through the hawthorn blows the cold wind'. It was friendly to touch the hedge or a tree trunk; to remember that I was journeying towards morning.

Sometimes I had visitors at Mistletoe Cottage. Once Miss Udall and Miss Hobbes came to see me, walking along the frozen lanes to Loxley. I knew they were coming and spent the morning making preparations, polishing up the furniture, and bringing in loads of wood for the fire, making scones to toast for tea, and preparing a casserole of chicken for lunch. Then I went to meet the guests, fearing that perhaps it was too cold a day to tempt them out to Loxley. But they were undaunted by the weather. They came around a bend in the lane. I remember it because of Miss Hobbes's colour and the sparkle in her eye; and Miss Udall's smile curling her lips; and because of their praise of the chicken. Miss Hobbes is not really interested in food, but Miss Udall relished a flavour as though it were a strain of music. The art of cooking! Taste! Taste included the primary pleasure of the palate with Miss Udall. She remembered special meals. There was a breakfast she had had in Scotland once; a fish she had eaten at . . . a duck at . . . She would say, 'You know, Treneer, I had a duck once . . .'. And my chicken was numbered among the occasion . . . 'That chicken of yours you know, Treneer . . . the day Hobbes and I came to Loxley.' It must have been not very long before Christmas, because I remember thinking the two came into the cottage as though they were holly and laurel, they were so decorative. They made everything kindle and sparkle and glow in the firelight, so that food was good, and to laugh was good, and to be warm was good, and time flowered.

11

BEARLEY

During that winter and spring, while I was living at Loxley, Martin Gilkes was ill, and I sometimes took his W.E.A. class at Stratford. This class brought me great good luck, for members of it were Mrs Oliver Baker, her son Geoffrey, and Miss Dorothy Amphlett who has since become Mrs Geoffrey Baker. It was Dorothy Amphlett who found me a cottage at Bearley. She called to me one morning from the steps of a Bank, when I was in Stratford, inwardly lamenting that at Easter I should have to give up my Loxley cottage. She asked me if I had found a cottage for the summer, and suggested that I should explore Bearley. It would be a good plan, she thought, if I bicycled to Bearley, called at the Stone House, and talked over cottages with Mrs Oliver Baker.

So I took my bicycle and set off up the road towards Henley-in-Arden. About four miles or so from Stratford I came to Bearley Cross where I turned right and went up a road with a farm-house and the old Vicarage on my right, and a little cottage, like a glorified and comfortable brick sentry box, on my left. Then I came to a minute green in which was a great, spreading, shady tree. From this green the church was reached, and a cottage where Miss Devy, the organist, lived with her cats. By the Church the road broke into three parts. One bore left to Manor Cottage, the Manor House with its lovely barn, and the village post-office-shop kept by Mrs Knight; the middle road went on towards Snitterfield; the third bore right; and went around so as to form a figure nine with a curly tail. On the curly tail were the Old Forge, and Old Forge Cottage. In the circular head of the figure were, nicely disposed, the Stone House, and three rows of cottages. Mr Kendrick's farmhouse was reached by a gate through a farm-yard. Bearley had nearly everything necessary for a delightful life: church, school—there was a village school down School Lane—fields and gardens in which to grow all manner of fruit, corn and vegetables; woods near at hand; and about two hundred varied people in the parish. A canal was near but, alas, there was no sea.

I went in quest of the Stone House and I quickly found it, set in a garden hedged with grey wooden palings. In the house was Mrs Oliver Baker. Mrs Baker had an ethereal strength. She looked fragile, but she could work in the garden all day, six days of the week. It was as though she went round saying: 'Grow, grow' to all the right plants, and to the wrong ones, 'Fly away'; for there was a peculiar harmony in the Stone House garden. Vegetables were less slow and placid, and flowers fuller of strength and scent than commonly. Although the vegetable garden was separated by bushes from the main flower-garden, flowers grew with the vegetables, and ripe apples dropped among the garden roses. When I first saw the garden it was March, and flowers were coming up in the places they had known for many years. They were at home in the garden, not newly set: late crocuses and early daffodils, snow-on-the-mountain, jonquils, polyanthuses, pheasant's eyes and long loose-shaking hyacinths. Between the stones grew all manner of small early flowers, garden daisies, and daisies returning to their single state.

Mrs Baker took me to see Novar Cottage opposite Mr Kendrick's farm. But Novar Cottage was too large for me. 'And I'm afraid Mrs Lott's cottage may be too small for you,' said Mrs Baker. But I thought no cottage could be too small. So we went to see Mrs Lott's cottage. It was like a child's house of bricks. In front was a hedge, a snow-ball and thorn hedge. It guarded the smallest of gardens, with enough grass for one person to sit on. Under the window there was a flower bed full of forget-me-nots, leant over by a flowering currant. On the right of the path was a plum tree. The cottage consisted of a stone-flagged passage, and a sitting-room, from which the stairs led up to two bedrooms, each with a casement window which opened out to give a view over the green fields and trees, with, in the far distance a faint line of the Malvern Hills. I knew instantly that I wanted the cottage—before I had seen the tiny scullery, and the small paved backyard in which there were a pear tree and two water-butts, one tall and slim, the other squat and fat. Mr Lott, a musician with an excellent voice, always referred to them as Carrie Tubb and Clara Butt. The cottage was furnished with tables and chairs, and beds, and pots and pans, and such things as dusters—all for fifteen shillings a week. Drinking water was from a well in Mrs Lott's garden. Down went a bucket; then I wound and wound and wound, and up came the pail again filled with the coldest cold clear water. Carrie and Clara provided me with rain water, and the yard in which they stood was so secluded, with high walls and elder bushes and the pear tree screening it, that I could run water into my tin bath, and bath outdoors in the summer mornings. Especially that was a refreshing way to wash when a soft warm rain was falling.

I concluded a pact with Mrs Lott by which I was to become the possessor of her cottage after the Easter holidays. Then I went to tea at the Stone House and met for the first time Mr Oliver Baker who had arrived from his shop in Sheep Street, where he sold antique furniture. Both he and Mrs Baker had been artists, and many were the pictures each had painted, and the sketching expeditions on which they had gone. But the public having stupidly (because modishly) come to like bare walls, and the sale of pictures consequently declining, the two had made use of Mr Baker's other asset, an altogether extraordinary knowledge of all things old, from churches and manors to black-jacks and leather bottles. Mr Baker had written a book on black-jacks and leather bottles. I learnt for the first time the difference between a black-jack and a bombard as I sat at the long table which ran along the dining-room window. I looked out on the birds and flowers, drank my tea, and listened to Oliver's discourse, feeling more like Alice in Wonderland than I had ever felt before. 'Yond same black cloud, yond huge one, looks like a foul bombard that would shed his liquor,' I quoted from *The Tempest* during the discourse on bombards; and I was immediately adopted by Oliver as a discerning person. He showed me all kinds of old implements which the house contained. He communicated their poetry, the poetry of things polished and worn by human hands. I discovered, too, that he was a Shakespearean scholar of an unusual kind.

By the time I was ready to leave for Loxley I felt as though I had known Mr and Mrs Oliver Baker all my life. At the gate I met their son Geoffrey. His hobby was any kind of machine—a machine driven by an engine preferably, but even a simple machine like a bicycle was immediately adopted by him. An ill-adjusted machine was almost as painful to his sensibilities as a mal-formed child. My Raleigh shocked him. I forget now what was the worst sin in it; but as far as I remember the front wheel wobbled, the handle-bars were askew, the bell would not ring, the tyres were soft, the lamp gave no light, there was no pump—and oil! The whole creature was crying out for oil, oil and more oil! It was a wonder the chain hadn't hopped off the wheel, and plunged itself into an oil-bath of its own initiative. Soaking! That was what it needed. Soaking in oil. Geoffrey had begun with the oil-can and ended with an overhaul of the entire bicycle. He had managed to renew the whole machine except for the lamp, of which the battery was dead.

'I'm used to riding in the lanes without a light,' I said, 'it will be all right for once.' At this, Oliver gathered himself together to deliver the first of the oracular sayings of which I was to hear many:

'You can't be killed twice,' he said slowly. Some light or other was contrived for me before I took my departure.

So began my association with Bearley, where I was to live happily for six years. The village had a quality which is hard to describe. It was partly that it seemed much more remote than it actually was. It was more accessible than Loxley, yet appeared to be less so. It was served by the little branch railway which connects Hatton Junction with Stratford: Hatton, Claverdon, Bearley, Wilmcote, Stratford-on-Avon. It was also connected by rail with Wootton Wawen and Henley-in-Arden. The station was about half a mile down the lane at Bearley Cross. I had to catch the morning train at 7.50, change at Hatton, where a slow barge might be seen passing up the canal amidst the buttercups, and so by stopping-train to Snow Hill. Then I made a dash through the arcades to New Street, and into school. When, after the Easter holidays, I first began my daily walk down Bearley Lane to the station, it was a dream of flowers and music. All the thorn trees were out, and I never heard birds sing more sweetly than in the Collins's garden which I passed on my right. They sang in the old Vicarage garden, too, which bounded the road on my left. But for some reason everything seemed to me to be more shadowy in the old Vicarage garden than in the Manor Cottage, where Major and Mrs Collins lived. Their garden had a honeyed richness enjoyed from the moment one passed the syringa and the lilac which overhung its little wooden gate. It was a long garden with depths of fruit and flowers, where bees hummed like mad, and every bird was jubilant. I had a feeling that all the birds and bees and butterflies of Warwickshire liked Manor Cottage garden, and the Stone House garden, better than any of the other gardens in the region; that they told each other about them; and so the hosts all came to see. It is rare to find gardens so secluded and hung in green leaves, and yet so sunny, as these two gardens.

There was considerable rivalry among the gardeners of Bearley and many good tales were told of plants obtained, and of prowess brought to happy blossoming. Some gardeners shared their successes and were free with cuttings; others were more guarded. The story I liked best concerned Mrs Vicarage.

Actually there was no Vicar of Bearley. The parish had been combined with Snitterfield, and was served by the Vicar of Snitterfield. The Vicarage had therefore come to be occupied by laymen and to be called 'old'. It was a pleasant brick house, set in a garden which always seemed to me a little gloomy. But every year Mrs Vicarage used to have the most wonderful display of lupins it has ever been my lot to see, towering lupins of more shades than there are colours in the rainbow. She gave me a bunch once which I set in a pitcher in my sitting-room, and they made the whole house glow.

Mrs Vicarage had several plants such as no other gardener in Bearley had; but one in particular was her treasure, her unique distinction. Once in a rash moment of unaccustomed generosity she gave Mrs Baker a choice offering for the Stone House garden. Mrs Baker could make any plant prosper, so, in a year or so's time, she asked Mrs Vicarage up to see how her scion had fared. It looked wonderful, and Mrs Vicarage had a sudden terrible misgiving as she walked towards it. Had she . . . had she . . .? But no. she gazed upon the splendour, first with a sinking of heart, and then with a rallying assurance, and Mrs Baker heard her mutter in the abandon of relief:
'Not my best.'

There was no house in Bearley without a garden; Dorothy Amphlett, who had a cottage in the lane leading to Snitterfield, had a good garden and tended it well; so had her neighbour Mrs Woodward from whom I had my eggs, and whose purple sprouts were almost as good, she said, as asparagus. It was Mrs Woodward who taught me to cook purple sprouts, and Mr Fawcett who taught me to cook nettles. 'Better than spinach,' he said. And truly nettles have more flavour than spinach, nice fresh young nettles, boiled in just as much moisture as sticks to the leaves after washing. Everything required for food could be obtained at Bearley. I pay tribute to Mrs Frank Hughes's lettuces. These lettuces had a shapely tenderness unsurpassed; a leafy texture crisp, not coarse; a delicate true lettuce greenness. I liked to make a salad simply of lettuce sprinkled with chopped chives or a hint of chervil from the Stone House garden. Some folk liked a dandelion leaf. Not I. Dandelion is bitter; and sorrel, though pleasantly sour, is either too thin and dry, or too tough a leaf for pretty eating. Parsley is as dry as a chip.

There was very little 'forcing' at Bearley. Our treats were seasonal. I was always invited to the Stone House for the first gooseberries and the first green peas. I used to bicycle into Stratford to get the first asparagus from Evesham. Strawberries, raspberries, black-currants, apples, pears—all these were abundant in their season; but above all Bearley was a village of delicious plums. My own little plum tree was one year so laden with golden fruit that a branch broke under the weight. All the gardens had one or two plum trees, fairy-like with blossom in spring, and rich with fruit in early autumn, so rich that there was a drunken smell of fallen plums about Bearley and the bees were almost too glutted to fly. A good deal of preserving was done, and jams and jellies were in favour. I used to go and pick the crab-apples, but Dorothy Amphlett made my jelly. Bottling and pickling were all the fashion, too; but there was not such a mania for preserving as to prevent extravagant eating of the fresh fruits as they came. Nowadays we seem to have reached a point when to pop plums into a bottle cold for Christmas is a greater virtue than to eat them sunned from the branch. We need to remember that the Children of Israel could not pick up manna to last them two days. They had to pick it every day. Ice and bottles are spoiling our palates.

Our manna was mushrooms. Some farmers said their mushroom fields were private property; they had put down spawn, they said, so one had to move circumspectly. I was once bicycling at some distance from Bearley when I spied a likely field. I got off, and, mounting the gate, sat on the top bar. I felt sure it was a mushroom field. I was just going to drop down to pick them, when I saw someone coming with a dog, so I sat still on my perch. The farmer came up and we began to talk. I put on as good a Birmingham accent as I could; for I thought he suspected my intent, and that, if I appeared townish and ignorant of all country knowledge, he would forget his fear. At last he said,

'There are some mushrooms in this field.'

'What, the kind of mushrooms you buy in the shops?' I said.

'Hardly worth the picking,' he said, 'for the price they're giving in Stratford.'

'I should dearly like to pick a mushroom,' I said. He looked at me, but I was staring wistfully into the misty air.

He said, 'Have you got a bag?'

I said, 'On my bicycle I have the bag I carried my lunch in.'

He said he would show me where some mushrooms were, if I liked to stay and pick some. They weren't, he repeated, worth the labour of picking for the price they were paying in Stratford. The shopkeepers got all the money. I said I was sure they did, and made the right exclamations of delight when he showed me my first mushroom really growing. He was convinced I'd never seen them with stalks in the earth before.

I shared my spoil with the Bakers. One Saturday morning, some days later, I was brushing my hair, and looking out of the window in a leisurely way, for I loved to feel leisurely on a Saturday morning, when I espied, on my handkerchief of grass in the front of my cottage, what surely were mushrooms— mushrooms growing. They were so certain that I liked them that they had come to grow in my minute plot! I leaned out of the window and regarded them tenderly. What an extra-ordinary thing! Four or five dewy buttons, in whom I divined the tender pink, and one upstanding, umbrella mushroom! I could almost feel my fingers peeling them. I ran downstairs and out. I stooped to them before I realized. And then, as Malvolio should have done, I heard a smile; Geoffrey had placed them there in the grass so cunningly that they looked more growing than actual growing mushrooms.

Another useful commodity, very easy to obtain in Bearley, was fire-wood. I enjoyed picking up sticks, or as they said in Bearley 'going wooding'. But Maria Woodward, who came up from Bearley Cross to work for an hour or two a day in my cottage, did not like me to go wooding on a Sunday. She showed much more genuine affection for my soul than one or two strict Plymouth Brethren I have known who, convinced that I was lost, and caring for me in a worldly way, were yet not altogether uncheerful at the thought that they had been elected for bliss and me for damnation. Maria was not a Plymouth brother; she went to church on Sunday nights. She lived alone in a tiny cottage with her hens as her beloved neighbours and friends. She planted her garden and did small jobs. I have never known anyone for whom the old age pension was a more splendid benefit when she reached the age of seventy and could draw it.

Maria was like an invisible beneficent fairy. Usually she had done her work and disappeared long before I got back from school. When we did meet she always called me Miss Treenix or 'Miss Treenix, Mum', never having been able to get her tongue round my proper name. But one Monday morning—Founder's Day Holiday at King Edward's—I was still in the cottage when Maria arrived. I had been out on Sunday and gathered a splendid pile of wood after a storm. Maria looked at my store in admiration.

'I got it in yesterday,' I said.

'Oh, Miss Treenix, Mum,' said Maria, 'you didn't go wooding on a Sunday!' I thought, as Bearley was a very respectable sort of place, that she was concerned because people must have seen me engaged in a job so menial as picking up sticks, so I said to please her, 'Oh, I don't think anyone saw me, Miss Woodward.' I always called her Miss Woodward, though I always thought of her as 'Maria'.

'Ah, Miss Treenix, there's an Eye above. He saw yeh, Miss Treenix, He saw yeh!' And before she went home she said to me, 'And don't go woodin' on a Sunday, Miss Treenix. I'll bring in all the wood you can want on Saturday rather than you should go wooding on a Sunday.'

Maria must have been brought up greatly to fear the Eye; she was always suspicious that I was suspicious of her honesty, and I have never met her equal at being sceptical of everybody else's virtue. I found her fear of being suspected very tiresome until I discovered the reason for it. When she was a little girl in the Infant School a penny had vanished. The teacher said it had been stolen and, searching the face of each child in the class with her terrible eye, she had asked: 'Which of you has stolen a penny?' And Maria had coloured up; poor Maria Woodward had coloured up in sheer, sympathetic fright at the awfulness of the drama. 'It is you, Maria Woodward; you have stolen the penny. I can see it in your face. Stand up.' Maria told me this story several times with all the burning resentment which makes unforgettable the scene of the child, Jane Eyre's, disgrace in Lowood Institution. I did my utmost afterwards not to leave money lying about the cottage for, until she knew me better, Maria actually believed that I left money in unlikely places deliberately to trap her. Her suspicion made me feel humiliated and despairing. When relations between simple human beings are so blind, what can be hoped of relations between enormous masses of people?

It was fear of being suspected of theft which made Maria so careful of my door-key. The key might have turned the lock of a church or a prison. It was a great iron key with a handle, a key which you would as soon have thought of slipping into your pocket as into a mouse-hole. I used to hide it in a flower pot by the door. Not so Maria, when the key was in her charge. During the holidays, when the first holiday came, I told Mrs Lott that she was welcome to use the cottage to sleep any visitors while I was away. But Maria would have none of it. She refused to give up the key without my written word. Her description to me of how, in spite of her refusal to give Mr Lott the key, Mr Lott himself slept in the cottage one night, was epical.

'He must have slipped back the catch of the window with a knife, Miss Treenix, Mum, or [more darkly] he has ANOTHER KEY! I went up early in the morning on purpose to catch 'un. "So you've broke in," I said . . .'

It was in vain that I told her that Mr and Mrs Lott were my friends, and were merely acting on a suggestion of my own, by making use of what was, after all, their own cottage furnished with their own furniture. Maria could not be persuaded. The cottage was my castle while I paid for it, and nobody in the world had right of entry but herself and me. Dear Maria! she did not live to enjoy her pension for so very long. I always picture her in winter bicycling slowly up Bearley Lane on an enormous great heavy bicycle, her face rosy with the cold above her red scarf. She always wore a scarf, an old one, on weekdays, and a fur necklet for the benefit of the Eye on Sundays. Her God was Milton's God—'Our Forbidder'—but I do not imagine that she ever thought of Him as off the watch with His spies called in. She could not believe for a long time that the pension had not some snag in it, and I could hardly persuade her to sign her name on the necessary form. To put her name to paper was an act she'd always been warned against. I imagine it has never been thought wise or proper by simple people to make too free a use of anything so intimately associated with their secret persons as their own names.

In Tudor times, as Oliver Baker often said to me, for a man to make his mark instead of signing his name did not prove him to be either ignorant or living in swinish conditions. He might append his name to one document and make his mark on another. This diversity of practice was an element in the thesis maintained by Oliver Baker in his book *Shakespeare's Warwickshire and the Unknown Years*. When I first came to Bearley the book was already nearing completion, but it was the fruit of a lifetime of love and learning. It was not a thin book, lean and gristly; but a book so full of good things that it was difficult to get it all between covers. Even on the verge of publication Oliver Baker was still adding note to note, still finding information which modified his earlier statements, still observing evidence in field, building, or inventory. As I became a friend of the Bakers I became vitally interested in the progress of the book; and I learnt through Oliver's conversation, and through reading his work in manuscript, to see the country between Snitterfield and Wilmcote, as well as the towns of Warwick and Stratford-on-Avon, as I could never have hoped to see them without such aids.

Oliver Baker approached Shakespeare's words through the land his ancestors cultivated, through their houses, the tools they handled, the life they lived in the changing seasons of the year, and through the wills they made when they died. To him an ancient inventory of goods was as illuminating as a poem to me. Writing of his intention towards the close of his long survey he said, 'In the foregoing pages I had no intention of writing a life of Shakespeare. The book was to have been a sketchy record of the surroundings and doings of the Shakespeares in Warwickshire, and I thought that one who lives between Snitterfield, where the Poet's father lived, and Wilmcote, where the Poet's mother was born, might venture to put down in black and white some of the facts which he had laboriously sought or fortuitously stumbled upon, in this interesting corner of England.' His book shows the Shakespeares and Ardens as cultivators of the soil by a system still visible to the initiated eye in the pattern of undisturbed landscape, in the carvings of misericords, in pictured encaustic tiles, in furniture, tools and utensils; for things outlast the men who made and used them. Oliver Baker loved these shapely, used things, and houses which fitted their surroundings; I have known no one else with such a passionate hatred of the intrusion of the ugly, the fake, and the smartly cheap. His book is rich in illustrations which send the reader to Worcester Cathedral, to Malvern Priory Church, and to many another ancient building in search of the originals. And, as one reads, many of Shakespeare's words and images, previously understood but vaguely, become suddenly concrete.

In his book, too, Oliver Baker brings home to the reader the pageants and progresses which the youthful Shakespeare, living within walking distance of Warwick Castle and of Kenilworth, might have witnessed. Quotations from contemporary writings and documents enliven such scenes. He stresses the neighbourhood of Coventry, then the foremost town of Warwickshire, and a town of standing in the realm. Everywhere he shows the pervasive influence of the representation of the dogmas of the Church in picture and figure. The stories of the Bible, the moral allegories shown on stained or on painted cloths, or worked into tapestries, were a part of daily life. With these were mingled illustrations of classical story. Thought and narrative were made visible; those who could not read, saw.

I was interested, too, in the second part of the book, the part which deals with the unknown years. Here it is a theory which is propounded; but a theory based on patient and toilsome research. The whole, though speculative, is worth most careful reading. It is grievous to think that so grand a book, published in 1937, is now out of print. Many copies were destroyed in the London fires, before the work had had time to make its full impact on scholars, or on the general reader. If I were a publisher of Shakespeariana I would leave the publishing of poor little handbooks about Shakespeare, books which are often a hash of discarded fact and half-baked opinion, to reprint this real book which has a lifetime of an artist-scholar's endeavour in it. It is also the author's own memorial; for Stratford's famous antiquary died not so very long after the publication of his book. His son, Geoffrey, carried on the well-known shop in Sheep Street, but the Stratford which Oliver Baker loved so well now sees his presence no more. I never handle his book, nor read a page of it, without re-living my days at Bearley, and remembering the evening parties at the Stone House which Mrs Baker's grace and hospitality made for ever memorable. I see Oliver Baker's fine features, and I hear his slow voice:

'Don't stop me,' Oliver once said to a young man who interrupted his leisurely progress through Bridge Street, 'don't stop me; I'm in a t-e-a-ring hurry.'

12

THE KING'S JUBILEE
AT BEARLEY

For a time, after reading *Shakespeare's Warwickshire*, I went more frequently to Warwick than to Stratford. Then an event happened which drew me oftener to Stratford again: Denne and Martin came to live at Stratford.

They took a place which was partly a house of two storeys, and partly a flat over Mason's grocer's shop in the High Street. It was a flat in front and a house with a walled garden behind. No one, seeing that house now, could possibly imagine what it looked like before Denne and Martin moved into it. The beauty of its gables from the High Street was visible to any eye; and the promise of the oak-panelled rooms within. But it had all the appearance of a house falling into decay. Its dark and dirty passages, its crooked stairs, its overgrown, neglected garden would have made any heart less brave than Denne's contract. But she took the house. She first made Martin's study habitable. Into it went his bookcases, his books, his armchair, his pipes, his desk and the Birth of Venus. Into it he moved himself, and shut the leaded casements that gave on to the High Street which he came to love so much. He loved its movement, its never-ending flow of people, cheerfully engaged in the business of the hour. But air—no; an unwholesome element, he said, impregnated with the damps of Avon. I've never known anyone so dislike the flow of air. My verse—his criticism was immensely helpful and he did occasionally praise—was too airy to please him; airy, watery and confoundedly lucid.

After making the study into a readily penetrable fastness—for Martin invited interruption—Denne turned to the next room along the wavy passage. This was a long, low, panelled room whose leaded casements were open except when Martin was there. Denne moved into this room her grand piano, her divan with the leopard skin, her bookcases containing her favourite George Moore, her favourite Proust and her Graham Robertson ready to hand. She made a room for M. J. and his railway and his books; then she turned to the kitchen and the cats. Both Denne and Martin cared for cats. Orange cats and Siamese cats were there; but there were also the shop cats which were not invited into the house and yet were frequently succoured.

Sfax is the cat I best remember. I am not devoted to cats; I am more devoted to Christopher Smart's idea of a cat. I see Sfax rather as I see poor Kit's Jeoffrey 'brisking about the life', or asleep on the grass plot in the back garden when there was 'nothing sweeter than his peace when at rest'.

There are few poems I enjoy with a more steadily renewable delight than Smart's 'Jubilate Agno'. Often I have comforted myself while listening to a ponderous speaker on education with: 'Let Eleazer rejoice with the Grampus, who is a pompous spouter.' I sometimes think that if one were sure of becoming as good a poet as Christopher Smart it might almost be worth while being mad. It is surprising how many poets since the fourteenth century have had to be mad. Fourteenth-century poets were not mad. Consider how sane Chaucer was! But many poets, since stingy Henry VII came to the throne, seem either to have had to be mad themselves or to invent mad characters as mouthpieces. Shakespeare's fools and mad persons speak some of the best poetry, 'with a hey, ho! the wind and the rain'. But Christopher Smart's 'Jubilate Agno' was written from his personal mad-house. In that poem how catly is his cat Jeoffrey! Mr T. S. Eliot's cats are human by comparison.

Perhaps it was the smell of savoury cooking which arose from the lower regions of the house in High Street which 'slocked', as we say in Cornwall, the cats. Denne is an inspired cook. She has the generous build and nature of a singer and a cook, combining in her own person the lyrical and the Falstaffian. Her cooking is careless, easy, original. 'Native woodnotes wild' is the phrase which springs to the mind—a handful of this and a pinch of that; no art by rule. And yet this phrase is not perfect. It needs a phrase more Keatsian, with a hint of Rabelais. 'Is that,' once said an honoured guest, arriving for dinner a little late, and walking to the table with the exaggerated care of one who knows his step might be unsteady, 'is that two chickens?' If ever I am on a raft in a wintry sea with the waves rising higher and higher, only half a ship's biscuit left to eat, and not even bilge water to moisten the sooty lips, I shall die in bliss with a vision of the warmth and goodness of Denne's kitchen. Heaven will welcome me with the words, 'We were hoping you would soon be here; we have a brace of pheasants . . . stay the night.'

I used to sleep in a bedroom in which there was so much criss-crossing of old oak that, when I woke up in the night, and the moon was shining in at the great casement window, I used to think I was sleeping in a roomy tree.

The coming of Denne and Martin to Stratford completed a good design for living. My pleasure in that design reached its height at about the time of King George V's Jubilee. There had been other royal occasions while I lived at Bearley. I remember a holiday for one royal occasion. I was bicycling idly along a lane near Norton Lindsey when I came to a cottage. Through the open doorway came the sound of music. I stopped to listen and the woman called to me to come in. She was ironing at the kitchen table, and listening to the service which was being relayed from the Abbey. It seemed a wonderful invention to me that could bring such a pageantry of sound to the wayside cottage. 'Father' was listening outside on a sunny bench. When the service was over, and I left the kitchen to sit with the old man on the bench, he delivered a lecture of some length on the Royal Family. I displayed ignorance. I hadn't remembered that Queen Mary had been engaged to the Duke of Clarence before she finally married King George V. 'I don't know what your parents were about,' said the old man, 'not to have told ye all about that.'

When the time drew near for the celebration of the King's Jubilee there was considerable difference of opinion expressed in Bearley Parish as to the form the celebrations should take. I went with the others, when a meeting was called, to the village schoolroom in School Lane; Major Collins was in the chair. Once gathered together, we seemed to have no differences at all. We carried with acclamation a proposal for a church service, to be followed by tea and games on the Manor Lawn. Mrs Percy Mills (now Lady Mills), appealed to at this point, welcomed, generous as ever, the entire Parish to her garden, and to the Manor Barn for a supper of ham and tongue, cider and beer. There was to be a bonfire on the high heathy field overlooking the Avon valley. Then the memento for the children was discussed. No mugs, we all said. Mugs were out of date. A brooch or medallion should be given. The meeting moved briskly to a close. Geoffrey Baker and Jack Collins thought they might be able to rig up a wireless with a loud speaker in the Manor Barn so that we might all hear the King's speech. There were votes of thanks. Major Collins closed the meeting. Then an old man from Bearley Cross arose at the back. He said:

'I want muugs, for the children. My grandfather had a muug, my father had a muug, I had a muug, my wife here had a muug, and we want our children to have muugs.' Major Collins re-opened the meeting. He put the motion, which dozens seconded; it was carried unanimously, and mugs the children had. I imagine that, except for the proposal to hear the King's speech over the radio, no item of the entertainment differed from what had been devised for rejoicing over the Jubilee of Queen Victoria.

For me the entire day, when it came, had an enchanted quality. There had been much talk of royal weather; when the morning dawned the weather was indeed royal. I lay in bed watching the pink roses as they looked in at my window, and listening to the sounds of passing feet. My feet, too, would have been pitter-pattering on any ordinary day. I should have been running down the lane with hardly time for a word with old Mr Cadd, as he swept the leaves, or hacked the weeds in the ditches. Today, instead of engaging in this breathless race, I was lying in bed. I heard Horace Washburne's steady pace as he set out for work; I heard Miss Kendrick click by on her high heels. I heard Geoffrey Baker starting up his car to go to Stratford; I heard Molly Collins drive off, taking the Major to the station; I heard the soft sound of Mr Lott's slippers padding in his garden. Then I got out of bed and, looking out over the fields, I smelt the fresh-cut hay, and saw the heat-haze over the Malverns. I bathed in my back-yard where, at this time of the year, Carrie Tubb and Clara Butt were overhung with flowering elder. This elder tree, with the pear tree, and other tall greenery, completely hedged me round, converting the little yard into an extra unroofed room to my cottage. Soon the cottage itself, when I had been up to the Kendricks' farm for milk and cream and eggs, was filled with the smell of my breakfast coffee. How delicious is a leisurely breakfast to those who are wont to dash down the lane with nothing but a piece of bread and butter to sustain them in health and wealth long to live! I blessed the King and Queen for the holiday, and spent the rest of the morning with Dorothy Amphlett in the wood; then we went to the Stone House where we pledged the royal healths in primrose wine of Mrs Kendrick's making. Mrs Kendrick was unsurpassed in the making of country wines: cowslip, primrose, dandelion, parsnip—I've seen them all working in the vat.

I remember the morning much more vividly than the afternoon and early evening. I went to the feast with the rest of Bearley, but one needs to be a child greatly to enjoy a feast. What I do remember is the barn at night, and the hush that fell on the company as Geoffrey's wireless arrangements proved themselves successful, and we heard the miracle of the King's voice. That personal, uniting note of thanksgiving and praise stirred in us emotion apt to be overlaid in tradeful times. Later, the blazing bonfire on the heathy field penetrated to something in us still more deeply layered over. The pyre had been well built. As the flames lit the darkness I caught glimpses of my ordinary friends transfigured. For me, as the fire died down to ashes, I could have leapt through the glow as my ancestors had gone leaping through the bonfires on bygone Midsummer Eves.

The Festival of the King's Jubilee was the peak of that period during which, in spite of unemployment and distressed areas, we felt a little blessed warmth in the midst of danger. The prancing and gesticulating hordes were circling round, not crashing through our territory. I felt cold when I saw men moving like automatons. Men of any nationality or race soever fill me with cold fear when I see them like dummies moving at command. They have surrendered something inherent to their humankindness—the right to control the movements of their own hands and feet. I saw these marching shadows in pictures. I heard mad voices shouting at them, telling them what to do; I saw them obey. I saw the horrible uniform-in-variety, making separate individual bodies look alike, but making groups of massed bodies look sharply different from other groups of massed bodies, so that hate might clash with hate and grab meet grab. And yet separately, each person needed very little. The air was wide enough; there was enough water; seeds produced a hundred-fold. We should die in time, but there would be much to enjoy before that. And not the entire self would die. Obviously it was as Sir Thomas Brown said: there was something in us which was before us and would be after us. Why not wait and see, holding on to and swaying the present, as I have seen a field-mouse, holding with his delicate hands a stalk of thrift, climb to the head, swing it over, and daintily eat the fruits? Field-mice have enormous ears in proportion to their size, yet that field-mouse did not hear me loom over him; he was too intent on eating. I suppose we were all like field-mice; but we darken of our own accord, by our own malevolence, the shadow looming over us. Our stupidity is crass. Why not at least seek to enjoy our seventy or so years, and then depart courteously with a grace for what we have received on our lips? If only all nations would give up showing the world and telling the world! The world is only bored in the long run with all showing off.

The abdication of King Edward VIII shook us. I was standing on Bearley station when I first opened my *Birmingham Post* and saw Bradford repeating what America had said. The hunt was up! How self-righteous, how smug we were! Smug! Smug! Smug! As a people, we are never so much to be detested as when we are expressing moral outrage. And what turncoats! Shakespeare, had he been alive, might well have compared the mob again to a flag (not a piece of bunting, but one of the sword-shaped leaves of the iris tribe) lackeying the flood. Those who had hurrahed loudest now hissed most serpently. Only the King's own speech of abdication came well out of that business; and the King's brother.

The Coronation of King George VI is the only state ceremony I have ever witnessed in London. Joan Holland and I went up to Town together. Joan was teaching mathematics at King Edward's. With one black eyebrow peaked higher than the other, she had one of the most amusing faces and minds I ever met. Like the absent-minded curate who, giving out the text of his sermon, prefaced it with, 'Stop me if you've heard this one before,' Joan had a fund of stories; but instead of, like so many stories, being boring, hers were sure to entertain. Anecdotes of her family and friends came into them. She loved quaint knowledge, antithesis and wit. Her mouth would curl, in narrating, into an expression of irresistible drollery. 'Oh, no, Holland, oh no!' Miss Udall would say, as she absorbed Holland's latest, putting down her coffee cup, to laugh at ease. Holland was tall. She loped along the corridors. She loped along Pall Mall, too, having at least her nose above most other bodies' noses, and in the free air; whilst I, unable to lope, but only to trot, seemed to be enclosed by towering humanity. We

went to a cocktail party with Mary Holland on the evening
before the Coronation then, emerging from it in the dim hours
of the morning, we made our way to Whitehall. Already people
were streaming in all directions. Many had stayed up all night.
We had no tickets for a stand. We stood, like Falstaff and his
company, on the pavement. The hours of waiting did not seem
long; there was so much to watch; so much to hear. Only once
did I wish I had not come, and that was when one of the bands
played a tune to which the whole crowd swayed. I had to sway
with it perforce, and that was a hateful sensation.

Standing by us on the pavement was an ex-sergeant of police
accompanied by his wife. They had brought mountains of food
and gave us some. The ex-sergeant was able to look right over
the heads of the crowd; but he pretended to be blasé about the
whole affair. He had only come up from Kidderminster for his
wife's sake, he said. He'd stood for half his life watching what he
didn't want to watch because he had to be there to keep the
crowds back. What he liked was his pipe and the *Daily Mail*.
Read it all in that, and no trouble to anybody. But Mrs Datchett
she would come up to London. We knew what women were!
Mrs Datchett said we mustn't mind Henry; he was inclined to
'run on'. And Henry said, 'Now, Mother!'

As the time drew near for the approach of the royal
procession expectation grew tense. We tried out our periscopes
on lesser attractions. There were several false rumours. It was
like being at a race meeting and waiting for the cry, 'They're
off!' At last the sergeant himself gave the word. He, from the
lofty tower on which his head was perched, announced,
'They're coming!' Immediately, his wife said, 'Henry, I'm going
to faint,' and she did. This fainting made me feel very unstable
myself, purely out of sympathy with Mrs Datchett. However,
the ambulance men came, the crowd making way for them as if
by some magic instinct. In a twinkling Mrs Datchett was being
borne off, Henry stalking behind her with official dignity. I took
heart again in time to see the horses and the colours, and hear
the bands, and to cheer madly as the King, the Queen and their
children passed by.

13

THE MOVE FROM NEW STREET

I found travelling to school daily from Bearley easy as long as King Edward's remained in New Street. It was very easy, too, for us all to go to the theatre and to concerts. We were within five minutes' of the Repertory theatre, and within five minutes' of the Town Hall. One might see a colleague teaching the young with enormous zeal in the morning, and behold her seated like a lady of leisure in the Rep on a Thursday afternoon. The Repertory, the Prince of Wales's Theatre, the Alexandra Theatre and the Crescent all provided me with memorable hours in Birmingham. Good friends on the staff used to invite me to a theatre and to a bed after it, thus providing a break in my daily journeying. And then there were organ recitals and orchestral concerts in the Town Hall. The only three Birmingham names I knew when I first went to the city were Dr J.D. Cunningham, Sir Barry Jackson and Leslie Heward. When I first asked my father what he thought of the idea of my teaching in Birmingham he said: 'You would be able to hear Cunningham's recitals and Leslie Heward is a fine conductor.'

Cunningham, the city organist, used to give lunch-hour recitals and to these, taking a little packet of sandwiches, we often went. When my brother Howard came up to see me he was all agog to try the Town Hall organ. I didn't think it likely that he could; but I remembered that Cunningham was, so to speak, an old parent, his daughter having been an Edwardian, though before my time. Miss Barrie said she could write me a note of introduction to Cunningham. So after a recital my brother and I strolled round and I presented my note. Cunningham had a long chin and long slender hands. He said, 'Are you a colleague of that wonderful woman, Miss Udall?' I said I was. He said to my brother, 'You try the organ if you like, dear, while I talk to your sister about King Edward's. My daughter, you know—Miss Udall made my daughter tidy. A wonderful woman! Still there?' So we talked, while my brother tried the organ, calling up all the little demons and all the deep demons that lie in organ pipes. That visit of my brother's—he stayed at the Bearley cottage—was also made memorable by a steak and kidney pie. I bought it at Barrow's for our supper, but pretended I had made it myself. Nest day in Birmingham my brother happened to walk by Barrow's window in Corporation Street, a window chock-a-block with pies similar to that which my fair hand had dished him out the night before, with a bottle of beer. It took me a long time to live down that pie.

When it was first suggested that King Edward's School should be moved from the centre of the city to the outskirts, we all thought with regret of our theatres, our concerts and the one o'clock train to town. I also thought of Snow Hill and Moor Street stations. There were, apart from our private satisfactions, advantages in having the school in the centre of the city. Its central position was part of its character. Children as well as staff could reach it easily from all directions. It had never been a local school, always a school available to the children of the entire city. The Boys' School was a feature of New Street. It was a school to work in. Working was our 'activity'. To work in the New Street building was satisfactory enough, except that it was rather dark. It was not, however, a school to play in. Pressure of numbers had caused the one-time play rooms, at the top of the school, to be impounded for other uses. The Girls' School playing field was at Canon Hill. I have never anywhere known a drearier tram-ride than from New Street to Canon Hill. I was in favour of the move to a more open place; yet, when we heard that the two schools had been sold, and that we should move to temporary buildings to be set up on the new site purchased in Edgbaston, we were all a little sad. Old boys were furious. The Boys' School in New Street embodied, they felt, a tradition which could not be separated from its stones. When it was suggested that some of the stones at least could be physically incorporated in the new building they were sardonic. Big school was big school; no building anywhere else would be the same thing.

Old girls, too, were attached to their building and opposed the move. Stairs! Splendid physical exercise. Darkness! Few Edwardians in the good old days ever wore glasses. No doubt the gloom had kept the muscles of their eyes taut. Traffic in New Street! No Edwardian had ever been killed, or had even broken a wrist, going to or coming from school. It was dodging traffic that had made Edwardians nimble, and contributed to their merit as the backbone of the nation. Edwardians, it must be admitted, do not tend towards the virtues of meekness and humility. They are a fine body of men and women, but they know it. Arguments surged to and fro. One could not settle down in the common-room to a quiet cup of tea and the *Spectator* without being hurtled over by flying words. 'In Miss Creak's day!' 'In Miss Major's day!' 'When Cary Gilson was alive . . .

But time rolled us inexorably towards a change which so many opposed with the whole might of their tongues. Even when it had been definitely decided that Edgbaston should be the site of temporary buildings and finally of new permanent buildings, it was hoped that the New Street building, at least the Boys' School building, might be preserved. It was a thousand pities that this was not managed. Birmingham is a wealthy city, a city with a strong sense of civic duty. Barry's building (the building in New Street was designed by Sir Charles Barry, architect of the Houses of Parliament) could have been useful in a variety of ways; it was a shame not to have kept it standing. New Street looks vapid without it. Nothing is more idle, to my mind, than to say that its destruction did not matter because the school was not a genuine old building, that it dated merely from 1837, that Barry's design was pastiche. Barry's building was a pleasure to the eye in its proportions and symmetry, just as Milton's poem is a glory to the ear; 'Come, come make passionate my sense of hearing.' Architecture and music are to be rejoiced in; their function is not to be confounded with the boring necessity of making a water-tight garage, or saying how-do-you-do, or quoting the prices of livestock. Birmingham's need is to be lightened with unexpected beauty; it is a ready city; its young people are eager and aware. But we watched the demolition of a piece of former work for which we should have angrily mourned if it had been knocked down by German bombs. We seem un-apt for splendour. Birmingham is a smothered city; even its Cathedral services do not soar. I would rather believe every miracle that every Saint's bones are ever claimed to have performed than father a religion in which the high hills never skip like rams or the little hills like young sheep.

Birmingham has had various ideas for improving its appearance and making itself seem spacious instead of merely big and sprawling. It lacks natural features. What a tremendous advantage a river is to a town, or hills within its boundary. There is no challenge to Birmingham builders; no stream to bridge, no heights to scale and link. I think the best walk in Birmingham is from Selly Oak to New Street by the bank of the Canal. I often walked that way in later years when coltsfoot was golden. I passed the University and distant Queen Elizabeth's Hospital, to where fields were green and trees were shapely. By the houses and gardens of once rich city merchants I passed under arches which spanned black water, and which would have been admired if they were in a Belgian city. As houses and factories closed in, I reached a strange place,

Dickensian in its picturesque squalor, a medley of heights and shapes. Dickensian indeed it was; for I was near the house of the 'wharfinger' in *The Pickwick Papers*.

It was in the neighbourhood of the University, near where Edgbaston joins Selly Oak, that land was purchased for building the new King Edward's Schools. It was a likely site, adjoining the open space of the golf course, with its beautiful crowning grove of trees. I wish a millionaire would give the school that grove for beauty's safety's sake. On one side it was bounded by the Edgbaston Park Road; on the other by Bristol Road. The permanent buildings were to be set well back from the Bristol Road; the temporary building was to stretch for nearly a quarter of a mile, right alongside that road and its tramlines. I forget how long the hutment took to build; it went up quickly. In many ways it was just the right arrangement for a school, as airy as a mushroom, but without, alas, the mushroom's grace, and dewy freshness. In spite of blue and yellow paint, and a plethora of coats-of-arms, the temporary building was as ugly as sin. One could see how nasty it would look as premature old age descended on it. Buildings not made to wear well are not for our climate; but of course the hutment was never intended to wear well. From quick birth to speedy death was its principle. By the time our last term in New Street had reached its close the temporary building was almost ready for occupation. We left New Street in July 1937; we were to reassemble at Edgbaston on September the eighteenth.

I had a delightful little hope budding in my breast. Surely the place would not be quite finished by September 18th. I knew Miss Barrie's unexpected passion for beginning on the tick of the first day of term, and losing no time. Always, before we dispersed for the holidays in July, every detail was ready for the beginning of the next session in September. Miss Barrie, with a complicated time-table to make, was a mathematician with a game of her very own to play. She settled down to it with the zest of a boy mending a clock, or a man playing with his son's Hornby trains. Spaces and times, mistresses and subjects, rooms, divisions, forms and parallel forms were better to her than a box of tricks. She turned it into a box of tricks. She used a board with colours on which she marshalled her pieces. I never understood the method, just as I never understood how marks were scaled in the Entrance Examination, graphs made, and order brought out of chaos. Trying to trace the fate of some child whose English examination had interested me, I would inquire what had happened to her, why hadn't she got in? Miss Barrie would produce evidence as to her fate in figures and graphs. 'You see,' she would say, getting out her ordered sheets, 'you see this? This becomes . . . and this becomes . . . and scaled that is . . . and with the age allowance . . .' 'Yes, Miss Barrie, I see,' I would murmur. And she would look up at me with her smile. She knew that I knew that she knew that I didn't understand a figure of it.

There were graphs, too, showing the relative merits in marks, of parallel forms, and of the performance of children at different stages of their school career. I might hazard some remark about a child's good progress when discussing the children of my form before reports were signed at the end of term. 'Oh! no! not good progress,' Miss Barrie might reply seizing her sheets. 'Elfride has gone steadily down. In the Upper IVa she—and in Lower IVb she—and in the Third Form she—and just consider how high up she was in the City Entrance Examination! Why [producing another sheet] she was nth out of x thousand. What's happening to her?' It was a swift way of keeping the records which mistresses now in all schools write laboriously out in long-hand, double entry, every term, on cards.

A time-table once made and committed by the senior mistress to paper—senior mistresses served for two years in King Edward's and then usually became headmistresses elsewhere—the whole thing was cut into strips, so that each mistress had two strips, her personal time-table and her form time-table, set out in such handy hieroglyphics that they were devilish easy to lose. If the strips were lost, one moved in a dark forest during the first two days of term, glancing nervously in at glass doors to find another mistress already in possession, racing down corridors, carrying the right books into the wrong place, getting later and later for each period. Even I, whatever else I lost, learnt not to lose my strips. I used to put them in a very safe place at the end of each term and tell a friend where the safe place was. But when the last term in New Street ended, and our strips were handed out as usual, I was really nonplussed. Where could I keep my strips? The old building to be dismantled, the new building with no lockers in yet! Finally, a trusted friend took my strips home with her own, promising to bring them on the first day of term. But would the first day of term be Tuesday, September 18th as I had stated on twenty-three reports? Surely not, I said to myself. Surely there must be more compressed partitions to set up, more cardboard walls to click together, more roofing to smack on, more staining, more painting—at least they couldn't have moved the girls' desks and the mistresses' platforms, and the staff-room carpet. Surely, surely we couldn't begin school in the old humdrum fashion on the correct date, after such an exciting event in the school's history as moving from New Street to Edgbaston. I composed a letter to Miss Barrie as the date of re-assembly drew nigh. I pointed out that I was staying at Lelant, a long way from Birmingham; it seemed a pity, I said, that I should travel so far, wasting the Great Western's steam, if school was going to re-open late owing to the Move. Could I, perhaps, have a telegram saying . . .

I had a postcard. It said: 'No nonsense, please; Staff meeting Sept. 18th at 9 a.m. Even a seagull . . .' and so it all turned out. Not a second of free time did we gain because of what I had imagined would be the turmoil. There was no turmoil. The builders had moved out, and Thorne, Twist, Gumery, Miss Barrie, Miss Jaques and the cleaners had moved in. Everything was prepared. The staff and children assembled ready for work. I was there, too; and my faithful friend handed me my strips.

14

FIRE IN THE TEMPORARY BUILDINGS

The prefects regretted the old building where, like the mistresses, they had enjoyed the privacy of a very secluded room of their own. There was no privacy in the Bristol Road. Outside, the trams clanked; within, every sound could be heard from room to room. If Lower IVa were two minutes late in greeting the belated arrival of the English mistress, the unavoidable scraping of their chairs as they sat down interrupted and incensed the French mistress next door who had begun punctually, and was fully launched on *celui-ci* and *celui-là*. 'Treneer, your form!' 'Treneer, your Joan, your Heather, your Ernestine, Hazel, Japonica!' What a business it was! For the juniors adored the temporary building. They flourished in its light and the length of its corridors. To them the delicate shades of pink, yellow or green with which the walls were so delightfully washed were a challenge to artistic endeavour. And the walls were so thin! I arrived one day to find a hole in one of my walls, an obvious hole in the back wall which divided this room from the next in the series. All the girls were standing still and most suspiciously silent as I went in. Their very silence directed my eyes to the hole.

'Who,' I said, 'has put her foot through the wall?'

'Please, Miss Treneer, I'm sorry, but I did,' said a popular member of the Junior hockey team whom we will call Annabel.

'What were you doing, Annabel?'

'Please, Miss Treneer, I was only swinging on my hands between the desks, and seeing how high up my toes could hit the wall, Miss Treneer.'

'I told you the walls were thin.'

'Yes; but please, Miss Treneer, I wasn't sure.'

Miss Barrie usually checked that spirit of destructiveness to property which occasionally descends on all high spirited children by making the delinquents pay to have the damage repaired or obliterated. It was effective; for either the money had to come in slow, small instalments out of the privy purse, or parents had to be asked for it, and thereby informed. Paying up is a necessary lesson in living; for pride in agreeable surroundings, so strong as girls grow older, is a slow growth. Few tender, delicate schools can have been occupied by congregated children for so long with so little deterioration in its appearance. 'Congregated' is the operative word; in a crowd, children and grown-ups too egg one another on.

Except for the noise of the trams, the thin partitions, and the meanness of its external appearance, the temporary building had real merit as a school. When the sun shone, we knew it was shining; we felt it warm on us. In the New Street building we had hardly known what the weather was like till we got out into the street. In Edgbaston, larks actually sang over our green quadrangles and playing fields. Hall, gymnasium and dining-room were spacious. There was a delightful sense of free movement everywhere. But changed conditions inevitably altered the pattern of school life as it had been laid down in New Street, a pattern which, for all its drawbacks, had been conducive, peculiarly conducive, I think, among pupils over the age of thirteen, to serious study. To work hard in the morning, to be free in the afternoon, to do some un-aided preparation in the evening, is a reasonable division of time. But in the new building there was no justification for the general closing down of school, except for voluntary and practical work, at one o'clock. Obviously, when city girls, often by long and devious routes, had reached this open space, it was better for them to remain in it as long as possible. More and more afternoon lessons crept into the time-table; more and more 'activities' were indulged in as the mornings were eased of work. Every mistress considered her own 'activity' most deserving of an award of time—I, of course, among the others. It was always the other fellow's demands on time which we wished to see curtailed. Having all gained a little of our own way we began to murmur. We were tending, we complained, to become like an ordinary school.

Had we been an extraordinary school before? I think we had. It is very difficult to describe what we felt we were in danger of losing: independence, quiet, recollection? I cannot exactly tell. The pattern of school life in New Street conduced to absorption; it seemed to promote a disinterested pleasure in learning, perhaps because it allowed the mistresses leisure to pursue their own studies in the subjects they taught. Energy is limited; if it is drained off in too many directions the current is weakened in the main. Teachers and taught ought not to see too much of one another. I think the present widespread mania for rather aimless discussion in education is debilitating to the immature mind, and enfeebling to the moral sense. Discussion where no knowledge is, is worse than a waste of time; it debases truth and heightens self-importance. Only informed persons can profitably discuss. In every branch of education I think we need to go back to the notion that a very important item in it is learning, and that learning, if laborious, is also delightful, strengthening and refreshing the mind, and renewing the vital spirits. Quite young children can experience this sense of mastery.

But I am indulging in digression. On the whole, we liked being in Edgbaston. But we were not to work for very long in our wooden and cardboard school without interruption. One morning, when I was coming up as usual in the train from Bearley, I heard somebody remark that there had been a fire at

King Edward's. I took no notice; I thought there had been some slight flare up in one of the laboratories. I had been preparing a lesson in the train; I had not opened my *Birmingham Post* and, as I was a little late, I met no children on the tram. I had nearly reached Edgbaston Park Road when I lifted up my eyes and saw, in place of the long line of the Boys' School—ashes. The Girls' School was standing, to outward appearance not greatly damaged. The flames had been checked just as they had begun to lick up that part of the buildings. The Boys' section they had devoured in a matter of minutes. No one knew how the fire had started; it was night, and so inflammable was our temporary treasure, that it had quite literally gone up in smoke before a book could be saved. The fire brigade had concentrated on checking the flames at the point where they threatened to lay hold of the Girls' School. Fire had swept through the corridors with a roar. Although the Girls' School was habitable, it was not considered right that such a building should be used by children until precautions had been taken against a recurrence of fire. The Boys' School had to be entirely re-fabricated. In the meantime both boys and girls had to be accommodated elsewhere. I forget what happened to the boys; but Miss Barrie, having explored the possibilities, accepted for the girls the hospitality of a Methodist Sunday school at Acocks Green.

I have always admired the Methodists for building that school. They had broken clean away from the tradition that a Sunday school can be a very poor thing compared with a day school, and yet prosper. They had built a school, a well designed school with an assembly hall, a little stage, and classrooms suitable for the numbers who came to Sunday school, but ill suited to the numbers of Edwardians who now came pouring in. I shall never forget teaching in that school. I have never in any other place lost my temper so many times in quick succession. The little fire-demon that had consumed the Boys' School at a gulp, seemed now to have found a lodging in my one time amiable bosom. I kept on blazing. Voices, voices, voices! Voices high, and voices low; voices using English,

French, German and Latin; Italian voices; voices spouting figures; geographical, historical, biological, chemical, scriptural and physics voices. I once read 'The Ancient Mariner' aloud against a choral background of voices which made it go something like this:

> It ceased; yet still the sails made on
> A pleasant noise till noon,
> A noise like to a hidden brook

In the leafy month of—if x equals 7 and Nehemiah did that which was evil in the sight of the Lord, if anyone hasn't a good figure look at mine while I go through it on the board, ecce! nein! Au clair de la lun-e, Mon ami Pier . . . You need the accusative . . . 1865 . . . Till noon we quietly sailed on.' Hazlitt talks, I remember, of 'the din and smithery of school learning'; but commonly we work in separate forges, and do not hear our fellow-smiths at the anvil.

On fine days some of us taught our little flock on the pavement so as to escape. We were ranged in circles, large prefects learning, as it were, at mother's knee. It is all very funny to look back on; but at the time we thought we were heroically performing our important task in difficult circumstances—we who had almost been through the fire. In our individual bosoms we anticipated what the women of the globe were to feel in swelling pride when told, during the tremendous disaster which was shortly to overwhelm the world, that they were being MAGNIFICENT. No word is large enough to express what I thought I was being while I taught my classes in that public fashion.

The lack of space reminded me forcibly of the days when I had taught in a primary school. Some Junior school buildings are excellent now; but many are still execrably bad. We spend thousands on one new building and deny a few pounds to make another barely habitable. And I know that no ability on the part of the teacher, no willingness, no enthusiasm—and I number teachers of genius among my friends in primary and secondary schools—can counteract the evil of herding children into cramped quarters and putting too many in charge of one person. I have said this before, but, like Mr T.S. Eliot in another context, 'I shall say it again'.

Ours was a kind of picnic inconvenience, with all that was possible being done to mitigate our temporary lot. Relations with the church authorities were happy. But we were glad when at last the Boys' School was reconstructed, the Girls' School cleaned and repaired, and both schools provided with means to make fire unlikely to spread if it broke out a second time. Each form-room was provided with a little flight of wooden steps, a handrail and a french window. Fire-drill was practised regularly. I can see myself searching madly for my register; for at the sound of the fire alarm we had to seize our registers, gallop out with the children, line up form by form, call the names, report to Miss Jaques that no one was missing—all in two minutes; or did it, perhaps, take a little longer than that? I used to feel 'some hurried' as we say in Cornwall, during the whole business. The girls rejoiced in fire-drill. Children and ponies have much in common, and fire-drill made them feel frisky. Next to fire-drill, they liked to open the fire doors and sit on the steps in the sun. You can always trust children to utilize anything in the nature of a ladder, even a tiny ladder, for their own convenience or pleasure.

It was originally intended that we should stay only a short time in the temporary buildings; but the period, we soon saw, was likely to be extended. Sometimes we went up to see how the permanent buildings were getting on. 'Very little progress has been made this term' would frequently have been our report on Mr Hobbis and his myrmidons if we had had the writing of terminal reports on them. Mr Hobbis, an Edwardian himself, was the architect who had been chosen to design the new schools. It was clear that he genuinely wished to build us a school in which we should enjoy teaching.

He did not disdain other people's special knowledge. So Miss Hobbes, head of the science side, was able to fight for what she considered was essential in the laboratories; Miss Jaques for the gymnasium; Mrs Hopkins for the domestic science room, and so on. Miss Barrie was in her element in the matter of the new buildings. From the first, she had been heart and soul for the move from New Street. Now she brooded over the elevation, the various plans, the prospect of good materials, and the likelihood of sound workmanship. The new school owes much to her; she had skill in conducting operations so as to get her own way. And the joke was that her skill consisted in seeming to have no skill. It was the same when she was dealing with parents and staff. With a straightforward, unsubtle, natural manner, and great equanimity, she was seldom deflected; she had a way of concluding an interview in which she had obtained all she wished with a memorable smile.

Her skill, no doubt, had grown with the years during which she had had relations with children of all ages, teaching staff, domestic staff, governors and parents. I only once saw her really nonplussed by a parent. There was a girl whom we will call Belinda Billing. We never quite knew how Belinda had managed to pass the admission examination; but she had passed it and, by the time she came to me, she was in her second year of enjoyment at King Edward's. Belinda could not be persuaded to do any work at all. The gears of her mind were constantly slipping. With homework seldom properly done, she was moving, towards the close of her second year, through a thickening haze in all subjects. But this lack of intellectual clarity had not in any way affected Belinda's gay spirits. I spent my time defending Belinda; for form-mistresses, like parents, are roused to defend their own. But I grew to dread the mention of her name. I used to forsee this opening gambit in every eye as Classics, French, Chemistry, Divinity swept down on me in turn: 'Treneer, your Belinda Billing!'

At last there came, as a climax to a year of bad reports, a report surpassing all others in pessimism as to Belinda's future prospects as a scholar. She must, the unanimous verdict declared, stay down a year; but Belinda was rather above the average age of the form she was already in, and she was very tall for her age. To keep her down would mean that she would be associating with girls a year younger than herself. Whatever good effect staying down might have in clarifying Belinda's notions of Latin and French, it could not seriously be considered, because of the ill effect it would have on her general development. The alternative seemed to be that she should leave King Edward's and go to a good boarding school. The parents were well off; Belinda was an only child. Miss Barrie invited Mrs Billing to come to school to discuss her daughter's future. After they had talked for a quarter of an hour or so Miss Barrie sent for me.

By Miss Barrie's desk I found Mrs Billing seated; she was well dressed and handsome, but looking warm and lost. I had met her before, and she had reminded me a little of Mrs Tulliver. You occasionally find, in Birmingham, George Eliot-like characters, women retaining a rural freshness of complexion, a country soundness in house-keeping, and a distrust of books; the whole only a little overlaid with town conformity to fashion. Dressed like other people, they remain very distinctly themselves. I knew that Mrs Billing considered that all this belittling of Belinda in her school reports was so much nonsense. You only had to look at the child to see that she was flourishing. A clear complexion like her mother's, and no fuss about helping with the washing-up, or doing a little shopping, such as some people had to put up with from their daughters. Mrs Billing had ceased to talk when I went into the room, and Miss Barrie was concisely recapitulating the arguments in favour of Belinda's leaving King Edward's and going to a boarding school. My part was to confirm this suggestion and to add a few words about Belinda on my own account. When we had both finished Mrs Billing looked from one to the other in a bewildered sort of way; then with her pleasant unspoilt smile she rose,

'Well, that will be all right, then, won't it, Miss Baarie?' she said, 'and Belinda will be staying on. She's so happy, Miss Baarie, with you and Miss Tremayne taking such an interest in her.' And suddenly she gave a kind of S-like heave, very comic in a fashionable figure and said,

'These suspender belts, Miss Baarie, uncomfortable, aren't they? How do you keep your stockings up?'

It was impossible to revert to the subject of Belinda's future. Mrs Billing took her leave. I walked with her to show her out of the front door, and, as we went, she thanked me in such a heartfelt way for all I was doing for Belle that I felt a worm. Then I went back to Miss Barrie's room. I found her standing as I had left her, and I inquired how she kept her stockings up. I have often laughed with Miss Barrie, but not more rollickingly than over our defeat at the hands of Mrs Billing. Belle, needless to say, completed the days of her school education with us.

I liked to tease Miss Barrie over her faith in intelligence tests. Once, after an argument, I waited until I knew she was in the midst of a mountain of work, and I went into her room—she kept her door invitingly open.

'Miss Barrie,' I said, rushing on with my words before she could speak, 'may I put to you a little intelligence test? A father duck, a mother duck and two ducklings went down to the river to bathe. It was a glorious day, the sun was shining, the birds were singing, and they had a wonderful swim. On their way up from the river they met a chicken and the duckling said, "We five have been down to the river for a swim, and the sun was shining, and the birds were singing, and the water was perfect." Why did the duckling say five?' Miss Barrie was vexed at being interrupted; but she wrinkled her brow for a second in thought, because she could never entirely ignore a puzzle. Then she said in her deepest tone,

'Well, what is it?'

I said, 'The duckling couldn't count,' and she said, 'GO AWAY!'

15

APPLICATIONS
ARE INVITED

At about this time, I decided to apply for a post as head-mistress. My motives were not very pure. I certainly wished to get back to Cornwall more than I wished to run a school; yet, in my secret heart, although I hardly admitted this apostasy even to myself, for I had always said I would never try to be a headmistress, I did begin to feel that there were some aspects of that work which I might enjoy. I fancied a Cornish school in a little Cornish town; a school to which the country children of the district would come by bus, or train, or on bicycles, or walking by the field paths and lanes; a school rather like St Austell Grammar School, to which I had gone myself, or like Camborne Grammar School, in which I had taught English for nine of the best years of my life. In *The Times Educational Supplement* I saw an advertisement for Penzance Grammar School. A headmistress was required.

I went to consult Miss Barrie. She was startled. Why did I wish to become a headmistress? I said that from the head-mistress's room at Penzance there was a fine view of St Michael's Mount. Miss Barrie said, 'You won't have time to look at St Michael's Mount.' She said she thought I hadn't the right talents for a headmistress, but added, on seeing my crestfallen appearance, 'I think you have other talents.'

I thought I could bend my talents to any purpose if only I could induce a committee to let me live where I wanted to. I like Mount's Bay. I have always had a fancy for living in the very narrowest part of Cornwall, so that I might stretch out one hand to the south and the other to the north coast. Miss Barrie did not think so ill of my prospects as not to support me. She gave me a testimonial, and I wrote to two other distinguished friends asking for their word in aid. I received back masterpieces of diplomacy. Miss Barrie had once remarked to me, when we were jovially going through applications she had received for the post of an assistant English mistress, that the way to read a testimonial was to look for what was left out. Reading the efforts of my three testifiers in this light gave me much beneficial amusement. I then went down to Cornwall to reconnoitre the school building. Was it so pleasant a spot as I remembered? I shall always recall with pleasure how I insinuated myself into the school precincts as the curfew tolled the knell of parting day. I did not think the situation was quite as fair as I had imagined. Buildings had sprung up which were not there when I had played hockey as a girl for St Austell against Penzance. But the night was balmy; the building was in the Treneere fields, a happy omen, I hoped. I wrote to the County Hall for a Form of Application.

I gazed upon this document in despair. On what committees had I served? I had avoided all committees like the plague. What had I done in the Great War? I had cut a few fields of 'milky disels' with a hook. I had to leave nearly all the little spaces blank or write, as in the income-tax form, NONE. In addition to filling in the form I had to write a letter of application. I bought some elegant writing paper so that I might appear a person of means and taste; I bought a new pen, and began to compose. I ask any competent critic whether the composing of a letter of application is not a test of style. To hit upon the exact mean! Not to praise oneself so highly as to be gross, but, on the other hand, not to grovel in self-depreciation. To decide between 'I beg to apply', 'I wish to apply' or, 'Look 'ee here! Don't 'ee miss this grand chance!' Was I merely the committees 'faithfully' at the close of my masterly little appeal to their sense of discrimination, or did I beg to remain theirs faithfully? My instinct is all for the most old-fashioned formulae. I regret the days of set ceremonial when Doctor Johnson could clinch the irony of his letter to Lord Chesterfield by signing himself his Lordship's most humble, most obedient servant, Sam. Johnson. Not without a hint of the Johnsonian rotundity of phrase which comes naturally to me when I am trying hard, I wrote the best letter I could; but just as I was folding it a friend happened along. I gave it to her to read. She said it was a handsome letter, but she suggested that there was character in hand-writing. My hand-writing revealed, she said, a carelessness ill becoming to a prospective headmistress. No i's dotted, no t's crossed. That kind of remissness would strike a committee at once. So I went through my letter again, carefully dotting every i and crossing every t. The result was funny. The application form looked a little funny too; I peered anxiously at the thin places where too vigorous an application of the ink eraser had nearly worn a hole. But I could not begin the whole tiresome business over again. I placed the letter on the form, attached the testimonials, folded the three-fold effort neatly, put it in a large envelope, posted it, and settled down to visions of myself as a headmistress gazing upon the Mount.

Weeks passed. Then I was invited to come to Truro for an interview. Immensely elated, I sought Joan Holland. She said I needed clothes which would give me a presence. We went shopping. It was good fun shopping with Joan. Instead of that feeling of intense depression which any form of shopping usually induces in me, I felt gay; I was mistress of an event, for Joan, having loped round me while I tried on half a dozen hats, came to a standstill, lifted her odd black eyebrow nearly to the level of her face's horizon, and announced that here, at last, was a Presence. We then bought a coat and skirt to live up to the hat, a pair of shoes to live up to the coat and skirt, and two pairs of stockings to live up to the shoes. One pair might ladder, Joan said, and a presence could not go before a committee of presences with laddered hose. The coat and skirt

were a bluish green or a greenish blue, according as to whether
you started with sky or sea in mind. I set off in the highest
spirits, for the Committee had had the splendid idea of holding
its meeting on such a day of the week that a week-end in
Cornwall was involved. I looked in at Exmouth and Exeter on
the way down to see what my father, and my sister Susan, and
my brother Howard thought of the idea of my becoming a
headmistress. My father said he shouldn't do anything which
involved extra work; my sister Susan said she'd like to look out
on the Mount herself; but my brother Howard was quite
serious, for him. He was very definitely in favour of my
becoming a headmistress. The difficulties of being head of a
school were vastly exaggerated, he said; he'd been a headmaster
for years, and he'd managed the clerical work involved without
losing any sleep, although he was no more methodical than I.
You could put your own ideas into action when you were a
head; it was exhilarating. The boys were the whole point—
the boys, in school and out. I could have a strong Scout
movement—take the whole school to camp. Girls! Well he
wouldn't want girls of course, but still! Committees! Far too
much silly talk about difficulties with committees. He'd never
had any trouble with his committee. I should be able to give
music its proper place on the timetable. Nobody understood
the importance of music . . . rhythm! My brother's refractory
lock of hair waved in the breeze, and his blue eyes waxed bluer,
as he told me what I could do for music in Penzance, and that
there was nothing so well worth doing in the world as running
a school for boys.

After enjoying my family at Exmouth and Exeter, I began to
enjoy my friends in Cornwall. Marjorie and Harold Harvey
met me at St Austell with their car, which had lost its silencer,
and we drove uproariously to Truro. It would be glorious, we
decided, for me to come back and live near them again. In the
evening I slipped down to St Ives to see some friends there.
One very dear old friend of mine at St Ives always called me
'Anne, my son'. She was very practical; deeply concerned
about my lack of bank-balance, and the reckless way I had

taken odd years off school, thus losing pensionable service. She said, 'What about the salary, Anne, my son?' I said it would be more than I had been getting at King Edward's. 'And the pension, Anne, would that be all right if you take this job?' She never doubted for a moment but that it would be a question of taking. I told her the pension would be more too. She said, 'Then I should go for'n.'

I did try to go for'n; but, by the time I reached the County Hall at Truro for the interview, a reaction from excitement had set in. The forward movement of the wave was spent, and I was in the back-wash. I felt my tide going out. As I talked to the other people who were to undergo the interview I reached low water. We were called in one by one. When my turn came, and I walked in, it seemed a very large committee. I thought perhaps I was seeing double or treble, though I had had nothing to drink. I kept on remembering a story a friend of mine had told me. She was the wife of a sea-captain and once, when she was very young, she went to Rouen to meet her husband on his return from a voyage. They went to a café and she drank wine freely; she was not used to it, but she found she liked it. Some days afterwards she asked her husband to take her again to the café in the wood. 'There was no wood,' he said. 'Oh, yes,' she said, 'there was a wood. Don't you remember all those trees as we came out?' 'Come and see,' he said to her. He took her back to the café, and she saw two little palm trees in tubs. The committee seemed to me to be multiplying like those little palms. At last I focused Mr C. V. Thomas and Mr Shopland, both of whom I knew.

'Why do you want to become a headmistress?' was the first question propounded. Professor Oliver Elton, who had been greatly entertained at the idea of my becoming a headmistress, had put me through a mock interview, and this was the first question he had asked.

'I should like to live at Penzance,' I said. I still think this was a pretty good reason. I knew I should be happy there, and happy persons' tend to make better headmistresses than unhappy ones. My strongest suit, I thought, was that I had had experience in primary as well as in secondary schools; but it did not seem worth while to say that. I had said it in the famous letter of application, a copy of which the committee members had in front of them.

'Would you be prepared to teach scripture?' I found this question very hard to answer. I could have written a thesis on it. If I were to have anything to do with the teaching of divinity I should have preferred, like my brother Howard, to be in a school directly associated with the English Church. The sacraments, the liturgy, the association of the Christian with the physical year, the provision made for the instruction of young people in the Faith, and for admission to share in its privileges—these things had been a more essential part of my own early education than secular learning. Without them I should not even have understood some of our choicest poetry. And these things cannot be taught as a mere adjunct to the study of literature. Cambridge University sets the candidates for entrance to its English school a paper entitled 'The Classical and Biblical Background'. But good teaching depends partly on the right reason for learning. You cannot teach the Bible in order that children may understand Biblical allusions. No; I have not the slightest doubt that man was born to praise and serve God, and that this service of praise and thanksgiving must be traditionally taught and lived; that all right education serves the underlying spirit of Christianity. And yet I was seeking to become headmistress of a secular school, with a syllabus of religious instruction, and provision for morning prayers, but nothing against which a child, untaught at home in the Christian faith, could lean on in times of danger or despair. I knew I was being inconsistent and confused. I said I thought that in a secular school divinity should be taught by a divinity specialist. This was the established practice at King Edward's, and I thought it as good a plan as could be devised. Traditionally, headmasters have taught divinity to their sixth forms; but traditionally headmasters have been Divines.

I do not remember any other questions except one which was put to me by Mr Shopland.

'Is it not a fact, Miss Treneer, that you prefer teaching to organization?'

It was a fact; I admitted it. But I nearly added as a rider that I thought altogether too much fuss was made over the great god, Organization. However, I just sat there looking meek. I looked meek, and felt shaken.

I was chosen with two others to go on to a second interview at Penzance. In the school itself we were to meet its Governors. As we motored down the main road between Truro and Penzance I was assaulted with doubts and fears, especially with regard to my motives. I have never been able to put school first in my life. I like children, and I like books; but I like just being alive better than either. I knew I enjoyed writing better than teaching, and teaching better than organizing. Was I trying to get to Penzance because I had begun a biography of Sir Humphry Davy, and wanted to live where he had spent his youth? Was I swayed by the desire for the Morrab library, and by the vision of the guarded Mount, and was my desire to be a headmistress quite spurious? I reached Penzance in a defeated mood. I smelt chlorine when I dashed to have a look at the harbour; I saw a swimming-pool instead of sea-weed. I hate swimming-pools. When it came to my turn to be interviewed by the Governors I said, 'No'. 'Oh, no!' and 'I'm afraid not' to pretty nearly every question they asked me. They must have thought me a fool ever to have applied. They did not appoint me. Mrs Arnold Forster, whom I knew slightly, told me afterwards that she thought poets and painters should not organize. Only one lady seemed to want me. She remarked, when I had said 'No' to a query about running school dinners, 'But surely, Miss Treneer, you could do a simple thing like that.' My heart warmed to her. She gave me several chances to make a better showing; but I felt dull, and dead, and obstinate, and anxious to get out of it all. I knew that I should never please my brother Howard by making music the animating principle of a school. Instead I went back to Birmingham feeling like a diminished seventh—an impossible figure of speech, I am told, but it expresses what I mean.

16

PLAYS, CAROLS AND BREAKING UP

I did not feel diminished for long. A school, like a family, wraps one comfortingly round. Children are conservative creatures, tending to like the people they know and are used to; and my friends on the staff made it delightfully clear that they were glad to welcome me back. In the teaching of English I rejoined my three immediate associates. Miss Baker, known to us familiarly as George, was tall, dark and handsome, with a wonderful eye for colour, whether in arranging flowers or wearing clothes. Her special love was drama, and children wrote well on the themes she suggested. Florence Bull was as fair as George was dark. She was an understanding person with thoughtful eyes 'as grey as glass'; her special talent lay in the teaching of language. Frances Stevens, who came from Plymouth, and could talk Cornish with me, had all the gifts, including a good singing voice. She taught Latin as well as English, but English was her true love.

We agreed with just the requisite amount of disagreement to keep our discussions from being flat. Our great discussions were about the books to be chosen for girls of different ages. At that time pupils at King Edward's bought their own books. There was a limit beyond which we might not go in expenditure per child—how naturally one says *per* in any official context! As a parent wrote to me once, 'Further to mine of yesterday, *re* Margaret.' Apart from being too extravagant, we might choose what books we would. What we wanted, and seemed never to be able to get in sufficient variety, were well-printed, attractively bound, complete texts. Solid notes on the right points—there is rarely a note on the real difficulties—are necessary in some books. But what I hate are school editions of the classical English texts, edited about 1908, hoary old creatures reprinted, reprinted and reprinted, getting more and more out of date in their scholarship every year. Even more I hate half the Language Courses and all the Comprehension Tests cumbering the ground. Some otherwise excellent series of novels are spoilt by the strings of questions and subjects for essays printed at the back. Their danger is that they tend to change the pleasure to be derived from novel-reading—the private enjoyment of a book for its own sake—by introducing the adventitious excitement, or boredom, of the quizz. Think of the books one devoured oneself as a child, and consider how one's pleasure would have been spoilt, and the reading instinct perverted, if one has been questioned on them. Apart from the study of the language and of prose other than fiction, drama is the branch of English most worth attending school for—drama and some kinds of poetry. They need, for their full enjoyment, the spoken word and a number of people; whereas narrative is best enjoyed alone and silently.

In the upper school at this time we started a play-reading society which long flourished. Our first reading was of the *The Admirable Crichton*, with Miss Barrie, who was Sir James Barrie's niece, taking part. For this reading we followed the practice, abandoned later, of having all characters on the platform sitting in a wide ellipse and each reading as her cue came. Later the school preferred to act the play with the characters taking their exits and entrances in due order, but all having books in their hands. I am sure this is a far less good arrangement; it needs time for rehearsal, and does not exercise the imagination as does a play intelligently rendered by a circle of readers where everything depends on the voice. In our first reading I recall Miss Thompson as the haughty daughter, and Elizabeth Ryder's Tweeny.

We joined the Drama League, and were thus able to obtain on loan copies of all kinds of plays to read; and we all took a turn at choosing and arranging. Some members of the sixth form were especially successful as producers, and at discovering readers with talent. Girls know one another better than the staff can ever know them.

As soon as the upper school had established a play-reading society, the junior and middle schools petitioned for something similar. But a reading society demands experience. Younger children only act well when unencumbered with books— indeed they act best when unencumbered even with set words. So we suggested, instead of a society, a dramatic competition. We chose a short play for each group up to, and including, the lower fifth form. As far as I remember, we gave no help at all in the first year. Each form elected a producer, a stage manager and a wardrobe mistress—children revel in technical words— and with the fewest possible rehearsals, staged a play. The English staff judged the heats in each set of forms, and gave some criticism and advice, of which the winning producers might avail themselves or not, for the final performance. The winning play in each group was acted before the school and before an external judge. It seemed at first sight unfair that a third form play should have to stand in competition with the lower fifths without some system of handicaps. In practice, it worked out well. The younger the children, the more unself-conscious they are, and the more ingenious at making-do. Invisible hands sprinkling torn-up white paper outside a 'window' made excellent snow in *The Tailor of Gloucester*; and Simkin was the perfect cat of story. Our first judge was Miss Grace Trenery; her warmth of imaginative sympathy communicated itself to the young actors. Of other good judges I remember in particular the grace and clarity of Margaret Leighton, and Elspeth Duxbury's power to impart some hint of the technical resources of her art. The Repertory Theatre was generous to us; organized parties to the theatre, especially after the benefaction of the Foyle Trust had made cheap tickets available to schools, became an entrancing aid to the teaching of English. Sir Barry Jackson himself came to lecture to us on the theatre. He told me afterwards that he had never been so frightened in his life as at the sight of so many girls. Girls' schools daunt the strongest man. When my brother Howard came to see me he peered in at a door, then fled for sanctuary to Miss Barrie's room.

Not all our work in drama was in the shape of dramatic competitions and readings. Perhaps the most fruitful use of drama in schools is in impromptu acting in the form-room; but of this I have already written. We also performed a school play at irregular intervals so as to set a standard and give enjoyment. On these occasions I put the play first and all other considerations second. I dearly liked casting, with the whole range of pupils to choose from; but there were difficulties over casting. My colleagues naturally tended to consider the effect of being given a principal part on the character of the chosen one. 'Why, Treneer, bring a girl like that forward?' someone would say. 'Goodness knows she is forward enough already.' The most wicked girls nearly always act best, their very wickedness being, indeed, a kind of play, an outlet for pent energies, and a desire to see what will happen in a contrived situation. Showing off! And then there was the trouble over accents. I am utterly inconsistent about a local accent. When I was teaching at Camborne in Cornwall, I used to choose for the best parts girls with the most Cornish voices; but for the life of me I could not help being prejudiced against a Birmingham voice and distorted vowels. It was an old Edwardian who reminded me that Birmingham, too, was loved. She was a distinguished doctor, and she told me that a patient of hers who had undergone a serious operation in a Liverpool hospital discovered that her doctor was from Birmingham. She said eagerly, 'Eh, Doctor, do you know the Pershore Road?' The heart attaches itself, whether to the Pershore Road or to Gorran Churchtown.

When I think of plays at King Edward's I watch, in imagination, the rehearsals; I go with Miss Baker and Miss Barnes to the acting cupboard to consider clothes; I hear us deciding once again to ask Miss Waterfield to lend us her Indian things with their glorious colours, and their shapes so easy to adapt. I see girls arriving with clothes made by mother or aunt to Miss Baker's specification; I find myself in despair at the last rehearsal. At the actual performance I still have a nightmare, someone has broken down in her part and nobody can find a prompt copy. 'Miss Treneer, how can you be *so calm?*' Fay Friend said to me once as she stood dancing with excitement in the wings. She was Tobias in *Tobias and the Angel*. She was a black-eyed imp of a child, with a genuine talent for acting. She had that spontaneity, that gift of mimicry, that bubbling over of the spirit of play, that drollness, for which there is no substitute in comedy.

Of other plays we did, I most vividly remember *Michael*, and an adaptation of the Coventry Nativity play. These plays were performed in the beautiful hall of the present building, in Edgbaston Park Road, where the stage, though small, is altogether better equipped than was the stage in New Street. The Nativity Play, like everything we did, had its imperfections. I am too impatient to produce that absolute beauty which should be unveiled by a religious play. But in a school which has on the staff many members appreciative of and creative in the various arts, and children eager and keen-witted, unexpected moments of genuine beauty can result from those elusive situations which make drama. In the Nativity Play Denne's music and Janet Crisp's sense of the pictorial combined to produce scenes evanescent, yet enduring in their effect on the beholder. Very few people can combine religious wonder with gaiety; one of the few was Denne. From the opening moment, when she sang 'Let all mortal flesh keep silence', to the close, when the school joined in the adoration, and the living picture glowed, the school hall, and those who daily assembled in it were in some sense transfigured. I remember especially the singing of Hugo Wolf's 'Nun Vandre Maria' as Joseph and Mary crossed the stage on their journey to Bethlehem; Pat Kent's voice in 'I sing of a maiden', during the Nativity scene; and the school singing in unison, 'Torches, torches, run with torches', as the procession of Kings and Shepherds and children came up through the hall with lighted tapers. Those tapers! I cannot forget how they were once forgotten. I forgot them; Denne forgot them; Grace Denley, the Daisy of our Cheltenham days, and our fast friend, scoured Birmingham at the last minute and came back in the nick of time, exhausted but triumphant, with a royal bundle. I have rarely blessed anyone more from my heart than I blessed Daisy when she put those tapers into my hands.

'Torches, torches,' was one of the carols which found a place at the traditional carol singing conducted by Denne each year. In New Street, in the Bristol Road, and in Edgbaston Park Road, I remember carol singing. A joyful spontaneity and gusto marked it, and yet it had intention. All the girls, excited and agog to sing, were in the hall; old girls, unrecognizable in their pretty clothes, drifted in at the back; Miss Barrie forsook all business to join the throng. 'They're beginning,' called a voice in the staff-room, and every mistress, however urgent the work she was doing, dropped pen or blue pencil to take her place with her form. Other occasions we might cut, but never carol singing. Denne divided the carols into groups. In the intervals between the groups, the holiday spirit bubbled over, but only to flow into the singing again, filling it out, lifting it up. The choir sang some carols; the girls who were learning German sang 'Stille Nachte'; Denne herself sang 'The Coventry Carol', and some carols the whole school sang. I remember 'There came three ships' with the youngest girls, in the front of the hall, beginning; then a fresh form would join in with each successive verse, the music growing and embracing ever fresh sets of voices until at last we came to, 'And all the souls on earth shall sing', and we were all in together with, 'Then let us all rejoice amain, on Christmas day, on Christmas day'. Of other carols and hymns, I recall especially 'King Jesus hath a garden', 'Personent Hodie', and the concluding hymn, 'Adeste fideles'. Even the youngest girls, those who were only beginning Latin, delighted in the moulded words. Standing in their places, seriously concerned with the pronunciation of each syllable, for Miss Hoggan was listening, they made the great hymn rise.

The school play and carol-singing came towards the end of the autumn term, just before we broke up for the Christmas holidays. Breaking up! What a whirl and swirl! I remember the fearful business of setting examination papers, the hush and solemnity of the examination room—pink blotting-paper, Cambridge paper, fresh-filled ink wells, and bits of string. We tied up sets of examination papers with string instead of using paper clips. I hated the heavy work of marking. There was a frightful occasion when I lost a set of papers for nearly a week, and found them in my bed. 'Miss Treneer, please, can't we have our marks today, please Miss Treneer?' 'Not today, I'm afraid, Rosamund.' And then Reports! I see them reposing in folders of blotting paper on the staff-room table. I always felt a certain subdued exhilaration when I began topping and tailing them— entering the name, form, age and average age at the top, filling in the date of re-assembly, and signing my name at the bottom. But before I had finished writing out reports I was always in such a temper that I could have heaved a book at anybody's head. I did not dislike making up reports; but I cannot copy out. For the life of me I cannot copy out correctly and, until Dr Smith came, and changed the system, we used to copy out in a fair hand all the reports we received from subject-mistresses on the girls in our forms. 'Julia will do better when she concentrates more.' She will, indeed, I used to think to myself grimly, making an error or dropping a blot as I wrote. I used to apply colourless liquids to my errors from two little bottles, labelled A and B. A drop of liquid A, applied with a glass rod, acted like magic in erasing the written word; but then the operation had to be repeated with liquid B, and I was generally too impatient to wait for A and B to dry on the page. I would begin to write over the damp spot too soon, and make such a mess that I had to tear up the report and begin all over again. I feel a kind of frenzy even as I recall this copying out. I would rather teach for a week than copy out for two hours. But how elegant Miss

Hoggan's completed reports looked, how exquisitely neat Miss Udall's! In addition to reports there were registers and address sheets to see to. I sometimes dream of address sheets in triplicate. It seemed as though end-of-term business would never be done; but the time came when the last report was signed, the last envelope addressed, and all the corrected examination papers were tied up in flat bundles and taken to Miss Carte's room. Miss Carte, always cheerful, always happily talking, had succeeded Miss Piper as secretary. She dealt with All. Registers? 'Take them to Miss Carte.' Health Tribute? 'Take it to Miss Carte.' Special buses? 'Ask Miss Carte.' There in the office she sat in the midst of forms and coins, not overwhelmed, never losing her temper, still talking.

Before Christmas all form-rooms were decorated, form vying with form in ingenuity; paper chains fighting the traditional evergreens. Secret signals became common, and there was heard the chink of money being counted under the desks. A pillar box was contrived, often with the powerful aid of 'Daddy', and set up in the form-room. At the last hour a postman was elected and went his rounds; cards piled up on the mistress's desk; girls thronged round exhibiting their Christmas cards. Then, mysteriously, all girls were back and standing in their places. It was the moment for the presentation of a joint gift to the form-mistress. Children are unbelievably generous, extraordinarily forgiving. No hard words, no injustice was remembered as they clapped and cheered. In the midst of the excitement the bell would ring for the breaking-up ceremony in the hall. Miss Barrie came tranquilly on to the platform to read the lists and present colours. As I wondered whether I should catch my train at New Street, a short service was read, a hymn was sung, and then the cheers were given. The head girl and three fellow prefects called for the different sets of cheers, their voices varying in pitch:

'Three cheers for Miss Barrie!'

'Three cheers for the Staff!'

'Three cheers for the School!'

'Three cheers for the HOLIDAYS!'

At the mention of the holidays the cheering reached a crescendo. There are no more rousing cheers than those for the holidays in a hard-working school. 'Work without end, Amen,' was how one little girl, newly admitted to King Edward's, rendered the close of the General Thanksgiving—after having touchingly addressed the Deity as 'Father of all Nursies.'

It is especially in the new building in Edgbaston that I remember proceedings subsequent to the breaking-up ceremony, because it was at Edgbaston that my anxiety to get to the station in time for my train always became paramount. I see myself diving through masses of surging girls, shaking outstretched hands, clutching my gift under my arm, clasping a bunch of flowers to my bosom, jumping into a waiting taxi at last, and so to New Street, to New Street, and into a train heading West.

17

AN ARTICLE FOR THE
BIRMINGHAM POST

During all this time I cherished grandiose thoughts about the books I would write. Teaching English should surely be compatible with writing it. Verse and verse translations I wrote for pleasure, showing my versions to Margaret Osborn, then a classical mistress at King Edward's, now High Mistress of St Paul's. She had a happy turn for verse translation herself. In addition to verse, which I wrote often to conjure up the physical sensation of Cornish pleasures, I had in mind two large books. I, who was no scientist, wanted to write a biography of Sir Humphry Davy; I also schemed to write a book on modern prose.

There was cunning in both my choices. I play a cat and mouse game with myself. Child of a good upbringing, I try to do my duty but, also, I dearly love pleasing myself. I like to be idle but feel working. My two proposed books gave me wide liberty. There was nothing written between 1770 and 1830, a favourite period of mine, which might not throw some light on Davy; there was nothing written between 1914 and the latest novel, or the current number of *The Criterion*, which might not come in handy for my masterpiece on 'Modern English Prose'. When I was reading James Joyce, Mr E.M. Forster, and Virginia Woolf I was not merely enjoying novels like everybody else, I was also 'working'. When I laughed over Bernard Shaw, or shared with the sixth form the moving drama of O'Neill's *The Emperor Jones*, or went to London to see Sara Allgood in *Juno and the Paycock*, I said to myself that not only here were works which re-created me, but also, what prose! Then, in quite another kind, there was the wit and rhetoric of Mr Churchill. To Mr Churchill, chronology was the life of prose; whereas my other masters and my mistress were seeking every device to get away from chronology. I read Churchill as I read Joyce, with a relish; but not only with a relish. I also said, 'All this will be splendid for my book on modern prose'. I could always go back to *Arabia Deserta*, too, and yet not feel too far removed from my new *opus*. It was *Arabia Deserta* which sent me to Lawrence's *Seven Pillars of Wisdom*—material also, I thought, for my book on modern prose. I always saw it like that: *MODERN PROSE*, by Anne Treneer, a nicely designed book, on elegant paper, with wide margins. How this projected masterpiece ended by becoming a single article of one thousand words, published in one column of the *Birmingham Post*, is a chastening tale.

I first read *Seven Pillars of Wisdom* in August 1935 soon after the work became available to ordinary readers. I began it not because of what I had heard or read of Lawrence, but because of my enduring love of *Arabia Deserta*. I cared for Lawrence because he had cared for Doughty.

I suppose this was the worst possible approach. A new book should be read for itself, regardless of connections, otherwise the first fresh taste is likely to be lost. But the first reading of *Seven Pillars* was not spoilt for me by *Arabia Deserta*. The books were too different. It was obvious that Lawrence was not Doughty, nor anywhere near him, either in humanity or as a maker. Lawrence was not a poet. But he had his own speed and luck, a story to tell of quick contemporary, dramatic and historical interest, with a capricious jinn at his command to help him tell it, and to transport his readers to the desert. There is an energy in Lawrence, some springing devil in himself, which preserved him to the end from blankness and officialdom. Heroes are said to end by being bores; Lawrence was too quick for his fate.

He lived his own fable. In Arabia he was contemplating a book as well as a campaign; he was even making a fairy tale. For there is a sense in which *Seven Pillars* is the thousand times repeated tale of the little man who defeats the big ones; the story of the youngest brother of no estimation who succeeds where his stupid elder brothers—the officers of the regular army—fail. Dynamite is his magic; he performs miracles of endurance; has recourse to tricks and disguises; unheard of cruelties are practised against him; he wins the undying devotion of some foreign tribes and blows up others without remorse; they are the Paynim. To over-emphasize this aspect of the book would be foolish, but it is there. It is the only thing which makes the horrors bearable. Even so, some are unendurable and must be skipped. That Lawrence himself recognized the fairy-tale side of his book is clear from his statement, a tricky statement no doubt, that he would co-operate in making a film based on his career if it were done in the manner and spirit of Mickey Mouse. He said it would lend itself perfectly to that treatment. Example: a Turkish troop train blown into the air in bits re-forms in space and, perfectly united, lands gracefully and proceeds merrily on its way. Treated thus, Lawrence said, his affairs would make a great picture. And they would. Colonel Ralph Isham, who relates this piece of conversation, says that Lawrence was talking at the time without any irony or bitterness, but beaming and chuckling. No doubt, in such a picture, Lawrence himself would have been shown as a kind of Brer Rabbit spitefully smiling at Bremond, or being spiny and high with General Barrow. The ending would be pure Lawrence with the hero disappearing in a cloud of dust on the horizon.

Lawrence the jester is an integral part of the various and elusive Lawrence of legend. Sober minds pooh-pooh the legend, but the essence of legend is that it provokes pooh-poohing. Lawrence himself is both legend and pooh-pooher, the story and the chorus, the hero and the scoffer, the romantic who is also a realist, taking us beyond the façade of victory, to the disillusion and horror when the dream of the crusader—of the knight and jester—is seen in 'the blank light of success'. In *Seven Pillars* there is a race between the drama and the self-despising critic of the drama, the one circling round and impinging on the other. Yet it cannot be said that the book is valuable as the revelation of a man rather than as the story of an action; it is the story which preserves the man. Lawrence's original elation, which kindles his story, is stronger than his most passionate protest against it, as story is always stronger than comment. He sees himself with an ironical eye, and the sub-title of his book, *A Triumph*, seemed to me to have a purely ironical ring, until I read in Lawrence's letter to Mrs Hardy, 'That day I reached Damascus I cried against all control for the triumphant thing achieved at last, fitly.' The main title, *Seven Pillars of Wisdom*, a perfect title in itself, is a strange one to indicate Lawrence's work. For that which it emphasizes, wisdom, is the weakest part of the book. No one was ever farther from the serenity of wisdom than Lawrence; his thinking is provisional, interesting as part of the colour of his character, but in no way interesting with the absolute interest of wisdom. His nihilism, his despising of the body, his dislike of physical life which he held in common with animals, his reflections on the subjugation of the personality to an ideal—all the ideas thrown out in relation to the discipline and devotion of his bodyguard are like an elementary theory of fascism—show him in an interesting light as a character, but they do not reveal him as a notable thinker. One excellent quality he had; he did not abide in any theory he threw out for himself, but passed beyond it. There is no better comment on the illusion inherent in a mystical devotion to the corporate state than Lawrence's:

> To our strained eyes, the ideal, held in common, seemed to transcend the personal, which before had been our normal measure of the world. Did this instinct point to our happily accepting final absorption in some pattern wherein the discordant selves might find reasonable, inevitable purpose? Yet

this very transcending of individual frailty made the ideal transient. Its principle became Activity, the primal quality, external to our atomic structure, which we could simulate only by unrest of mind and soul and body, beyond holding point. So always the ideality of the ideal vanished, leaving its worshippers exhausted: holding for false what it had once pursued.

Lawrence was not wise; perhaps he was too honest to be wise. The struggles of his honesty with the involutions of his disposition and character, blown big by circumstance, are intensely interesting even when his honesty is baffled, as it often is. He was never a charlatan to himself; and that is one of his claims to greatness, and it is that which redeems what he feared he had lost, his essential integrity. He enjoyed seeing himself in a romantic or in an ambiguous situation; but he knew his weakness and owned it and despised himself for it, despised himself too much. He has the harshness towards himself of a religious making a self-examination. One would, perhaps, have guessed, even if one had not read it, that for a short period his education was in a Jesuit school; many of his instincts are those of a mystic and an ascetic—the total subjugation of the body to the cruel force of the will, the attempt to transcend the personality through devotion, though it was not the devotion of a saint.

His discussion of atonement, his realization that his 'preferring of the unknown to the God was a scapegoat idea, which lulled only to false peace', his desire to accept a life of rule and abnegation, all have parallels among great men of action in the past who have retired into monasteries. Yet Lawrence's desire was in part the very opposite of theirs. Far from severing himself from life, he went into barracks partly because he desired a share in common human life from which he felt his form of education had mysteriously cut him off. A similar impulse made 'bourgeois' writers seek for 'proletarian' material in the same decade—as though a man could not write unless he had been born in a slum. Lawrence never abnegated his desire for expression. He was a writer all his life. He realized the vital part the Air Force would play in war, but also, immediately after joining the Air Force, he was planning a book about it. He saw that a modern Haklyut would some day collect narratives of great flights; he said he longed to keep the log of a master voyager through the air; he felt that only by experiencing what he wrote could he get actuality into phrasing and feeling.

If comparisons must be made, Lawrence is comparable with Hopkins rather than Doughty, who had an undivided soul, a wholeness by birthright which the others sought at great price, Hopkins the more intensely and, for all that he never went through a physical war as Lawrence did, with greater agony; for with Lawrence the whole man was never engaged, so was never quite purified either by suffering or joy. Half himself was always aloof watching the other half. And so it comes about that we never feel and know Lawrence directly as we feel and know Hopkins and Doughty. They use strange words, strange rhythms; Lawrence current words, common rhythms; yet it is they who stand clear and naked, and Lawrence who is seen through a literary haze. But he was possessed of a great demon, an authentic flame. He was one of the magnetic personalities of our age. Perhaps one of his greatest claims to respect is that after his Arabian experience and his disenchantment, he did not seek to exploit further his personal power. In *Seven Pillars of Wisdom* he had speculated whether an idol, strengthened by the prayers breathed into him, and the wonders performed in his name, might not become in some sort a god. He himself was a popular idol; but, mercifully, his power of self-analysis was too incisive to allow him to become either a Leader or a Duce.

To me Lawrence's writing gave the satisfaction of communicating with a contemporary mind altogether more splendid and far-reaching than, yet not too remote from, my own. I wrote at great length on Lawrence, pretty nearly a monograph, although it was only intended to form part of a chapter on 'The Prose of Action' in my masterpiece on 'Modern Prose'. I wrote at similar length on Virginia Woolf for my contemplated chapter on 'The Prose of the Novel'. With my proposed chapter on 'The Prose of the Short Story' in mind I was able to read, with the clear conscience of an earnest worker, pretty nearly every enjoyable modern short story ever written. I adored H.E. Bates. But for all my lively effort my great work refused to get under way. It lay about in isolated parts. I felt like Robinson Crusoe when he had cut down tree trunks and made so heavy a boat that he could not get it to the water. Perhaps, I thought, I needed the stimulus of print. So I put aside my heavier efforts, wrote an article of a thousand words on *Seven Pillars of Wisdom*, and sent it to the Editor of the *Birmingham Post*. I had long had my eye on the weekly Tuesday column headed *Books and Writers*. When my article appeared I hugged my success in secret as far as school was concerned. Only Alex Makin spotted A. T. at the foot of my masterpiece. I was secret at school; but I rushed to tell all my friends in Bearley, puffing and swelling as I received their pleasant praise. We all read the *Birmingham Post* in Bearley.

I set to work to evolve another article. This effort was refused; but an essay on Santayana, based on the newly published novel *The Last Puritan*, was accepted. Again my hopes rose high; but my next attempt met refusal. An essay on Hartley Coleridge which I greatly enjoyed writing was taken; a better one, as I thought, on the lyrical quality of Virginia Woolf's prose was returned. With it I received the first of the assistant editor's notes, written in green ink. Mr Hadley suggested that I should submit suggested topics to him before writing the actual article. This practice, he said, would prevent me from sending in essays which he could not possibly use in a daily newspaper. Even literary articles must, as a general rule, be slung on to some peg of topical interest—centenaries and so forth. I think the centenary business is very boring, and that it has had an ill effect on that ephemeral kind of writing pleasantly called *Belles Lettres*. However, I did my best to comply with Mr Hadley's command. I greatly liked receiving his scrawled comments on such topics as I suggested. I never met either him or Mr Record; I did not call at the office in New Street; I did not even venture to use the telephone when suggesting my subjects. I wrote notes in my best handwriting, and received back scrawls in green ink, often very illuminating and sometimes dryly humorous. I grew to know my assistant editor's taste and even to divine some of his habits. He had spent some holidays at Porthgwarra, he said, with reference to some Cornish remark of mine, and had heard a fisherman say, he was glad he hadn't lived in his granfer's day when, as far as he could hear, they had 'nawthin to ate but they old fairmaids [cured pilchards] and tatties'.

I did not write a great many articles for the *Birmingham Post*, as I had time to do them only at long intervals, and sometimes, by the time I had completed my article, it was no longer news, and had to be abandoned. The one I most enjoyed writing was on the translations of Arthur Waley. I wrote it during one holiday in Cornwall, the 'peg' being the newly published translation of *The Book of Songs*. Arthur Waley's translations of Chinese poetry had been my well-beloveds ever since I had picked up *170 Chinese Poems* at Thornton's, in Oxford. Later I bought *More Translations from the Chinese* and *The Temple and Other Poems*. Miss Hoggan (who had, by this time, become my friend 'Dorcas') introduced me to *The Tale of Genji* by the earliest of the women novelists of the world, the Japanese writer Lady Murasaki, born about A.D. 978. Arthur Waley's translation of this novel, which is six volumes in one—*The Tale of Genji, The Sacred Tree, A Wreath of Cloud, Blue Trousers, The Lady of the Boat* and *The Bridge of Dreams*—enchanted us both. We read it during a winter term, telling each other, when we met for coffee, how we were progressing, and discussing the inter-twinings of the narrative and the flowering of character and poetry. These stories of love, and of hate which can kill by 'possessing' the victim, so that malice and jealousy are deadly sins in an extended and literal sense, held our attention partly because of their setting in the natural year, with its festivals of flowers and snow, its scents and colours, and partly too, because of the English of the translation. It was the same with the translated Chinese poems. We relished not only the reflective humanity of the Chinese poets, but also the skilful unrhymed verse, with its varying line-lengths, of the English translator. It was interesting, too, to see how some dreams of the third century fitted with Lawrence's dream in the twentieth:

> I wanted at a stroke to clear the Yang-tze and the Hsiang,
> And at a glance to quell the Tibetans and Hu.
> When my task was done, I should not accept a barony,
> But refusing with a bow, retire to a cottage in the country.

I wrote with a proselyte's zeal of the translations of Arthur Waley; I overflowed with zeal; I overflowed the column, and had to curtail. Writing for the column improved my prose. My tendency is to be flowery; I dearly love a word or a phrase. I always argued secretly, whatever my various teachers said to me, and they said a good deal, that it was, after all, a matter of taste. But I could not argue even secretly with Mr Record and Mr Hadley. I had to fit their space or perish; so I fitted it, growing less and less rotund until, at last, I was so spare I could have jumped through any hoop.

The improvement in my prose effected by Mr Hadley illustrates that most difficult paradox in the teaching of any art or craft; that those who do not mean to teach, teach best. It is the casual hint, dropped by the master of an art to a person struggling by practice to learn, which is assimilated.

I had at this time correspondence also with Mr Edward Garnett. He had written me first about the manuscript of my book on Doughty in which, he said, he had been particularly interested in the chapters on style and words. Later he was shown some samples of my own verse-making, and I received the following letter:

> 19 *Pond Place*,
> *Chelsea, S.W.*3.
> *Sept.* 28, 36

Dear Miss Treneer: Yes. You are a poet and you have found your own individual way to enshrine, delicately and finely, sensations and feelings not commonly discerned and centred so truthfully. I like all your poems except the Epilogue. I am left speculating whether you may go further along the track and become known as the Poet of the Body's Feeling—by extending the field of your perception and analysing your sensations and emotions in the same aerial, delicate, flying style.

Here your strength lies in the fine exactness of your perceptions and the grace and beauty of your phrasing.

So you have the chosen medium ready should you wish to extend your boundary.

I can conceive a sequence of poems dealing with the development of the Body's States from Childhood onwards. And if recorded by a woman the development might mirror the states of Virginity, of Womanhood and Motherhood. I emphasize this merely to say that we have had no Woman poet yet to centre her perceptions on her Body's feelings, though hundreds have spoken for the Soul, the Mind and the Heart.

Your poems ought certainly to be published. Perhaps some have been printed in the press? You might send a few to *The London Mercury*, 10 G Turnstile, Holborn, London, W. and mention my name. But of course that is only a chance. Nobody buys books of poems. If you can think of an illustrator of genius, a book of Poems and Drawings might possibly tempt some Private Press, such as the Golden Cockerel, but the outlook for poets is over unpeopled lands.

However this may be, I congratulate you on your Poems.

Sincerely,
                                                    EDWARD GARNETT

This was by far the most exciting letter I ever received in relation to any work of mine. I soon knew it by heart and preserved it as a talisman against despondency. I sent some samples of my excellence to *The London Mercury*, and my spirits soared as morning followed morning and I received no reply. Surely Mr J.C. Squire—or was he Sir John by then?—must be meditating acceptance. Morning after morning stretched into week after week and month after month. Each month I hastened to Cornish's for a copy of *The London Mercury*, hoping that, as I opened the orange covers on my way to Snow Hill . . . But no; never any elegant appearance on the part of the Woman Poet. After about a year I ceased to hope. Only *Time and Tide,* by occasionally printing some offering of mine, kept a little warmth in the veins of the languishing versifier.

A P.E.N. CONFERENCE
IN PRAGUE:
HENRY NEVINSON

During my years at King Edward's I had not given much thought to dangers, disasters, politics and European affairs. Hitler bored me. When members of the sixth form came back from visits to Germany and talked excitedly of enthusiastic demonstrations and mass displays in which the emotions of the Many found expression in the One I could have hit them on the head. I loathed all the talk about the need for transcending the self, and devoting the energies to a cause. I hated even my dearly beloved Yeats when he made a marching song, an execrable marching song, and wrote other verse with the pen of a tainted Fascist. The stupid possessed the earth with their shouted slogans, so we who thought ourselves the wise began to shout back. I, in my tiny feeble way, began to imagine that the only thing worth doing was so to teach English literature to a few Edwardians that they at least should be able to think and feel and resist the hated potted catchwords. In fact I almost became zealous. I sometimes entered into that dangerous state, forgetting that the lovely gifts of inherited treasure which I had to offer to the young must never be perverted to any end other than themselves. If they are forced into a deliberate educational purpose they lose their bright lustre. It is perilously easy to become a propagandist, or a counter-propagandist, to try to sow immature minds with ideas instead of opening them, and tilling them, so that they may become receptive of beauty and diligent for truth.

By this time I had joined the London P.E.N. Club, with Edward Garnett as my sponsor. The letters P.E.N. stand for Poets, Playwrights, Essayists and Novelists, and the Club is an international society of writers. It seemed, and still seems to me, a fair society, in which members bind themselves to the principle of liberty of the mind, that principle on which there has been so concerted an attack in our day. The P.E.N. stands for freedom of thought, conscience, and expression in all countries. It is also, for the isolated writer, a help against provincialism and a ground for finding friends. All societies have their dangers. The P.E.N. has needed all the patience and tact of its late General Secretary, Hermon Ould, himself a poet and playwright, and a man most selfless, unprejudiced and compassionate, to preserve it from the contending tentacles of fanatics. Its very principles lead it again and again into a dilemma which is also the dilemma of our time. We seek the right; but by abrogating politics, we have abrogated power actively to promote what we consider right; Nevinson, speaking at a P.E.N. Conference, at the time of Munich, seemed to me the image of intellectual despair. His speech was profoundly moving.

I cannot claim to have known Henry Nevinson very well personally, but I knew his mind. Before I met him I had read *Changes and Chances*, that great autobiography; I had also read many of his essays, and a few poems. When I met him he seemed to me more like his writing than any other writer I had known. There was no barrier between himself and his books. I was first introduced to him at a London dinner—one reason why I liked the P.E.N. was that, in the old days, its monthly meetings were monthly feasts. I was no sooner introduced to Nevinson, in the crowded reception which preceded the dinner at Frascati's, than I managed, before he had time to sheer off, to pronounce the name of Martin Gilkes. Nevinson was arrested. He stood still, he was so large and I was so small that we seemed to be standing on a little rock with people like the sea flowing round us, but not touching us.

'Martin Gilkes,' he said, 'you know Martin Gilkes?'

I said I did indeed. He began to describe to me the great height of Martin's father, Dr Gilkes, headmaster of Shrewsbury School, and later master of Dulwich. Nevinson forgot me and he forgot Frascati's while he indulged in reminiscence of the man to whom he felt he owed so much. Hereafter, I was always safe when I went to a P.E.N. reception; whoever else might have forgotten who I was, Nevinson never had. And whoever else I might not be able to distinguish, I could distinguish Nevinson like a lighthouse. His height and massiveness, his head with its thick, white hair, the clipped beard which added length to a broad face, his sanguine complexion and blue eyes always reminded me of Chaucer's Franklin. I suppose this was really because, when I knew him, his beard was white 'as is the daisy'. There was a strength in the way he planted his feet—he had the least wavering of presences—which drew me towards him. He was always ready to talk. I enjoyed his talk, as I enjoyed his prose, not because he was a pacific man who had been a famous war-correspondent; nor because of his championship—his almost indiscriminate championship—of the weak against the strong; but for the zest of life in his works. *Fire of Life* was just the right title for the shortened version of *Changes and Chances.* I liked, too, in his prose the very discursiveness which is its danger. Nevinson's writing was and is immensely readable; it is surely time it came into its own again. He lacked the artistic intensity to shape perfectly a little action; he dashed on to the next adventure or the next crusade and wrote of that. When I said to him once that he must have led a most exciting life he replied, 'I took my chances, my dear, take your chances.'

I cannot remember whether or not, at the time of the P.E.N. Conference at Prague, Nevinson was President of the Club. Perhaps he presided; perhaps Storm Jamieson presided;

perhaps Wells was still President. Certainly Wells was there, communicating in his thin high voice his strong unwavering convictions. Wells could always make us listen, whereas most of us, when most people spoke, felt a strong sympathy with the eighteenth-century lady who said, 'I began to be horribly in the vapours.' I nearly always begin to be horribly in the vapours at meetings, for my ears will not let me sleep.

I especially enjoyed the journey to Prague, and during that journey Nevinson was at his best. He was at that time feeling acutely the limitation set on his physical activities by advancing age. I have never known anyone else, except my own mother, who so keenly resented growing old. He fiercely arraigned his body's failing powers. But during the journey to Prague the train bore us all along, and he had not to envy us our power to walk, and to repine at his own loss. He talked freely with any member of our company. It was during that journey, when I happened for a time to be sitting next him, that he said he considered Tolstoy to be the most remarkable of the eminent men he had met. Tolstoy had most in him, he said, of genius; of a quality which was not merely an intensification of the spirit informing all men, but animation by a spirit altogether beyond other men's range. He described vividly his meeting with Tolstoy; Nevinson talked very much as he wrote, in telling words with quick, vivid detail, and as though he himself enjoyed what he was saying.

In eastern Europe he was as much at home as in England. No English writer was more a citizen of the world. Yet he enjoyed the beauty of Prague freshly again, and watched the marching squares of scarlet-clad children with never-wearied interest. We were in Prague during the Sokol Festival. In the streets loud speakers blared the Czech national anthem until I felt I should die of it. Children had been brought in from the far country districts to salute their country's capital and to be cheered in their turn. The girls were in short scarlet skirts and white blouses; they marched with bands playing and flags flying, sometimes with companies of women in national dress, sometimes with bands of men in uniform adorned with the falcon crest, sometimes with athletes in white. Crowds cheered and waved; but after a time the marching seemed aimless, and I pitied tired children. Most spectacular was the performance of physical exercises in a vast open stadium. Here there was no hint of drooping or weariness or of vacant wonder. In every district of the land these exercises had been so taught and practised that, with only a brief rehearsal, thousands took their places in the Stadium, and moved in concert. The rhythmical movements of girls in blue, and boys in scarlet and white like poppies, can never be forgotten by those who witnessed them; nor the flutter of the waved handkerchiefs as friends and parents applauded at the close; nor the fervour of the salute to Benes who presided. Only, in the bright sunlight, it seemed ominous that the shadow of an aeroplane, hovering overhead, was etched black upon the great garden of coloured human flowers. I can still hear the faint rustle of feet as the boys moved, and see their raised hands and undefended arms; and hear above the human rustle, at intervals, the drone of the machine. The pathos of the vulnerability of the human body, and the beauty of its perfect functioning, were strongly felt.

National feeling was running high in Prague, but this was the period when it was being freely said that many of Hitler's tanks were faked, that the whole war machine had jammed on the way to Vienna, and that the menace of his power was a phantom menace which would collapse when straightly challenged. Fear of Hitler, but also disdain of Hitler, were part of the climate of Prague. It was the summer before Munich. Reliance on England was especially strong among the common people—and a desire to learn English. When the lift boy at the Hotel where I was staying discovered that I was English he learnt a sentence which he said to me each day: 'Gut morning; you haf gut sleeping?' The boatmen from whom I hired a boat to row for an hour in the early mornings drank to England when they bade me goodbye. They invited me into their shed, and filled tall glasses with beer, and raised their glasses and said 'England'. I drank to Czechoslovakia and squinted down my lowered eyelids at the amber liquid which seemed hardly to diminish in my glass however valiantly I swallowed. The most startling two words which I heard uttered in broken English were spoken by a baby of three. I had been to a bathing place on the Danube and was sun bathing when a Czech woman with a baby running about naked and brown came to talk to me. She spoke bad English with the unembarrassed energy which reminded me of what someone said of Bernard Shaw speaking French, 'Monsieur Shaw ne parle pas bien, mais il parle avec une telle énergie qu'il s'impose.' She told me that she wanted her little girl to speak English from babyhood and added that the child, whose name was Ruth, already knew a word or two. She called to 'Root' in her own language, evidently inviting her to come and say her English to the lady. 'Root' came and stood, looking indescribably cheeky and gay in the strong yellow sunlight. Her mother spoke to her again in Czech, and the child came nearer to me, stood with legs apart gazing up at me, and said, 'O Kay, Boy!'

The hospitality of the Czech P.E.N. whose guests we were, was so heart-warming and generous that to recall it is like looking back upon a burnished age. It was not merely that we were refreshed with food and wine. The beauty of the city refreshed us, a beauty enhanced by drama and music, and by the quality of its people. Since, in this darkened age, to name names is ever dangerous, I will name only Karel Čapek, whom no venom can reach. How easy, how friendly, how entirely without consciousness of his own great merit he was. I had heard Professor Oliver Elton, who had translated many of Čapek's short stories into English, read his own versions aloud. I admired greatly the poetic quality of Čapek's imagination, a singing, folk quality. And here, in his own city of Prague, he mingled very freely with us. He, like Nevinson, had the modesty which lends a bloom to intellectual and artistic distinction. I have never been able to assign an exact meaning to the apparently simple words, 'Blessed are the poor in spirit for theirs is the Kingdom of Heaven', but I think the Kingdom of Heaven is possessed, was even then possessed, by Čapek. Of the artistic performances offered for our delight many will remember music in the city which nurtured Dvořák; but for myself I remember most vividly a performance of *Romeo and Juliet* in a Czech translation. It was performed at night in the garden of a floodlit palace. The whole length of the palace terrace was the stage, so that the action was rapid, and fluid, and yet given depth; since the preparations for the wedding-feast, and the terrible fear possessing Juliet before she drank the potion, were seen contemporaneously. I have seldom witnessed a scene more touching than when the girl Juliet, deserted by all experienced people—by father, mother and nurse—determined to drink the potion, but imagined the possible horror of awaking too soon in the charnel house. I had always thought that Shakespeare's plays depended in large part on their verbal felicity; the Czechs acted *Romeo and Juliet* in such a way as to prove that this play was a lyrical tragedy of possessing beauty, pitiful above all, even when spoken in words of which I directly understood not one syllable. I followed the sense of the words because I knew the play almost by heart, but for me there was no sensuous appeal in the harsh foreign syllables. I began to think I had written a great deal of nonsense, and talked a great deal of nonsense in school, about the delicate chiming of consonants and the colour of the vowel sounds in the appreciation of poetry and drama. Here, I perceived, the play was the thing.

In Prague the question of the Sudeten Germans was constantly and openly discussed; in Bratislava, to which we went later, the cleavage between the Czechs and Slovaks was felt, but not talked of. The cleavage is audible in the awkward juxtaposition of two names in Czechoslovakia; perhaps the Slovaks resented the lack of a capital letter. Compare such a compound with names like Tuscany or Menadarva. Everywhere in the neighbourhood of Bratislava we were wonderfully fêted, as we were in Prague. But I remember very vividly, after being feasted on roast goose in a village, and being treated to a wonderful display of dancing and peasant dresses, climbing with two fellow members of the P.E.N. a nearby hill. You could not call it a mountain. Yet it led to remoteness, up in the air. At one point, when I was at some distance from my two companions, I saw a girl, with the broad face of the Slavs, standing and gazing over the distant prospect. I tried to greet her in the way we greet our fellows in Cornwall if we meet in lonely places. She looked at me and then, deliberately turning her back, she fixed her eyes anew on the far-stretching land below. I felt cheap. I knew that she had hated the dressed-up show in the village, that she hated us all, and wanted only her own solitude.

In the Tatra Mountains, where some of us spent a few days, I walked—again it was walking rather than climbing—with friends to the top of a peak and looked down on Poland. Then I walked for three days alone in the foothills, putting up at night in the huts of which I had been told. I had no German, only English and French. At one place we did not understand a word of one another's language; yet I managed to procure good wine and food and a feather quilt to sleep under. The scattered country people were wonderfully friendly. They were very poor, but they had air and sunshine; they grew their food, and embroidered their dresses. I thought they were better off than folk with more money in Birmingham. And they did not seem to be possessed with the cursed notion of improving the world out of existence.

The Czechs showed extraordinary gaiety, energy and great good will. The Masaryk tradition was strong; yet the Czechs were not able to reconcile, not even by generosity, their German, Polish and Slovak neighbours, any more than England has been able to reconcile her southern Irish neighbour. In that summer of 1938 there seemed some hope of a settlement with the Sudetens; by the autumn Munich had happened. Many Englishmen then who had spent their lives in seeking to weaken the power of Britain cried out with all their hearts for Britain to wield the power she no longer possessed.

My visit to Czechoslovakia brought home to me, with a force I had never felt before, how very much I had, all my life, taken liberty for granted in my own country. I had been born free, I had lived essentially without fear, wandering alone wherever I chose without a thought of danger, and loudly voicing my opinions without a thought of being penalized for them. In eastern Europe I began really to perceive that liberty was a precarious gift, hard to win, harder still to maintain, easy to lose; for a dark tyranny advances as imperceptibly from minute to minute as night on day. I think the other thing which most remains with me, and which gives me cause always to grieve, is the memory of the eager zest, the intellectual delight, and the joyousness in their art of certain writers from countries in eastern Europe which became self-governing after the Treaty of Versailles—writers from Estonia and Latvia. They were of the first fruits of liberty, and must have perished with the rotting of it.

In England after Munich, in the early months of 1939, as the hope of avoiding war grew fainter, arrangements were made to evacuate all English schools in danger areas should necessity arise. King Edward's girls, we learnt, would go to Cheltenham, and share a school building with Pate's Grammar School; the boys would go to Repton. Miss Barrie, with Miss Jennings, headmistress of Pate's, and members of the two teaching staffs, went fully into questions of billets. Before the end of the summer term 1939 the plans were complete; the girls even had strong paper bags, cement bags or sugar bags, in which they packed such books and stationery as might be immediately required should the signal to move be given during the holidays.

19

EVACUATED TO CHELTENHAM

During August, my father, my sister Susan and I were living at Readymoney Cove, Fowey; and, for part of the time, Joan Holland was our guest at Beach Cottage.

It was Joan who persuaded my father to let her drive him to Gorran and Caerhays. He had not revisited these villages since his retirement. It would be too sad, he had always felt, to go back to a place where so many people he had cared for and who had cared for him were no longer alive. He had come to Gorran within two years of leaving College. He had spent all his working days in Gorran and Caerhays and had brought up his family there. As soon as he retired from teaching he had left Caerhays and had never gone back. Now, through the hot August lanes, Joan drove cautiously. My father was enchanted to see again Mevagissey harbour from Polkirt Hill. We lingered a while outside Gorran School House, but did not enter. The only building we went into was Caerhays Church, which my father, unlike my mother, had cared for more than St Goran. From the churchyard we looked across to St Goran tower; then we drove back to Fowey by Faircross, Hewas Water, Higher Sticker, St Austell and Par. It was one of the days we most enjoyed before the war was upon us. Soon of all the happy folk who had lounged and played in Readymoney Cove only one old lady remained knitting unperturbed, in a deck chair on the beach. Even in times of looming public calamity people's immediate preoccupations and solicitudes are private. Susan and I were concerned to get my father home before train journeys became too difficult; yet we were loath to lose one of the precious weeks for which we had paid to stay at Readymoney. When, from a neighbour's wireless, I heard that all Birmingham teachers were to return to their schools at once, I felt caught. I had delayed too long in coming back to Cornwall to live. I knew that I should have to stay in Birmingham now until the end of the war, not only because it would be right and fair to stay with the children who knew me, but because I knew that I should be afraid of being thought afraid, if I now left the Midlands.

How strange the word evacuation sounded to us then; how horribly familiar it was to become. None of us doubted that the big industrial cities would be attacked from the air at once; we knew King Edward's children could not stay in Birmingham in the inflammable wooden huts. The plans which had been made to move to Cheltenham worked with complete smoothness. Carrying hand luggage and raincoats, and wearing winter uniform, the girls assembled; carrying hand luggage, raincoats, first-aid outfits and water-bottles, each form-mistress paraded with her form. We all wore old clothes except Miss Udall, who cheered us by appearing arrayed in her choicest apparel. She would have answered in the affirmative the query of a dear old friend of mine who, when the evacuation of his house was ordered in the middle of the night, because a time bomb had been dropped in the lane, said to his wife as he sat on the bed in his nightshirt, 'Had I better put on my best boots, Mother?'

Lorries took the cement-bags of books to Cheltenham. We all went by slow train via Evesham. The fact that they were in full winter uniform and wearing stockings on a sweltering hot day bothered the girls more than did the machinations of Hitler and Stalin. At four o'clock we arrived, the guests of Pate's Grammar School. We assembled in the hall of the old building, a building pervaded with the smell of hops. There was a brewery opposite. Someone, addressing the assembled girls from a platform began, 'This—is a great adventure.' Miss Barrie, returning thanks at her briefest, ended with, 'But I think they are all wanting their tea.' I went, with a member of Pate's staff, to see my form into billets, and found the temporary billet provided for myself.

Then the greatest piece of luck befell me. In the business of moving schools which rapidly became like a grand chain, everyone moving somewhere, Cheltenham College was sent to Shrewsbury. Philip Taylor, organist and master of music at Cheltenham, was moved to Shrewsbury with the school, and his wife was left alone in their pleasant house. She telephoned Pate's and said she could put up one of the King Edward's staff. Miss Jaques thought of me. So to Dalhousie in Sydenham Villas Road I was transferred, and my personal happiness in Cheltenham was assured. No one could have failed to be happy with Kitty Taylor. Perhaps musicians have a special grace. She was a 'cellist; she was also a most harmonious human being. The musicians' world is a closely associated one; I discovered that Kitty and Philip who, fortunately, soon returned to Cheltenham, knew my friend Denne; we drove to Stratford to see her, and this excursion seemed a miracle. I had thought when war broke out that I should never see my friends again.

Cheltenham citizens in general, and the headmistress and staff of Pate's Grammar School in particular, were extraordinarily kind to us. Yet many children found it difficult to settle into billets. What seemed on the surface the nicest of homes were sometimes the most unhappy. It is strange how many people, charitable, and even indulgent, to dogs, are intolerant of children. Such people do not even seem to have the kind of dogs children take to. Absence of their own pets was almost as hard for some children as the absence of their parents. I went to see one member of my form in bed one night towards the end of the first month of our stay in Cheltenham. Louise was crying in bed, her friend had privately told me. I found her in a pleasant house with a hostess anxious to be kind. I pointed out these advantages to Louise. 'I know, Miss Treneer, I know. It's a nice billet; I'm not crying, really I'm not crying. But at home we had the dog and cat, and tortie in the garden, and I had a little mouse, but he died.' Tears would come as she spoke of the animals, though she went on protesting she wasn't crying.

Being billeted bore most heavily on the most dutiful and sensitive of the girls. To be always a guest, and always trying to be good, was liable to lead to an outburst of wickedness in the gentlest. The happy-go-lucky were the support of the more imaginative. Imagination bred anxiety; secret fears for the safety of fathers and brothers in the forces, and for mothers and home in the event of bombs falling on Birmingham were the most difficult things to deal with. Many of the children settled down easily and happily, accepting what came, as children will; and the majority of the foster-parents really fostered, with warmth of heart, or from a sense of duty, their unbidden guests.

We were by no means the only school to be billeted in Cheltenham. Other schools, and many expectant mothers, also sought the Spa. No doubt some of the children who arrived there were dirty; but Catherine Mielke was a little startled when, at a meeting she had been invited to attend, a Cheltonian turned to her and said: 'Tell me, are your children verminous?' Catherine replied that they were not, as far as she knew, verminous yet; but that many were beginning to miss in Cheltenham the baths to which they had been accustomed in Birmingham. I felt sorry for Cheltenham, over-run by the varied hordes. As an old lady said to me sadly, as we waited side by side for a bus, 'We do miss our quiet Saturday morning shopping, don't we, with all this influx.' I had to admit that I was influx; but I was sorry to be influx; it has always seemed to me a thousand pities when a place which has acquired an essence of its own through years of slow growth, or even of slow stag- nation, is imperilled by swarms of people indifferent to what they are killing. Cheltenham is a polite place, a conversation piece; a place in which Emily Brontë would have been stifled, and which Jane Austen would, with delicate malice, have enjoyed. It is one of the very few places in which I have found it attractive to shop. Perhaps it is the unwonted combination of trees with shop windows. I liked to saunter down the shady Promenade on those first hot September mornings. Sunshine was almost as fierce, and shade as violent, as in Italy. The trees were stately in their dark late-summer leaves. In the squares the Georgian houses kept their discreet distance. I trembled, when we were all bent on sacrifice—casting down our aluminium saucepans before the Lord—for the delicate tracery of ironwork on the balconies. As a nation, we are not merely careless of beauty; we are almost spiteful towards it. We have destroyed more than our enemies have destroyed.

Part of the charm of Cheltenham is that it is a cultivated town so near the bare Cotswolds; not altogether bare, for the Cotswolds themselves embrace an immense variety of country. Once out of the Cheltenham hollow, and on the heights, and off the roads, I could walk by turfy ways and stony hedges, or drop down into hidden villages. I remember best the swerve of the hills, and the clear brightness of little flowers. When I first began to explore, a few harebells were still in bloom. These flowers, set on their slender wiry stalks, unsappy, unluscious, fragile yet enduring, their colour watchet-blue, have a fairy grace, a form ethereal as music. If I were Ariel I would rather lie in a harebell than a cowslip. On sunny days, where harebells grow, the air has a thin, spare radiance which makes the body light. Usually I had girls with me, and as we walked over the scented, rounded hills, it seemed ironical that it should have taken a war to bring city girls to this benefit. They forgot to be homesick when they were soaked in the sunshine of the hills. Sometimes Kit Taylor and I bicycled to Cranham. I shall never forget Cranham as I saw it in springtime. Herbert's line 'a box where sweets compacted lie', springs to my mind. The grey, yet honey-warm houses and their gardens were at the foot of a rising beechwood where the leaves, sprinkling the layered branches, contrasted with the trunks grey as elephants, and with the bright brown of the scales of winter-buds strewn below. There were lilies of the valley to be found in Cranham Woods at Whitsuntide I was told. But I never found them. I found garlic. If, instead of the woods, we wished for bare uplands, we needed only to walk from Cranham five minutes or so in the opposite direction to be up in the fresher air. Are there water-meadows between Cranham and lovely Painswick? I seem to remember them crowded with cowslips.

A favourite walk with all of us was to Withington, by way of Seven Springs. I once saw air cure a person on the way to Withington. Our chemist, Doris Brown, was very low after a bad attack of influenza in the early spring. A tireless golfer and swimmer when in ordinary health, now she could hardly totter. But she would not postpone the walk. She was out of bed, so she could be out of doors. We set off at a pace suited to the weak. She was vexed with her body; what could be the matter with it that it could not respond to her urging? I kept on saying that there was no need to go all the way to Withington; we could have a little walk; I liked short strolls, I said. And then, when we had got out of the suburbs, and had rested at Seven Springs and were going by naked ways and clumps, the air quickened, and she began to pick up. By the time we had found some snowdrops beyond a water-splash, and then an orchard full of snowdrops, her own rhythm was beginning to take possession of her. Before we reached Withington she was moving in her customary effortless way. Tea and hot buttered toast completed the cure. We came back laughing and talking and swinging along as though she had never been ill.

Perhaps it was the bitter cold of that winter which made us all liable to illness, and made us irascible too. Every man is a rascal when he is sick, according to Dr Johnson; and certainly if I have as much as an aching finger the devil enters into me. We had a spell of biting weather. I have never seen other ice like that ice, or felt colder than in that piercing air. Yet this cold spell must have been in spring, for I remember clear ice encasing winter buds, so that they were like ships in bottles. Smooth ice sheeted the ivy leaves; splinters of ice barbed the brambles; I heard a birch tree, its slender buds hung with icy drops, tinkle as the wind shook it. In the wood, huge trees were split by the frost and crashed. I struggled out to a wood where the icicles took fantastic shapes, and where walking on the paths was like walking on crunchy glass. Every form was sharpened; death glittered all around us.

We felt the cold in Pate's Grammar School. Soon after our arrival in Cheltenham it had been decided to move both King Edward's and Pate's to the new unfinished building on the hill not far from Prestbury. I was glad; I hated the smell of beer that clung about old Pate's. New Pate's was a splendid building. From its great staircase window it seemed as though you could take survey of all the world. I thought the whole school delightfully planned. I remember how much I liked the quadrangle, and the open corridors. I continued to like them even when the wintry gusts whirled our skirts around our heads as we went out of one form-room into another. Open-air schools are not really suited to our climate in winter, but as we used the building from 2 o'clock to 6.30 we noticed the cold more than people occupying the place during normal school hours. Cheltenham children worked from 9 o'clock till 2, and Birmingham children worked from 2 o'clock till 6.30, during the year we shared the school. As the hall was still unfurnished, Miss Barrie read prayers at night in the open quadrangle; this meeting together under the sky took away all perfunctoriness from school prayers and made them intentional. We are different when not roofed in. Old girls, with whom I have talked of our stay in Cheltenham, always remember prayers in the quadrangle, Miss Barrie's good night, and their own 'Good night, Miss Barrie.'

When, in imagination, I return to Cheltenham I see especially in my mind's eye Ailsa Jaques, who was in charge of the billeting from our side, and her friend, Grace Denley, known to us affectionately as Daisy. Daisy worked for love. She became an honorary member of the common-room; and she not only eased our legs by driving us hither and thither when, without her, we must have trudged, but she eased many a tension by making the parties laugh.

I know, from stories told me by some of my friends evacuated in hard circumstances, how intolerable was the strain placed on many teachers. For ourselves, we suffered no great hardship; and yet, at the end of the year, when we were told that King Edward's permanent buildings were sufficiently advanced for our return, there was general satisfaction. I was one of the very few who would have preferred to remain in Cheltenham.

20

WE ENTER THE NEW BUILDING

When we got back to Birmingham, Cecil Waterfield, who, by this time, was the lucky possessor of a little house in Selly Oak, invited me to live with her during the school week. I could no longer live at Bearley: I had had to give up my cottage; even if it had been vacant I could not have risked the delays likely to be caused in those days by a train journey plus a tram ride through Birmingham. Cecil's house was not very far from Edgbaston Park Road where the new permanent buildings of King Edward's School had been built.

We found that Mr Hobbis had provided us with a building rather roofy-looking to the eye from without, but uncommonly well adapted to the purposes of teaching from within. All the form-rooms were sunny; they had great windows which could be pushed out so that we could be as airy as we chose; but the form-room doors opened on to closed corridors, not on to open corridors as at Pate's Grammar School. There was no need to be cold. The quadrangles, which have now become charming gardens, gave the school, even then, a great sense of spaciousness and light. I was very sorry the library was on the north side, and tended to be cold; I have never liked to read in it quite as much as I liked to read in the New Street library.

The roof is too heavy; and, although the high lights admit some afternoon sunshine, and although the main windows are well-placed and elegant, the room lacks goldenness. On the other hand we had a stage incomparably better than the New Street stage in a hall of quiet beauty. Its proportions, its floor, its oak panelling, its tall door-windows which can stand open in summer so that the sunlight falls in patterns, all help to make a hall in which to assemble is pleasant. Many a child must, I think, have derived unconsciously a notion of harmony from the hall.

The two staff common-rooms, one for working in, and one a very attractive sitting-room, pleased us greatly. Our only aversion was a Latin tag which Mr Hobbis had had carved on our otherwise dignified oak chimney-piece. We tackled him on the subject of this text as soon as he paid us a visit. We said it was worse than GOD IS LOVE or HOME SWEET HOME. He was astonished at us. He said he had meant to please us with his sound Latin motto. When we said he hadn't pleased us at all, that we couldn't bear it, he smiled. He temporized. He said he would have it planed off. Our pleasure was his. But DOCENDO DISCIMUS! What could be better? What indeed? Its truth is irrefutable. I should never have learned half I know if I had not had to teach. But we did not want to be reminded of a truism every time we drank our tea. It irritated us; it became a focus for wrath. And then, as time went on, we forgot all about it. As telegraph posts become invisible so, unless some visitor remarked on it, did Mr Hobbis's little joke cease to operate on our spirits. I always think he laughed to himself as those letters were being carved.

Human beings are fatally adaptable. Given time to habituate themselves the eye ceases to see, the ear to hear, the tongue to taste, the nose to be nauseated. We can breathe ourselves to death in tainted air without, it seems, a pang of protest. For me, my eye accustoms itself more readily than my ear. I hate noise; and now noise was my portion. King Edward's was completed about our naked ears. Bangings, sawings, gratings, whingings, whangings, scrapings, screechings—we endured them all. But how we wished that we could, at least, have left the boys behind in New Street:

> Two paradises 't were in one
> To live in paradise alone.

It was not that I failed to admire the O.T.C. Far from it. I never saw its members without a sense of shamed compunction. I felt that if I'd been a young man I might have shirked the O.T.C., and what would have become of us if we had been a nation of shirkers? No: I admired the O.T.C. with all my heart. When, after the war, General Slim came to inspect it, I cheered madly. But the band of the O.T.C.! Nothing has ever made me lose my temper like the band of the O.T.C. That *Ta-ta-ta-tat; ta-ta-ta-tat!* That *Bang, wang, wang!* I understand murder because of the band of the O.T.C.

The bombardment, first of Coventry then, night after night, of Birmingham from the air, began not so very long after our return from Cheltenham. That was one of the chances of war. No amount of foresight or planning on the part of those in charge of evacuation could have prevented that. Further plans had been made for those girls who wished to be taken to Kidderminster. Not very many chose to avail themselves of the offer; but a small number did wish to go, and there had to be mistresses to go with them. In staff-meeting Miss Barrie asked those of us who did not desire this lot to state any urgent reason why we should not go. In an impulsive moment, thinking that I did not want to go still further away from Cornwall, I said I did not wish to go any further north. There was laughter in court. It took me a long time to live down that little utterance. Dear Joyce Martin, our geographer, met me outside the staff room with an atlas.

It is impossible for a civilian, and a woman civilian at that, to describe war impersonally and objectively. I think a woman is chiefly obsessed with the incredible folly of it. I cannot even set down with any exactness what I personally felt during air raids over Birmingham. I remember, on the first night, from the comparative safety of Selly Oak, peering through the blackout curtains of my bedroom window, and viewing as a spectacle the flashes and flares and flake of fire when so much of the business centre of the city was destroyed. Flame and crash, darkness and fury. I remember my shame when, for the first time, my knees seemed to turn to water at the approach of danger; I remember discovering that it was literally true that the scalp crept and the roots of the hair moved, and I remember my relief when custom made knees and scalp more reliable. Cecil Waterfield was as valiant as a lion; I only once saw her a little rattled, and that was when she once made a dash for home on her bicycle after completing her period of fire-watching, and heard death pinging on her tin hat. We had a shelter which, for some reason, reminded me of a little Wesleyan chapel, in our back garden. But when it was not my turn to fire-watch I liked to withdraw into the recesses of my person, and stay warm in bed during a night raid. I am comparatively courageous when warm, and a coward when cold. I felt that I would rather be blown to pieces in a warm bed than escape in a cold Morrison. The most ignominious thing which happened to me was when we were lingering by the fireside after the siren had gone. We just could not make up our minds to move. Our arm-chairs held us snugly; the fire blazed; the divan piled with the various books on which we had been working, stretched between. The blue curtains with border of many colours, which Cecil had woven, hid the ugly black-out, so that we were in a little hollow of genial glow and quietness amid the forest of black bangs. Then, in place of dull opaque thuds, there came a crack that shook our boundaries. I tried to dive under the settee, but it was one of those upholstered to the floor. I could not even stick my head in. I just crouched and cowered under the arm.

Fire-watching in the school building meant going in, in winter time, at nine o'clock one morning, and not coming out until four o'clock or so next day. A terribly long spread of time this seemed to me, but fire-watching night meant having a good dinner. This was due to Mrs Thorne, wife of Mr Thorne the caretaker. They lived, with their dog, in the lodge at the entrance to the Girls' School. Mrs Thorne proved that even in war-time, and on Birmingham fish, a generous disposition could work wonders. It was not only that she was a capable shopper and a good cook, but she never once gave us the impression that we were anything but welcome to her dining-room, to its heartening fire, to her skill, and to her bounty. 'A merry heart goes all the way'—that saying was exemplified in Mrs Thorne. Every night she was there, always her cheerful self, bringing in something which smelt uncommonly good. The men fire-watchers from the Boys' School shared this meal with the women on duty in the Girls' School. I must admit that I was glad we had not left the Boys' School behind in New Street when it came to fire-watching. Custom soon made me comparatively unafraid; but being both clumsy and, although I listened and tried to do as I was told, stupid, in face of the fires of Tophet, I let my imagination dwell with comfort when the siren went in the dark vast and middle of the night, on the thought that there were men about.

The school felt eerie at night. Two of the Girls' School staff in rotation were on duty together. I shared duty with Cecil Waterfield. It already seems strange to look back at the blackout, our torches, our tin-hats and our gas-masks. In spite of all our elaborate precautions, it happened that Thorne was pretty nearly alone in the building when incendiary bombs fell and burnt out the music room. He went round putting the fires out. Once, we arrived at school to find Miss Barrie and Miss Jaques at the gate warning us not to come in. We were to have a holiday while a time bomb was being removed from the precincts. The school had another lucky escape of which we were at that time unaware. Several years afterwards an unexploded bomb was discovered in the grounds; it was removed and detonated. What courage it must have taken to deal with live bombs in cold blood! Yet squads took this duty for granted.

At the time when explosive incendiaries were first being dropped I was having breakfast at Mrs Thorne's with one of the masters from the Boys' School. He had been to a film a couple of nights before, a film explaining how best to deal with these bombs. As I did not want to have to go to the film, I inquired about the treatment, and the master obligingly told me about the suggested procedure, illustrating his lecture by moving the tea-pot, the sugar-basin, and the milk-jug as occasion demanded: 'This tea-pot is the bomb; this sugar-basin is you. Now, don't rush out and play water on the thing. You see this milk-jug? That's the wall. Well, the basin will retire behind the wall thus, until . . .' A week or so later, going on a short railway journey with Edna Hobbes, I wiled away some time in a carriage too dimly lit for reading, by telling her, in a low voice as I thought, the story of this little lecture, imitating the master to the best of my ability, so as to try to make her laugh. She was anxious about her parents and her home in Bristol at that time. When I had finished, a sergeant who, we thought, was asleep in the other corner of the carriage, opened his eyes, sat up, and said 'Moi advice to you, Miss, if you have to deal with any one of them bombs, is not to worry about no tea-pot nor no milk-jug. Just retoire, and stay retoired.' 'Retoire, and stay retoired', became a catch word with us until a fresh saying ousted it.

It was amazing how gay and unperturbed the children remained unless they had actually witnessed carnage in their home or street. Children are secretive; but I should say that, as long as grown up courage safely bridged them, they went their playful way. I remember one morning, when we had been in the shelters for an unusually long time, I was thinking to myself how bad this must be for the girls. My reverie was broken by the 'all clear'; a couple of merry faces were turned to me and a lively voice said, 'Oh, Miss Treneer, isn't it lovely? We've missed maths and French; and I hoped we were going to miss English, too didn't you?' We tried to get some work done in the shelters; books were taken down. But in junior forms great ingenuity in paper games was displayed.

When one was out of doors the sound of a siren made for sociability. I was bicycling home at about four o'clock one

November evening, along the wide road which goes by the Queen Elizabeth Hospital, when I was forced to dismount and take shelter under the wall of a building near the road on my left. Almost immediately a door opened, a woman looked out, and a voice said, 'Coome in, Luvie, coome in out of it.' I found, when I had accepted the invitation with alacrity, that the building was the hospital laundry. I shared the shelter, I shared a cup of tea, and when the 'all clear' sounded I was shown over the laundry and admired its machinery and equipment. That 'Coome in, luvie,' was typical of the opposite to war. Friendly and fiendly were a couple of Old English antonymns. Any little evening festivity, any hospitality, when the hostess had procured some delicacy once common but now rich and rare, was enjoyed with a zest heightened by a journey through the black-out. I always associate Alex Makin, classical scholar, and vice-president of the Musical Society, with such parties. I remember once going to her house through the snow when the wail of sirens sounded like wolves howling. Then came the slipping through the black-out into Alex's welcoming house. Of all the parties I went to in Birmingham, Alex's carol parties are most vividly present to me. This was an occasion when she invited all her friends, and we really sang. The parties were not solemn; they were joyous. Each of us had to bear a part; we had to be like Pepys when confronted with a piece of music, and we felt a seventeenth-century satisfaction when our voices chimed. More than any other single phrase 'Green grows the holly' brings back to me the heart-warming side of being a member of King Edward's staff. We learnt that carol at one of Alex's parties, and I have never sung it elsewhere.

In school and out of school I think what struck me most in Birmingham during the war years was the steadfastness of other people's endurance. I was humbled by it. I find it easy to do well in short spurts. But Birmingham was saved from chaos by those who went on doing more than their duty for years. After a bad night, what a reassuring quality was given to morning by the appearance of the milk bottle on the door-step! It would have been so easy for the distributors to have given up the attempt some mornings. But no. Milk was brought. The water system was repaired. Gas and electric light came on again. The trams and buses were kept running. Girl conductors punched tickets as though nothing had happened. And in school the bell went for prayers; we sang, we proceeded with the daily time-table, that time-table which I had so often cursed, but which had now become, if not a blessing, an anodyne.

21

ON THE
MALVERN HILLS
(I)

I was lucky during the war to be out of Birmingham for many week-ends. On the first Friday evening after our return from Cheltenham I set out by bus, with a knapsack, determined to find a pleasant refuge beyond Worcester in which to spend my Saturdays and Sundays. I was sitting in the front seat of a double-decker, and surveying the landscape, when a voice said, 'Is it draughty there in front?' I said it wasn't; and there came and sat beside me a lady who was to make all the difference to my life during the war years and, indeed, during the rest of my stay in Birmingham.

She was elegant, slender, with a white face, dark eyes and hair, and a forehead whose bony structure reminded me of a high ecclesiastic. She might have stepped out of a Florentine picture. She noticed my knapsack. I should get out of the bus, I explained, as soon as we came to a place which attracted me. She asked where I was going to sleep. I said I didn't know.

'Quite mad,' she said, 'quite mad. You won't find anywhere to sleep. The whole district is swarming with soldiers and evacuees.' I said I thought in the Malvern area . . .

'Worst place possible,' she said. 'Bob-tail and rag-tag from all over England at Malvern.'

We exchanged a few desultory remarks as our journey proceeded, and then she said abruptly,

'Better come home with me for the night. Quite mad to think of finding a bed. We shall get out a stage beyond Great Malvern.'

When we reached this stage her clear voice went ringing down the bus.

'Darling, we have a kind of evacuee for the week-end.'

I was startled. I had thought she was alone.

'Yes, Audrey; yes, dear, of course,' a voice replied.

Audrey's escort, like Audrey herself, had a personal distinction becoming rare in these days. He stood with head a little thrown back. He had a habit of speaking each word as though he cared for its excellent rightness; and yet he was always a little absent and unready, as though his real presence were elsewhere. We got out of the bus, and walked down a very steep narrow lane almost in silence, except that Audrey told me that she and her husband had rented, furnished, No. 13 the Lees. They had rented it from one of the masters of Malvern College, Malvern having, with the 'All Change' watch-word which governed all schools during the war, been sent to share quarters with Harrow.

We were met at the door of No. 13 by 'Holly', who gave me a more shrewd scrutiny than my host and hostess had bestowed. We had arranged that I should leave my knapsack, go out to supper in Malvern, and come back for the night. Audrey explained that she herself always took breakfast in bed, but that I could breakfast with Sebastian. My room would be ready by the time I came in.

It was not until breakfast time that I learnt Sebastian's surname; and then I discovered it by looking at the mark on my table napkin. It was *Meynell*. I asked if he were related to Alice Meynell. He was her eldest son. I had remembered that there was a Viola, for I had greatly admired one of Viola Meynell's short stories, as well as her biography of her mother. Now I also recalled Sebastian. Alice Meynell's poetry, and her essays, had been one of my pleasures; I admired Coventry Patmore's

Odes tremendously; when I was young, George Meredith's poetry had been part of my life. It felt very strange to me to be at breakfast with one who had grown up among the old and the young poets. There is hardly a greater pleasure than suddenly to be talking with a stranger whose literary affections are akin to one's own; to me it is almost as good as meeting, in a distant place, someone who has been brought up in Gorran village, someone who remembers the pennyworts by the stile in Crooked Lane, and the sea-gulls, all looking into the wind, on the chimney-tops in Mevagissey.

After breakfast I set out for a day on the hills. Holly had cut me some sandwiches; I had been invited to supper with my new friends, Mr and Mrs Sebastian Meynell as I had now discovered them to be. That invitation to supper seemed to me particularly alluring when, on my way back, just before I reached the Wyche, it began to rain, a soft busy rain, a rain nourishing to plants, but damping to the spirits of man. It grew darker. I did not mind the dark, for I was going down the cutting and over the common to friends and a fire and supper. I associate Audrey and Sebastian especially with a glowing fire, a curtained room, books and something delicate to eat, an omelette, a little wine. I, who do not commonly note such things, remember also Audrey's clothes. Everything about her was vivid—her intellect, her affections, her anger, her clothes. Often she wore black with white, or something brilliantly coloured. She hated half tones, the thick, the clumsy, the blurred, the art-and-crafty, half-baked notions, all that was slurred or slick, coarse food, every kind of gross exaggeration or stupidity. Her wit was pictorial. I remember when she was accused of breaking the black-out regulations, she went to court; it was a question of the staircase window. Audrey detested this window, with its fifteen or so fussy divisions, and its suburban edging of coloured panes. Black-out curtains had been fitted; but we were accused of having turned on the light in the hall, just after black-out time, and before these curtains had been drawn. 'Light blazed', Audrey was told, 'from fifteen stained-glass windows.' 'Do you think I live in a cathedral?' was her reply. The curl of her voice on the final syllable of cathedral as she related to me this story is my chief reminder of the fury which swept us all when we were arraigned for any infringement of the black-out regulations. I suppose it was a psychological necessity that we should talk almost humorously of the tragedy of the blitz, and give our anger vent over some little thing, some minor interference with our immemorial right to put up what curtains we liked and draw them when we chose.

But this tale of the black-out came, of course, much later. What I remember especially of the first night is the blessedness of communion. Enisled as we are in ourselves, our means of signalling to each other so imperfect, it is a deep satisfaction to meet fresh people who understand what you mean, and who take it for granted that you will understand what they mean. All explanation is tedious; all directness enlivening. I love ease of intercourse. If I had met Audrey and Sebastian only for that one night, I should have remembered the night as an oasis in the wilderness of war; but I was to know them for many nights.

For on Sunday morning, before I set off again for the hills, Audrey proposed a plan. She took me up to the top of the house and showed me a large attic room, with a french window opening on to a balcony railed round with little palings. The attic had been a nursery, and the palings had been put up to keep small children from falling into the garden below. Beyond the trees of the garden, and of the green enclosure round which the houses of the Lees were set, the eye travelled wide and free over the plain to Bredon; it was a spacious prospect. To my astonishment Audrey said I might have this room for a nominal rent, and come to it whenever I chose. I could use the bath-room, I could transform the landing into a little wash-up place, I could make arrangements for a little simple cooking, and live as free as air. The generosity was as boundless as the view. It has always seemed a miracle to me that one whose life was a constant struggle with severe pain, and that in the organs of a sense so precious as eyesight, should have had the impulse to make a perfect gift to another who had had little acquaintance with pain of any kind, and who cared only to be out on the hills. But so it was. I had sufficient grace to be grateful and to recognize, with humility, a nature richer than my own. Audrey discussed the furniture as though the room were to be for her own delectation. I need get nothing. She had some of her own furniture in store at Malvern—pretty rugs, a table, chairs, a bed, a coverlet—all were to be mine to use. I might bring my books. I went back to Birmingham on Monday morning, rising in the dark at six o'clock, and creeping downstairs with my shoes in my hand. I caught, near Bell Vue Terrace, the red double-decker bus which carried me to the Gun Barrels, a three minutes' walk from King Edward's School.

During the week, the Malvern story seemed more like a fairy tale than an actual happening; I wondered whether, by the time I went again, Audrey, Sebastian, Holly and all the houses of the Lees would have vanished together. But no; there they all were when the next week-end came. The room was furnished and arranged, and it became my favourite among the many rooms I have lived in. It was high and lifted up, yet I could walk out of it into the air; it was a room with a view; it was a private room, but not too private. Audrey and Sebastian were in the house and the pleasure of their company often crowned the pleasure of my days on the hills.

Malvern is essentially walking country. I came to know it as you can only know country your feet have trodden in successive seasons of successive years. In trying to describe this neighbourhood of the wavy hills I am like Yeats' father, the painter J.B. Yeats, who could never let a picture of a place alone. He visited the scene again and again as the year advanced, adding touch upon touch, until December's snow filled his June roses. But although I should try through all the months of the year, I could not convey the beneficence of the Malverns. I cannot convey the sparkle in the air, nor the taste of the water quenching my thirst, nor the pleasure to my eye of the shadows moving over the plain; nor tell how sounds came from vast distances to my ear in the quiet of nightfall. I have been on the hills of a still evening when I have fancied a dog's bark might come from the Clee Hills, or the lowing of a cow from the region of Far Forest.

The bodily senses are more acute on the hills than in the plain; but especially on the Malverns, because the range is long and thin. From North Hill to Chase End is a distance of eight or nine miles; but at no point is the range wider than a mile across. I like to think of the extent of the chain; to say over the names of successive heights, and see, as I name them, their rise and roll. Not all the peaks seem to have names; there are twenty or so greater and lesser peaks, but the only names of heights that I know are: North Hill, the Sugar Loaf, Worcestershire Beacon, Herefordshire Beacon, Tinkers Hill, Hangman's Hill, Swinyard Hill, Midsummer Hill, Hollybush Hill, the Raggedstone and Chase End.

The three counties, Worcestershire, Herefordshire and Gloucestershire, meet in the valley of the White-leaved Oak.

For the pedestrian it is a great piece of luck that the Malvern chain runs south. To walk from the Worcestershire Beacon to Chase End when a soft air is flowing is the most exquisite of pleasures. The wind slips gently round the body, lending it wings. One moves with the air and for the sun. It is rare to walk so long a distance, shored by the air on both sides, with so little attention diverted to one's feet. In this region the feet place themselves except in the steep stony places, or on the wooded slopes, where they need some direction. For much of the way the turf is short and springy. The Malverns, surely, are Shakespeare's 'turfy mountains where live nibbling sheep'; his 'flat fields thatched with stover' are in the Severn Plain. I like to think that he saw himself standing on the Malverns when he wrote:

> Full many a glorious morning have I seen
> Flatter the mountain tops with sovereign eye,
> Kissing with golden face the meadows green,
> Gilding pale streams with heavenly alchemy;

I have seen the sun gild the pale streams, and have seemed to catch the very accent of some of Shakespeare's people in Herefordshire, on the confines of Wales.

North Hill and the Worcestershire Beacon look worn and shabby as you survey them from their peopled base; they are worn and shabby, cut with paths and roads, and deeply quarried. We care so little for what serves to make our spirits mount that we are quite ready to blast the hills, bottle the waters, and make the holy wells hideous with brick and marble. But it is useless to repine among the houses. The remedy is to get to the top of the nearest height the quickest way. From the top of North Hill you have the best view of the little subsidiary heights which lie on the further side of West Malvern; but from whatever point I view these little hills I am absorbed and satisfied by them. They have not great heights, but they have line and movement. In the day time they seem to sweep forward; towards sunset they appear to reel away from the gathering dark towards the new light which will come with morning.

Next to North Hill by way of the Sugar Loaf is the highest peak of the range, the Worcestershire Beacon, with its topo-scope on the summit. I liked to look at the toposcope, a map engraved on a bronze plate set flat on the top of a little pillar. It is a means by which to locate oneself in space. It depends on the weather, of course, how far the eye can range—a radius of sixty-six miles at the finest, and with the best eyes, it is said; a radius of sixty-six miles and over fifteen counties, some aver. I cannot say that I have ever been able to spy with my little eye all that the indicator indicates; but it is splendid to think that one might. The toposcope is a rendezvous. Sometimes I used to stand near it in pretended abstraction to listen to people saying what they could see. I have heard people beholding the three cathedrals—Worcester, Hereford and Gloucester—at every point of the compass; pride lends us all long sight. 'There's Tewkesbury Abbey, look! There's Clee; there's the Lickey Hills; fifteen counties, fifteen counties and bits of two or three more; eighteen counties, and there's Birmingham smoke, look! Eh! That's Birmingham smoke.'

Often, when I let my fancy roam, I walk again, in imagin-ation, from the Worcestershire Beacon, and its Indicator, to

Chase End. First I run down the slopes of the Beacon to the Wyche. An immediate and rewarding section of the hills lies between the Wyche and the British Camp. Even if I walk the Pyx path, just above the Jubilee Drive, it is good; but that allows the eye to wander only over the fields and orchards of Herefordshire on my right. The thing to do is to walk the crests. Roughly I keep to the Red Earl's Dyke; then what a prospect to view on either hand! With a turn of the head I may see the Severn Plain to the Cotswolds, and Herefordshire to Wales. On the crests I have a God-like eye; I look about and think I have done very well in making the world. Then I go from the pointed heights down to the round foothills, I cross the road at Wynd's Point, and so along the flank of the Herefordshire Beacon between the lake water of the reservoir and the British Camp. At the saddle there is a whole new revelation, and I feel a quickening glee. Down by way of Clitters Cave I go, up the processional wide grassy slope to the head of the Gullett, and from there I scramble down by the quarry borders into the green depths. Then I climb up Midsummer Hill, hop over the Holly Bush with its twin peaks, and crawl with the penitential monk up the Raggedstone, peak of ill omen.

And so I come at last to where the hills die away into valley which leads to the last gentle hill of Chase End. The country about Chase End reminds me of that rich third of his Kingdom which Lear originally bestowed upon his daughter Goneril:

> Of all these bounds, even from this line to this,
> With shadowy forests and with champains rich'd,
> With plenteous rivers and wide-skirted meads
> We make thee lady.

The peculiar glory of walking the Malverns is a sensation as of riding the hills; although actually I was a-foot, I used often to feel as though I were riding, not a horse, but the hills themselves. All the lowlands seemed fluid, and over them the hills seemed to move, carrying me on their backs. I have mounted them in every kind of weather, in every season of the year. I have ridden them morning, evening, noon and night, never without excitement. There is perpetual change. Although the chain runs south, some peaks tip back, some stand still, some have long slopes forward, some plunge sheer down. To the west the flanks may fall in a series of gentle declivities, while to the east the fall may be abrupt. I tried to convey the sensation of being astride the hills and of being carried forward by them in the following lines:

> My horses stand, their shoulders high
> Thrusting to their great thoroughfare;
> Green scent of bracken in my nose,
> And the wild wind lifting my hair,
> I mount my beasts, until astride
> I stand, and with no slackening rein
> Horsed between earth and air, I ride
> The swift-winged shadows of the plain,
> And the slow portents of the sky.

22

ON THE
MALVERN HILLS
(II)

I did not often walk the whole length of the hills; usually I chose some nearby haunt in which to linger. Even in winter, when the sun was out, a warm covert or a slope especially favoured could be found. One such favoured spot was to the right of Clitters Cave, above Walms Well. I remember in particular an early February day when the sun fairly rippled over me, as I sat on the slope, with my back comfortably ensconced in a curly tree-trunk, and ate my sandwiches. It was the day I found the first primroses for that year.

I knew the daisies were out, but I did not expect to find primroses, though I had seen some in the garden at the Lees. Except that the wing petals of the furze were the clear lemon colour of shells, I had seen little colour on the hills, which rose, dun or tawny, against the green fields of the plain, and their darker hedgerows. When I had finished my lunch, I went down the slope to the black five-barred gate at the foot. I saw old man's beard, grey and hoary, reminding me of Miss Haversham's wedding cake in *Great Expectations*; old man's beard has that dusty look, as though no tender green will ever again rejoice the eye. I think it was its frosty air which made me think winter would last for ever. Then I climbed over the gate, and went up the sunken path almost like a river bed, filled nearly to the brim with crisp, veined, dead leaves, sweet chestnut leaves. I was walking up the path, shuffling the leaves with my feet, when I saw among the moss in the steep bank the crinkled primrose leaves and, among the leaves, in the secretest, warmest place, at the heart of the plant, the delicate stalks and folded buds of new primroses.

Very early in the year dog's mercury covers the slopes of the wood; then, while the bluebell leaves are only thrusting their way up through the cover, the wild daffodils bloom. I used to watch the slender buds hooded with green, then see the pale greenish gold showing, and then, as the buds bent their heads to protect the fragile cups, the flowers were out. 'Trumpet' is hardly the right word to use of the lent-lily's cup; garden daffodils have trumpets. Wild lent-lilies are near the earth. They grew plentifully in the wood by Walms Well; they grew also in the woods through which the Ridgeway runs to Eastnor; and beyond Ledbury, in Masefield's country—Masefield was born at Ledbury—they grew at Dymock.

For snowdrops, I think some of the loveliest I ever saw were growing at Hope End. I set out for Hope End one Sunday morning. Audrey and I had been reading *Aurora Leigh*, and I had a desire to see the place where Elizabeth Barrett Browning had spent some years of her childhood, and in which she had set the early scenes of her long novel in verse. She had made her heroine lament the tameness of this park-like country with its folded hills, after the multitudinous mountains of Italy; yet some of the best descriptions of this same countryside are in *Aurora Leigh*. I walked to the Wyche and along the Pix Path to The Kettle Sings; then I dropped down through the wood to Colwall Green and took the Ledbury Road. I went along the road till I came to a kissing gate on the right which led by pathway fields to a dingle and, by a little lane, to a lodge with locked gates. Through these gates I could not pass. Instead I went up a path by the wood into a field and so, by way of a rookery, up to Wellington Heath. I reached a cottage overlooking the wide sweep of Frith Wood, and was directed to the upper lodge of Hope End. If I called at the House, I was told, Mrs Hewitt would certainly direct me to the ruin, or take me herself. No; it wouldn't be considered an intrusion.

I went up the drive. The trees were dramatic; and at one point snowdrops flowered in sheets as snowdrops should flower. I approached what seemed itself a ruin; for the existing house had been partially destroyed by fire in 1910, and the owners were living in the unburnt wing. I asked for permission to see the stables of what had once been Moulton Barrett's house and was guided by Mrs Hewitt herself. We went back part of the way I had come, past the great pointed cypresses, the monkey puzzles, and the clump of sweet chestnuts, to the old drive. This led to the low-lying site of the original house at Hope End. Moulton Barrett's house must certainly have been sheltered; but shut in, cold and dank. Frost lingers in that hollow where now only a massive gateway, the stables, and other outbuildings remain of the house which Elizabeth Barrett knew. In the stables are the racks and the mangers, and two strong splendid wagons. The stables, in warm red brick, were in use almost to the present day; but the stones of the old house were used to build the present one in its airy gay position; Italian cupolas remain, indications of the taste of Mr Barrett. I went past huge American redwood trees. My guide told me that her father-in-law had planted most of these trees about 1870. They grow rapidly to perfection; but when the roots touch the rock they die. I suppose they starve to death. There lay, not far from the old house, the mighty skeleton of a tulip tree. Before she left me, Mrs Hewitt gave me permission to explore the woods and grounds at my pleasure and when I chose. I might also pick some snowdrops; I picked a bunch, some double and some single, and then I dived under the branches of trees, or hopped over dead trunks, so as to follow the old moss-grown drive to the lower lodge, and the lane to old Colwall. From one point at Hope End I caught a most fluid and rhythmic view of the Malverns. They ran in a huge semi-circle, in swerves and points and counter-points against the sky.

Clouds were coming up, and the hills were arrayed in sumptuous purple.

On my way home I made a détour so as to call in at Colwall Church before the evening service. I like to go to Colwall Church and read on the spot the booklet *Colwall Church*, by Allan H. Bright. He helps me to see something beyond the half-open wooden porch, and the Victorianly comfortable interior. On this particular day I had a fancy to look again at the encaustic tile of which Oliver Baker had told me, a tile on which was represented the month of March. It shows a man digging with vigour, and seeming at the same time to turn his head as though to shout at somebody. The church dates from the twelfth century or even earlier, but the chancel was entirely rebuilt in the mid-nineteenth century. I can always absorb myself in the history of this church. Allan Bright, in his limited space, takes me back, as no general history book does, to the days when Colwall Church was the church of the manor of Colwall, one of the manors appertaining to the see of Hereford. In medieval days the bishop of Hereford used to travel round his see, putting up at each of his manors in turn. He came with a great retinue, and lived until the store of good things was exhausted. Then he moved on. A splendid way of life this seems to me, the kind of life I should like to live if I were a bishop.

When, as occasionally happened, I spent a week-end at Eastnor at the Somers Arms, I used to find my mind slipping back to the days when the whole region was forest. There are a thousand ways to Eastnor. Sometimes I walked along the Ledbury road from the British Camp and, turning left at the lodge, walked along the Ridgeway dark with yews, and through the golden gates to the Park; or I walked up the pass from Hollybush; or I went through the woods by Deddyman's Thorn from Ledbury; or from Wynd's Point I walked to Obelisk Hill and dropped down through the Park. These are the four main themes; one can dance them with as many variations as feet can find.

All months of the year are good for Eastnor and the pleasant town of Ledbury. I have come walking up the Hollybush pass

by Bronsil Castle in November, and seen a stag standing
watching, his antlers branched formally against the sky; and I
have seen the herd moving off towards cover when, in the dim
light, all the brake seemed endowed with life. No other
creatures move as slimly as deer. They hardly appear to
displace the air. Perhaps they have been hunted through the
long centuries until they are familiar with all the intricate
corridors of space and so they never break, but slip through.
They are eloquently suggestive of the past, when the five wild
beasts of venery—the hart, the hind, the hare, the boar, the
wolf—lived in Malvern Forest.

I liked to spend an occasional week-end at the Somers Arms.
It is an inviting example of an inn, though it has no bar; a
former lady of Eastnor Castle put down the bar, I have heard
say. I associate the Somers Arms with crimson and scarlet; it
never looks better than when the scarlet geraniums are out, or
when the walls are covered with reddening virginia creeper.
Eastnor itself is at its best in June when the glorious lime
avenue to the church is in flower, or a little earlier when the
scent of lilac is in the air.

My favourite book about the Eastnor neighbourhood had its
abode at the Somers Arms, and was always lent me by my
hostesses, the Misses James, to read in bed. The title was
Eastnor and its Malvern Hills, written by Henry L. Somers-
Cocks, and published in 1923. In this book, so firmly localized,
I read not only of the early history of the hills, but also of the
later masters of Eastnor, the Somers-Cocks family, by whom
the existing castle (modern baronial) was built in the early
nineteenth century. The valour of the Somers and the Cocks in
the eighteenth, nineteenth and twentieth centuries is
commemorated by the obelisk, on Obelisk Hill, and by the
lovely gift of Midsummer Hill to all who care to go and stand
on it. My favourite Somers-Cocks is James, Ensign of the
Guards, the date and occasion of whose death is inscribed on
the south side of the obelisk. The relations between this
youthful James and his guardian Charles Cocks, who was also
his heir, would be matter for a novelist. It is clear from the

correspondence quoted in *Eastnor and its Malvern Hills* that Charles Cocks strongly opposed the enlistment of James, and yet, after James had been killed, Charles was bitterly blamed for allowing him to join the army. But how could he have refused his hard consent after receiving such a passionate plea as the following, in which the accents of a living voice are heard as in few historical novels and documents? It is the climax of a series of appeals and reads as follows:

From Jas Cocks to Charles Cocks Esq. M.P. to be left at Tom's Coffee House, Devereux Court nr Temple Bar, London en Angleterre,

The Hague
Sept. 13, 1757

Dear Cousin,

... I take this opportunity to repeat what I said in the latter end of my last letter leaving the history of my journey till I see you in England, which I hope will be very soon, as I propose setting out by Saturday's Pacquet. What I there said to you and what I now repeat was that as you had promised me that when I had been a fortnight or three weeks in campaign with the King of Prussia if I still continued my resolution to go into the army you would immediately apply for a commission for me, I expect though I have not been that time with him I shall find my commission if not obtained at least applied for when I reach England or at least that you should immediately tell me that you absolutely not permit my going into the army at all which tho' I assure you most solemnly I shall never forgive, I shall take much more kindly than any put-offs you can use. For upon my honour that way in which you have always treated me, not only as if I was a child but an Idiot hurts me more than anything in the world can do, and I cannot bear with it any longer ... In the name of God if you have any the least regard for the ease and happiness of my whole life, do not put it off any longer for if I am not a soldier I shall never be happy, I know enough of myself to be assured of it, and I shall curse the

author of my disappointment I am afraid even with my last
breath

I am dear cousin
Your affectionate friend and obedient
humble servant,
J. COCKS

It is clear from other letters written from James to Charles
that Charles gave his permission for his ward to join the army
only with the greatest reluctance. But the permission was
finally obtained and James had his way. He became an ensign
in the Grenadier Guards and took part in the expedition to St
Malo. He landed near there on September 7th, 1758, and was
killed at St Cas on September 12th. Charles inherited his
ward's patrimony and men said he had abused his trust. The
south side of the obelisk on Obelisk Hill is thus inscribed:

> Inscribed to the memory of James Cocks, Ensign of the Guards;
> he was the surviving issue of James Cocks Esq. eldest nephew of
> Lord Chancellor Somers, and of Ann, sister of the late Lord
> Berkeley of Stratton. Possessed of an ample patrimony, he
> preferred honour to security, and before he had attained the age
> of twenty, fighting for his country, fell in battle at St Cas, on the
> coast of France, A.D. 1758.

The books I read introduced me to a variety of legends of
the hills, and taught me something of their history. But no
other book supplanted the poem which I had read long before I
set eyes on the Malverns: *The Vision of William Concerning Piers
the Plowman*. The visions of this poem move far away from the
scene of the poet's first dreaming and yet, because there is pure
poetry in the scanty references to the hills, the Malverns and
the so-called William Langland have become closely associated
with one another. I remember coming across, in an unexpected
book shop, the scholarly *New Light on Piers Plowman* by the
same Allan H. Bright whose history of old Colwall Church I
have mentioned earlier in this chapter. *New Light on Piers
Plowman*, which removes William's birthplace from Cleobury
Mortimer to Ledbury, locates a field for centuries known as

Longland or the Longlands in the vicinity of the Herefordshire Beacon and of 'Primeswell'. It is a book to read slowly with the poem at hand, and then to take out for field days on the hills. Allan Bright's thesis is disputable, but his book and R. W. Chambers's essay on *Piers Plowman* in *Man's Unconquerable Mind* show what a fascinating pursuit, and how rewarding, research in English can be.

Piers Plowman is a hard poem; it can be dull, bitter, crowded, clouded, vividly realistic or cluttered with abstractions; its verse can ding in your ears until you wish you were deaf. But the visions are not false; though denunciation is fierce, a way out of the welter of evil is the motive of the poem. Piers is Christ, and Christ is truth and charity—and Holy Church. I expect, like most moralists, Langland was often railing against himself. It is pretty clear that this denouncer of time-wasters was himself a 'spill-time'. Perhaps poets need to be spill-times. But Langland was a man of faith as well as one who could make a phrase ring. I forget who said, 'Until a phrase begins to ring there is no speech.' Langland had the gift and, amidst much clumsiness, the skill. I have remembered since the first time I read the poem, as a student, the lines in *Dobet*, when Easter day dawns, and men ring in the resurrection, and the poet calls to Kitte his wife and to Kalote his daughter:

> Arise and reverence God's resurrection,
> Creep to the cross on knees, and kiss it as a jewel,
> For God's blessed body it bore for our bote,
> It frightens away the fiend, for such is its might,
> May no grisly ghost glide where it shadoweth.

I have remembered, too, the fairy enchantment of a fourteenth-century May morning on Malvern Hills, when Long Will first slept and dreamed:

> But on a May morning on Malvern Hills,
> Me befell a ferly, of faery it seemed;
> Wearied out with wandering I went me to rest
> Under a broad bank by a burn side,
> And as I lay and leaned and looked on the water,
> I slumbered in a sleeping, it sweyed so merry.

Piers Plowman has in it an exalted strain of religious feeling, unecclesiastical, and reaching, in its humanity and its faith in God, to what is profound in us all and common to us all. I think this strain accounts for the great popularity and influence of the poem in its own day. But I, being earthly, love the poet of the Visions most of all when he makes us feel the weather, and see the flowers in the frith, and hear the brook, and marvel at the birds' nests. Even in his satire a swift memory of mist on the Malverns will help him to expression. Of the lawyers in their hoods of silk he says that you could more easily measure the mist on Malvern Hills than get a mum of their mouths unless money was shown. To describe the glory of love after strife he writes:

> After sharpest showers, quoth Peace, most sheen is the sun,
> Is no weather warmer than after watery clouds . . .

He describes the effects of a south-west gale that blew one Saturday evening in the fourteenth century so vividly that it seems as though we felt that wind but now. We, too, have seen pear trees and plum trees 'puffed to the earth', and beeches and broad oaks 'turn upward their tail'. Poor Will was often exposed to the weather; few gave him charity without charge. I can feel his coldness when he wandered wetshod; and I remember the time when he woke meatless and moneyless in Malvern Hills, for I once woke meatless and moneyless in Malvern Hills myself.

23

MIDSUMMER HILL
ON MIDSUMMER EVE

My meatless state was partly the result of a wager proposed to me by Martin Gilkes; he bet me five pounds I would not sleep out on the Long Mynd and tell him afterwards what I had seen. I had not accepted this challenge; the Long Mynd made my heart refrain. But Midsummer Hill beckoned me; I needed no prospect of five pounds to make me decide to sleep out one Midsummer Eve on Midsummer Hill.

Audrey and Sebastian were away. There was no one in the house in the Lees but myself, so no one would be surprised if I failed to come back on Saturday night. I went up the Wyche Cutting and over the tops of the hills to Wynd's point. The bracken fronds were spreading full out, except for a few which retained their delicate curled tips. On the black patches, where the bracken had been burnt back in swaling time, new bracken necks, bent double for strength, as a man's back bends to a load, or to heave up a weight, were forcing their way up; their grey-green, with coppery hairs taking the sun on the curve, was vivid against the black waste. Wild thyme was out in the turfy bays of the bracken, or bordering the paths; wild thyme, white bedstraw, and brilliant yellow cinquefoil. To go bare-foot over wild thyme is as exquisite a sensation to the feet as is a fine flavour to the palate.

It is easy to walk considerable distances on the Malverns in one's feet. 'I shall take off my shoes and walk in my feet,' I heard a child say once. Shod, a foot is just a foot; but take the shoe off and each toe does its separate delicate duty. I was deciding to go bare-foot for the rest of my life when I came to a furzy, earthy, stony piece of path; the soles of my feet shrank and I put my shoes on.

I crossed the Ledbury road at Wynd's Point, took the path round the flank of the Herefordshire Beacon, went over the saddle and up the clear way which leads to a point above the Gullet. From this point one best sees the wooded skirts of Midsummer Hill. To the left, the blue-green of ash and willow predominates; to the right the golden translucence of oaks. Nothing is lovelier than to watch the wind in these trees, twinkling every leaf, swaying some slender trunks throughout their lengths, catching the sheen of summer at some fresh point in every second of time. I scrambled down to the Gullet, but I did not yet go up among the trees to the top of Midsummer. That was the final pleasure of the day, to be kept as a climax. Instead I went round the hill to Hollybush and had tea at Westfield.

Westfield garden was a riot of roses red and white; clove pinks were out, a tiger lily and gay sweet-williams. After tea in the garden I went to the western base of Midsummer Hill where, by a sunken lane, I passed into a deserted orchard. I could spend any number of hours on the grass of this old orchard, where only a dozen or so twisted fruit trees remain. It is more like a meadow, a square pulled out of shape. Holly, willow, hazel and wild rose help to screen it from all eyes. All manner of flowers grew among the tall grasses; clover, red and white; bird's foot trefoil, which we used to call boots-and-shoes; self-heal; and small burnished buttercups set up, like church lights, on their last tall branchings. The meadow slopes southwest to the rolling Herefordshire country, and the gap into Wales.

I returned to the Gullet and began to climb up the face of Midsummer Hill. I never go up Midsummer twice the same way. There are two clear paths, but there are others, hardly tracks at all, and into these I deviate. I like to keep the path nearly opposite the quarry until I have reached that strange sight—an oak, an ash and a thorn growing as though in one. Kipling recovered the magic of oak, ash and thorn in *Puck of Pook's Hill*. I often wonder whether he had seen this trinity-in-unity of trees on Midsummer Hill. A living thorn clasps the oak hard on one side, and two great limb-like roots of an ash enfold it serpent-wise on the other. All the branches mingle; now you are looking at a thorn tree, now at an oak, now at a plumed ash. The ash trees on this side of the hill are of unusual size and beauty, like green-playing fountains. Of other forest trees on Midsummer Hill the finest are sycamore and oak. I had seen crab-apple and thorn in blossom earlier in the year; now elder was in the last stage of its blossoming; its astringent, rather sinister scent came to my nostrils. Honeysuckles leap the tall trees on Midsummer Hill. I have never, even in Cornwall, seen more splendid bowers of these honied bacchanals. They fling themselves upwards, and fall in cascades of bloom; and yet each flower is so placed that it looks up through the sprays towards the sun; and every floret on each head is delicately set in right relation to the sun and to its fellows so as to ensure its own perfection in time.

The scent of honeysuckle takes a sovereign prize; but even its scent does not equal in indescribable subtlety the scent of wild rose. The white roses and the pink were past their prime on Midsummer Hill, but a few remained. Their scent must be breathed right from the centre of the freshly opening bud. The nose must press in among the clustered yellow anthers, ripe and trembling on their threads. No words can describe the scent directly; even Keats's poetry, so full of the sensuous spell of summer, cannot quite evoke that sprite of a scent, a faery's child. Garden roses are earthly girls in comparison, and some are court ladies.

When I passed beyond the trees to the bare summit of the hill, and reached the Somers-Cocks memorial shelter, the sun was still fairly high; I lay and watched the clouds. They were not moving fast; the drama was in their shape and texture, and in their size. They were luminous, full, soft and billowy; to ride on the curled clouds scarcely seemed a fable. I was almost a cloud myself sailing through space among kindred phantoms. Two chariot-horses raced neck and neck; a polar bear rode a bluish iceberg; a tremendous snowball was capped with stone like a cromlech. Below them lay the plain stretching to Bredon and the Cotswolds. Turning towards the west I saw that the sun was entering a sphere of banked cloud, and was sending out broad straight rays, a great fan of rays, earthward. But when the sun had plunged right into the region cloud, the earthward rays faded, and rays were sent out in the reverse direction, fanning upwards, towards the meridian. As the light faded, space narrowed. To the obelisk on the opposite hill it now seemed but a step; the heads of the high hills crowded nearer, Hangman's Hill, the Herefordshire Beacon, and the Worcestershire Beacon seemed close grouped; the subsidiary hills were still visible, but night was welling up in their folds. It was a sombre sunset with no vivid display of colour. The sun withdrew himself; he did not sink.

But before the sun went out in the west, the moon was up in the east between Bredon and the Cotswolds. She was nearly full. She went up the sky, dim while the daylight lingered, then shining bright. I meant to stay awake all night. I meant to watch every change in the ritual of the sky, and to test the mysterious powers of Midsummer Eve. I lay down on my ground sheet, but I kept my eyes open wide. I listened to all the little rustlings that haunt the night and make the heart beat faster. But sleep is maddeningly perverse. Try to sleep, and you keep awake; try to keep awake and you go to sleep. I went to sleep, and when I woke up I was cold. I cared no longer for Midsummer Hill, I cared only for my cold feet. I tried to snuggle them under my skirt, but it was the period of miserably short, skimpy skirts. I crept under the bracken and wished for day, and day came stealing on me at last without magnificence. I have often elsewhere watched the sun rise in full glory; but on this early midsummer morning he loitered invisible in his vapoury tent.

Now until very late did he appear to fight the mists until they 'smitten with amazement fell'. The wraiths could hardly have been smitten and dispersed more epically; yet I remained out of heart. I had imagined myself being warmed by the sun hours earlier, and I had imagined myself delightfully breakfasting. Alas! I had left my precious packet, all my little store of food, in one of my resting places of the previous day.

I went about among the trees on the lower slopes of Midsummer Hill until well after midday, when I set out for Wynd's Point. Two friends of mine, Mr and Mrs Dick Hawkes, were at that time renting a cottage at the foot of the Herefordshire Beacon, not very far from the gate leading to the Ridgeway, on the Ledbury road. I knew my friends would invite me to have tea with them, and before tea I knew I could ask for a bath. How good are friends! How delightful their hot water, how delicious their tea and themselves. Talk has seldom seemed to me more heart-warming than on that afternoon, nor tea a more gracious feast. My first sip of that fragrant brew will not be forgotten, nor my first bite of a delicate sandwich which had as a filling cream cheese, a little crisp lettuce, a hint of salad-dressing and chopped dates. The sun, I thought, may disappoint his worshippers, but a good friend abideth for ever.

I have never been in the Malverns at harvest time, nor seen the stooks set up in the fields of the plains. By the time harvest was in full swing I was always in my proper place, in Cornwall. I was at Malvern for several Whitsuntides; that is why I associate the hills with the scent of hawthorn. The hawthorn trees above Little Malvern are particularly accessible to the nose; as you are going down the hills towards Little Malvern Priory your head is sometimes on a level with the top layers of a thorn planted lower down the slope. I remember going down past the thorns in full flower once when Whitsuntide fell early. I went to sing 'Come Holy Ghost, our souls inspire' in Little Malvern Priory Church. More than any other church in the neighbourhood, more than the beautiful Priory Church at Great Malvern, more than the steadfast aspiration of Worcester, I think Little Malvern Priory Church fosters, so as to hand down to those yet unborn, the spirit of Christian worship.

I remember one wonderful autumn day which ended in this little church. I woke in my room at the Lees to find the autumn sun rising red, a little to the left of Bredon, which lifted its whale's back out of the mist, and seemed to swim. When I went up the hill the mist had thinned; the distance was blue-violet. It had rained in the night, but now the sky was clear with cloud on the horizon. As I stood looking, with the sun behind me, at the webs on the furze bushes, they turned iridescent—blue, green and rose gauze; the water-drops were rainbows. The world was grey, or coloured and shining according to the angle of my eye. By the time I reached my favourite point above the Gullet, I felt the sun warm on me as I watched the trees on Midsummer Hill. Hardly touched, as yet, by autumn, the main effect was grey-green, green, or dark green where shadows lurked—as though night hid, and awaited his turn. Every now and then the sun would seem to set an aureole on the tall poplars. In a medieval painting they would be in the circular glory; but here they moved with the wind which surfed through them. The sound, as I closed my eyes, seemed to be the sound of waves on Hemmick beach. Now all the world was pied. Just as, near at hand, a withering frond of fern would burn gold, or a velvet moss patch turn more than elfin green, so, in the distant plain, among the glooms, a field would take the sun so vividly that, against this green, the shadows of the trees rested as strong as summer.

I had my lunch on the little southern slope above the quarry of the Gullet, and then went down to Castle Morton Common. October! The very sound of the month is red and gold. On the common I saw an old countryman wearing the dun-coloured clothes which might belong to any period, but with a red-brown scarf wound round his neck. He leaned on his stick by a gate and watched the ducks. He seemed a symbol of October manhood, just as a horse-chestnut near at hand, its great fan leaves touched with yellow and gold, symbolized October in the trees. After a chat with the countryman, I walked the low lands until I came to Little Malvern Priory Church. Two perfect little crab apples in the porch indicated that it was the time of harvest thanksgiving. The church is exactly the right size and shape for harvest decorations. There is room for fruit and flowers and vegetables on the side ledges, and the screen is right for Michaelmas daisies. On the font were Michaelmas daisies, dahlias, and trails of scarlet bind-weed berries, with apples heaped at the base. Apples were expansive everywhere, and with them were carrots and vegetable marrows; cabbages mingled with the marigolds. On the altar was bread, food of man's body, and symbolic food of the soul; token sheaves of wheat were on the rood screen where a vine is carved.

I sat in the chancel in one of the old monk's stalls. The chancel is a little chapel in itself; indeed it is the original chancel which now serves as a parish church. The tower stands; but there are only indications of the nave and side chapels. Little Malvern must have been at its most enchanting in the twelfth century when it was only a hermitage founded by two monks from Worcester. When, in 1170, the hermitage developed into a priory, it was 'one inseparable body with the church of Worcester', and no person was admitted to the Monastic habit in Little Malvern 'without the consent of the bishop, prior, and convent of Worcester'. It must have been very hard for a hermit to become a member of a community; but I suppose by the time the hermitage became a priory the two founder hermits were dead. I hope so. Very different from a hermitage was a priory built on the same site in the fifteenth century; the domestic buildings escaped destruction at the time of the dissolution of the monasteries, and form part of Little Malvern Court today, with its fish-ponds and ancient trees and ancient peace.

Autumm is a peculiarly lovely season in the Malverns; but winter, too, has its cold revelry. I saw a strange effect one rainy November day. I went up Worcestershire Beacon by way of St Anne's Well; when I was high enough up to oversee, for some distance, the roads and roofs, they seemed all turned to water. The roads were slate-blue rivers; the roofs lost all substantiality; only the hills themselves retained their form as the grey clouds broke in the west, and the sun sent out broad spokes of radiance; I tried to express the effect in the following verse:

> With streaming flanks the hills alone
> Abide the dissolution;
> Past liquid roads and roofs they strain
> To where the great sun once again
> Shoots his broad beams, to stabilize
> This shifty earth, these vaporous skies.

Snowflakes falling on the hills isolate the passenger from earth and heaven. One Saturday when I set out from Great Malvern a little snow had already fallen, but it only sprinkled the hills. Uncovered patches looked black against the whiteness as I went up the Worcestershire Beacon. I went up by St Anne's Well, sheltered at first. I might have been on a ship. The air was thick and leaden; the plain below was quickly lost to view. The flakes that began to dance round my head appeared to have nothing else to fall on. At the summit the air was icy, but there was not wind enough to blow away the murk. Except that I no longer had the flank of the hill on my right I might have been climbing still. There was no release, none of that fling of the spirit one usually feels on top. Instead the atmosphere had closed in; only the snowflakes could fly. They went with me along the ridge and down to the Wych cutting; they swarmed round me like bees. I did not walk further that day; but next morning, when the fall was over, I went directly to Wych and walked through the deep snow along the Pix path to Wynd's Point, and from there I went up the Herefordshire Beacon. On the Malverns a south wind caresses the body, an east wind shrivels it up, but a north wind seems to ignore the creature, man, cutting right through him as though he were not. Sometimes I seemed to stick to the earth by the tips of my toes. The wind was moving through the hill fortress, and hissing in the grass as I had been used to hear it hiss in Chûn Castle in West Penwith, or on Bodmin moor. I never felt a stranger in the Midlands when I was on the Herefordshire Beacon. There my spirit was both in Cornwall and Herefordshire. I was not out of place. No snow lay on the exposed side of the hill; that was where I could hear the wind whistling through the grass. But on the more sheltered side snow lay light and soft in the trenches, and in the deep ditch under the 'citadel'. When I escaped from the camp into the more sheltered woodland, I saw the armed and glossy hollies, with leaves 'smooth and glib' from which the snow had slipped; and the slippery ivy leaves with their black fruits, each having 'a small sharp pointall'.

It was from such cold excursions as these that it seemed especially good to return to the house in the Lees, and to Audrey and Sebastian. Neither was well enough, at this time, to walk on the hills; but Audrey knew them even better than I. Her father had been, at one time, Curate of Colwall, and she had frequently returned on visits to friends. Colwall to her was like Gorran to me. She liked to hear of my visits to places she could picture in her mind's eye, and I, in my turn, liked to hear of her wrestlings with war conditions. Though these were hard and wearing, she made them sound funny. I remained a permanent tenant in my room at the top of the house; but to the ground floor came a succession of persons of whom I saw little except through Audrey's eyes. She had a gift for swift portraiture and, although delicate physically, an unquenchable spirit and quick impulses. I lived in imagination the saga of the Lees, so different from the life I led during the week at King Edward's. At King Edward's, happenings had the kind of results one would expect; there seemed to be logical consequences in spite of the impact of war. At Malvern all was unexpected, encompassing terrific ups and downs, gulfs and peaks. With Audrey, all creatures intensified their innate selves. Even the hens which she added to the establishment were more henly, if one can coin a word of Chaucerian formation, than ordinary hens. Whether they were Buff Orpingtons or Rhode Islanders I forget, but they were aristocratic hens of handsome appearance. Audrey loathed mediocrity even in hens. A sense of style was of the essence of her nature.

It is curious, when looking back upon Time spent, how frequently minutes which seemed wasted prove more rich in purchase than those carefully laid out. Among these were the minutes I spent in Malvern near the Belle Vue on Monday mornings waiting for the Birmingham bus. The bus stop was well placed in relation to the Malvern Priory Church; my eyes, resting idly on it in seven o'clock light throughout successive seasons and states of sky, gathered a precious store of pictures. Sometimes, on fine mornings, I left time to mount the steps leading to the hills. Looking back from the various landings as the steps twisted I saw the light turn the Priory tower golden, and gild even the heterogeneous buildings of the town. I saw a series of pictures framed against the tender blue of Malvern distance. Then the jumble of high and low roofs, with the cream, or pink, or brickish, or yellow walls, was transfigured. The whole became other than the tiresome Great Malvern of the shopper. The priory church lifted itself with ease above the earthlier dwellings. I used to remember Piers Plowman: 'The sweet red rose that spicers desire . . . out of a ragged root and a rough briar springeth and groweth'.

24

'THE WAR IS OVER'

How sustaining in the years of war seemed the prospect of peace—peace with victory. But that is the reason for the ultimate purposelessness of all wars: not all the combatants can have victory with their peace. We had victory, but we hardly tasted it. For when at last victory came in Europe we put off our mood of elation, and elation cannot be postponed. The poverty and exhaustion of our minds were reflected in the naming of our high day by mere letters—V.E. Day. Perhaps if all the nations of the world had overflowed with blessed relief, and if we had spontaneously shut shop and school and factory for a week and run mad with joy, we might have secured a better peace. Perhaps we had grown used to not reacting until we were allowed—a terrible condition, the basis of evil; perhaps it was the knowledge that we were still at war with Japan. But we waited to rejoice. We hung on to the wireless to know when.

Two disappointments of my own, one of them comic, reflect a certain flatness in the general tendency. I was at Malvern on the Friday night when, from the nine o'clock news, it seemed certain that V.E. Day would be either on Saturday or Monday. In either case it would mean for me a long week-end, and suddenly, as I sat listening with Audrey and Sebastian to the Voice, it seemed absolutely essential that I should spend this weekend with my sister Susan in Exmouth. Was there a night train?

'Quite mad,' said Audrey; 'but you can ring up the station inquiry office.'

There was a train at 9.55. I borrowed money from Audrey, put on a coat, and went running down to Malvern station. Catching that train was at least an act. I sat in the dim carriage, and we went a long way round to Bristol by way of the Severn tunnel. At Bristol I waited on bombed Temple Meads; at Exeter I waited again; the Great Western and the Southern railway companies were a twain which never met.

It was drizzling in Exeter; at Exmouth it was raining great drops; it was half-past six and a hungry morning. But I was sustained by the thought of Susan. I would surprise her in bed. I would make coffee and toast, and take it up to her room, and we would rejoice together. Soon I was going up the street, thinking what fun it would be, and how grand it was to have a sister. I ran the last bit of the way. I reached the house and rang the bell. All was still. I rang again. No one stirred.

'Is there anybody there?' said the traveller. But no voice replied from the leaf-fringed sill. Susan, obviously, was not at home. I have seldom felt more flat.

I put back the catch of a window with my hair-slide and stepped bleakly in. She must, I thought, have gone to Exeter. I had meant to go to Exeter with her and surprise Howard and Mary. But the edge of the adventure was blunted. Susan's excited welcome was what I had most looked forward to, the sudden unexpected being together. I put on the kettle to make myself a cup of tea; it was no good filling the house with the aroma of coffee if there was no one to share it. The next moment I heard a small voice from upstairs saying: 'Is that someone in the house?' Susan was there. She had been asleep.

'I'm here!' I said, and went dashing up the stairs. It was very good; but there had been the little preliminary shock of disappointment; and when we heard that V.E. Day was to be neither on Saturday nor Monday, which meant that I must go back to Birmingham on the Sunday train, we both felt that V.E. Day had played us false.

When the Day was finally announced, I spent it with Cecil Waterfield, with whom I had lived during the Blitz. We wanted to drink to Churchill in the presence of the couch under which I had once vainly tried to poke my head when a burst of destruction, more than usually near, had prompted me to play the ostrich. A wine merchant had promised us a bottle of good sherry for V.E. Day, but when I went to claim it, Miss C.— usually so kind to us—was quite out of countenance. She hadn't a drop of wine left in the shop, she said. I muttered that I'd like a box of matches, knowing that, although I'd been denied matches for three weeks, a box would now be forthcoming as balm for my disappointment over the sherry. Silently I was handed a box, as silently I was turning away, when Miss C. said: 'Wait a minute, I'm not sure I haven't one bottle of Something left below.' Like the funny man disappearing in a Pantomime, she went down through a trap-door, and emerged bearing her trophy by the neck. She wrapped it up well. 'Don't let anybody see it,' she said, 'or they'll all be in.' I didn't let anybody see; I hadn't even seen, myself. In high feather I smuggled my prize into my bicycle-basket and pedalled back to Cecil and Nina who had come over from Burton to celebrate with us. And when we unwrapped that well-wrapped bottle we found it was invalid port.

The day of celebration was officially calculated; but there was nothing official in our nation-wide and immediate response to the news that war had ended in Europe. This response, which waited for the fixing of no official day, was one of confused thankfulness to God. Churches overflowed with people whose emotion prompted them to a general thanksgiving, and who gathered together to express it in buildings consecrated to worship. Not in my lifetime had I experienced anything like it. The secular rejoicings, the teas and the bonfires, had no great heart in them; but the churches, cathedrals and abbeys opened their doors to a concourse of people moved by a common impulse. Service followed service throughout the day. Exeter Cathedral, I was told afterwards, was filled with relays of folk from morning until late at night. The pigeons were amazed. In all lands there must have been similar demonstrations of desire to unite and to sing. If only that common heart of hope could have given some effective means to effective action. But the ordinary people of each country never seem to be able effectively to meet; arid channels of communication are established, and magnanimity is drained away as policy replaces kindness. Not only the pity of it, but the damned folly of it is bitter to contemplate—the dumbness of mankind.

I walked along Severn bank from Worcester to Tewkesbury on the second day of the V.E. school holiday. The weather was warm with a soft south wind, and the sky was over-cast, but so thinly that the sun could be felt through the veil, and every now and then sailed clear into lakes of blue. I caught the bus to Worcester, went into the Cathedral to experience again its soaring glory, and then went by College Walk to the river. The wind freshened. The sky was now deep blue with here and there cloud castles, or cloudy mountains, winged angels and flying monsters. My spirits livened as I went by the industrial banks where even today hammers were clinking, and kept the path by the fields to the grove of pollard willows. Then the trees on the steep red banks came almost to the water's edge—horse-chestnut trees, their candles still alight; sycamores heavy with green-winged fruits; waving ash trees; two soaring poplars. Now the path wound under the arching boughs of the trees beyond which the river showed in blue glimpses; now I came to meadows gold with buttercups, or green with corn still running in lines. Delicate lady's lace waved white and green on the banks. May trees gave their scent, though some of the flowers had been blighted by the bitter east wind which had blown in April.

By the Yachting Club I paused to listen to the news coming through a loud speaker—the joy in Moscow, the gloom in Berlin. Then I walked on to the lovely grove of trees, mainly white poplar, by Kempsey village. The wind was in the leaves 'airy abeles caught in a flare', as Hopkins has it. I went past a garden into Kempsey Church—a very wide church. I have never examined the traces of a Camp from which Kempsey is said to be named. I walked round the great loop of the river by

Kempsey and followed the path where it lost itself half way down the bank. I could look down through grey-green willows to the water. The undergrowth grew rank. Here lady's lace grew so tall that it reached my head; here were white dead nettle, and comfrey, and giant stinging nettles which stung my legs as I pushed through. On the principle, I suppose, that what hurts must in some mysterious way be good for one, it has been said that stings from stinging nettles will prevent rheumatism. For my part, I thought, I would rather risk rheumatism in the future than court nettle-stings in the present. Through an orchard which had recently shed its blossom I came out into an open meadow again.

All this time the Malvern Hills had been playing a game with me. Sometimes I saw the whole melodious line blue in the distance; sometimes the entire chain disappeared altogether; sometimes North Hill alone reared a head. Try as I would I seemed unable to out-pace North Hill. When I reckoned I had reached a point opposite Midsummer Hill, a winding of the river would set me once more in chase of North Hill. The high hills must have been skipping like rams and the little hills like young sheep.

I passed Clevelode and came opposite the Rydd with its towering red banks looking like a Devon cliff. It was now a long time since I had eaten my lunch in a buttercup meadow, and I had had nothing to drink with it. Thirstier and thirstier I grew. I was sitting on the bank for a rest, and thinking how thirsty I was, and fancying draughts of various delicious fluids, when I saw a yacht, with all its victory flags flying, come gaily down the Severn. It anchored not far below me. I swear that I made no effort to communicate the fact that I was thirsty; I did not even hear the chink of cups. Yet I was quick to catch a voice which said, 'Would you like a cup of tea?' I said, 'Yes, please,' with alacrity. I never tasted better tea, nor ate a better slice of chocolate cake than that day on Severn bank when I partook of the bounty of the owners of the *Dolphin*. The name of the yacht I read; but the owners and I were not named to each other. I, poor thirsty tramp, was the receiver of the loving cup at their Victory tea.

I went on past a cattle shed, the ruin of a cattle shed, yet most handsome in itself, built of brick raised on piles, with shingle roof. It might have been almost worth while to be a cow to live in it. A vast number of cows were grazing in the next meadow, but I did not like the look of them. With dignity, for I did not run, I quickened my pace, and came to the sight of Severn Stoke Church tower.

I went up the road to Severn Stoke, admiring the placing and appearance of its houses. Then, with an old lady leaning over the churchyard gate, I fell into talk. She was from one of the almshouses nearby, and with almshouses I have an affinity. I fancy I shall end my life in a nice little almshouse. I could do worse than Severn Stoke. These almshouses were made lovely with peonies and early honeysuckle, and the first great poppy buds. My old lady pointed to her husband's grave on which she had placed a few white flowers. 'Not that he liked flowers,' she said. I asked if it was only on graves he hadn't liked flowers. 'He hated all flowers,' she said, 'all flowers except cauliflower, but I put a few on his grave all the same. Nineteen years since he died. He can't be lingering about now to care one way or the other, and I like flowers meself.' Her bearded chin waggled; under her bristled eye-brows she shot out a glance that triumphed over him. She said she had two sons at the war, and both went before they had to. They weren't going to be slackers, they said. One had been in Egypt most of the time, and the other was in Holland. Wanted to get to Berlin, he did, but those Russians, they fairly burst along. He had enjoyed himself on the whole; there were some things he wouldn't have missed for anything, though there were some he'd give the world never to have set eyes on. Liked the Dutch, he did. Fine people, the Dutch; real good to our boys, they were.

She said there had been a fine number of people at church for the Thanksgiving Service. More than a hundred, a big lot for a little place. But it had been a funny sort of service to her mind; not the right prayers, but made-up ones. And then afterwards there hadn't been anything much to do till the evening when her daughter-in-law came to fetch her and they all went to the Local. Nobody needed to be without a young man. One member of the Air Force had said, 'Come on, Gran, have a drink,' and she'd enjoyed herself all the evening and it never cost her a penny. And her daughter-in-law said: Jack, he was enjoying himself in Holland, and she was going to enjoy herself in the Old Bull. One time she had her arms round the necks of two, but there wasn't any harm in any of it; and when they came out they found the people in the Local had put a double row of fairy lights right across the road.

From Severn Stoke I took a bus back to Birmingham, but on Saturday I was again on the banks of the Severn. I took the bus to Severn Stoke so as to resume my walk just where I had left off on Wednesday. The day was warm; the sun too hot for May. At Worcester I had been caught in a thunder shower, and as I left Severn Stoke and went down the lane and across the field to the river bank, I could feel myself teeming and growing with the other plants. A few horse-daisies were out in the meadow, their scent acrid and strong as August.

Again among the buttercups of the meadow I ate my lunch, and took my way along the lightly worn path where the flowers seemed to crowd thickest, making a track of sprinkled yellow. Unlike celandines, which vary in the number of their petals, buttercups have always five, unless the flower is double. I found one such rosette, made to the pattern of a double primrose. The buttercup-pollen made my feet yellow; I was wearing sandals, and the pollen lodged between my toes. In the days when the land was all fulfilled of faery I might have turned into a buttercup.

The sun had the scalding quality of thundery weather, and the river looked sleek, unlike Severn water. Only on the off bank, ripples broke the reflections. North-west the Malverns wavered, insubstantial; south-east the long flank of Bredon would come into view and disappear again behind the trees. The walk from Stoke to Upton is in no way exciting or dramatic; it is pastoral and easy. Here is land to live in and live on; a countryside fully humanized, although I met no person until I saw the spire at Upton, and went, in loving memory of Tom Jones, to take tea at the Lion. I was rewarded for my piety.

The maiden who seemed to be in sole charge had no townish, war-time airs. She said the dining-room was being done up, but if I didn't mind tea in the kitchen, I was welcome. The kitchen was old and big, but fitted up with useful modern stoves and appliances. On a corner of the long kitchen table a cloth was laid, and good bread and butter and cake set out, with tea of better quality than is common in an enormous teapot. While I was having my tea I mentioned Tom Jones to the maiden, but she said that, although it was true Mr Jones owned the place, he didn't actually live there.

I walked at ease to Tewkesbury, until I came to a world drowned in water. The Severn seemed no longer able to sort itself from the Avon. I pretty nearly swam in to Tewkesbury, and when I arrived none of its many hotels liked the look of me when I proposed myself as a guest for the night. It is base ingratitude that I cannot remember which grand establishment finally took me in and bestowed on me what Coleridge called 'the wide blessing of sleep'. On Sunday, I went to the solemn Service of Thanksgiving at the Abbey; it could not have that urgency of half-inarticulate praise, forcing itself into some sort of expression, which had marked the brief service I had attended in Birmingham on the Day. But the glory of the building, the historic memories it enshrined, the sunshine, the music, and the assembled people worked that bond between souls which made me think of the trees above the Pix path of Jubilee Drive on a Sunday morning. I have seen them aspiring to a single point as though, if men fell silent in praise, even the trees would cry out.

That August, my sister Susan and I set up tents, and camped at Hemmick, in Cornwall, a mile or so from Gorran Schoolhouse where we were born. I heard of the atom bomb at London Apprentice. I was bicycling to St Austell to change our library books at Smith's in Fore Street. I had passed Pentewan, and was nearing London Apprentice when, on the left, by a path leading to a cottage some distance up a steep slope, I perceived a notice which read 'Sweet Apples Sold Here'. I left my bicycle and went up steps into a green and cool recess. There was a house among the tree-tops, and, seated in the porch of the house, was another visitor who also had come for sweet apples. The lady of the house, this visitor said, had gone to the orchard to pick the apples up, and had I heard about the atom bomb? I said I hadn't. At first when she began to tell me what an atom bomb was, I hardly took in what she was saying. I was thinking of other things. I imagined, as I listened vaguely, that it was only some new kind of incendiary. Then suddenly I began to listen, and in about ten bald words I was told what had happened. How confused were our reactions to the news of the destruction caused by the atom bomb! It is easy now to say that our blood ran cold, and that we at once condemned this appalling climacteric of wickedness. But I know that I did not at once condemn it; that my immediate reaction was one of astonished relief. I rejoiced to think that the sailors, soldiers and airmen who were risking, or about to risk, their lives in what we still called the Far East might now be spared: that my brother Maurice's only son, serving with the American Marines, would go back to Indiana, and my brother Wilfrid's second son, serving in the Royal Navy, would return to London. My heart cannot embrace the world. I think only Hermon Ould's heart was true to the whole world.

When the cessation of war with Japan was announced the news was brought to my sister and me by John Grose of Penquarry. He came down through the steep field which divided his house from our tents, and stood on the hedge amidst the brambles and bindweed and purple loosestrife. I was washing up our breakfast cups and plates.

'Don't 'ee do any washing up today, Anne,' he said.

'Must do a little bit o' washing up even in camp, John,' I replied, 'though sometimes I do just stream 'em out in the brook.'

'Don't 'ee do any washing up today,' he repeated. 'The war is over.'

25

OFF AGAIN

After the war was over, I, like everybody else, found it very hard to settle down steadily to work. I had never before taught for so many years at a stretch. My scheme had always been to teach until I had saved enough money to buy myself some free time; then, when time and money were spent, teach again. In this way I had constantly secured that slack should follow stress, slack follow stress, as it must in any rhythmical progression. If I have no spring in me I cannot teach.

At King Edward's, because the atmosphere prevented fatigue, I had taught for a long time without feeling exhausted. Miss Barrie never seemed busier than she was nor wanted us to seem so. She had in a rare degree a quality of restfulness, a largeness of mind and an absence of pettiness in themselves refreshing. We had said goodbye to her very regretfully when she retired in 1943. But her retirement did not change the nature of the school. Dr Sybil Smith who succeeded her was quite unlike Miss Creak, Miss Major or Miss Barrie; but she brought her own wisdom to her task, her own quick helpfulness, her faculty of not being dismayed, and her rare power of combining perception with patience in seeking to remedy faults of youthful character and bearing. For all her pupils Dr Smith will take infinite pains; and the school is not so big but that she can know all the dwellers in it. She has guided the school, too, in changeful times, in such a way that, while taking count of modern needs, and sympathizing with experiment and advance in education outside the limits of King Edward's, she has striven to maintain and promote the school's traditional characteristic. I think that characteristic is best summed up in a phrase of Henry James's, 'the spirit of fine attention'.

The change was not in the school—though we all worked harder than before the war—but in myself. Unlike the teachers I admire, unlike born teachers such as my brother Howard who, as they grow older, retain and deepen their enthusiasm, I have always had among the properties of my nature a little seed of reluctance to teach. This little seed now grew and grew. I think I can honestly say that, once in the class-room, I never longed for my lessons to end; but I became daily more reluctant to begin.

I looked about for a remedy. I thought, perhaps, repetition was dulling the faculties, and I wondered if I could give up teaching and write for a living. I had not executed the weighty works I had planned; but I had won a good deal of delightful praise for a book about my childhood at Gorran in Cornwall, a book which I had called *School House in the Wind*. The book had been suggested to me by my brother Maurice when he was in England in 1939. After reading a children's story of mine he had said, 'Why do you make it all up? Why don't you write down exactly what we used to do at Gorran when we were children?' I had carried out this suggestion, and had greatly enjoyed doing it. During the war it was impossible for me to travel from the Midlands to Cornwall as often as formerly, but I found that, by writing a page or two of *School House in the Wind* I could whisk myself into Cornwall, into my country childhood. When the book was published, it appeared that it had power to whisk other people too. But I had written chiefly for pleasure; it would not be pleasure to write for a living.

I decided that what I really wanted was to go back to work in Cornwall. I was no longer a stranger in the Midlands; I had friends; I knew of lovely places to go to; but more and more I longed for the sea. I began to scan the columns of advertisements in *The Times Educational Supplement* and, at last, I applied once more for a job in Cornwall. This time I was interviewed and was offered the post; I accepted it with alacrity on the spot, and then refused it over the telephone.

Why I refused it I can hardly say. It was a job I should greatly have enjoyed, and I could have lived almost where I would in Cornwall. And yet I refused it. I can only conclude that, after all, I did not want to work. I expect I wanted to go to Cornwall just to lie among the sea-pinks; and I knew that a spell of such flower-cushioned ease was possible. For, while awaiting a reply to my Cornish application, I had asked Dr Smith if she thought it possible that she and the Governors would grant me a year's leave of absence without pay from King Edward's. She had been sympathetic; she had approached the Governors for me; and I knew that a free year was within my grasp. The Governors would grant me leave if I wished it.

How much I wished it! I have written a great deal in praise of King Edward's; it is a happy school for teachers and taught; yet I was delighted to flit away from it. A friend, meeting me in the corridor after the grant of a year's leave of absence had been confirmed, hissed in my ear, 'Anne, take that grin off your face.'

When my free year began it was April, and I went first to Gorran and Caerhays. As I have already described elsewhere the beauty of Roseland, and of these parishes bordering Roseland, I will say no more except that, as I breathed the salty air over Dodman, and the primrose-scented air of the lane which leads from Polgrain to East Portholland, I felt renewed in all my fibres. Later, Phyllis Angove, an old Camborne pupil of mine—there are great advantages in having been a teacher— lent me the cottage which she rented from Mr Roberts at Little Trevarrick, not so very far from the wonderful summit of Trencrom. There my sister Susan came to stay with me. My father, alas, had died in 1943; no longer had my sister and I to confer anxiously about the amenities for him before choosing a cottage. We only wished now that we had so to do. I visited my brothers in their homes: I visited Stan and Kate, and Wilfrid and Edith; and then, while I was staying in the Choristers' School at Exeter, where Howard and Mary put into practice with cheering result those principles of education from which they have never swerved, I received a letter from my American brother, Maurice, inviting me to spend a holiday with him and Helen in Indiana. I should be their guest from the start, even aboard the *Queen Elizabeth*; and, as a preliminary to my American tour, my brother would fly with me from New York to Bermuda—that still British possession. We often tease each other about our respective nationalities, British and American, my brother and I. He has become an American citizen. The thought of Bermuda added the final touch to my pleasurable anticipations. I went out murmuring:

> He hangs in shades the orange bright,
> Like golden lamps in a green night.

Then I looked out my passport, booked my passage on the *Queen Elizabeth*, and went up to London to get a visa. This was at the beginning of 1947, when America was as a distant celestial city to displaced persons. I was merely a tripper; but the golden gates were straitly guarded, even against trippers. I was surprised when I learnt later the inscription on the Statue of Liberty. As I filled in forms, I found myself longing to state that I had been in prison most of my life, was at death's door, had no Affidavit of Support, and was intent on overthrowing the American Constitution. When I joined the queue in London I realized faintly, as I sympathized with the anxieties of my fellows, most of whom spoke foreign English, what it must be like to be country-less. I fiercely detested the petty clerks who gave me contradictory directions and reminded me that a dog's obeyed in office. What seemed so comic and reassuring was that, when I had been bandied about, my fingerprints taken, and all details of my past and present typed by robots on to an important looking document—when all this had been done, and I had reached at last the holy of holies, or the spider in the centre of the web, the presence of the American Consul, all inhumanity vanished. The genial representative of America was telephoning. He sat, magic tube in hand, on one side of an enormous desk and, motioning me to a chair on the other side, he held a conversation with the unseen:

'Is that you, Woo Woo?'

'Rash all gone?'

'Good girl.'

'Temperature down?'

'Fine.'

'Taking your medicine like a good girl?'

'Swell.'

'Yeah.'

'Bye bye, Woo Woo!'

America surrounds herself with a barbed entanglement of forms; but, once I was through, I found that her characteristics were informality and generosity.

When the time came for me to board the *Queen Elizabeth* it seemed glorious to be off on my travels again after the long confinement of the war years. I was to meet my brother Maurice and my sister Helen in New York; I was to fly to Bermuda with my brother; I was to see something of the United States and, I hoped, of Canada. How wholesome to see myself and my country once more in proportion and relation to the whole! I remembered the story told me by a Canadian friend. He said he was talking to a woman in a remote part of Ontario about England and she said, 'Is England swamp or hard-wood country?'

I love England, and I adore Cornwall; but I dearly like to be heading away from both for a change; I like schools well enough, and I am interested in education, but how dearly I like, how very dearly I have always liked, to shake the chalk from off my fingers, and kick the blackboard into the sea.

ANNE TRENEER

A Biographical Sketch

by Brenda Hull

ANNE TRENEER was born at Gorran in Cornwall on 30th January, 1891. Cornwall remained of supreme importance to her throughout her life; even when living and working away she returned to it frequently, until she retired early to live at Gerrans, near Portscatho, a few miles along the coast from her birthplace. Her happy childhood in a county as yet untouched by the changes brought about by modern life and by tourism is described in *School House in the Wind* which she dedicated 'To Cornwall, great rocky scroll, graved by the wind, cut by the bright blades of the sea'. Habits and interests formed in that childhood characterize her work: above all, a love of beauty both in the natural world and in the use of language. She remained happiest out of doors. In fact, her published work would probably have been even more extensive had it not been for her need to escape on to the cliffs or into the countryside whenever possible.

In 1906 she began at the Pupil Teachers' Centre at St Austell which became St Austell County School, where the distinguished Cornishman, Dr A.L. Rowse was also a pupil. It is described by him in *A Cornish Childhood* (Cape, 1942). From there began what was at that period an unusual progression towards academic qualifications and honours. It was all the more extraordinary when one considers not only, as she wrote, that she 'drifted into teaching' but also that she was not driven by powerful ambition. Her attitude contrasts strongly with Dr Rowse's bitterness at his lack of opportunity. She trained to be a teacher at the Diocesan Training College in Agar Road, Truro. After working first at

Treverbyn Council Mixed School and then at Exmouth Church School, as described in *Cornish Years,* she enrolled at Exeter University College, later to become the University of Exeter. The result of her study was an external degree from the University of London. The pattern that her subsequent life was to follow was thus established—teaching interspersed with periods of further study. She was now 27, but she went on to write a thesis on George Meredith for an MA degree from London, and followed that by a year at Liverpool University as a Research Fellow, writing *The Sea in English Literature.* Finally, in 1929, came two years at Lady Margaret Hall, Oxford as a research student, working for a B.Litt and writing her book on Doughty. She was deliriously happy at Oxford: research was not work; it was pure pleasure. In the Bodleian Library she felt 'a sense of private possession in the jointly held', the same feeling that she had in the Morrab Library at Penzance.

Perhaps one of the explanations for her escapes from teaching was her view that: 'No one ever is good enough to teach—and everyone is too good to teach all the time' and 'For a teacher, research in her own subject is an essential if she is to retain freshness.' Another reason is that she hated to be tied down for too long. Freedom was of supreme importance: she travelled light. That she did 'retain freshness' is evident from tributes by former pupils at Camborne County School. They describe her as 'a wonderful teacher', 'inspiring' and 'stimulating'. She passed on to those she taught a love of language and of poetry. Some, now elderly, retain a vivid memory of her lessons. One wrote: 'Invariably, as she entered the classroom, she would be carrying a book, often the *Golden Treasury'* (of poems, F.T. Palgrave, Oxford University Press, first published in 1861, with many subsequent editions) and her first words would be a little reading from it. She loved the sound of words and the richness of the English language'. She was particularly fond of Shakespeare and of amateur dramatics, and would produce plays, both in and out of doors, in which she often took a leading role herself. Her views on education in the autobiographies and in her articles in *Out of Doors* are of great interest, and surprisingly apposite today.

Her personal charm and zest for life endeared her to all those with whom she came into contact. Everyone loved her, and yet even close friends had to respect her privacy when she felt the need to withdraw. Although she chose as the title of her third book of autobiography *A Stranger in the Midlands,* she did not remain a stranger for long. Tributes in the King Edwards' school magazine after her death reveal how much loved and valued she was by the staff as well as the pupils. However, during her time there, she made frequent visits to Cornwall. In her broadcast 'On Being Made to Feel a Fool', she describes dashing down to Cornwall from Birmingham for a weekend: 'As I looked out over the sea and felt again that lively air I knew that it had been worth the dash to New Street station, worth being turned out in the middle of the night to kick my heels at Temple Meads. I was in my proper place'. In that broadcast in 1950 she had recounted various occasions on which she had been scatterbrained. Once, she was going by train from Birmingham to Brearley when she travelled on to Warwick by mistake, so she went to see the castle. Having hurried back to the station, she put up her hand to stop the London train. Similar occurrences were so frequent that she described herself as 'pixie-led'.

Anne Treneer retired from teaching in 1948 after having taken time off the previous year to visit her brother Maurice and his wife Helen in America at Elkart in Indiana. She particularly enjoyed the many lakes in the area and read whilst she was there *Winesburg, Ohio: Intimate Histories of Everyday Life* by Sherwood Anderson (Cape, 1922). She always tried to match her reading to her surroundings. On her retirement she wrote to Herman Ould: 'Did I tell you I've given up my teaching job. I have. Every morning I wake in heaven!'. She went to live first at Exmouth where her sister Susan was still living, their father having died in 1943. There, she finished *Cornish Years;* in order to write this she had turned down the offer of a job as a sessional tutor in Cornwall which Dr F.L. Harris had been instrumental in getting offered to her.

It was not until 1956 that she and her sister Susan moved to Gerrans to a bungalow which brother Maurice helped them to buy, and where they remained until her death. Maurice had become rich in America, having invented Alka-Seltzer. Whilst living in Exmouth, Anne had spent a good deal of time in Cornwall, staying with friends or in cottages lent to her by them. Much of these visits was spent walking, particularly in West Penwith, but she also, for example, presented prizes at Truro High

School speech day in December 1951, opened a book exhibition in Truro and acted as Chairman of the West Country Writers' Association. Whilst walking near Ludgvan one day, she ate her lunch by a stream: 'As I ate my pasty I watched the small, slim trout curve and dart in the water as swallows dart in the sky. Creation is so wondrous that one need only sit and watch an hour to forget all the trivial cares of daily living'. On another occasion: 'I went out one morning early in March to be for a couple of hours with the birds . . . the larks go lilting above the Towans and the curlew call over the mudflats, two contrasting expressions of Cornwall, one of joy and one of melancholy'. This could well be a description of contrast not only in Cornwall but in Anne Treneer herself. She had courage and a sense of adventure, but also the sensitivity of a poet.

During this time, she also wrote articles and poems for magazines and newspapers and made her broadcasts. She had been elected a Bard of the Cornish Gorsedd in 1945, her bardic name being Flogh Plu Woran—Child of Gorran. Although she could speak in broad Cornish dialect, she did not wish to learn Cornish. She did, however, think that a knowledge of it was useful for understanding place-names. She had also been elected a member of the PEN Club in 1936, proposed by the poet Edward Garnett and seconded by the General Secretary, Hermon Ould, and attended its meetings both at home and abroad. She was writing *The Mercurial Chemist* and planning a second book of poetry, for she had written poems all her life, and a biography of Coleridge. At Gerrans, she entered into village life, even becoming secretary of the cricket club. She would often switch to Cornish dialect when in contact with the indigenous inhabitants.

Anne Treneer died on 22nd August, 1966. On the same day as the private funeral service at Plymouth Crematorium taken by her nephew, the Revd Cyril Treneer, there was held a memorial service at Gerrans. The Revd Robert MacDonald, rector of Gerrans, who conducted the service, described her as 'A delighted person who gave delight'—a fitting epitaph.

* * *

Of the many obituaries which appeared after her death, the most informative and sympathetic was by Arthur Gibson, published in *The Cornish Review* (Autumn 1967, pp. 18–23).

A Descriptive Bibliography
of the Writings of Anne Treneer,

compiled by Brenda Hull

George Meredith.
Thesis for M.A. Examination,
University of London. June, 1922 (unpublished).

Anne Treneer's second attempt at an M.A. was successful. One spring she returned to her first effort: 'I fell upon it with energy and spite. I cut and scraped, and polished, and white-washed. I ruined it with white-wash. I hid its joints, I modified its forthrightness, and I attached a list of authorities to its tail'. (*Cornish Years*, p. 314). In it Treneer discusses Meredith's poetry, novels, and prose with sections on tragedy and comedy. She observes his reticence in terms which are resoundingly modernist: 'Meredith was reticent on the subject of personalities and never wearied of telling the collectors of personal details and the seekers after pictures and autographs that the best of him was to be found in his work. "I cannot refer you", he writes to a would-be interviewer "to any published account of the personal me. Our books contain the best of us. I hold that the public has little to do with what is outside the printed matter, beyond hearing that the writer is reputedly a good citizen." ' (M.A. thesis, p. 6)

The Sea in English Literature from Beowulf to Donne
(University Press, Liverpool; Hodder & Stoughton, London, 1926)
pp. xvii 299.

Dedicated to 'my Father and Mother'. Notes her debt to the School of English at Liverpool University and especially Professor O. Elton. Very professional over her writing: 'In translating from

Old English I have consulted many existing versions; I can only regret my failure to make more fruitful use of them and my inability to produce anything which adequately represents the beauty of Old English sea poetry'. She ends the introduction with the sentence: 'One would like to tumble the treasures of early English Literature pell-mell at the feet of those who are too constant to the moderns; but I have tried to proceed soberly and in a good fashion, looking up the dates'. Her humour is revealed again in the first chapter on the sea in Old English literature: 'Colouring much of the verse is a restlessness as of the sea itself— the feeling in human beings which makes the Cornish saying true—"You'm never happy unless you be where you bain't." '

Charles M. Doughty
A study of his prose and verse (Cape, London, 1935) pp. 350.

A reviewer in the *Birmingham Post* wrote: 'Miss Treneer's theme is Doughty the writer more than the traveller. She considers him too as "a poet who wrote one great piece of prose who, unfortunately, also wrote long poems." '

This World's Bliss
(Cornish Brothers, Birmingham, 1942) pp. 22.

Cornish Brothers were publishers to the University of Birmingham. Anne Treneer paid for the publication herself. The B.D.W. to whom the book is dedicated was Miss Wright, the English lecturer at the University College of Exeter, who had persuaded her to study there full-time and who encouraged her writing of poetry. When Anne Treneer died, she was preparing another volume for publication.

School House in the Wind
(Cape, London, 1944) pp. 142.
Subsequent editions: Travellers' Library 1950 pp. 220; 1953 pp. 220;
Anthony Mott Ltd. 1982 pp. 224.

The best known of the volumes of autobiography, and the only one to have been reprinted. In it, Anne Treneer describes a childhood blessed with both security and freedom: security in a loving family and a framework of church festivals and seasonal pursuits, and freedom to roam in a beautiful county with little crime or traffic. Much of her time was spent out of doors but books were greatly appreciated at home, so she grew up not only conscious of the beauty of her surroundings but also able to describe that beauty for future generations.

Cornish Years
(Cape, London, 1949) pp. 284.

Second volume of autobiography. Dedicated to her sister Susan. The events covered in this volume are more varied. Anne Treneer goes from teaching in a primary school to Exeter University College and then on to teaching at Camborne County School for Girls (later known as Camborne Grammar School for Girls), with interludes at Liverpool and Oxford. Each chapter is headed by one of her own poems and the main themes remain the beauty of her surroundings, friendships and literary associations, with the addition of theories of education. Its republication is to be welcomed; a Book Society non-fiction choice, it is at least as fine a book as the better-known *School House in the Wind.*

Happy Button and other stories
(Westaway Books, London, 1950), pp. 222.

Dedicated to Howard and Mary (her brother and his wife). Short stories set in Cornwall, some in Cornish dialect. Almost half of them had previously been published in *The West Coutry Magazine* ed. J.C. Trewin. A reviewer wrote that they had 'the authentic Cornish flavour . . . they will delight the Cornish heart . . . they also have the quality of universality that every good short story must possess. Miss Treneer changes from gay to grave with equal skill'. However, although demonstrating her sense of humour and her mastery of Cornish dialect, it is the least successful of her books.

A Stranger in the Midlands
(Cape, London, 1952), pp. 224.

Third volume of autobiography. Dedicated to Helen and Maurice (her brother and his wife). This last volume covers the period from 1931, when Anne Treneer arrived in Birmingham to teach at the distinguished King Edward's High School for Girls, until her retirement in 1948. One reviewer wrote in *The West Country Magazine* 'if any West Country readers should fear that Anne Treneer has strayed too far from home in this her third instalment of autobiography, it should be remembered that she carries Cornwall with her wherever she goes, loyally, nimbly and gracefully, even bringing some of her county's light into the streets of Birmingham'. But that did not prevent her from appreciating the country around Birmingham and also Cheltenham, to which the school was evacuated from 1939 until 1940. Her most interesting observations on education continue to be as relevant now as they were then.

The Mercurial Chemist
A Life of Sir Humphry Davy (Methuen & Co., London, 1963),
pp. xvi 264.

Dedicated to 'My Friends in the Hundred of Penwith'. Anne Treneer had been interested in Sir Humphry for many years, not least because of his connection with Penzance. She writes in the preface: 'This book had its origin in a paper "Sir Humphry Davy and the Poets", read before a small Cornish Society [audience] and broadcast in part in the West Region [of BBC radio]. Davy's early life was as intensely and vividly local as his later life was cosmopolitan'. The evocation of Cornwall in the late eighteenth and early nineteenth centuries is the most successful part of the book.

Books published under the name of S.K. Ensdaile

Philippa at School (Black's Boys' and Girls' Library, London, 1928), pp. vii 241.
Marceline Goes to School (Partridge & Co., London, 1931), pp. 320.
Discipline for Penelope (A. & C. Black, London, 1934), pp. v 249.
Puck of Manor School (F. Warne & Co., London & New York, 1938), pp. 288.

The only people who knew about the publication of these books were her own family and her god-daughter and family. They are typical girls' boarding school stories, though better-written than most. Anne Treneer tried not to use current slang which she knew would date. They include interests of hers such as form plays, camping and motorbikes.

ARTICLES

Birmingham Post

While at King Edward's, Anne Treneer contributed a series of literary essays to the *Birmingham Post* between 1935 and 1937. These were found in the British Library newspaper section at Colindale, and copies obtained by Susan Palmer. There are eleven articles altogether on such diverse subjects as Mr Pickwick, Chinese Poetry and Medieval Spring.

The West Country Magazine
(ed. J.C. Trewin).

Many diverse articles and poems between 1946 and 1952, including an evaluation of various versions and translations of 'Tristram and Iseult'.

Old Cornwall
Articles and poems, 1946–1962.

Out of Doors
The magazine of the Open Air, incorporating *Countrygoer*.

A series of twelve articles 1951–1953 entitled 'Walking Round the Village', the first ten of which are illustrated by line drawings by Clifford Russell. Descriptive and evocative essays on areas of West Penwith, Cornwall. They combine description of natural beauty and musings about human nature, education and literature.

Anne Treneer also contributed articles and poems to such publications as *Time and Tide* and *The Western Morning News*. It is probable that there are many which have not yet been discovered.

BROADCASTS

Anne Treneer made three radio broadcasts for the BBC West of England Home Service between 1950 and 1953: 'On Being Made to Feel a Fool'; 'Spring Holidays in Cornwall' and 'Gorran and Gorran Haven'. The last one was part of a series called 'Coast and Country' which included talks on Padstow by Claude Berry; St Just in Penwith by Arthur Caddick; and Bude to Morwenstow by Charles Causley.